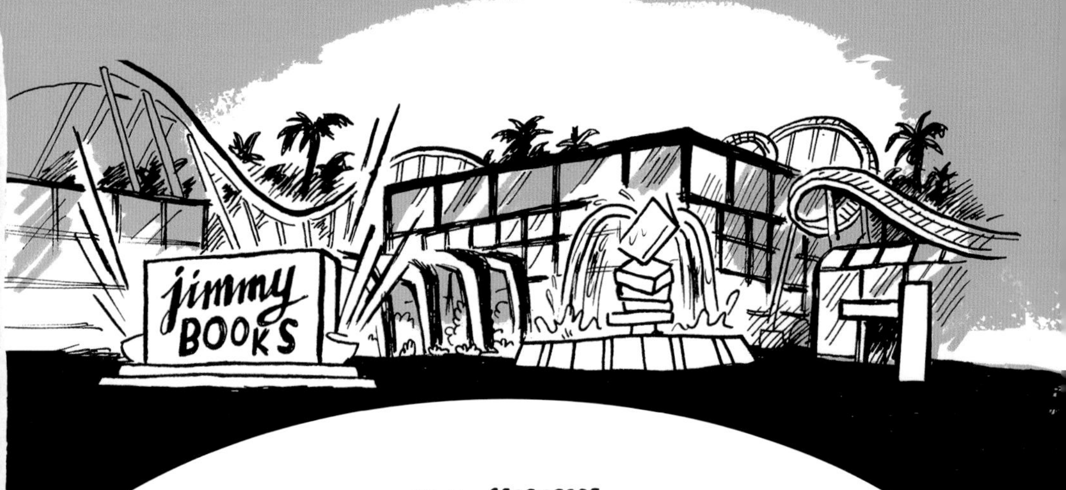
jimmy BOOKS

Hi, I'm JIMMY!

Like me, you probably noticed the world is run by adults.

But ask yourself: Who would do the best job

of making books that *kids* will love?

Yeah. **Kids!**

So that's how the idea of JIMMY books came to life.

We want every JIMMY book to be so good

that when you're finished, you'll say,

"PLEASE GIVE ME ANOTHER BOOK!"

Give this one a try and see if you agree.

(If not, you're probably an adult!)

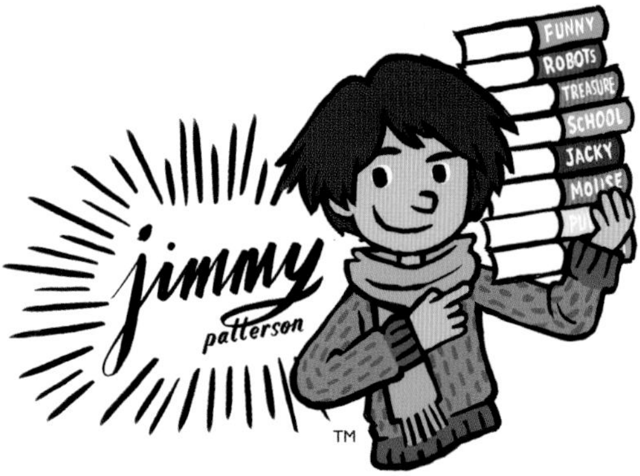
FUNNY
ROBOTS
TREASURE
SCHOOL
JACKY
jimmy
patterson
TM

JIMMY PATTERSON BOOKS FOR YOUNG READERS

James Patterson Presents

Sci-Fi Junior High by John Martin and Scott Seegert
Sci-Fi Junior High: Crash Landing by John Martin and Scott Seegert
How to Be a Supervillain by Michael Fry
How to Be a Supervillain: Born to Be Good by Michael Fry
How to Be a Supervillain: Bad Guys Finish First by Michael Fry
The Unflushables by Ron Bates
Ernestine, Catastrophe Queen by Merrill Wyatt
Scouts by Shannon Greenland

The Middle School Series by James Patterson

Middle School, The Worst Years of My Life
Middle School: Get Me Out of Here!
Middle School: Big Fat Liar
Middle School: How I Survived Bullies, Broccoli, and Snake Hill
Middle School: Ultimate Showdown
Middle School: Save Rafe!
Middle School: Just My Rotten Luck
Middle School: Dog's Best Friend
Middle School: Escape to Australia
Middle School: From Hero to Zero
Middle School: Born to Rock
Middle School: Master of Disaster

The I Funny Series by James Patterson

I Funny
I Even Funnier
I Totally Funniest
I Funny TV
I Funny: School of Laughs
The Nerdiest, Wimpiest, Dorkiest I Funny Ever

The Treasure Hunters Series by James Patterson

Treasure Hunters
Treasure Hunters: Danger Down the Nile
Treasure Hunters: Secret of the Forbidden City
Treasure Hunters: Peril at the Top of the World
Treasure Hunters: Quest for the City of Gold
Treasure Hunters: All-American Adventure

The House of Robots Series by James Patterson

House of Robots
House of Robots: Robots Go Wild!
House of Robots: Robot Revolution

The Daniel X Series by James Patterson

The Dangerous Days of Daniel X
Daniel X: Watch the Skies
Daniel X: Demons and Druids
Daniel X: Game Over
Daniel X: Armageddon
Daniel X: Lights Out

Other Illustrated Novels and Stories

Ali Cross
Katt Vs. Dogg
Dog Diaries
Dog Diaries: Happy Howlidays
Max Einstein: The Genius Experiment
Max Einstein: Rebels with a Cause
Unbelievably Boring Bart
Not So Normal Norbert
Laugh Out Loud
Pottymouth and Stoopid
Jacky Ha-Ha
Jacky Ha-Ha: My Life Is a Joke
Public School Superhero
Word of Mouse
Give Please a Chance
Give Thank You a Try
Big Words for Little Geniuses
Bigger Words for Little Geniuses
Cuddly Critters for Little Geniuses
The Candies Save Christmas

For exclusives, trailers, and other information, visit jimmypatterson.org.

To my dearest dad: love always. —B.T.

Copyright © 2020 by James Patterson
Illustrations by Betty C. Tang

Hachette Book Group supports the right to free expression and the value of copyright. The purpose of copyright is to encourage writers and artists to produce the creative works that enrich our culture.

The scanning, uploading, and distribution of this book without permission is a theft of the author's intellectual property. If you would like permission to use material from the book (other than for review purposes), please contact permissions@hbgusa.com. Thank you for your support of the author's rights.

JIMMY Patterson Books / Little, Brown and Company
Hachette Book Group
1290 Avenue of the Americas, New York, NY 10104
JamesPatterson.com

First Graphic Novel Edition: May 2020

JIMMY Patterson Books is an imprint of Little, Brown and Company, a division of Hachette Book Group, Inc. The Little, Brown name and logo are trademarks of Hachette Book Group, Inc. The JIMMY Patterson Books® name and logo are trademarks of JBP Business, LLC.

The publisher is not responsible for websites (or their content) that are not owned by the publisher.

The Hachette Speakers Bureau provides a wide range of authors for speaking events. To find out more, go to hachettespeakersbureau.com or call (866) 376-6591.

ISBN 978-0-316-49195-2

Library of Congress Control Number 2019957380

10 9 8 7 6 5 4 3 2 1

Printed in China

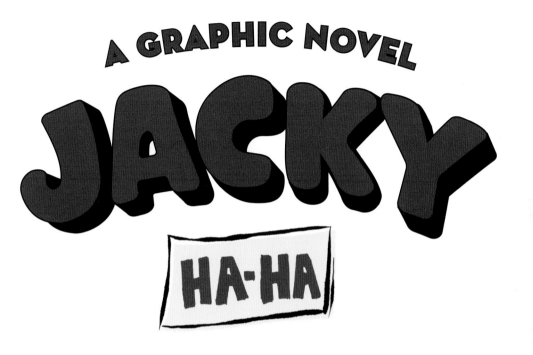

A GRAPHIC NOVEL

JACKY

HA-HA

JAMES PATTERSON
AND CHRIS GRABENSTEIN

ADAPTED BY ADAM RAU
ILLUSTRATED BY BETTY C. TANG

JIMMY Patterson Books
LITTLE, BROWN AND COMPANY
NEW YORK BOSTON LONDON

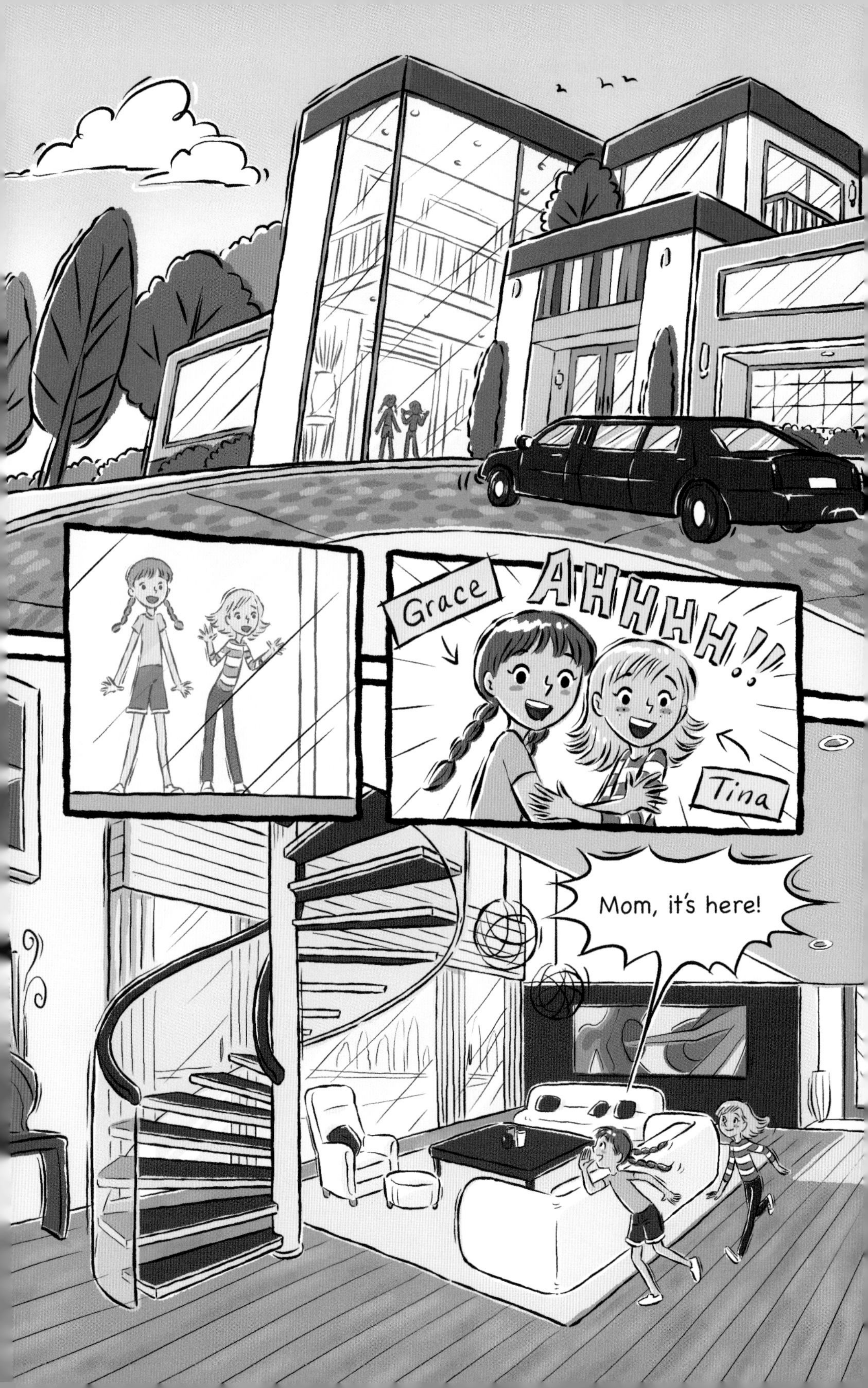
Grace
AHHHH!!
Tina
Mom, it's here!

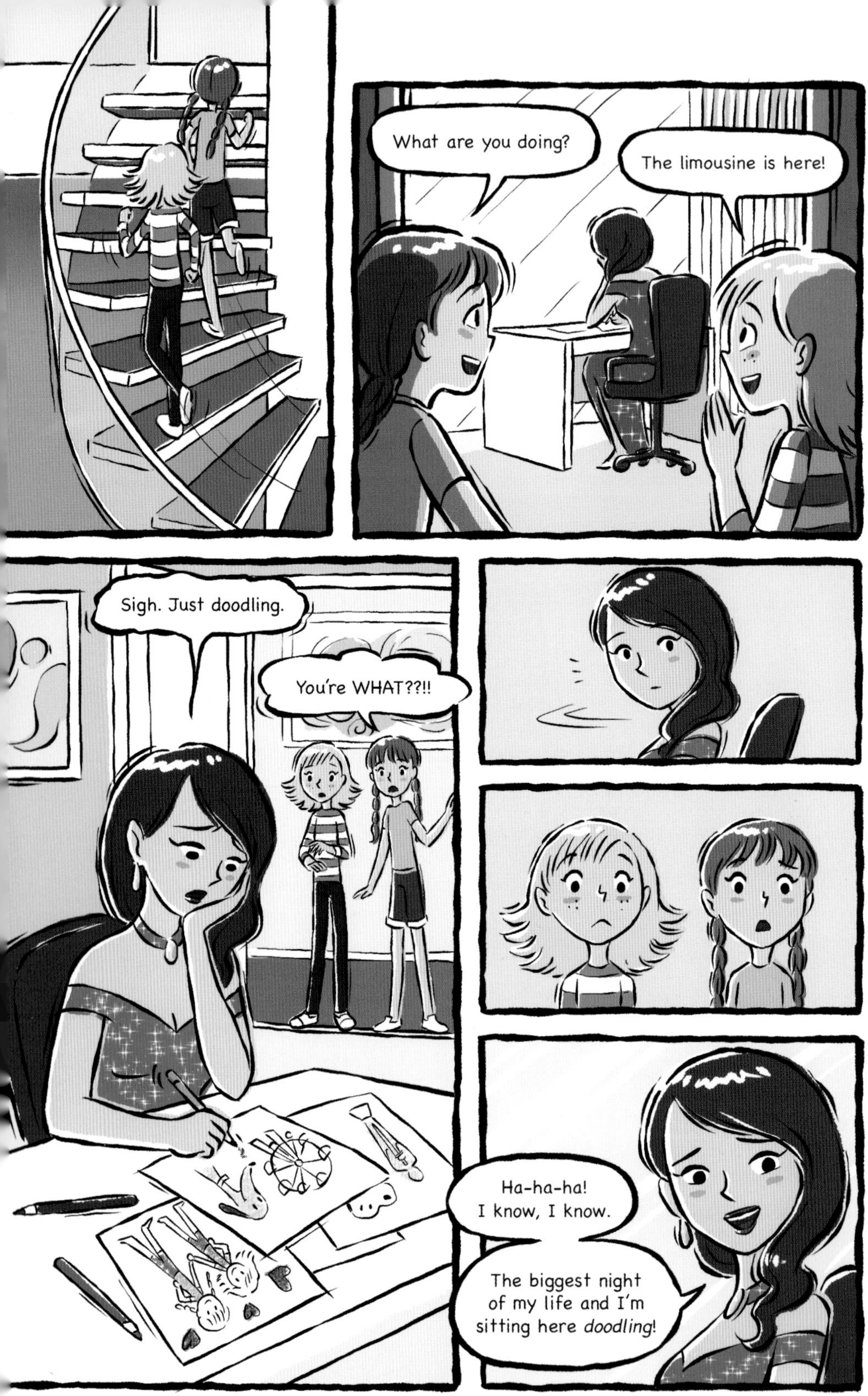
What are you doing?
The limousine is here!
Sigh. Just doodling.
You're WHAT??!!
Ha-ha-ha!
I know, I know.
The biggest night of my life and I'm sitting here *doodling*!

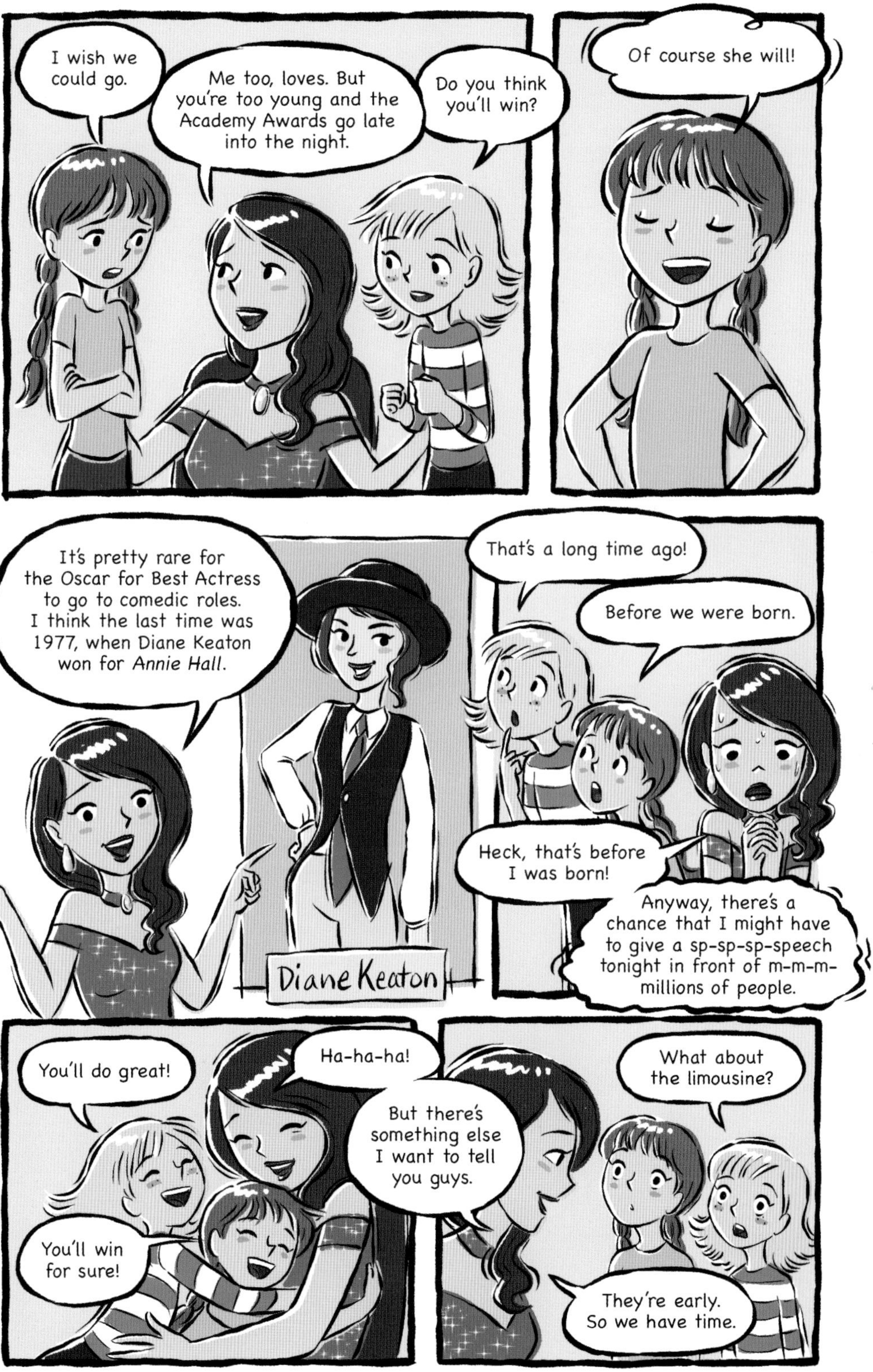

I wish we could go.
Me too, loves. But you're too young and the Academy Awards go late into the night.
Do you think you'll win?
Of course she will!
It's pretty rare for the Oscar for Best Actress to go to comedic roles. I think the last time was 1977, when Diane Keaton won for *Annie Hall*.
Diane Keaton
That's a long time ago!
Before we were born.
Heck, that's before I was born!
Anyway, there's a chance that I might have to give a sp-sp-sp-speech tonight in front of m-m-m-millions of people.
You'll do great!
Ha-ha-ha!
You'll win for sure!
But there's something else I want to tell you guys.
What about the limousine?
They're early. So we have time.

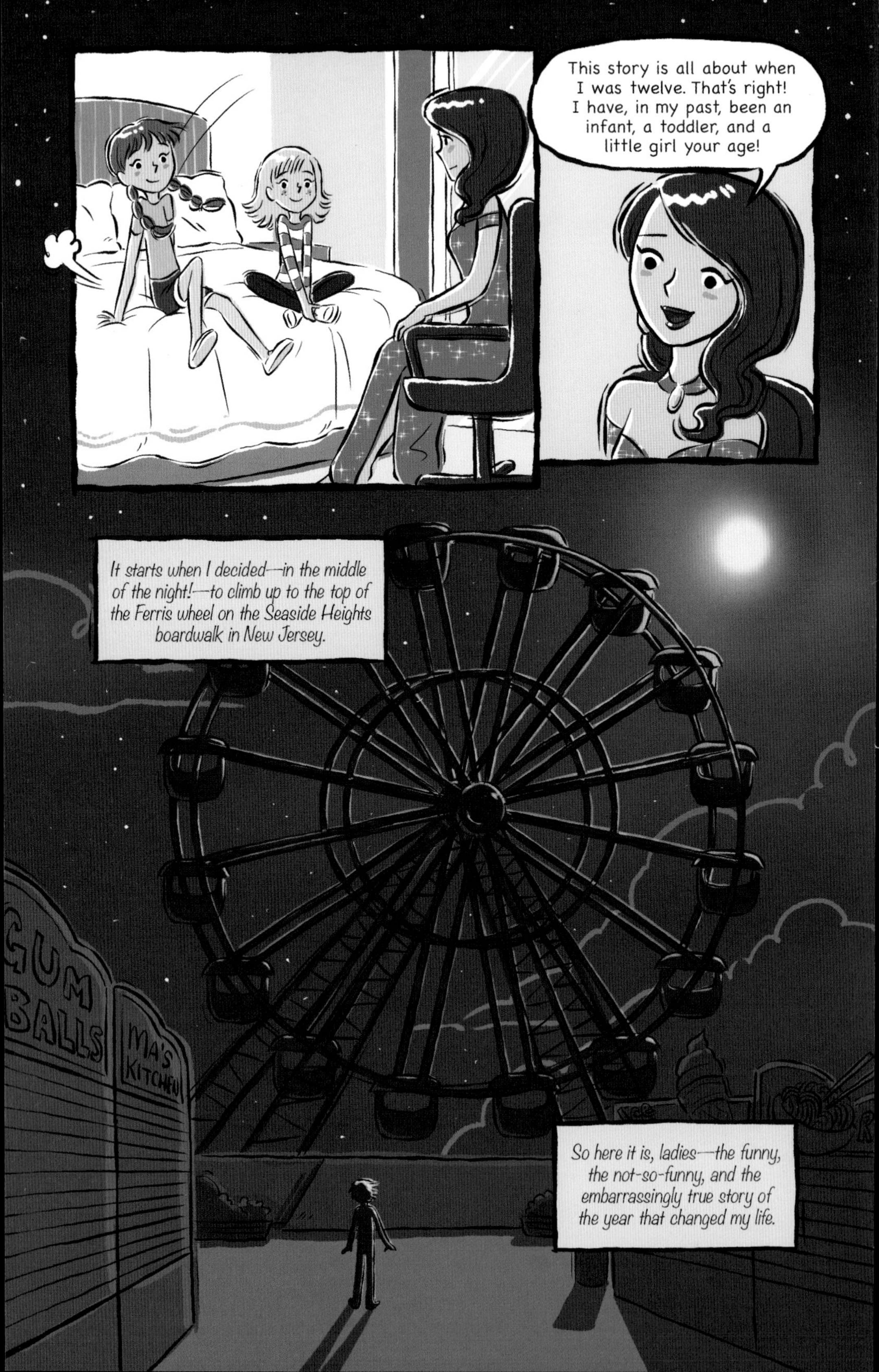
This story is all about when I was twelve. That's right! I have, in my past, been an infant, a toddler, and a little girl your age!
It starts when I decided—in the middle of the night!—to climb up to the top of the Ferris wheel on the Seaside Heights boardwalk in New Jersey.
GUM BALLS
MA'S KITCHEN
So here it is, ladies—the funny, the not-so-funny, and the embarrassingly true story of the year that changed my life.

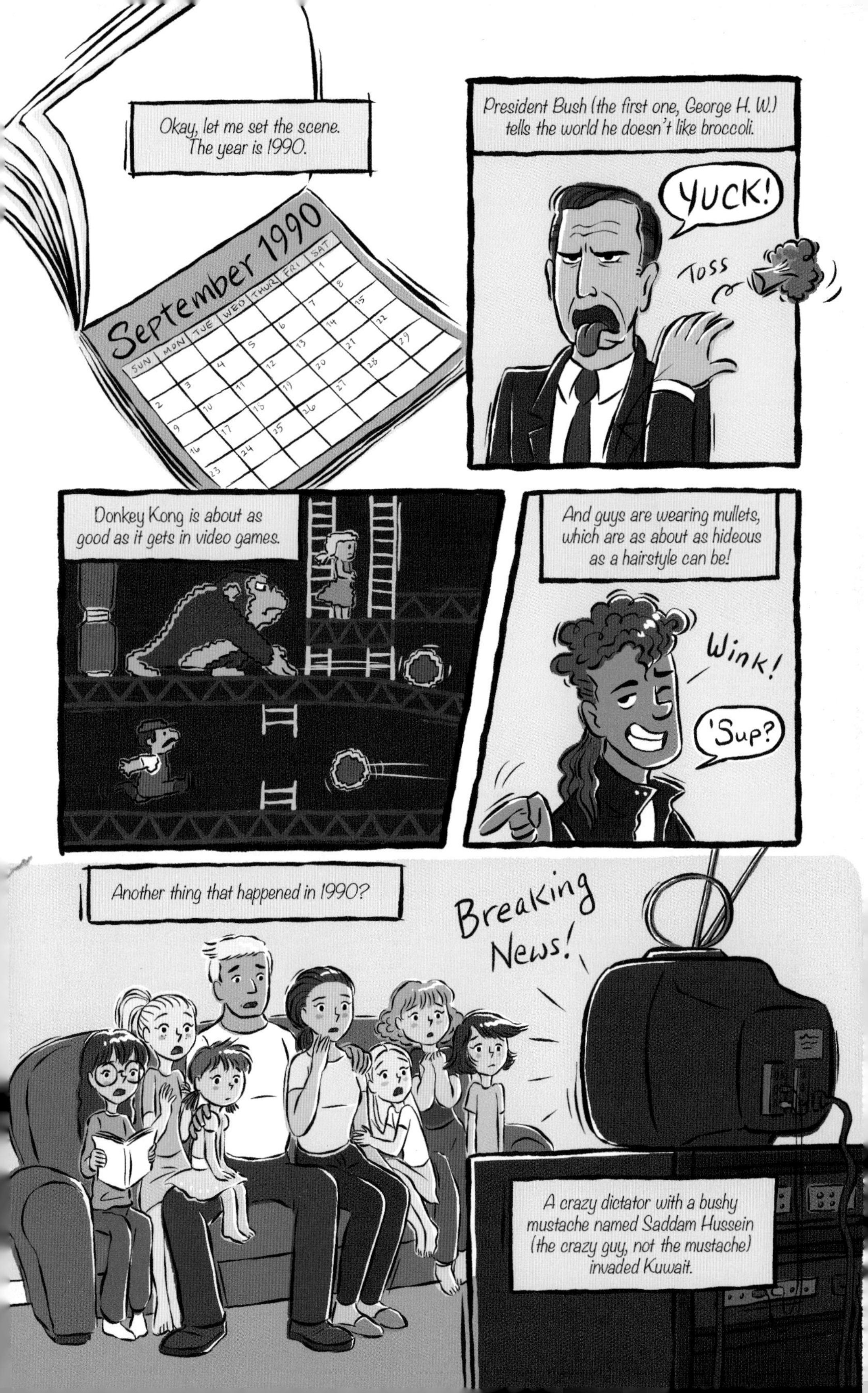

Okay, let me set the scene. The year is 1990.
September 1990
SUN MON TUE WED THUR FRI SAT
President Bush (the first one, George H. W.) tells the world he doesn't like broccoli.
YUCK!
Toss
Donkey Kong is about as good as it gets in video games.
And guys are wearing mullets, which are as about as hideous as a hairstyle can be!
Wink!
'Sup?
Another thing that happened in 1990?
Breaking News!
A crazy dictator with a bushy mustache named Saddam Hussein (the crazy guy, not the mustache) invaded Kuwait.

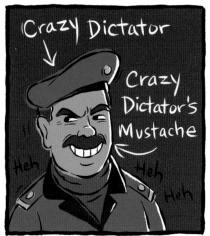

Crazy Dictator

Crazy Dictator's Mustache

Heh Heh Heh Heh

So in early 1991, President George H. W. Bush ordered the start of Operation Desert Shield.

Just two hours ago, allied air forces began an attack on military targets in Iraq and Kuwait...

Mom (your grandmother) was a staff sergeant in the Marine Corps. So she had to pack up her gear and ship out for Saudi Arabia.

Mom's HERE

WE'RE HERE

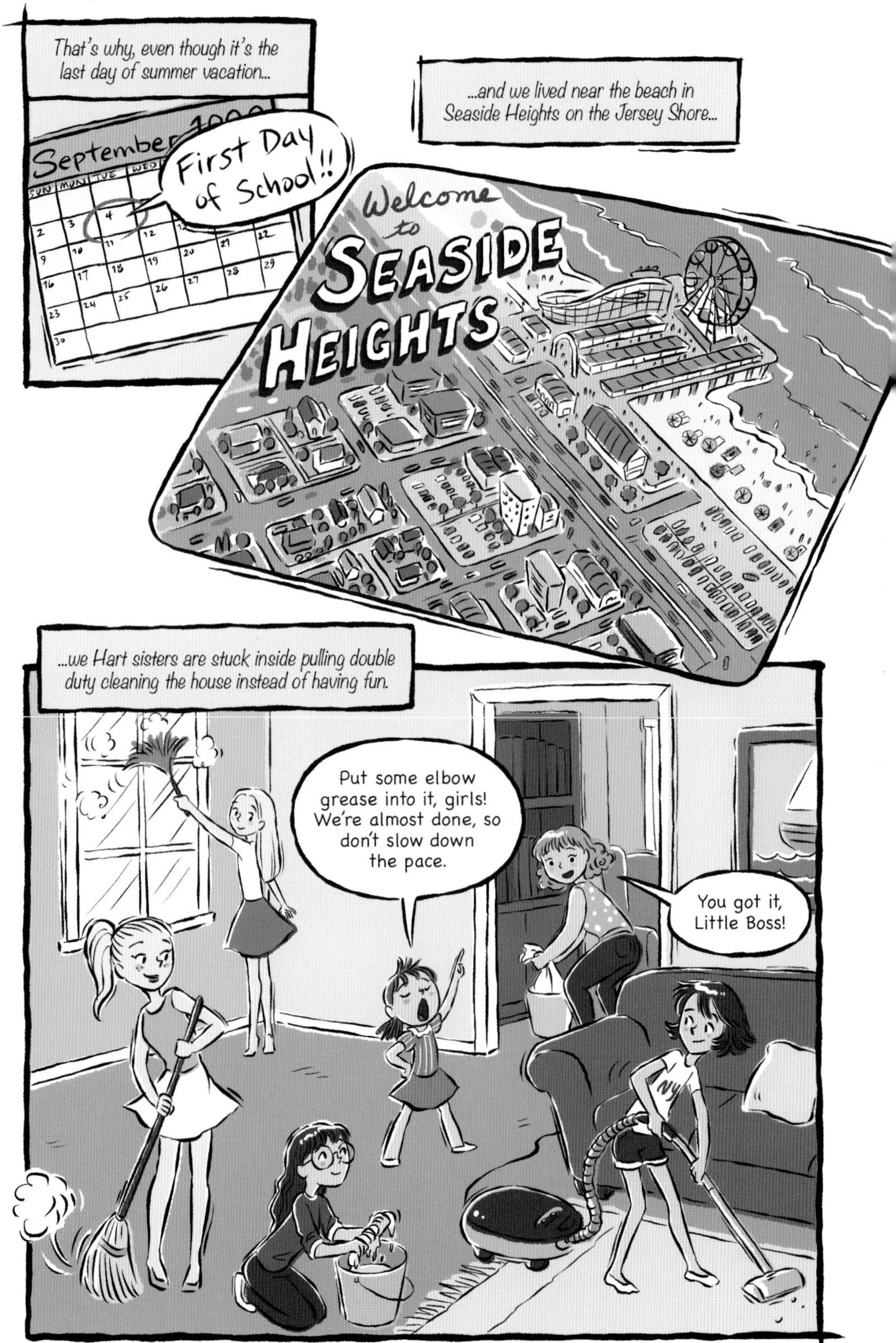

That's why, even though it's the last day of summer vacation...
September
First Day of School!!
...and we lived near the beach in Seaside Heights on the Jersey Shore...
Welcome to Seaside Heights
...we Hart sisters are stuck inside pulling double duty cleaning the house instead of having fun.
Put some elbow grease into it, girls! We're almost done, so don't slow down the pace.
You got it, Little Boss!

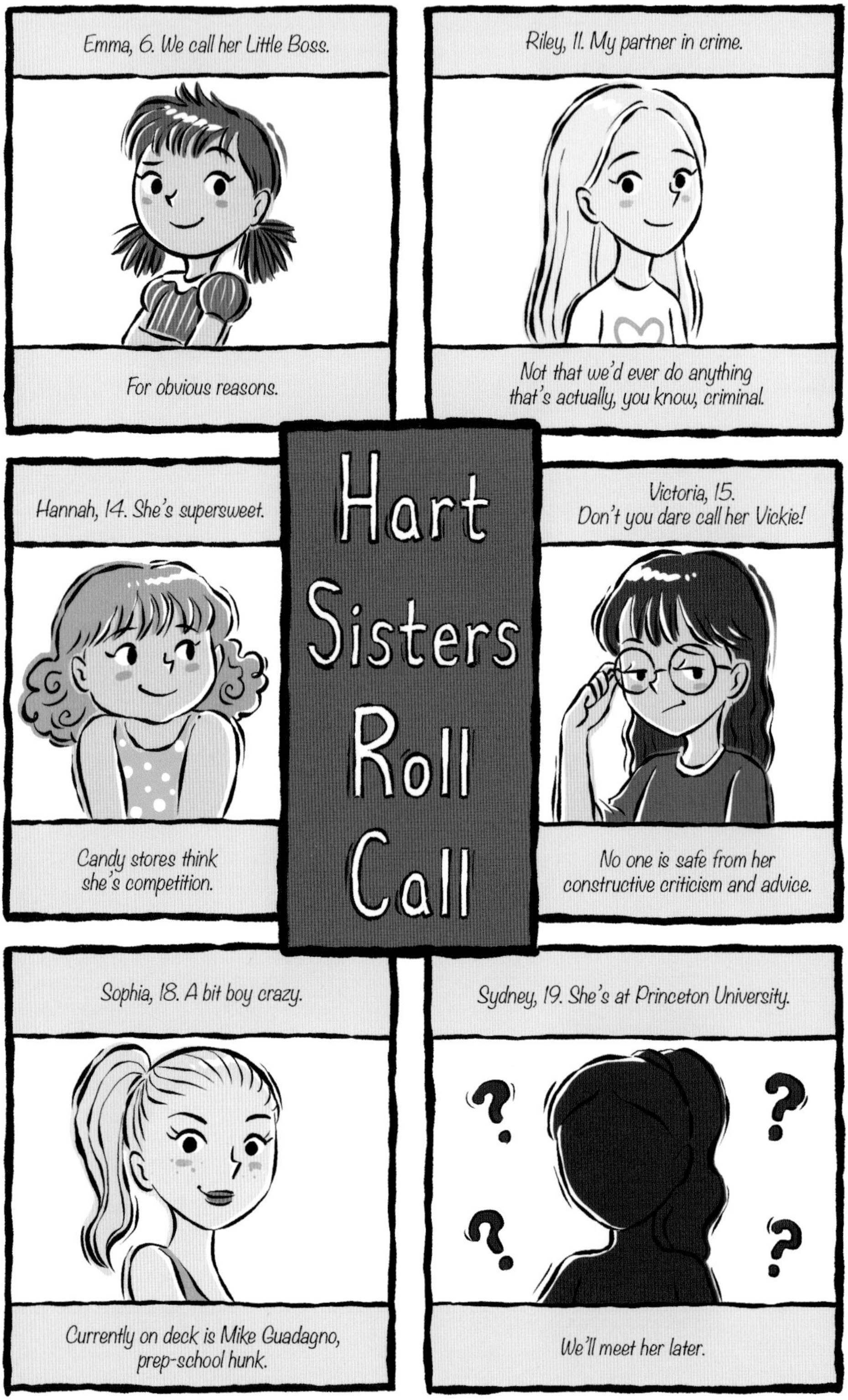

Hart Sisters Roll Call
Emma, 6. We call her Little Boss.
For obvious reasons.
Riley, 11. My partner in crime.
Not that we'd ever do anything that's actually, you know, criminal.
Hannah, 14. She's supersweet.
Candy stores think she's competition.
Victoria, 15. Don't you dare call her Vickie!
No one is safe from her constructive criticism and advice.
Sophia, 18. A bit boy crazy.
Currently on deck is Mike Guadagno, prep-school hunk.
Sydney, 19. She's at Princeton University.
We'll meet her later.

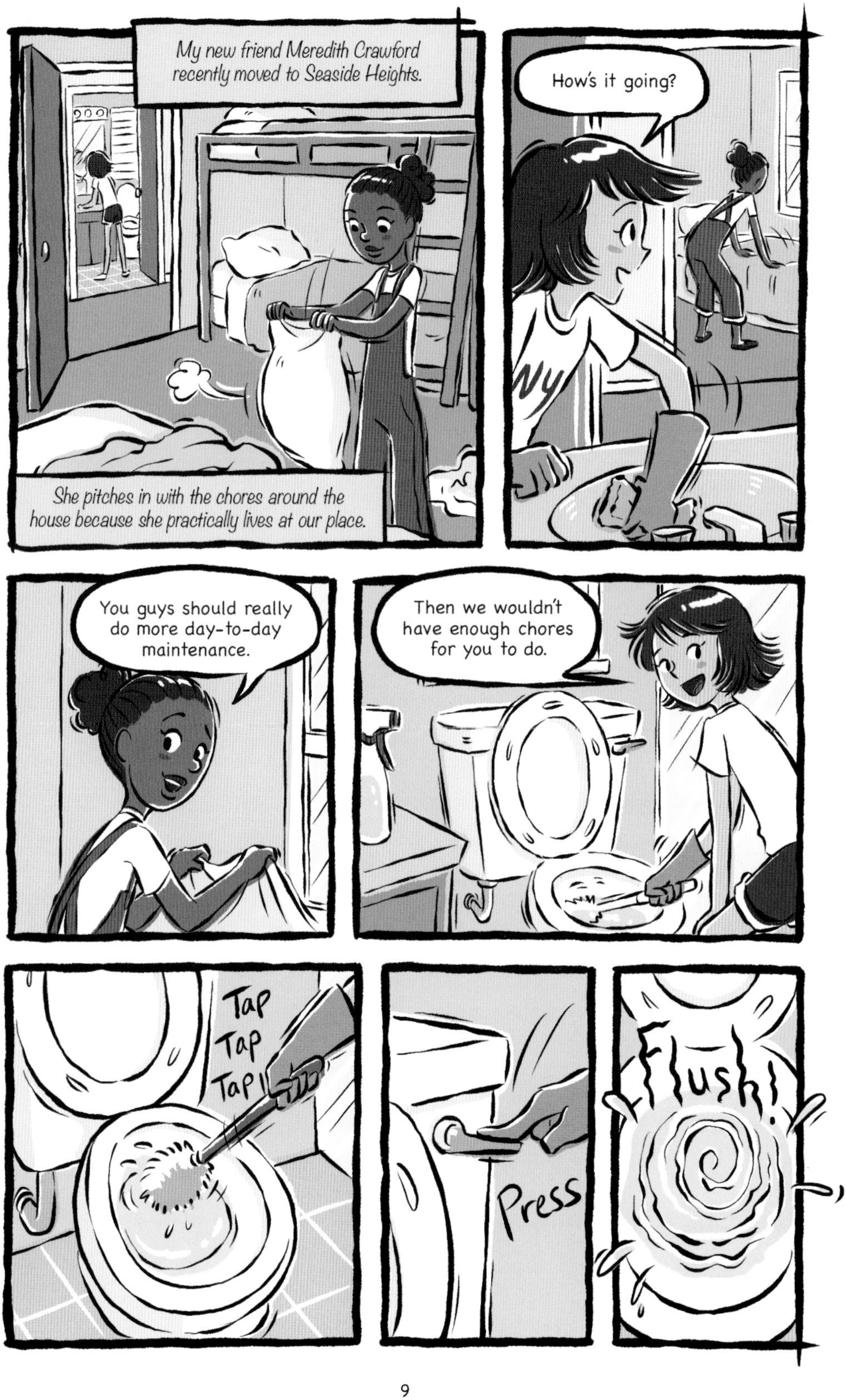
My new friend Meredith Crawford recently moved to Seaside Heights.
She pitches in with the chores around the house because she practically lives at our place.
How's it going?
You guys should really do more day-to-day maintenance.
Then we wouldn't have enough chores for you to do.
Tap Tap Tap
Press
Flush!

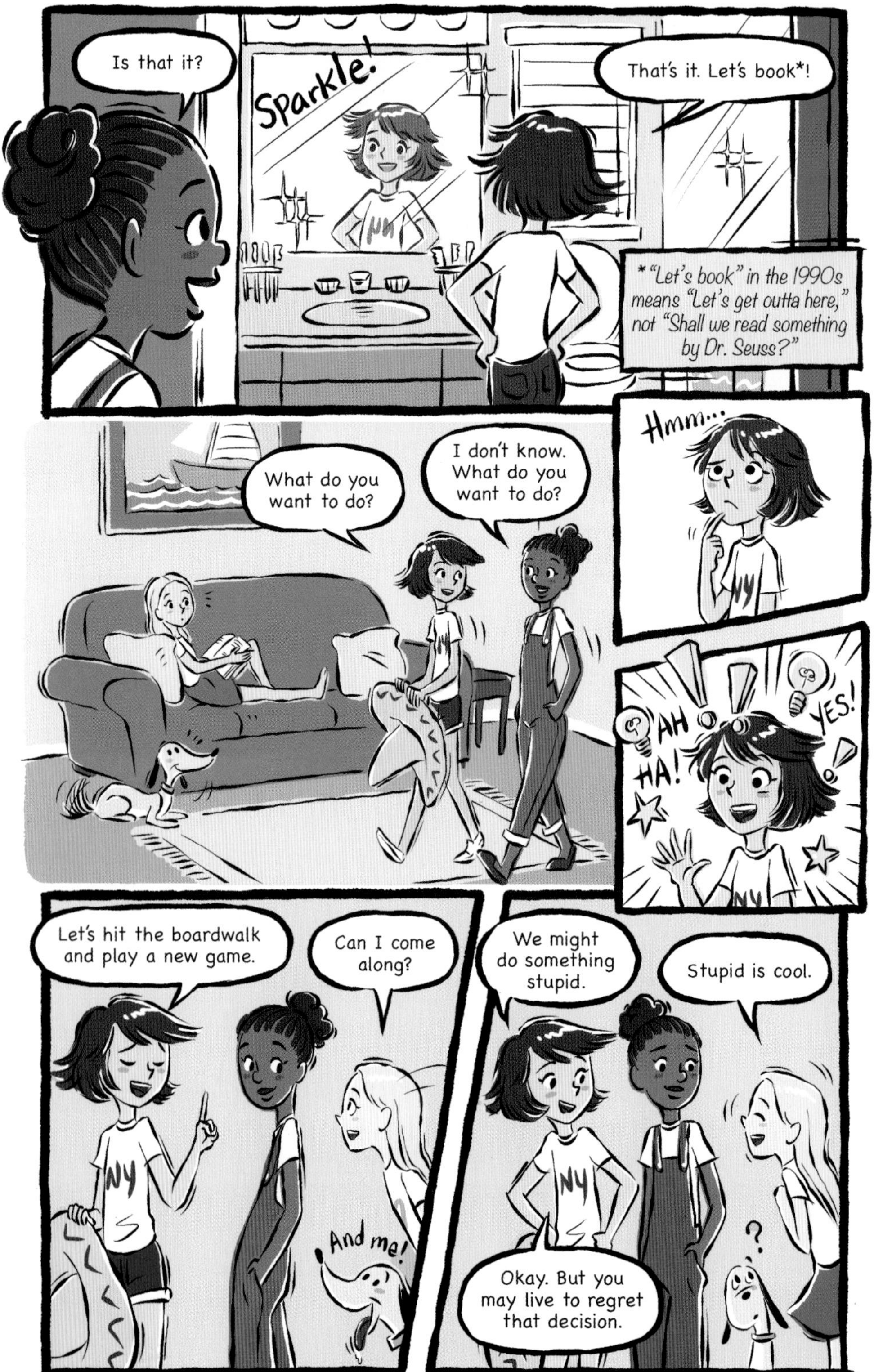
Is that it?
Sparkle!
That's it. Let's book*!
* "Let's book" in the 1990s means "Let's get outta here," not "Shall we read something by Dr. Seuss?"
What do you want to do?
I don't know. What do you want to do?
Hmm...
AH HA!
YES!
Let's hit the boardwalk and play a new game.
Can I come along?
And me!
We might do something stupid.
Stupid is cool.
Okay. But you may live to regret that decision.

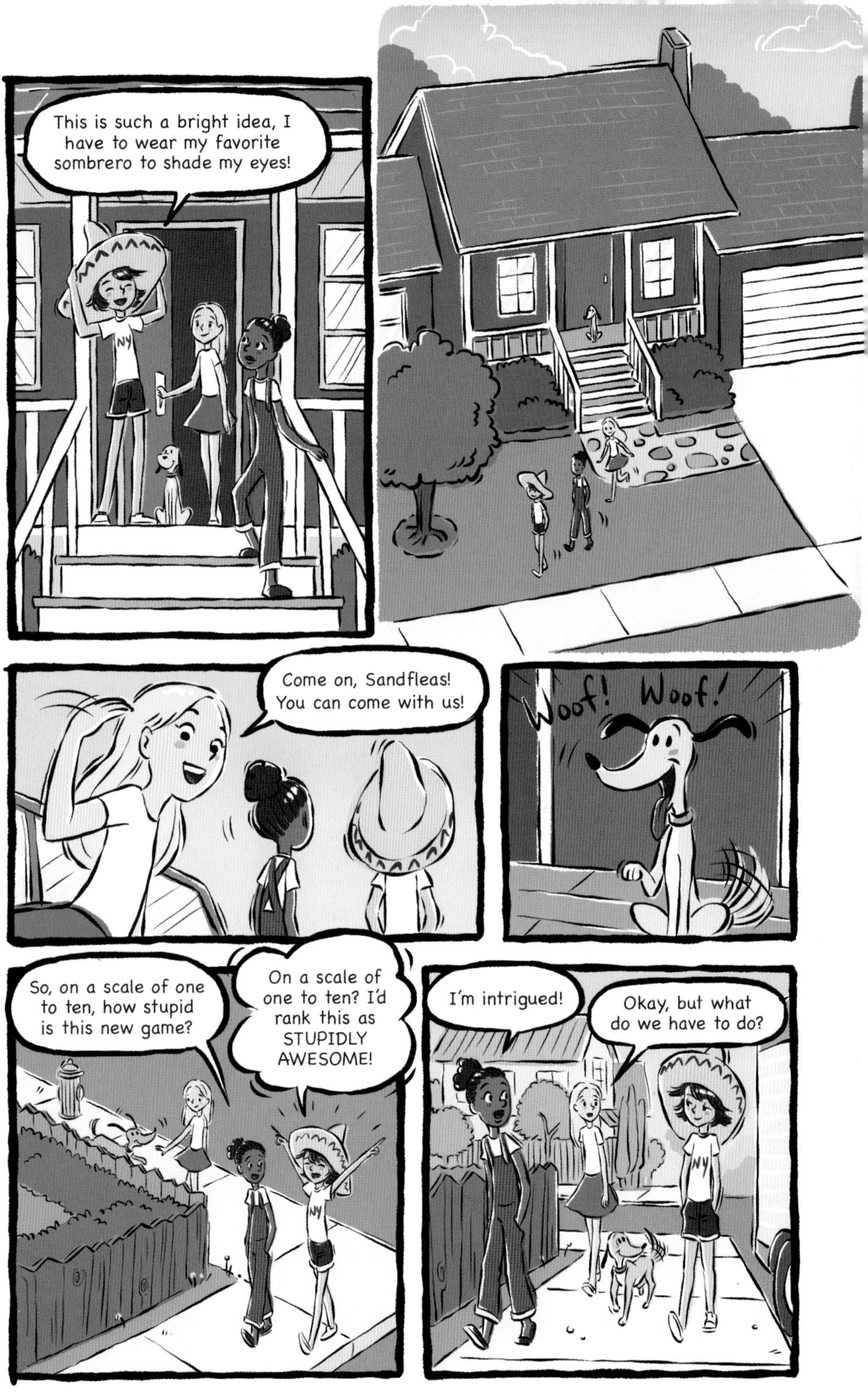
This is such a bright idea, I have to wear my favorite sombrero to shade my eyes!
Come on, Sandfleas! You can come with us!
Woof! Woof!
So, on a scale of one to ten, how stupid is this new game?
On a scale of one to ten? I'd rank this as STUPIDLY AWESOME!
I'm intrigued!
Okay, but what do we have to do?

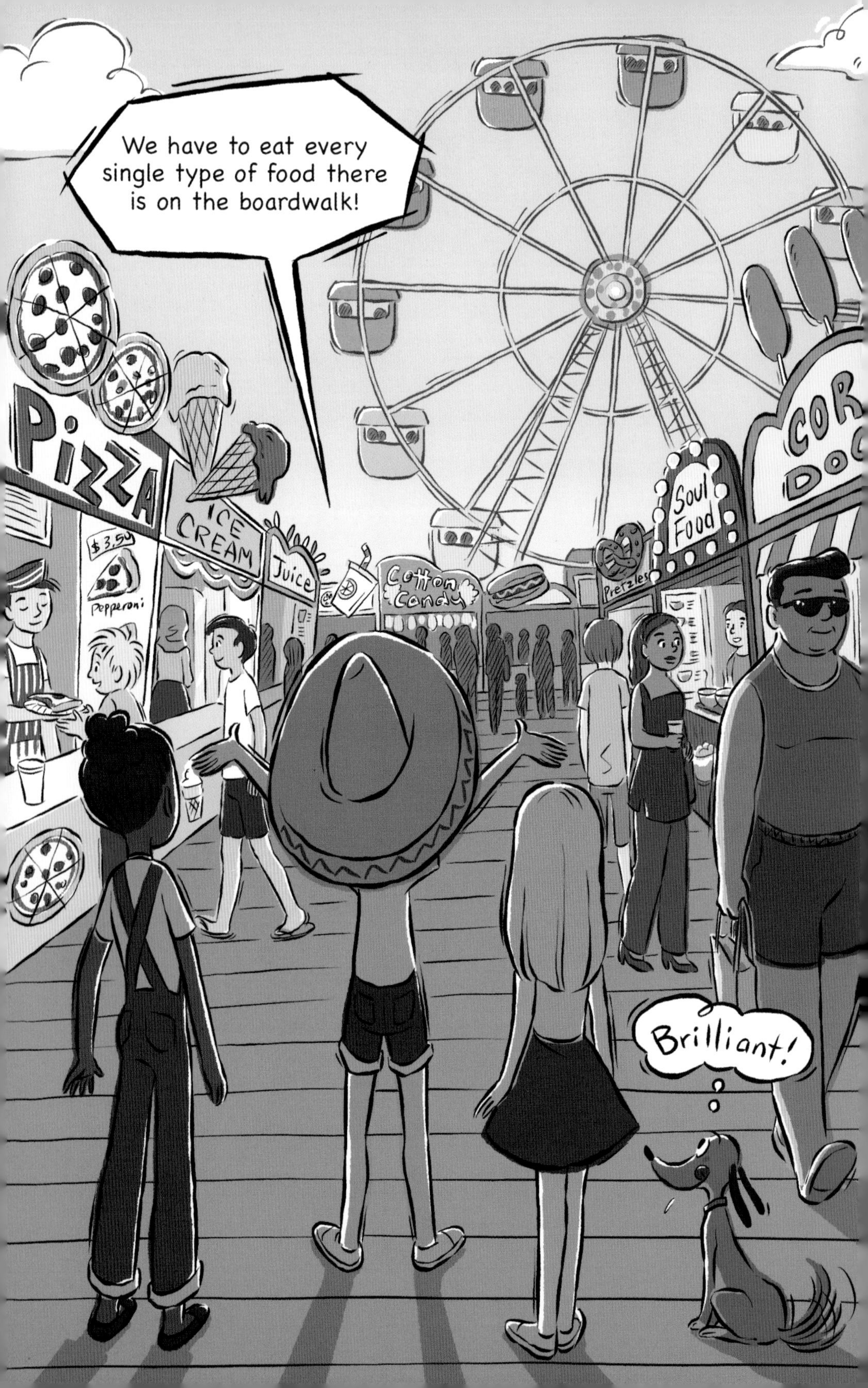
We have to eat every single type of food there is on the boardwalk!
PIZZA
$3.50
Pepperoni
ICE CREAM
Juice
Cotton Candy
Pretzles
Soul Food
COR DO
Brilliant!

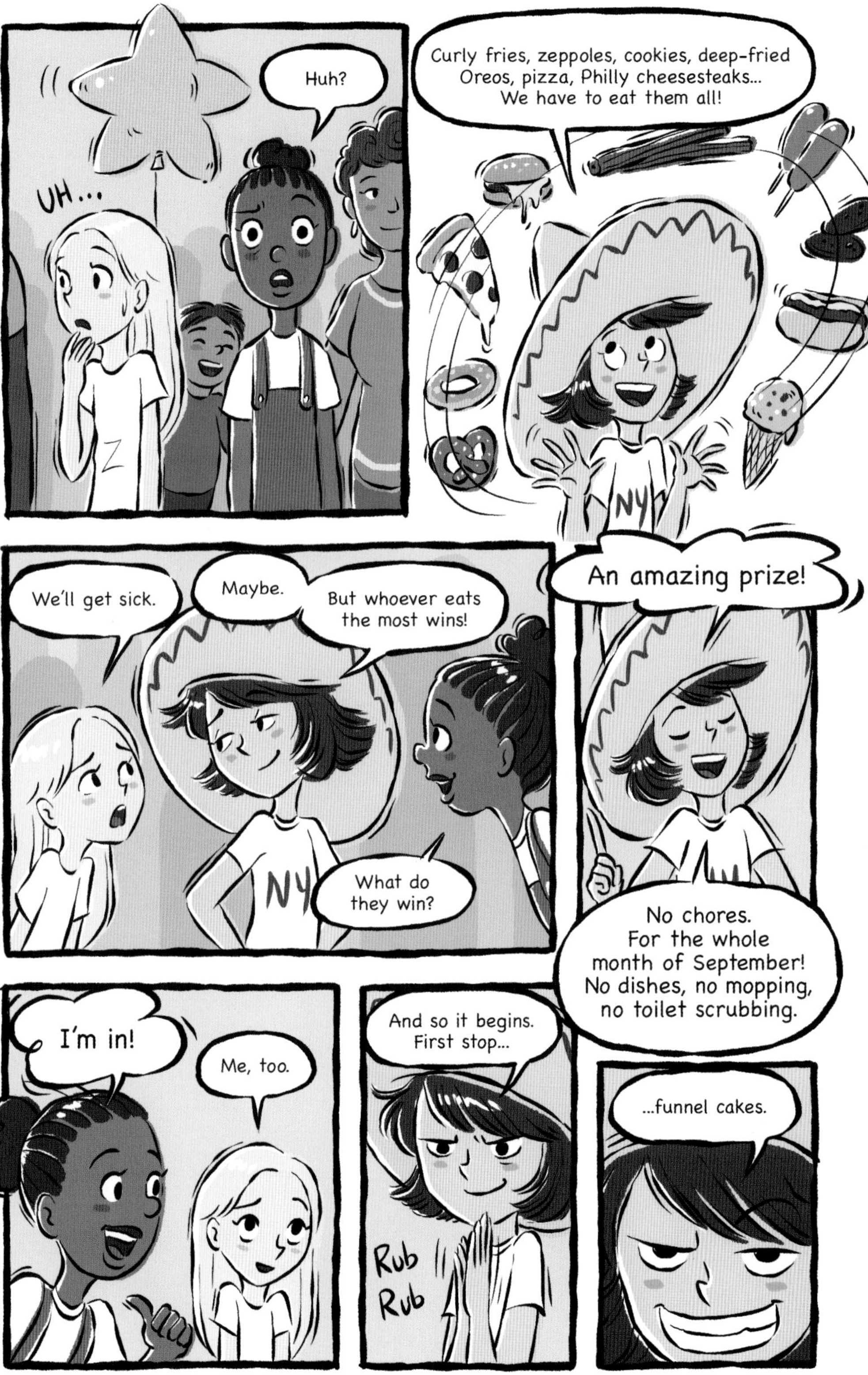
Huh?
UH...
Curly fries, zeppoles, cookies, deep-fried Oreos, pizza, Philly cheesesteaks... We have to eat them all!
We'll get sick.
Maybe.
But whoever eats the most wins!
What do they win?
An amazing prize!
No chores. For the whole month of September! No dishes, no mopping, no toilet scrubbing.
I'm in!
Me, too.
And so it begins. First stop...
Rub Rub
...funnel cakes.

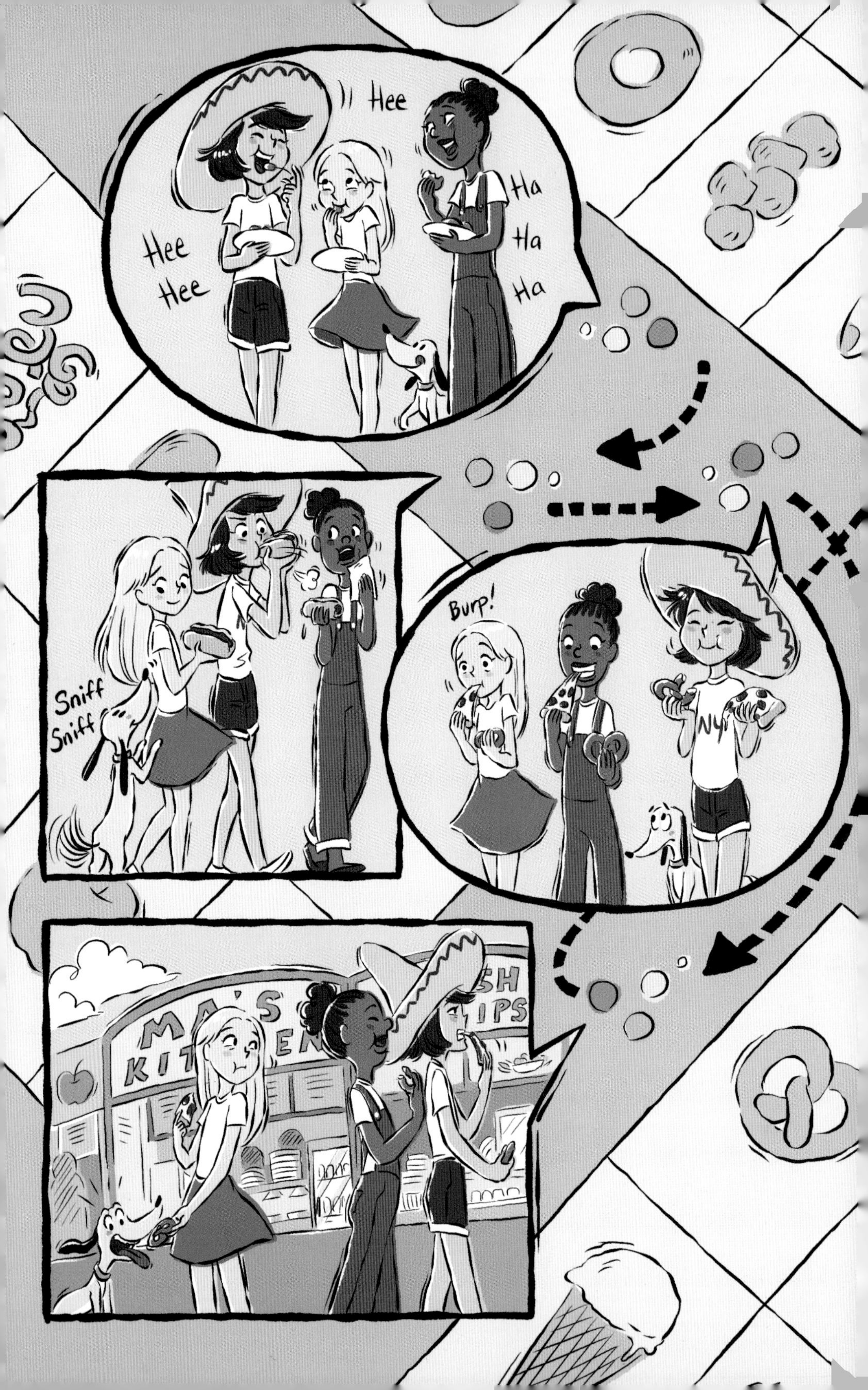
Hee
Hee Hee
Ha Ha Ha
Sniff Sniff
Burp!
MA'S KITCHEN
SH IPS

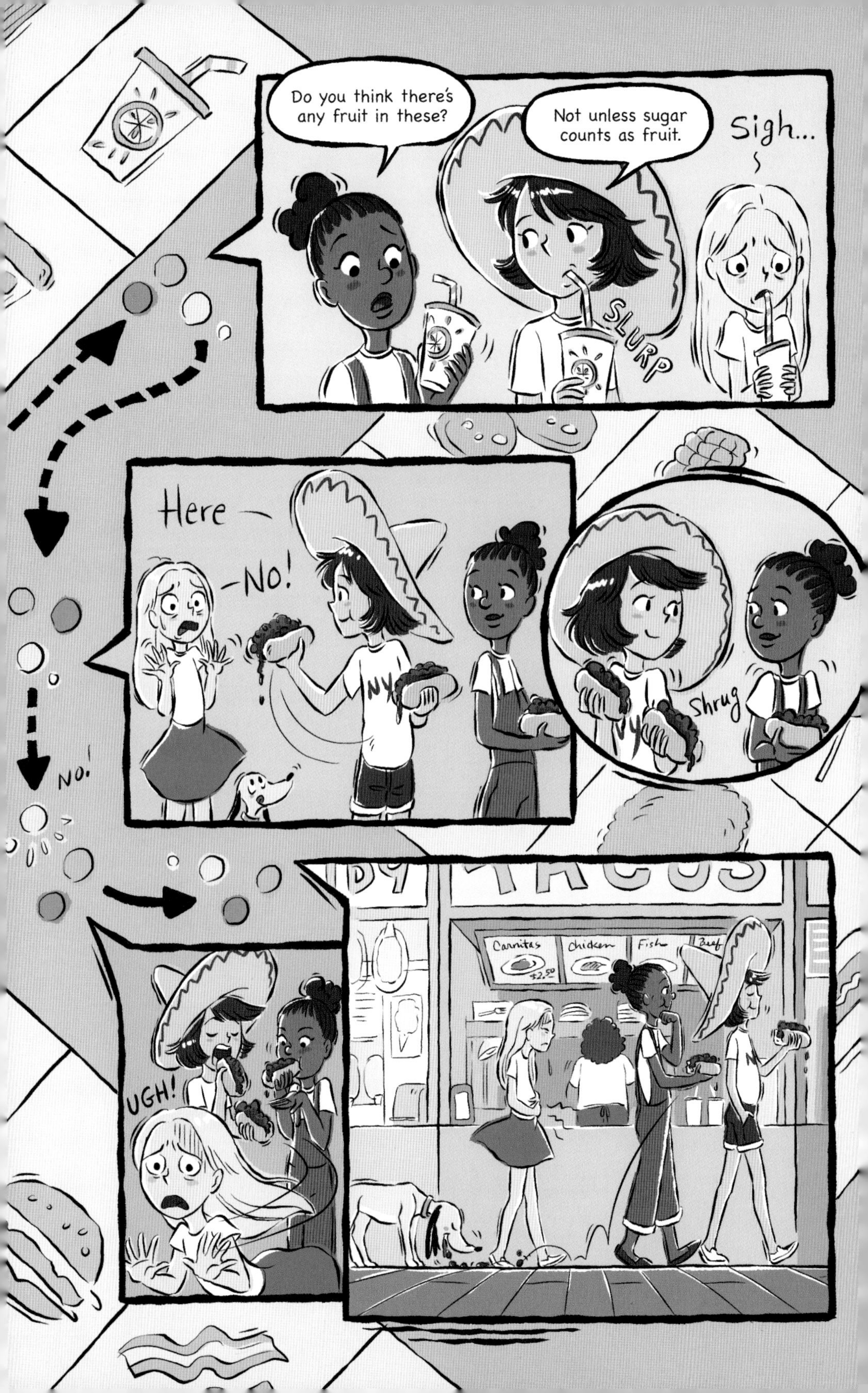
Do you think there's any fruit in these?
Not unless sugar counts as fruit.
Sigh...
SLURP
Here —
—No!
Shrug
NO!
TACOS
Carnitas
Chicken
Fish
Beef
$2.50
UGH!

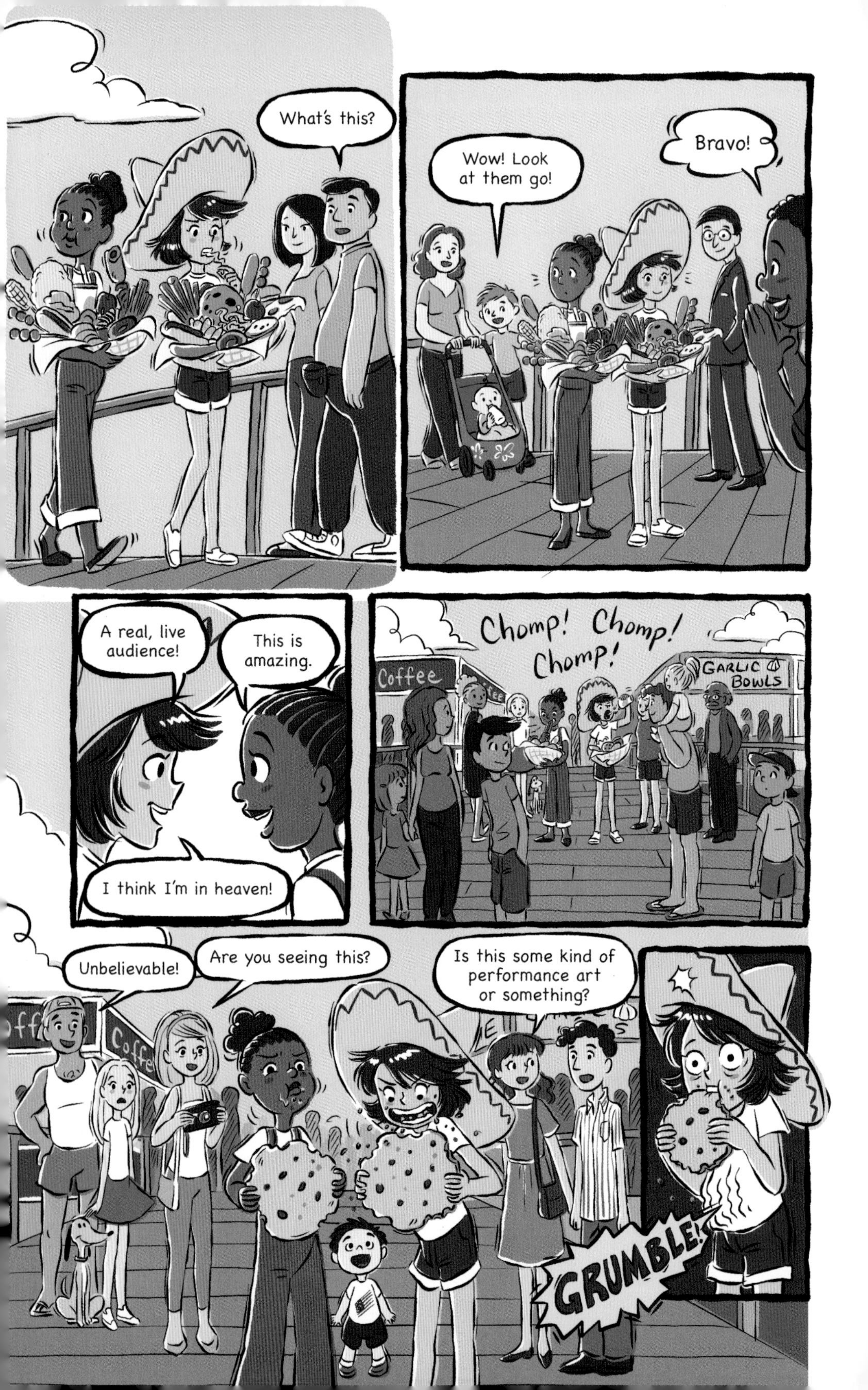
What's this?
Wow! Look at them go!
Bravo!
A real, live audience!
This is amazing.
I think I'm in heaven!
Chomp! Chomp! Chomp!
Coffee
GARLIC BOWLS
Unbelievable!
Are you seeing this?
Is this some kind of performance art or something?
GRUMBLE!

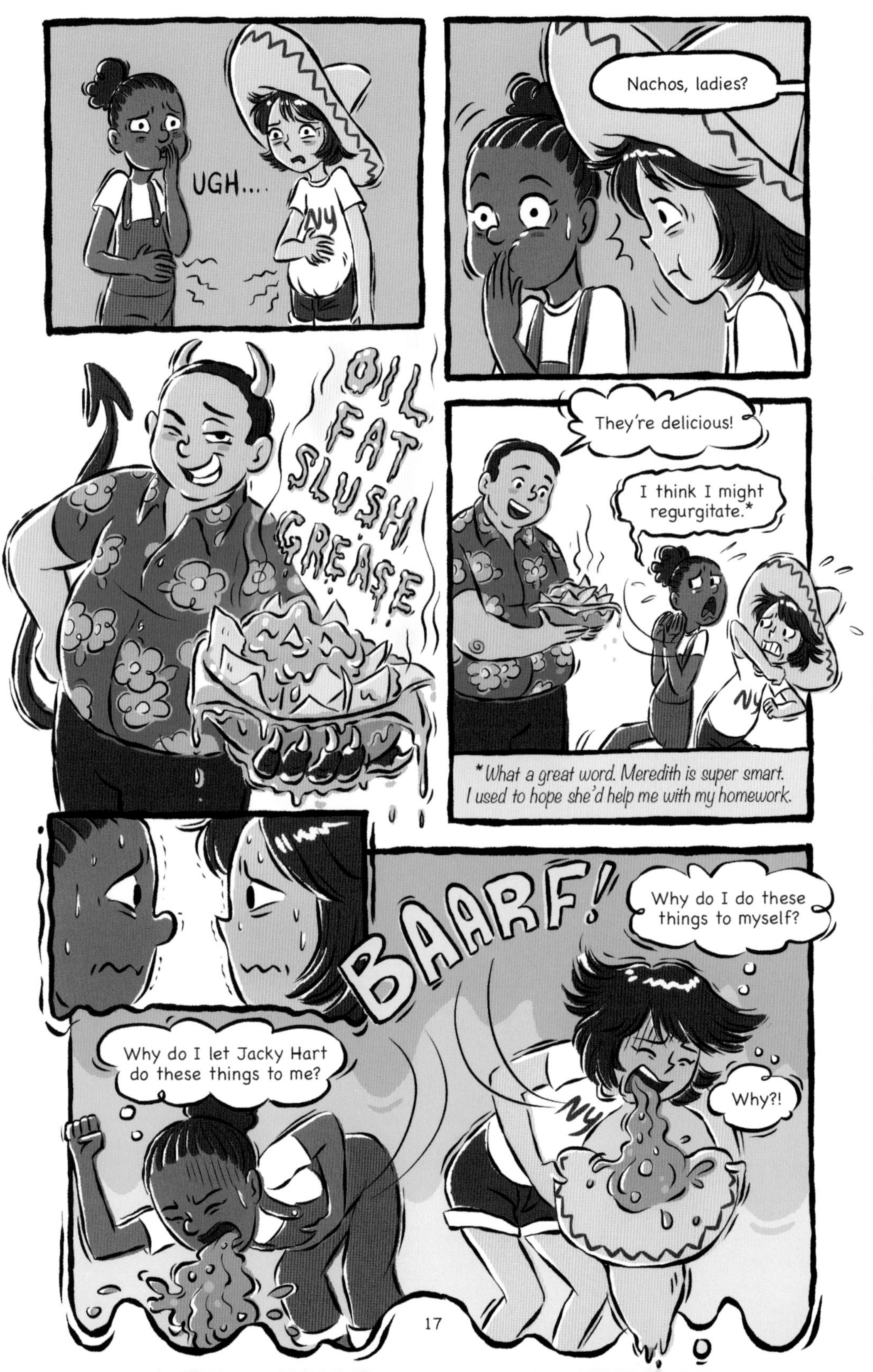
UGH....
Nachos, ladies?
OIL
FAT
SLUSH
GREASE
They're delicious!
I think I might regurgitate.*
*What a great word. Meredith is super smart. I used to hope she'd help me with my homework.
BAARF!
Why do I do these things to myself?
Why do I let Jacky Hart do these things to me?
Why?!

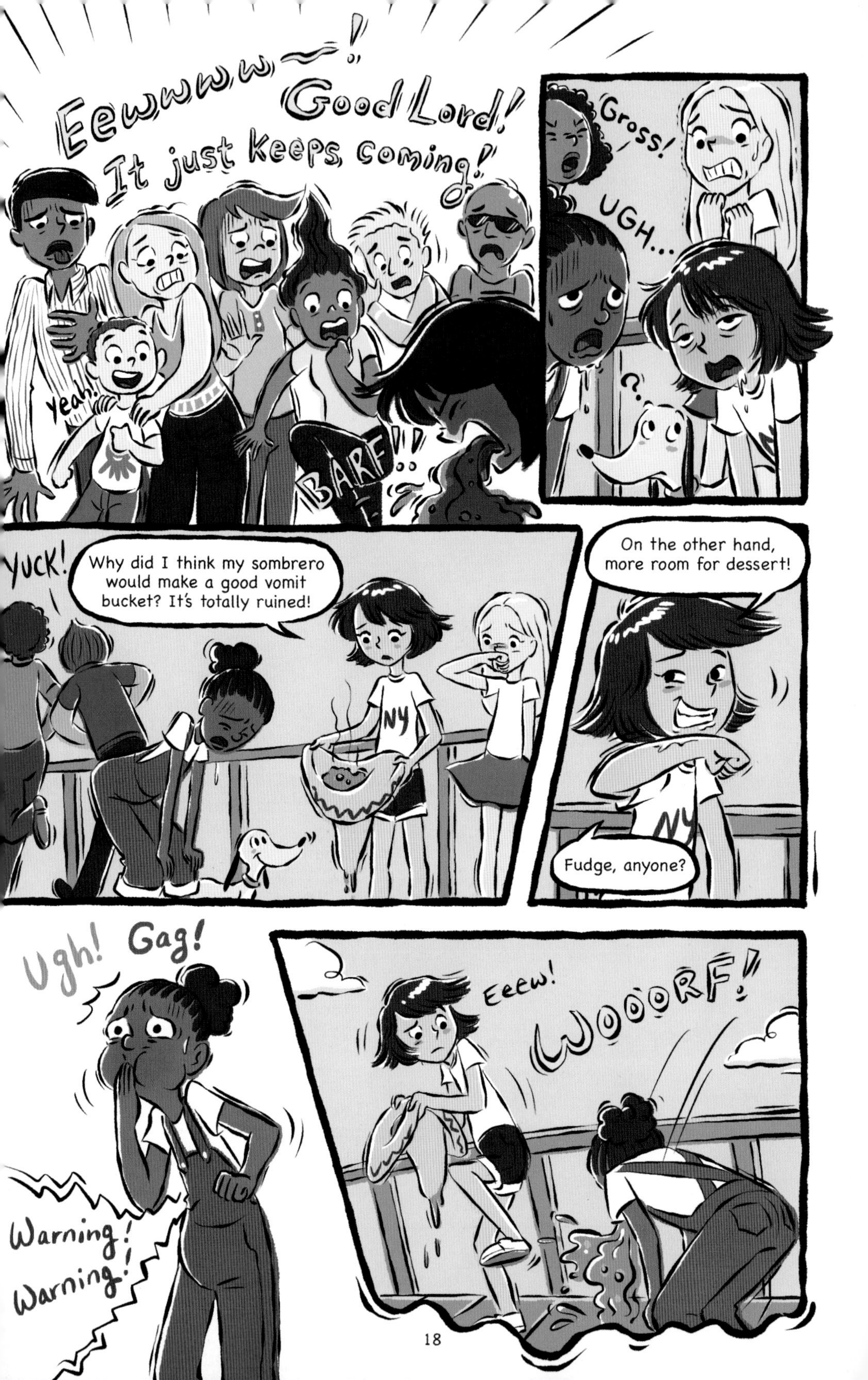

Eewwww~~!
Good Lord!
It just keeps coming!
Yeah!
BARF!!
Gross!
UGH...
?
YUCK!
Why did I think my sombrero would make a good vomit bucket? It's totally ruined!
On the other hand, more room for dessert!
Fudge, anyone?
Ugh! Gag!
Warning! Warning!
Eeew!
WOOORF!

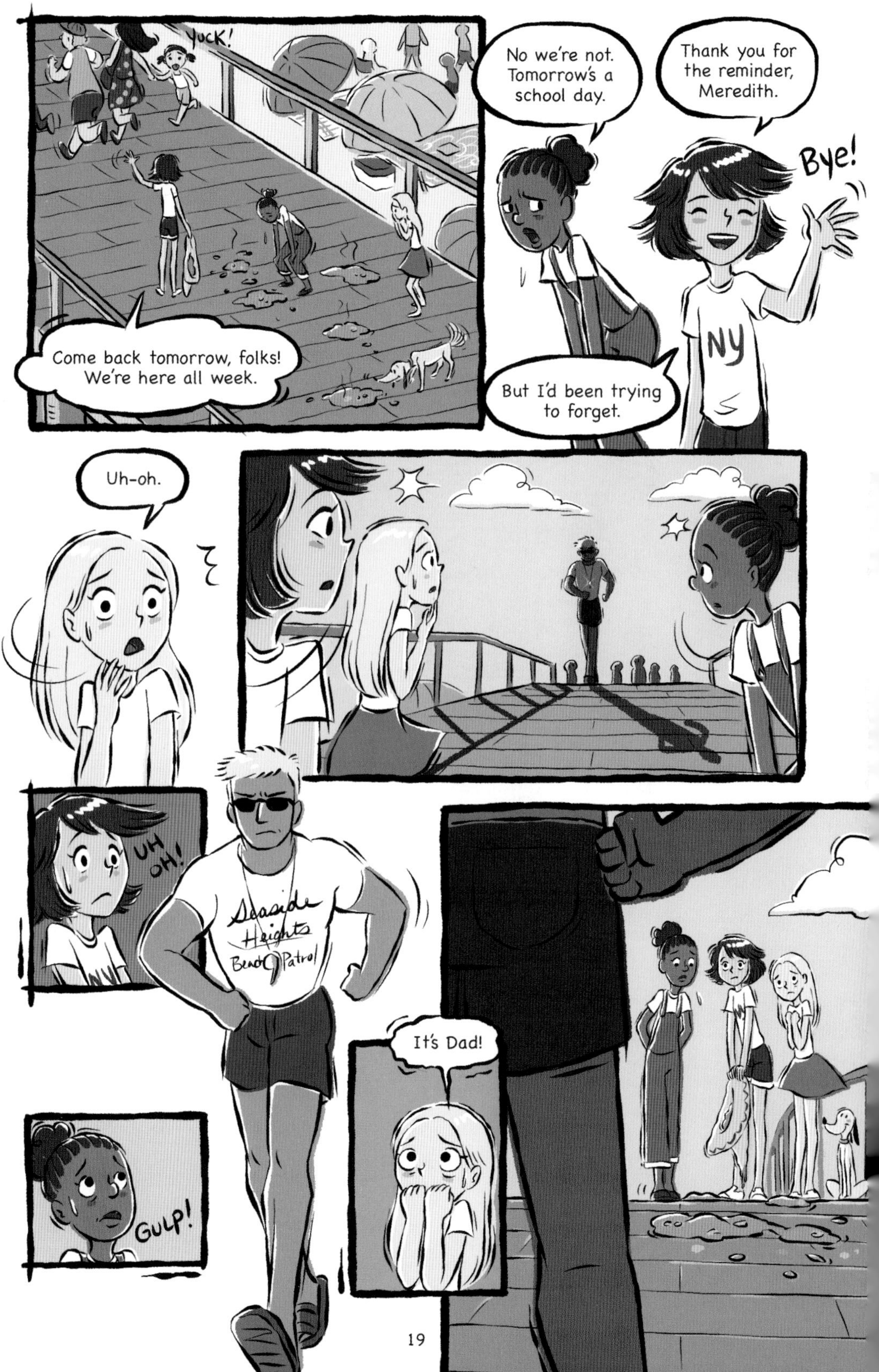
YUCK!
Come back tomorrow, folks! We're here all week.
No we're not. Tomorrow's a school day.
Thank you for the reminder, Meredith.
Bye!
But I'd been trying to forget.
Uh-oh.
UH OH!
Seaside Heights Beach Patrol
GULP!
It's Dad!

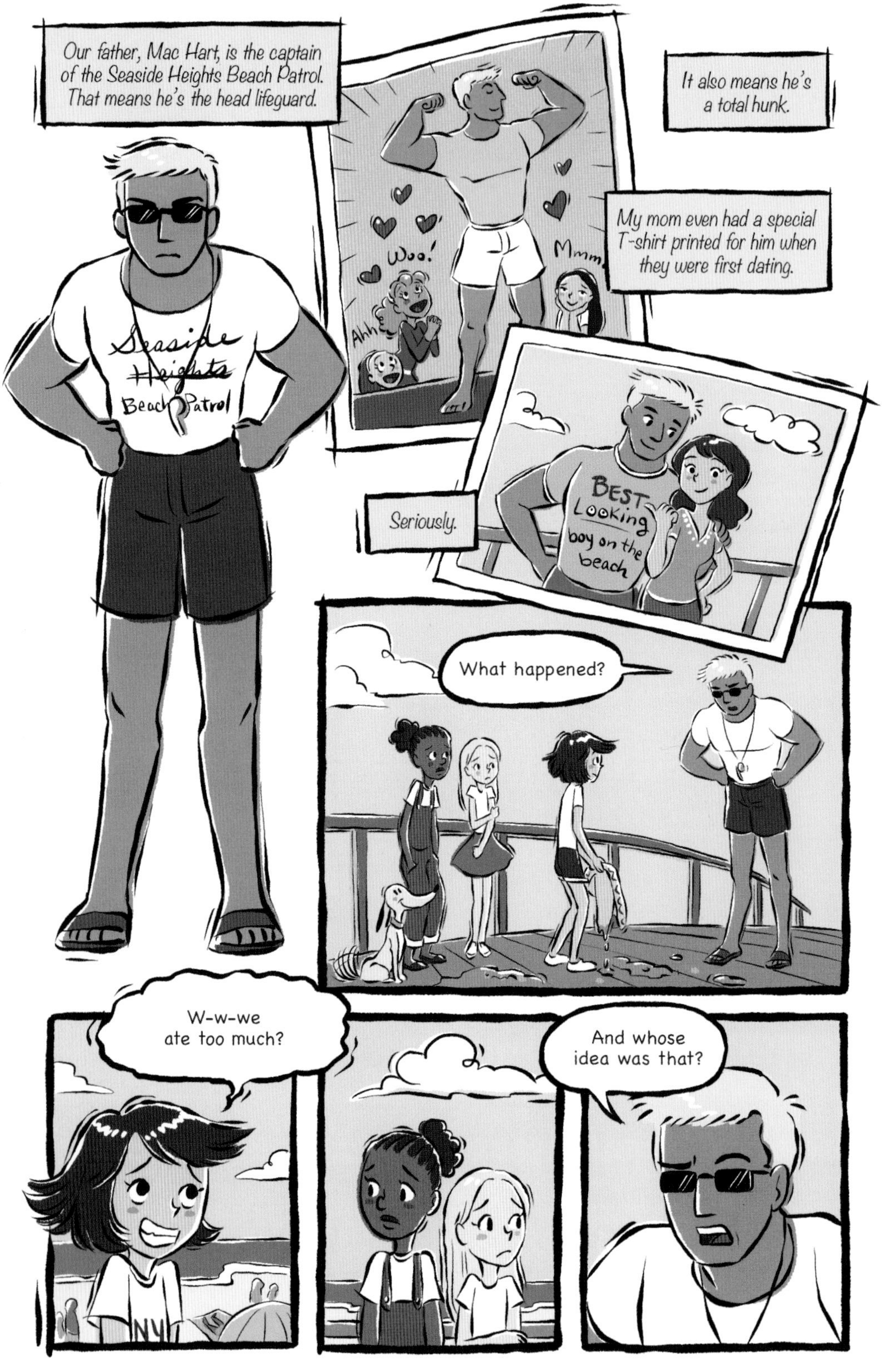
Our father, Mac Hart, is the captain of the Seaside Heights Beach Patrol. That means he's the head lifeguard.
Seaside Heights Beach Patrol
Woo!
Ahh
Mmm
It also means he's a total hunk.
My mom even had a special T-shirt printed for him when they were first dating.
BEST Looking boy on the beach
Seriously.
What happened?
W-w-we ate too much?
And whose idea was that?

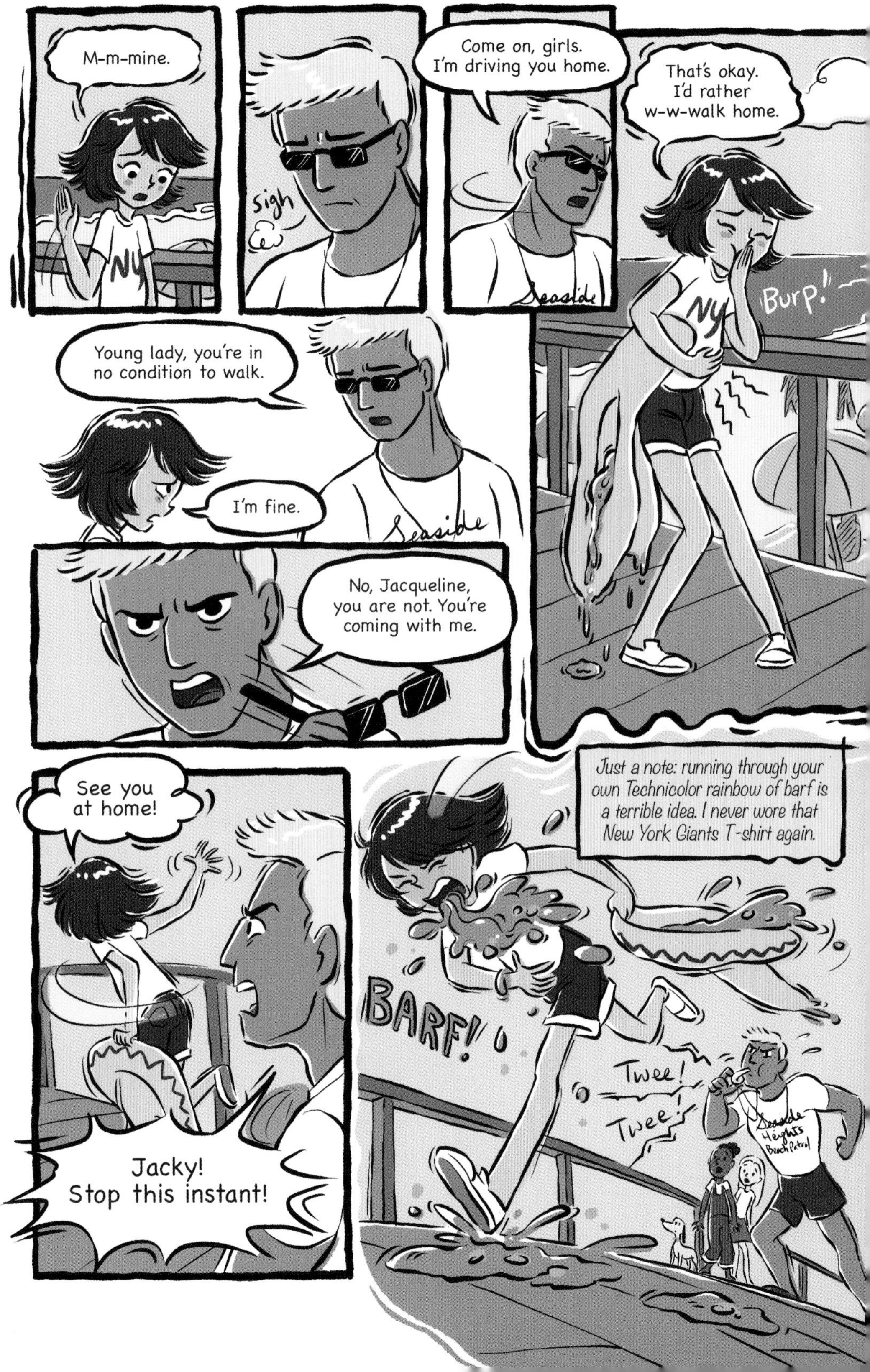
M-m-mine.
Sigh
Come on, girls. I'm driving you home.
Seaside
That's okay. I'd rather w-w-walk home.
Burp!
NY
Young lady, you're in no condition to walk.
I'm fine.
Seaside
No, Jacqueline, you are not. You're coming with me.
See you at home!
Jacky! Stop this instant!
Just a note: running through your own Technicolor rainbow of barf is a terrible idea. I never wore that New York Giants T-shirt again.
BARF!
Twee!
Twee!
Seaside Heights Beach Patrol

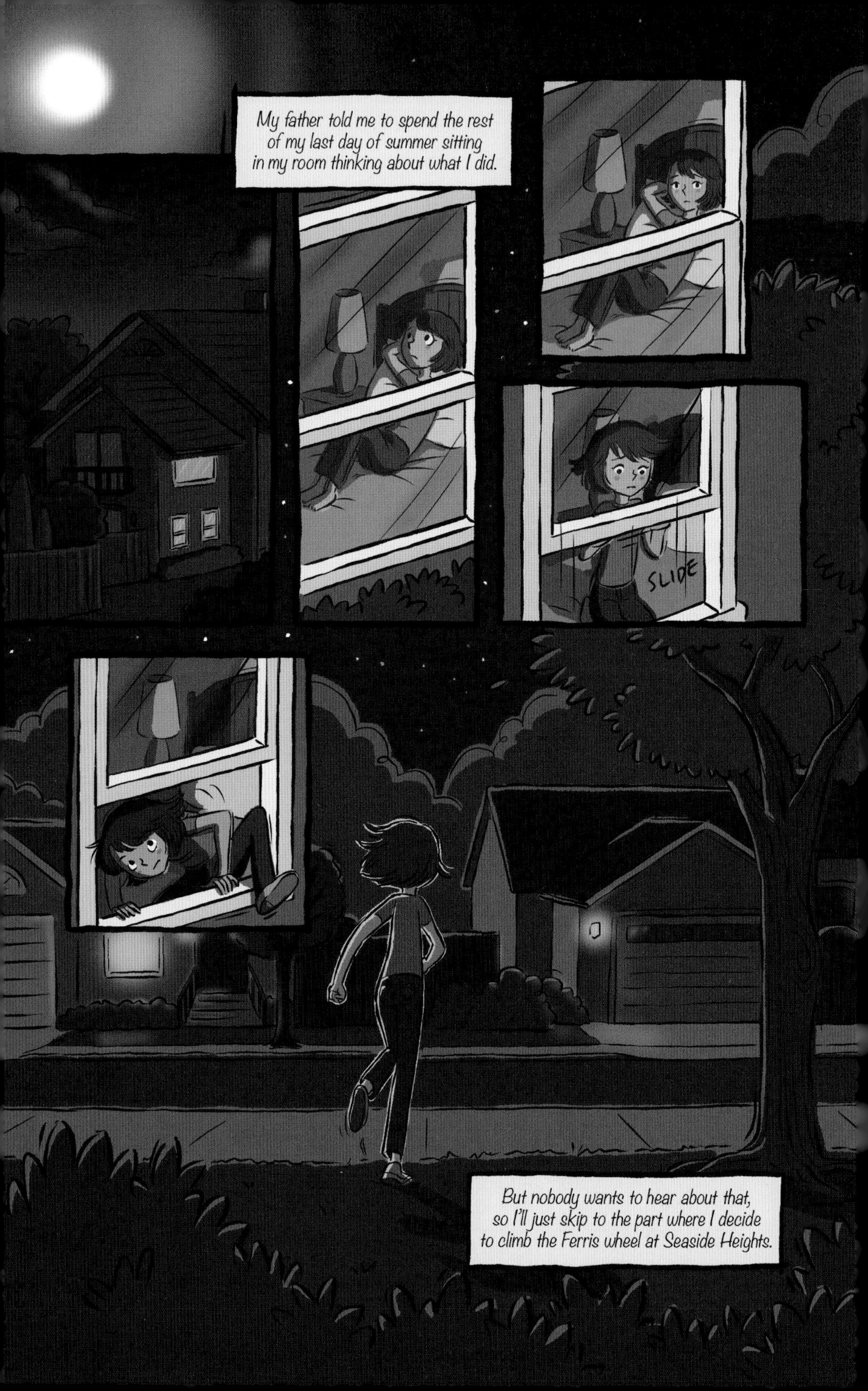
My father told me to spend the rest of my last day of summer sitting in my room thinking about what I did.
SLIDE
But nobody wants to hear about that, so I'll just skip to the part where I decide to climb the Ferris wheel at Seaside Heights.

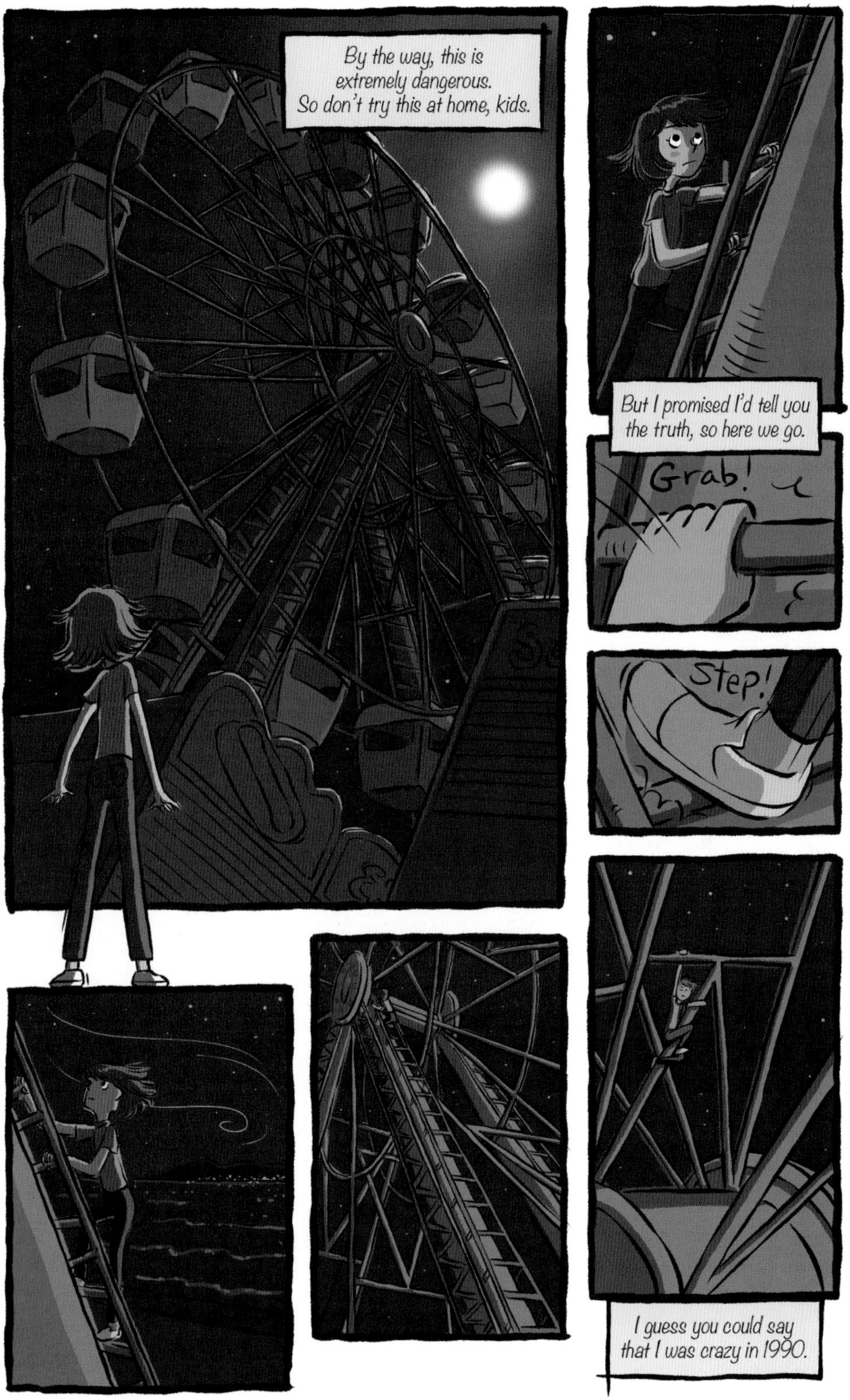

By the way, this is extremely dangerous. So don't try this at home, kids.
But I promised I'd tell you the truth, so here we go.
Grab!
Step!
I guess you could say that I was crazy in 1990.

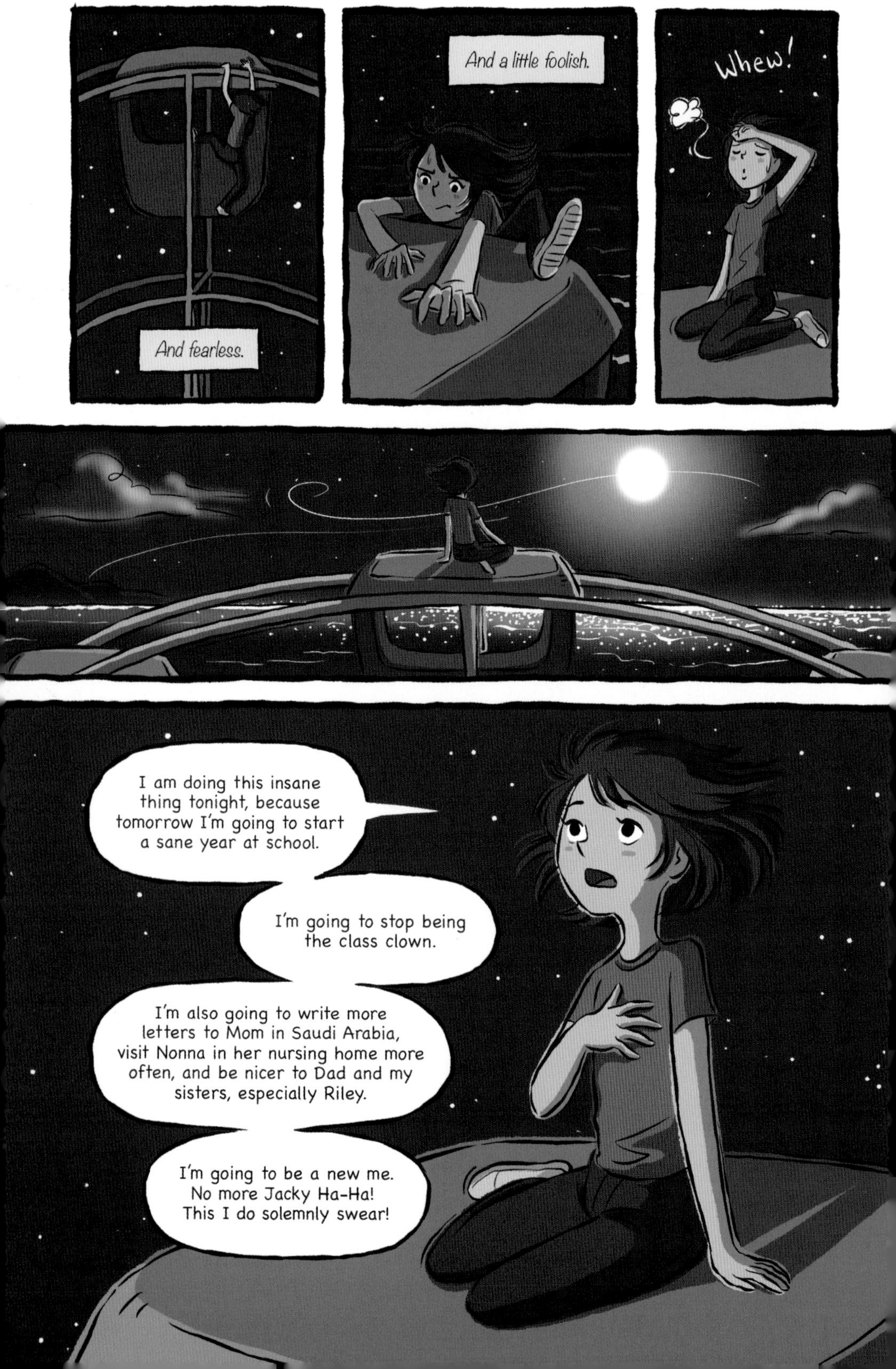
And fearless.
And a little foolish.
Whew!
I am doing this insane thing tonight, because tomorrow I'm going to start a sane year at school.
I'm going to stop being the class clown.
I'm also going to write more letters to Mom in Saudi Arabia, visit Nonna in her nursing home more often, and be nicer to Dad and my sisters, especially Riley.
I'm going to be a new me. No more Jacky Ha-Ha! This I do solemnly swear!

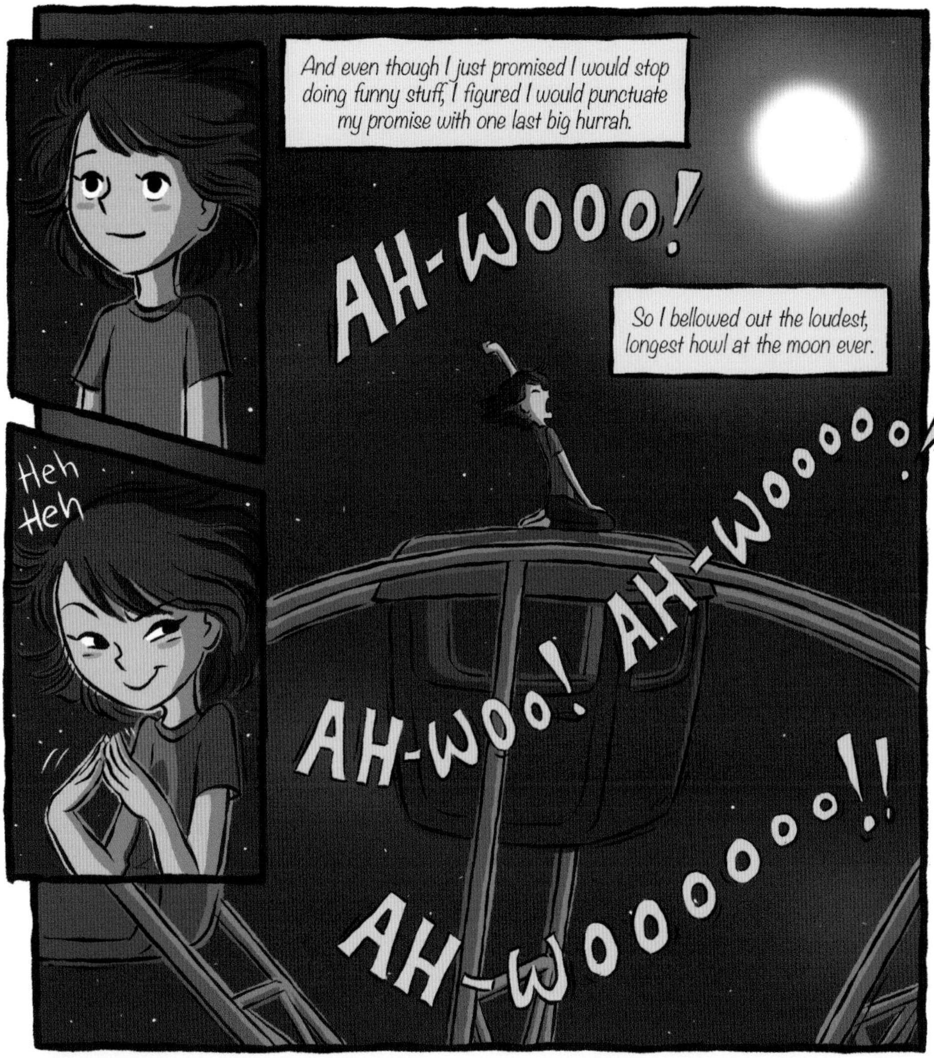
And even though I just promised I would stop doing funny stuff, I figured I would punctuate my promise with one last big hurrah.
Heh Heh
AH-WOOO!
So I bellowed out the loudest, longest howl at the moon ever.
AH-WOO! AH-WOOOOOO!
AH-WOOOOOOOO!!

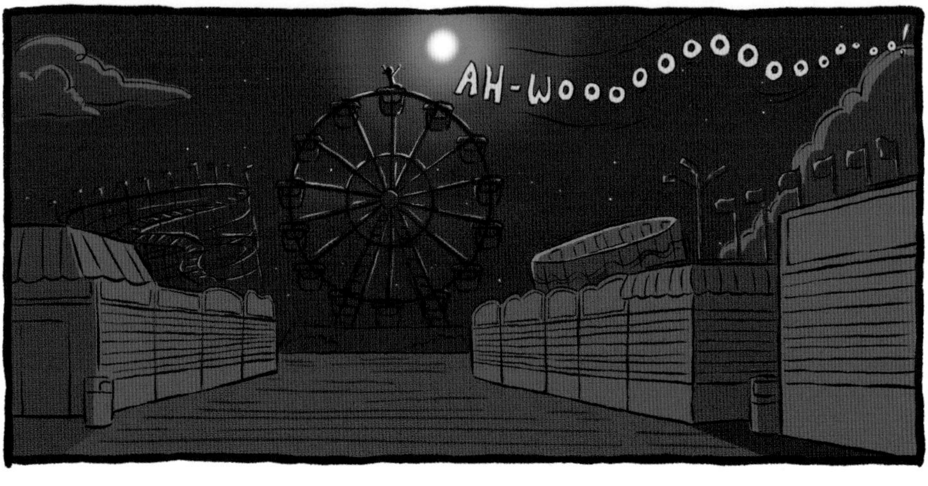
AH-WOOOOOOOOOOOOOOO!

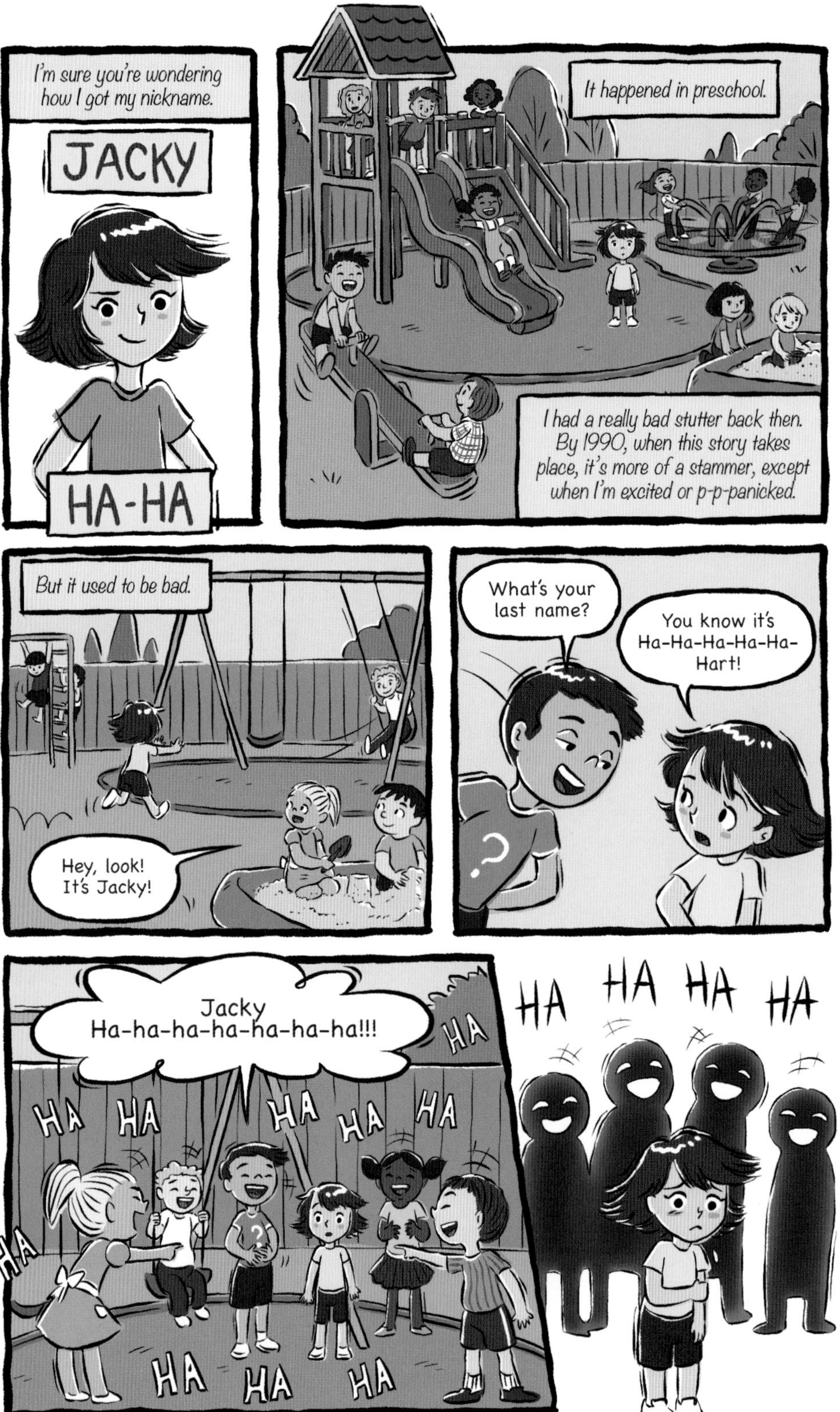
I'm sure you're wondering how I got my nickname.
JACKY
HA-HA
It happened in preschool.
I had a really bad stutter back then. By 1990, when this story takes place, it's more of a stammer, except when I'm excited or p-p-panicked.
But it used to be bad.
Hey, look! It's Jacky!
What's your last name?
You know it's Ha-Ha-Ha-Ha-Ha-Hart!
Jacky Ha-ha-ha-ha-ha-ha-ha!!!
HA HA HA HA HA HA HA HA HA HA HA HA
HA HA HA HA

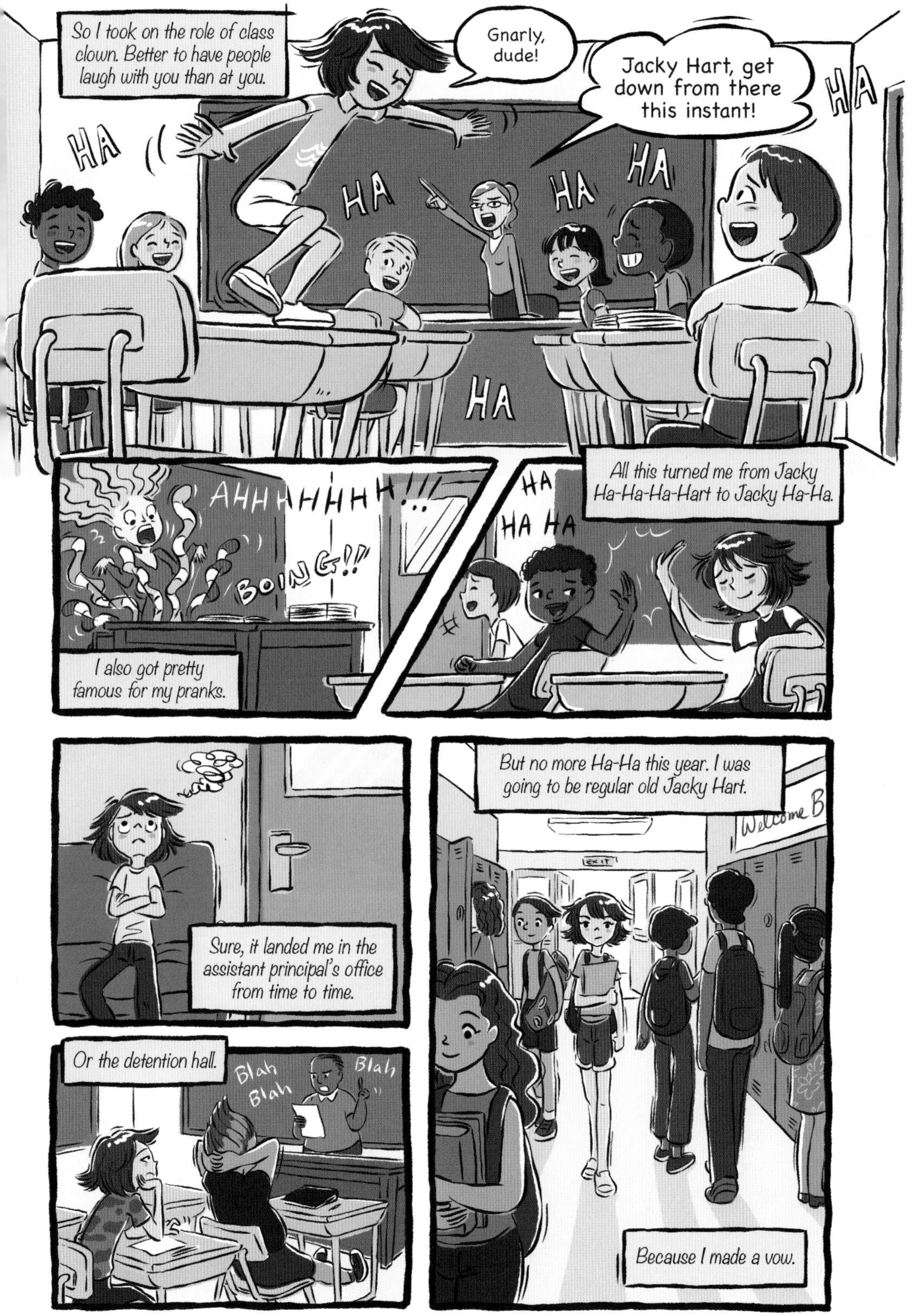

So I took on the role of class clown. Better to have people laugh with you than at you.
Gnarly, dude!
Jacky Hart, get down from there this instant!
HA
HA
HA
HA
HA
HA
HA
AHHHHHHHH!!!
BOING!!
I also got pretty famous for my pranks.
HA
HA HA
All this turned me from Jacky Ha-Ha-Ha-Hart to Jacky Ha-Ha.
Sure, it landed me in the assistant principal's office from time to time.
Or the detention hall.
Blah
Blah
Blah
But no more Ha-Ha this year. I was going to be regular old Jacky Hart.
EXIT
Because I made a vow.

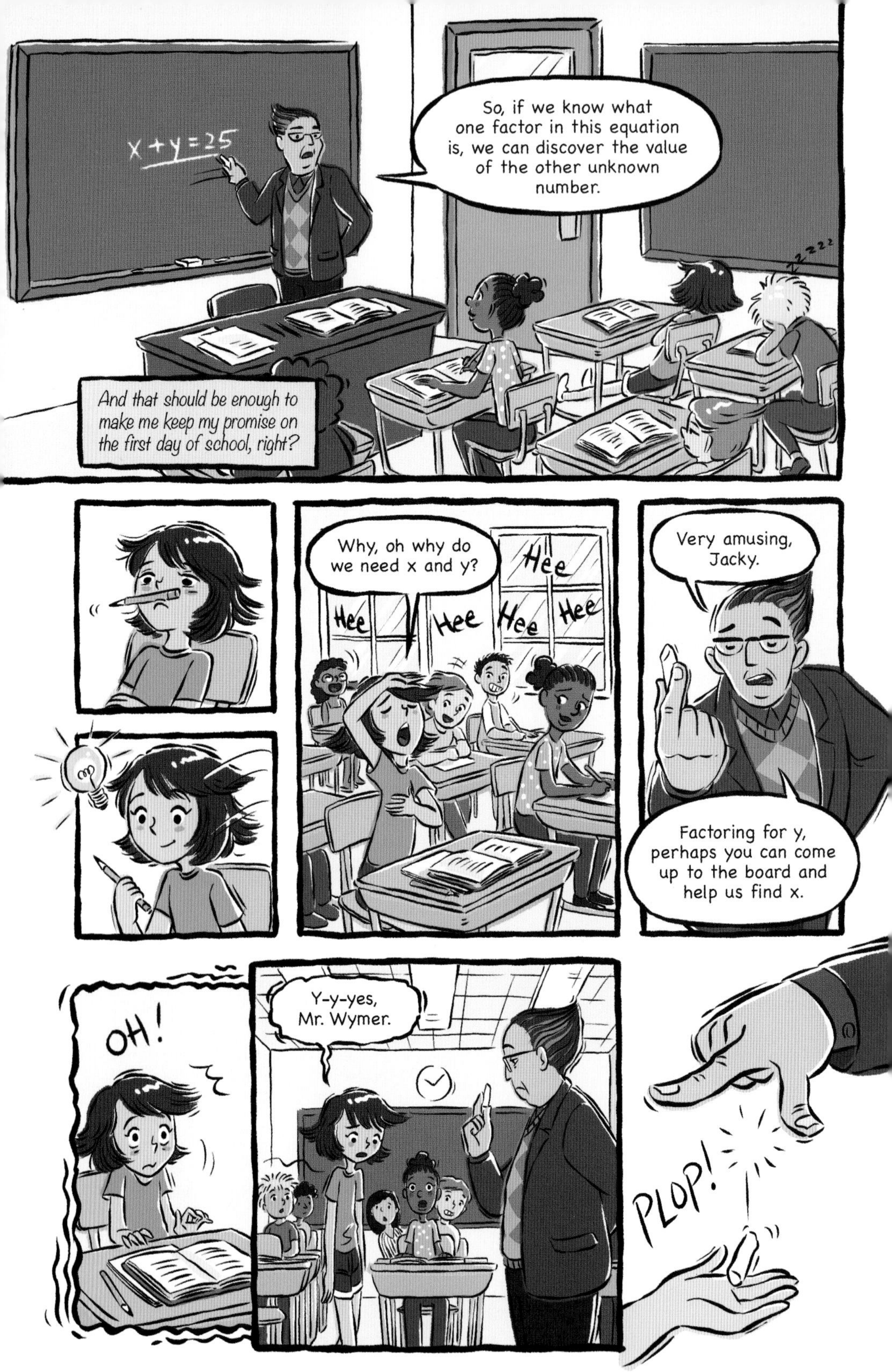

x + y = 25
So, if we know what one factor in this equation is, we can discover the value of the other unknown number.
And that should be enough to make me keep my promise on the first day of school, right?
Why, oh why do we need x and y?
Hee
Hee
Hee
Hee
Hee
Very amusing, Jacky.
Factoring for y, perhaps you can come up to the board and help us find x.
OH!
Y-y-yes, Mr. Wymer.
PLOP!

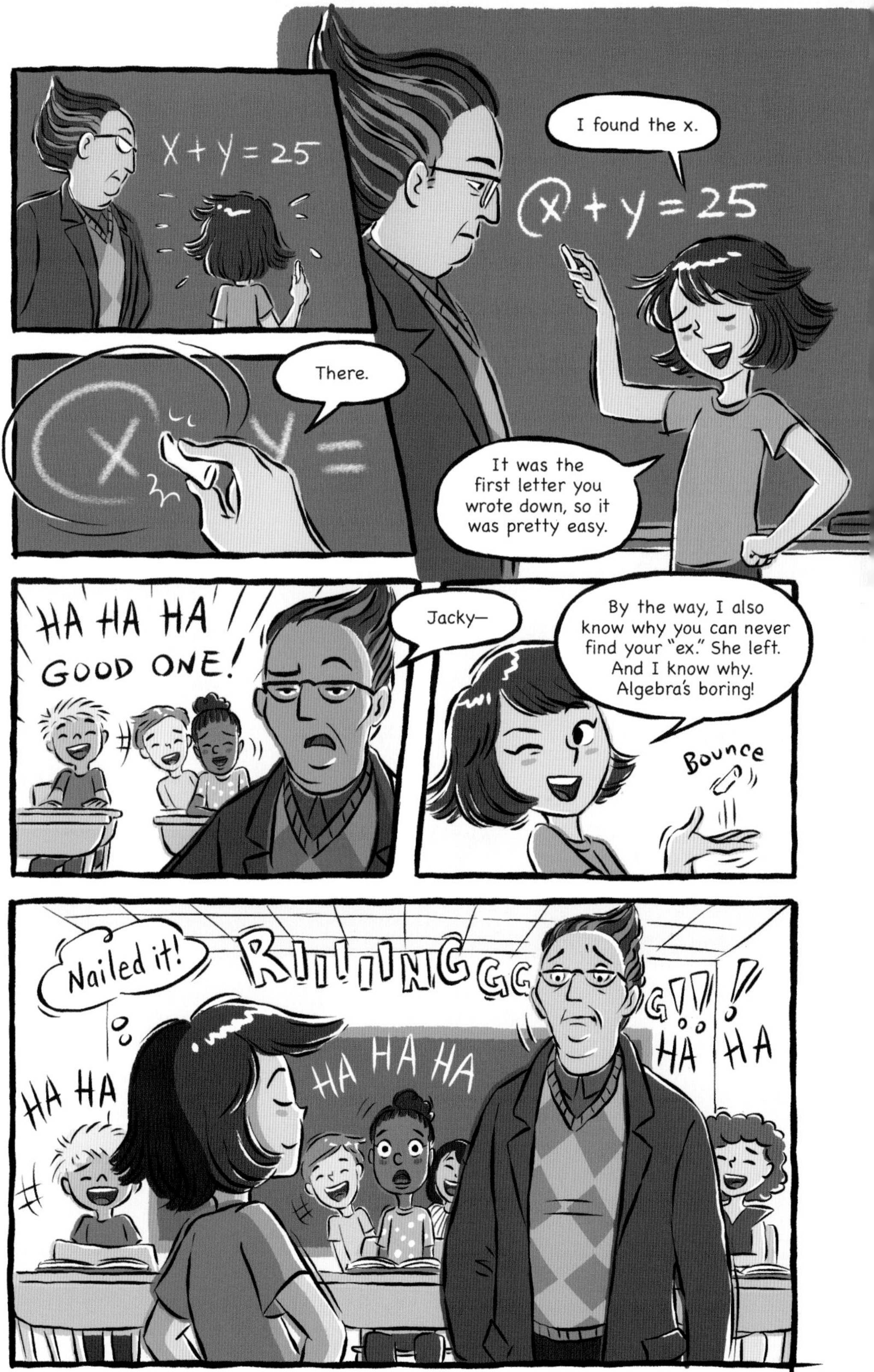
X + y = 25
I found the x.
There.
It was the first letter you wrote down, so it was pretty easy.
HA HA HA
GOOD ONE!
Jacky—
By the way, I also know why you can never find your "ex." She left. And I know why. Algebra's boring!
Bounce
Nailed it!
RIIIINGGGG!!!
HA HA
HA HA HA
HA HA

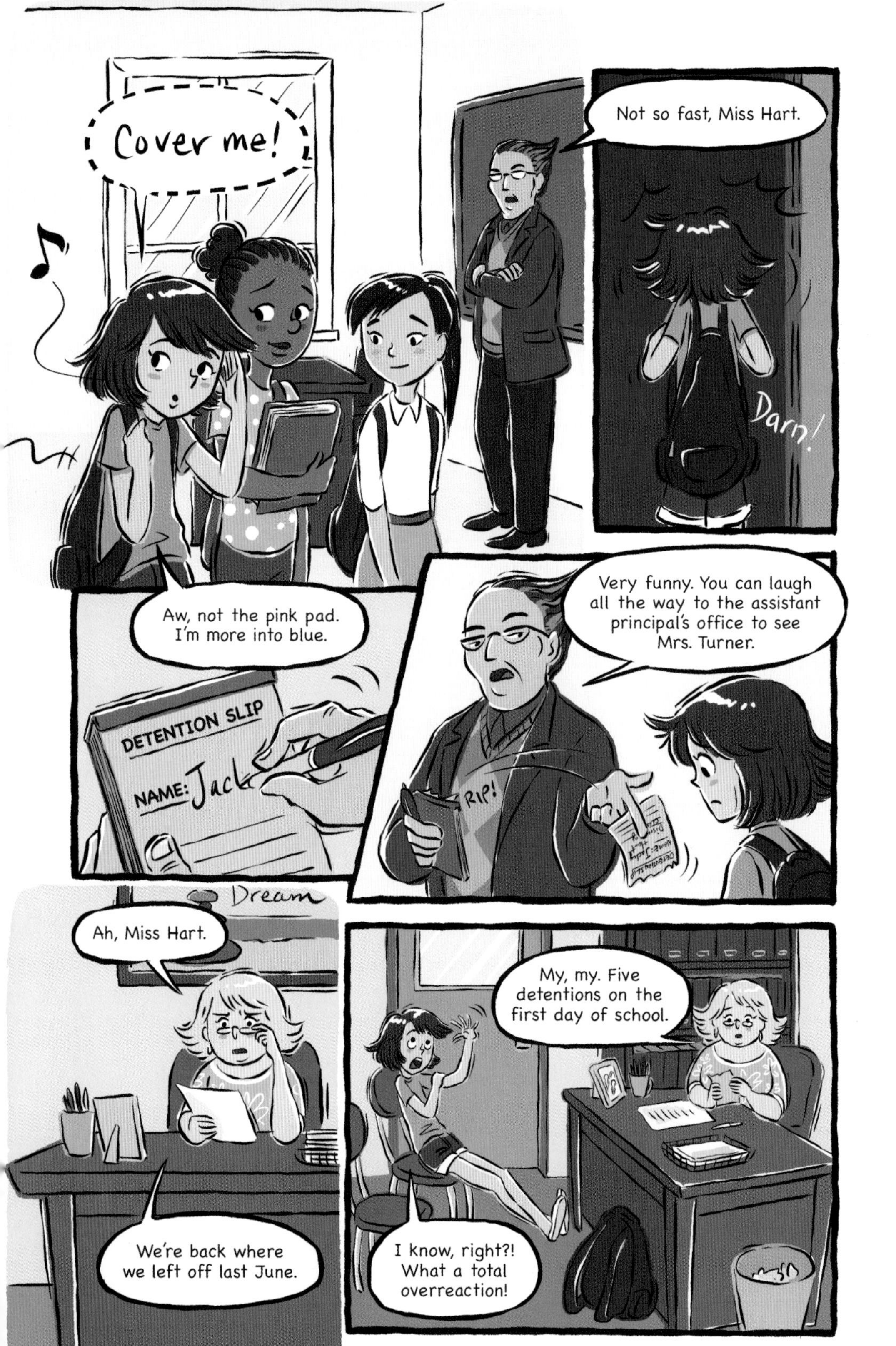
Cover me!
Not so fast, Miss Hart.
Darn!
Aw, not the pink pad.
I'm more into blue.
DETENTION SLIP
NAME: Jack
Very funny. You can laugh all the way to the assistant principal's office to see Mrs. Turner.
RIP!
Dream
Ah, Miss Hart.
We're back where we left off last June.
My, my. Five detentions on the first day of school.
I know, right?! What a total overreaction!

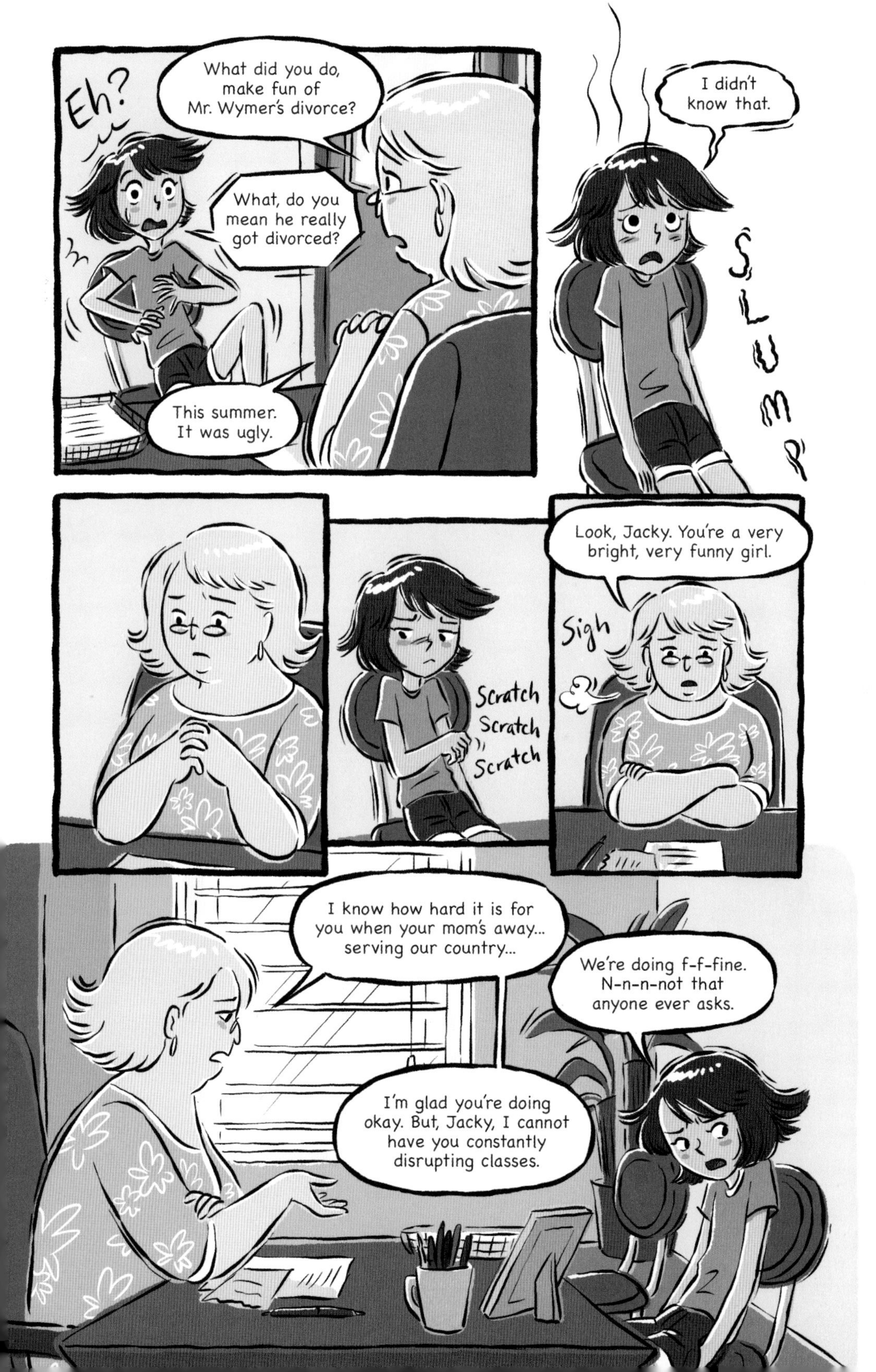
Eh?
What did you do, make fun of Mr. Wymer's divorce?
What, do you mean he really got divorced?
This summer. It was ugly.
I didn't know that.
SLUMP
Scratch
Scratch
Scratch
Look, Jacky. You're a very bright, very funny girl.
Sigh
I know how hard it is for you when your mom's away... serving our country...
We're doing f-f-fine. N-n-n-not that anyone ever asks.
I'm glad you're doing okay. But, Jacky, I cannot have you constantly disrupting classes.

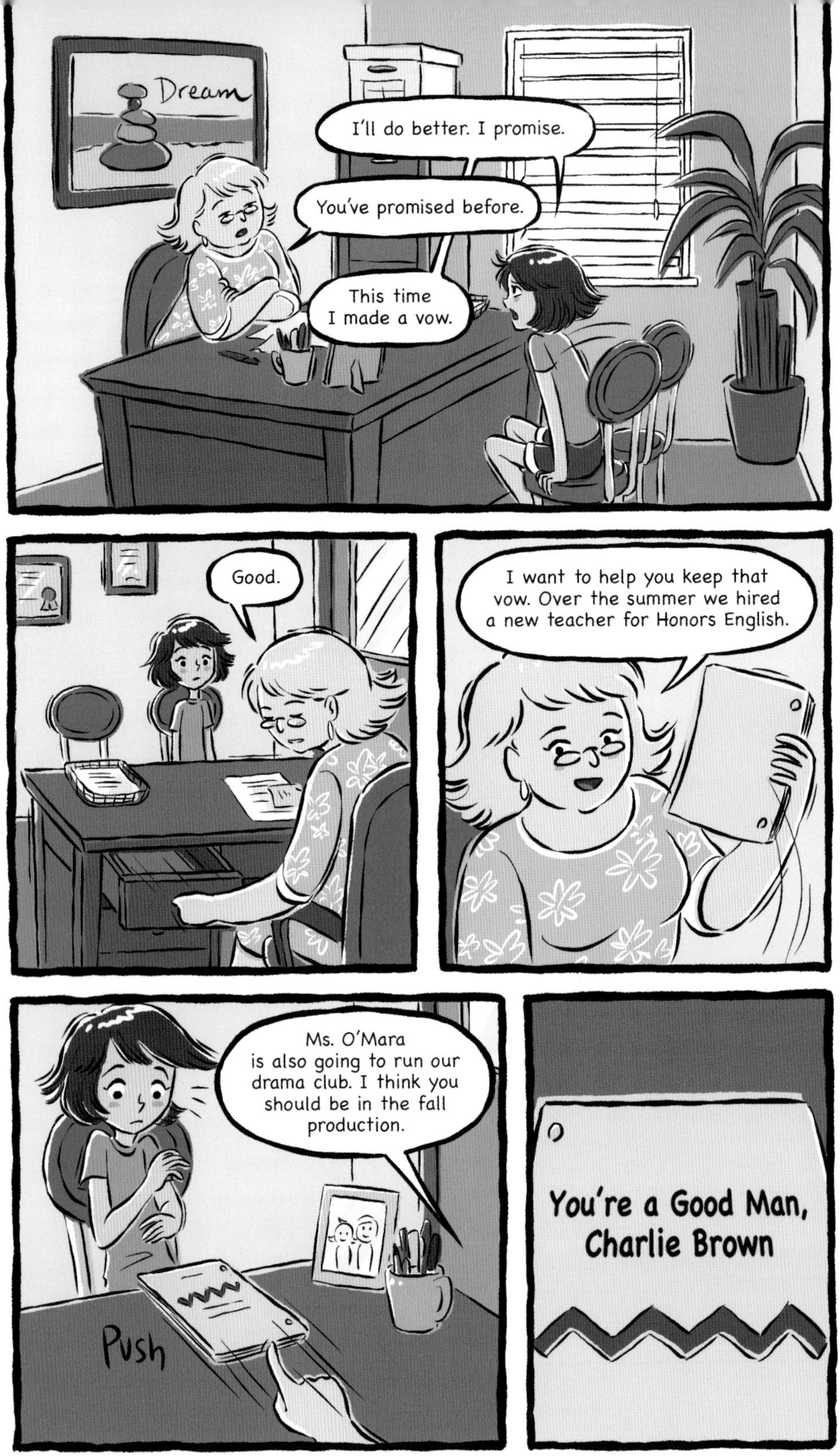
Dream
I'll do better. I promise.
You've promised before.
This time I made a vow.
Good.
I want to help you keep that vow. Over the summer we hired a new teacher for Honors English.
Ms. O'Mara is also going to run our drama club. I think you should be in the fall production.
Push
You're a Good Man, Charlie Brown

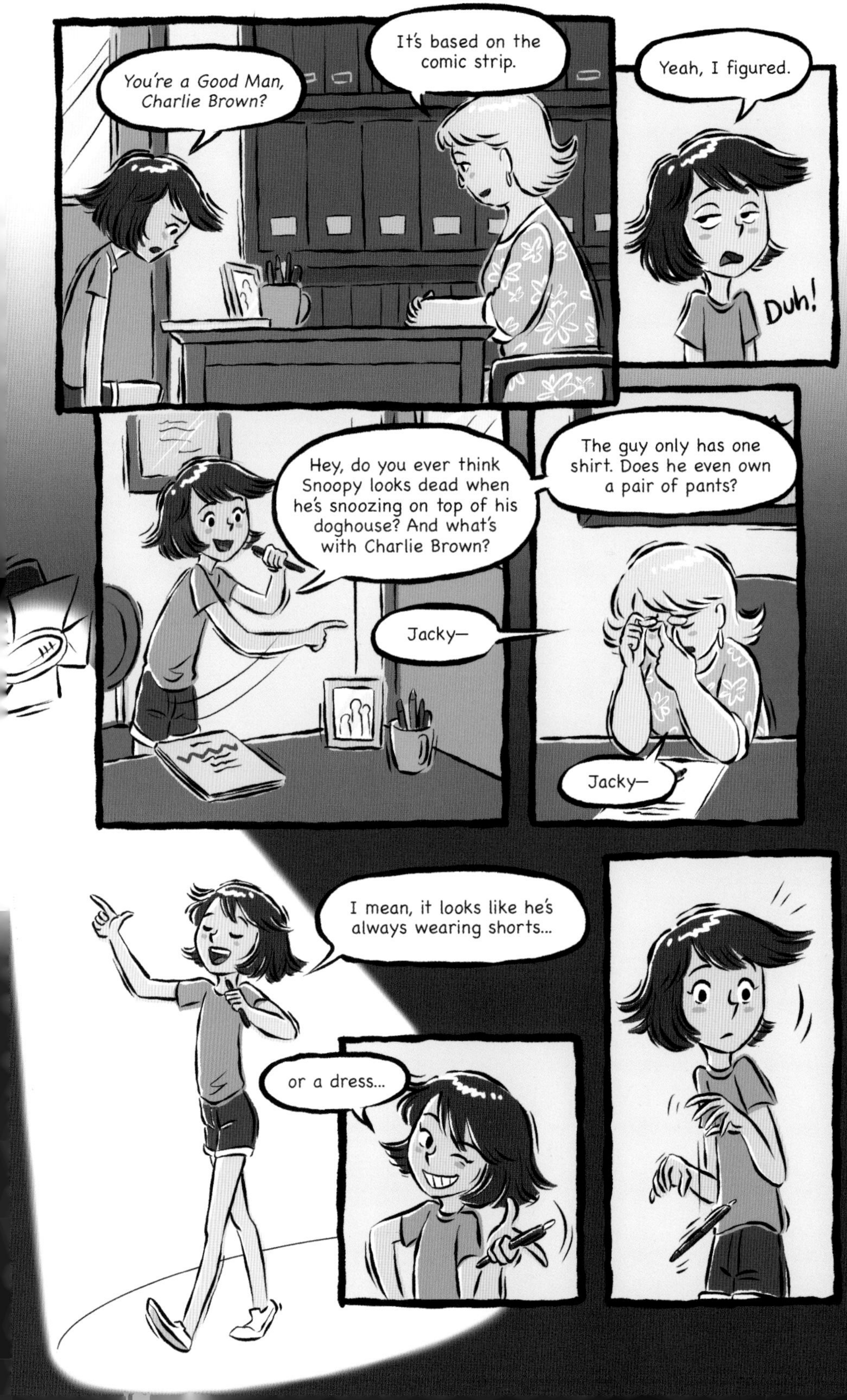
You're a Good Man, Charlie Brown?
It's based on the comic strip.
Yeah, I figured.
Duh!
Hey, do you ever think Snoopy looks dead when he's snoozing on top of his doghouse? And what's with Charlie Brown?
The guy only has one shirt. Does he even own a pair of pants?
Jacky—
Jacky—
I mean, it looks like he's always wearing shorts...
or a dress...

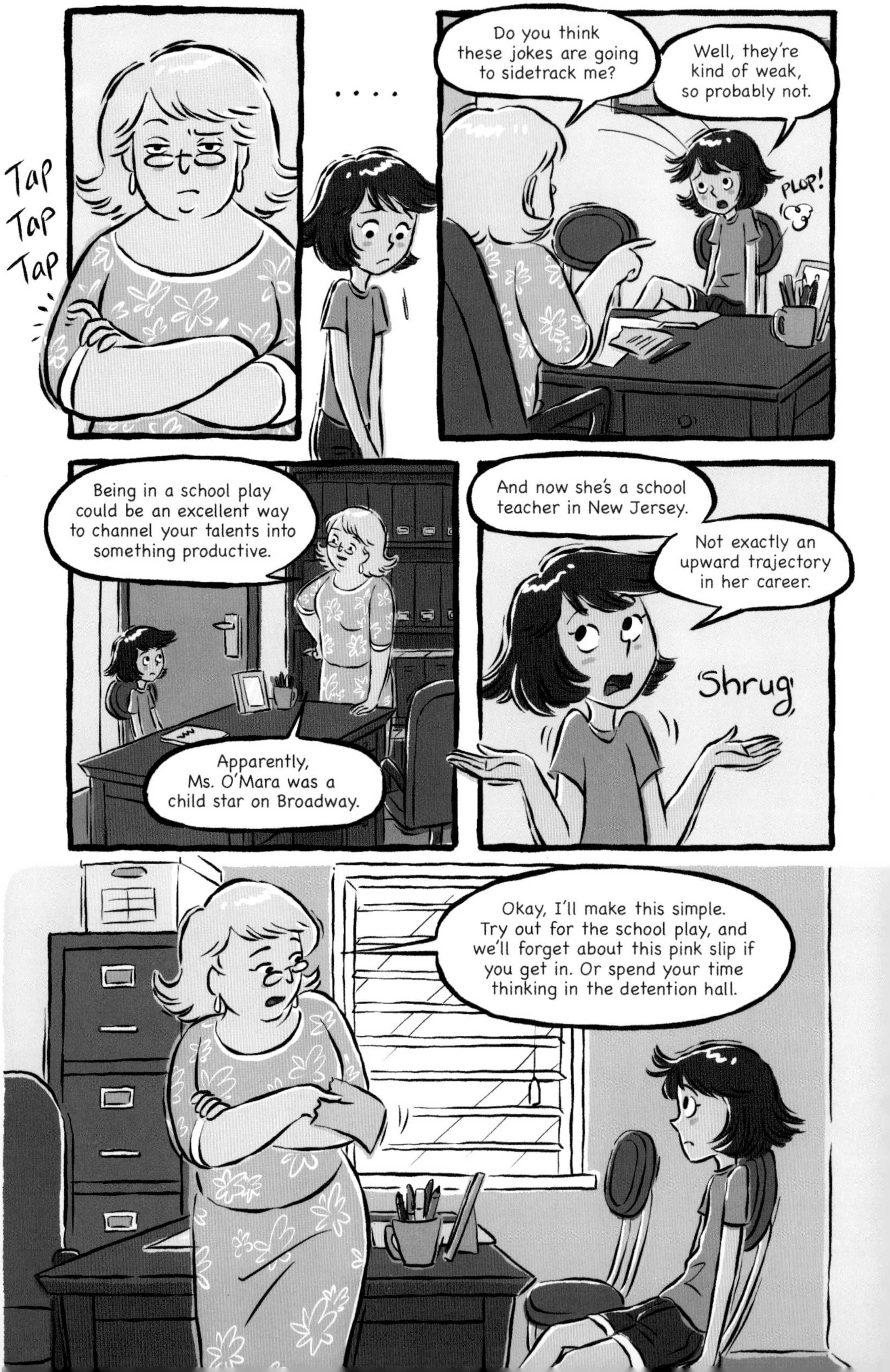
Tap
Tap
Tap
. . . .
Do you think these jokes are going to sidetrack me?
Well, they're kind of weak, so probably not.
PLOP!
Being in a school play could be an excellent way to channel your talents into something productive.
Apparently, Ms. O'Mara was a child star on Broadway.
And now she's a school teacher in New Jersey.
Not exactly an upward trajectory in her career.
Shrug
Okay, I'll make this simple. Try out for the school play, and we'll forget about this pink slip if you get in. Or spend your time thinking in the detention hall.

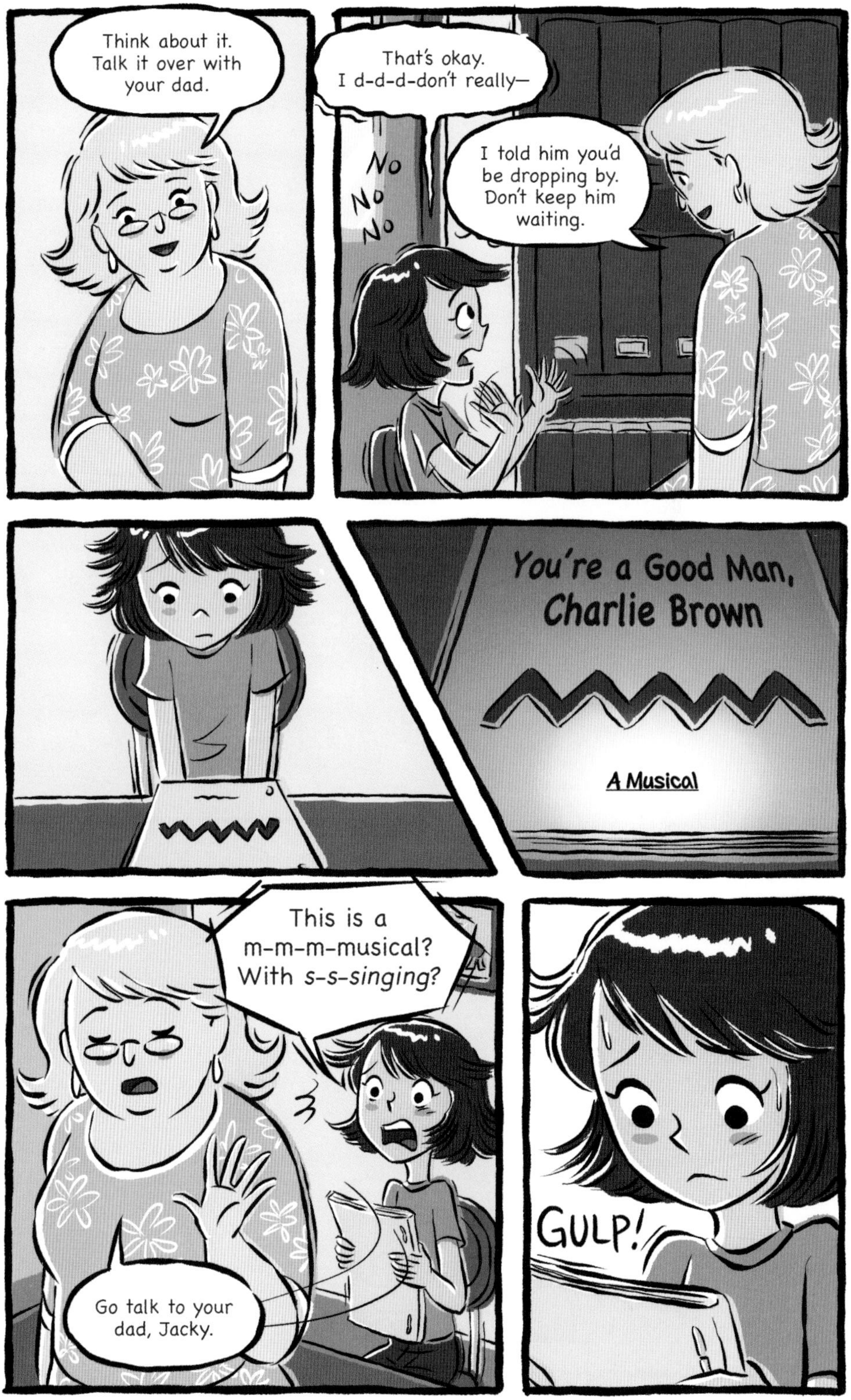

Think about it. Talk it over with your dad.
That's okay. I d-d-d-don't really—
NO NO NO
I told him you'd be dropping by. Don't keep him waiting.
You're a Good Man, Charlie Brown
A Musical
This is a m-m-m-musical? With *s-s-singing*?
Go talk to your dad, Jacky.
GULP!

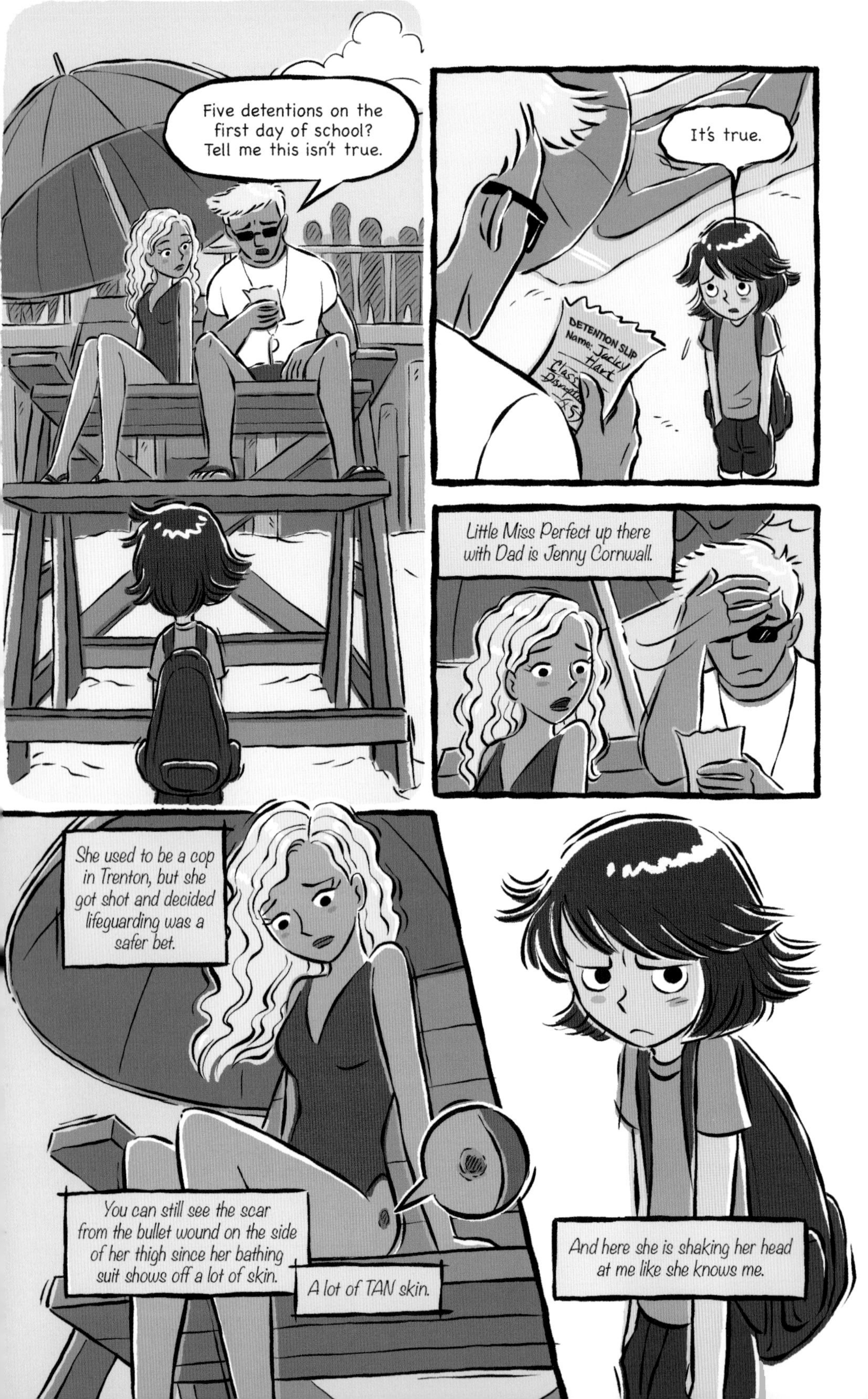
Five detentions on the first day of school? Tell me this isn't true.
It's true.
DETENTION SLIP
Name: Jacky Hart
Class Disruption (x5)
Little Miss Perfect up there with Dad is Jenny Cornwall.
She used to be a cop in Trenton, but she got shot and decided lifeguarding was a safer bet.
You can still see the scar from the bullet wound on the side of her thigh since her bathing suit shows off a lot of skin.
A lot of TAN skin.
And here she is shaking her head at me like she knows me.

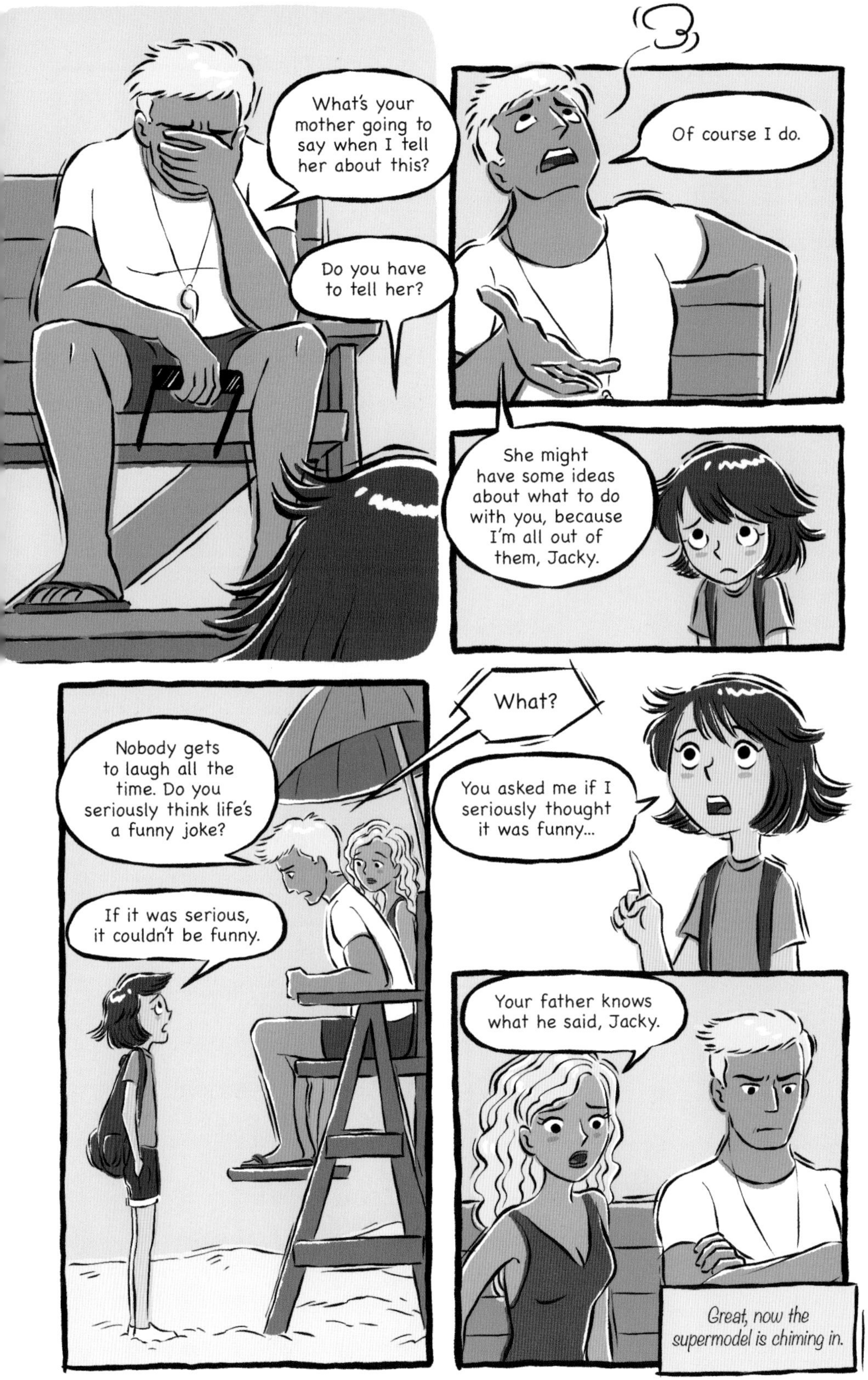
What's your mother going to say when I tell her about this?
Do you have to tell her?
Of course I do.
She might have some ideas about what to do with you, because I'm all out of them, Jacky.
Nobody gets to laugh all the time. Do you seriously think life's a funny joke?
If it was serious, it couldn't be funny.
What?
You asked me if I seriously thought it was funny...
Your father knows what he said, Jacky.
Great, now the supermodel is chiming in.

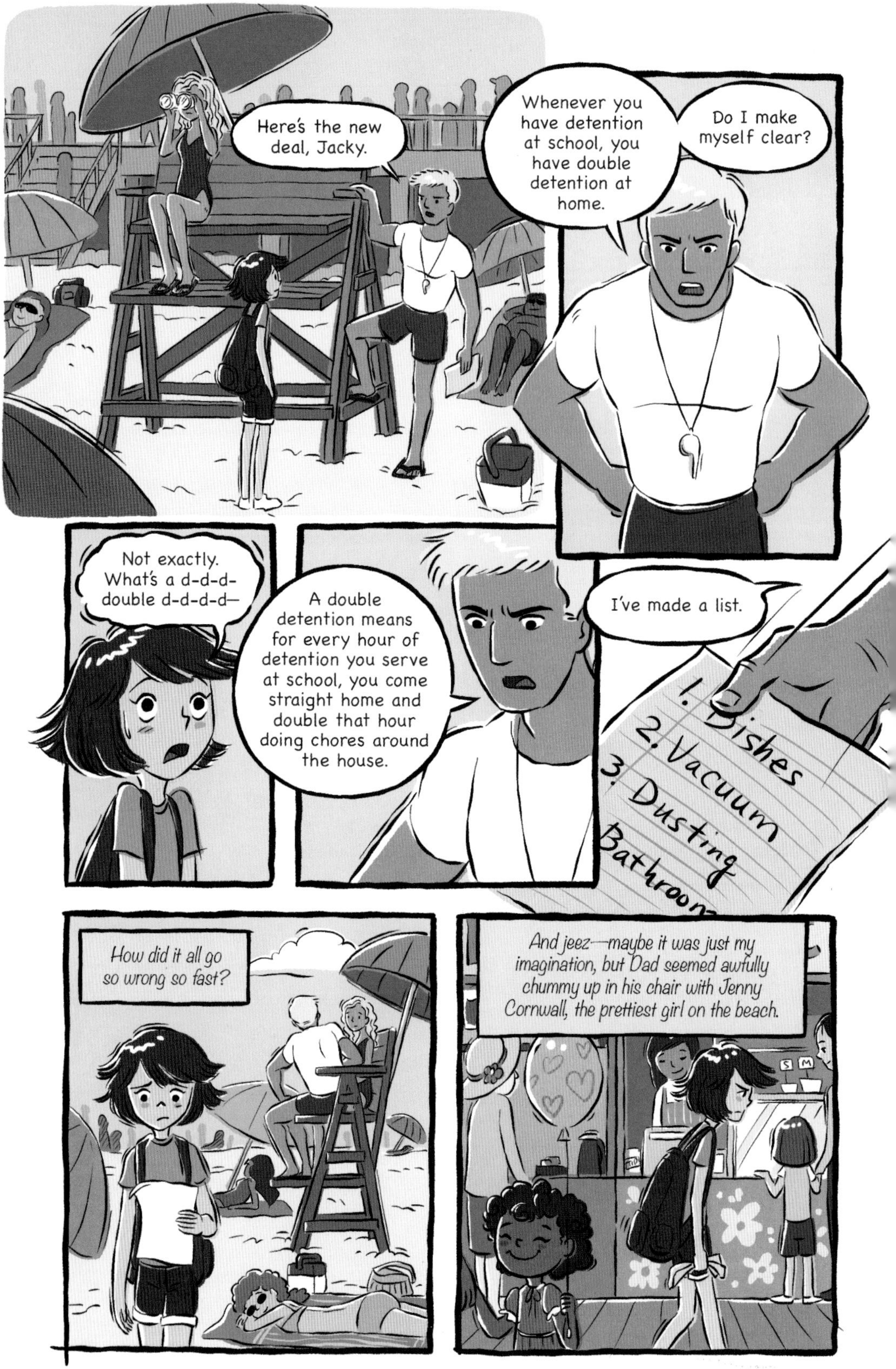

Here's the new deal, Jacky.
Whenever you have detention at school, you have double detention at home.
Do I make myself clear?
Not exactly. What's a d-d-d-double d-d-d-d—
A double detention means for every hour of detention you serve at school, you come straight home and double that hour doing chores around the house.
I've made a list.
1. Dishes
2. Vacuum
3. Dusting
Bathroom
How did it all go so wrong so fast?
And jeez—maybe it was just my imagination, but Dad seemed awfully chummy up in his chair with Jenny Cornwall, the prettiest girl on the beach.

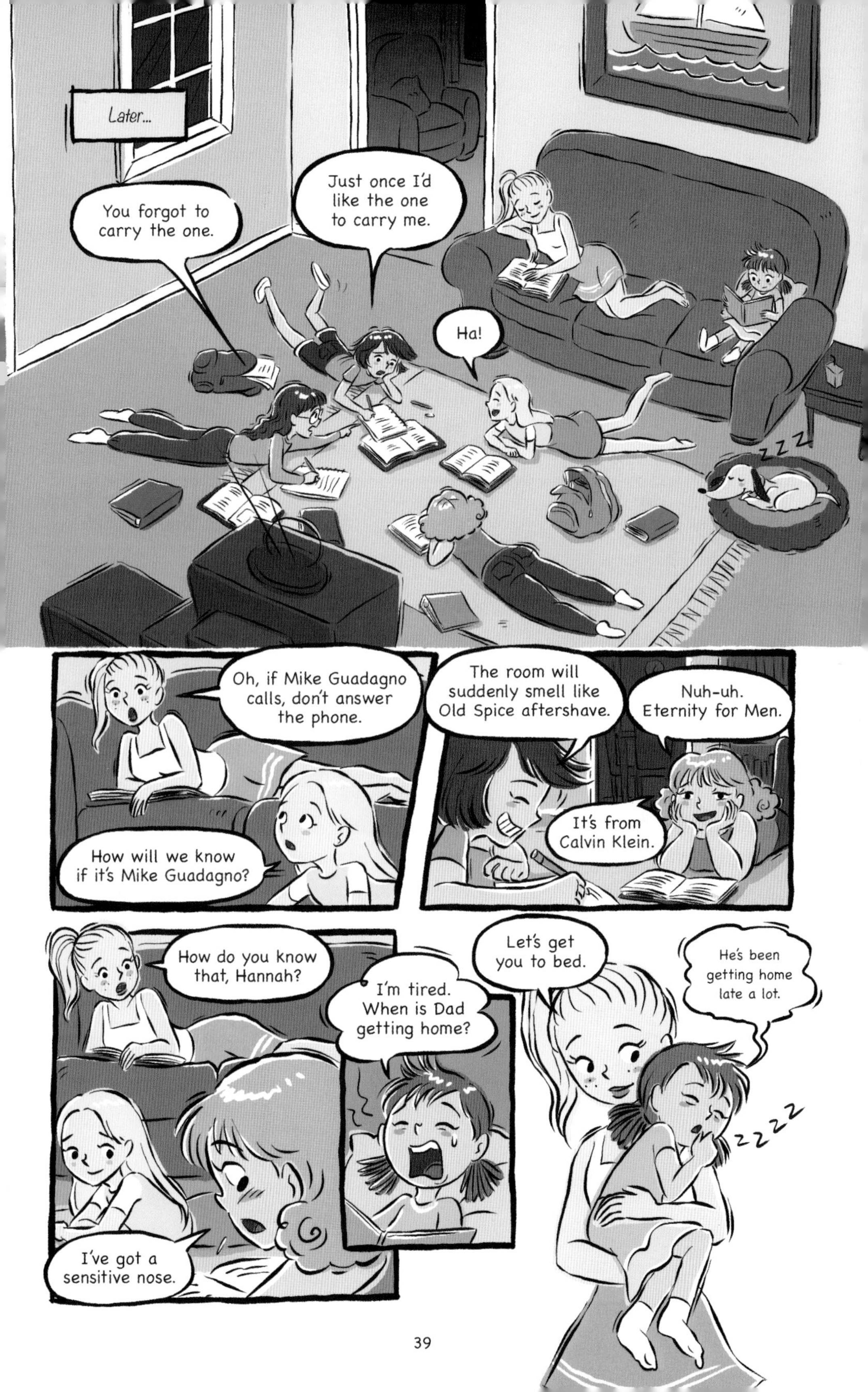
Later...
You forgot to carry the one.
Just once I'd like the one to carry me.
Ha!
Oh, if Mike Guadagno calls, don't answer the phone.
How will we know if it's Mike Guadagno?
The room will suddenly smell like Old Spice aftershave.
Nuh-uh. Eternity for Men.
It's from Calvin Klein.
How do you know that, Hannah?
I've got a sensitive nose.
I'm tired. When is Dad getting home?
Let's get you to bed.
He's been getting home late a lot.
ZZZZ

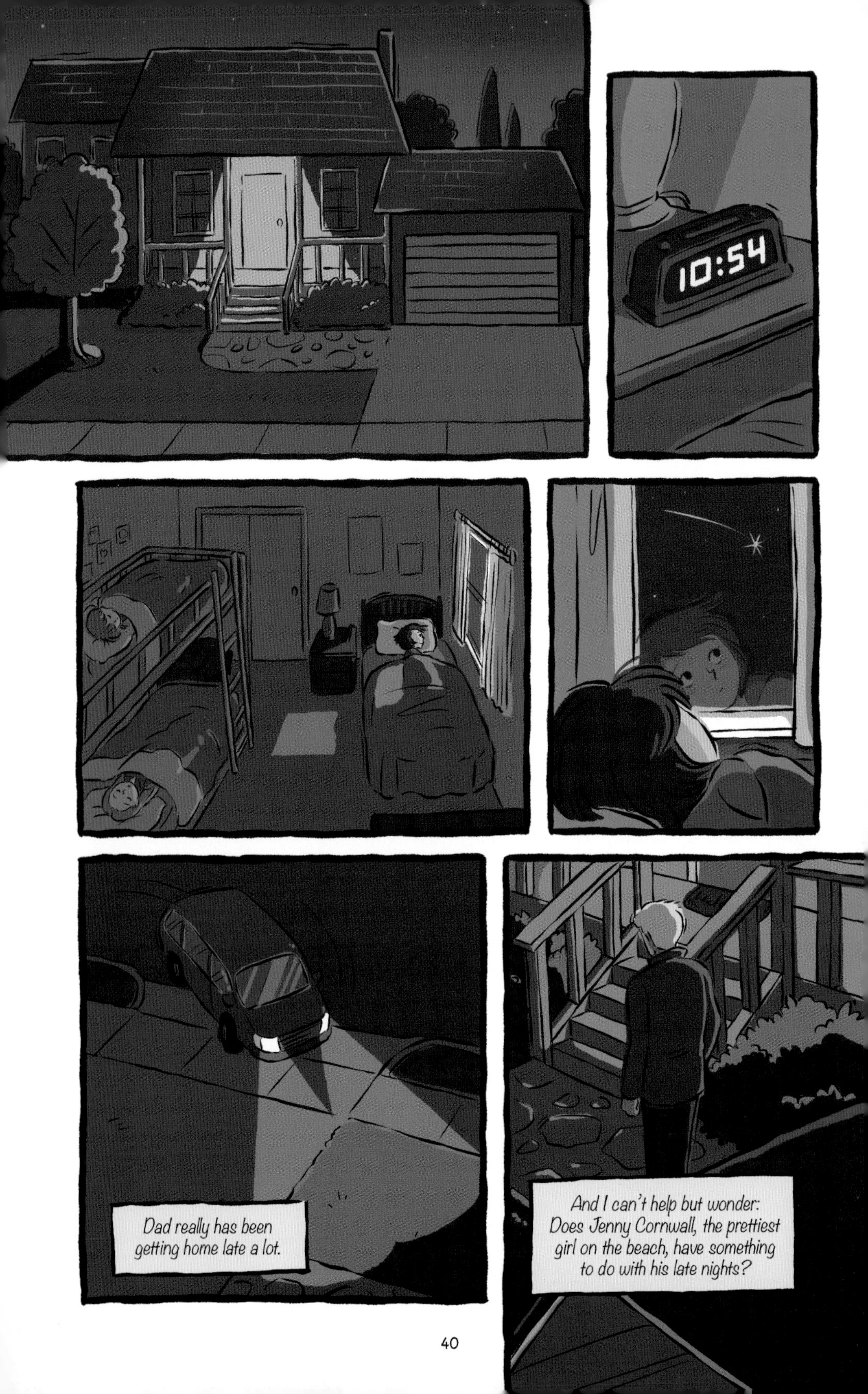
10:54
Dad really has been getting home late a lot.
And I can't help but wonder: Does Jenny Cornwall, the prettiest girl on the beach, have something to do with his late nights?

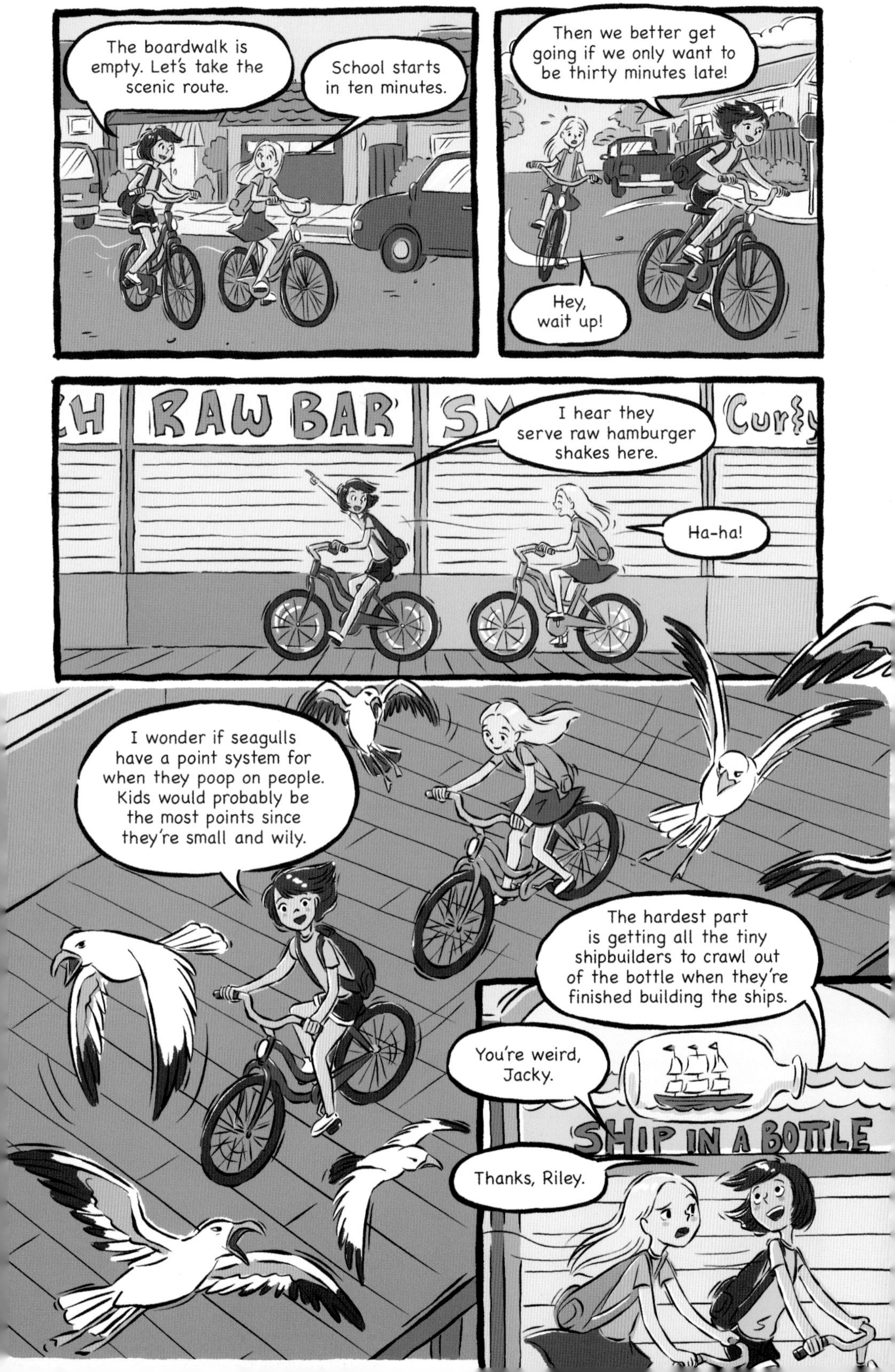
The boardwalk is empty. Let's take the scenic route.
School starts in ten minutes.
Then we better get going if we only want to be thirty minutes late!
Hey, wait up!
RAW BAR
I hear they serve raw hamburger shakes here.
Ha-ha!
I wonder if seagulls have a point system for when they poop on people. Kids would probably be the most points since they're small and wily.
The hardest part is getting all the tiny shipbuilders to crawl out of the bottle when they're finished building the ships.
You're weird, Jacky.
SHIP IN A BOTTLE
Thanks, Riley.

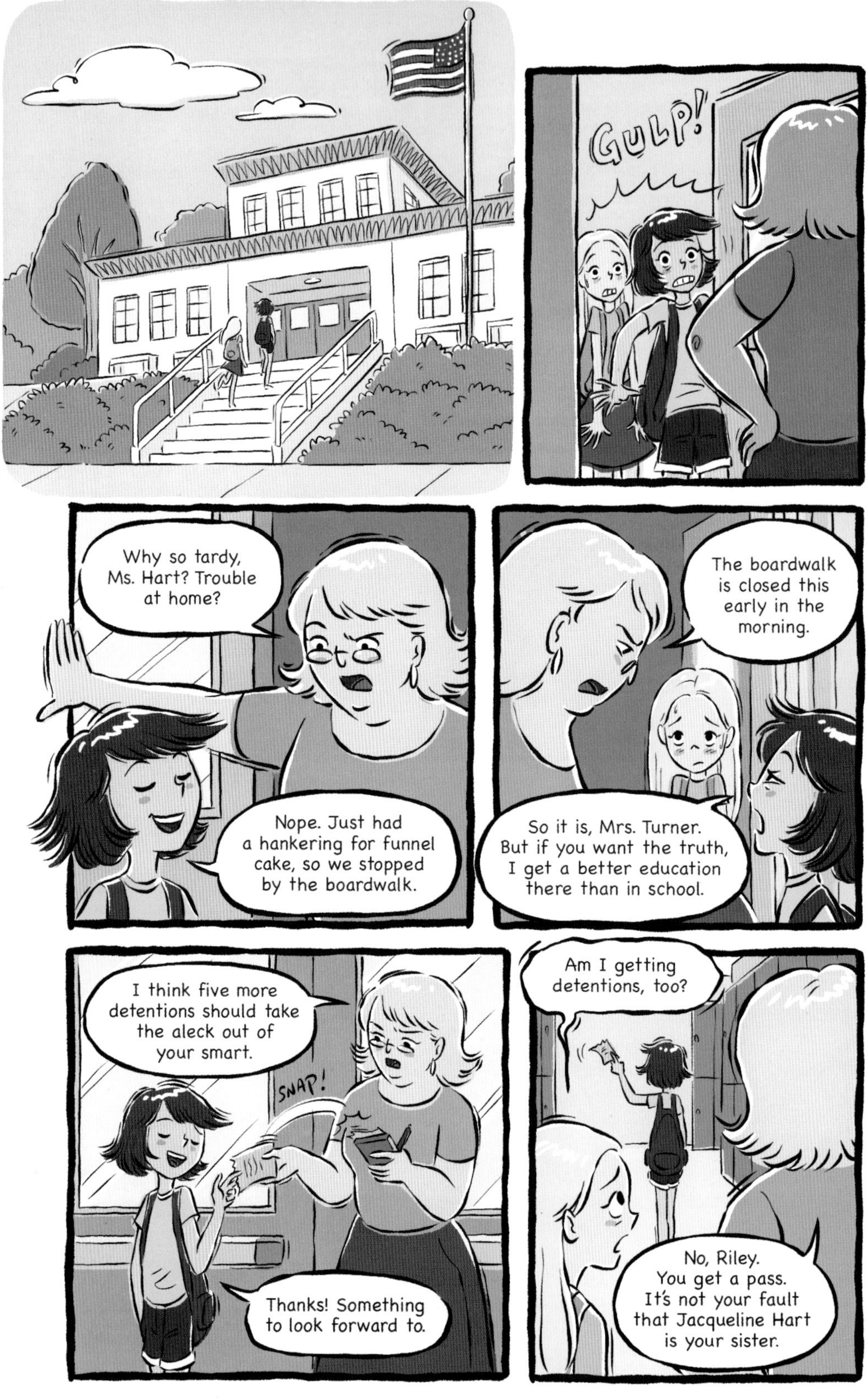
GULP!
Why so tardy, Ms. Hart? Trouble at home?
Nope. Just had a hankering for funnel cake, so we stopped by the boardwalk.
The boardwalk is closed this early in the morning.
So it is, Mrs. Turner. But if you want the truth, I get a better education there than in school.
I think five more detentions should take the aleck out of your smart.
SNAP!
Thanks! Something to look forward to.
Am I getting detentions, too?
No, Riley. You get a pass. It's not your fault that Jacqueline Hart is your sister.

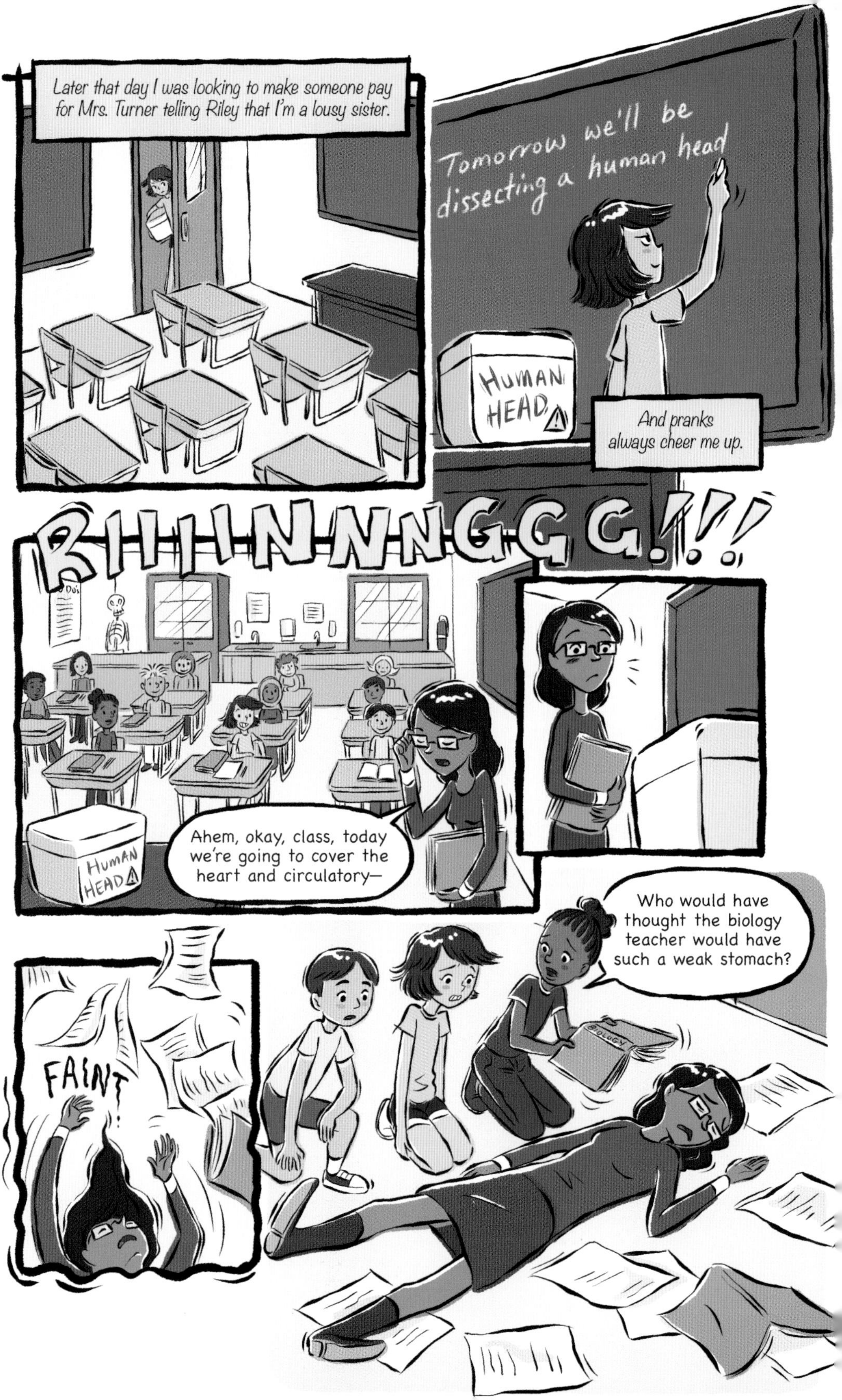
Later that day I was looking to make someone pay for Mrs. Turner telling Riley that I'm a lousy sister.
Tomorrow we'll be dissecting a human head
HUMAN HEAD
And pranks always cheer me up.
RIIIINNNGGG!!!
DO's
HUMAN HEAD
Ahem, okay, class, today we're going to cover the heart and circulatory—
FAINT
BIOLOGY
Who would have thought the biology teacher would have such a weak stomach?

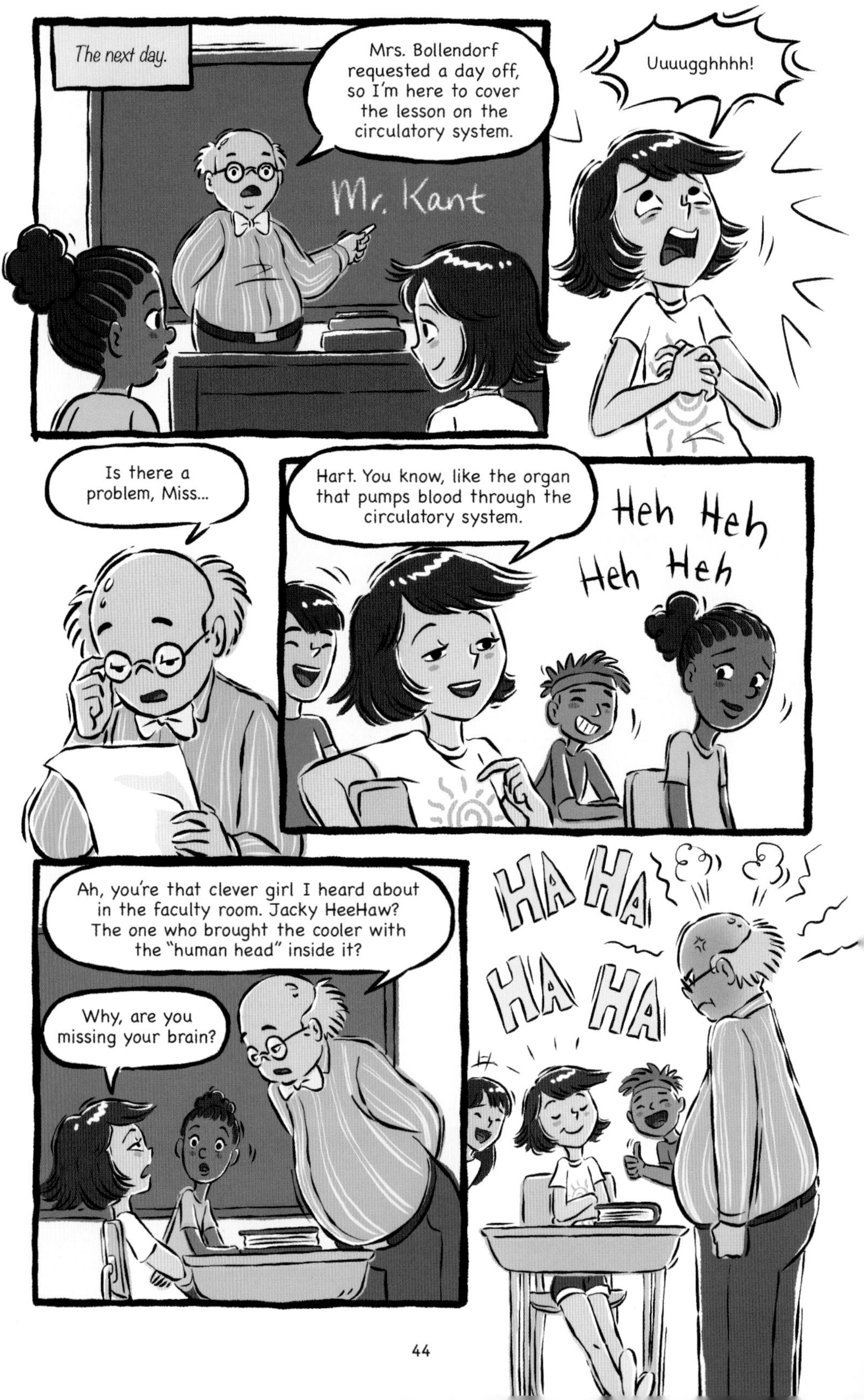
The next day.
Mrs. Bollendorf requested a day off, so I'm here to cover the lesson on the circulatory system.
Mr. Kant
Uuuugghhhh!
Is there a problem, Miss...
Hart. You know, like the organ that pumps blood through the circulatory system.
Heh Heh
Heh Heh
Ah, you're that clever girl I heard about in the faculty room. Jacky HeeHaw? The one who brought the cooler with the "human head" inside it?
Why, are you missing your brain?
HA HA
HA HA

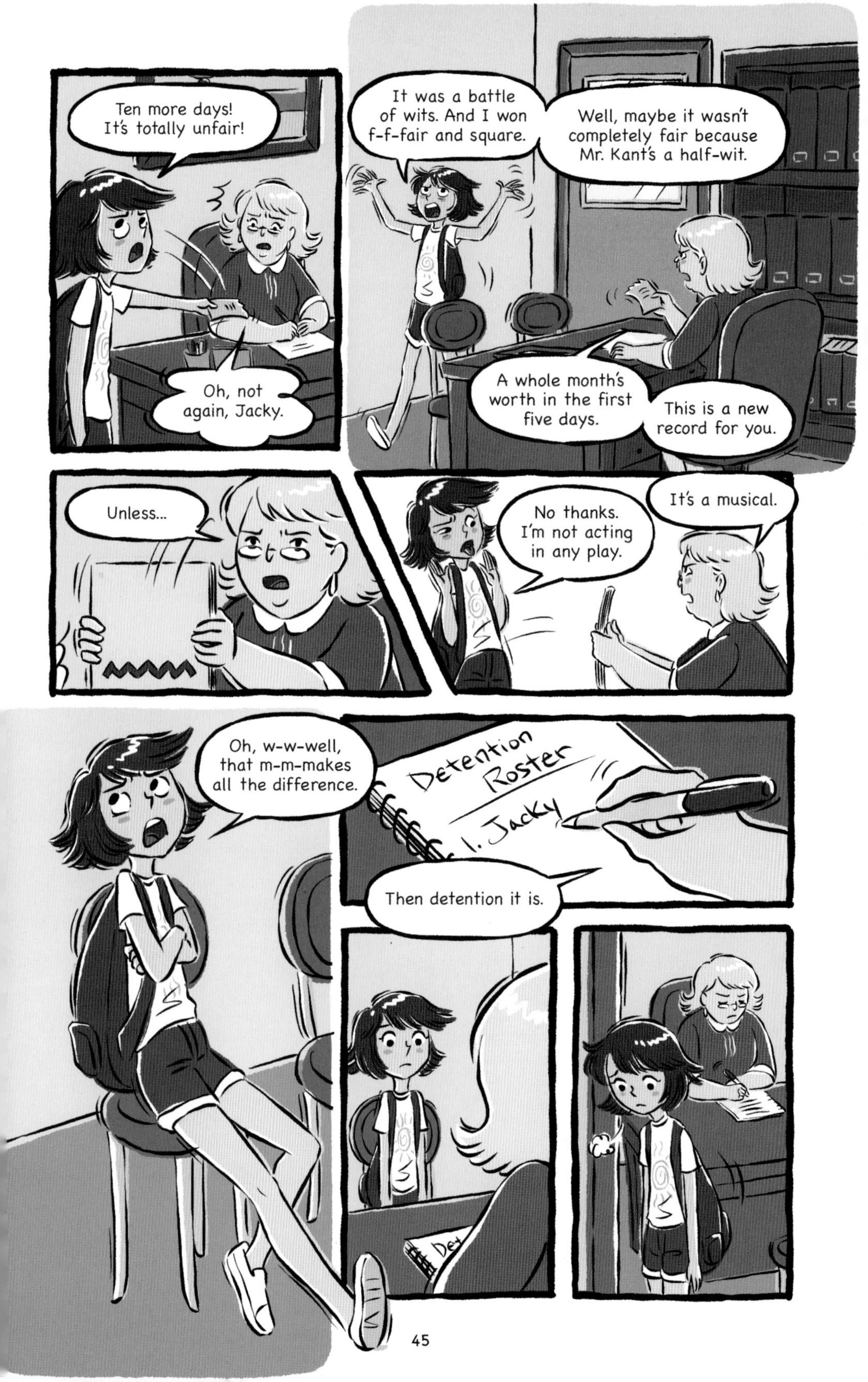
Ten more days! It's totally unfair!
Oh, not again, Jacky.
It was a battle of wits. And I won f-f-fair and square.
Well, maybe it wasn't completely fair because Mr. Kant's a half-wit.
A whole month's worth in the first five days.
This is a new record for you.
Unless...
No thanks. I'm not acting in any play.
It's a musical.
Oh, w-w-well, that m-m-makes all the difference.
Detention Roster
1. Jacky
Then detention it is.

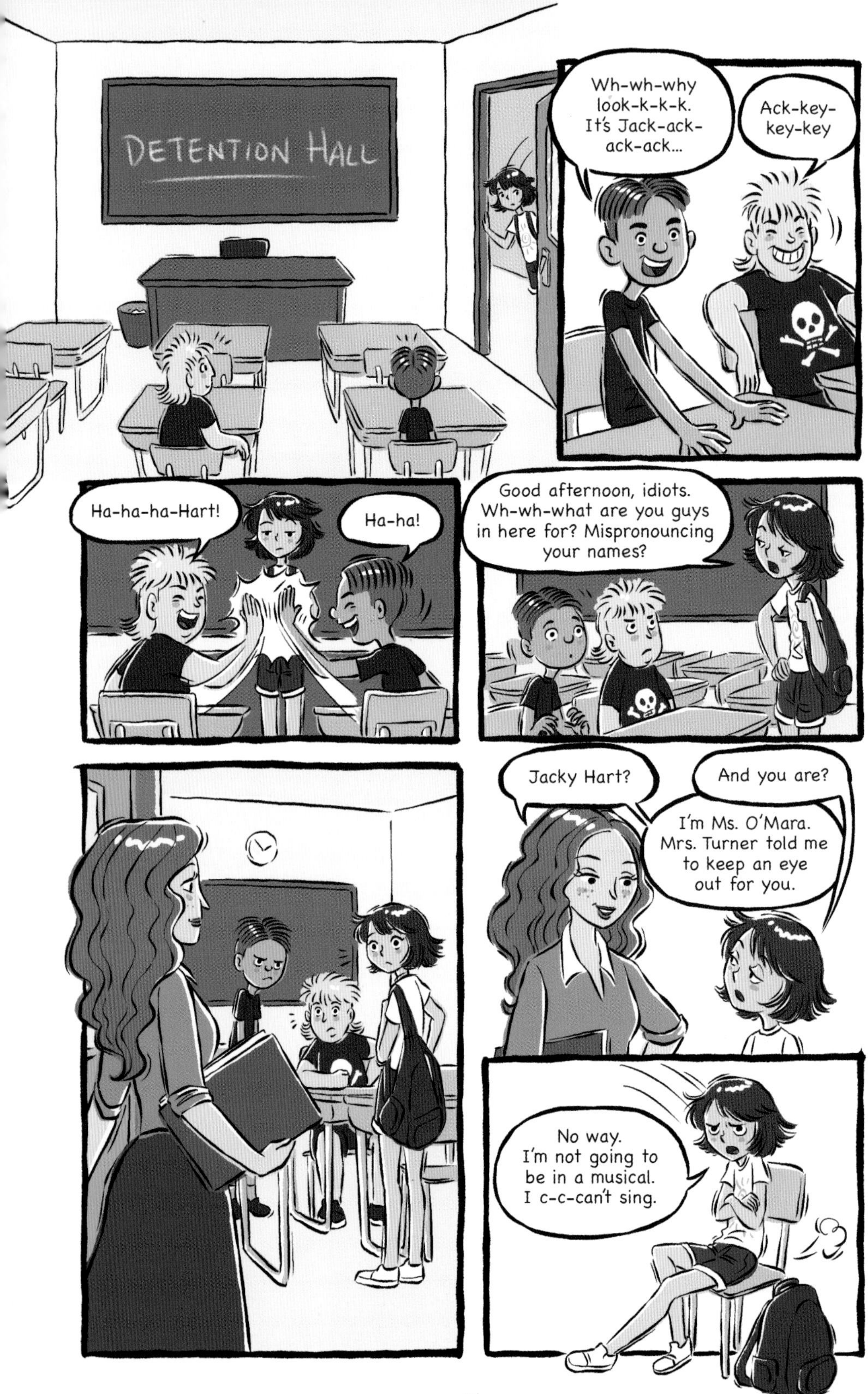
DETENTION HALL
Wh-wh-why look-k-k-k. It's Jack-ack-ack-ack...
Ack-key-key-key
Ha-ha-ha-Hart!
Ha-ha!
Good afternoon, idiots. Wh-wh-what are you guys in here for? Mispronouncing your names?
Jacky Hart?
And you are?
I'm Ms. O'Mara. Mrs. Turner told me to keep an eye out for you.
No way. I'm not going to be in a musical. I c-c-can't sing.

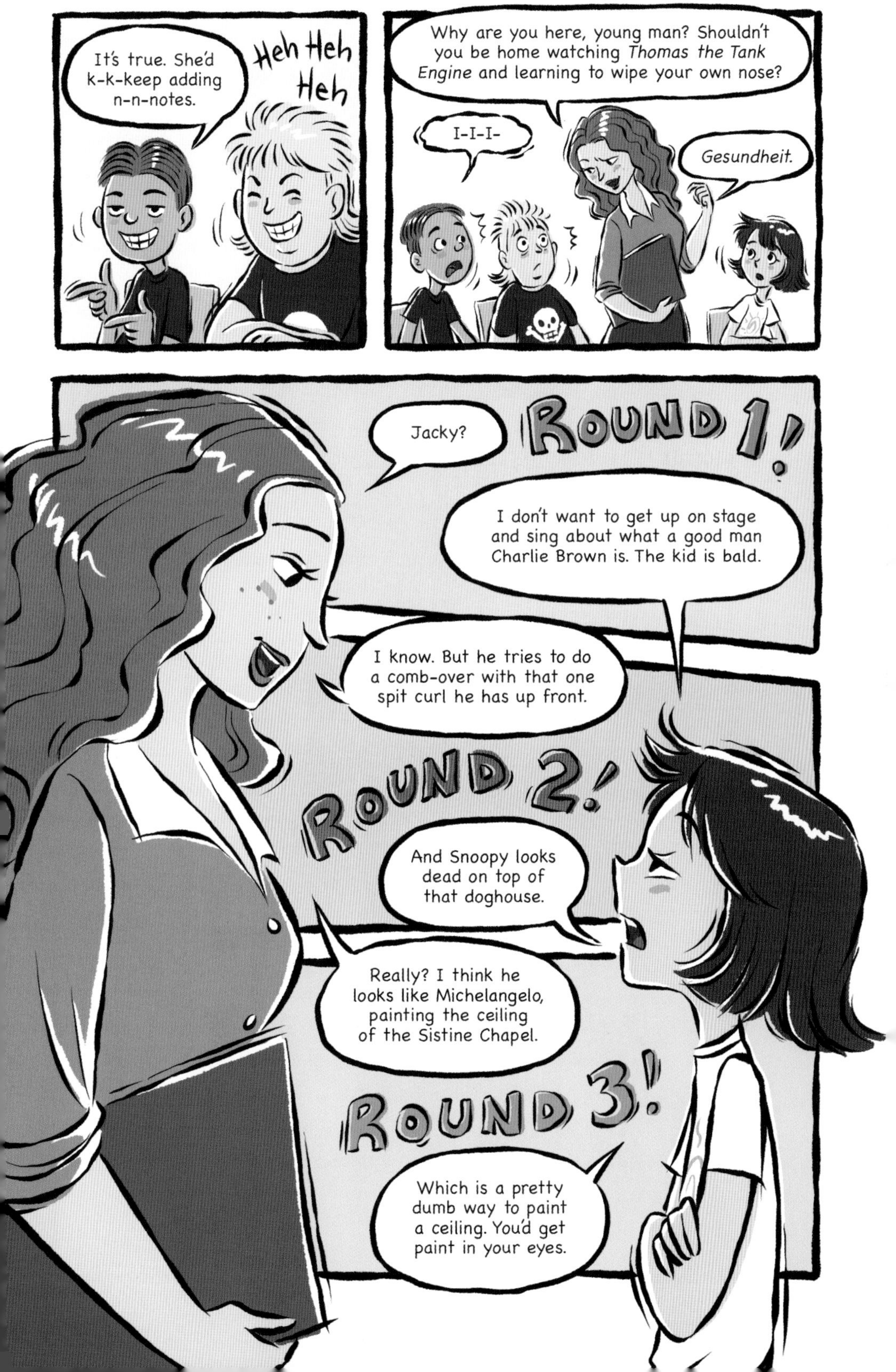

It's true. She'd k-k-keep adding n-n-notes.
Heh Heh Heh
Why are you here, young man? Shouldn't you be home watching *Thomas the Tank Engine* and learning to wipe your own nose?
I-I-I-
Gesundheit.
Jacky?
ROUND 1!
I don't want to get up on stage and sing about what a good man Charlie Brown is. The kid is bald.
I know. But he tries to do a comb-over with that one spit curl he has up front.
ROUND 2!
And Snoopy looks dead on top of that doghouse.
Really? I think he looks like Michelangelo, painting the ceiling of the Sistine Chapel.
ROUND 3!
Which is a pretty dumb way to paint a ceiling. You'd get paint in your eyes.

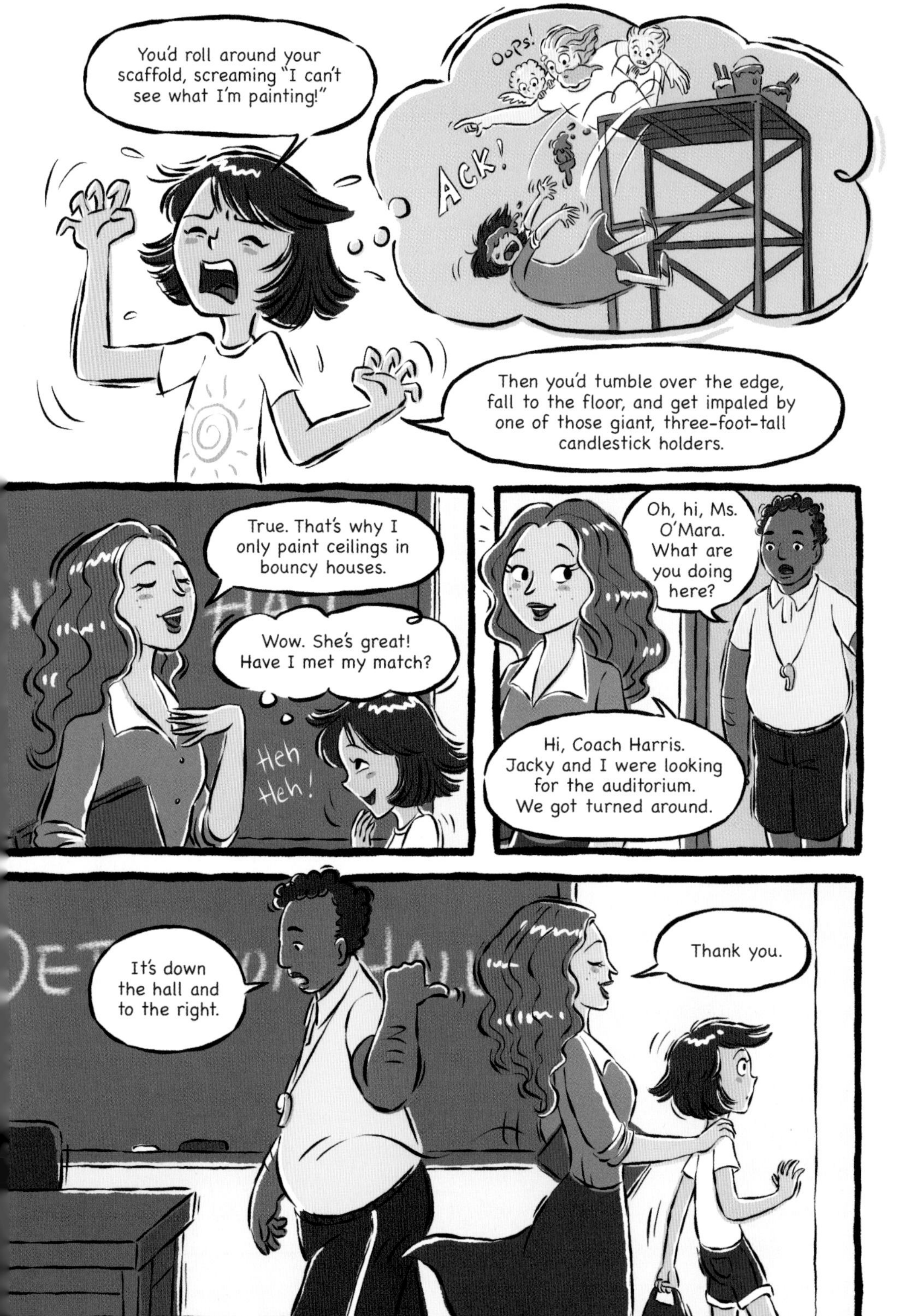
You'd roll around your scaffold, screaming "I can't see what I'm painting!"
OOPS!
ACK!
Then you'd tumble over the edge, fall to the floor, and get impaled by one of those giant, three-foot-tall candlestick holders.
True. That's why I only paint ceilings in bouncy houses.
Wow. She's great! Have I met my match?
Heh Heh!
Oh, hi, Ms. O'Mara. What are you doing here?
Hi, Coach Harris. Jacky and I were looking for the auditorium. We got turned around.
It's down the hall and to the right.
Thank you.

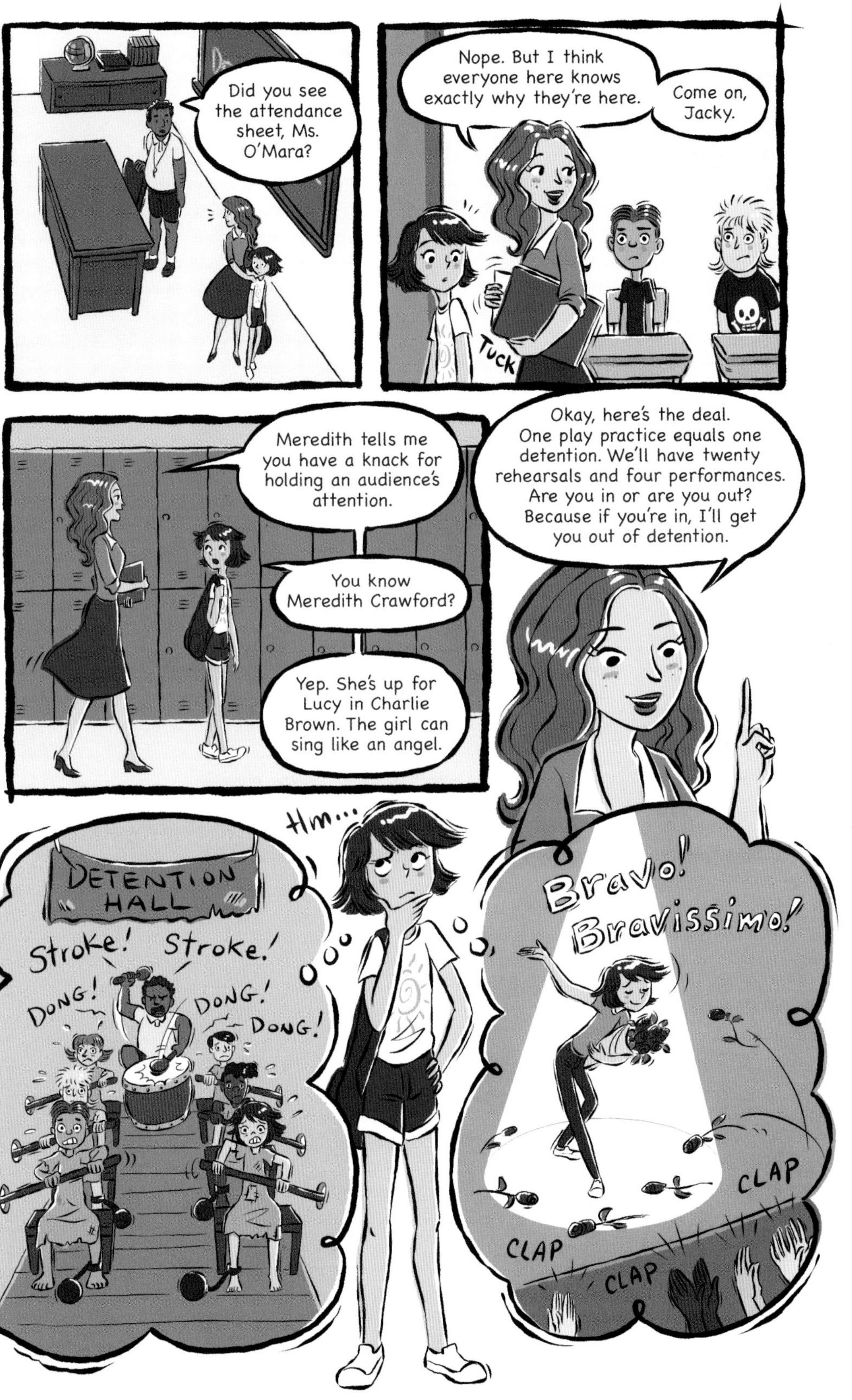

Did you see the attendance sheet, Ms. O'Mara?
Nope. But I think everyone here knows exactly why they're here.
Come on, Jacky.
TUCK
Meredith tells me you have a knack for holding an audience's attention.
You know Meredith Crawford?
Yep. She's up for Lucy in Charlie Brown. The girl can sing like an angel.
Okay, here's the deal. One play practice equals one detention. We'll have twenty rehearsals and four performances. Are you in or are you out? Because if you're in, I'll get you out of detention.
Hm...
DETENTION HALL
Stroke! Stroke!
DONG! DONG! DONG!
Bravo! Bravissimo!
CLAP
CLAP
CLAP

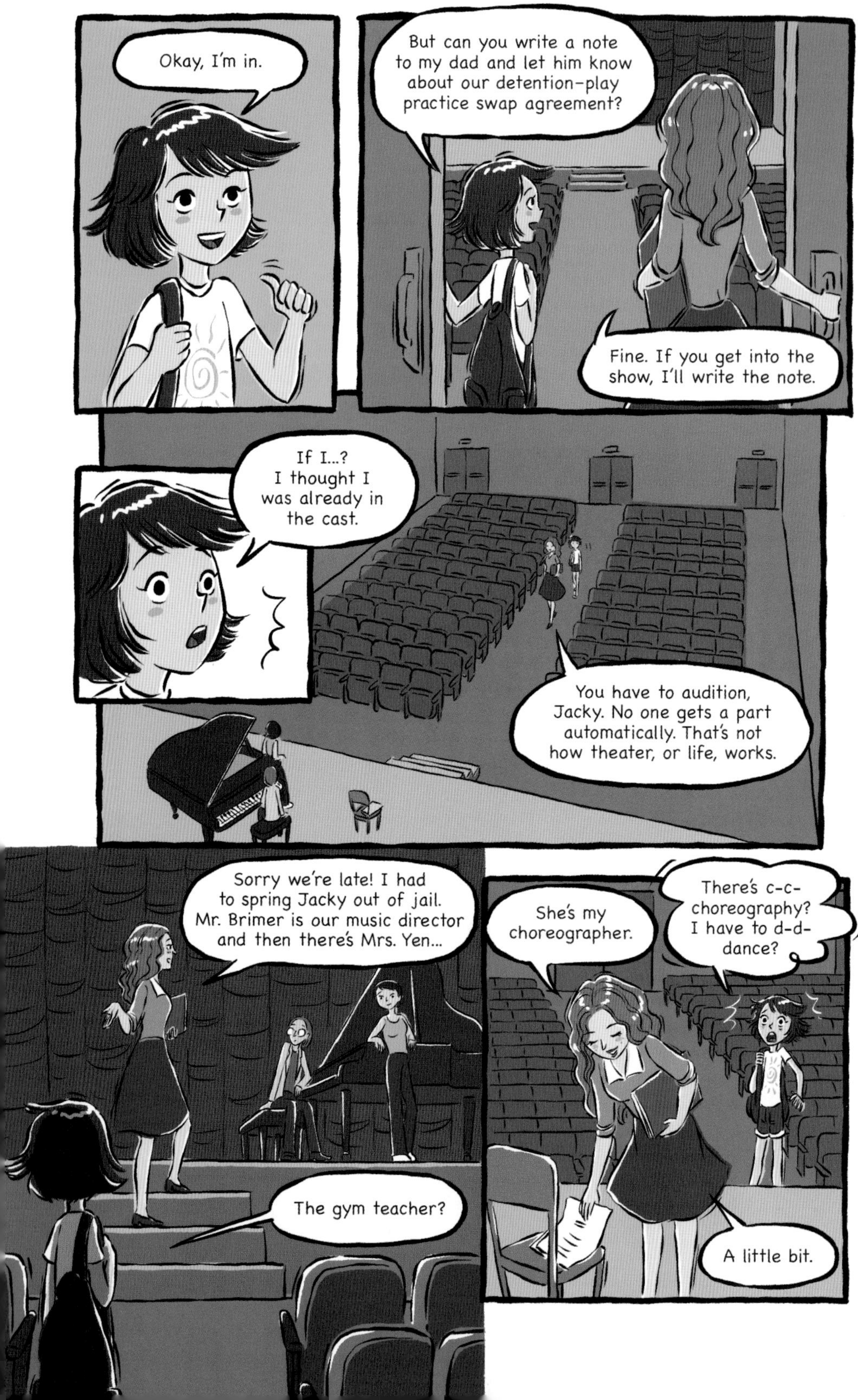
Okay, I'm in.
But can you write a note to my dad and let him know about our detention-play practice swap agreement?
Fine. If you get into the show, I'll write the note.
If I...? I thought I was already in the cast.
You have to audition, Jacky. No one gets a part automatically. That's not how theater, or life, works.
Sorry we're late! I had to spring Jacky out of jail. Mr. Brimer is our music director and then there's Mrs. Yen...
The gym teacher?
She's my choreographer.
There's c-c-choreography? I have to d-d-dance?
A little bit.

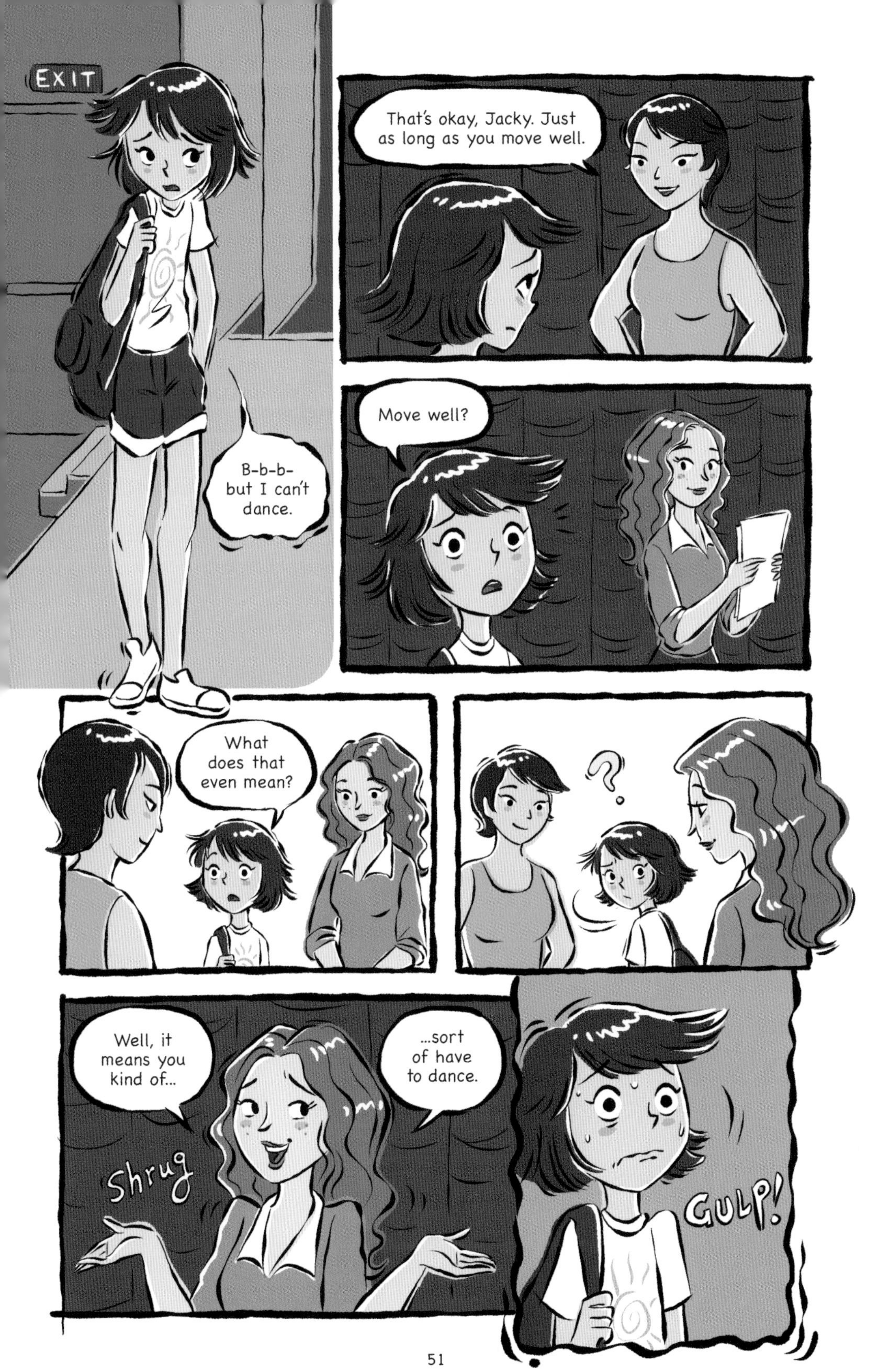
EXIT
B-b-b-
but I can't
dance.
That's okay, Jacky. Just
as long as you move well.
Move well?
What
does that
even mean?
?
Well, it
means you
kind of...
Shrug
...sort
of have
to dance.
GULP!

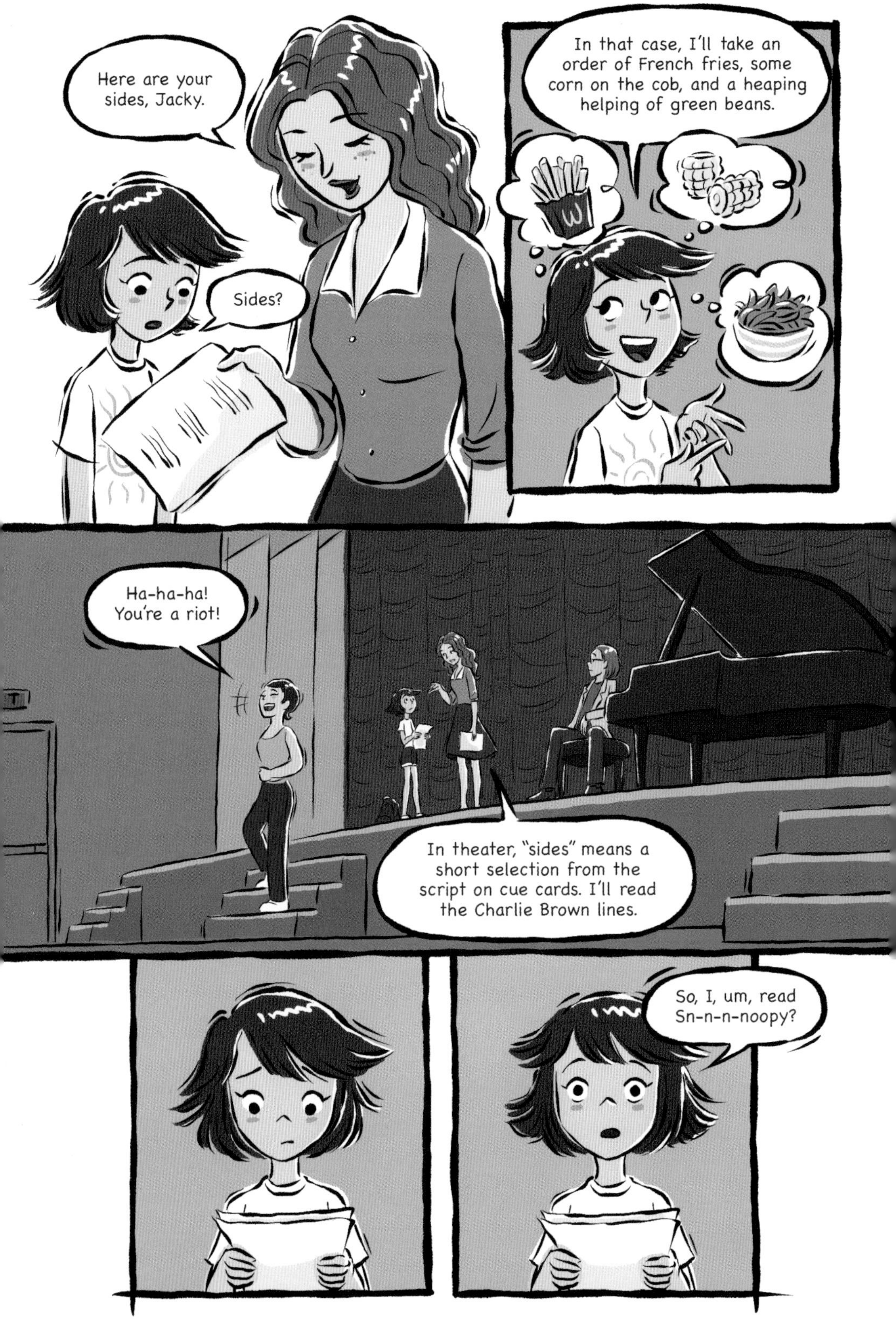
Here are your sides, Jacky.
Sides?
In that case, I'll take an order of French fries, some corn on the cob, and a heaping helping of green beans.
Ha-ha-ha! You're a riot!
In theater, "sides" means a short selection from the script on cue cards. I'll read the Charlie Brown lines.
So, I, um, read Sn-n-n-noopy?

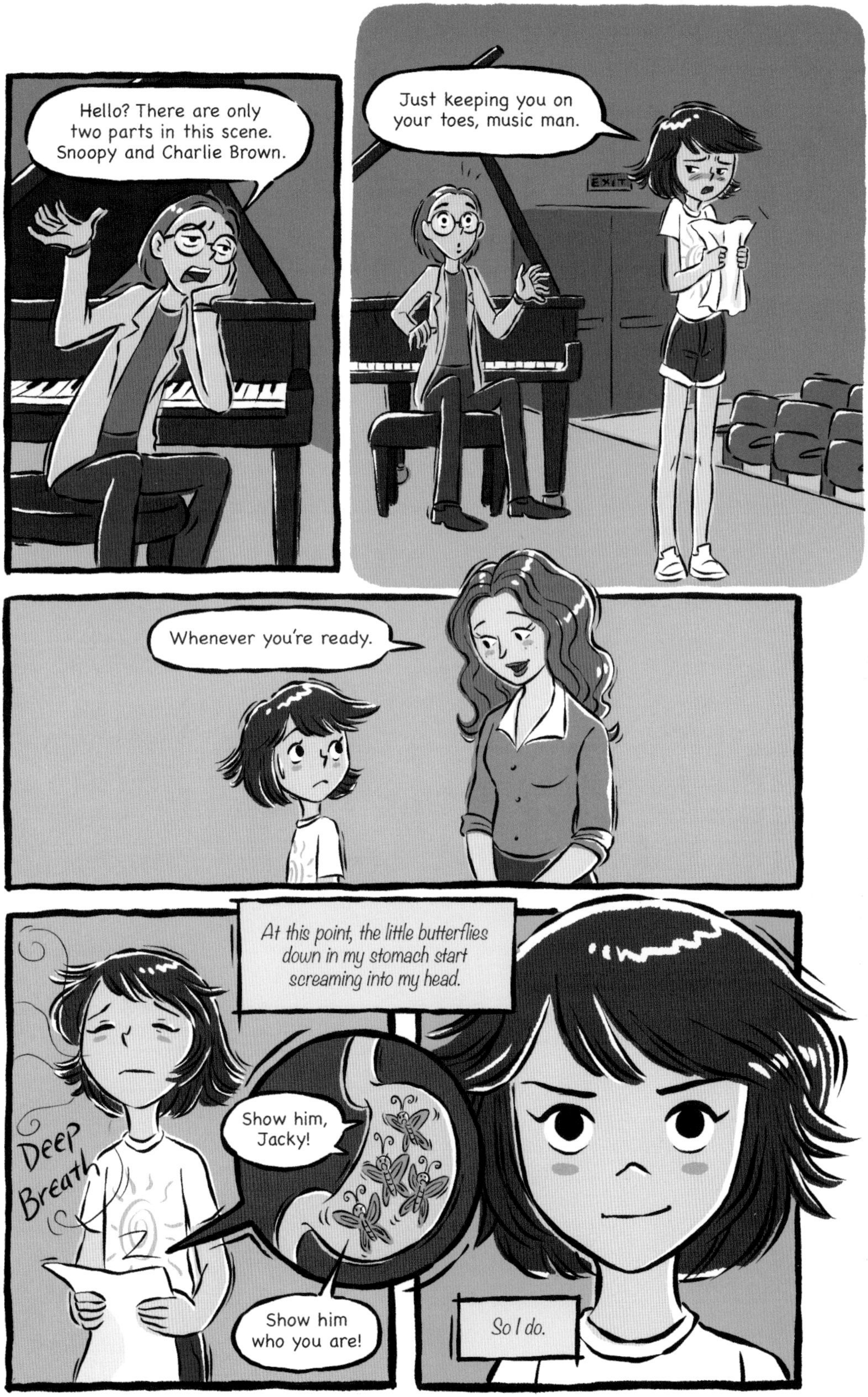
Hello? There are only two parts in this scene. Snoopy and Charlie Brown.
Just keeping you on your toes, music man.
EXIT
Whenever you're ready.
At this point, the little butterflies down in my stomach start screaming into my head.
Deep Breath
Show him, Jacky!
Show him who you are!
So I do.

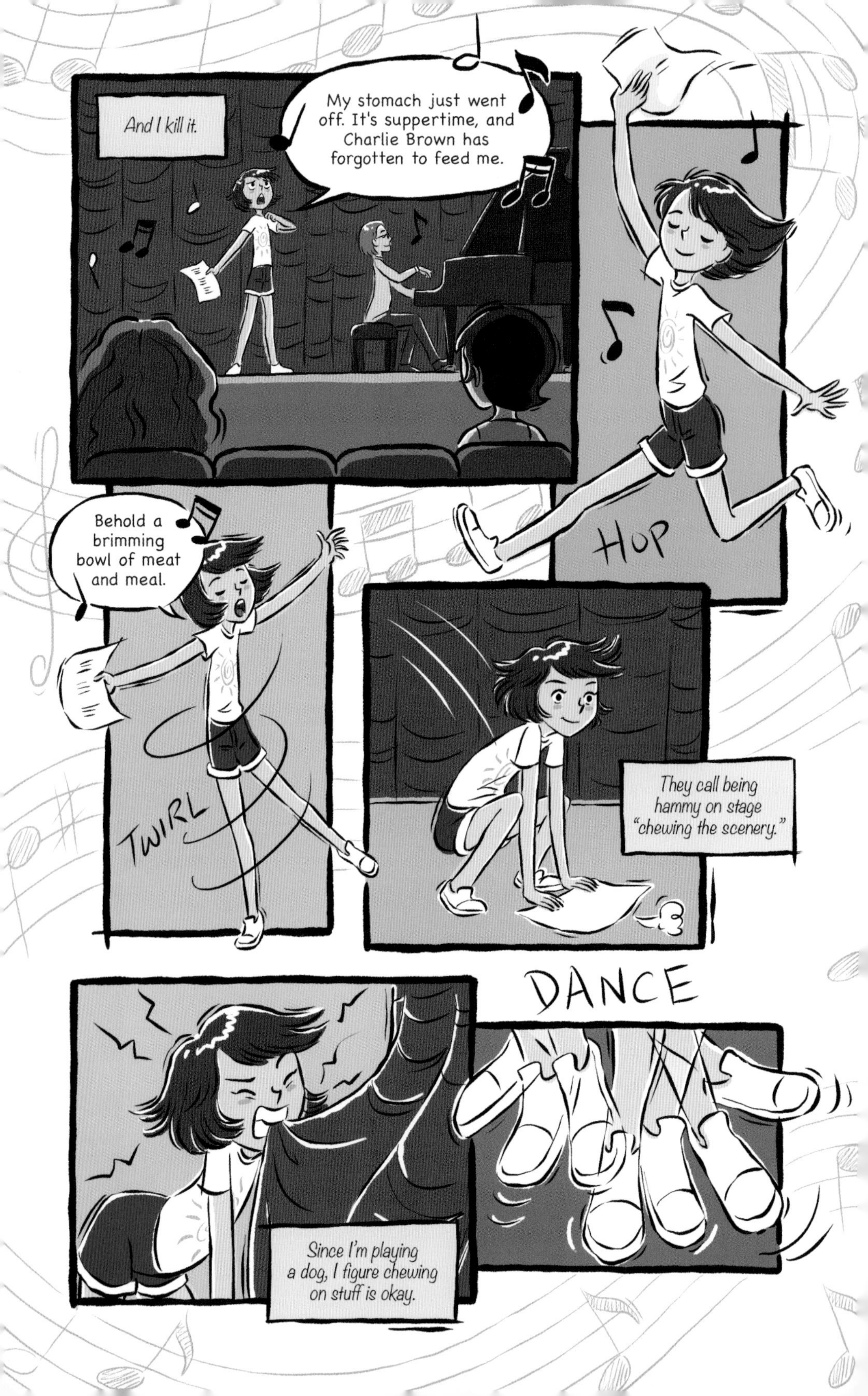
And I kill it.
My stomach just went off. It's suppertime, and Charlie Brown has forgotten to feed me.
HOP
Behold a brimming bowl of meat and meal.
TWIRL
They call being hammy on stage "chewing the scenery."
DANCE
Since I'm playing a dog, I figure chewing on stuff is okay.

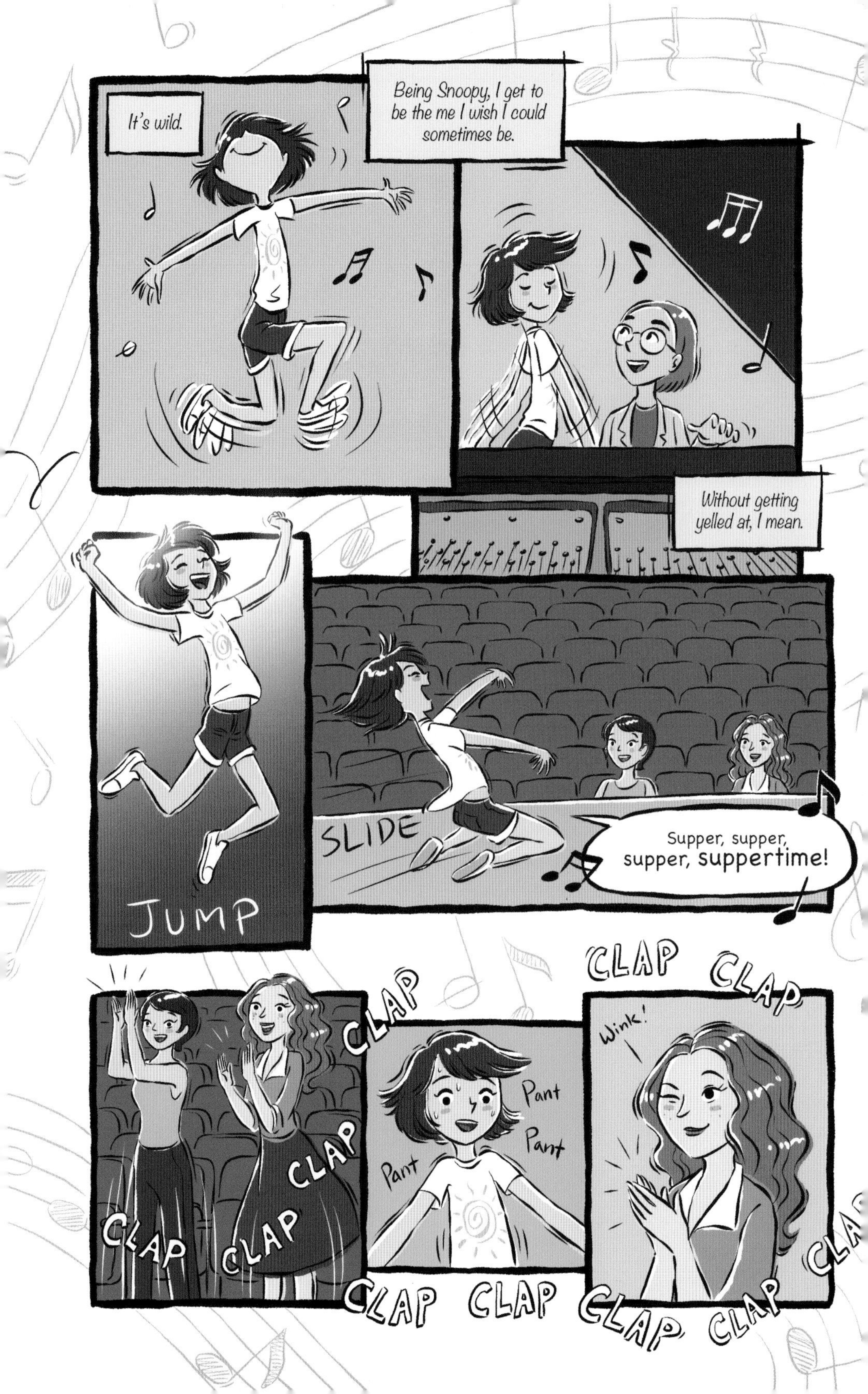
It's wild.
Being Snoopy, I get to be the me I wish I could sometimes be.
Without getting yelled at, I mean.
JUMP
SLIDE
Supper, supper, supper, suppertime!
CLAP
CLAP
CLAP
CLAP
CLAP
CLAP
CLAP
Wink!
Pant
Pant
Pant
CLAP
CLAP
CLAP
CLAP

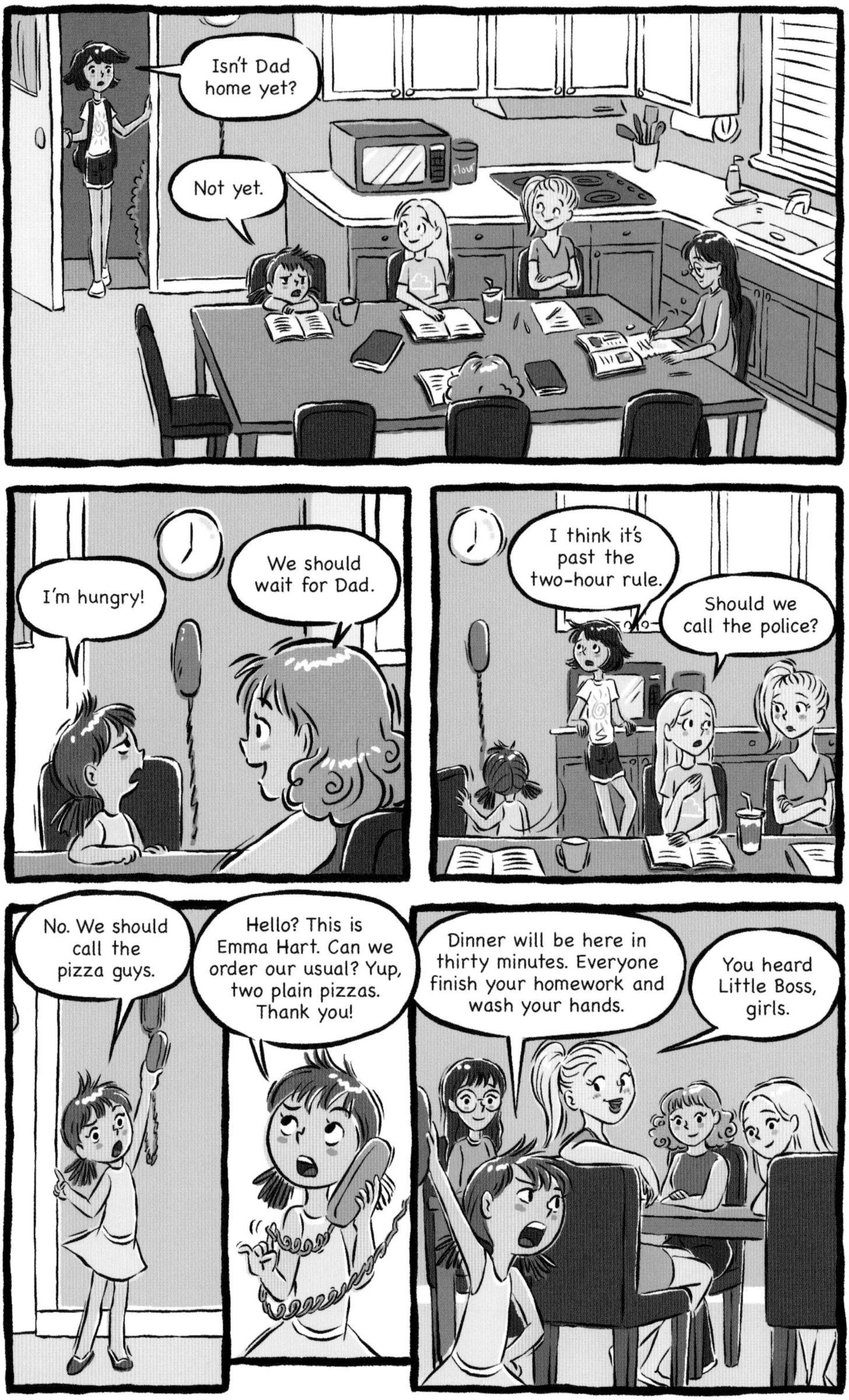
Isn't Dad home yet?
Not yet.
I'm hungry!
We should wait for Dad.
I think it's past the two-hour rule.
Should we call the police?
No. We should call the pizza guys.
Hello? This is Emma Hart. Can we order our usual? Yup, two plain pizzas. Thank you!
Dinner will be here in thirty minutes. Everyone finish your homework and wash your hands.
You heard Little Boss, girls.

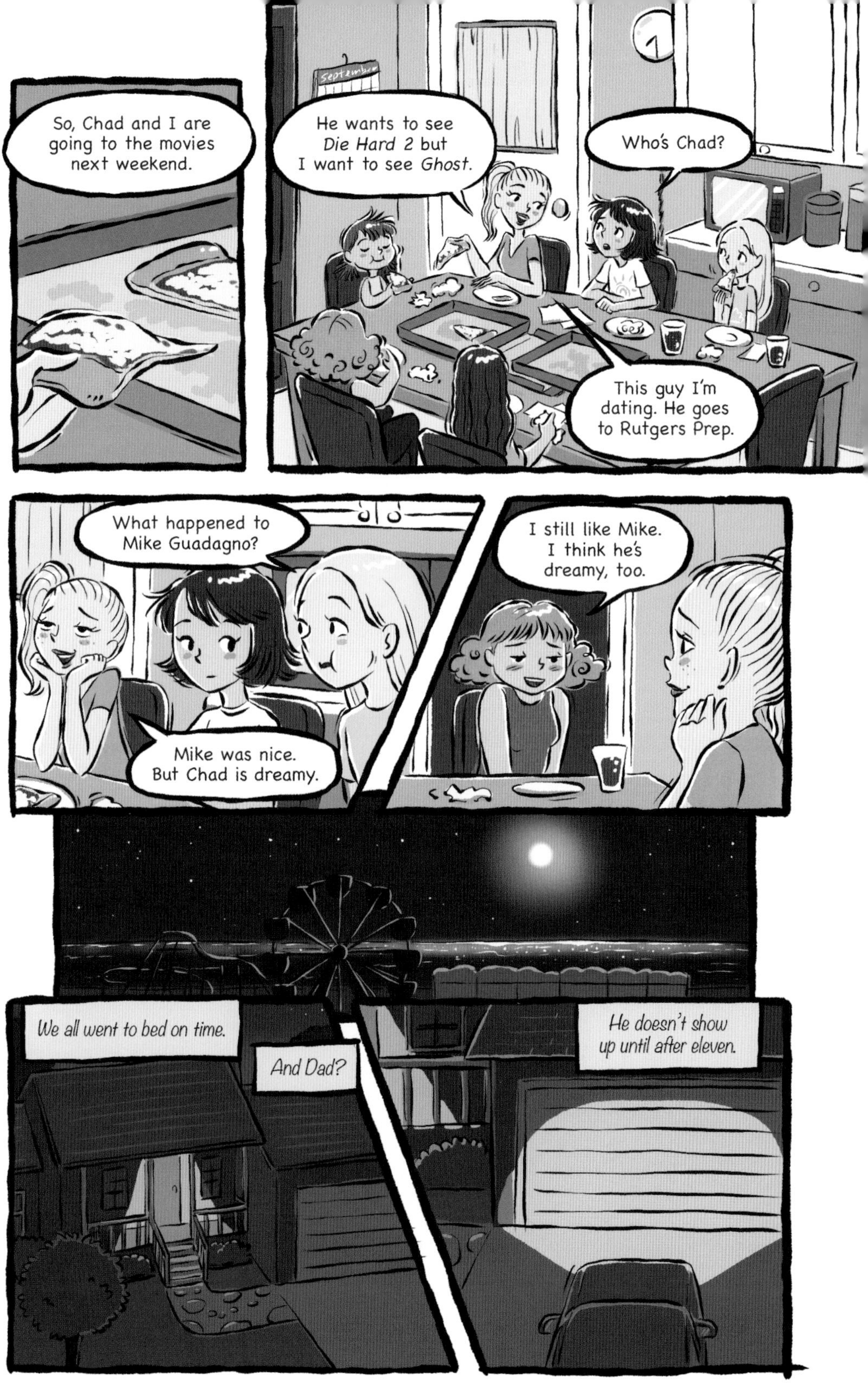
So, Chad and I are going to the movies next weekend.
He wants to see *Die Hard 2* but I want to see *Ghost*.
Who's Chad?
This guy I'm dating. He goes to Rutgers Prep.
What happened to Mike Guadagno?
Mike was nice. But Chad is dreamy.
I still like Mike. I think he's dreamy, too.
We all went to bed on time.
And Dad?
He doesn't show up until after eleven.

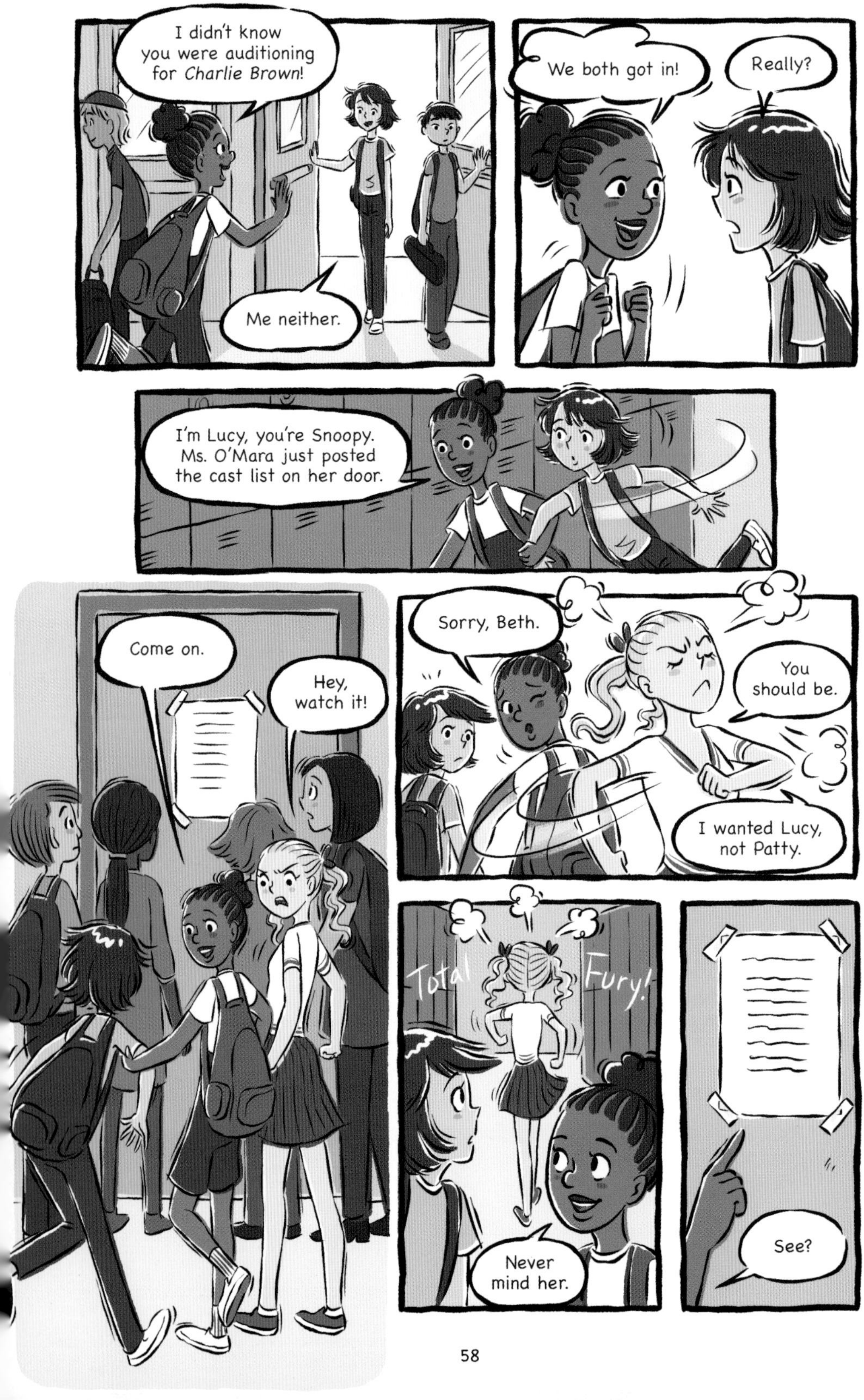
I didn't know you were auditioning for *Charlie Brown*!
Me neither.
We both got in!
Really?
I'm Lucy, you're Snoopy. Ms. O'Mara just posted the cast list on her door.
Come on.
Hey, watch it!
Sorry, Beth.
You should be.
I wanted Lucy, not Patty.
Total Fury!
Never mind her.
See?

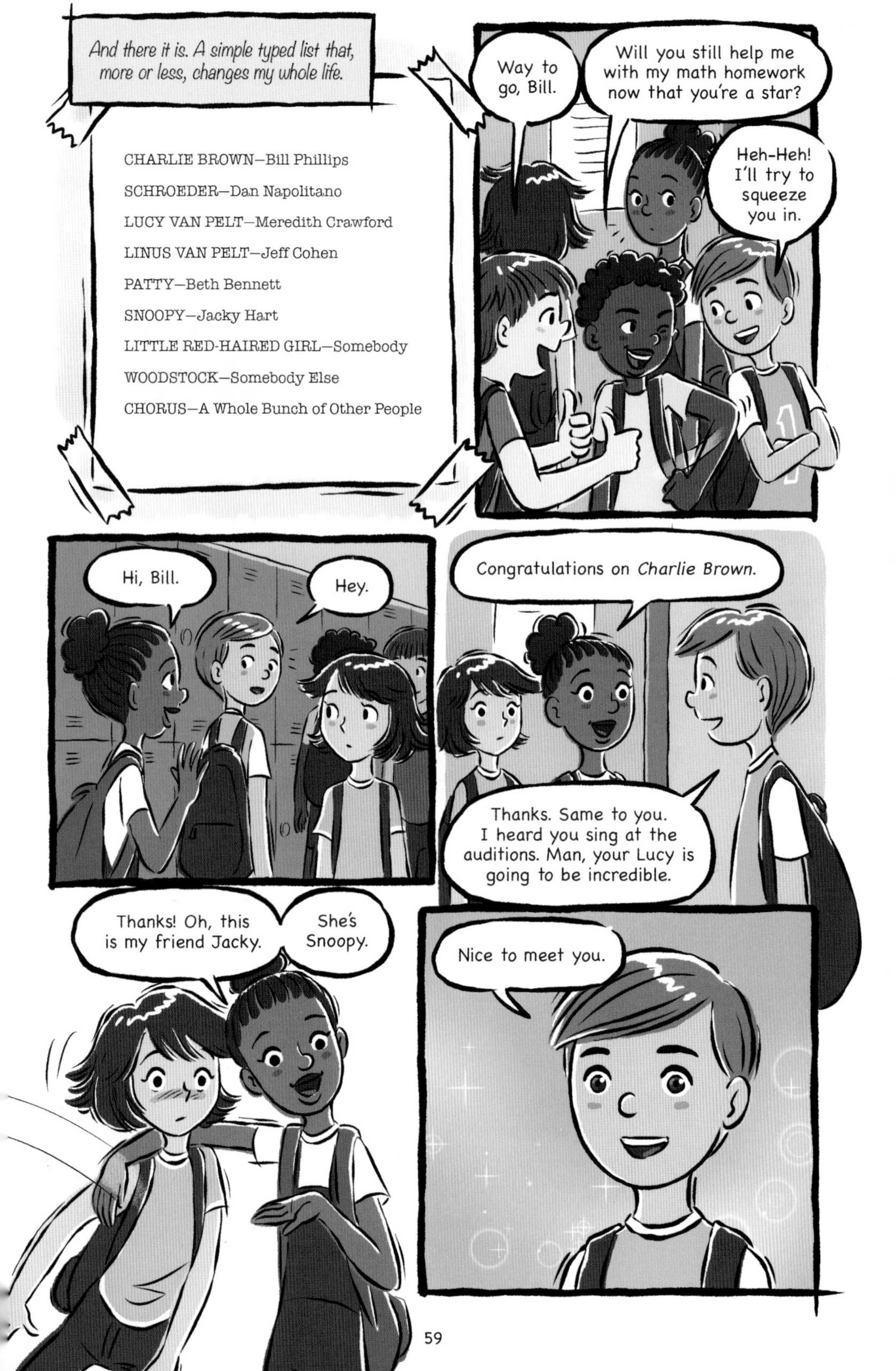
And there it is. A simple typed list that, more or less, changes my whole life.
CHARLIE BROWN—Bill Phillips
SCHROEDER—Dan Napolitano
LUCY VAN PELT—Meredith Crawford
LINUS VAN PELT—Jeff Cohen
PATTY—Beth Bennett
SNOOPY—Jacky Hart
LITTLE RED-HAIRED GIRL—Somebody
WOODSTOCK—Somebody Else
CHORUS—A Whole Bunch of Other People
Way to go, Bill.
Will you still help me with my math homework now that you're a star?
Heh-Heh! I'll try to squeeze you in.
Hi, Bill.
Hey.
Congratulations on *Charlie Brown*.
Thanks. Same to you. I heard you sing at the auditions. Man, your Lucy is going to be incredible.
Thanks! Oh, this is my friend Jacky.
She's Snoopy.
Nice to meet you.

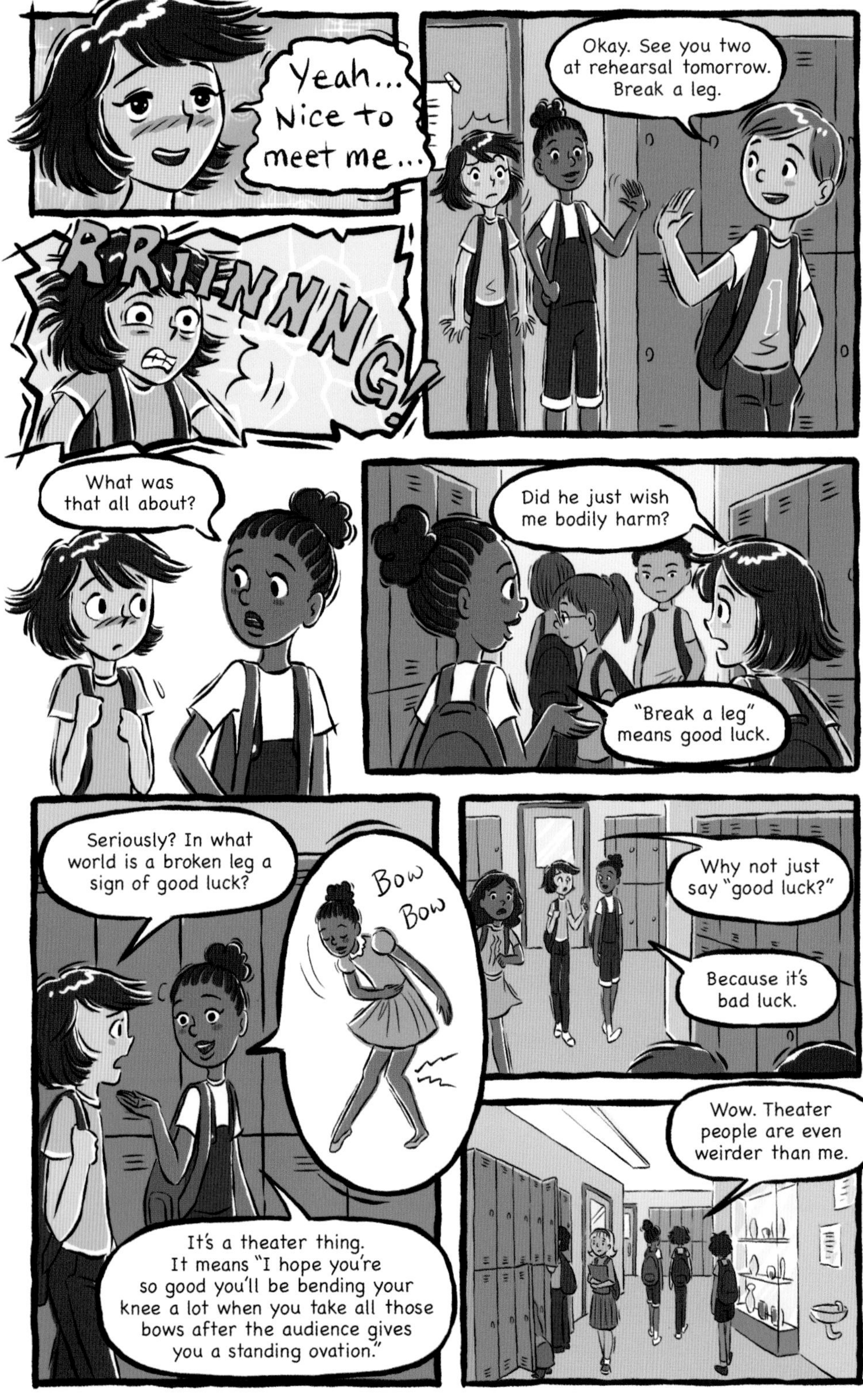
Yeah... Nice to meet me...
RRIINNNG!
Okay. See you two at rehearsal tomorrow. Break a leg.
What was that all about?
Did he just wish me bodily harm?
"Break a leg" means good luck.
Seriously? In what world is a broken leg a sign of good luck?
Bow
Bow
It's a theater thing. It means "I hope you're so good you'll be bending your knee a lot when you take all those bows after the audience gives you a standing ovation."
Why not just say "good luck?"
Because it's bad luck.
Wow. Theater people are even weirder than me.

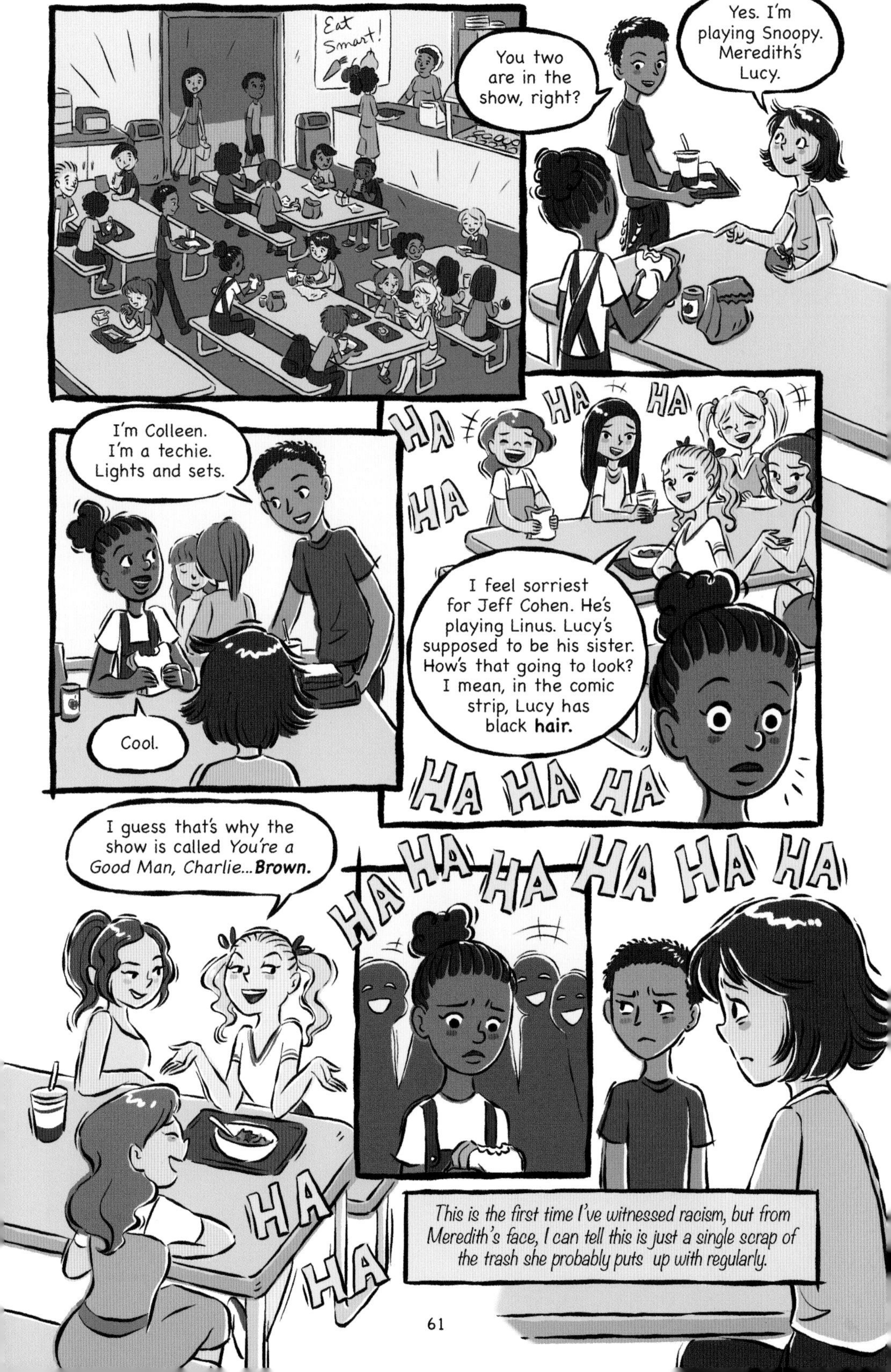
Eat Smart!
You two are in the show, right?
Yes. I'm playing Snoopy. Meredith's Lucy.
I'm Colleen. I'm a techie. Lights and sets.
Cool.
HA HA HA HA
I feel sorriest for Jeff Cohen. He's playing Linus. Lucy's supposed to be his sister. How's that going to look? I mean, in the comic strip, Lucy has black **hair.**
HA HA HA
I guess that's why the show is called *You're a Good Man, Charlie*...**Brown.**
HA HA HA HA HA HA HA
HA HA
This is the first time I've witnessed racism, but from Meredith's face, I can tell this is just a single scrap of the trash she probably puts up with regularly.

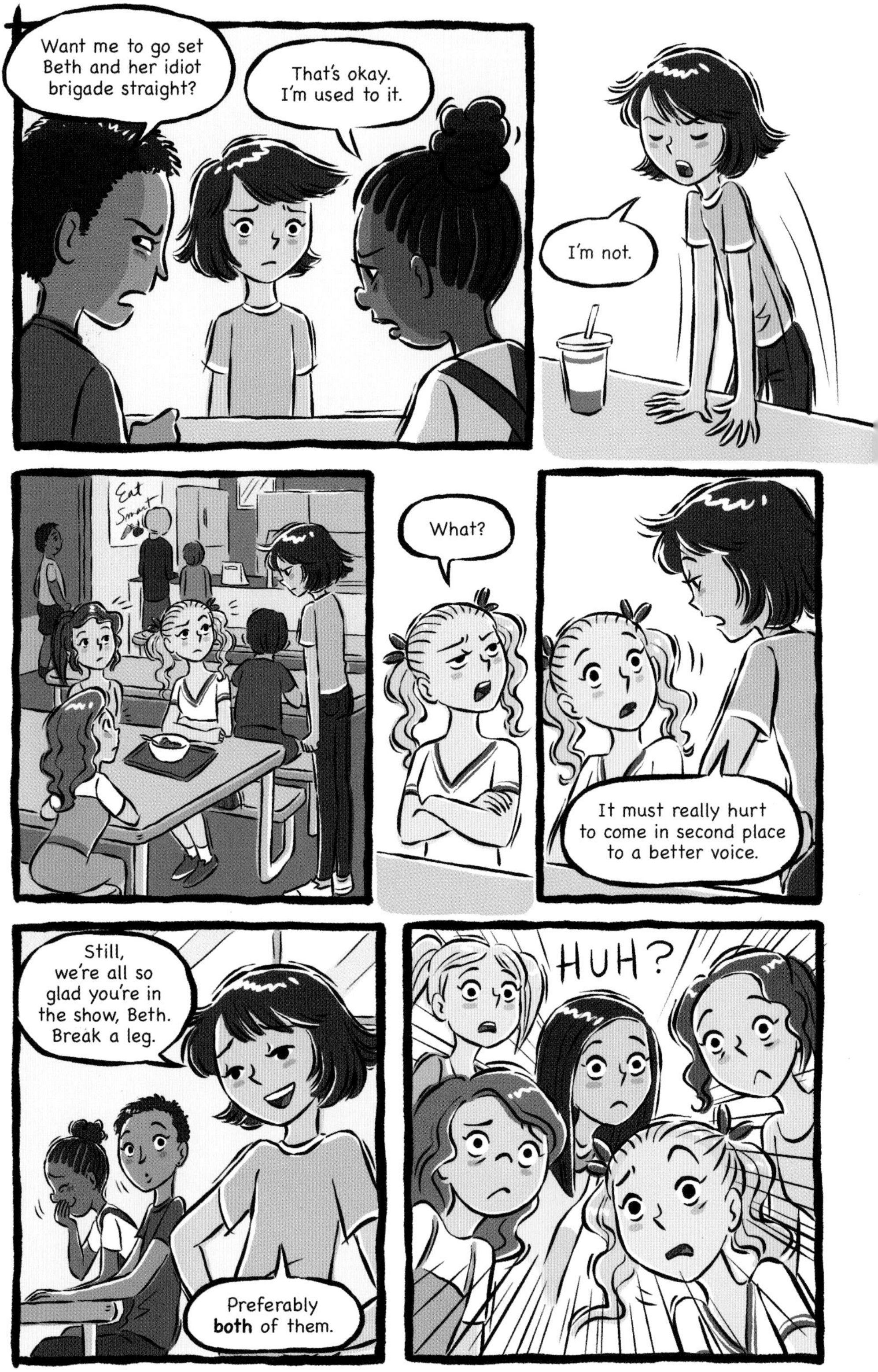
Want me to go set Beth and her idiot brigade straight?
That's okay. I'm used to it.
I'm not.
Eat Smart
What?
It must really hurt to come in second place to a better voice.
Still, we're all so glad you're in the show, Beth. Break a leg.
Preferably **both** of them.
HUH?

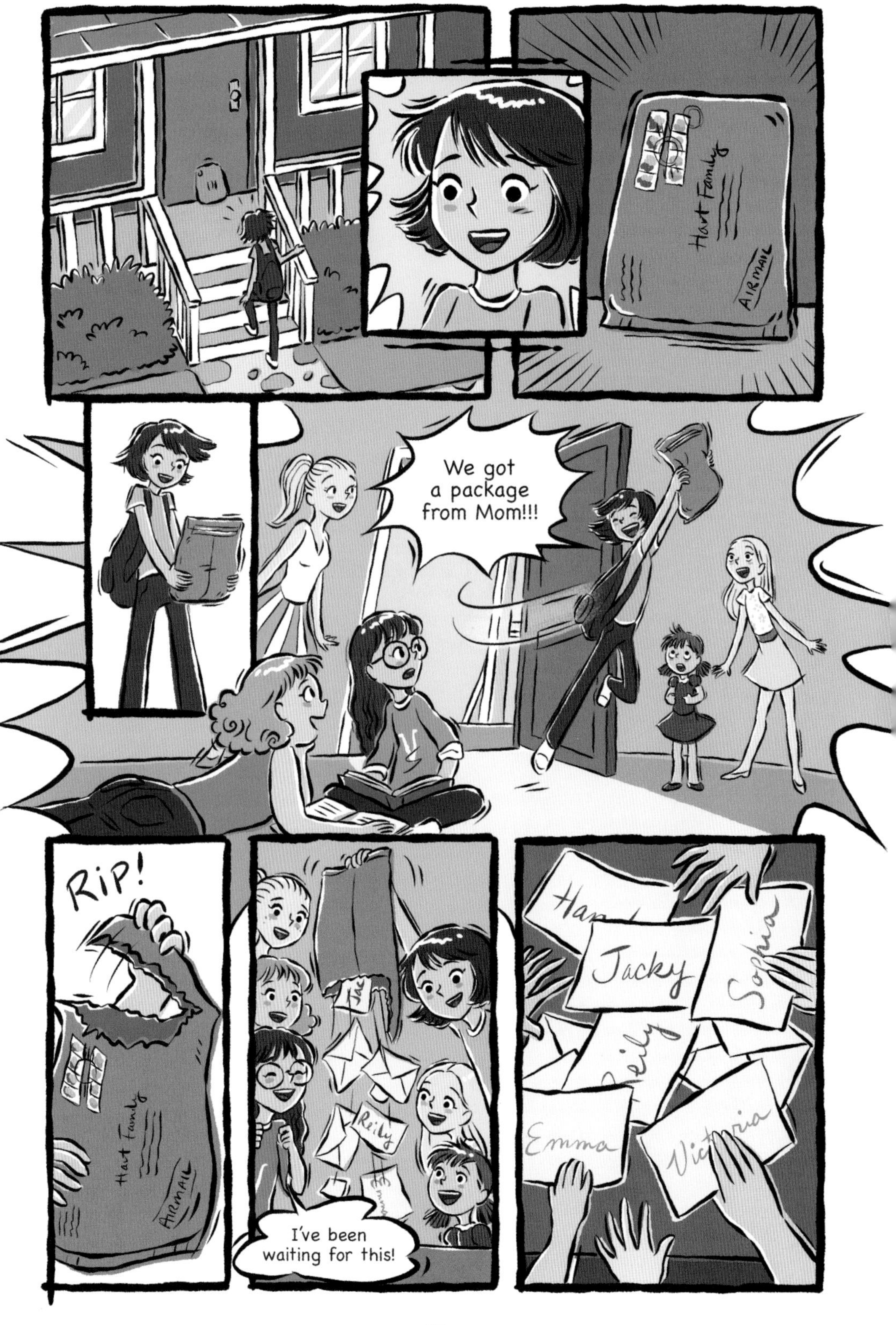
Hart Family
AIRMAIL
We got a package from Mom!!!
RIP!
Hart Family
AIRMAIL
Reily
I've been waiting for this!
Jacky
Sophia
Emma

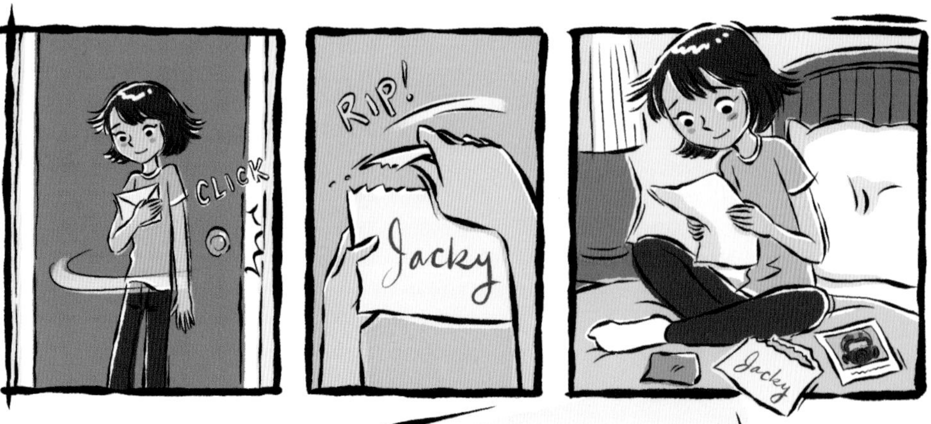
CLICK
RIP!
Jacky
Jacky

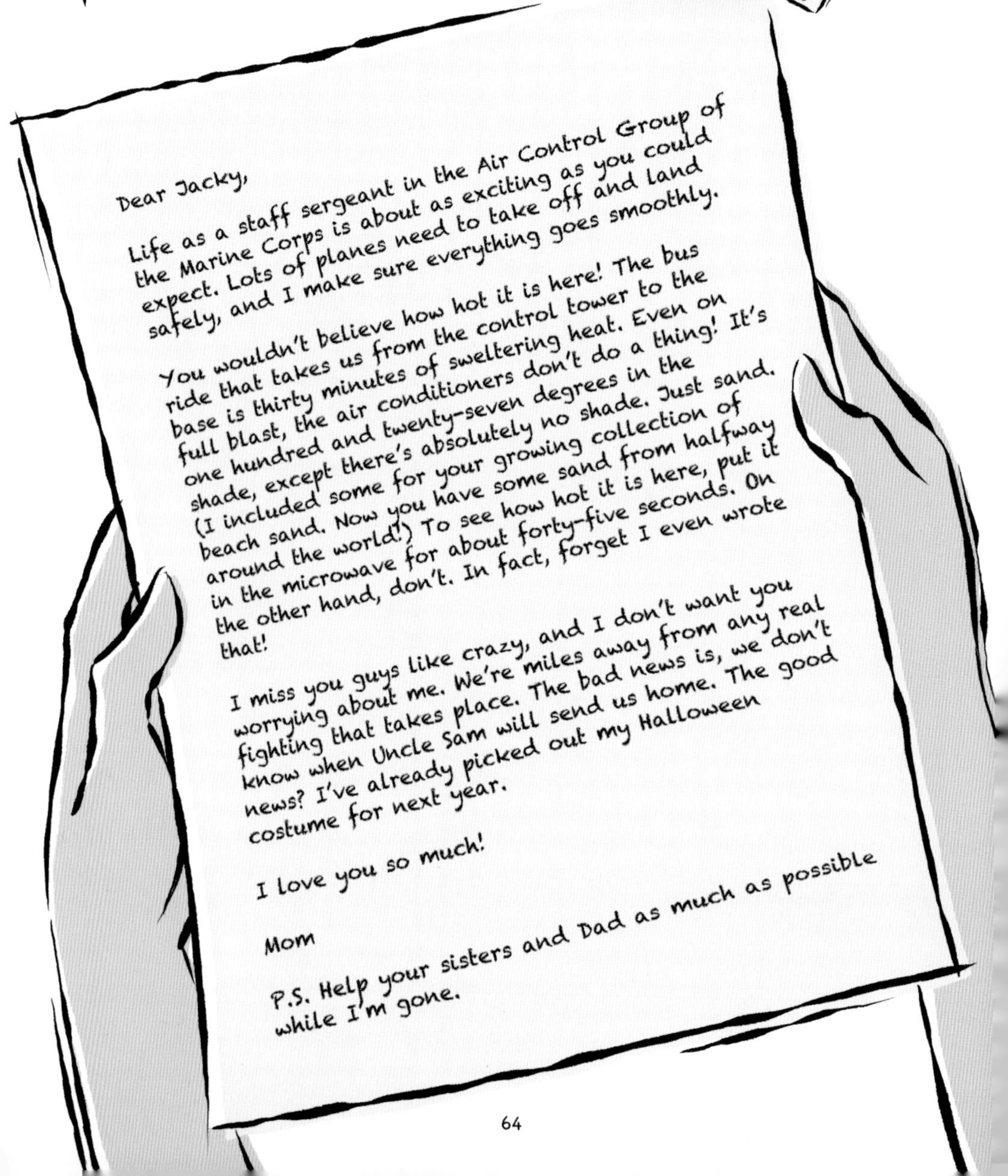

Dear Jacky,

Life as a staff sergeant in the Air Control Group of the Marine Corps is about as exciting as you could expect. Lots of planes need to take off and land safely, and I make sure everything goes smoothly.

You wouldn't believe how hot it is here! The bus ride that takes us from the control tower to the base is thirty minutes of sweltering heat. Even on full blast, the air conditioners don't do a thing! It's one hundred and twenty-seven degrees in the shade, except there's absolutely no shade. Just sand. (I included some for your growing collection of beach sand. Now you have some sand from halfway around the world!) To see how hot it is here, put it in the microwave for about forty-five seconds. On the other hand, don't. In fact, forget I even wrote that!

I miss you guys like crazy, and I don't want you worrying about me. We're miles away from any real fighting that takes place. The bad news is, we don't know when Uncle Sam will send us home. The good news? I've already picked out my Halloween costume for next year.

I love you so much!

Mom

P.S. Help your sisters and Dad as much as possible while I'm gone.

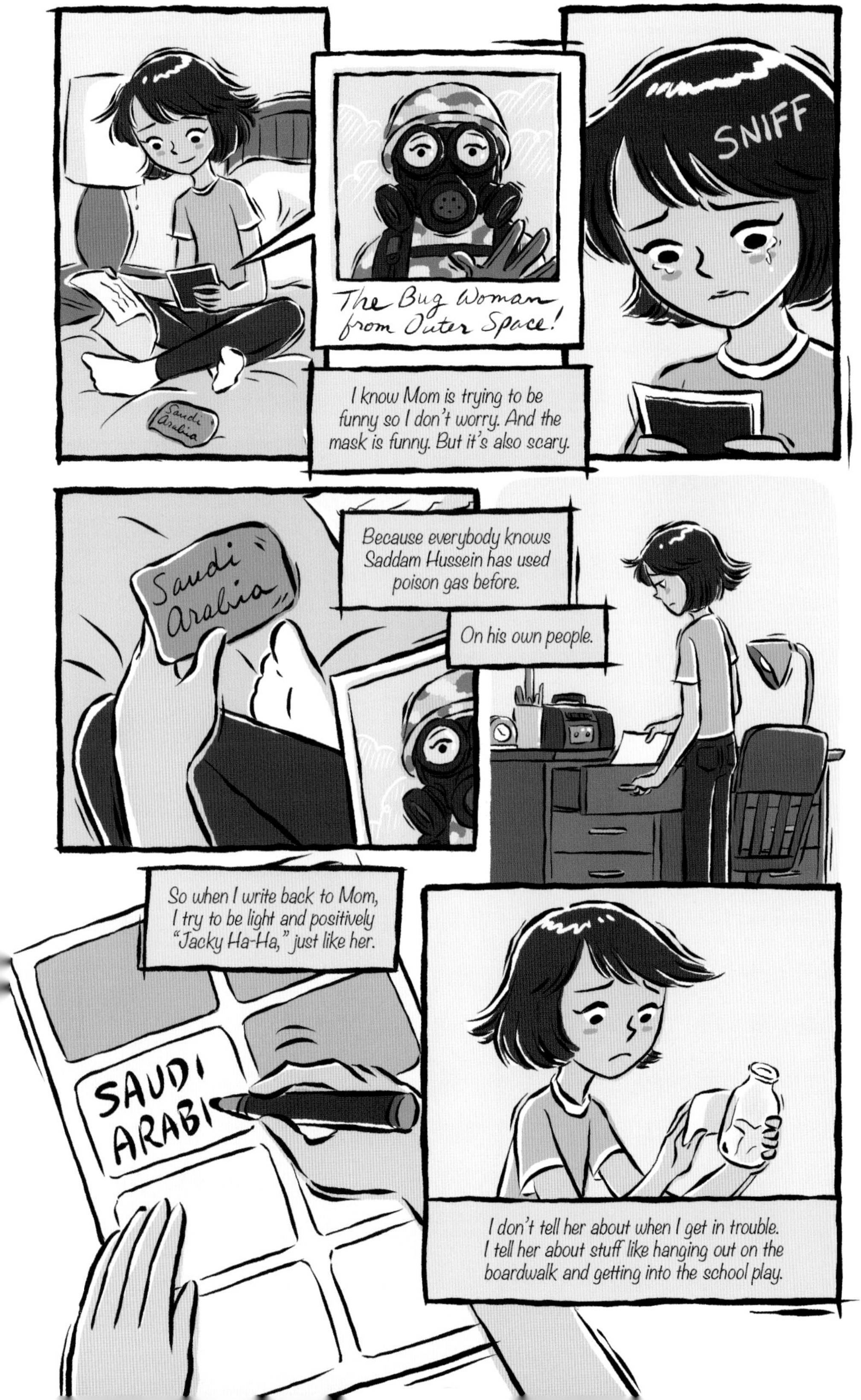

Saudi Arabia
The Bug Woman from Outer Space!
SNIFF
I know Mom is trying to be funny so I don't worry. And the mask is funny. But it's also scary.
Saudi Arabia
Because everybody knows Saddam Hussein has used poison gas before.
On his own people.
So when I write back to Mom, I try to be light and positively "Jacky Ha-Ha," just like her.
SAUDI ARABI
I don't tell her about when I get in trouble. I tell her about stuff like hanging out on the boardwalk and getting into the school play.

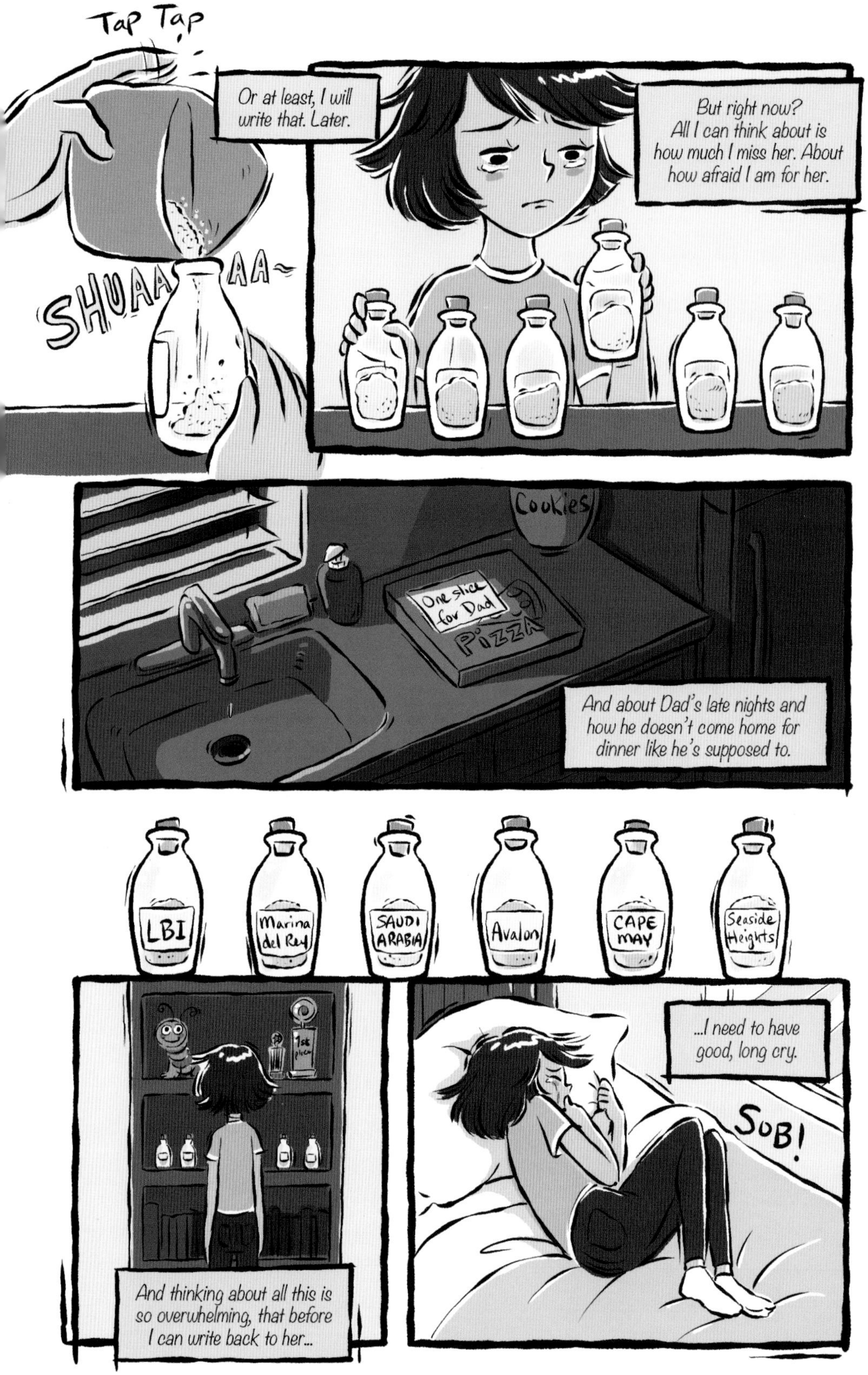
Tap Tap
SHUAAAA~
Or at least, I will write that. Later.
But right now? All I can think about is how much I miss her. About how afraid I am for her.
Cookies
One slice for Dad
PIZZA
And about Dad's late nights and how he doesn't come home for dinner like he's supposed to.
LBI
Marina del Rey
SAUDI ARABIA
Avalon
CAPE MAY
Seaside Heights
1st place
And thinking about all this is so overwhelming, that before I can write back to her...
...I need to have good, long cry.
SOB!

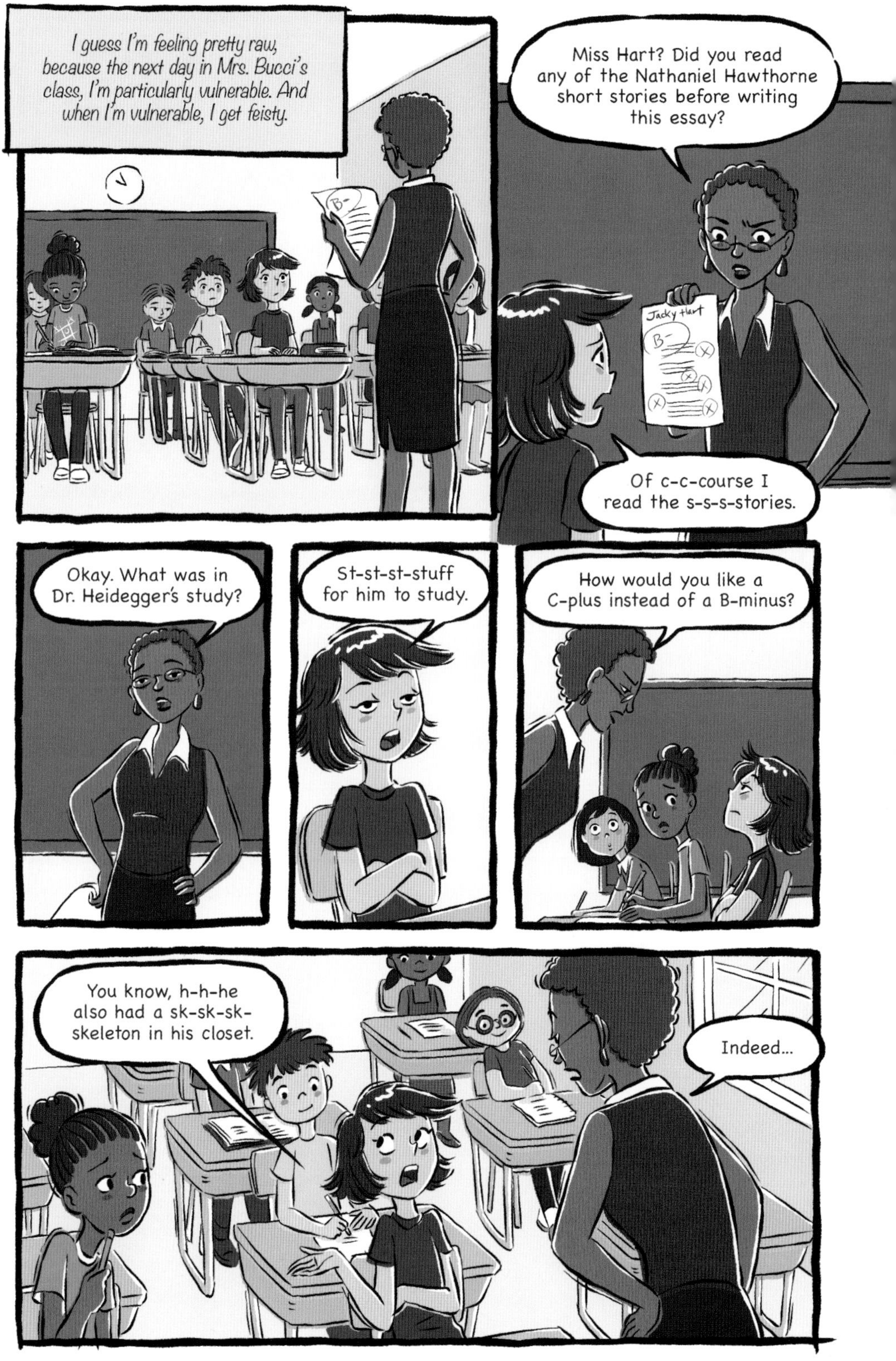

I guess I'm feeling pretty raw, because the next day in Mrs. Bucci's class, I'm particularly vulnerable. And when I'm vulnerable, I get feisty.
Miss Hart? Did you read any of the Nathaniel Hawthorne short stories before writing this essay?
Jacky Hart
B-
Of c-c-course I read the s-s-s-stories.
Okay. What was in Dr. Heidegger's study?
St-st-st-stuff for him to study.
How would you like a C-plus instead of a B-minus?
You know, h-h-he also had a sk-sk-sk-skeleton in his closet.
Indeed...

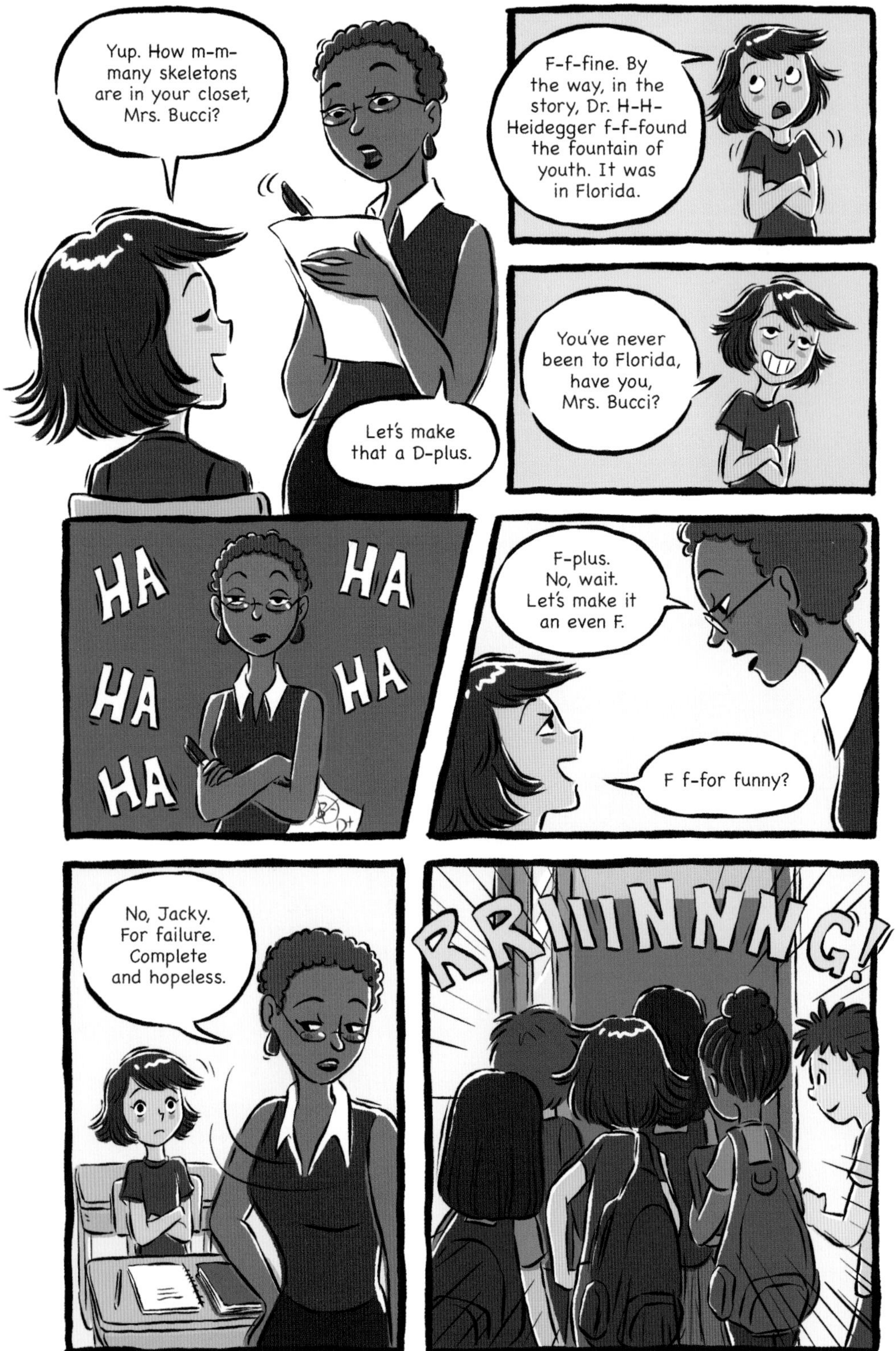

Yup. How m-m-many skeletons are in your closet, Mrs. Bucci?
Let's make that a D-plus.
F-f-fine. By the way, in the story, Dr. H-H-Heidegger f-f-found the fountain of youth. It was in Florida.
You've never been to Florida, have you, Mrs. Bucci?
HA HA HA HA HA
F-plus. No, wait. Let's make it an even F.
F f-for funny?
No, Jacky. For failure. Complete and hopeless.
RRIIINNNG!

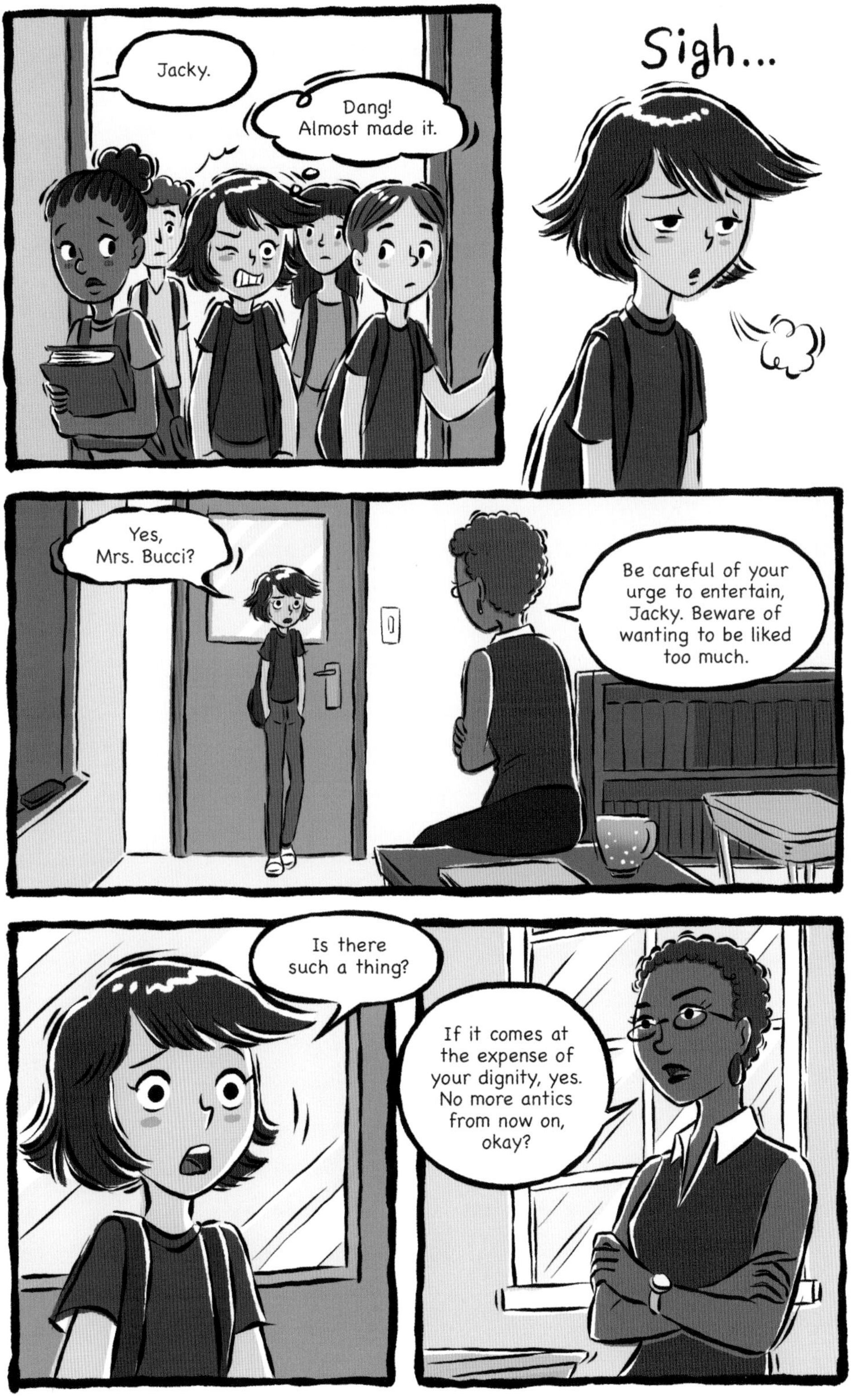
Jacky.
Dang! Almost made it.
Sigh...
Yes, Mrs. Bucci?
Be careful of your urge to entertain, Jacky. Beware of wanting to be liked too much.
Is there such a thing?
If it comes at the expense of your dignity, yes. No more antics from now on, okay?

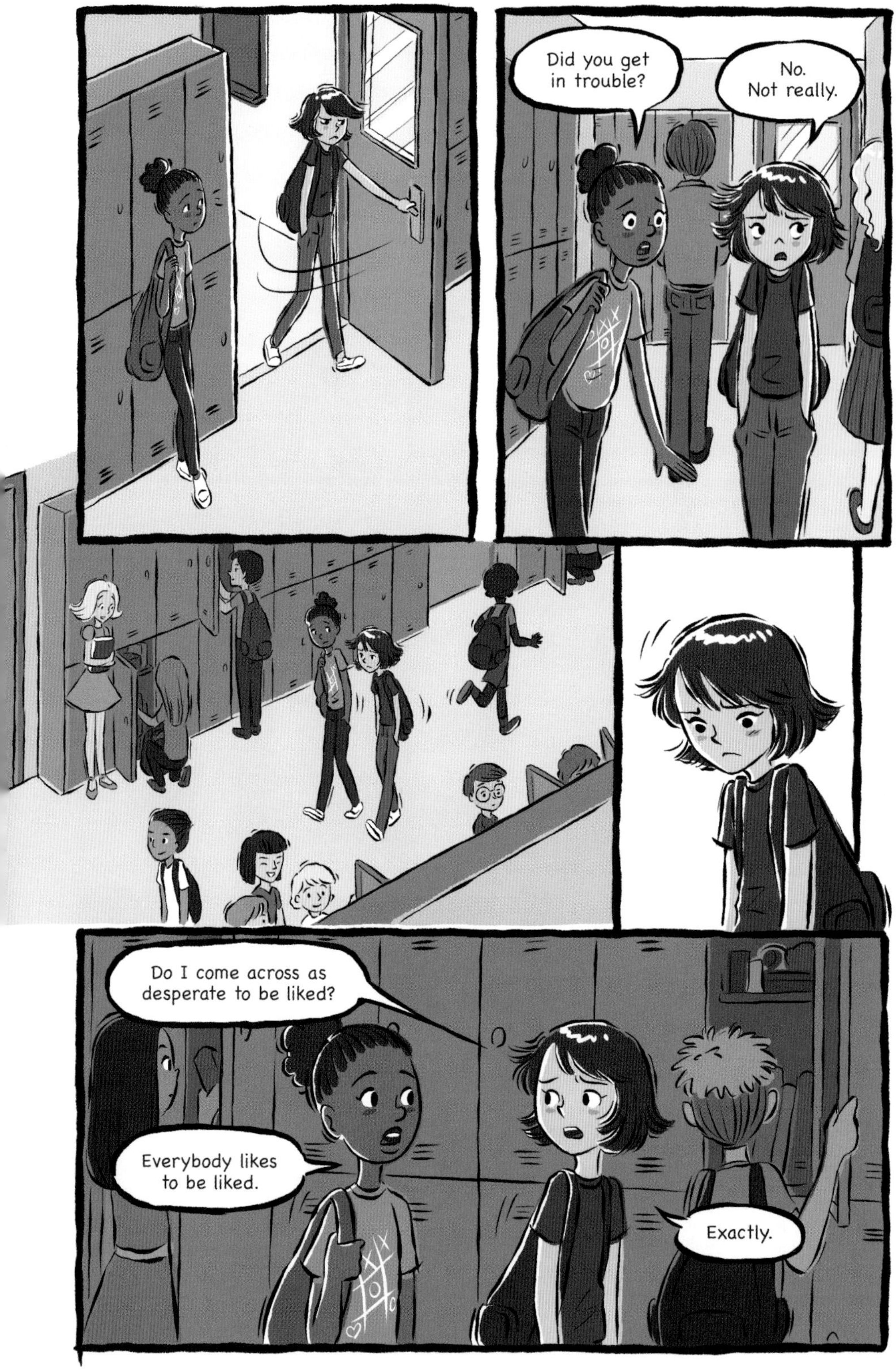
Did you get in trouble?
No. Not really.
Do I come across as desperate to be liked?
Everybody likes to be liked.
Exactly.

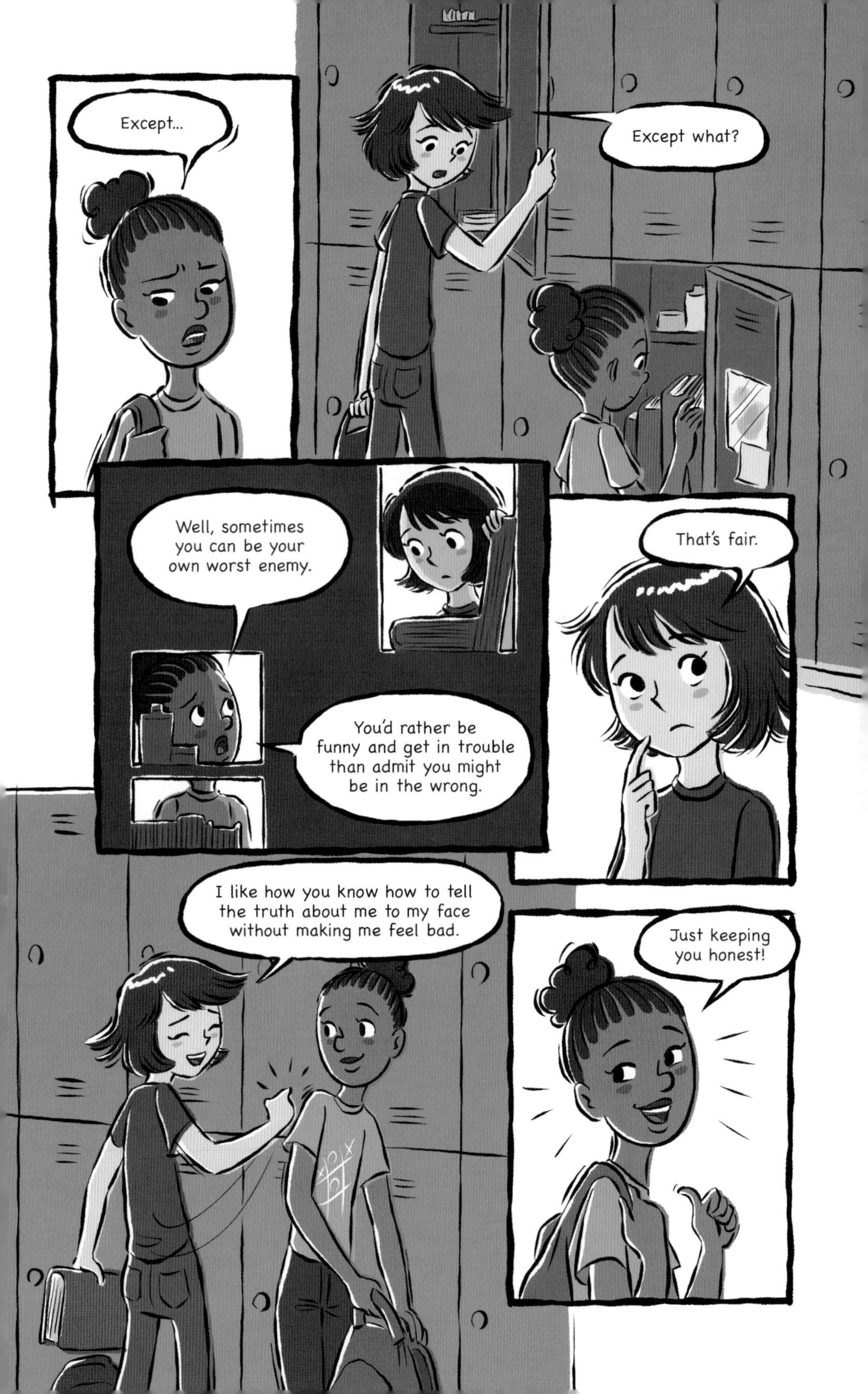
Except...
Except what?
Well, sometimes you can be your own worst enemy.
You'd rather be funny and get in trouble than admit you might be in the wrong.
That's fair.
I like how you know how to tell the truth about me to my face without making me feel bad.
Just keeping you honest!

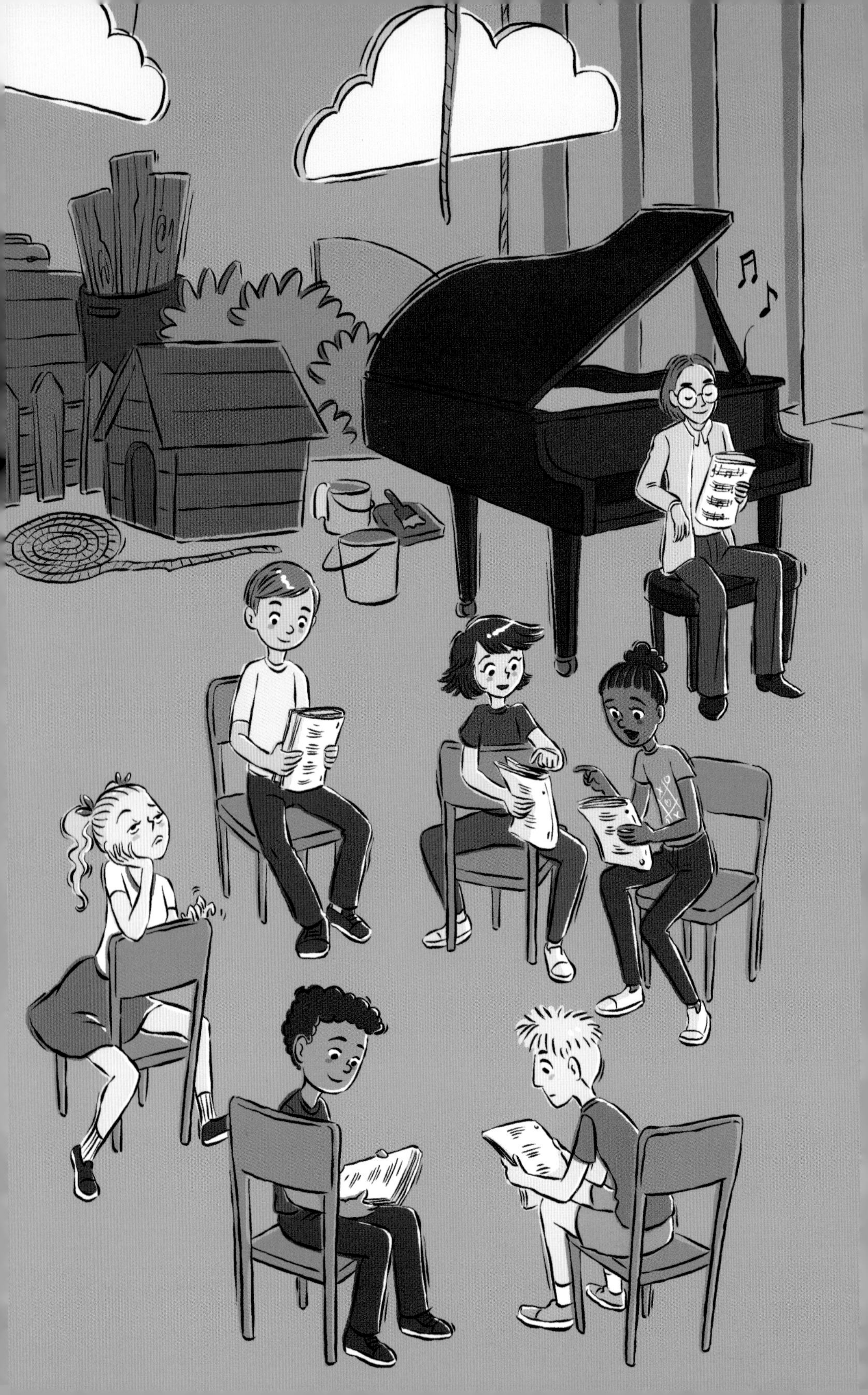

Good afternoon, everybody. And congratulations. The competition for these six roles was pretty intense. So give yourselves a round of applause.

CLAP CLAP CLAP

Before we start our first read-through, I want to warm up your ears.

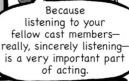

CLAP CLAP CLAP CLAP

Because listening to your fellow cast members—really, sincerely listening—is a very important part of acting.

Meredith?

Yes, Ms. O'Mara?

I don't mean to put you on the spot, but would you sing your Schroeder song for us?

Right now?

If you don't mind. I want the cast to hear it.

To really listen to it.

73

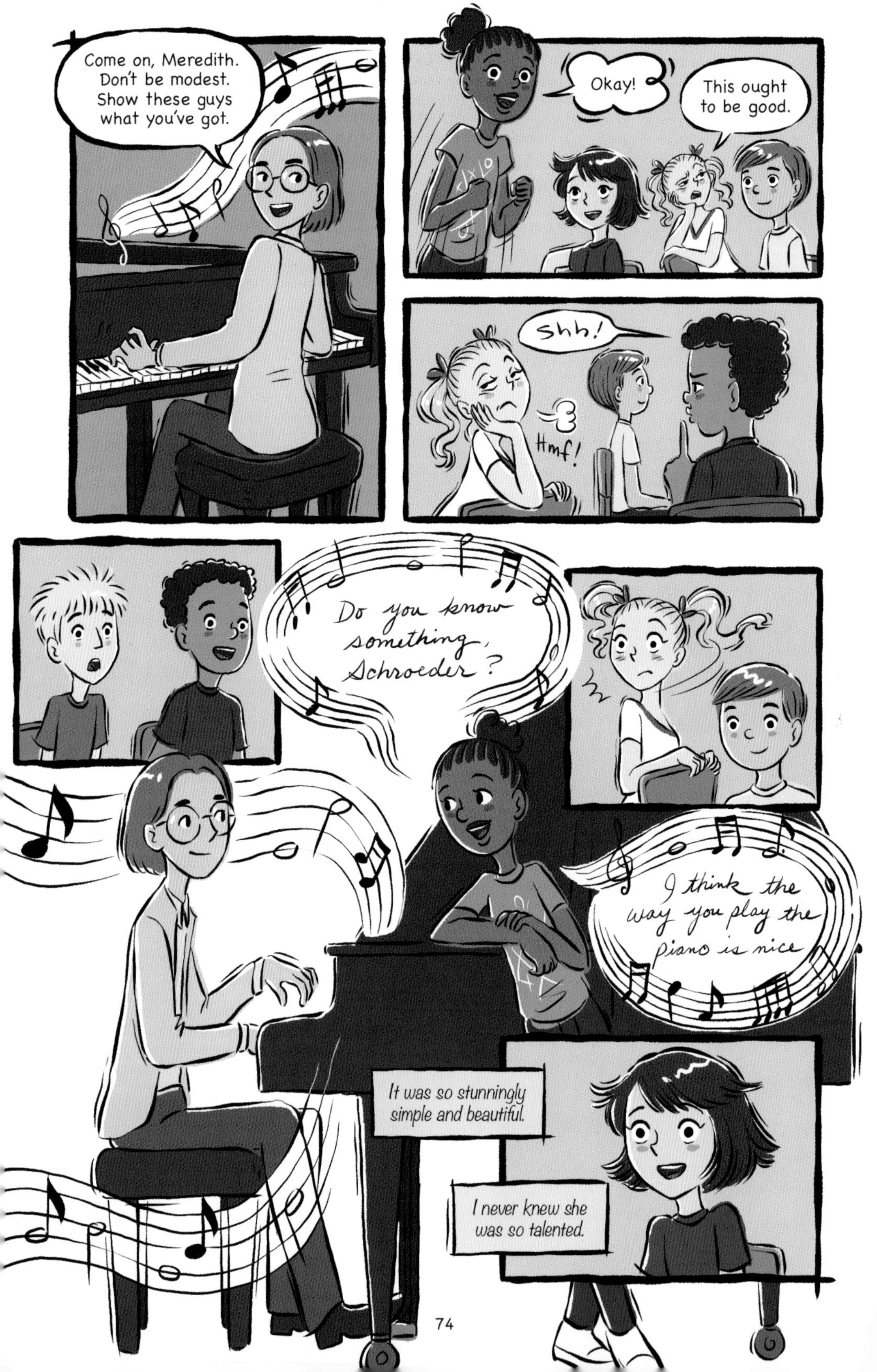
Come on, Meredith. Don't be modest. Show these guys what you've got.
Okay!
This ought to be good.
Shh!
Hmf!
Do you know something, Schroeder?
I think the way you play the piano is nice
It was so stunningly simple and beautiful.
I never knew she was so talented.

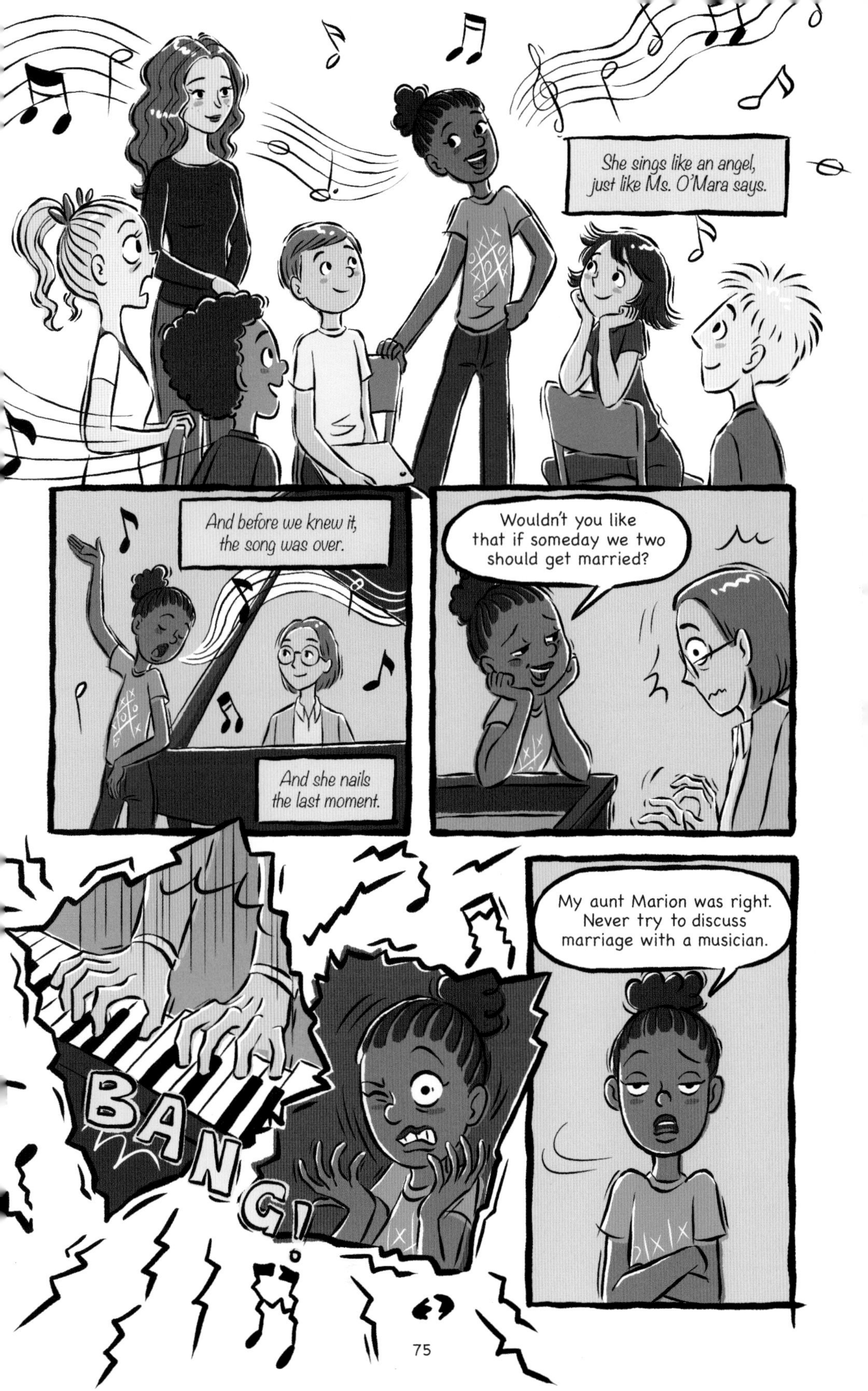

She sings like an angel, just like Ms. O'Mara says.
And before we knew it, the song was over.
And she nails the last moment.
Wouldn't you like that if someday we two should get married?
BANG!
My aunt Marion was right. Never try to discuss marriage with a musician.

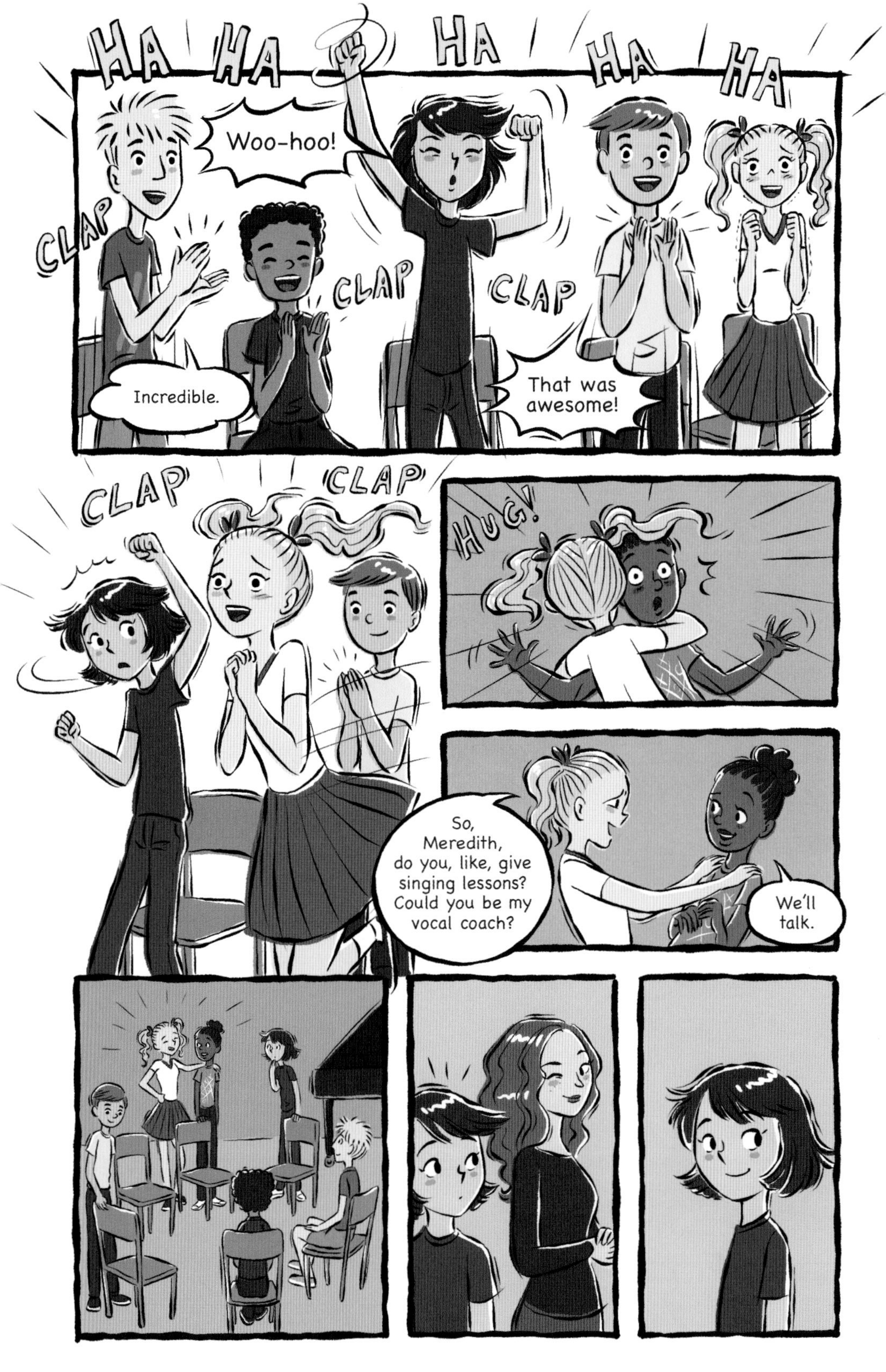
HA HA HA HA HA
Woo-hoo!
CLAP
CLAP
CLAP
Incredible.
That was awesome!
CLAP
CLAP
HUG!
So, Meredith, do you, like, give singing lessons? Could you be my vocal coach?
We'll talk.

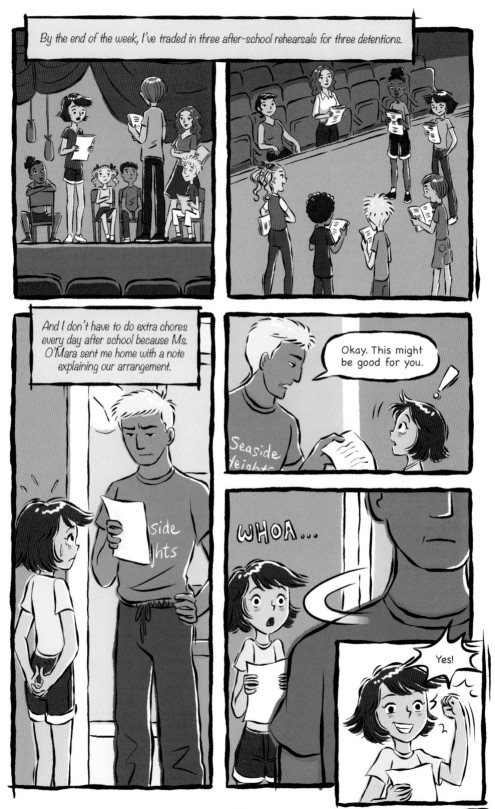

By the end of the week, I've traded in three after-school rehearsals for three detentions.

And I don't have to do extra chores every day after school because Ms. O'Mara sent me home with a note explaining our arrangement.

Okay. This might be good for you.

WHOA...

Yes!

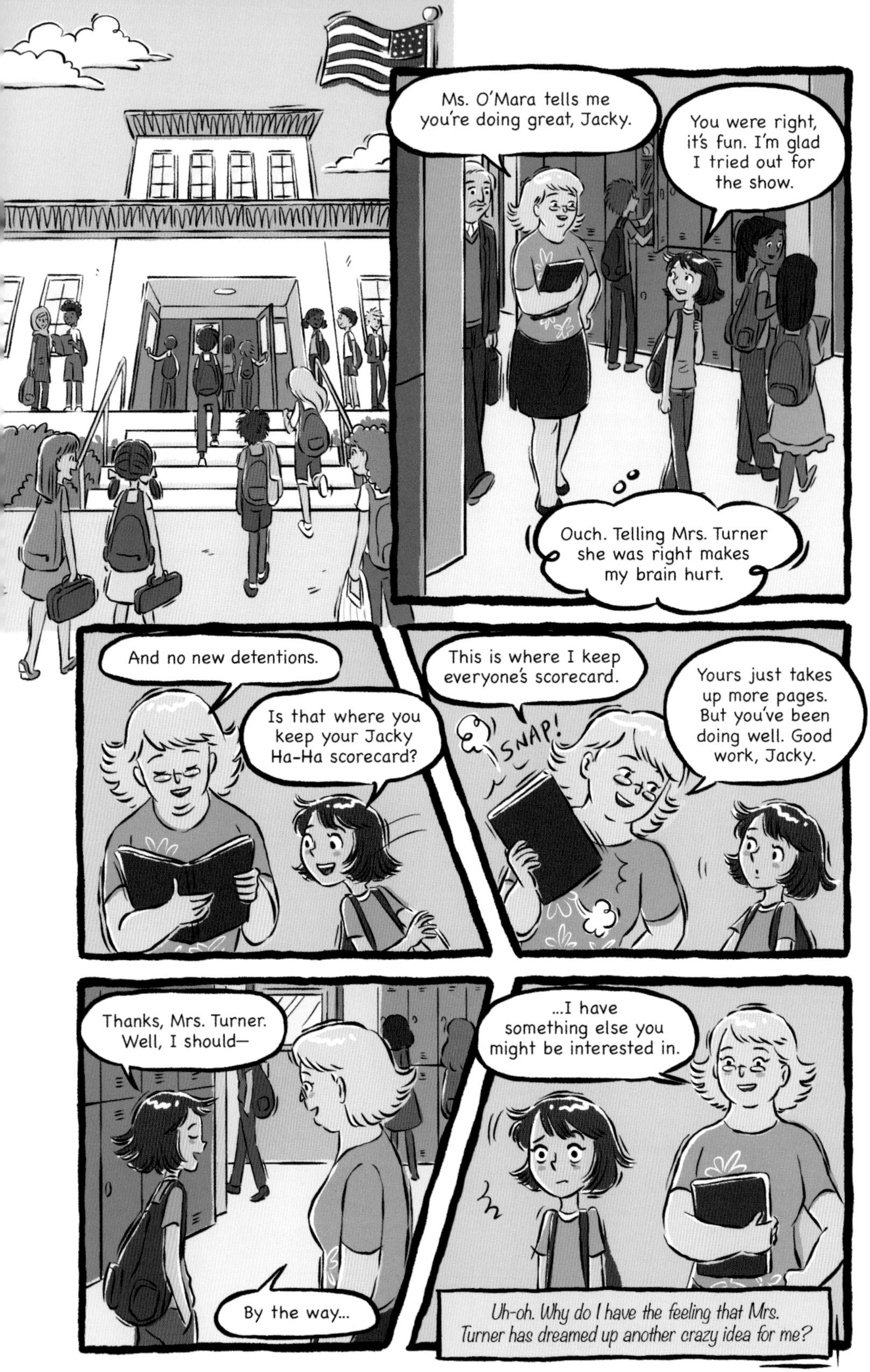
Ms. O'Mara tells me you're doing great, Jacky.
You were right, it's fun. I'm glad I tried out for the show.
Ouch. Telling Mrs. Turner she was right makes my brain hurt.
And no new detentions.
Is that where you keep your Jacky Ha-Ha scorecard?
This is where I keep everyone's scorecard.
SNAP!
Yours just takes up more pages. But you've been doing well. Good work, Jacky.
Thanks, Mrs. Turner. Well, I should—
By the way...
...I have something else you might be interested in.
Uh-oh. Why do I have the feeling that Mrs. Turner has dreamed up another crazy idea for me?

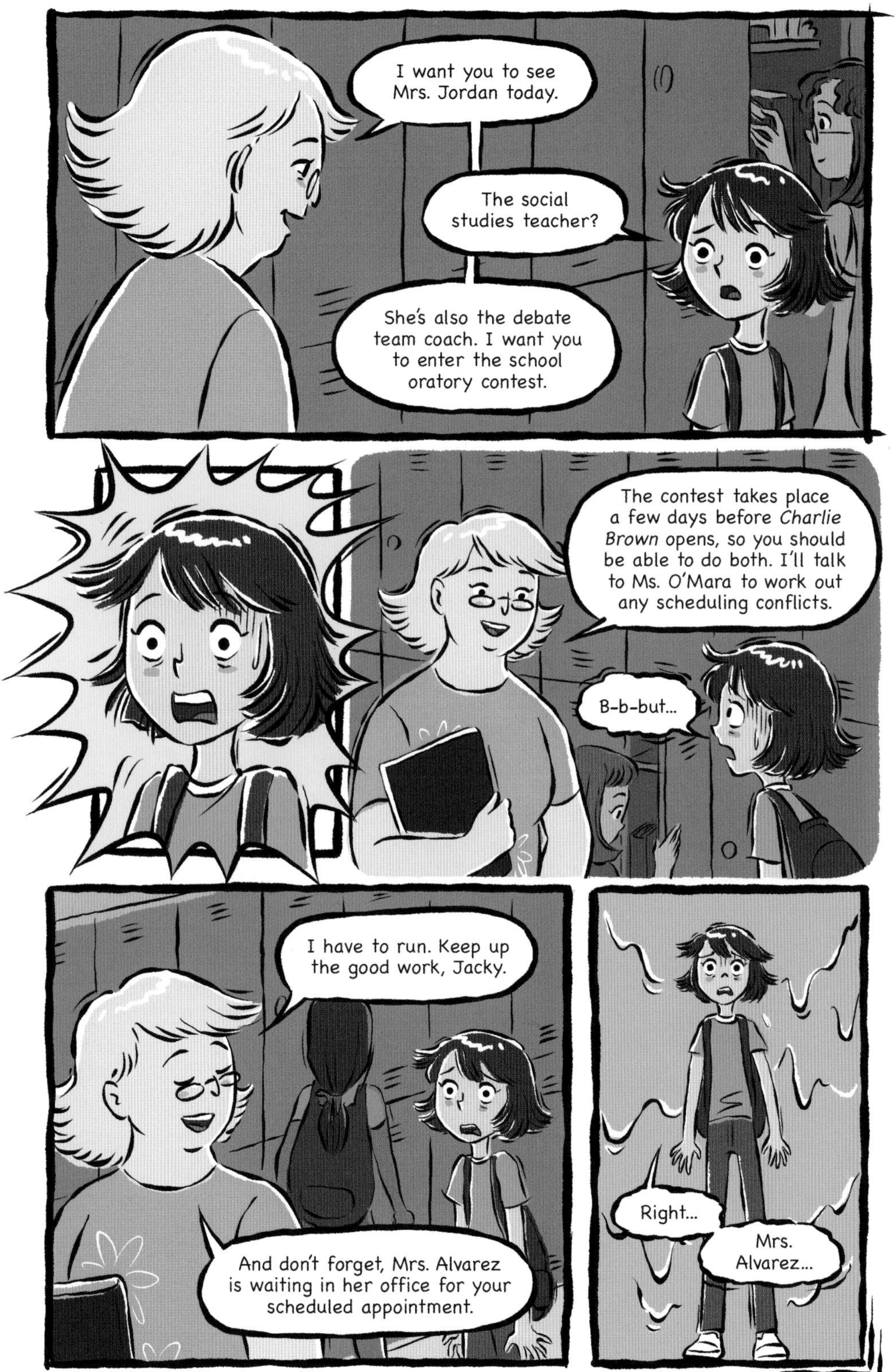
I want you to see Mrs. Jordan today.
The social studies teacher?
She's also the debate team coach. I want you to enter the school oratory contest.
The contest takes place a few days before *Charlie Brown* opens, so you should be able to do both. I'll talk to Ms. O'Mara to work out any scheduling conflicts.
B-b-but...
I have to run. Keep up the good work, Jacky.
And don't forget, Mrs. Alvarez is waiting in her office for your scheduled appointment.
Right...
Mrs. Alvarez...

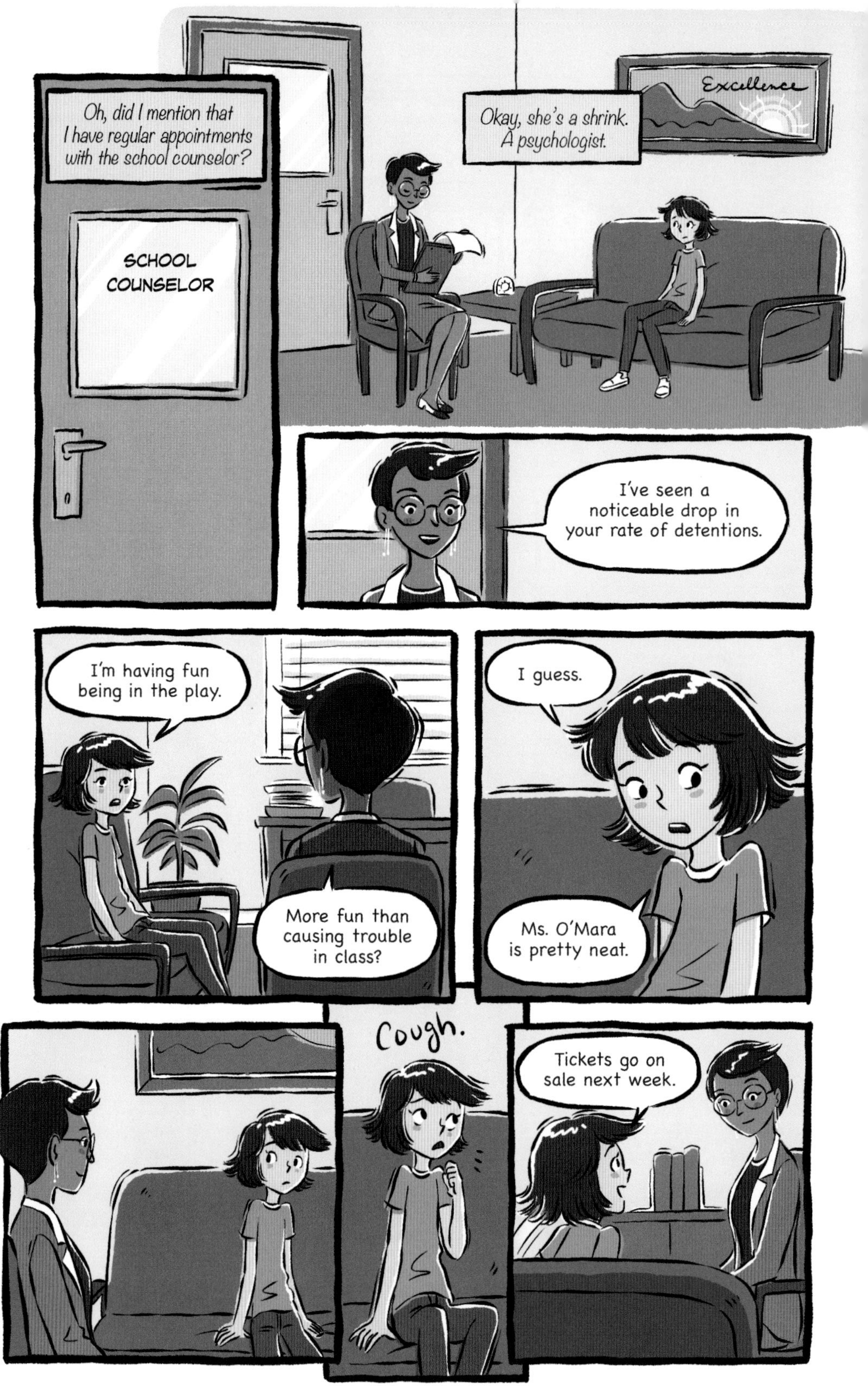
Oh, did I mention that I have regular appointments with the school counselor?
SCHOOL COUNSELOR
Okay, she's a shrink. A psychologist.
Excellence
I've seen a noticeable drop in your rate of detentions.
I'm having fun being in the play.
More fun than causing trouble in class?
I guess.
Ms. O'Mara is pretty neat.
Cough.
Tickets go on sale next week.

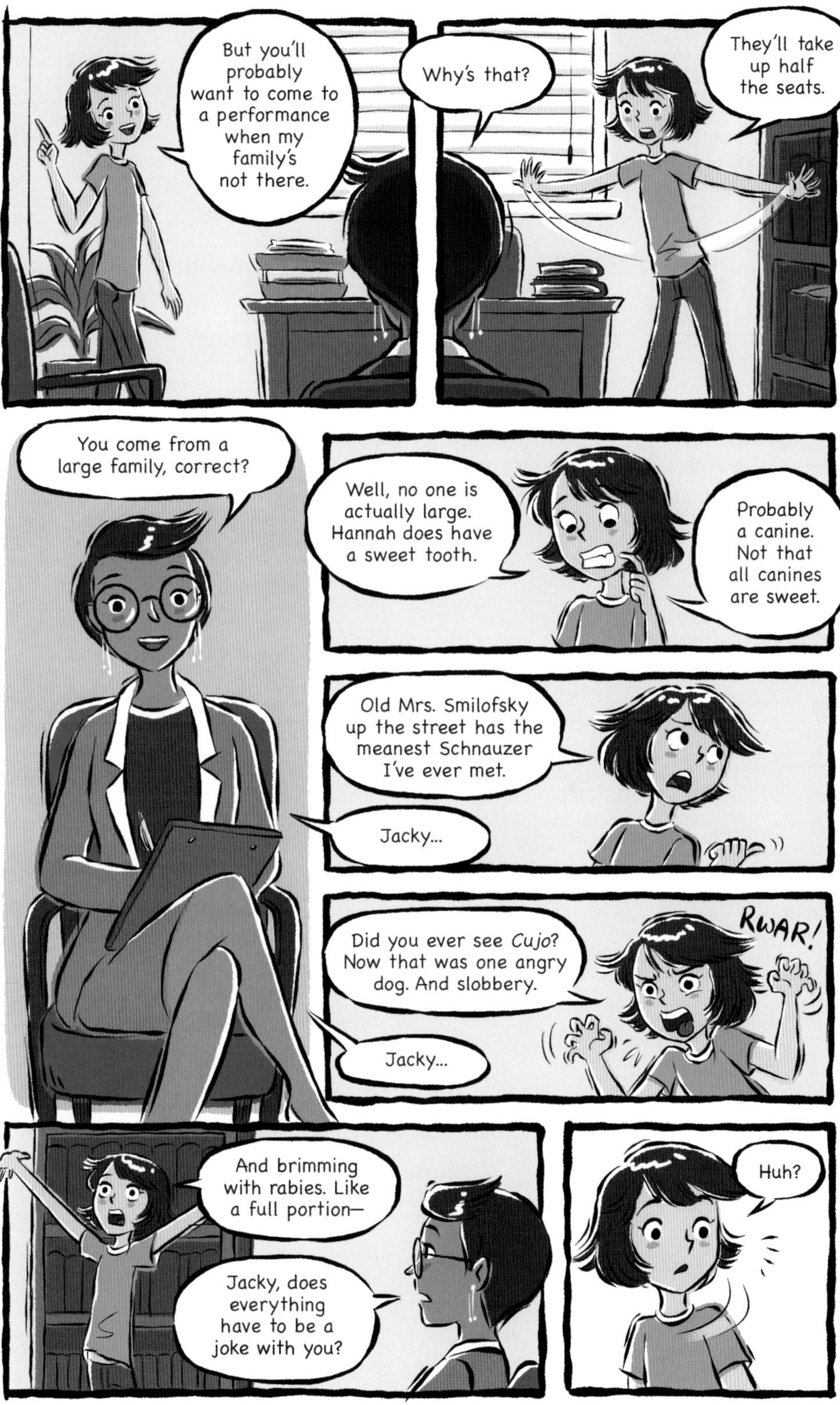
But you'll probably want to come to a performance when my family's not there.
Why's that?
They'll take up half the seats.
You come from a large family, correct?
Well, no one is actually large. Hannah does have a sweet tooth.
Probably a canine. Not that all canines are sweet.
Old Mrs. Smilofsky up the street has the meanest Schnauzer I've ever met.
Jacky...
Did you ever see *Cujo*? Now that was one angry dog. And slobbery.
RWAR!
Jacky...
And brimming with rabies. Like a full portion—
Jacky, does everything have to be a joke with you?
Huh?

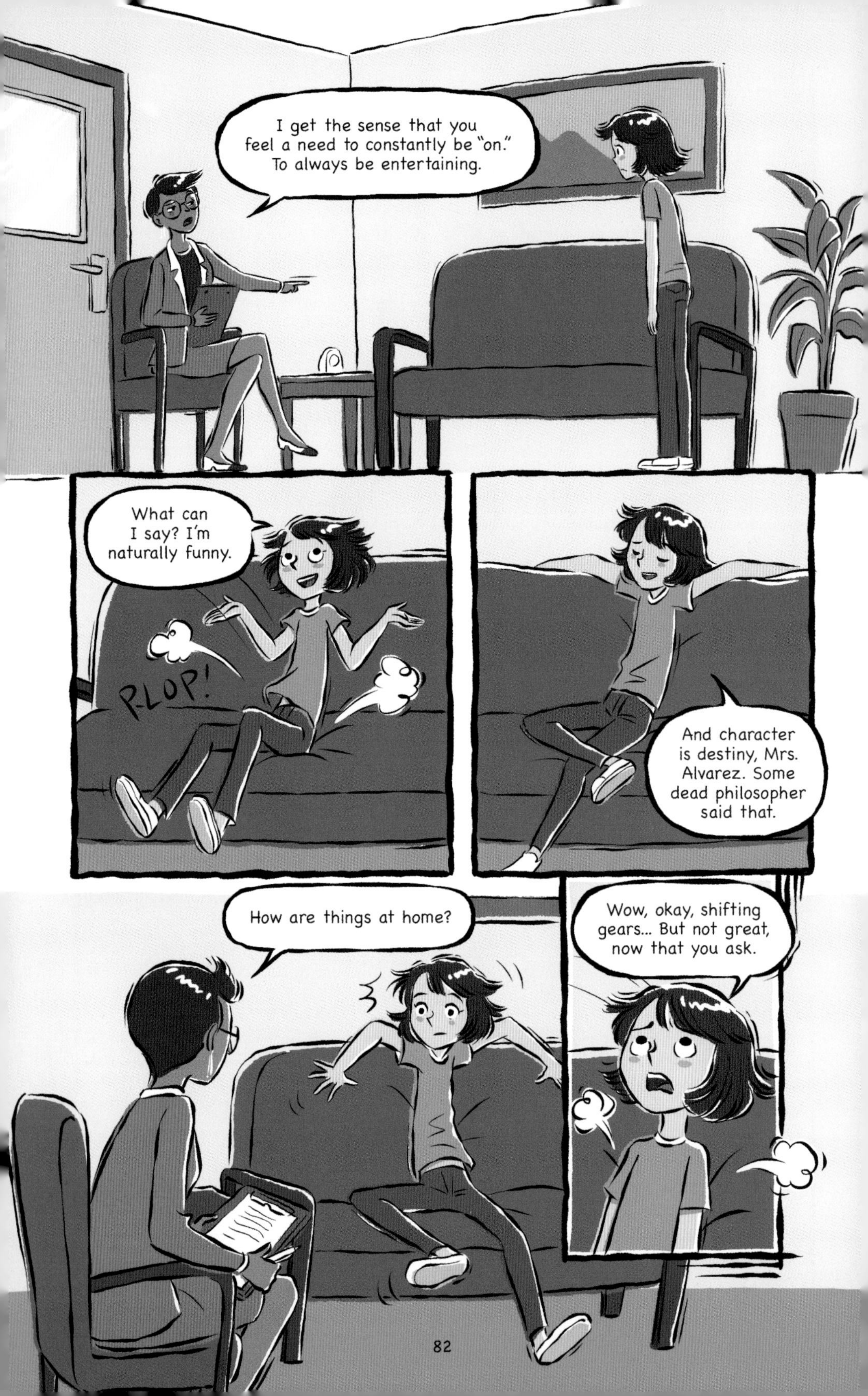
I get the sense that you feel a need to constantly be "on." To always be entertaining.
What can I say? I'm naturally funny.
PLOP!
And character is destiny, Mrs. Alvarez. Some dead philosopher said that.
How are things at home?
Wow, okay, shifting gears... But not great, now that you ask.

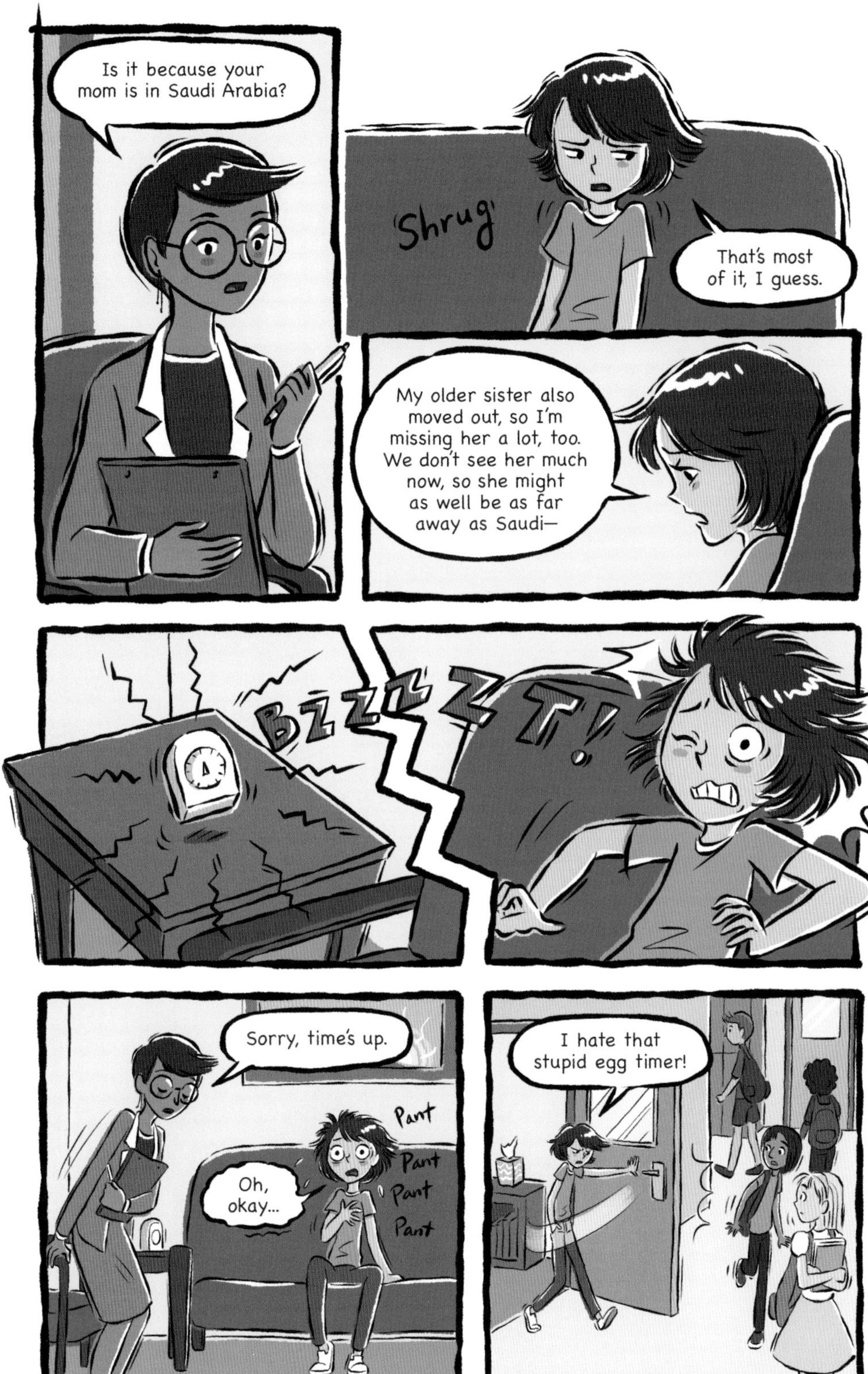

Is it because your mom is in Saudi Arabia?
Shrug
That's most of it, I guess.
My older sister also moved out, so I'm missing her a lot, too. We don't see her much now, so she might as well be as far away as Saudi—
BZZZZZT!
Sorry, time's up.
Pant
Pant
Pant
Pant
Oh, okay...
I hate that stupid egg timer!

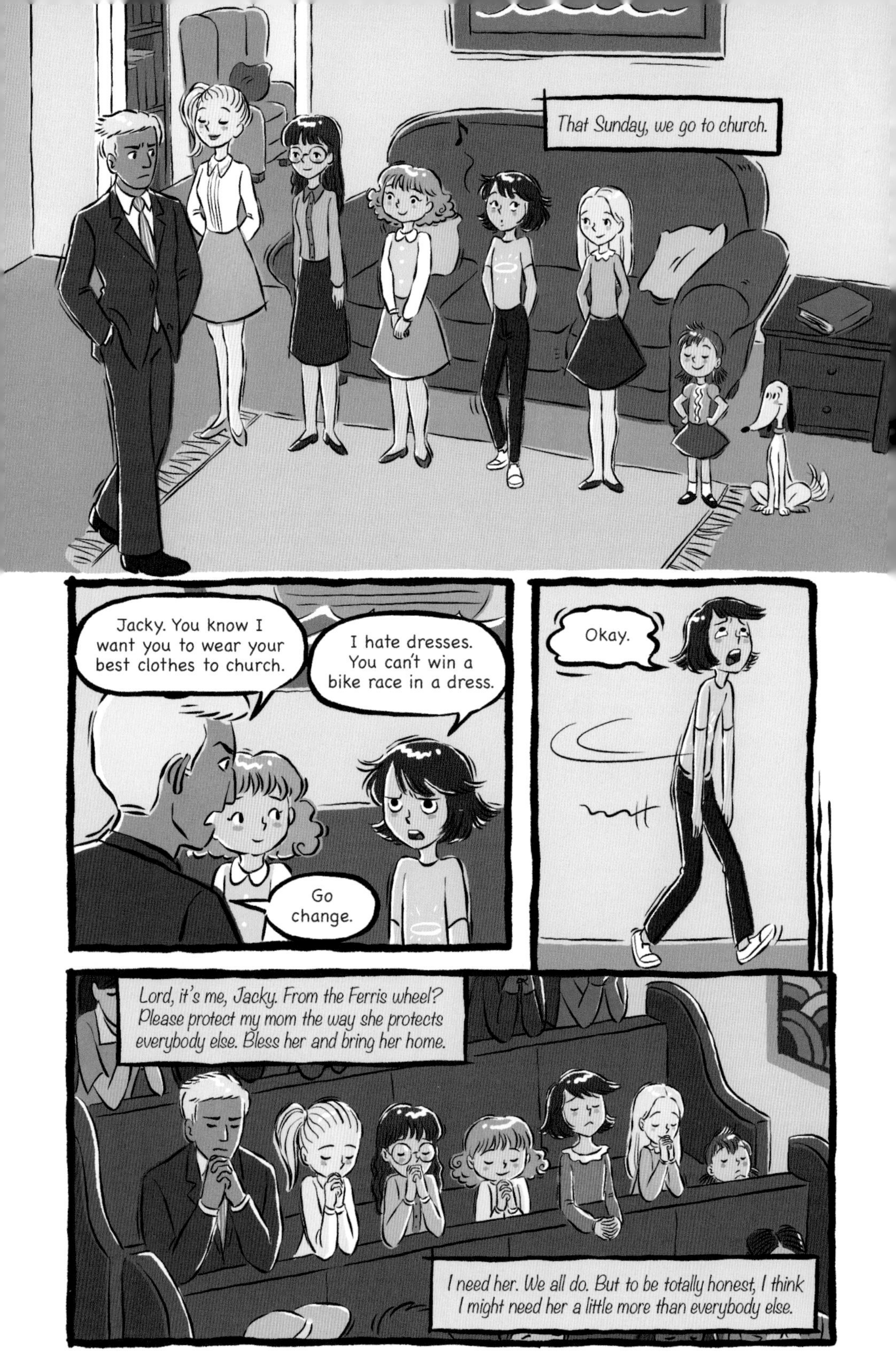
That Sunday, we go to church.
Jacky. You know I want you to wear your best clothes to church.
I hate dresses. You can't win a bike race in a dress.
Go change.
Okay.
Lord, it's me, Jacky. From the Ferris wheel? Please protect my mom the way she protects everybody else. Bless her and bring her home.
I need her. We all do. But to be totally honest, I think I might need her a little more than everybody else.

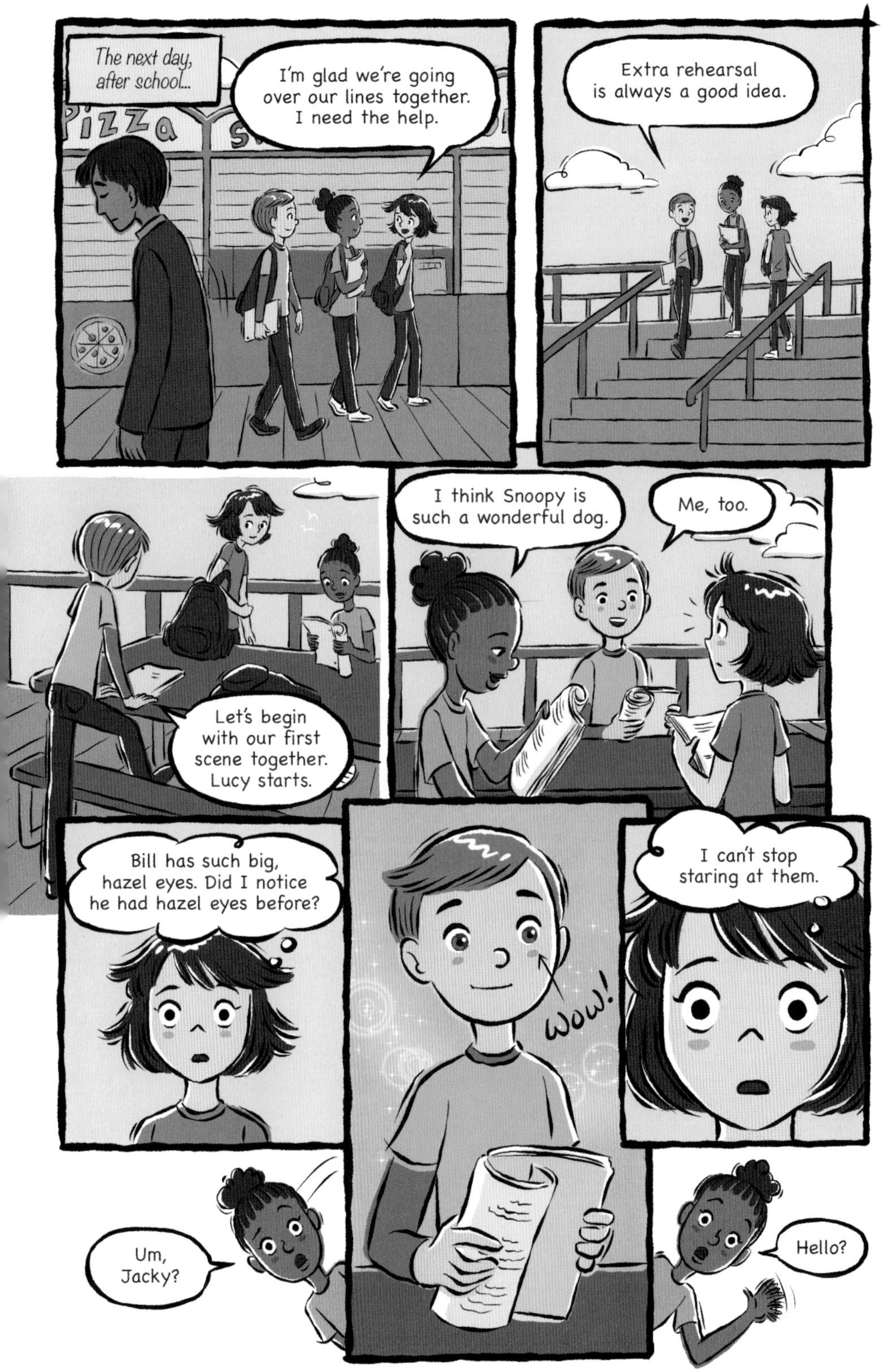
The next day, after school...
I'm glad we're going over our lines together. I need the help.
Pizza
Extra rehearsal is always a good idea.
Let's begin with our first scene together. Lucy starts.
I think Snoopy is such a wonderful dog.
Me, too.
Bill has such big, hazel eyes. Did I notice he had hazel eyes before?
WOW!
I can't stop staring at them.
Um, Jacky?
Hello?

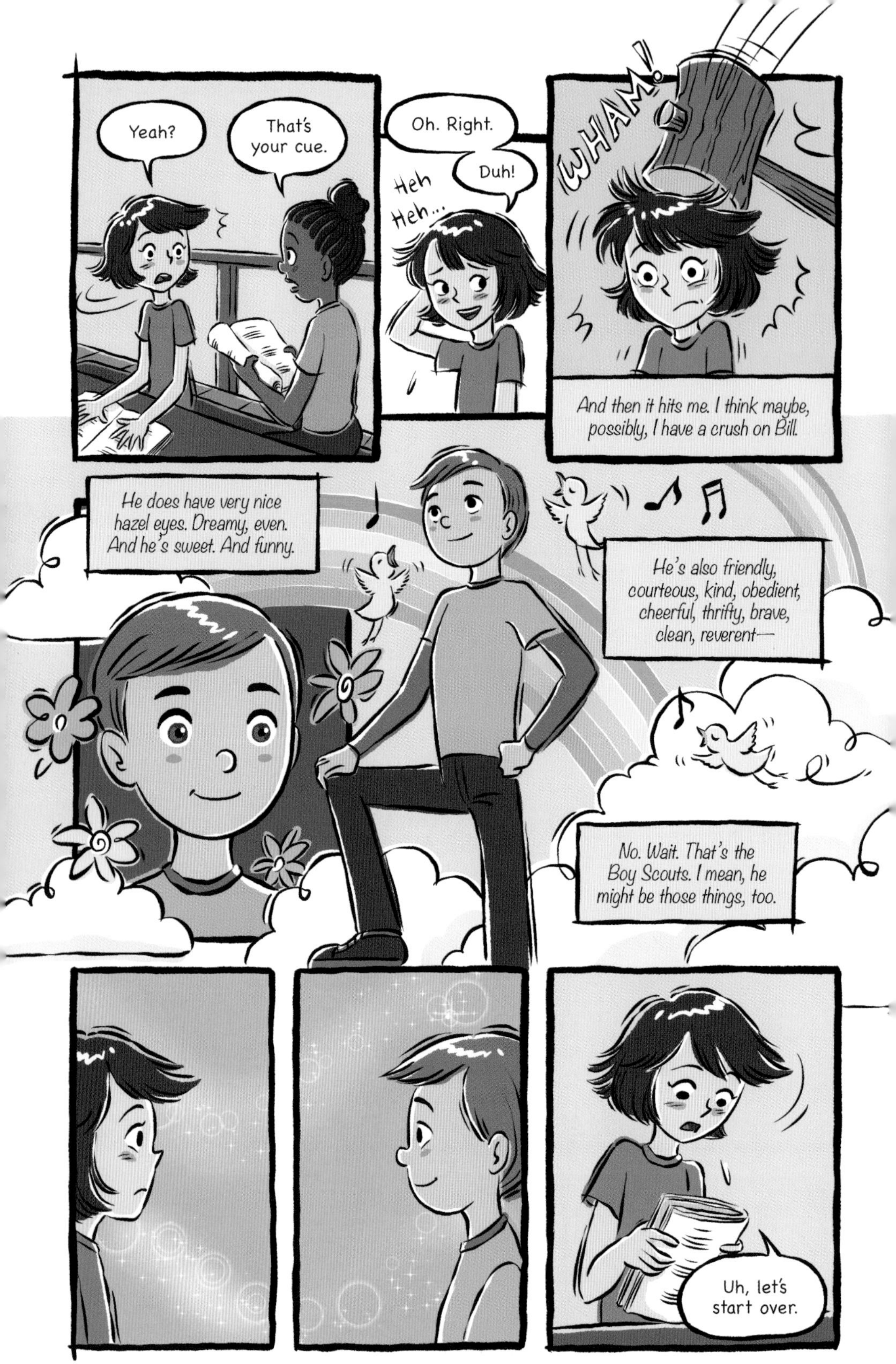
Yeah?
That's your cue.
Oh. Right.
Heh Heh...
Duh!
WHAM!
And then it hits me. I think maybe, possibly, I have a crush on Bill.
He does have very nice hazel eyes. Dreamy, even. And he's sweet. And funny.
He's also friendly, courteous, kind, obedient, cheerful, thrifty, brave, clean, reverent—
No. Wait. That's the Boy Scouts. I mean, he might be those things, too.
Uh, let's start over.

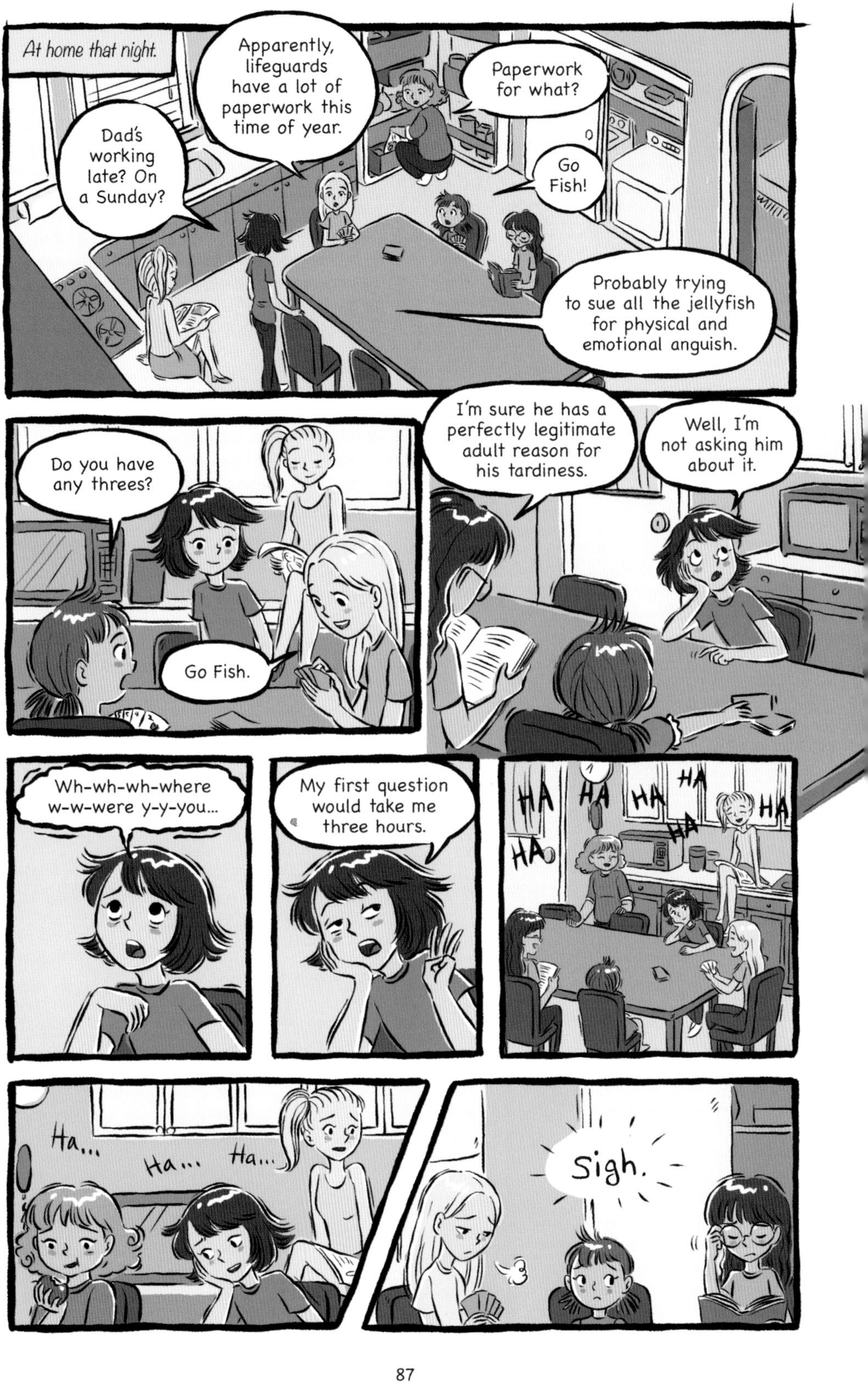
At home that night.
Dad's working late? On a Sunday?
Apparently, lifeguards have a lot of paperwork this time of year.
Paperwork for what?
Go Fish!
Probably trying to sue all the jellyfish for physical and emotional anguish.
Do you have any threes?
Go Fish.
I'm sure he has a perfectly legitimate adult reason for his tardiness.
Well, I'm not asking him about it.
Wh-wh-wh-where w-w-were y-y-you...
My first question would take me three hours.
HA HA HA HA HA HA HA
Ha... Ha... Ha...
Sigh.

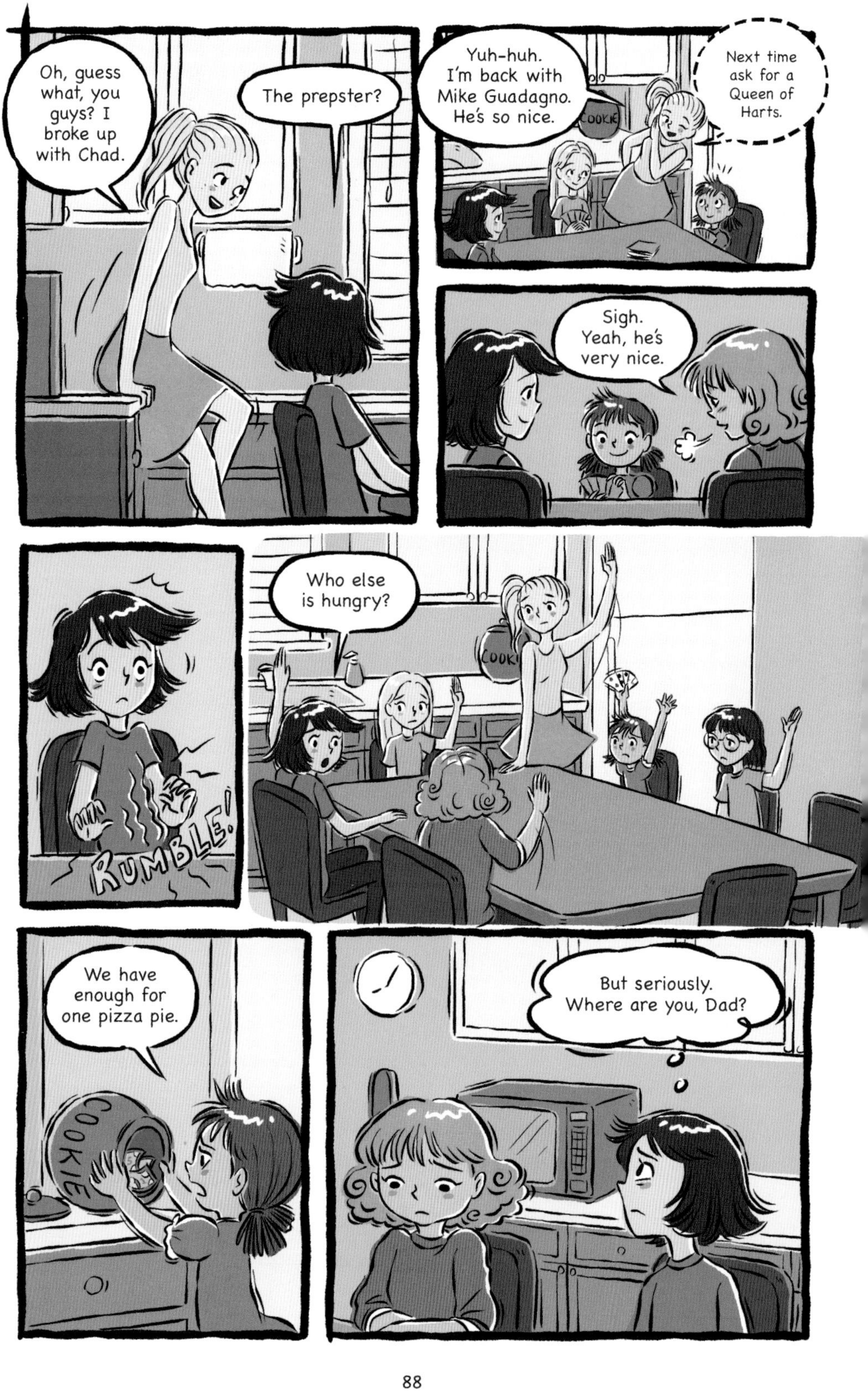
Oh, guess what, you guys? I broke up with Chad.
The prepster?
Yuh-huh. I'm back with Mike Guadagno. He's so nice.
COOKIE
Next time ask for a Queen of Harts.
Sigh. Yeah, he's very nice.
RUMBLE!
Who else is hungry?
COOKIE
We have enough for one pizza pie.
COOKIE
But seriously. Where are you, Dad?

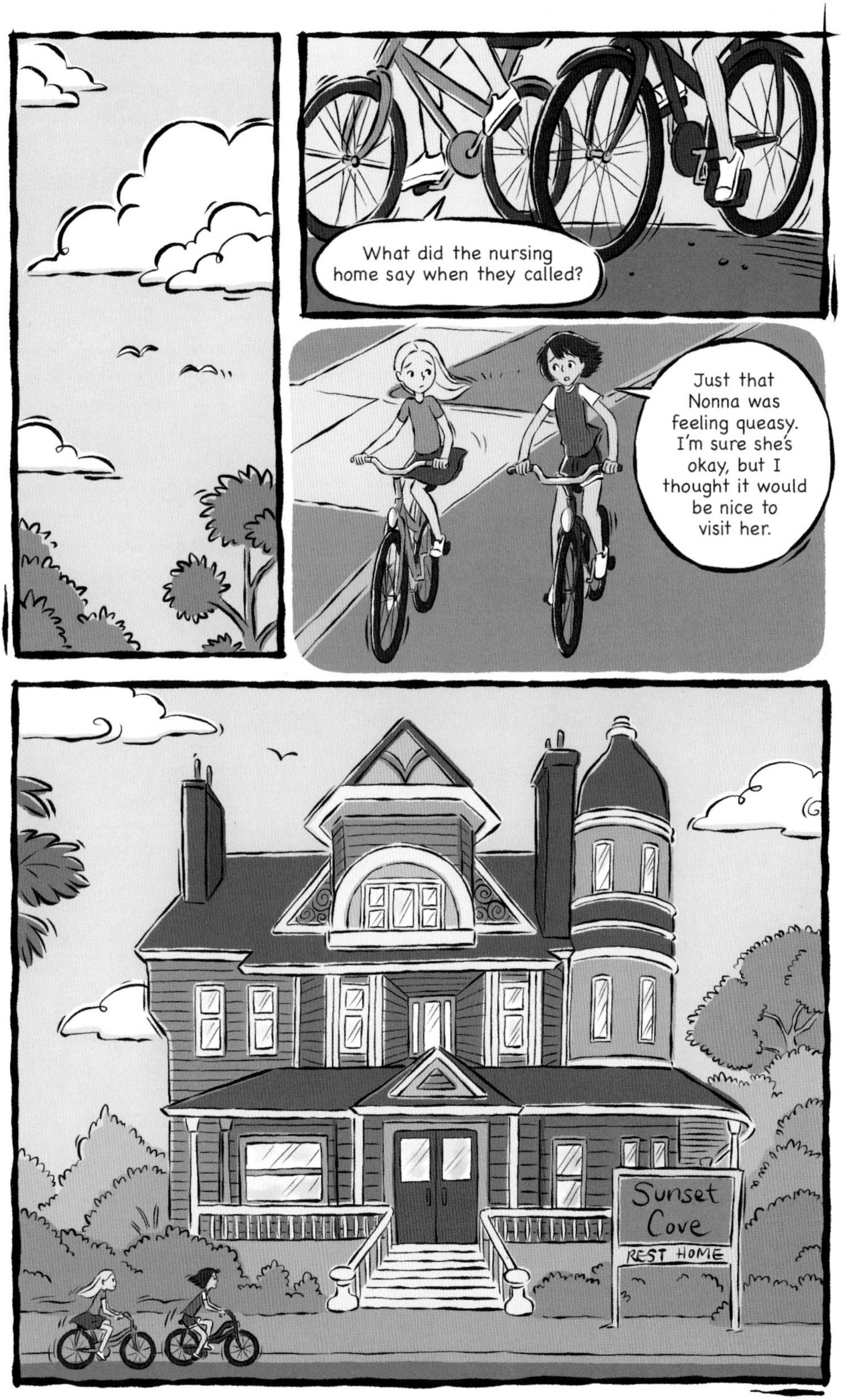
What did the nursing home say when they called?
Just that Nonna was feeling queasy. I'm sure she's okay, but I thought it would be nice to visit her.
Sunset Cove
REST HOME

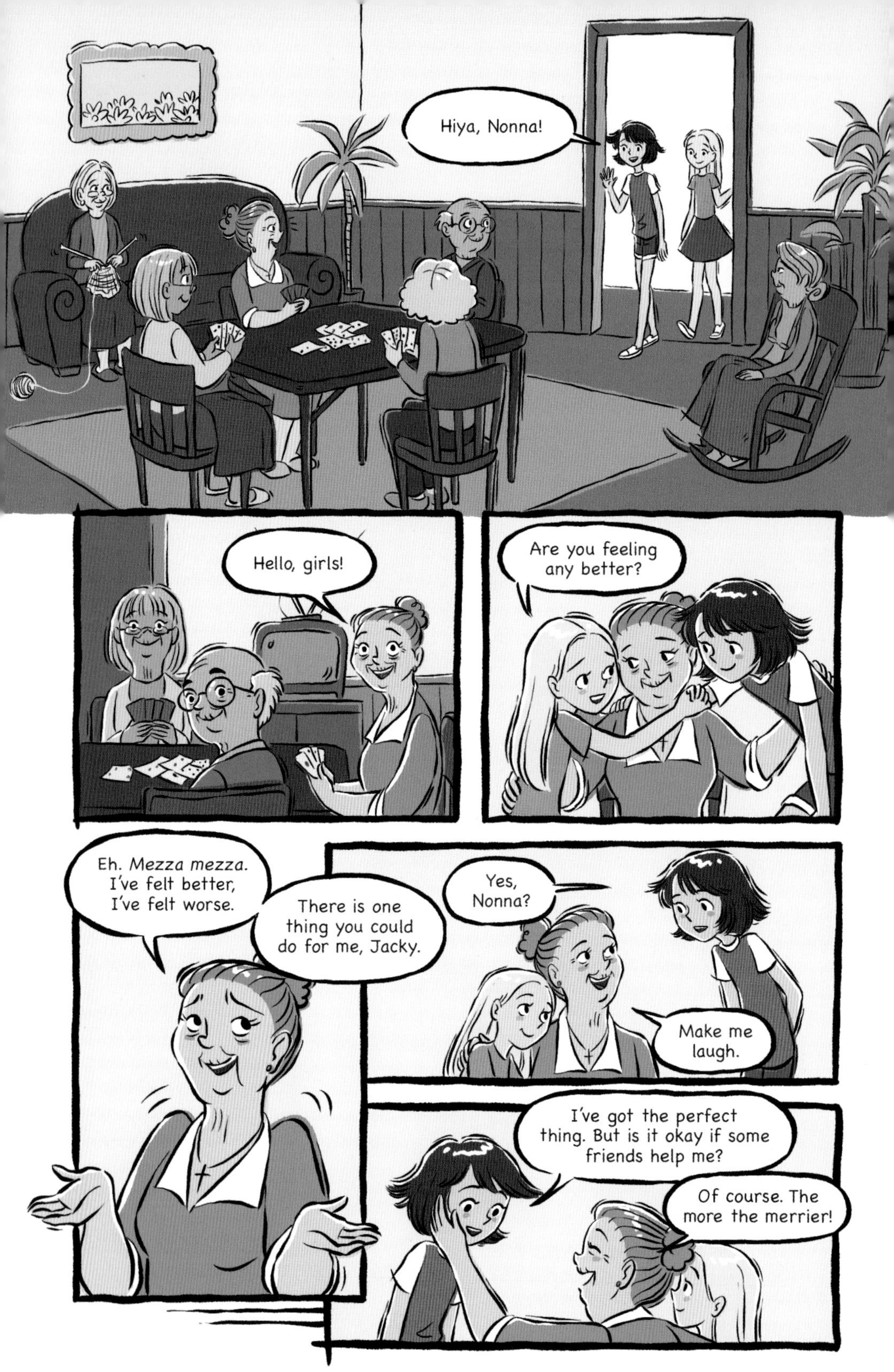

Hiya, Nonna!
Hello, girls!
Are you feeling any better?
Eh. *Mezza mezza.* I've felt better, I've felt worse.
There is one thing you could do for me, Jacky.
Yes, Nonna?
Make me laugh.
I've got the perfect thing. But is it okay if some friends help me?
Of course. The more the merrier!

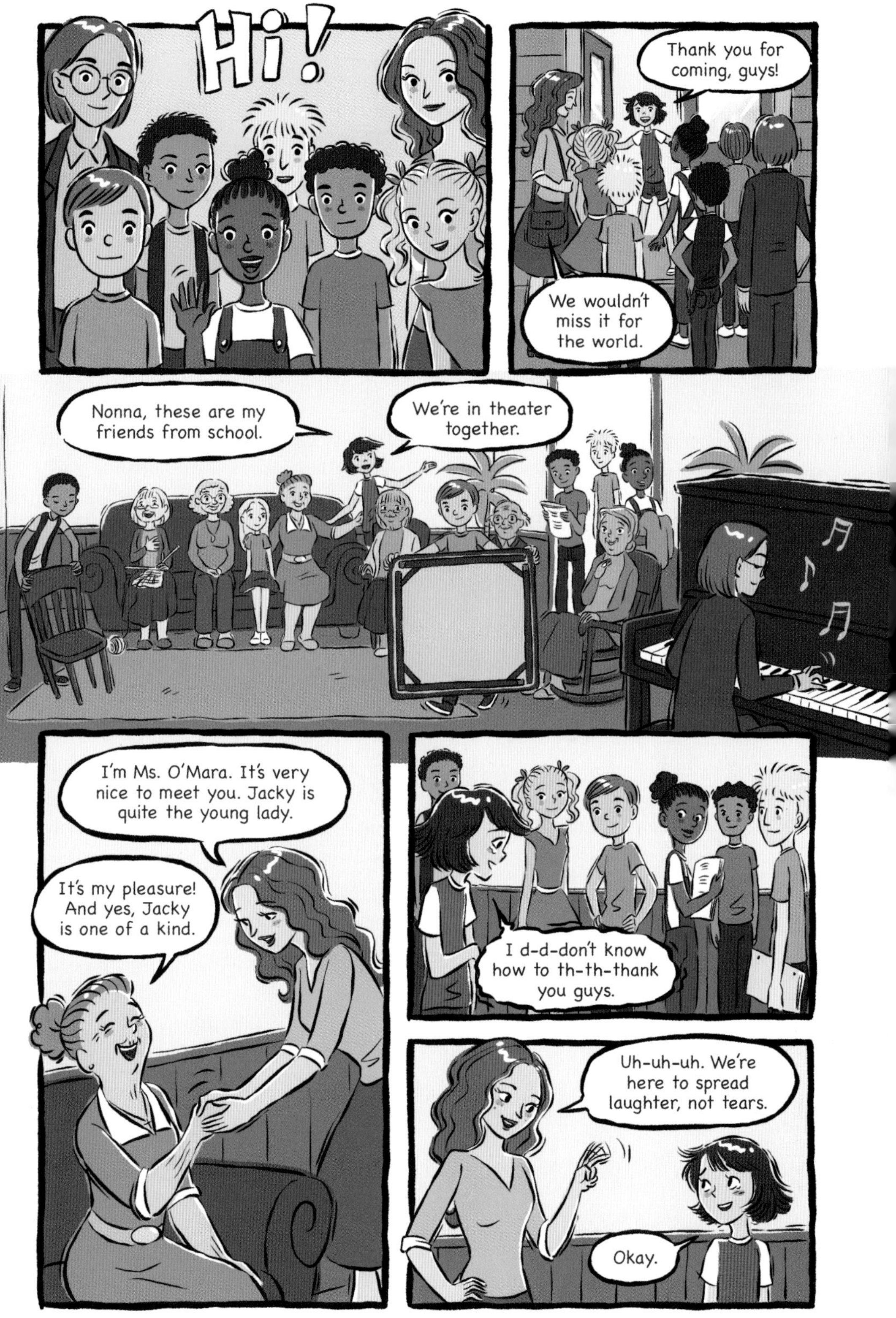
Hi!
Thank you for coming, guys!
We wouldn't miss it for the world.
Nonna, these are my friends from school.
We're in theater together.
I'm Ms. O'Mara. It's very nice to meet you. Jacky is quite the young lady.
It's my pleasure! And yes, Jacky is one of a kind.
I d-d-don't know how to th-th-thank you guys.
Uh-uh-uh. We're here to spread laughter, not tears.
Okay.

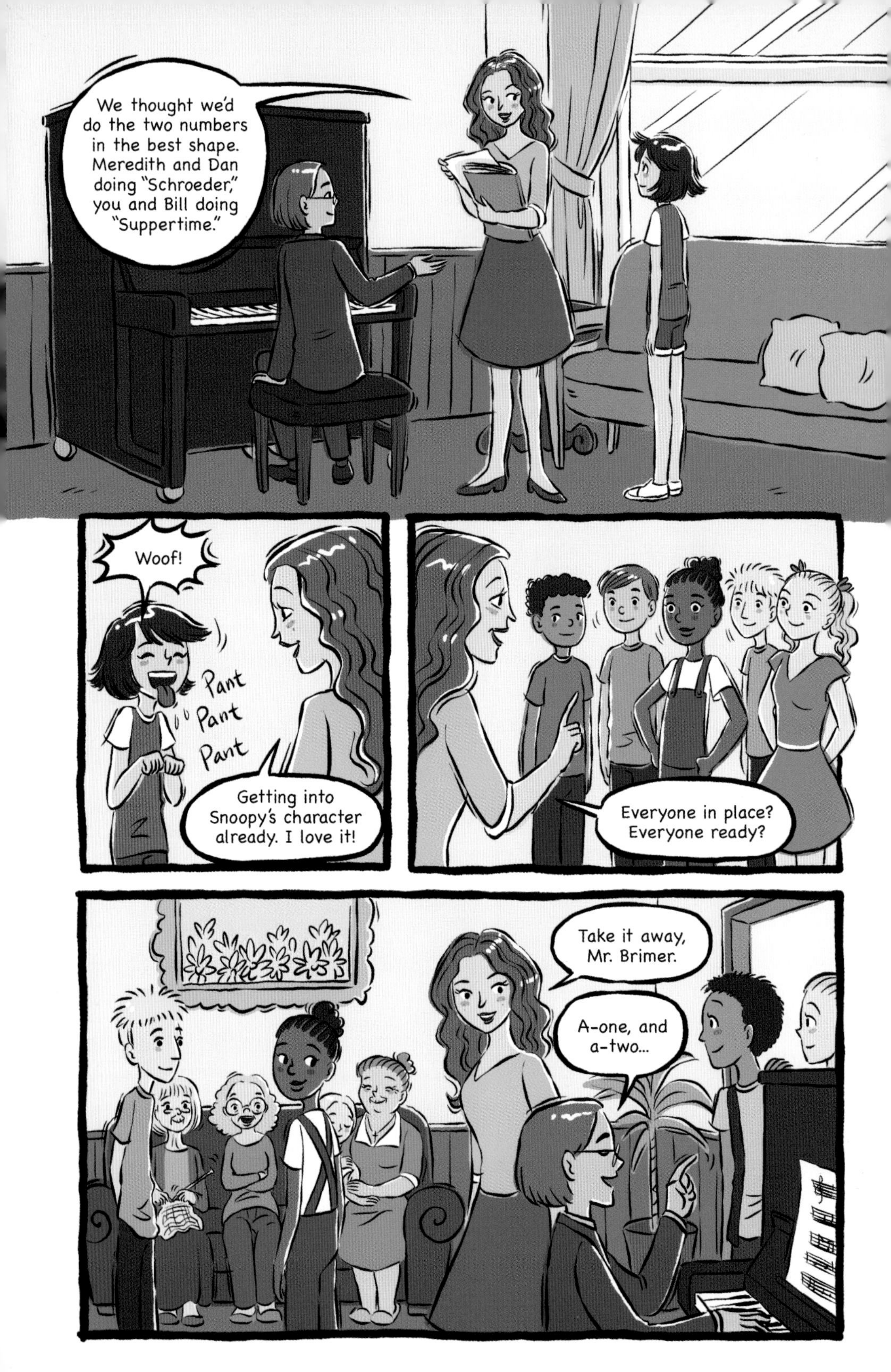
We thought we'd do the two numbers in the best shape. Meredith and Dan doing "Schroeder," you and Bill doing "Suppertime."
Woof!
Pant Pant Pant
Getting into Snoopy's character already. I love it!
Everyone in place? Everyone ready?
Take it away, Mr. Brimer.
A-one, and a-two...

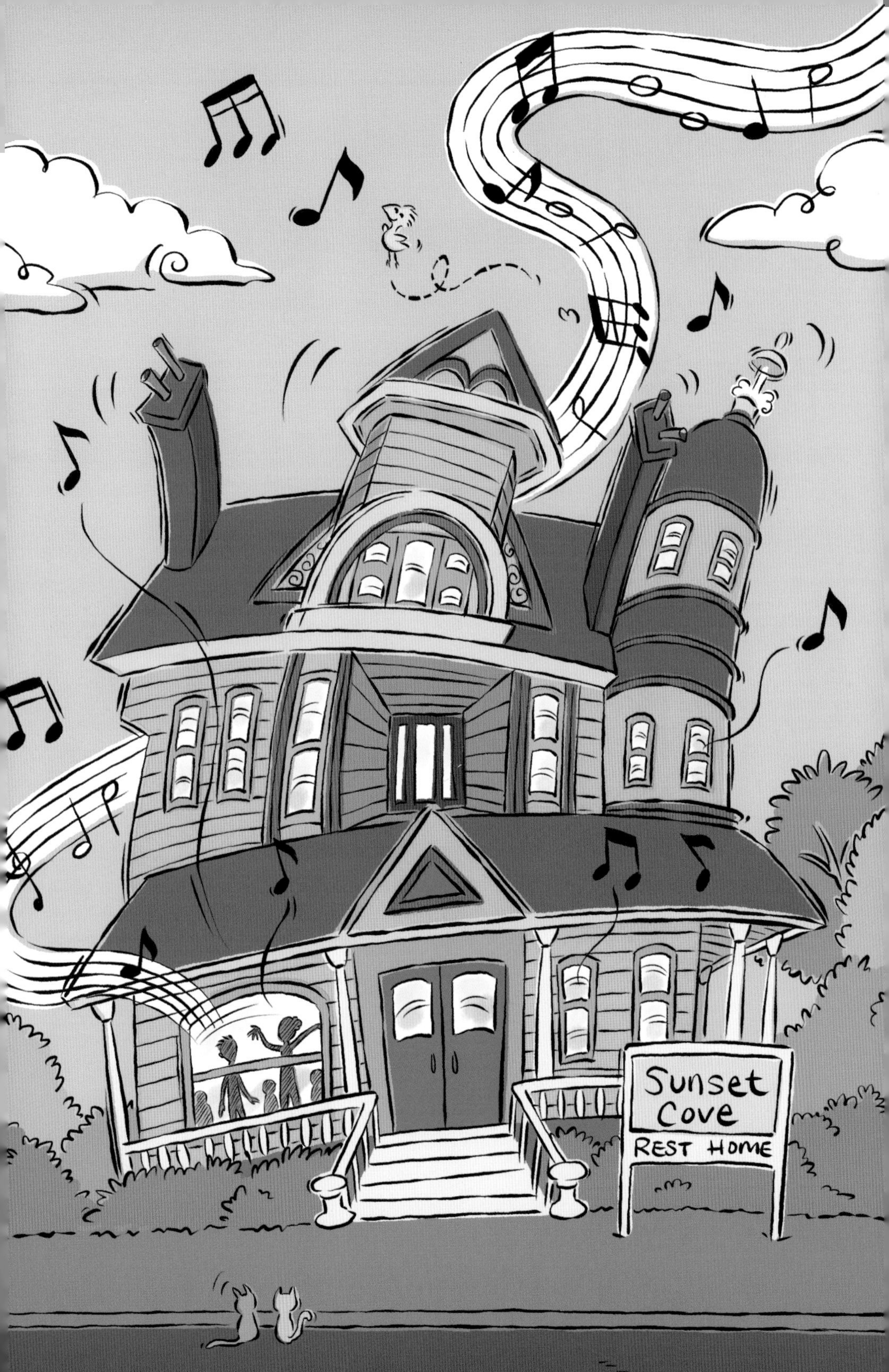
Sunset Cove
REST HOME

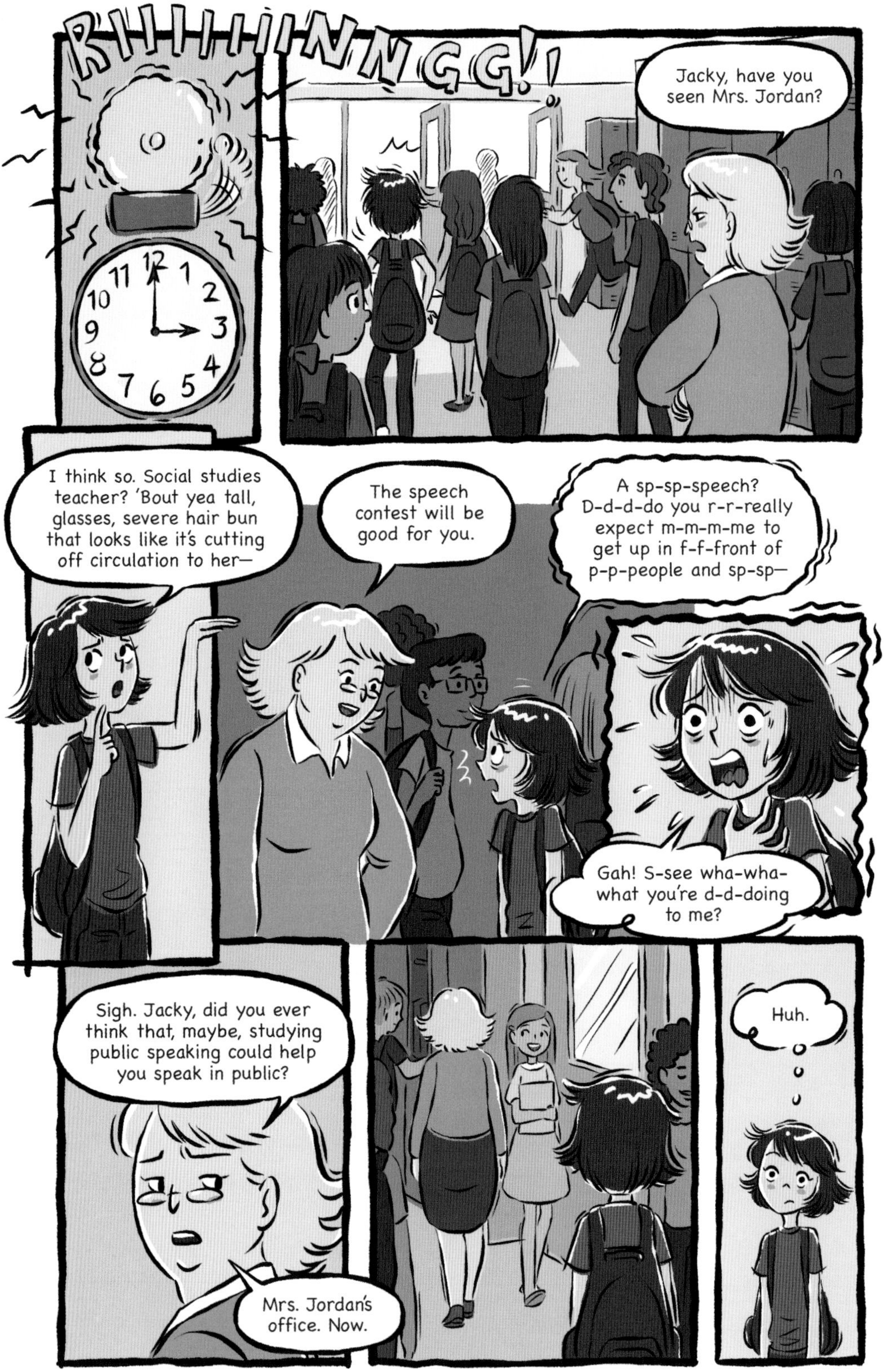
RIIIIIINNGG!!
Jacky, have you seen Mrs. Jordan?
I think so. Social studies teacher? 'Bout yea tall, glasses, severe hair bun that looks like it's cutting off circulation to her—
The speech contest will be good for you.
A sp-sp-speech? D-d-d-do you r-r-really expect m-m-m-me to get up in f-f-front of p-p-people and sp-sp—
Gah! S-see wha-wha-what you're d-d-doing to me?
Sigh. Jacky, did you ever think that, maybe, studying public speaking could help you speak in public?
Mrs. Jordan's office. Now.
Huh.

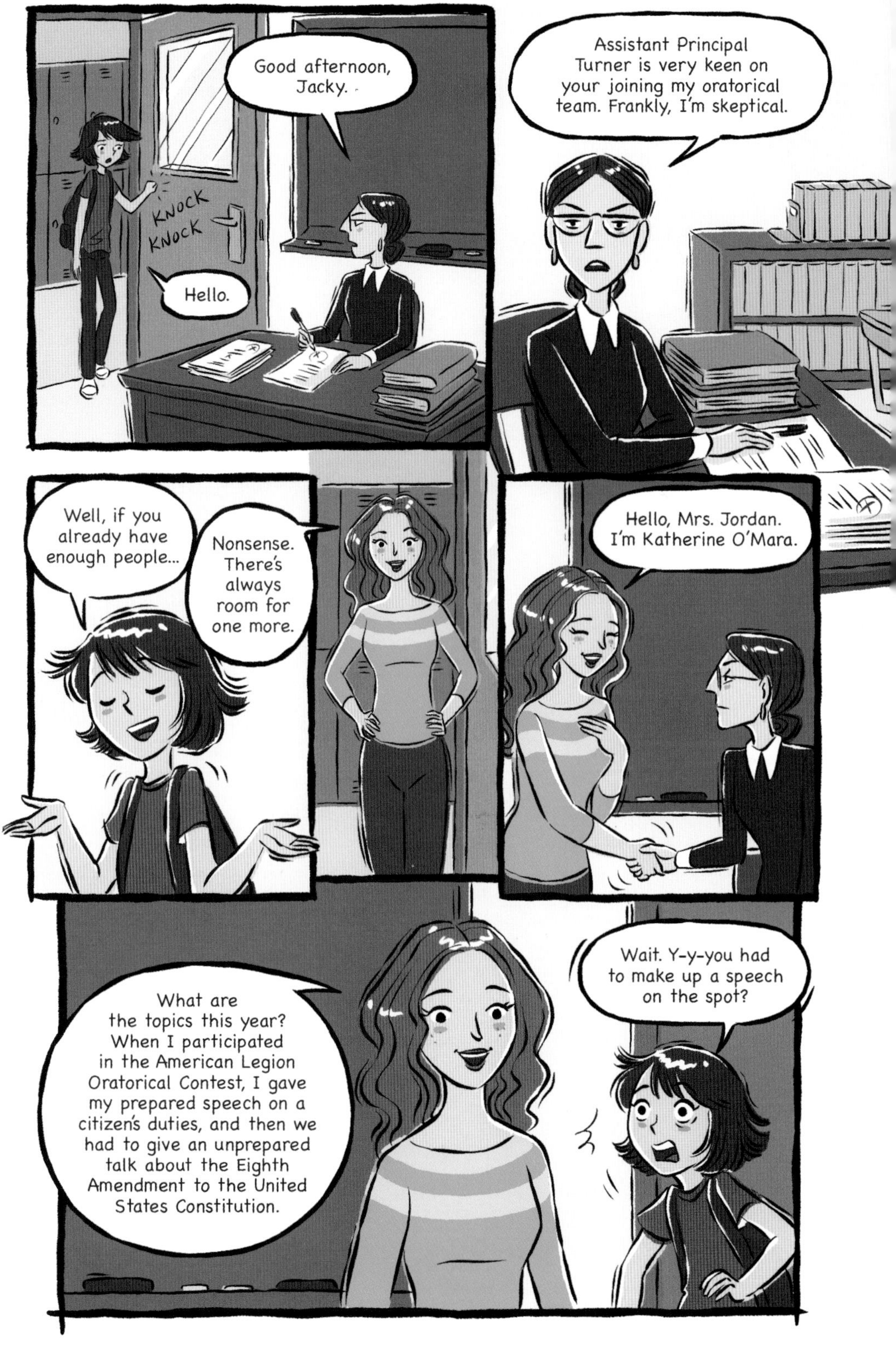
Good afternoon, Jacky.
KNOCK KNOCK
Hello.
Assistant Principal Turner is very keen on your joining my oratorical team. Frankly, I'm skeptical.
Well, if you already have enough people...
Nonsense. There's always room for one more.
Hello, Mrs. Jordan. I'm Katherine O'Mara.
What are the topics this year? When I participated in the American Legion Oratorical Contest, I gave my prepared speech on a citizen's duties, and then we had to give an unprepared talk about the Eighth Amendment to the United States Constitution.
Wait. Y-y-you had to make up a speech on the spot?

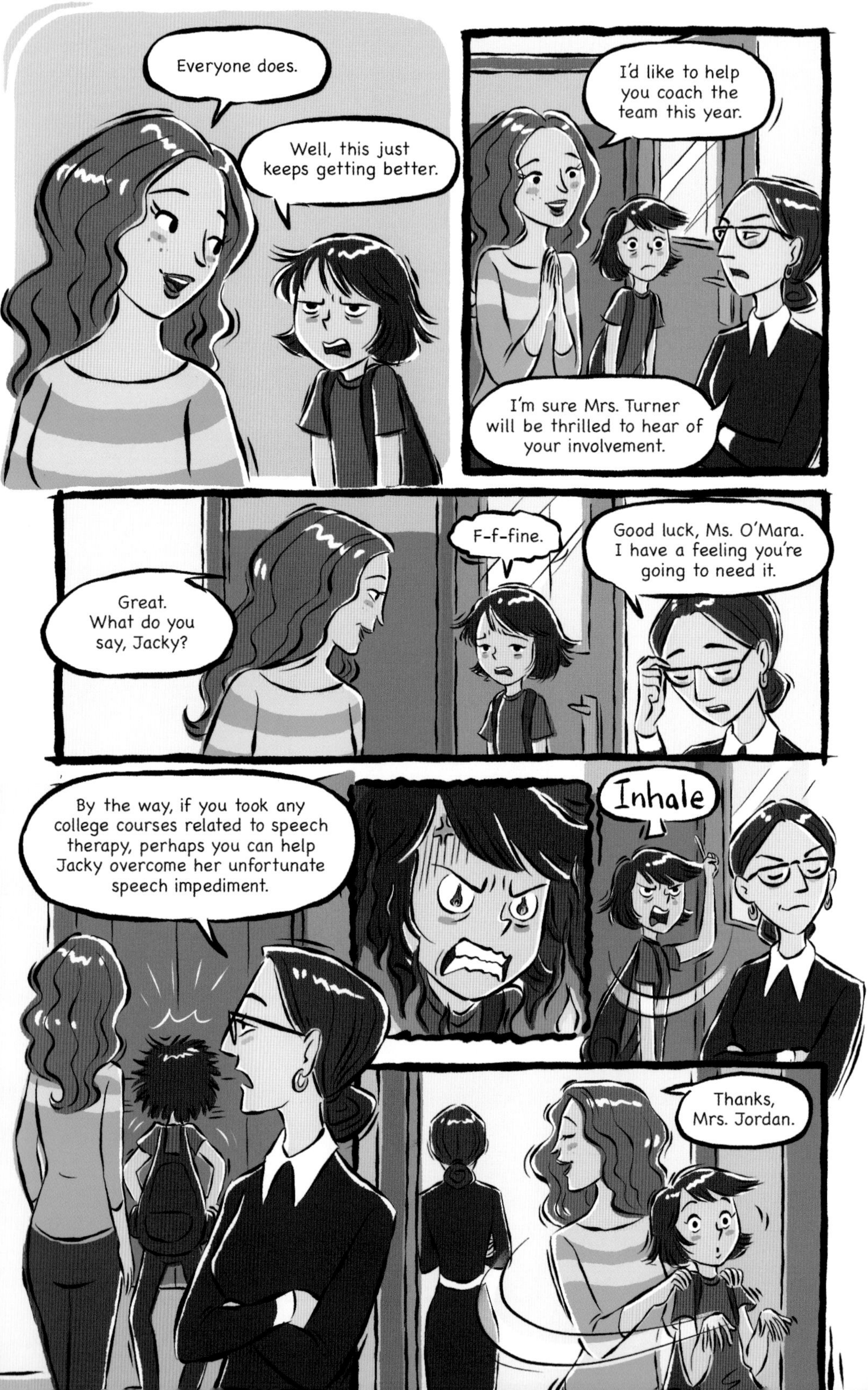

Everyone does.
Well, this just keeps getting better.
I'd like to help you coach the team this year.
I'm sure Mrs. Turner will be thrilled to hear of your involvement.
Great. What do you say, Jacky?
F-f-fine.
Good luck, Ms. O'Mara. I have a feeling you're going to need it.
By the way, if you took any college courses related to speech therapy, perhaps you can help Jacky overcome her unfortunate speech impediment.
Inhale
Thanks, Mrs. Jordan.

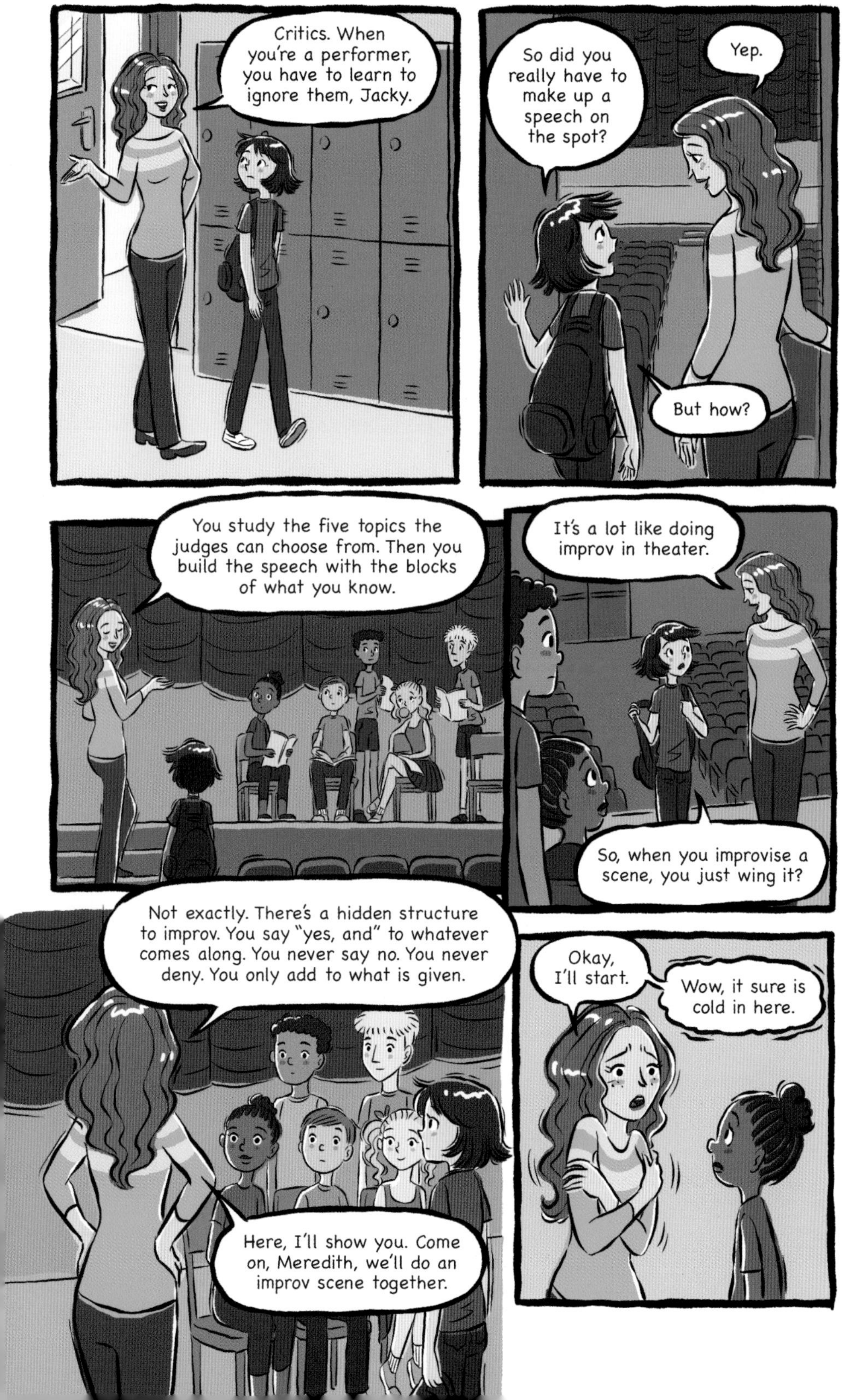

Critics. When you're a performer, you have to learn to ignore them, Jacky.
So did you really have to make up a speech on the spot?
Yep.
But how?
You study the five topics the judges can choose from. Then you build the speech with the blocks of what you know.
It's a lot like doing improv in theater.
So, when you improvise a scene, you just wing it?
Not exactly. There's a hidden structure to improv. You say "yes, and" to whatever comes along. You never say no. You never deny. You only add to what is given.
Here, I'll show you. Come on, Meredith, we'll do an improv scene together.
Okay, I'll start.
Wow, it sure is cold in here.

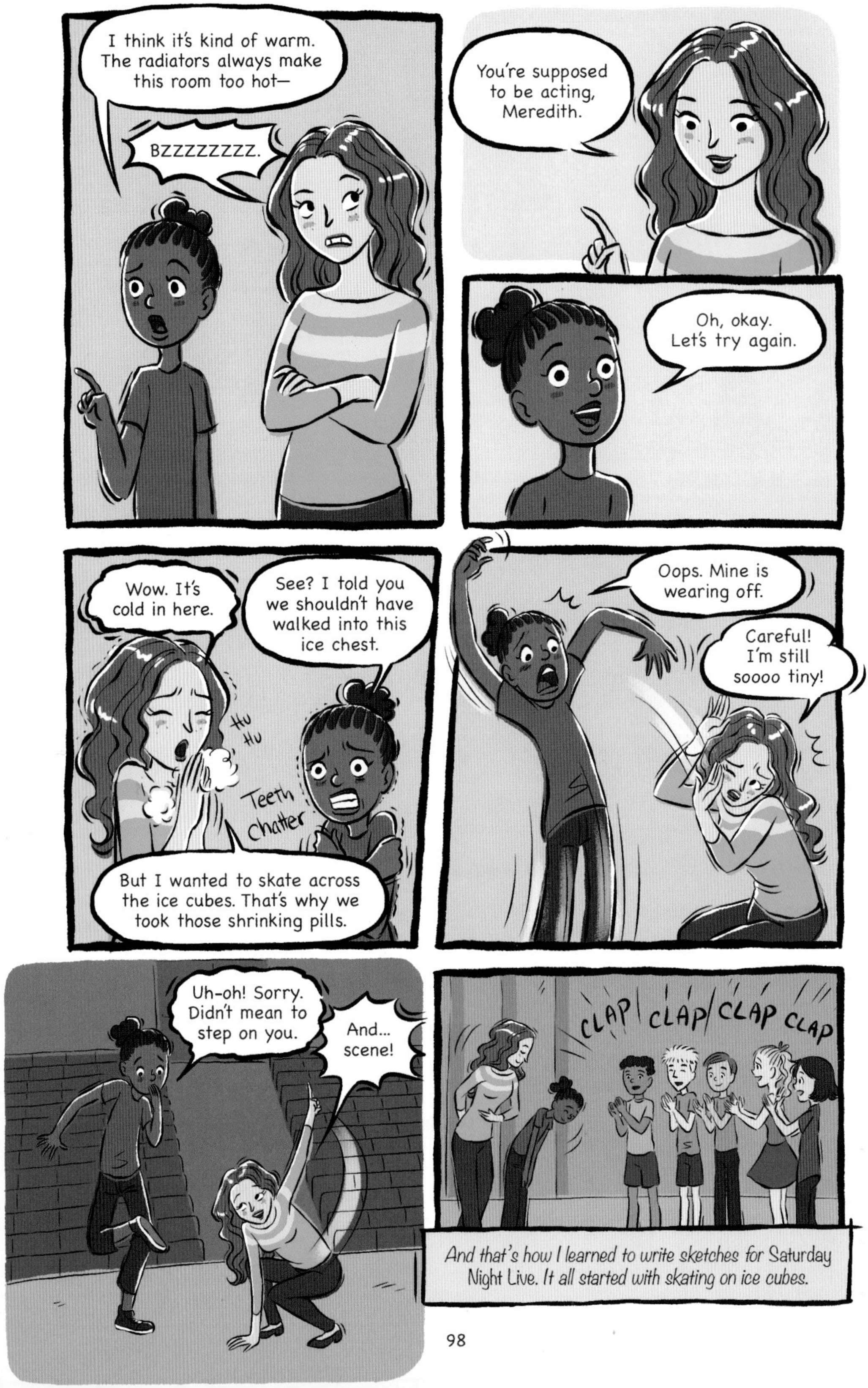
I think it's kind of warm. The radiators always make this room too hot—
BZZZZZZZZ.
You're supposed to be acting, Meredith.
Oh, okay. Let's try again.
Wow. It's cold in here.
See? I told you we shouldn't have walked into this ice chest.
Hu Hu
Teeth chatter
But I wanted to skate across the ice cubes. That's why we took those shrinking pills.
Oops. Mine is wearing off.
Careful! I'm still soooo tiny!
Uh-oh! Sorry. Didn't mean to step on you.
And... scene!
CLAP CLAP CLAP CLAP
And that's how I learned to write sketches for Saturday Night Live. It all started with skating on ice cubes.

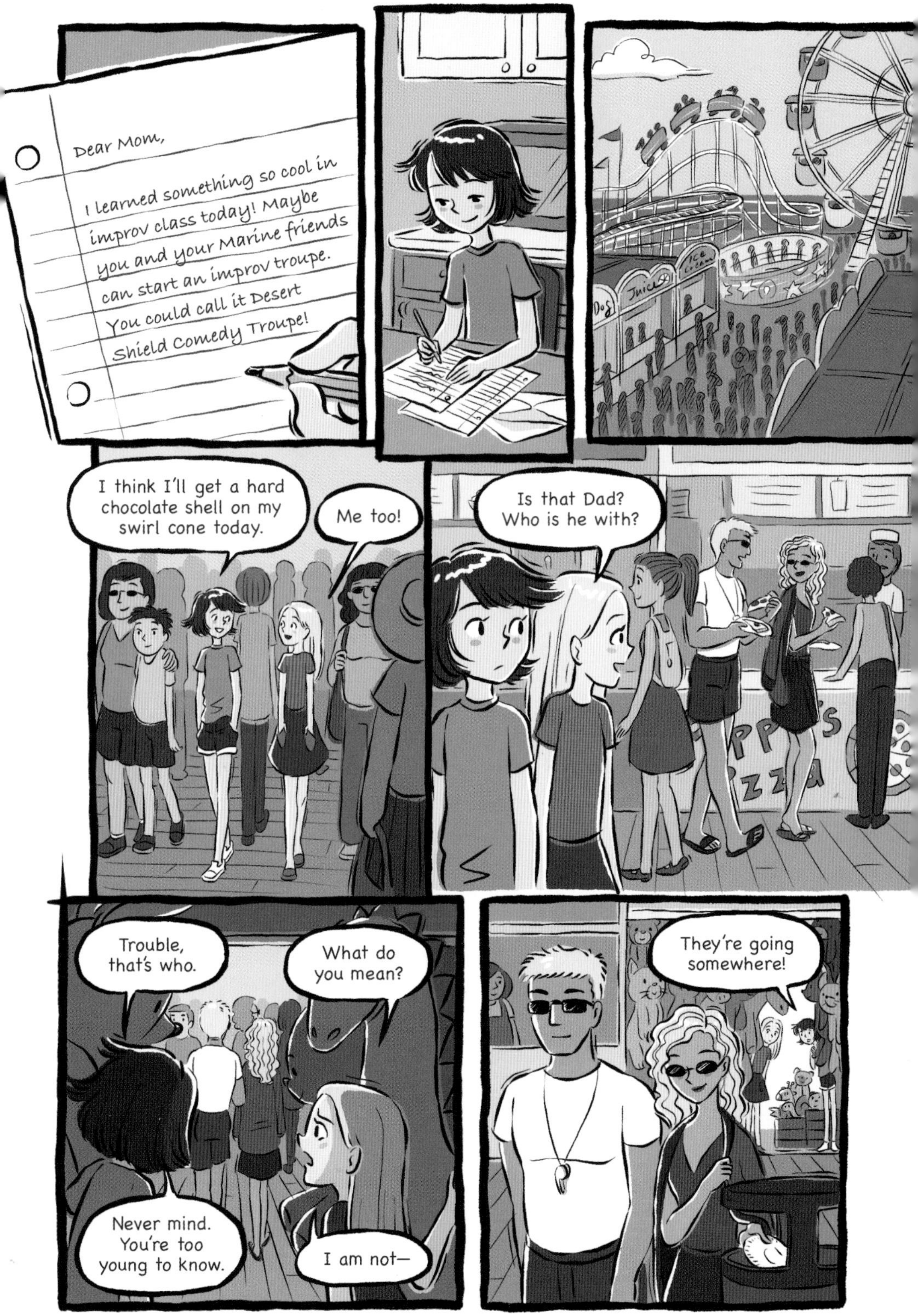
Dear Mom,
I learned something so cool in improv class today! Maybe you and your Marine friends can start an improv troupe. You could call it Desert Shield Comedy Troupe!
Dog
Juice
Ice Cream
I think I'll get a hard chocolate shell on my swirl cone today.
Me too!
Is that Dad? Who is he with?
Trouble, that's who.
What do you mean?
Never mind. You're too young to know.
I am not—
They're going somewhere!

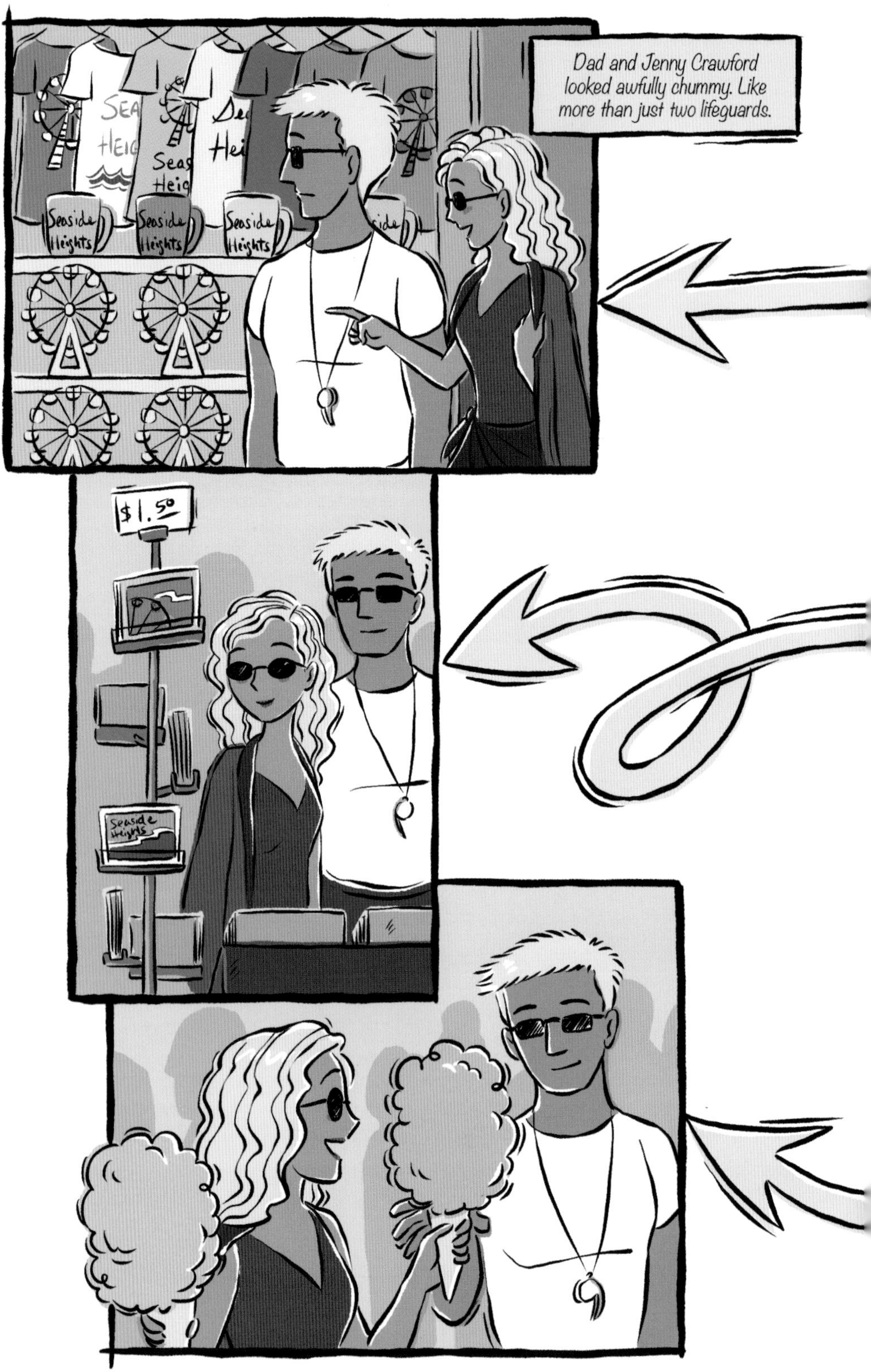
Dad and Jenny Crawford looked awfully chummy. Like more than just two lifeguards.
Seaside Heights
Seaside Heights
Seaside Heights
$1.50
Seaside Heights

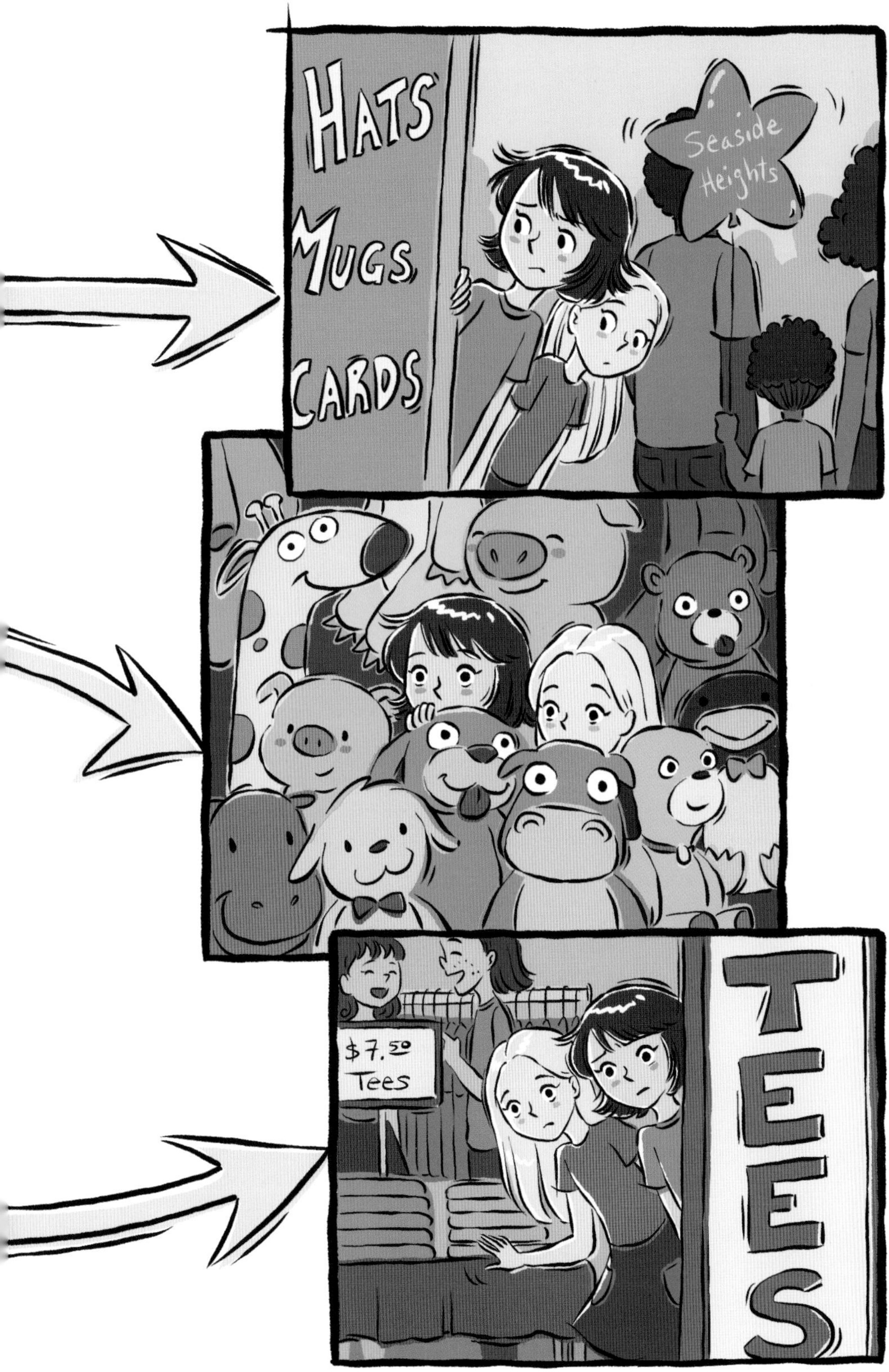
HATS
MUGS
CARDS
Seaside Heights
$7.50
Tees
TEES

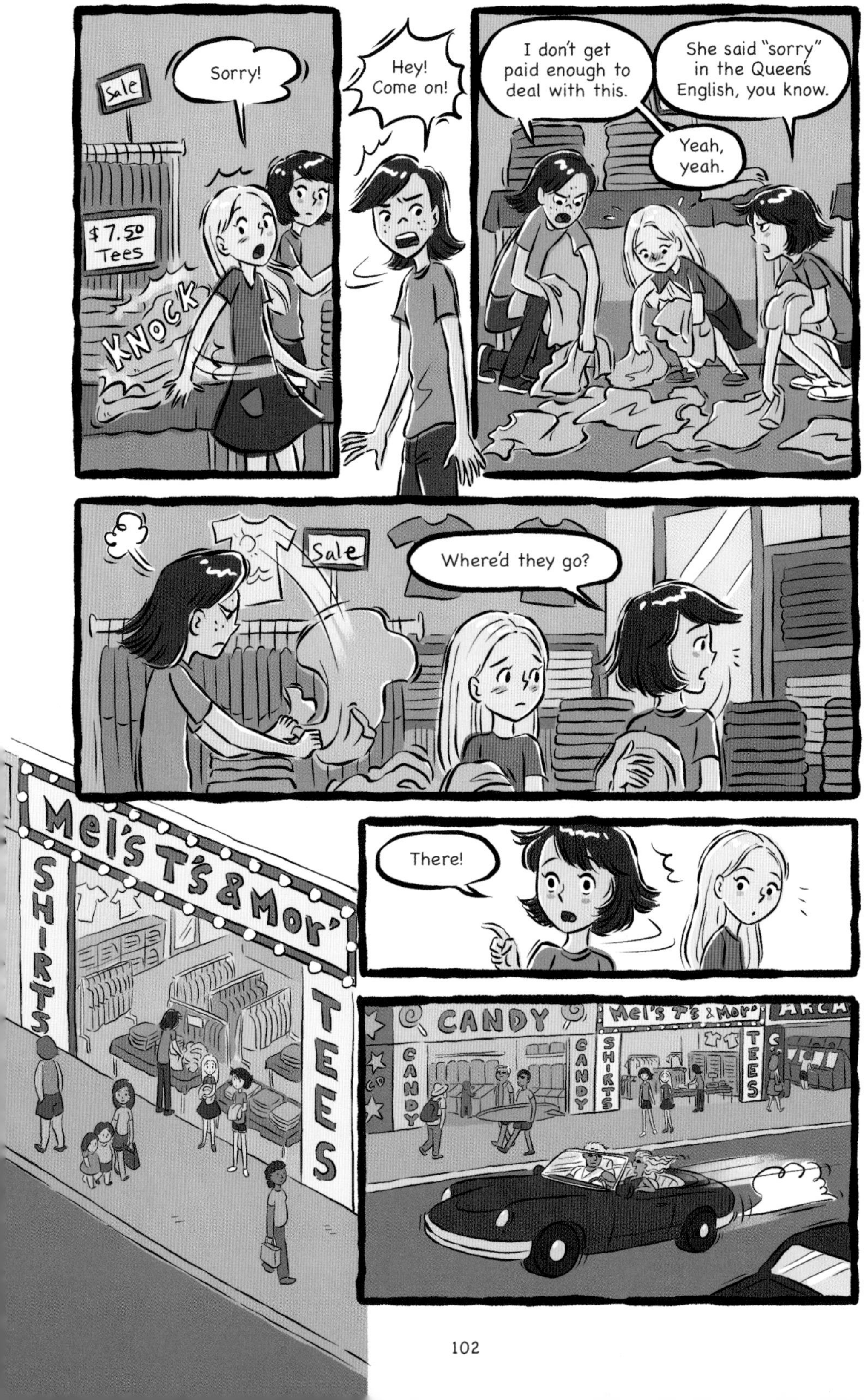
Sale
$7.50 Tees
Sorry!
KNOCK
Hey! Come on!
I don't get paid enough to deal with this.
She said "sorry" in the Queen's English, you know.
Yeah, yeah.
Sale
Where'd they go?
Mel's T's & Mor'
SHIRTS
TEES
There!
CANDY
CANDY
CANDY
Mel's T's & Mor'
SHIRTS
TEES

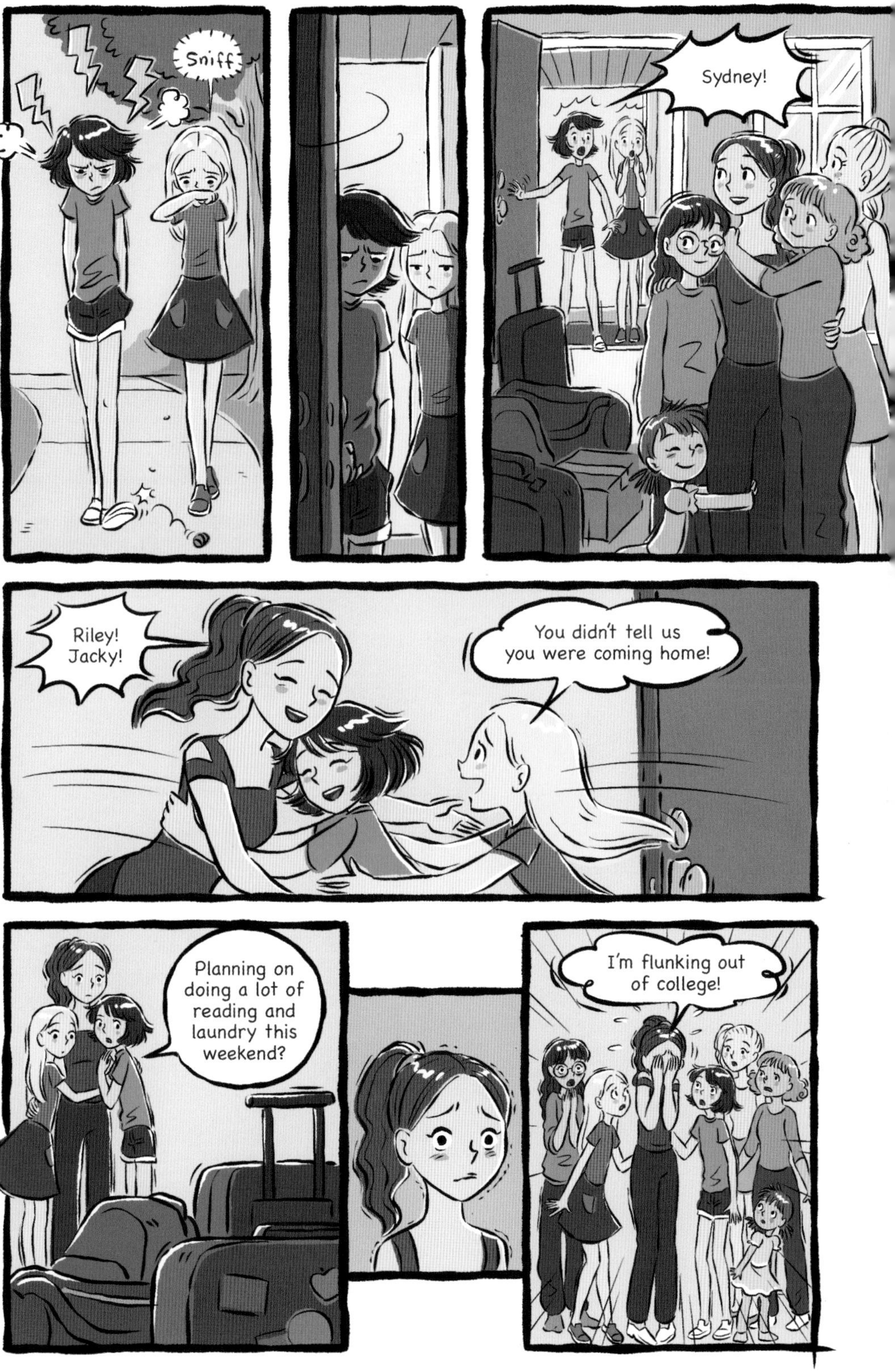
Sniff
Sydney!
Riley! Jacky!
You didn't tell us you were coming home!
Planning on doing a lot of reading and laundry this weekend?
I'm flunking out of college!

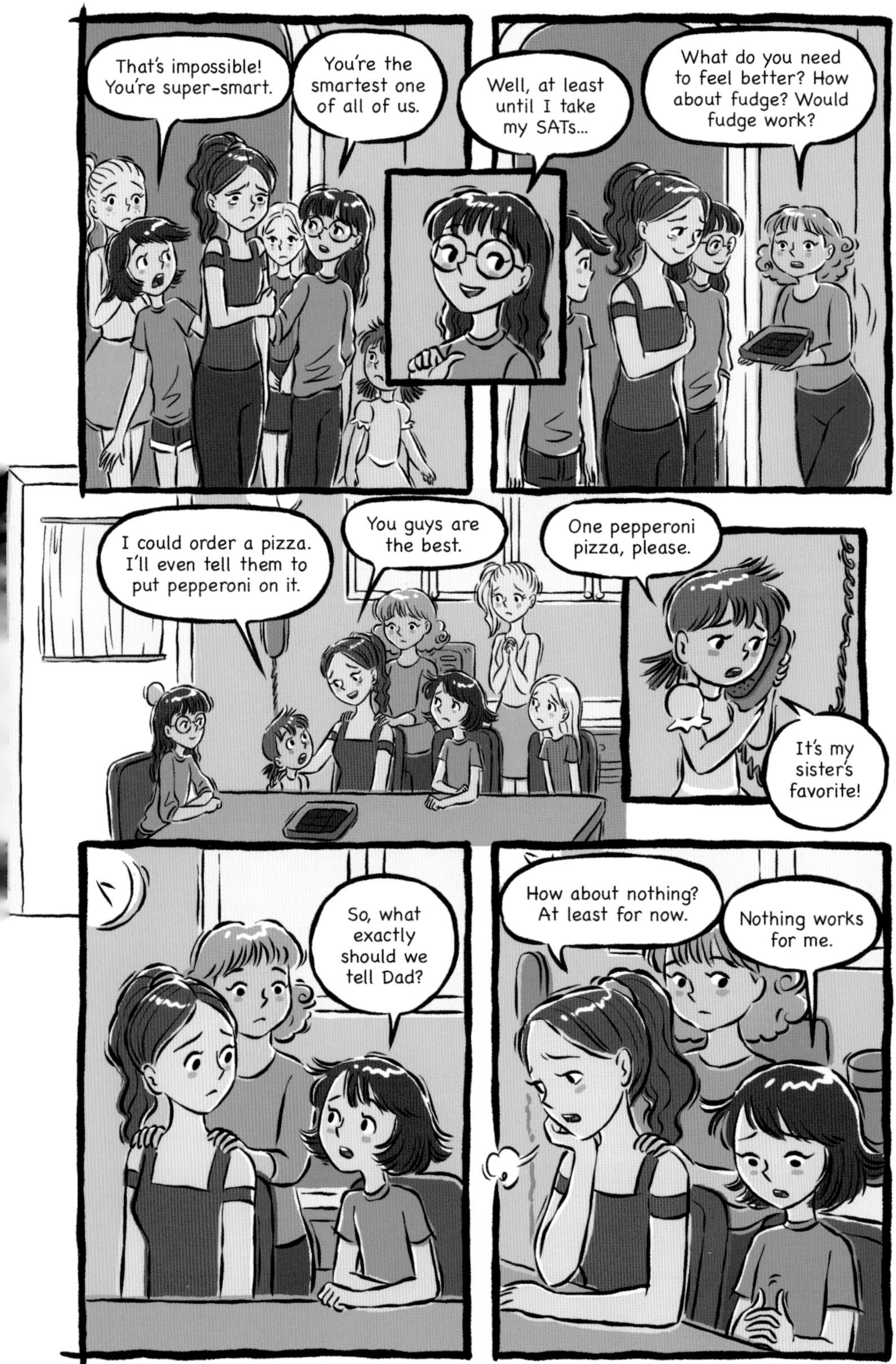
That's impossible! You're super-smart.
You're the smartest one of all of us.
Well, at least until I take my SATs...
What do you need to feel better? How about fudge? Would fudge work?
I could order a pizza. I'll even tell them to put pepperoni on it.
You guys are the best.
One pepperoni pizza, please.
It's my sister's favorite!
So, what exactly should we tell Dad?
How about nothing? At least for now.
Nothing works for me.

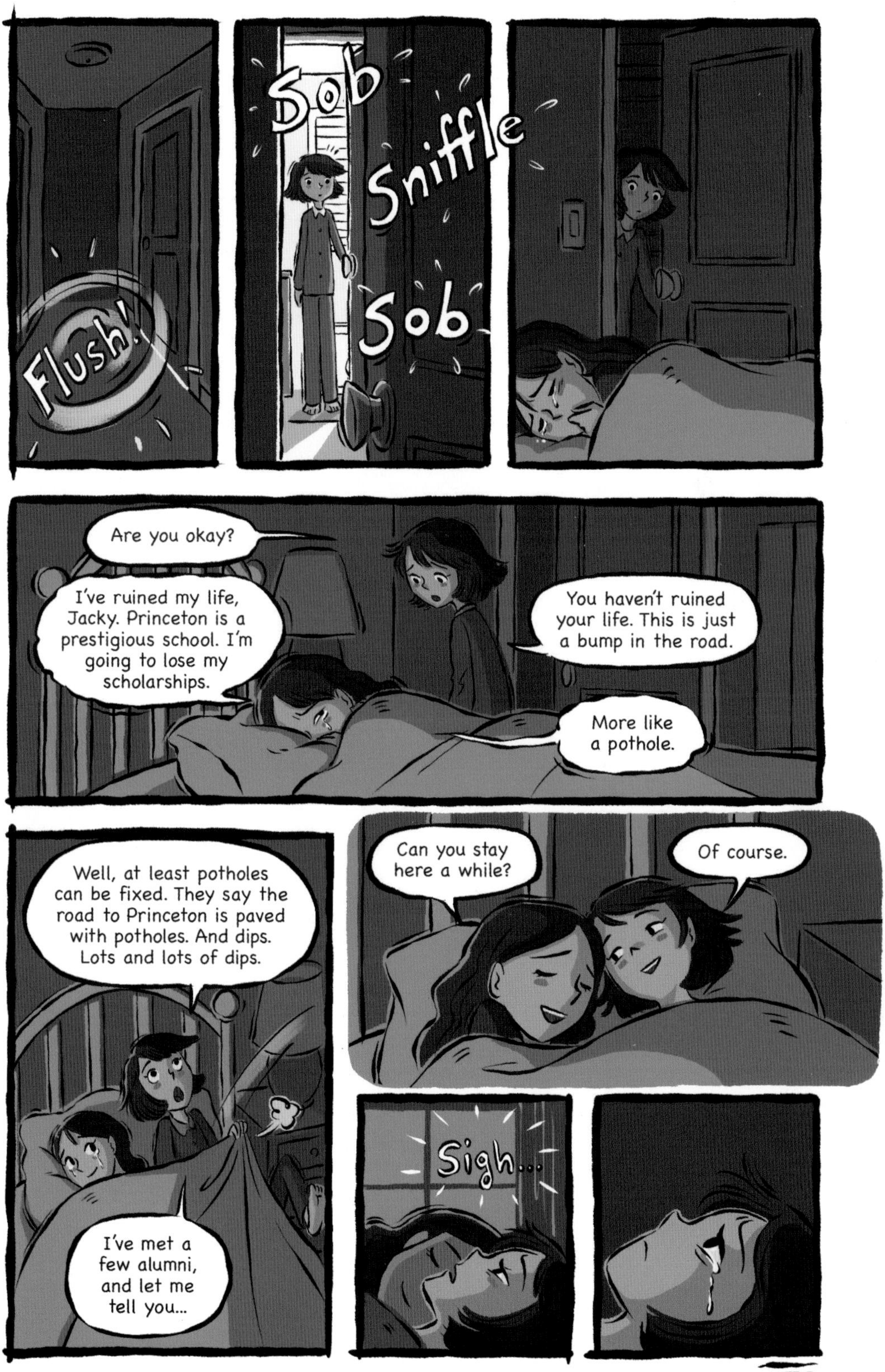
Flush!
Sob
Sniffle
Sob
Are you okay?
I've ruined my life, Jacky. Princeton is a prestigious school. I'm going to lose my scholarships.
You haven't ruined your life. This is just a bump in the road.
More like a pothole.
Well, at least potholes can be fixed. They say the road to Princeton is paved with potholes. And dips. Lots and lots of dips.
I've met a few alumni, and let me tell you...
Can you stay here a while?
Of course.
Sigh...

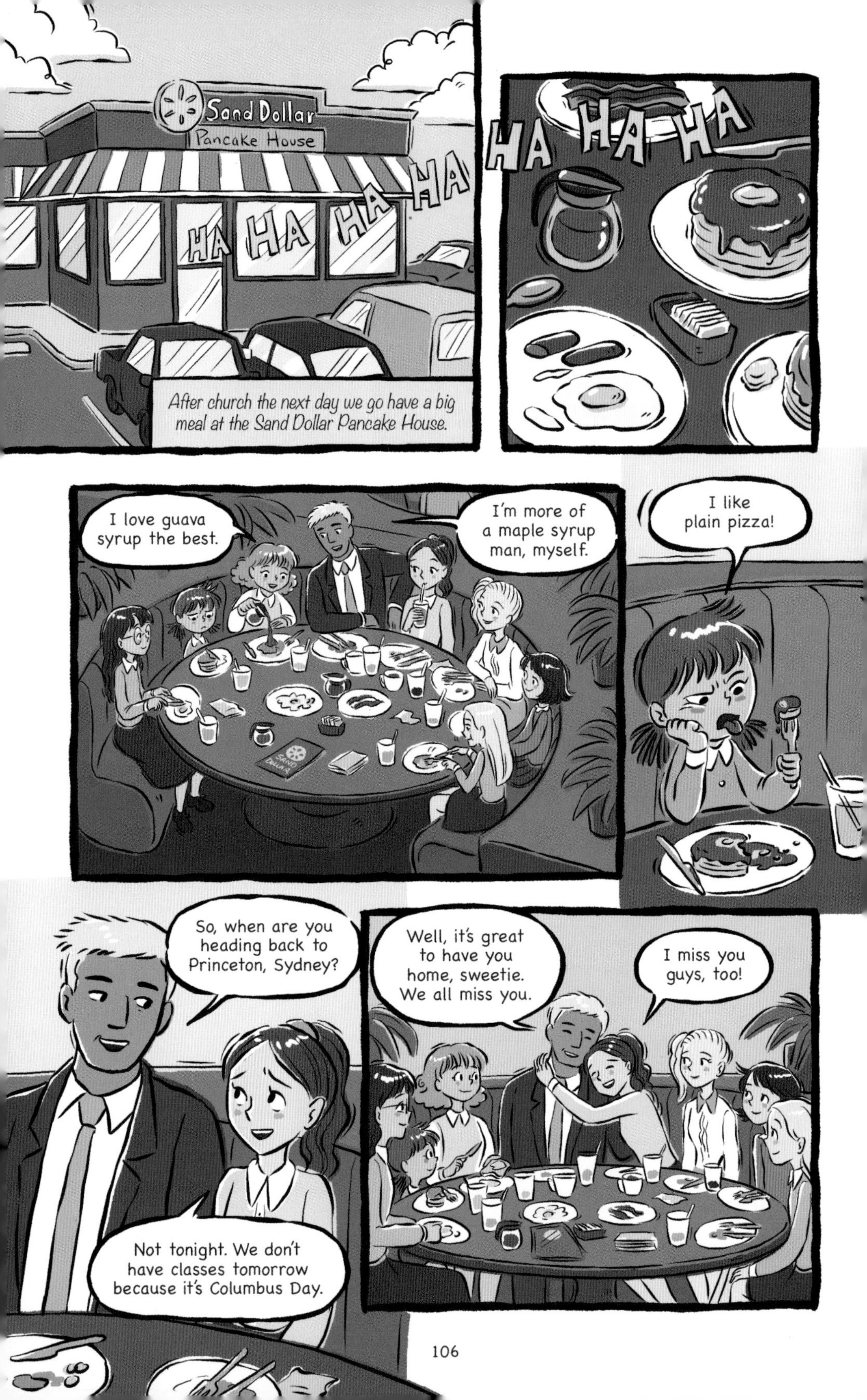
Sand Dollar
Pancake House
HA HA HA HA HA
After church the next day we go have a big meal at the Sand Dollar Pancake House.
HA HA HA
I love guava syrup the best.
I'm more of a maple syrup man, myself.
I like plain pizza!
So, when are you heading back to Princeton, Sydney?
Not tonight. We don't have classes tomorrow because it's Columbus Day.
Well, it's great to have you home, sweetie. We all miss you.
I miss you guys, too!

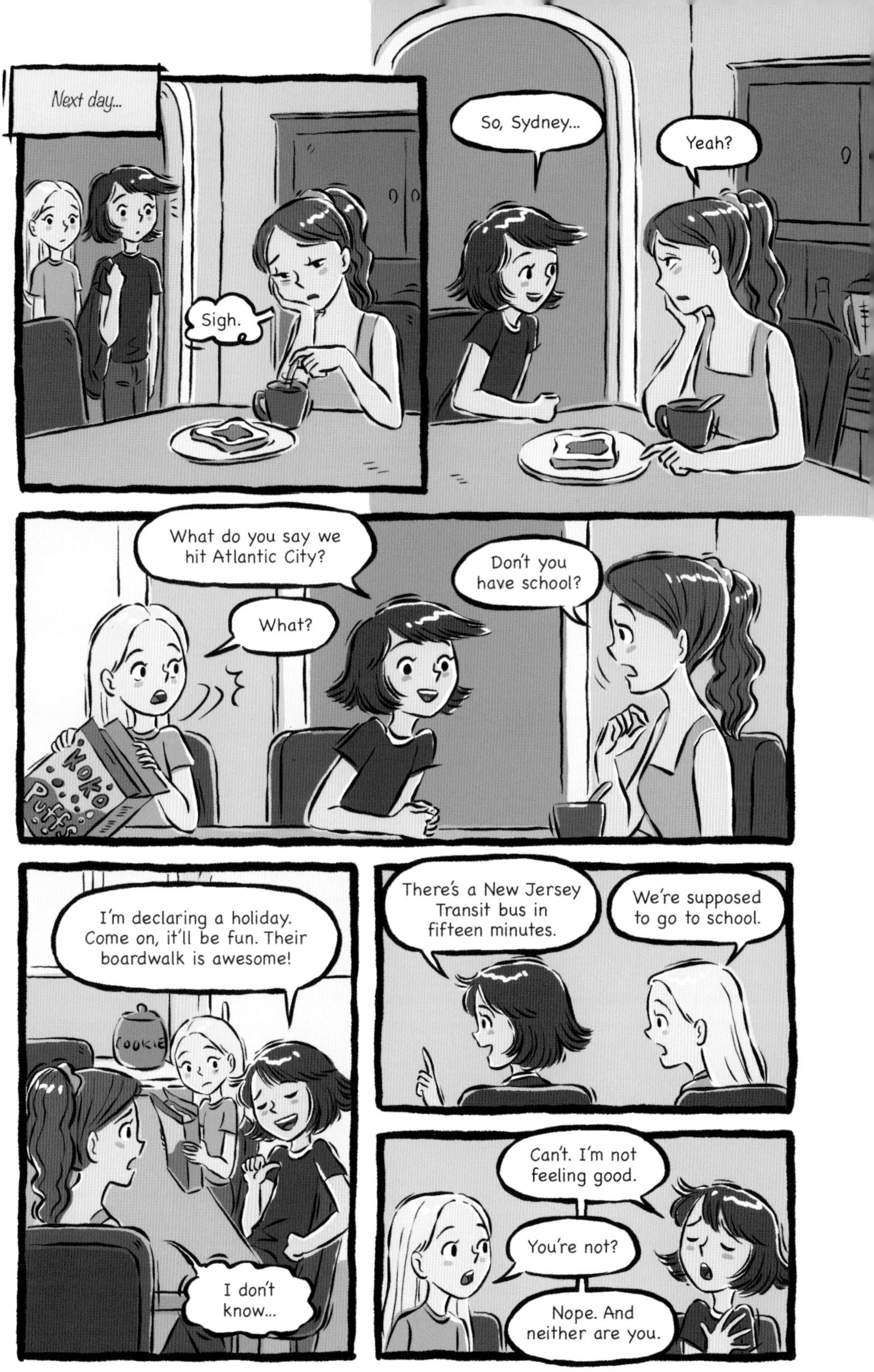

Next day...
Sigh.
So, Sydney...
Yeah?
What do you say we hit Atlantic City?
What?
Don't you have school?
KOKO Puffs
I'm declaring a holiday. Come on, it'll be fun. Their boardwalk is awesome!
COOKIE
I don't know...
There's a New Jersey Transit bus in fifteen minutes.
We're supposed to go to school.
Can't. I'm not feeling good.
You're not?
Nope. And neither are you.

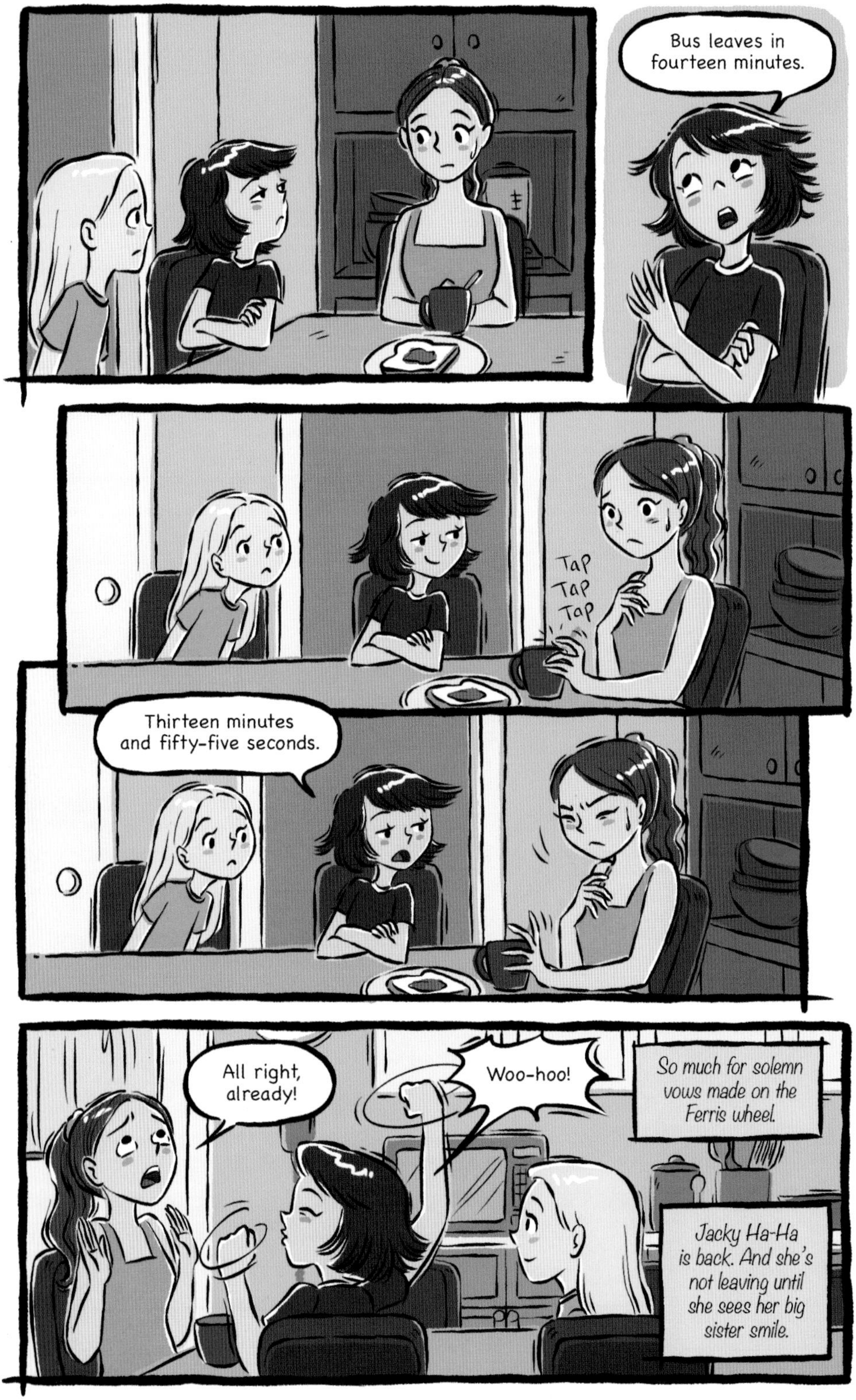
Bus leaves in fourteen minutes.
Tap
Tap
Tap
Thirteen minutes and fifty-five seconds.
All right, already!
Woo-hoo!
So much for solemn vows made on the Ferris wheel.
Jacky Ha-Ha is back. And she's not leaving until she sees her big sister smile.

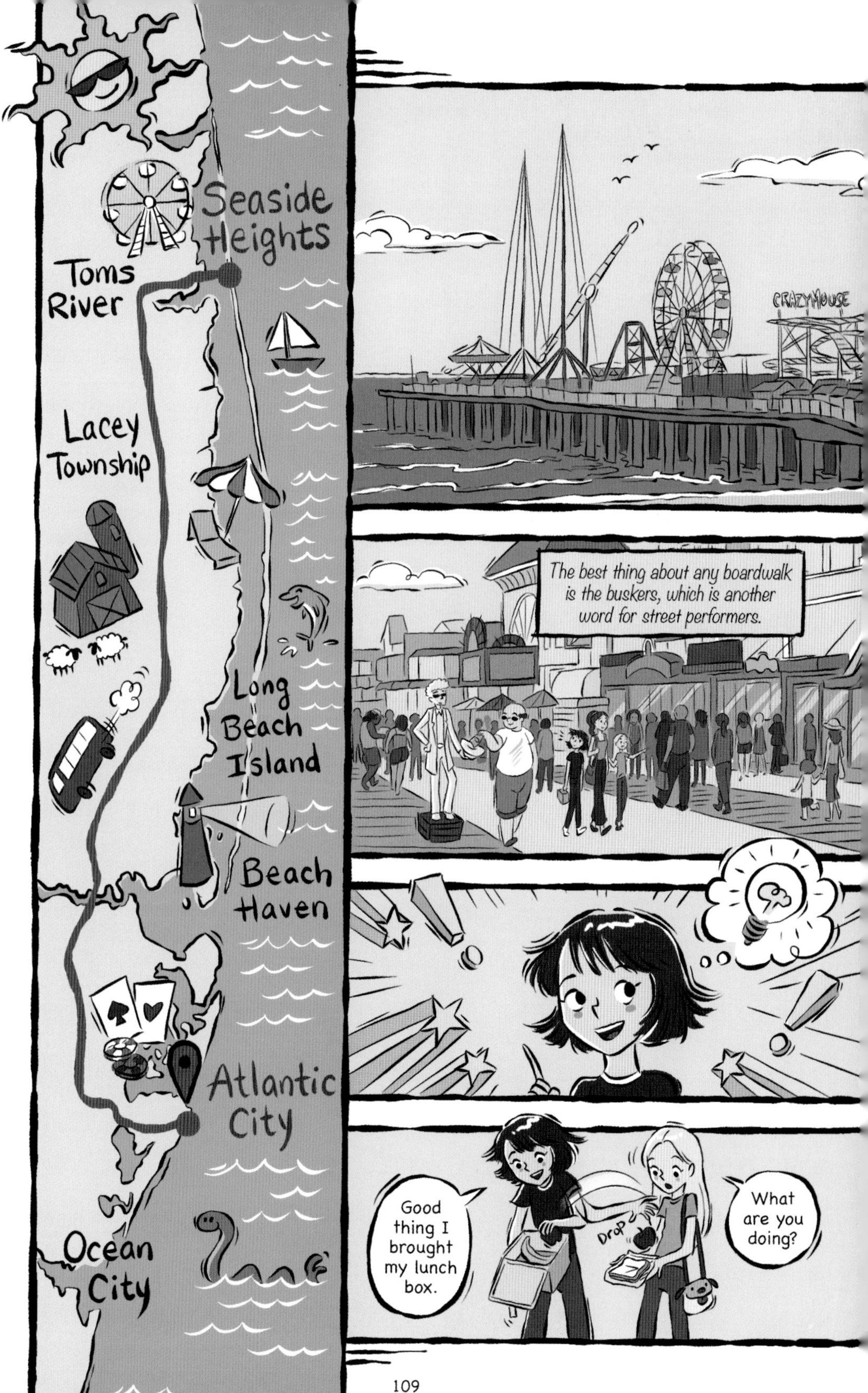
Seaside Heights
Toms River
Lacey Township
Long Beach Island
Beach Haven
Atlantic City
Ocean City
CRAZY MOUSE
The best thing about any boardwalk is the buskers, which is another word for street performers.
Good thing I brought my lunch box.
DROP
What are you doing?

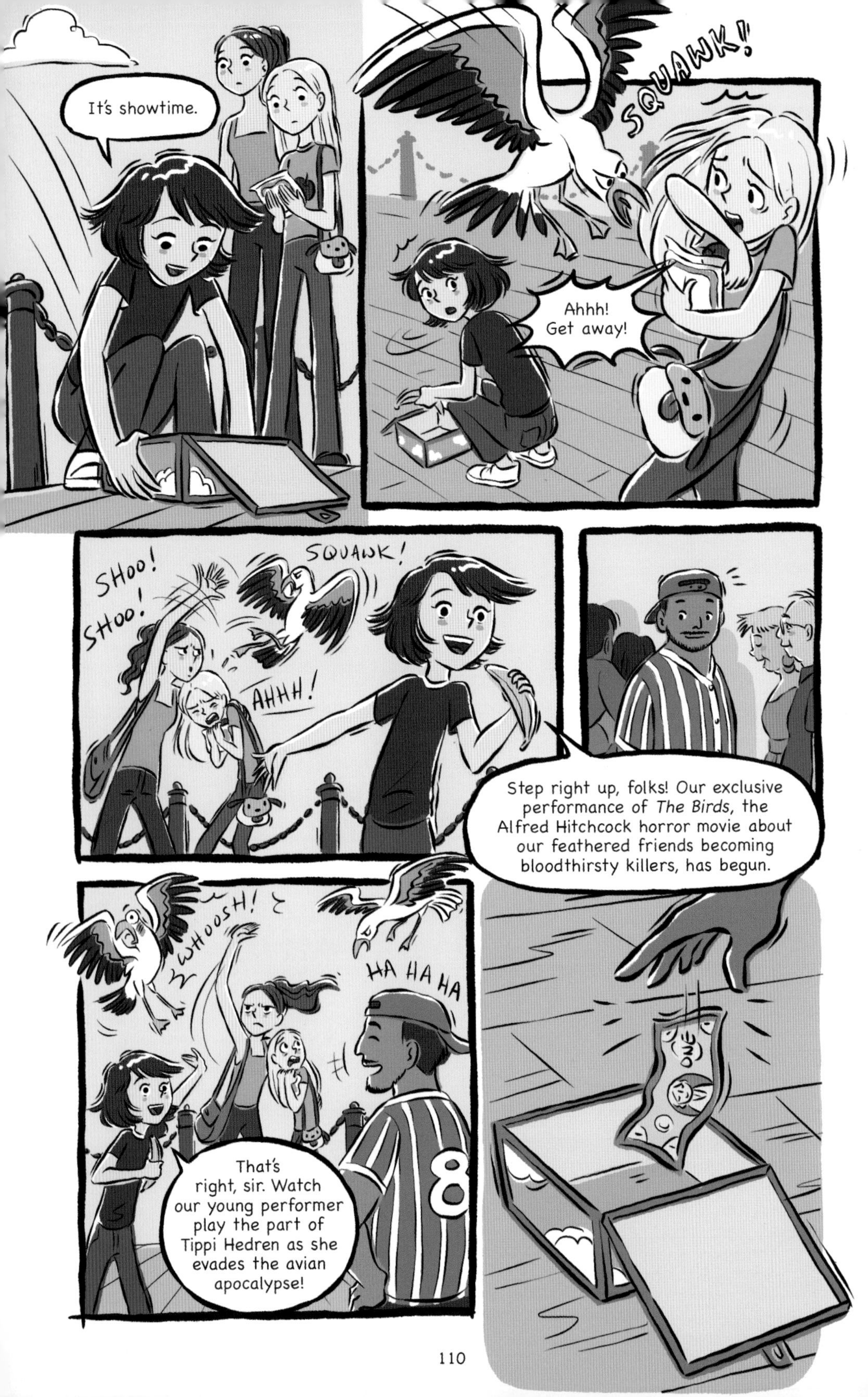
It's showtime.
SQUAWK!
Ahhh! Get away!
SHOO! SHOO!
SQUAWK!
AHHH!
Step right up, folks! Our exclusive performance of *The Birds*, the Alfred Hitchcock horror movie about our feathered friends becoming bloodthirsty killers, has begun.
WHOOSH!
HA HA HA
That's right, sir. Watch our young performer play the part of Tippi Hedren as she evades the avian apocalypse!
ONE

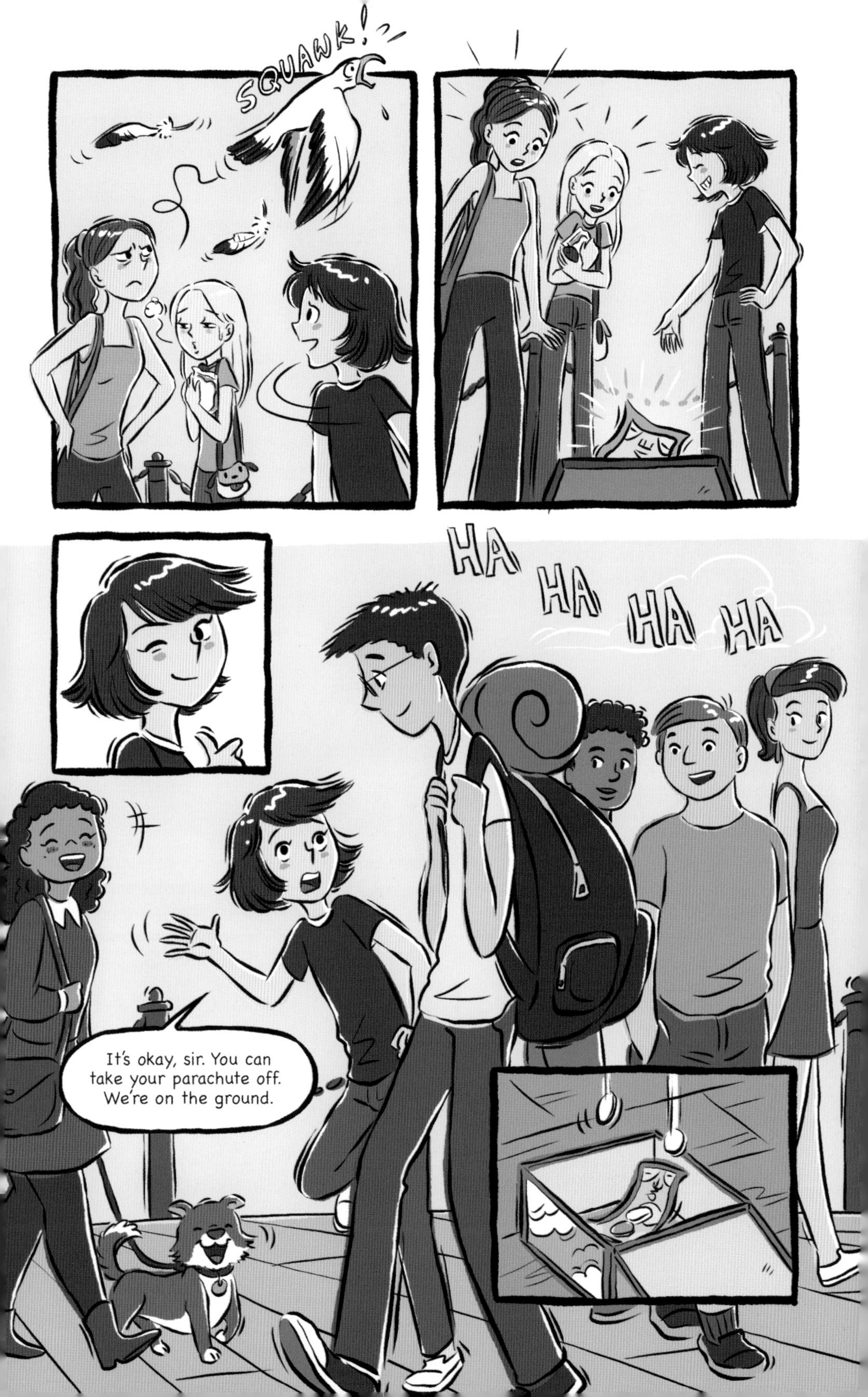
SQUAWK!
HA HA HA HA
It's okay, sir. You can take your parachute off. We're on the ground.

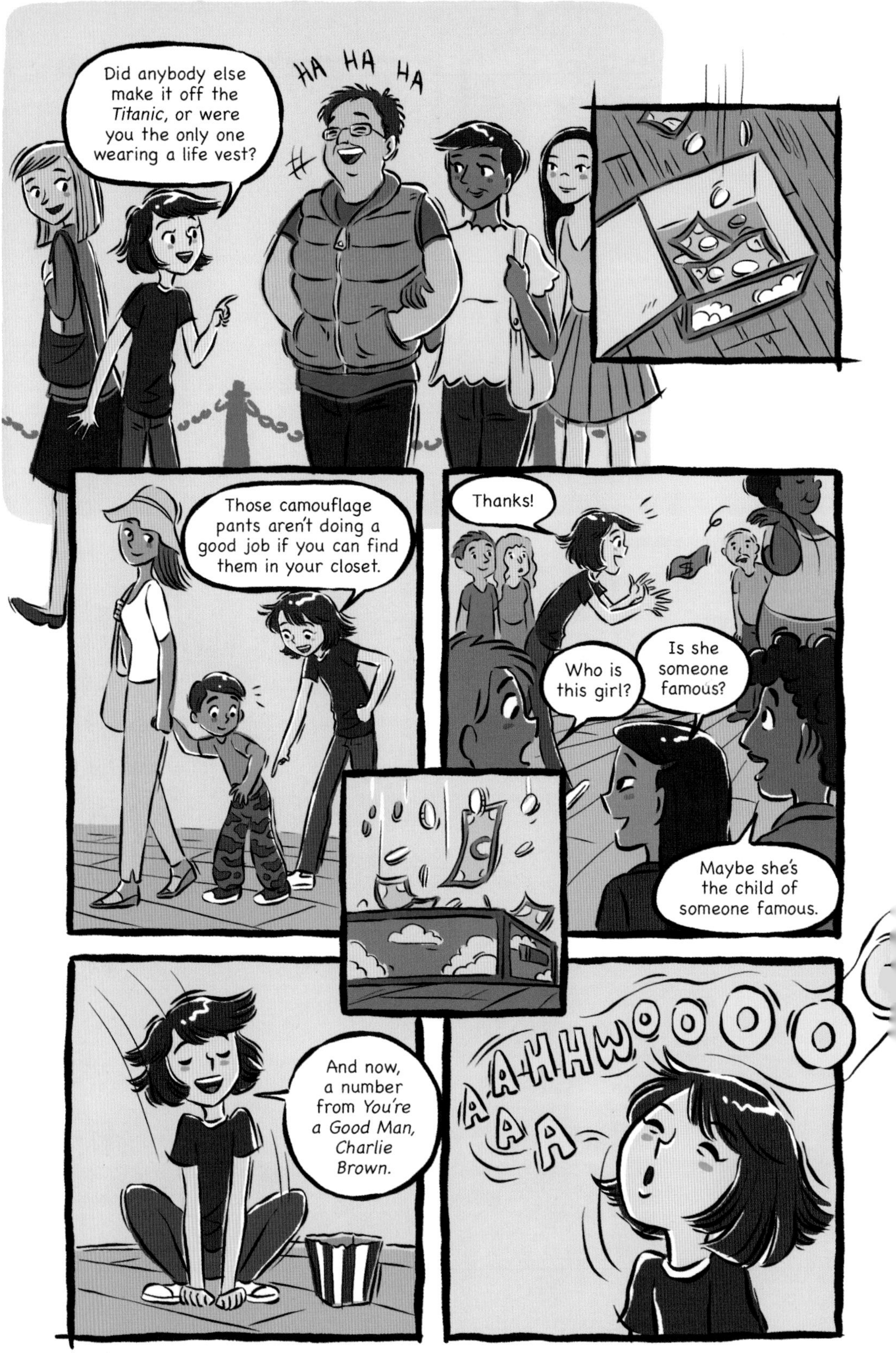

Did anybody else make it off the *Titanic*, or were you the only one wearing a life vest?
HA HA HA
Those camouflage pants aren't doing a good job if you can find them in your closet.
Thanks!
Who is this girl?
Is she someone famous?
Maybe she's the child of someone famous.
And now, a number from *You're a Good Man, Charlie Brown.*
AAAHHWOOOOO

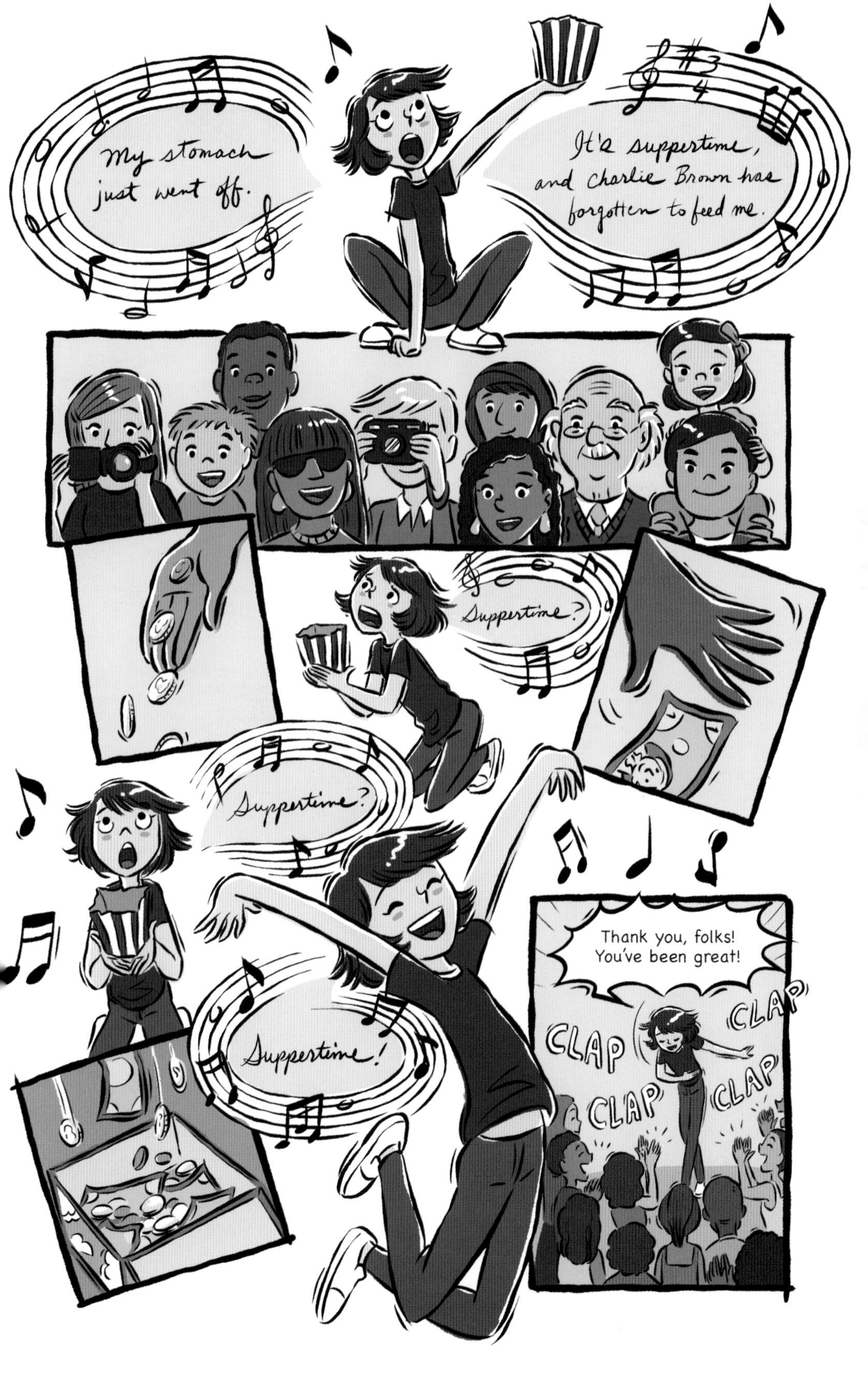
My stomach just went off.
It's suppertime, and Charlie Brown has forgotten to feed me.
Suppertime?
Suppertime?
Suppertime!
Thank you, folks! You've been great!
CLAP
CLAP
CLAP
CLAP

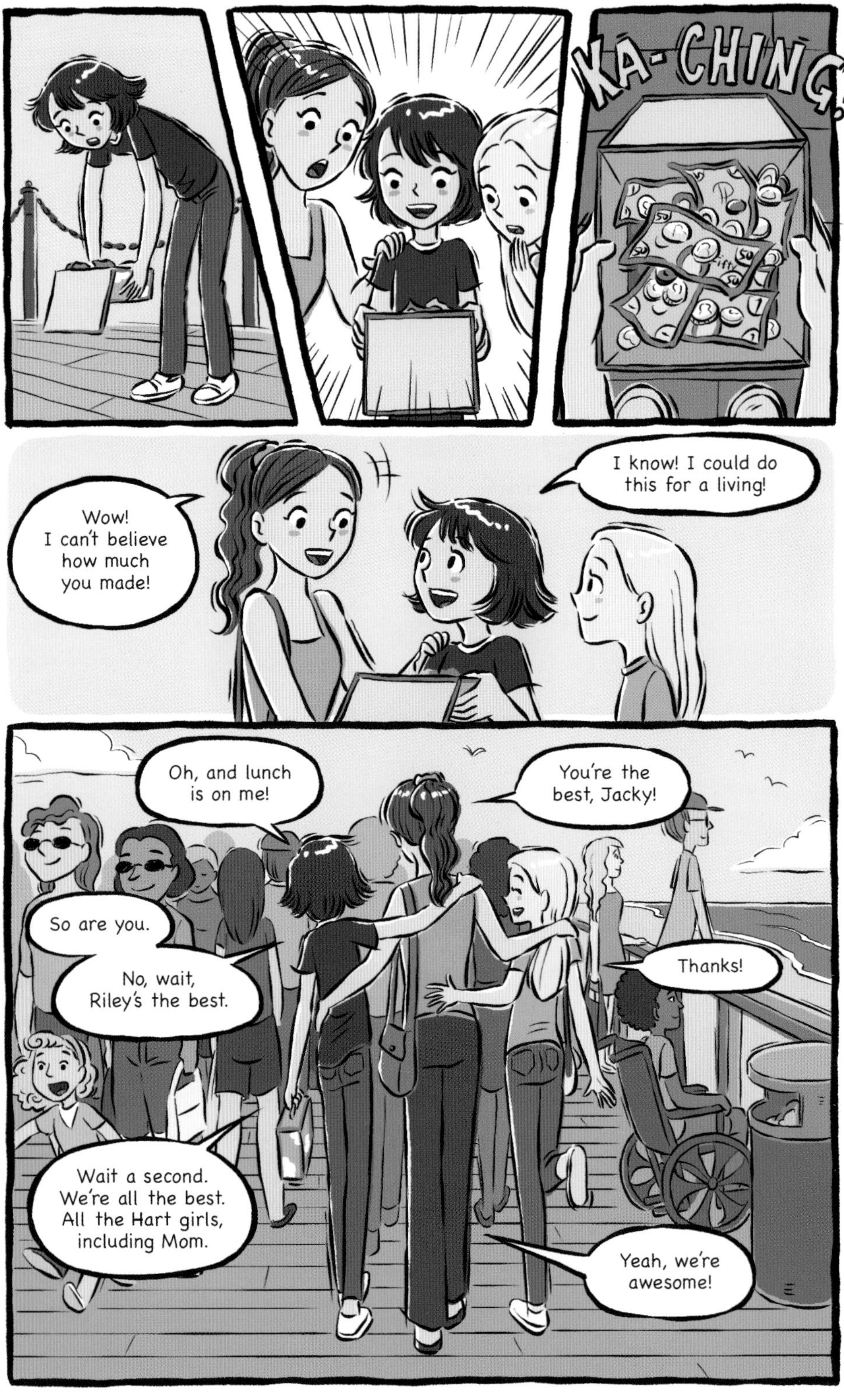
KA-CHING!
Wow!
I can't believe
how much
you made!
I know! I could do
this for a living!
Oh, and lunch
is on me!
You're the
best, Jacky!
So are you.
No, wait,
Riley's the best.
Thanks!
Wait a second.
We're all the best.
All the Hart girls,
including Mom.
Yeah, we're
awesome!

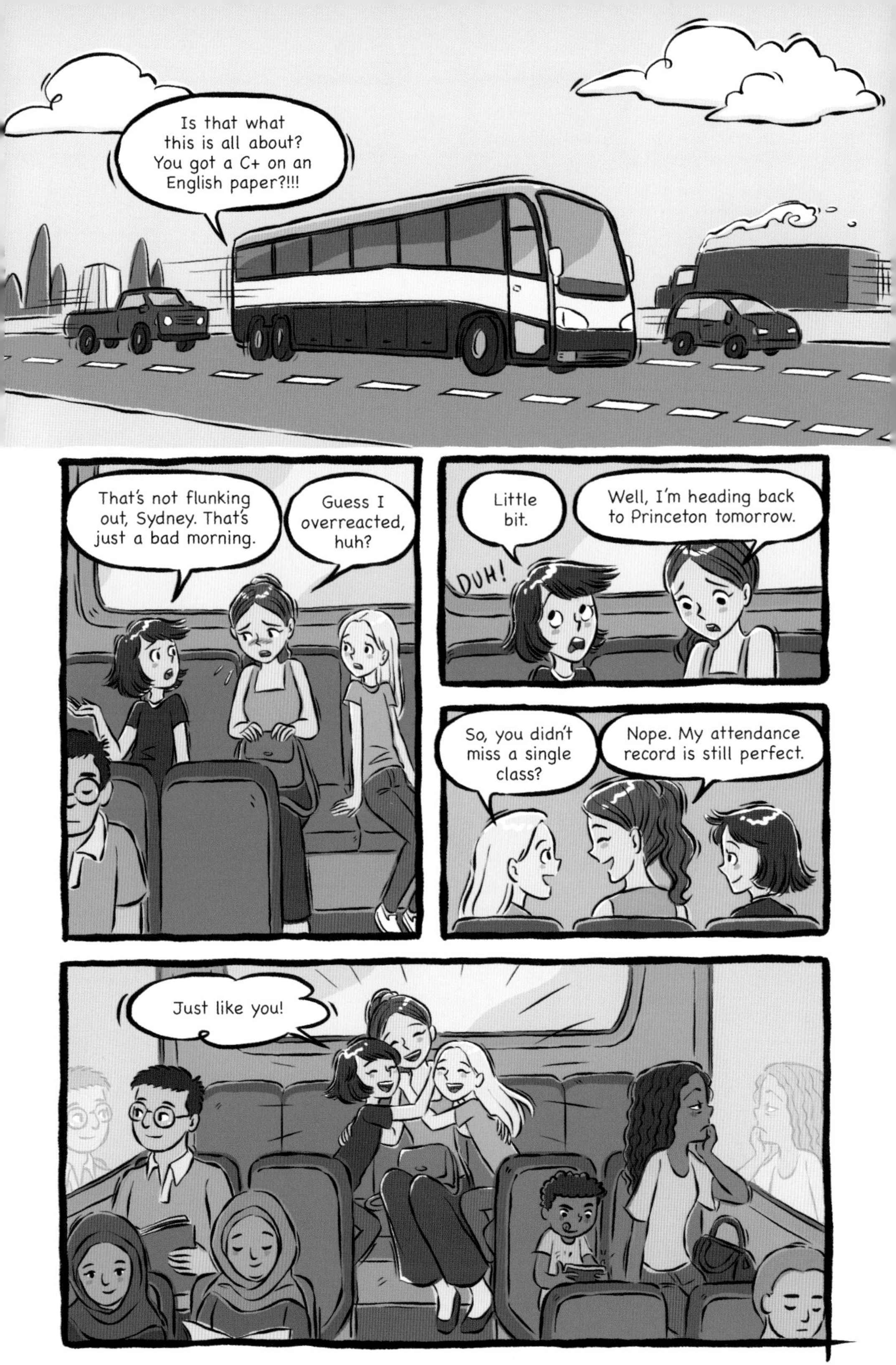
Is that what this is all about? You got a C+ on an English paper?!!!
That's not flunking out, Sydney. That's just a bad morning.
Guess I overreacted, huh?
Little bit.
DUH!
Well, I'm heading back to Princeton tomorrow.
So, you didn't miss a single class?
Nope. My attendance record is still perfect.
Just like you!

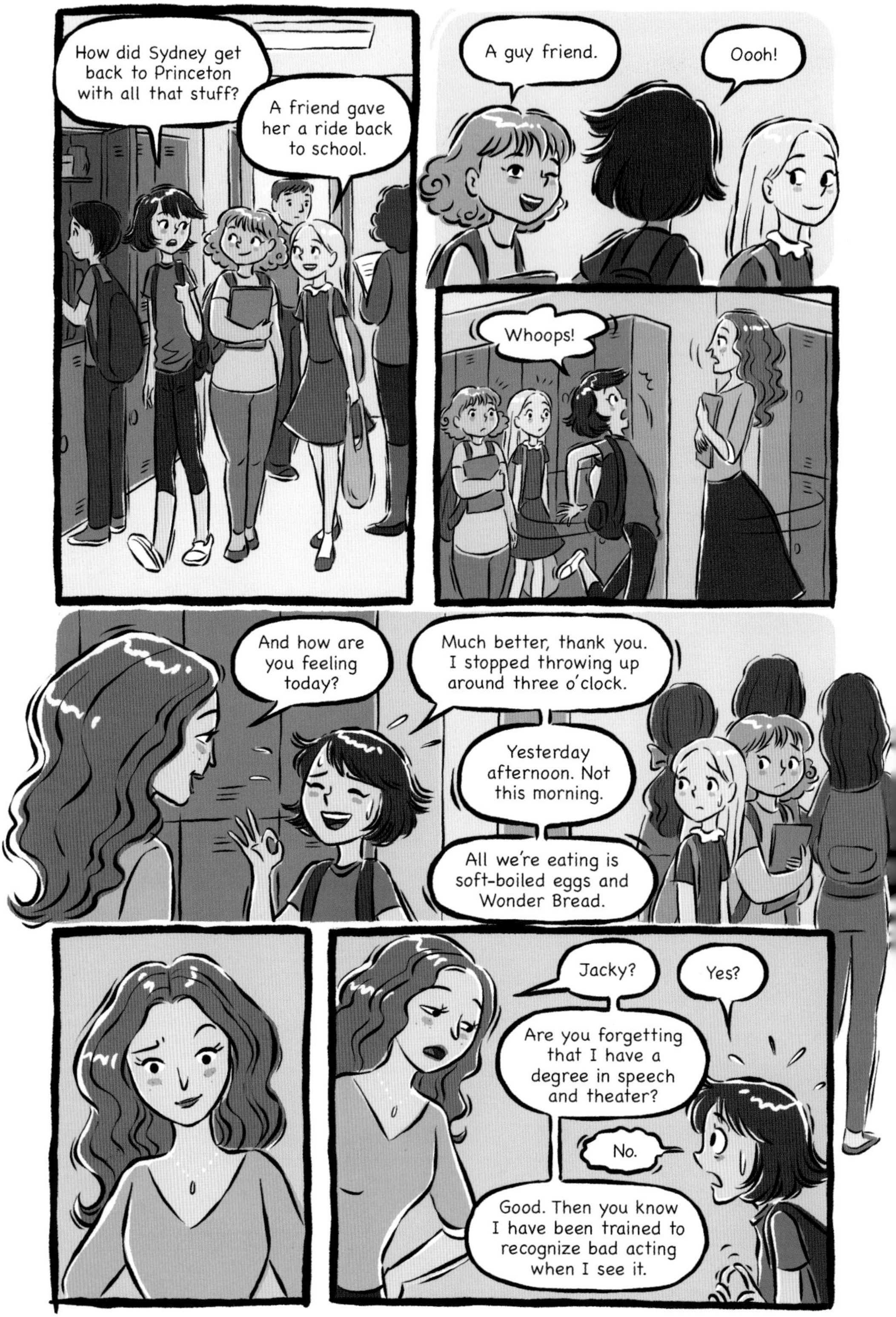
How did Sydney get back to Princeton with all that stuff?
A friend gave her a ride back to school.
A guy friend.
Oooh!
Whoops!
And how are you feeling today?
Much better, thank you. I stopped throwing up around three o'clock.
Yesterday afternoon. Not this morning.
All we're eating is soft-boiled eggs and Wonder Bread.
Jacky?
Yes?
Are you forgetting that I have a degree in speech and theater?
No.
Good. Then you know I have been trained to recognize bad acting when I see it.

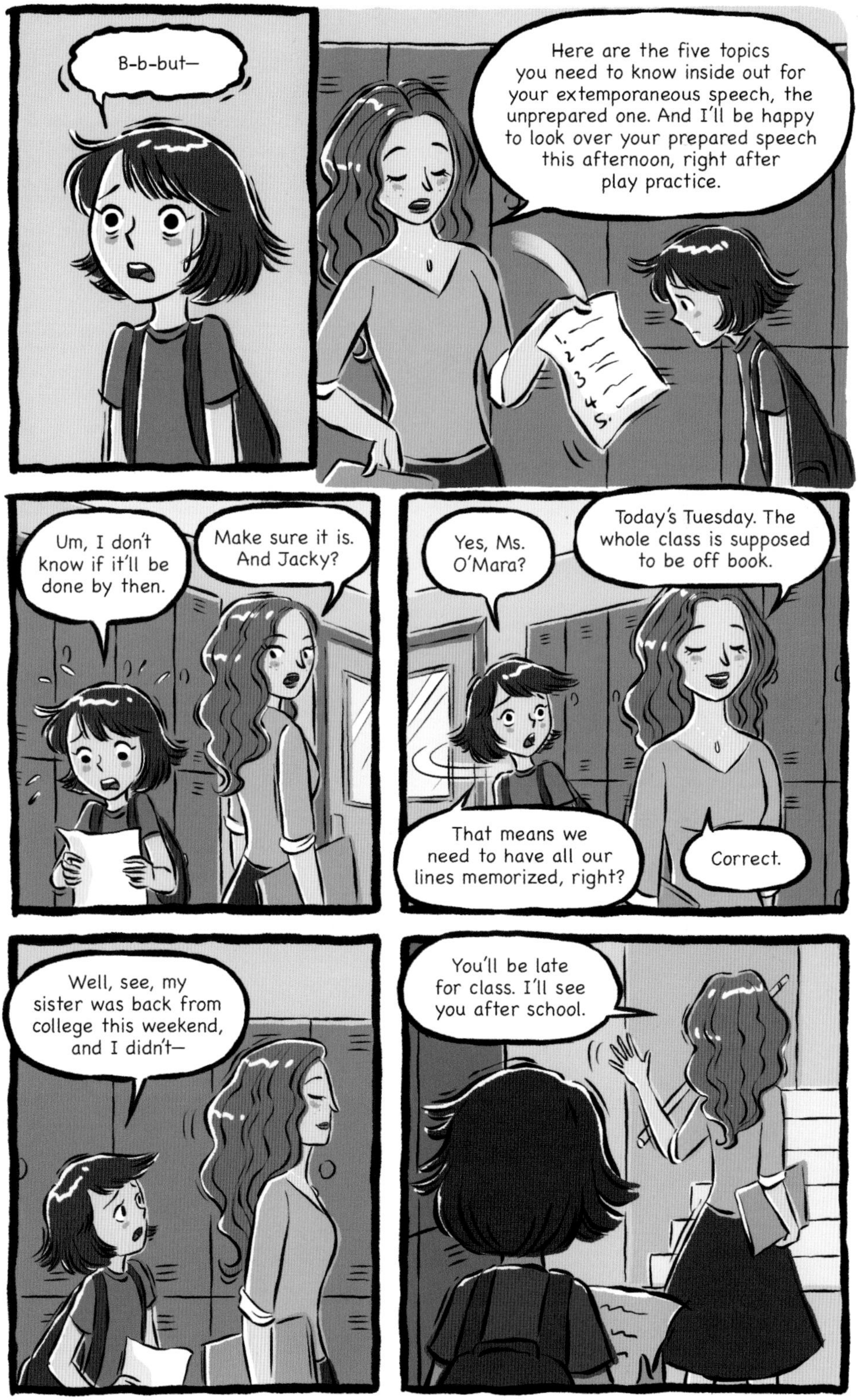
B-b-but—
Here are the five topics you need to know inside out for your extemporaneous speech, the unprepared one. And I'll be happy to look over your prepared speech this afternoon, right after play practice.
1.
2.
3.
4.
5.
Um, I don't know if it'll be done by then.
Make sure it is. And Jacky?
Yes, Ms. O'Mara?
Today's Tuesday. The whole class is supposed to be off book.
That means we need to have all our lines memorized, right?
Correct.
Well, see, my sister was back from college this weekend, and I didn't—
You'll be late for class. I'll see you after school.

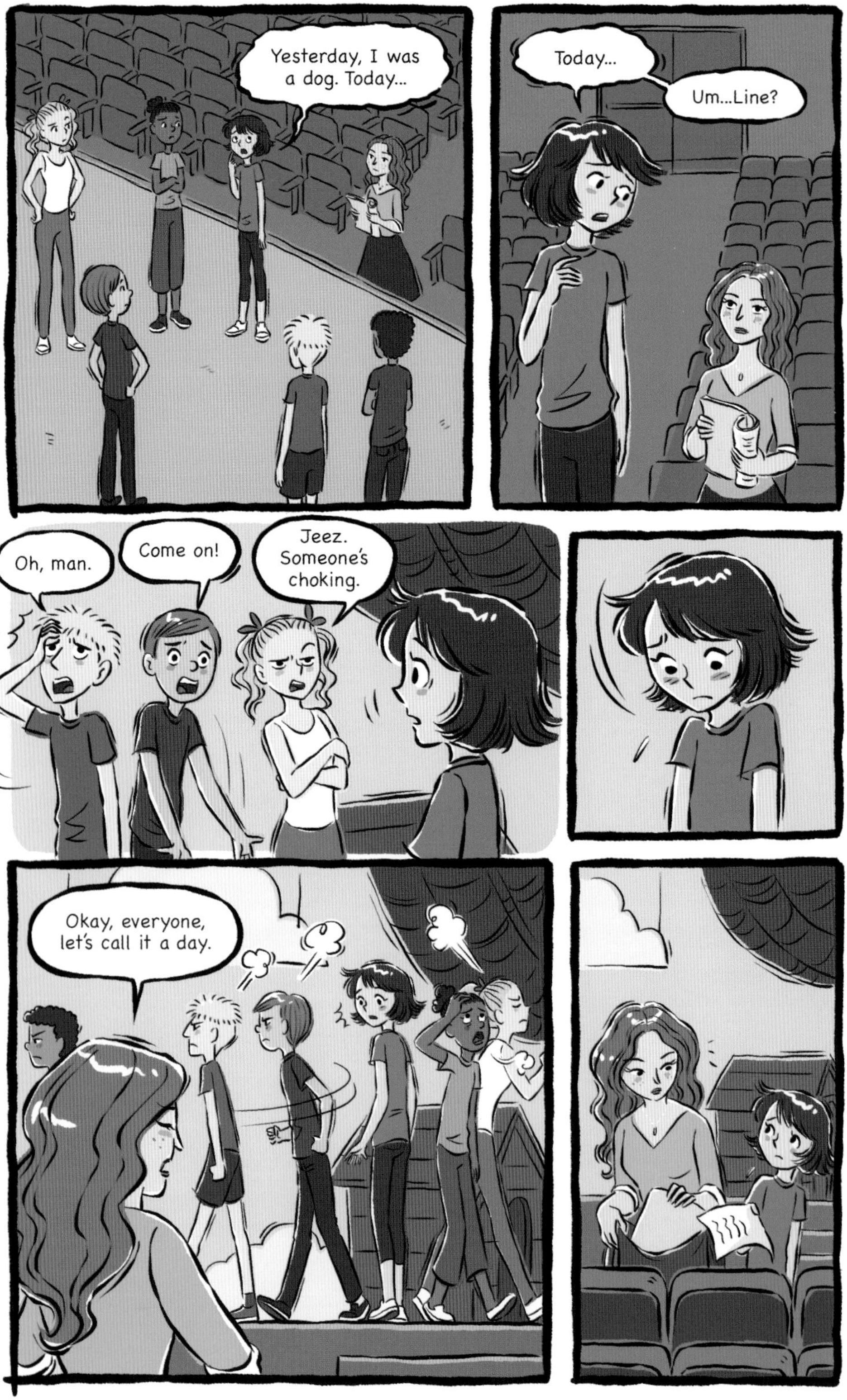

Yesterday, I was a dog. Today...
Today...
Um...Line?
Oh, man.
Come on!
Jeez. Someone's choking.
Okay, everyone, let's call it a day.

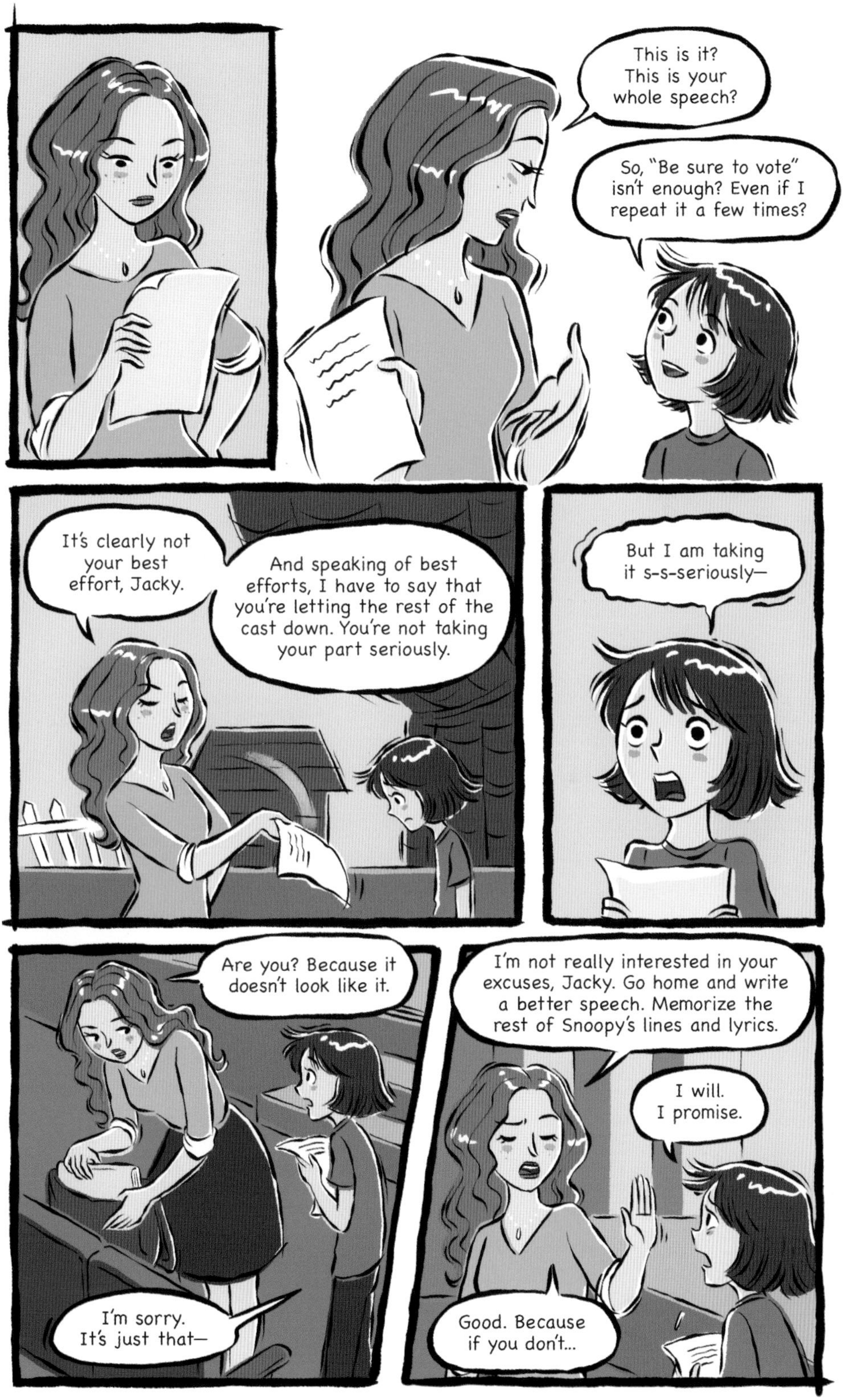
This is it? This is your whole speech?
So, "Be sure to vote" isn't enough? Even if I repeat it a few times?
It's clearly not your best effort, Jacky.
And speaking of best efforts, I have to say that you're letting the rest of the cast down. You're not taking your part seriously.
But I am taking it s-s-seriously—
Are you? Because it doesn't look like it.
I'm sorry. It's just that—
I'm not really interested in your excuses, Jacky. Go home and write a better speech. Memorize the rest of Snoopy's lines and lyrics.
I will. I promise.
Good. Because if you don't...

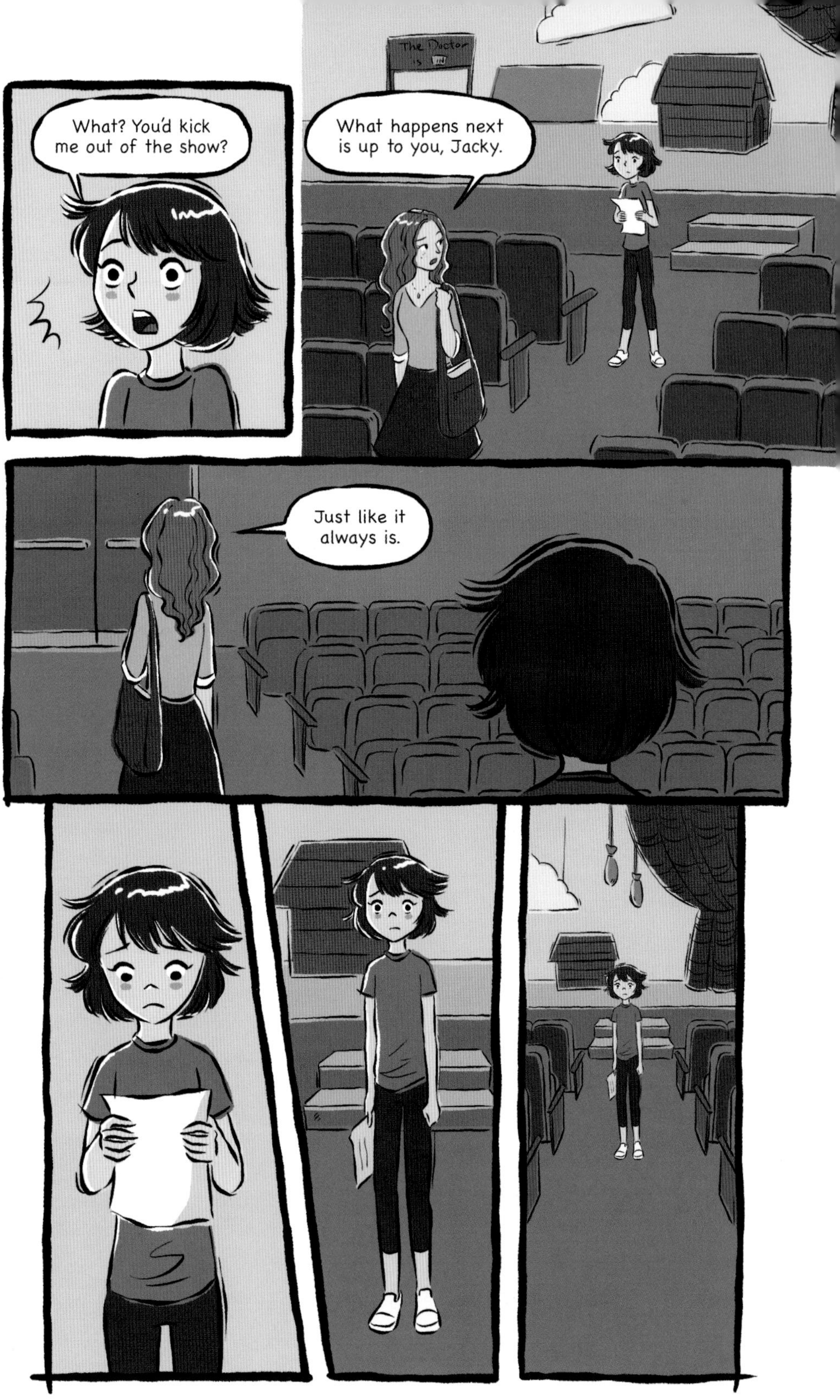

What? You'd kick me out of the show?
What happens next is up to you, Jacky.
Just like it always is.

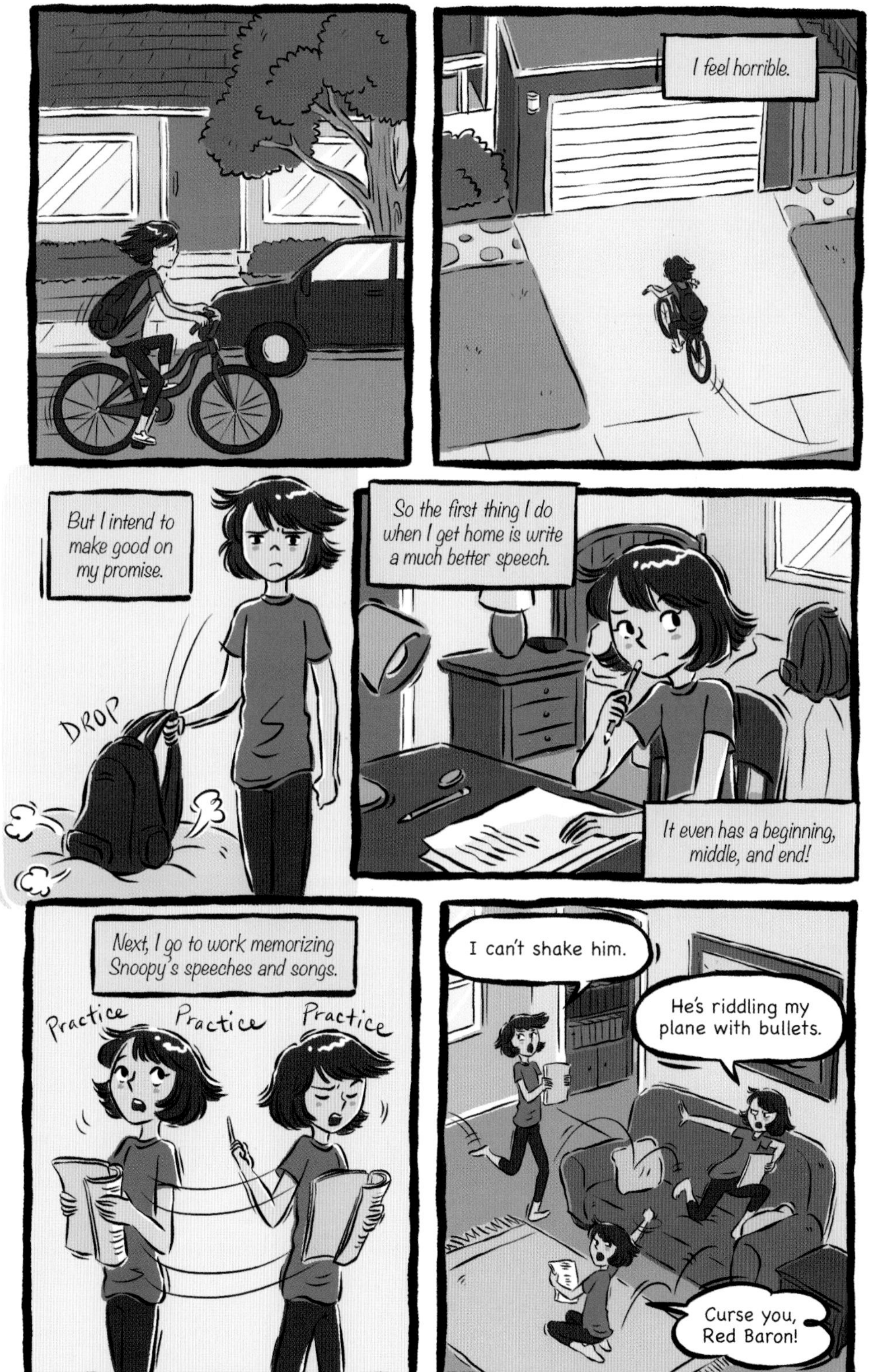

I feel horrible.
But I intend to make good on my promise.
DROP
So the first thing I do when I get home is write a much better speech.
It even has a beginning, middle, and end!
Next, I go to work memorizing Snoopy's speeches and songs.
Practice
Practice
Practice
I can't shake him.
He's riddling my plane with bullets.
Curse you, Red Baron!

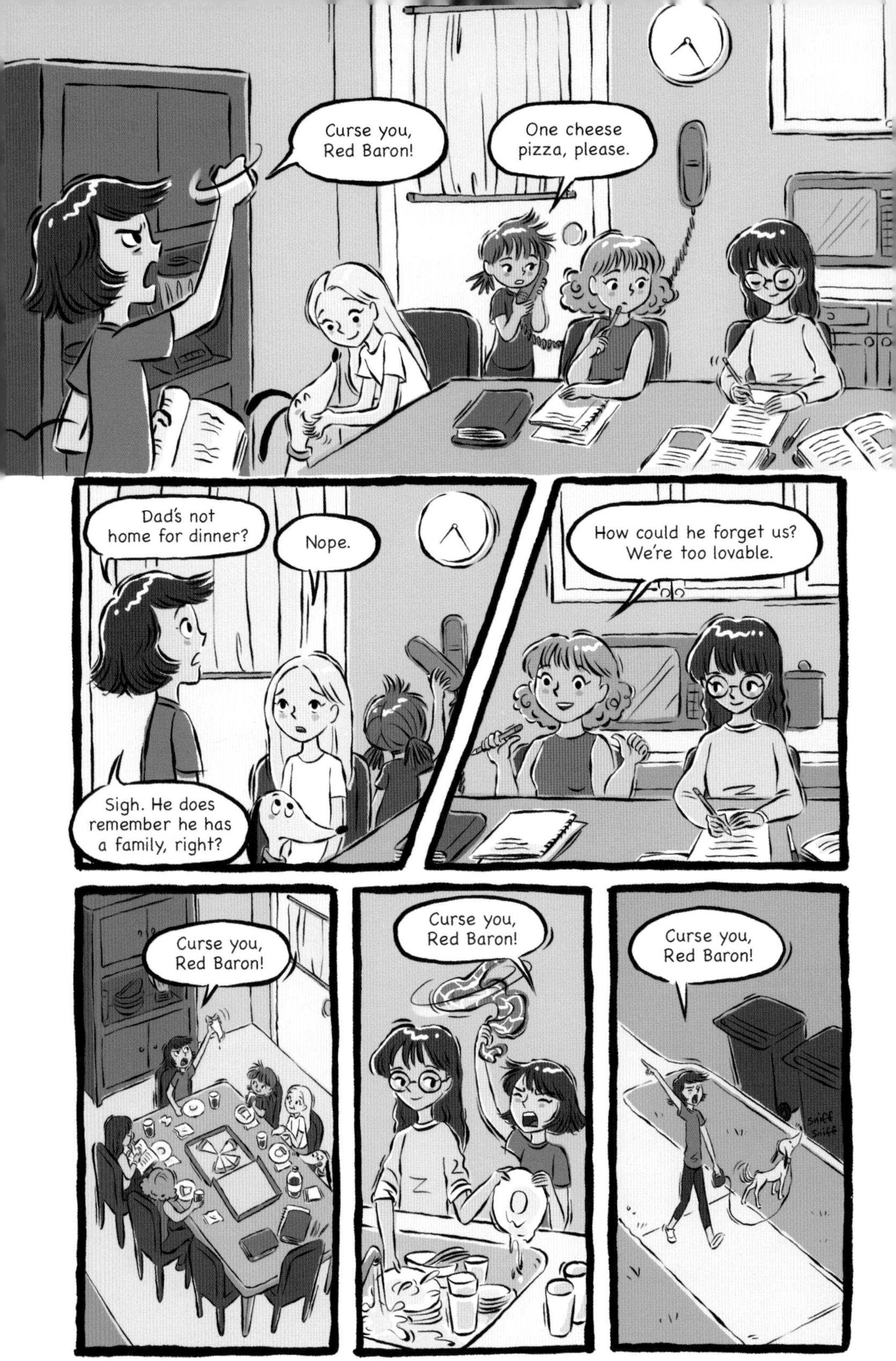

Curse you, Red Baron!
One cheese pizza, please.
Dad's not home for dinner?
Nope.
Sigh. He does remember he has a family, right?
How could he forget us? We're too lovable.
Curse you, Red Baron!
Curse you, Red Baron!
Curse you, Red Baron!
Sniff
Sniff

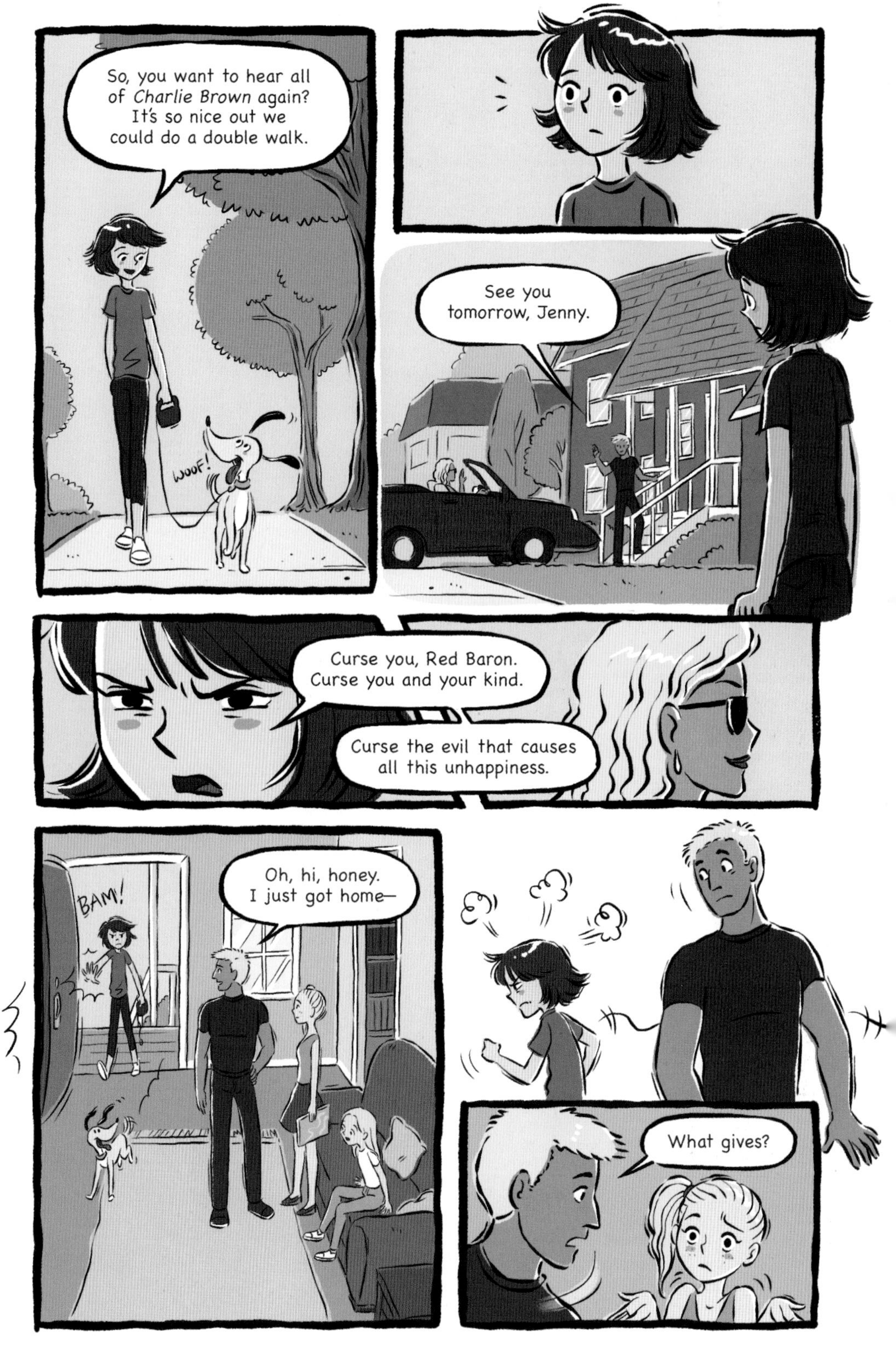
So, you want to hear all of *Charlie Brown* again? It's so nice out we could do a double walk.
WOOF!
See you tomorrow, Jenny.
Curse you, Red Baron. Curse you and your kind.
Curse the evil that causes all this unhappiness.
BAM!
Oh, hi, honey. I just got home—
What gives?

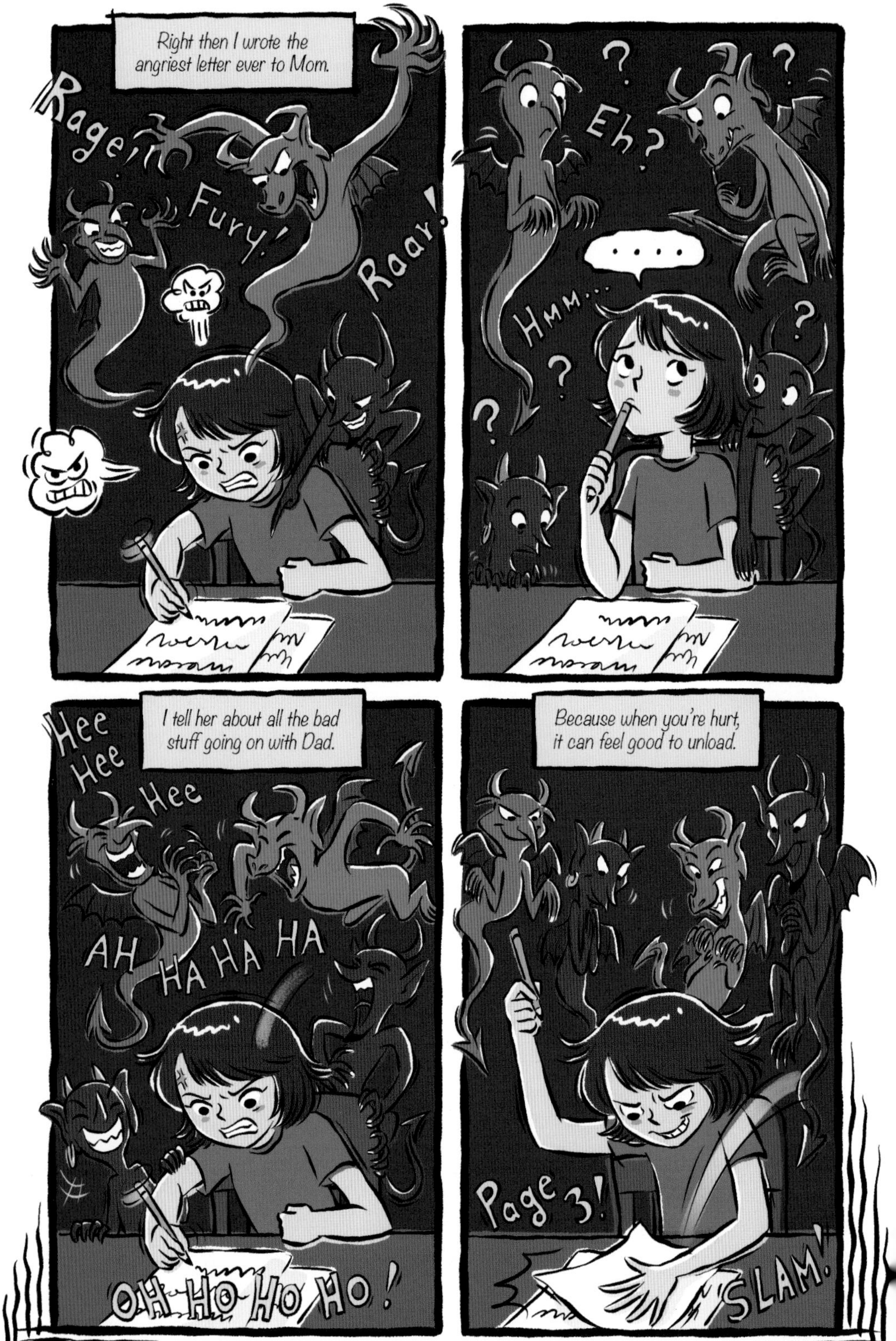
Right then I wrote the angriest letter ever to Mom.
Rage!!
Fury!
Raar!
Eh?
Hmm...
....
I tell her about all the bad stuff going on with Dad.
Hee Hee Hee
AH HA HA HA
OH HO HO HO!
Because when you're hurt, it can feel good to unload.
Page 3!
SLAM!

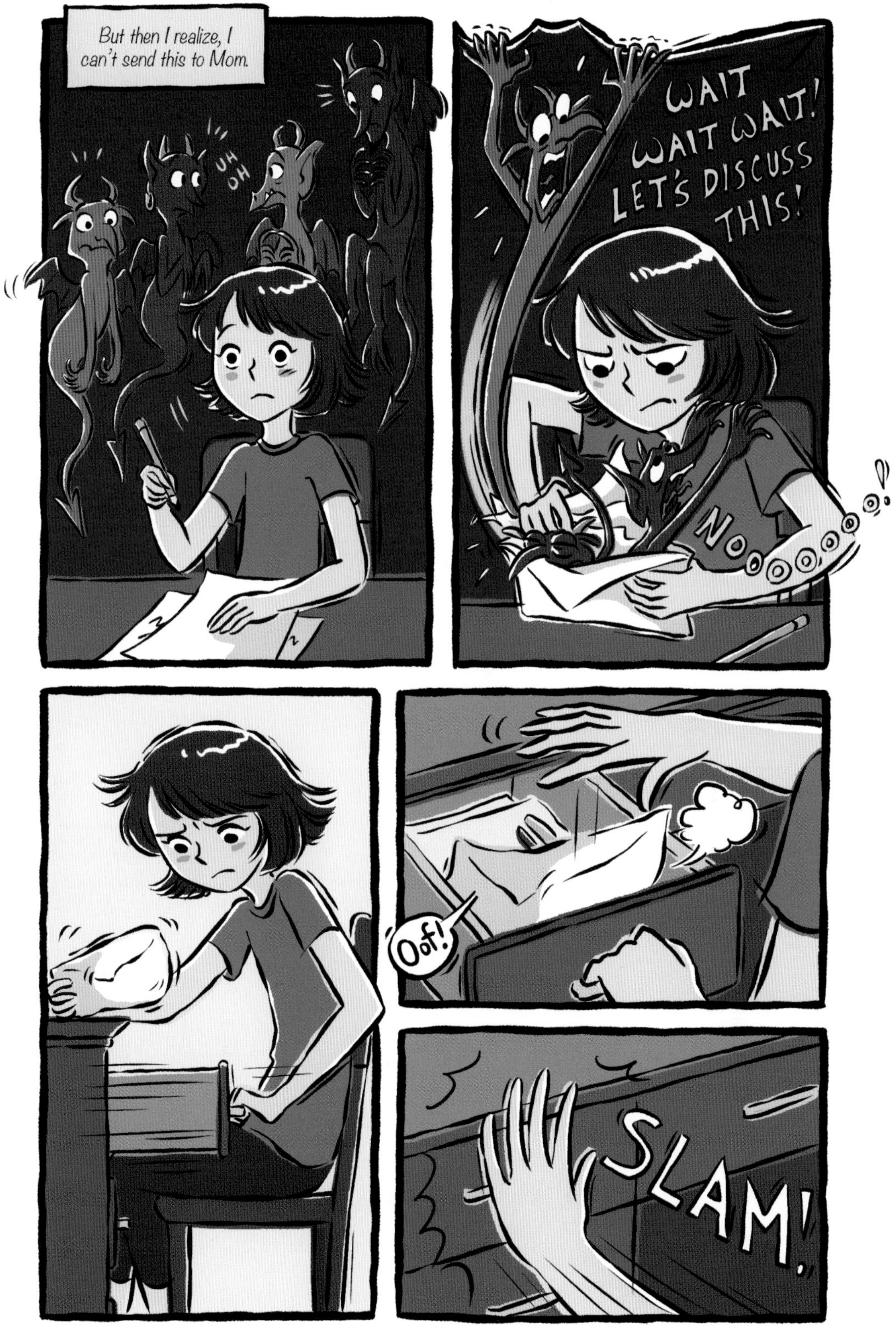

But then I realize, I can't send this to Mom.
UH OH
WAIT WAIT WAIT! LET'S DISCUSS THIS!
NOOOOOOOO!
Oof!
SLAM!

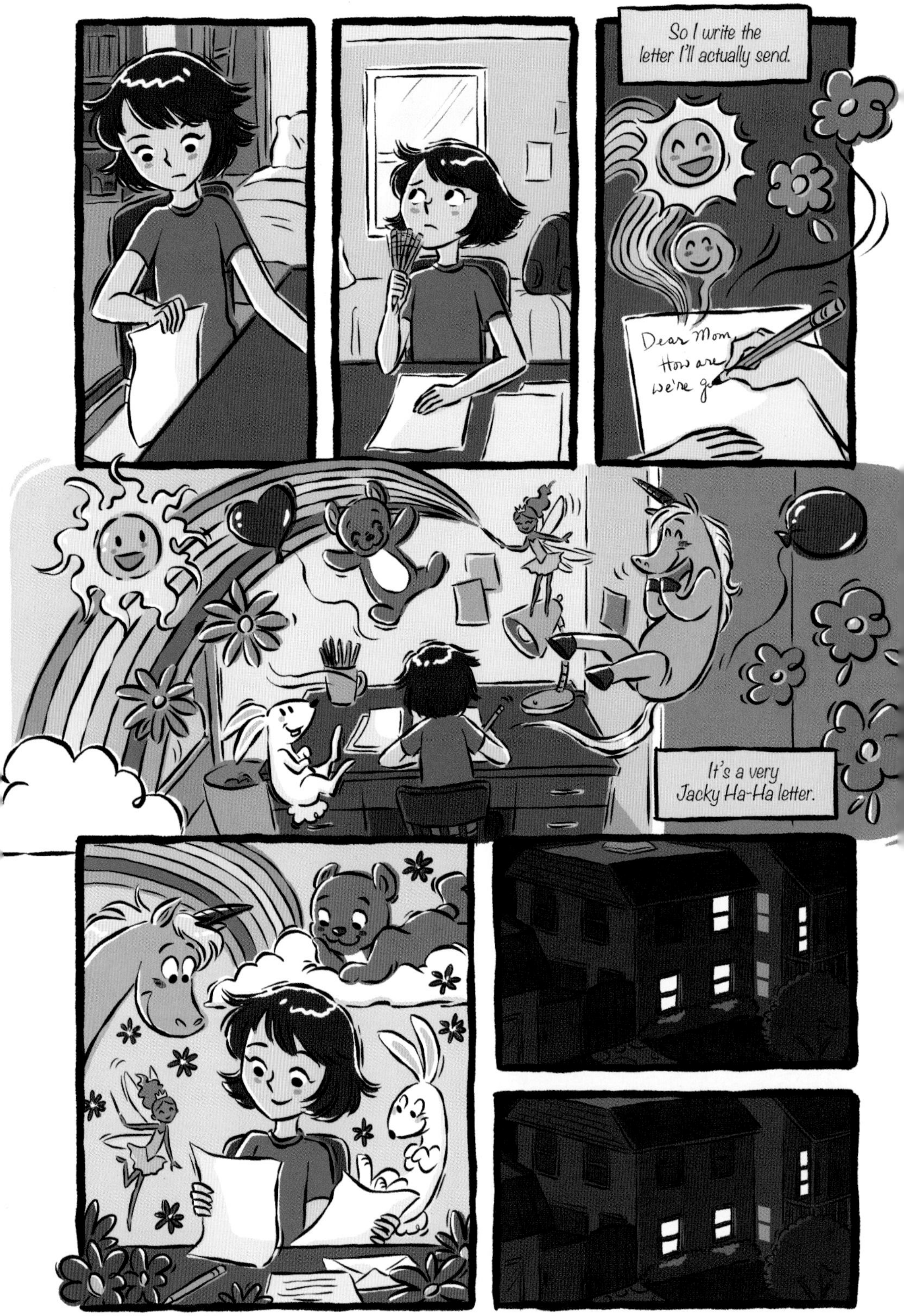
So I write the letter I'll actually send.
Dear Mom
How are
It's a very Jacky Ha-Ha letter.

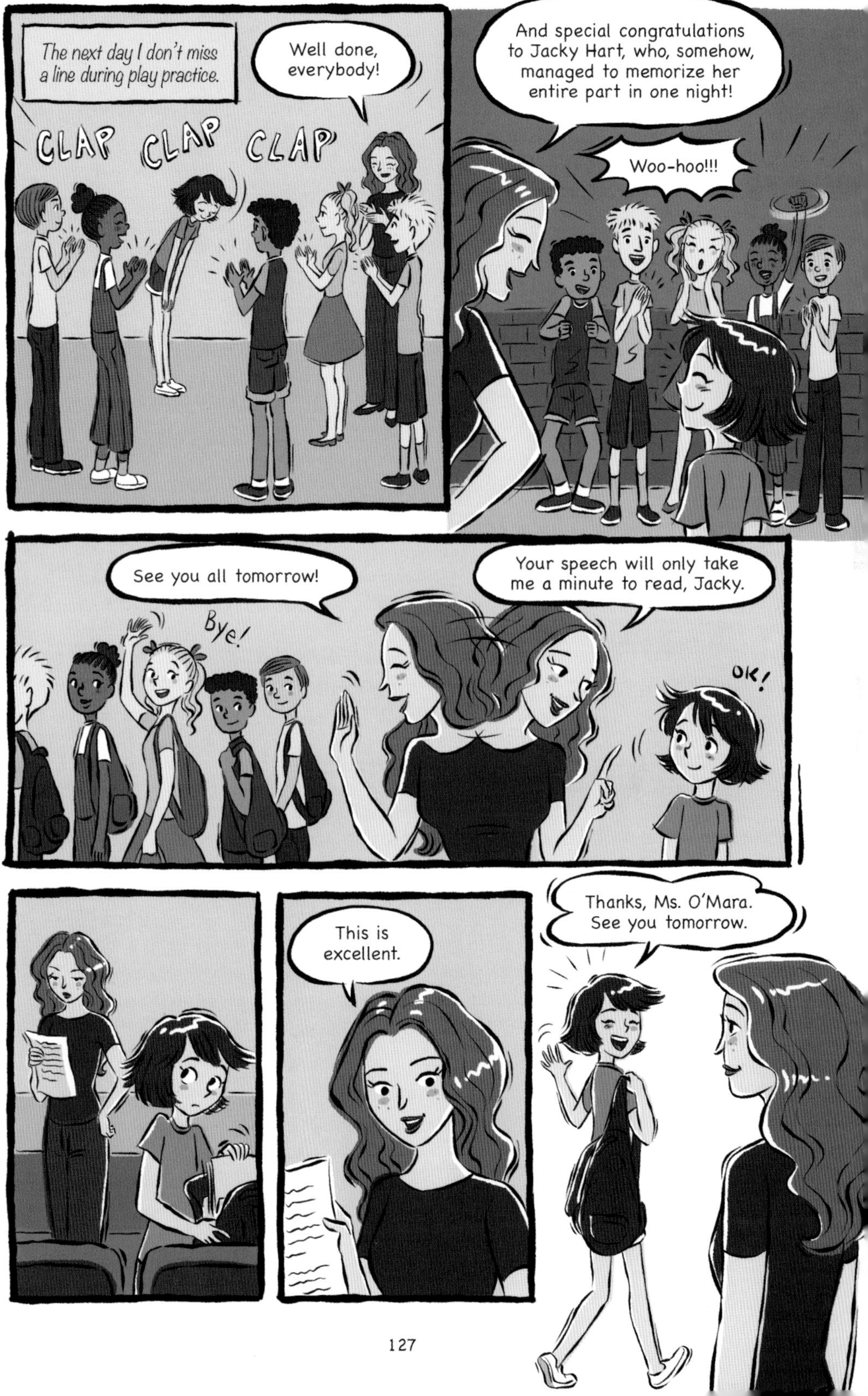

The next day I don't miss a line during play practice.
Well done, everybody!
CLAP CLAP CLAP
And special congratulations to Jacky Hart, who, somehow, managed to memorize her entire part in one night!
Woo-hoo!!!
See you all tomorrow!
Bye!
Your speech will only take me a minute to read, Jacky.
OK!
This is excellent.
Thanks, Ms. O'Mara. See you tomorrow.

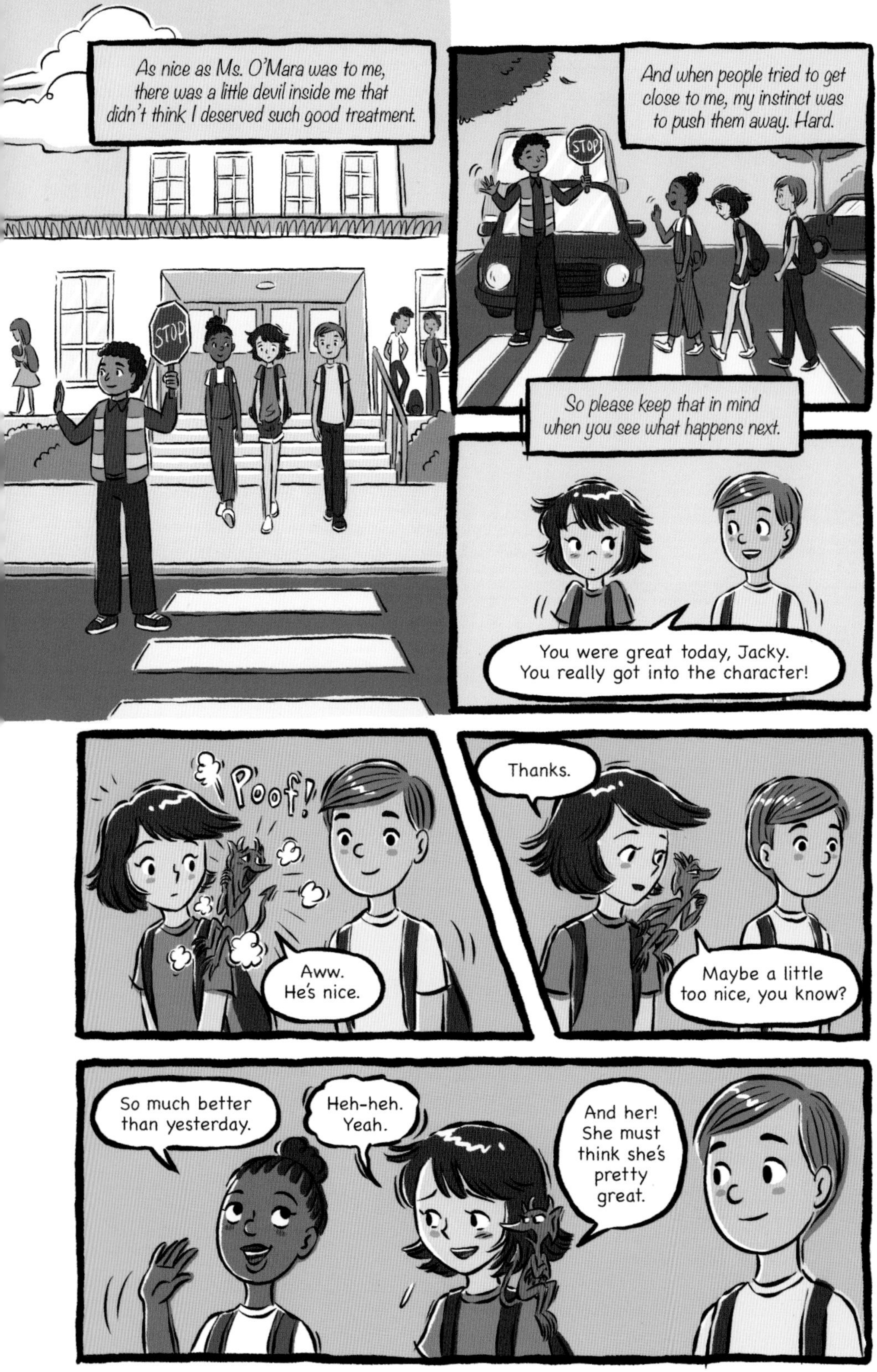
As nice as Ms. O'Mara was to me, there was a little devil inside me that didn't think I deserved such good treatment.
STOP
And when people tried to get close to me, my instinct was to push them away. Hard.
STOP
So please keep that in mind when you see what happens next.
You were great today, Jacky. You really got into the character!
Poof!
Aww. He's nice.
Thanks.
Maybe a little too nice, you know?
So much better than yesterday.
Heh-heh. Yeah.
And her! She must think she's pretty great.

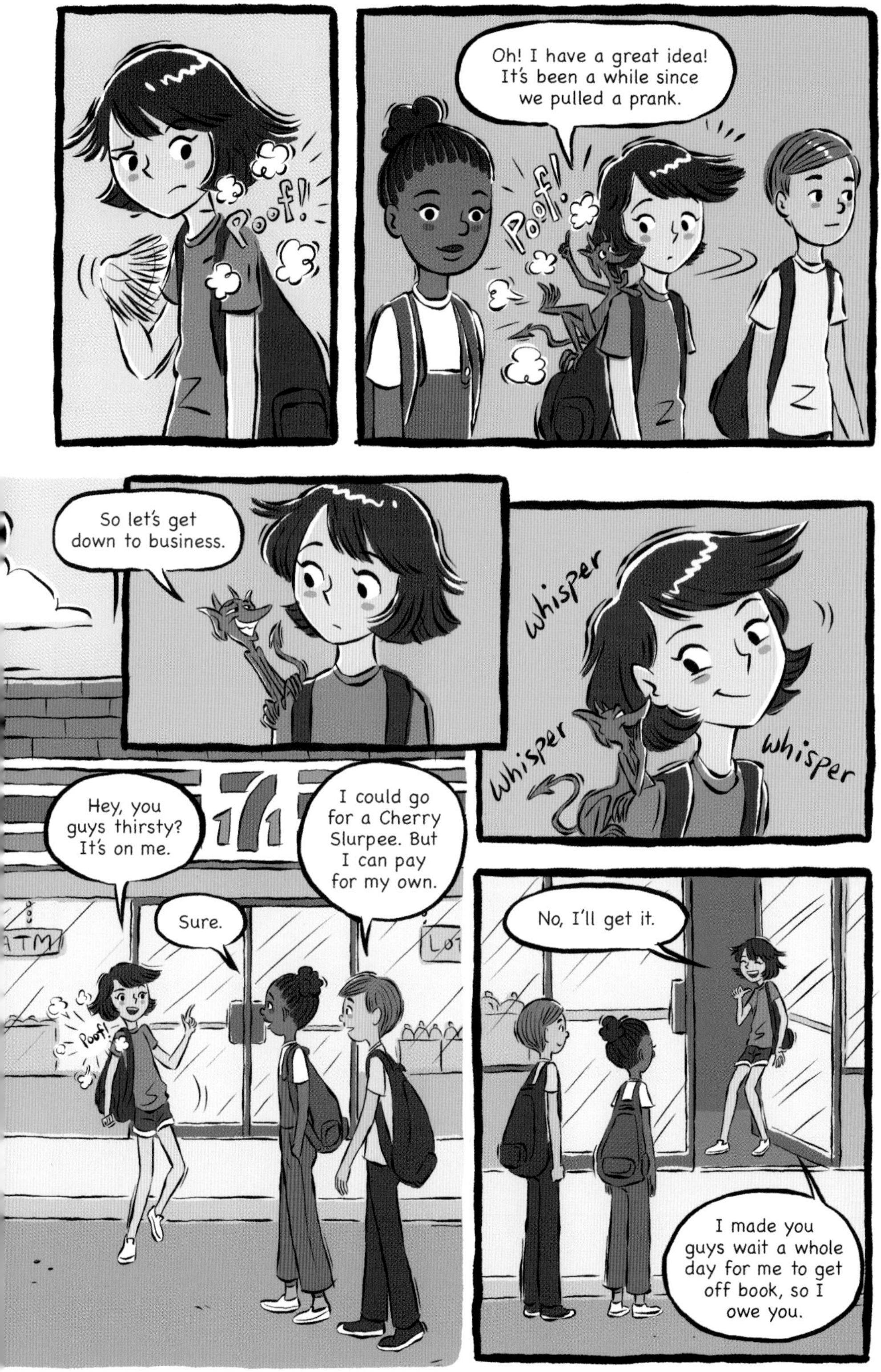
Poof!
Oh! I have a great idea! It's been a while since we pulled a prank.
Poof!
So let's get down to business.
whisper
whisper
whisper
Hey, you guys thirsty? It's on me.
Poof!
Sure.
I could go for a Cherry Slurpee. But I can pay for my own.
ATM
No, I'll get it.
I made you guys wait a whole day for me to get off book, so I owe you.

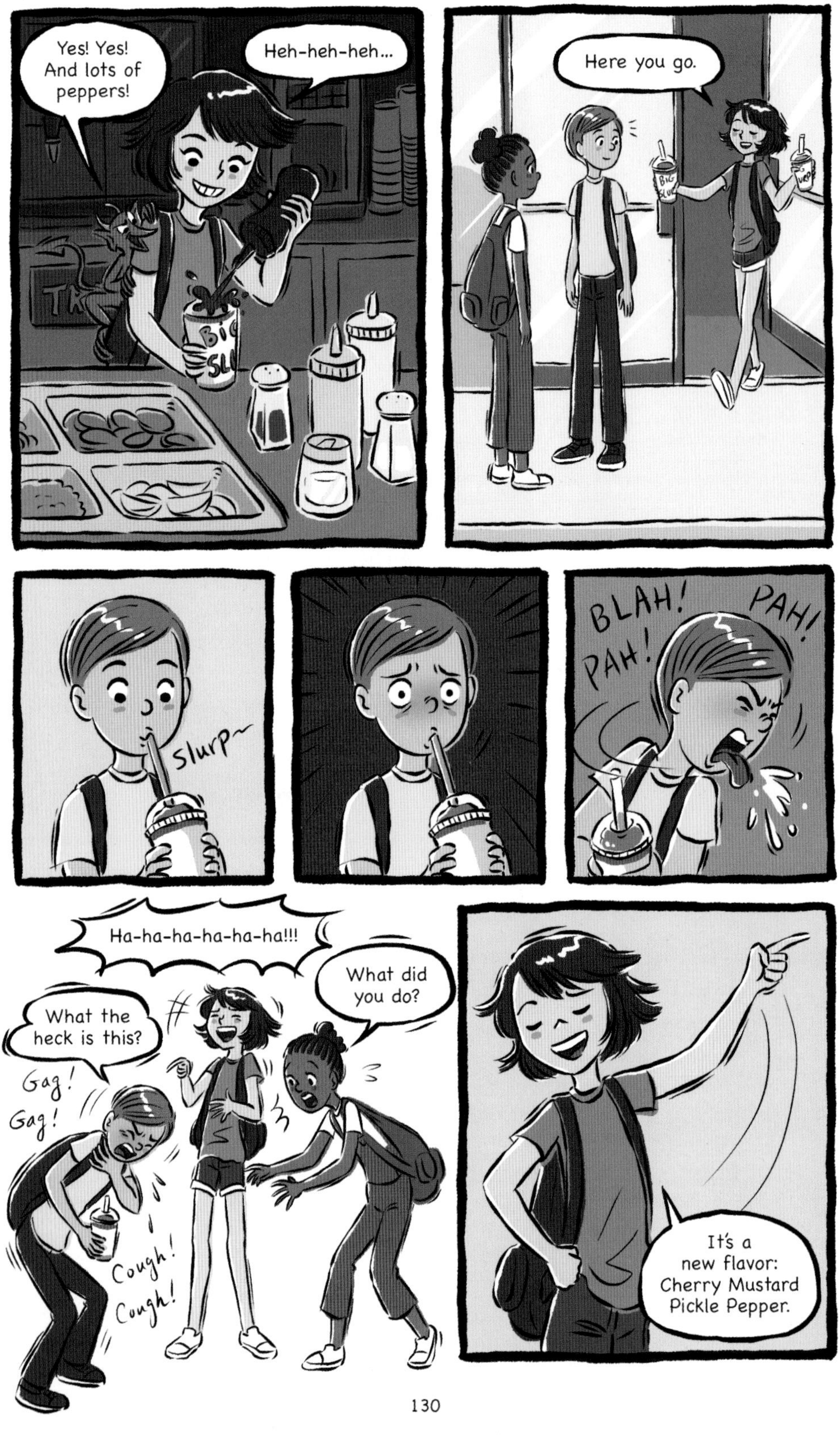
Yes! Yes! And lots of peppers!
Heh-heh-heh...
TK
BIG SLU
Here you go.
BIG SLU
Slurp~
BLAH!
PAH!
PAH!
Ha-ha-ha-ha-ha-ha!!!
What the heck is this?
What did you do?
Gag!
Gag!
Cough!
Cough!
It's a new flavor: Cherry Mustard Pickle Pepper.

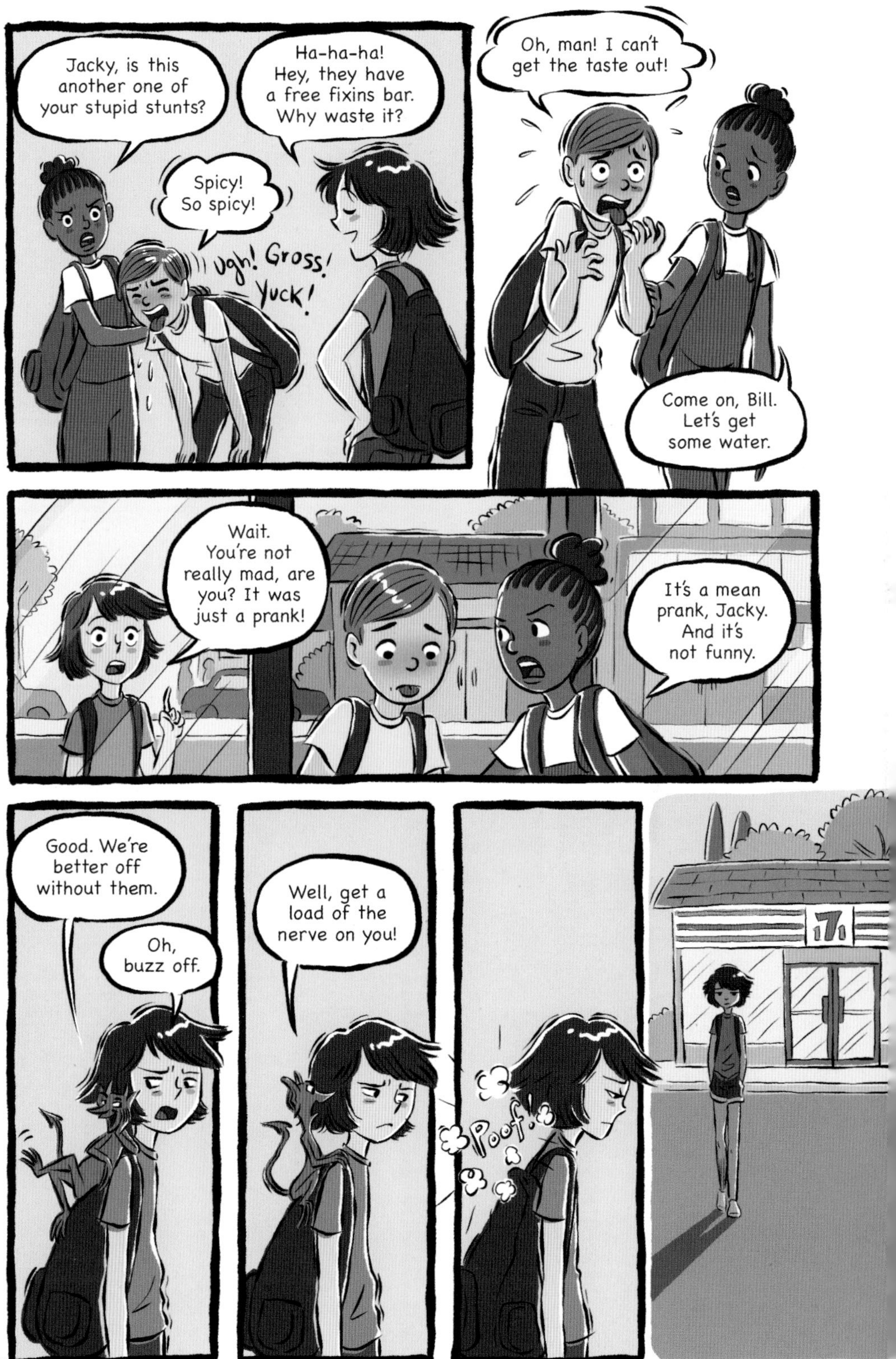
Jacky, is this another one of your stupid stunts?
Spicy! So spicy!
Ha-ha-ha! Hey, they have a free fixins bar. Why waste it?
Ugh! Gross! Yuck!
Oh, man! I can't get the taste out!
Come on, Bill. Let's get some water.
Wait. You're not really mad, are you? It was just a prank!
It's a mean prank, Jacky. And it's not funny.
Good. We're better off without them.
Oh, buzz off.
Well, get a load of the nerve on you!
Poof!

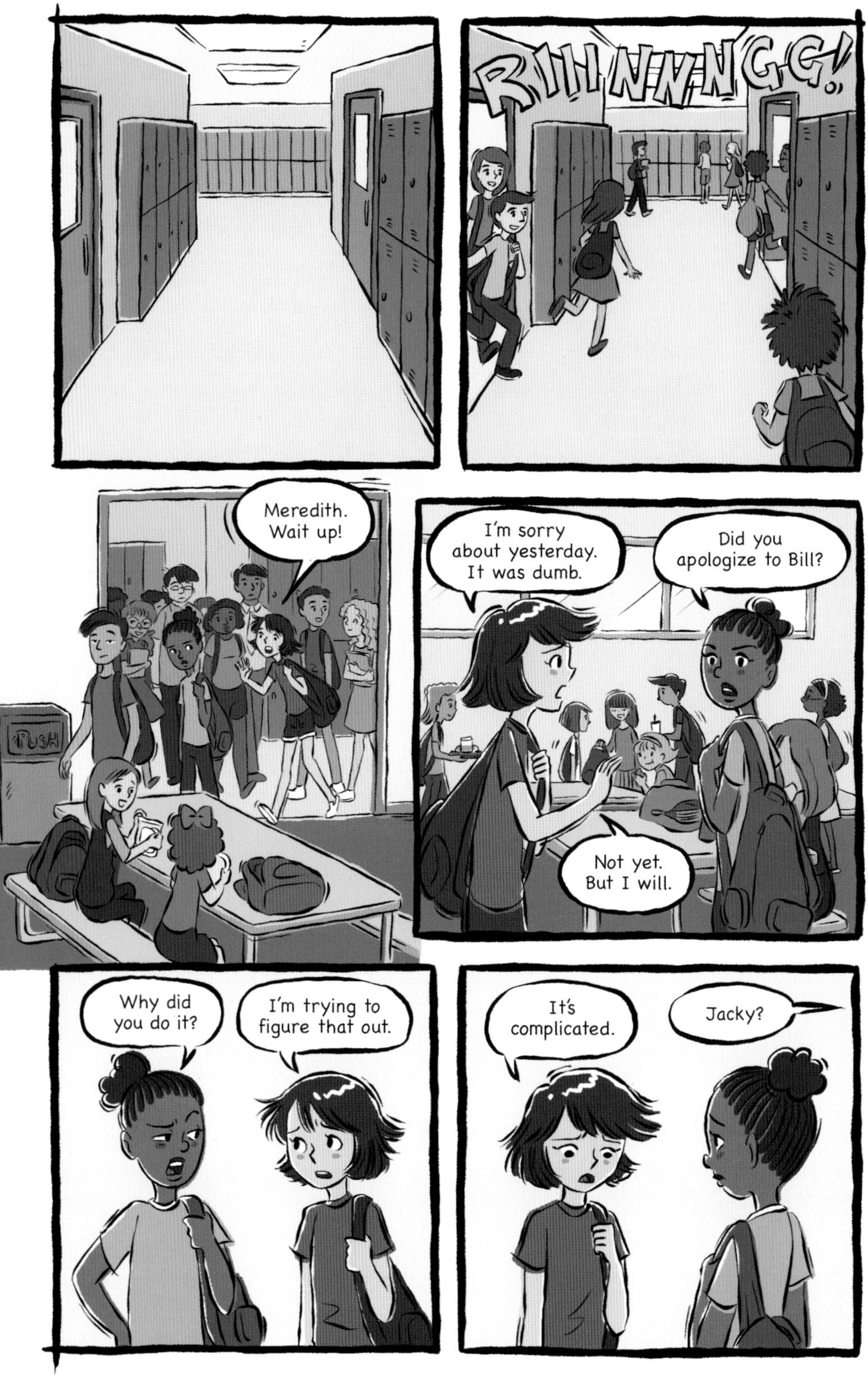
RIIINNNGG!
Meredith. Wait up!
I'm sorry about yesterday. It was dumb.
Did you apologize to Bill?
Not yet. But I will.
Why did you do it?
I'm trying to figure that out.
It's complicated.
Jacky?

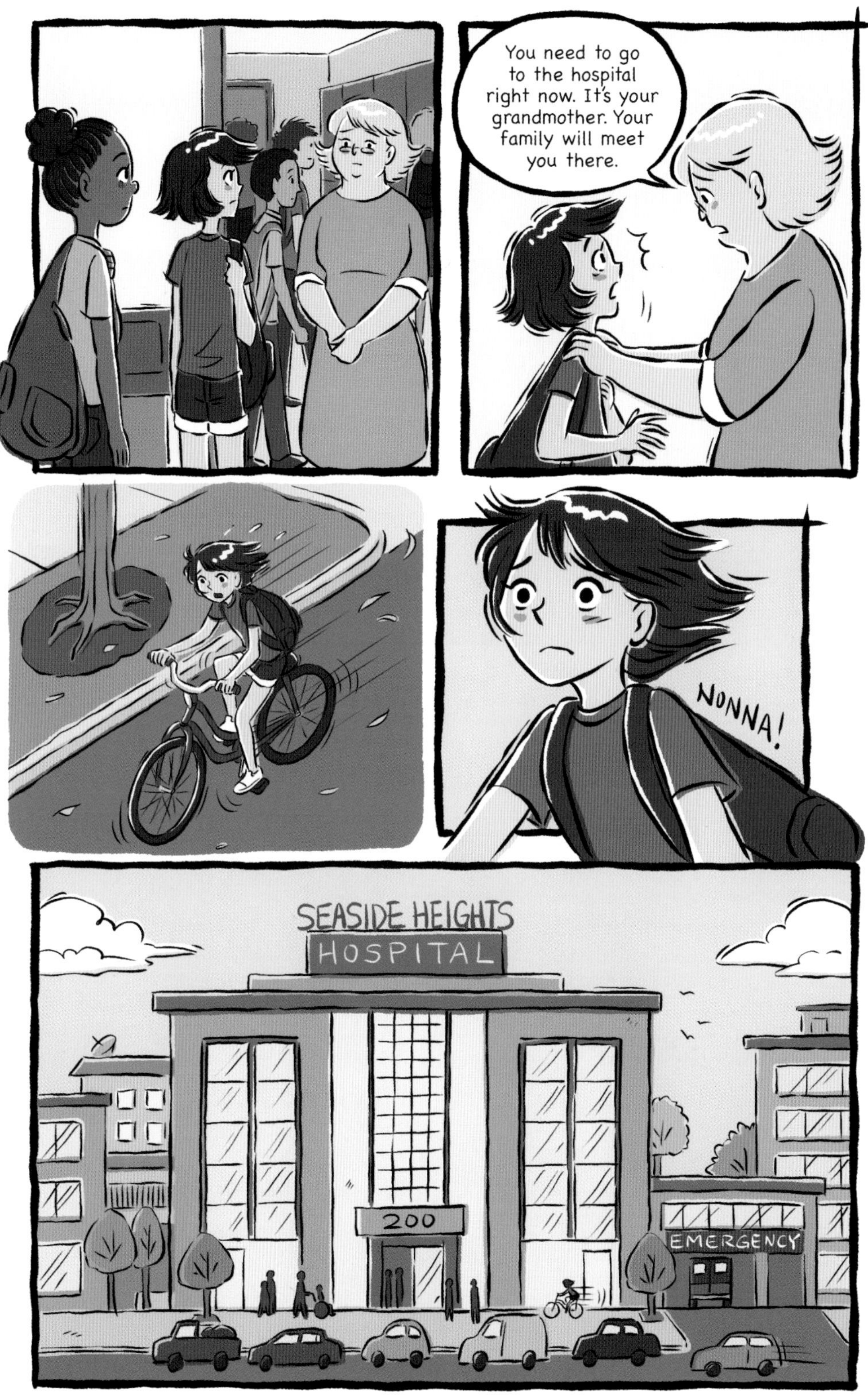
You need to go to the hospital right now. It's your grandmother. Your family will meet you there.
NONNA!
SEASIDE HEIGHTS
HOSPITAL
200
EMERGENCY

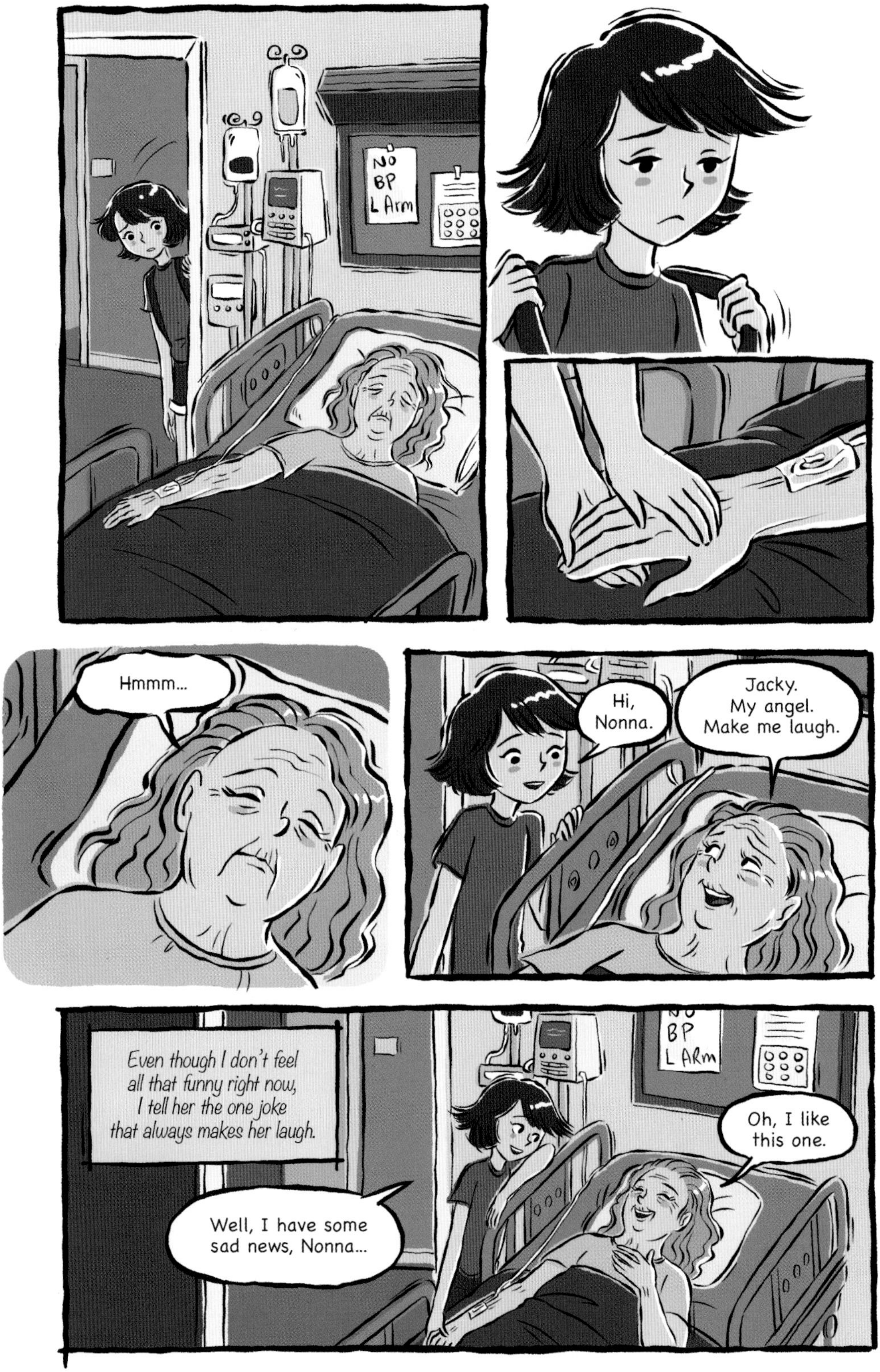
NO
BP
L Arm
Hmmm...
Hi, Nonna.
Jacky. My angel. Make me laugh.
NO
BP
L Arm
Even though I don't feel all that funny right now, I tell her the one joke that always makes her laugh.
Oh, I like this one.
Well, I have some sad news, Nonna...

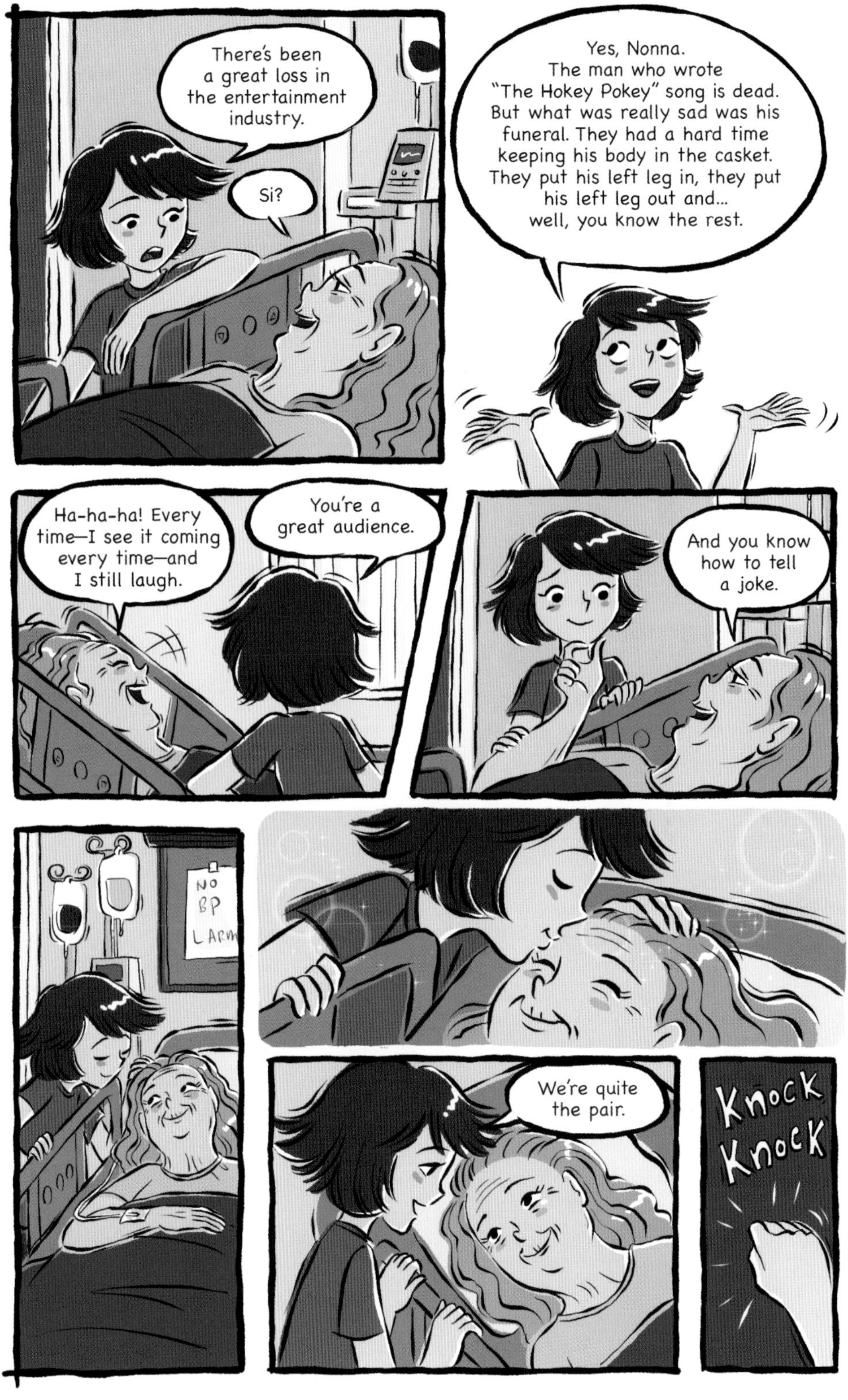
There's been a great loss in the entertainment industry.
Si?
Yes, Nonna. The man who wrote "The Hokey Pokey" song is dead. But what was really sad was his funeral. They had a hard time keeping his body in the casket. They put his left leg in, they put his left leg out and... well, you know the rest.
Ha-ha-ha! Every time—I see it coming every time—and I still laugh.
You're a great audience.
And you know how to tell a joke.
NO BP LARM
We're quite the pair.
Knock Knock

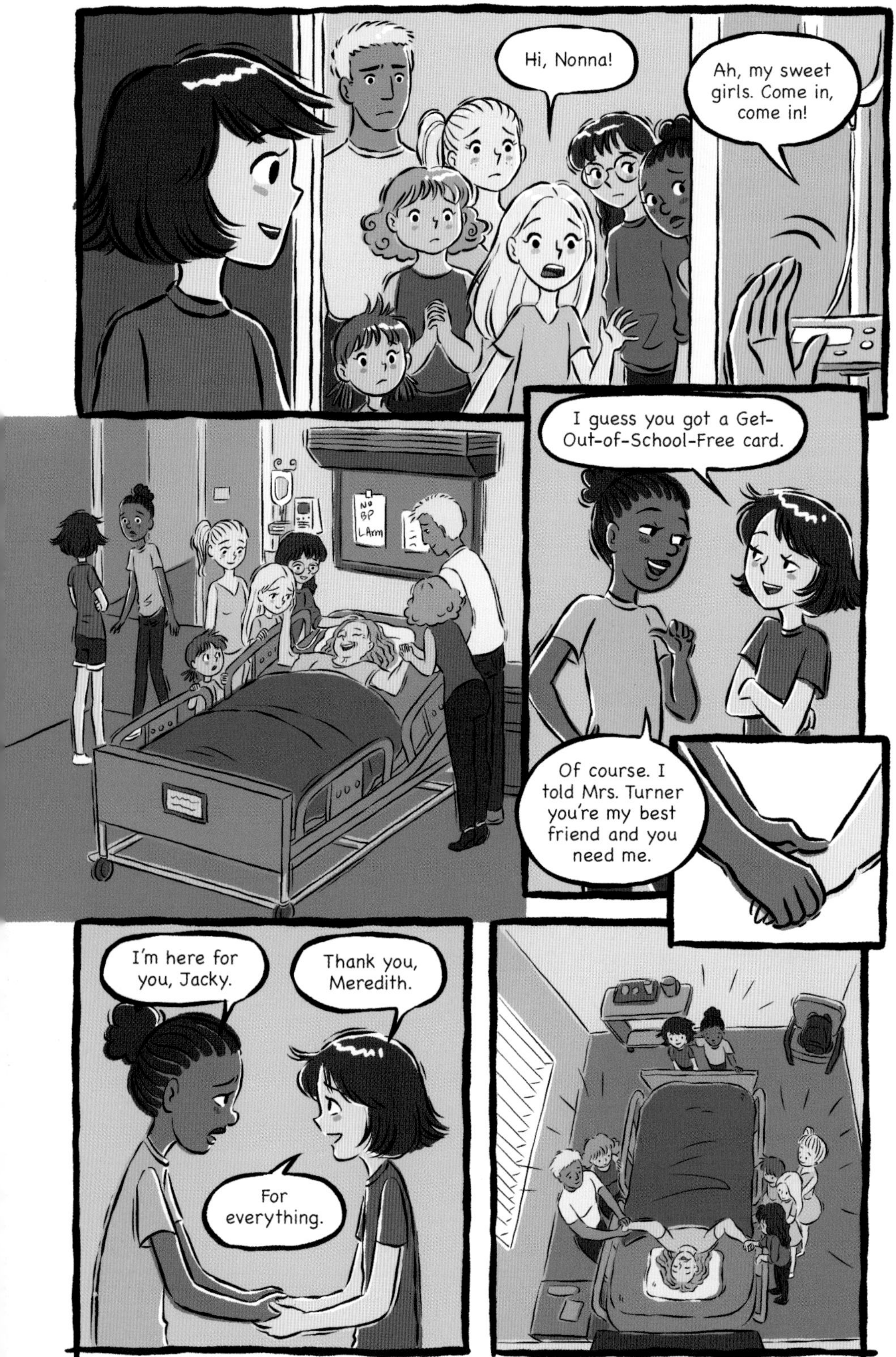
Hi, Nonna!
Ah, my sweet girls. Come in, come in!
NO BP L Arm
I guess you got a Get-Out-of-School-Free card.
Of course. I told Mrs. Turner you're my best friend and you need me.
I'm here for you, Jacky.
Thank you, Meredith.
For everything.

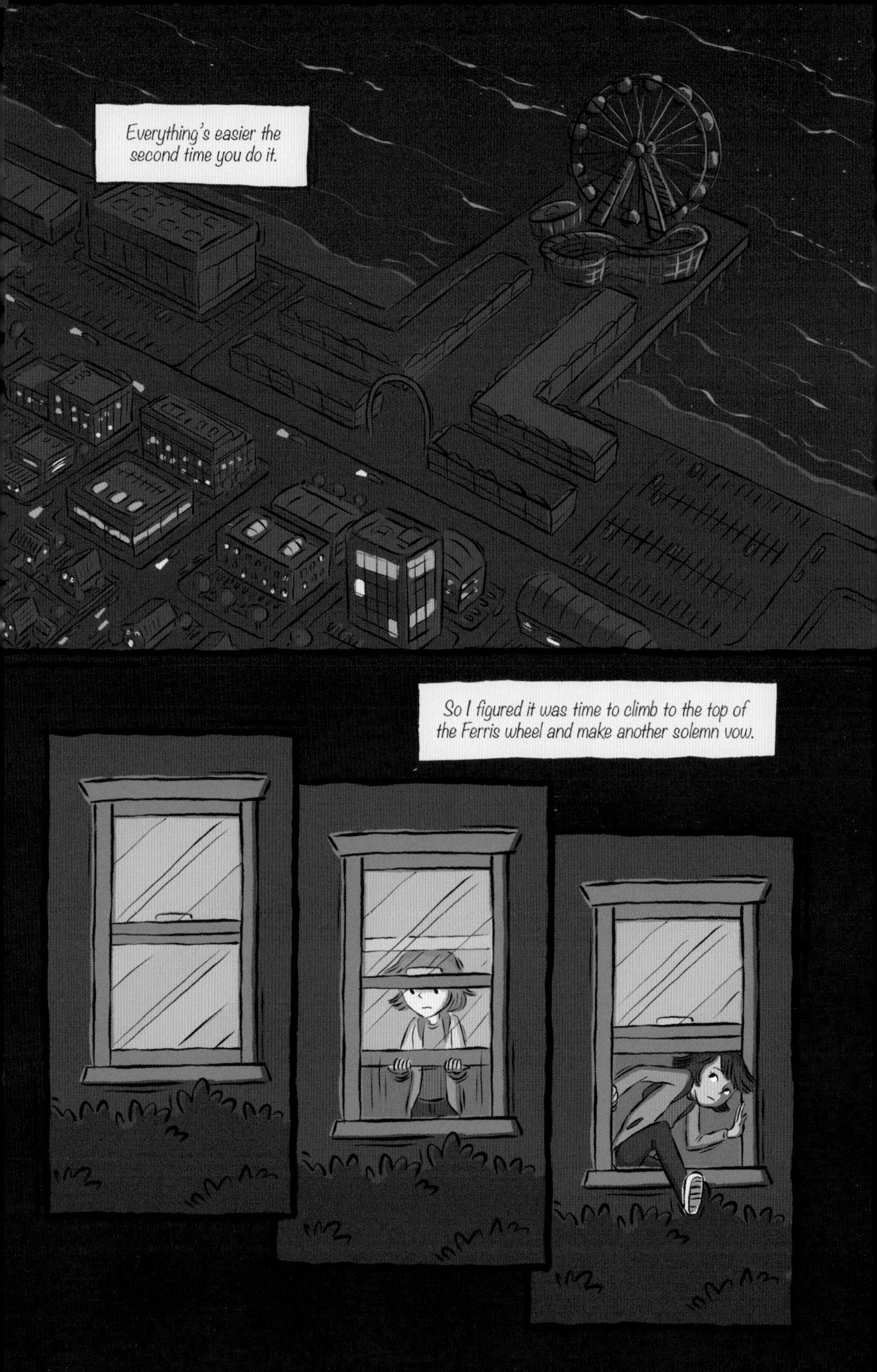
Everything's easier the second time you do it.
So I figured it was time to climb to the top of the Ferris wheel and make another solemn vow.

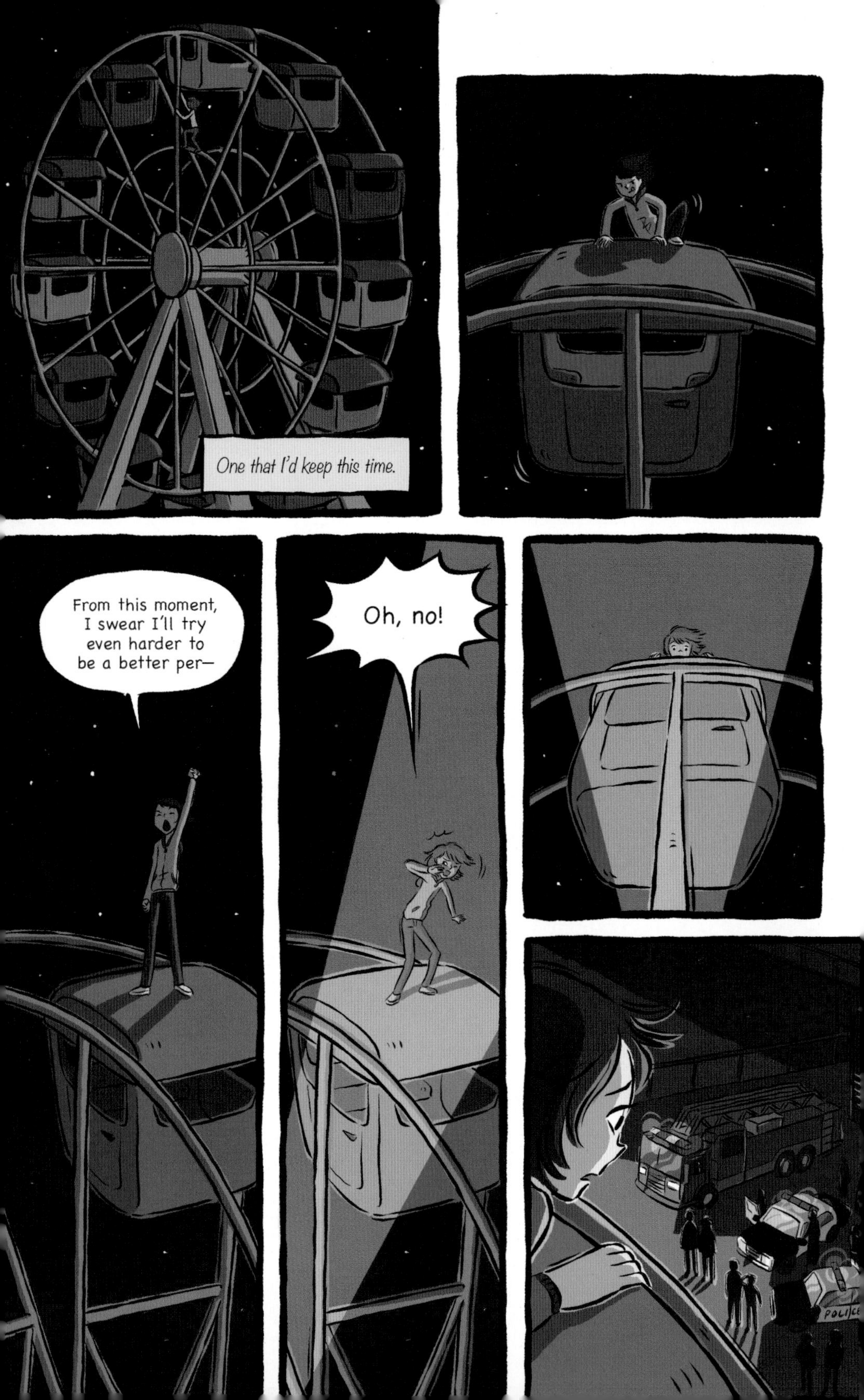
One that I'd keep this time.
From this moment, I swear I'll try even harder to be a better per—
Oh, no!
POLICE

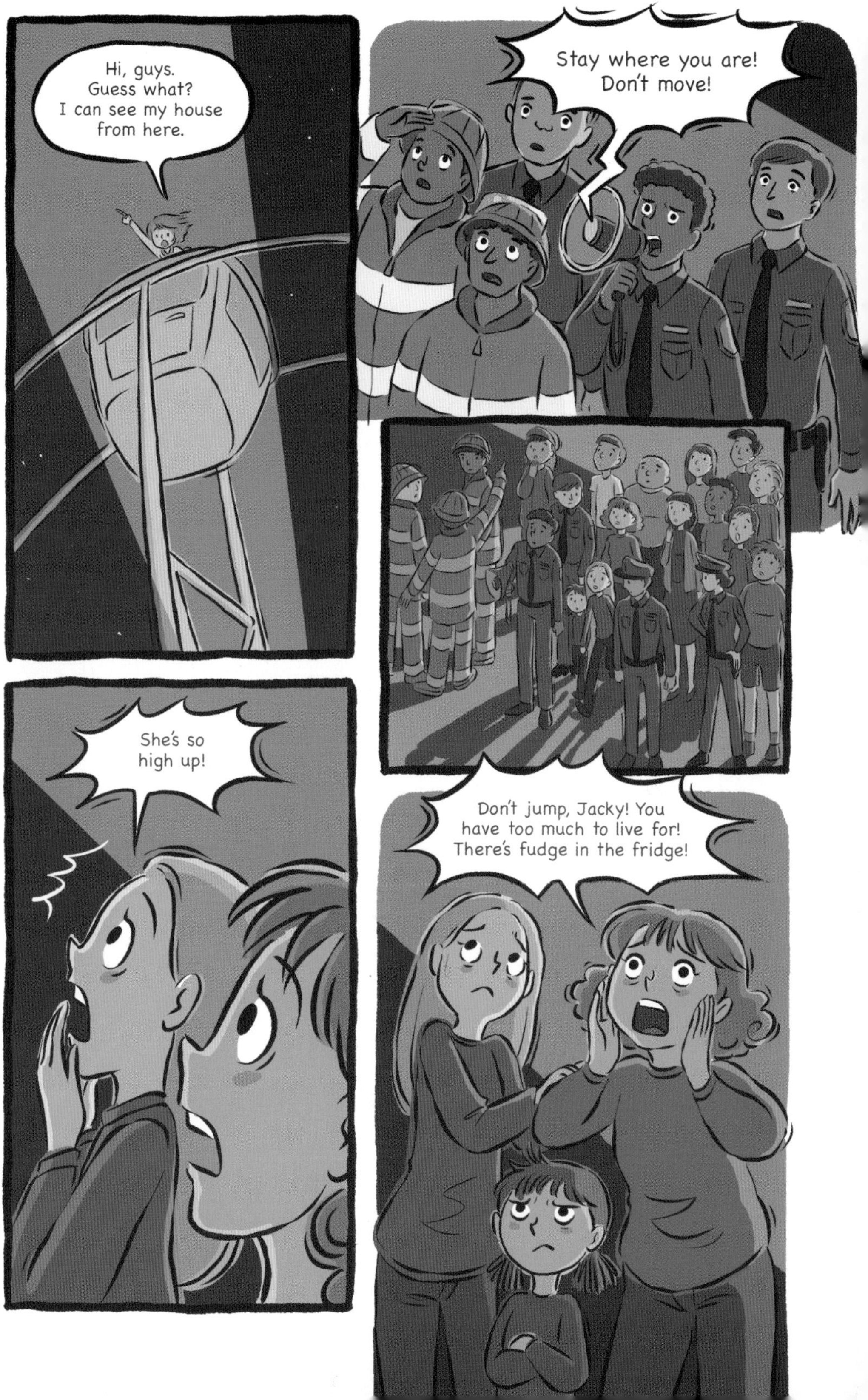
Hi, guys. Guess what? I can see my house from here.
Stay where you are! Don't move!
She's so high up!
Don't jump, Jacky! You have too much to live for! There's fudge in the fridge!

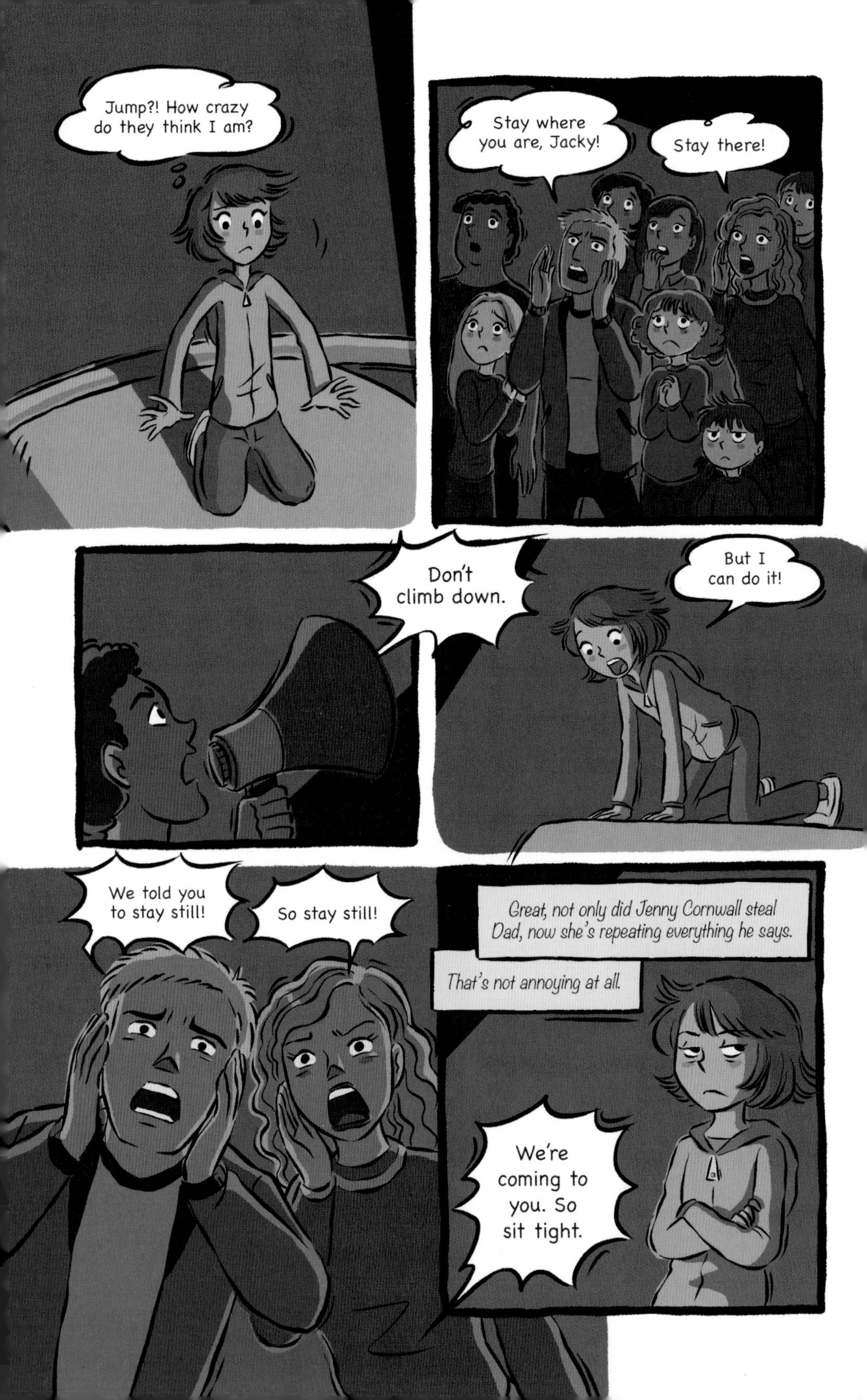
Jump?! How crazy do they think I am?
Stay where you are, Jacky!
Stay there!
Don't climb down.
But I can do it!
We told you to stay still!
So stay still!
Great, not only did Jenny Cornwall steal Dad, now she's repeating everything he says.
That's not annoying at all.
We're coming to you. So sit tight.

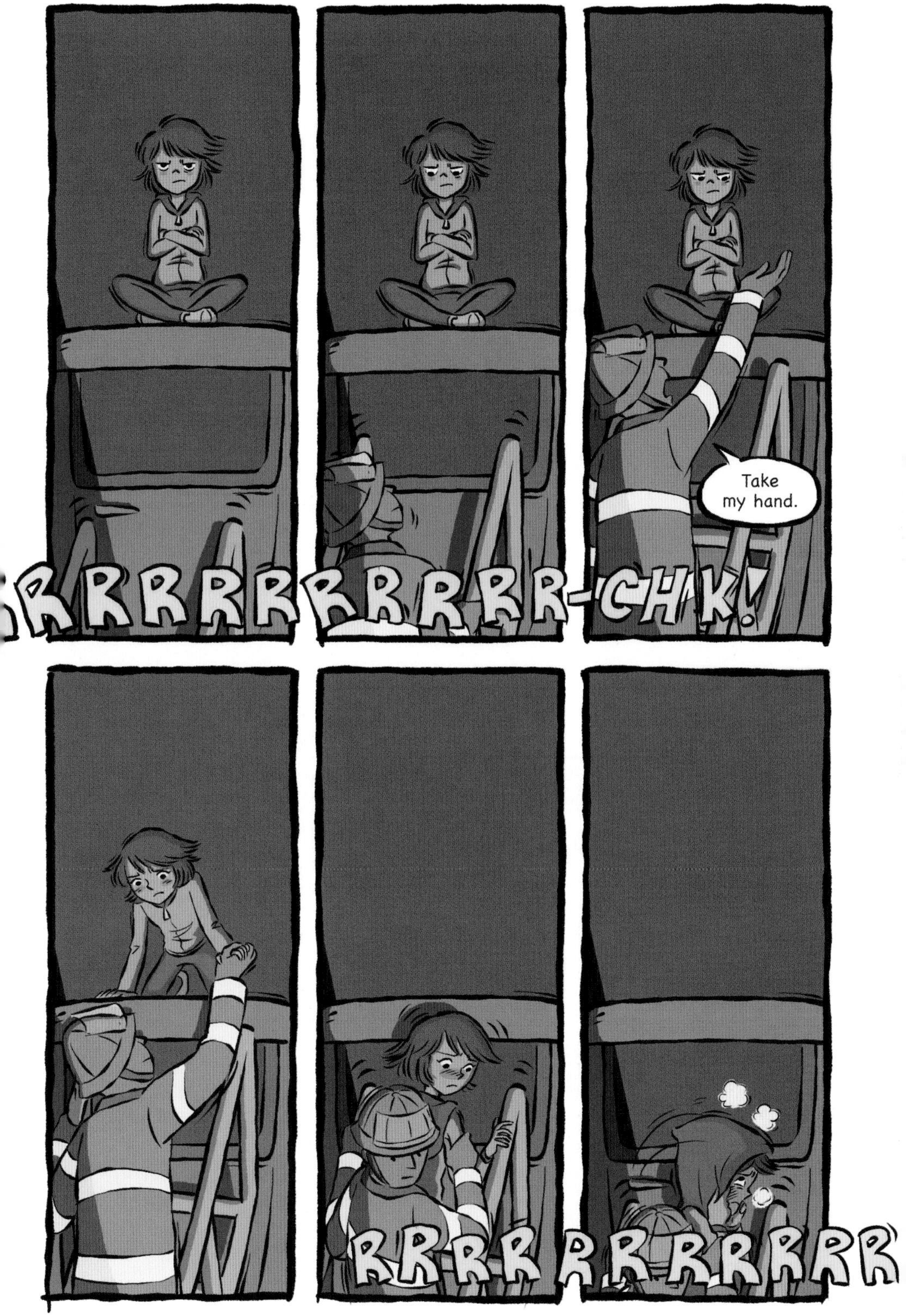

RRRRRRRRRR-CHK!
Take my hand.
RRRRRRRRRR

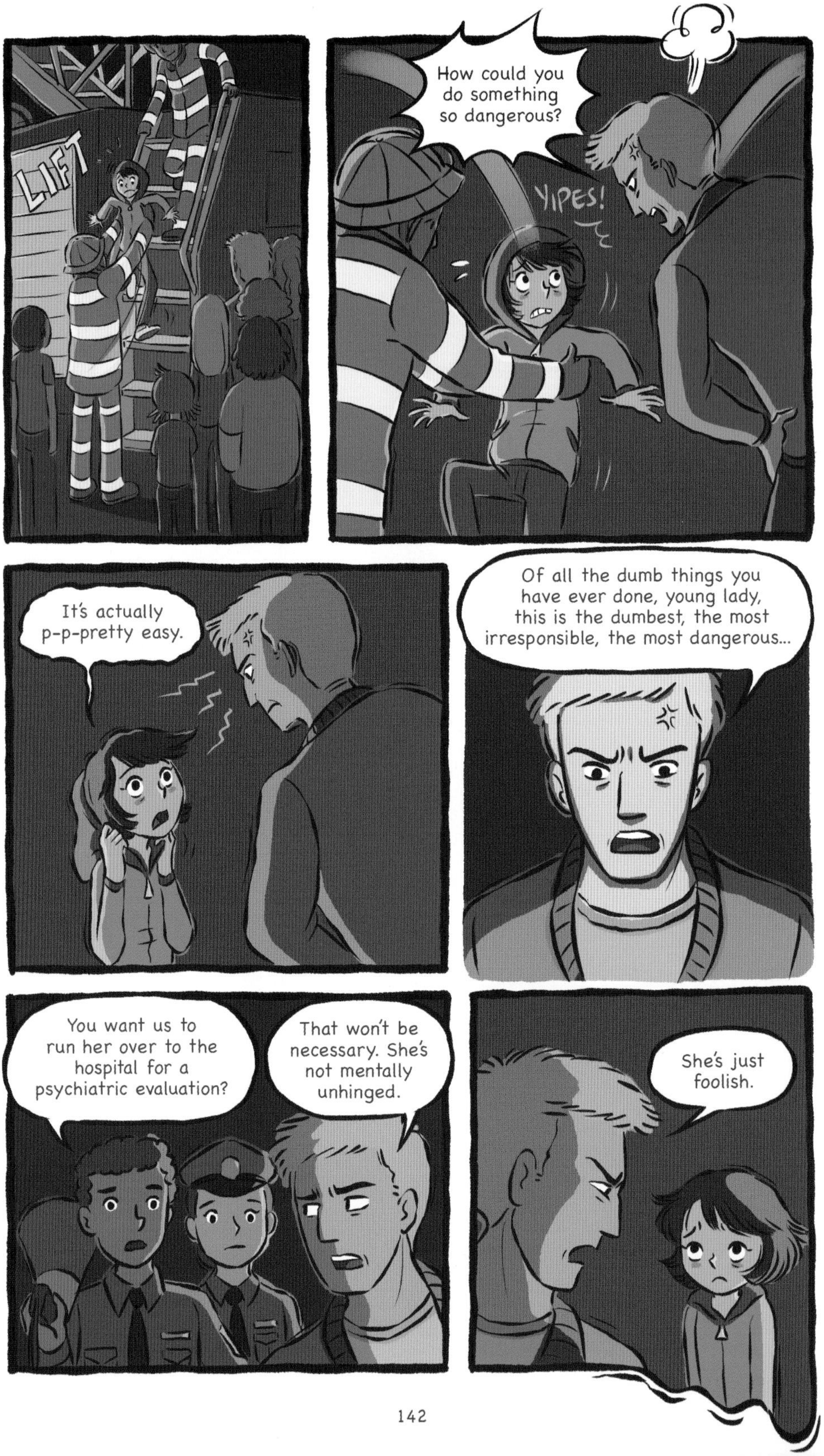
LIFT
How could you do something so dangerous?
YIPES!
It's actually p-p-pretty easy.
Of all the dumb things you have ever done, young lady, this is the dumbest, the most irresponsible, the most dangerous...
You want us to run her over to the hospital for a psychiatric evaluation?
That won't be necessary. She's not mentally unhinged.
She's just foolish.

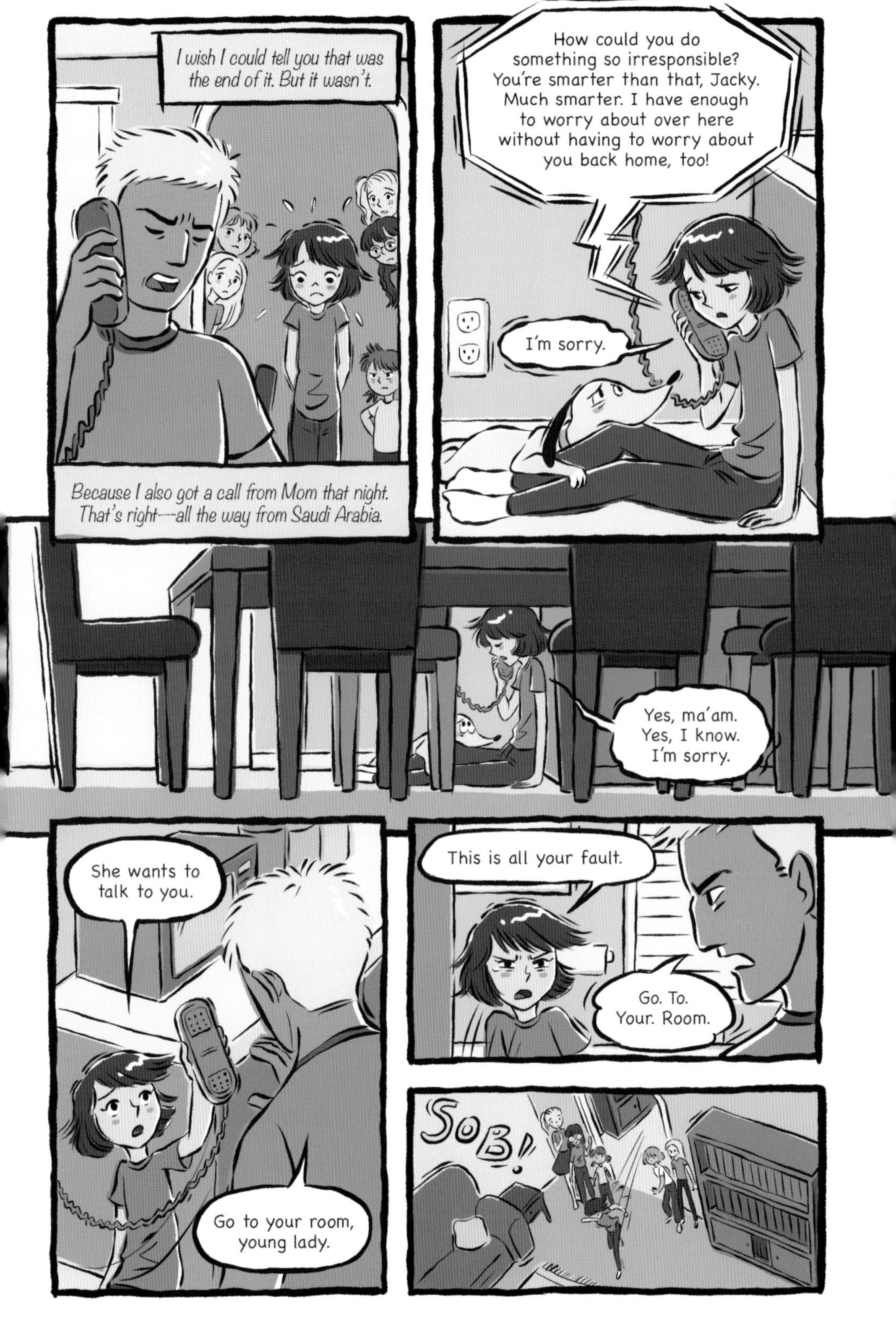
I wish I could tell you that was the end of it. But it wasn't.
Because I also got a call from Mom that night. That's right—all the way from Saudi Arabia.
How could you do something so irresponsible? You're smarter than that, Jacky. Much smarter. I have enough to worry about over here without having to worry about you back home, too!
I'm sorry.
Yes, ma'am. Yes, I know. I'm sorry.
She wants to talk to you.
Go to your room, young lady.
This is all your fault.
Go. To. Your. Room.
SOB!

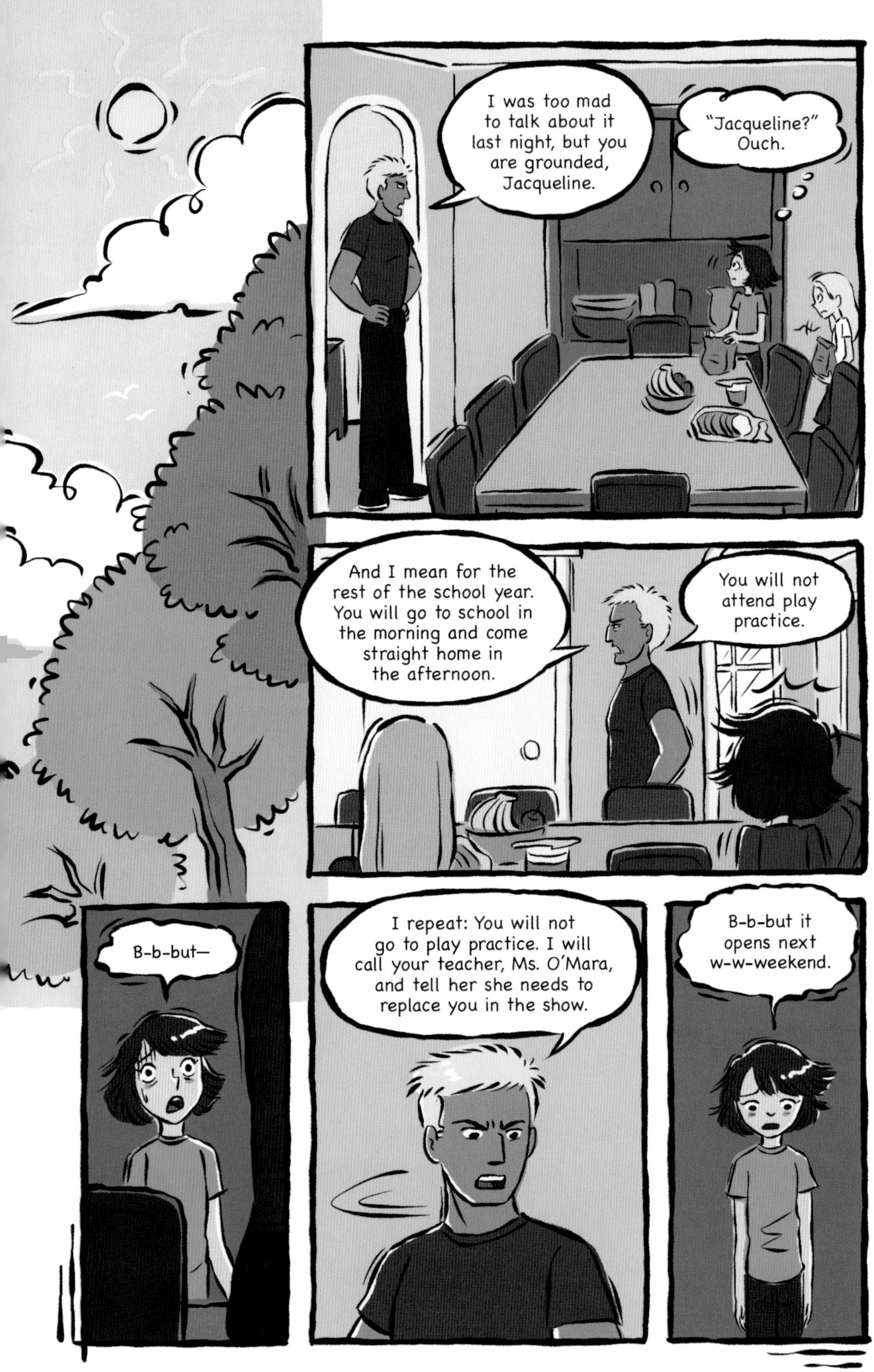
I was too mad to talk about it last night, but you are grounded, Jacqueline.
"Jacqueline?" Ouch.
And I mean for the rest of the school year. You will go to school in the morning and come straight home in the afternoon.
You will not attend play practice.
B-b-but—
I repeat: You will not go to play practice. I will call your teacher, Ms. O'Mara, and tell her she needs to replace you in the show.
B-b-but it opens next w-w-weekend.

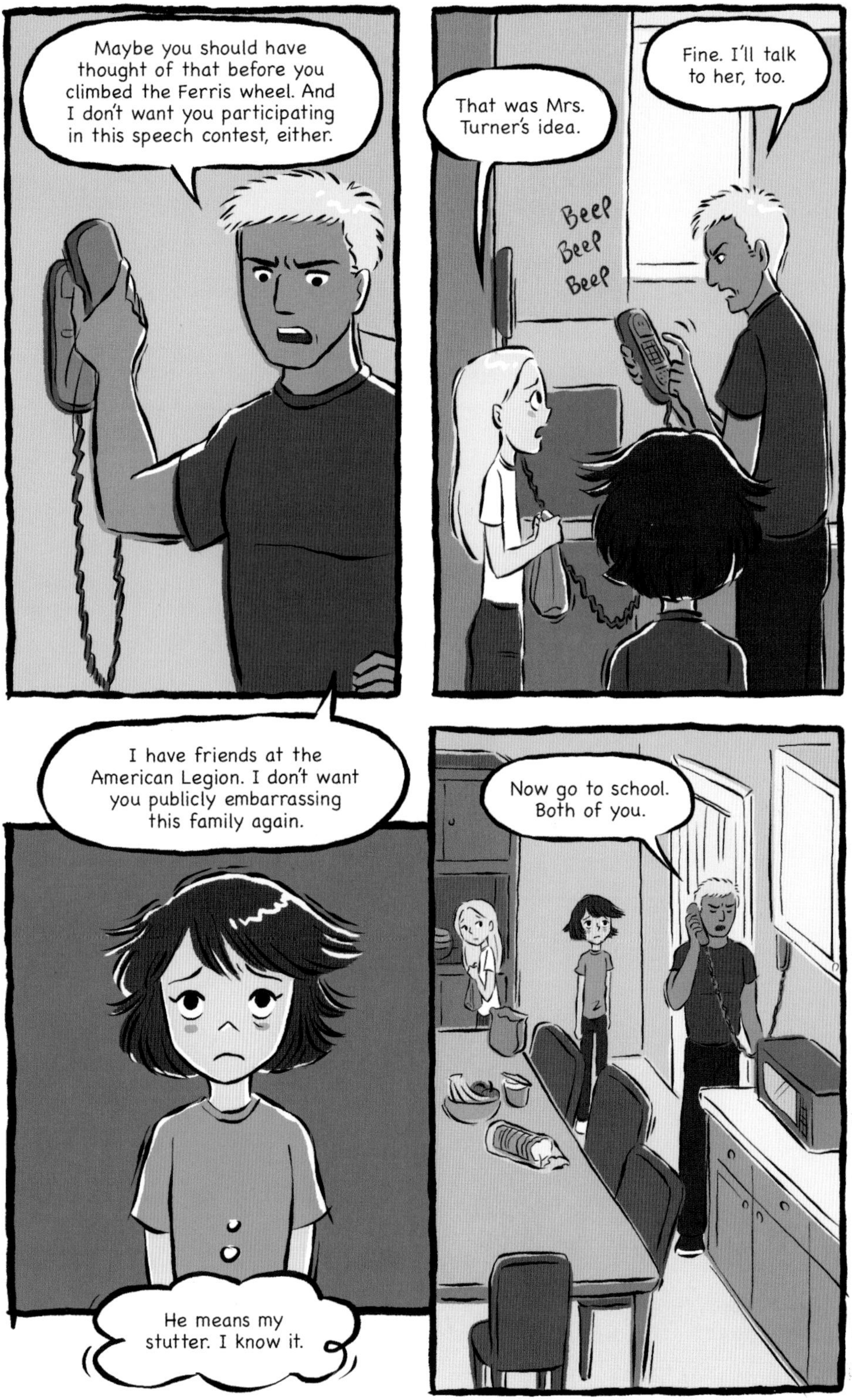
Maybe you should have thought of that before you climbed the Ferris wheel. And I don't want you participating in this speech contest, either.
That was Mrs. Turner's idea.
Beep Beep Beep
Fine. I'll talk to her, too.
I have friends at the American Legion. I don't want you publicly embarrassing this family again.
He means my stutter. I know it.
Now go to school. Both of you.

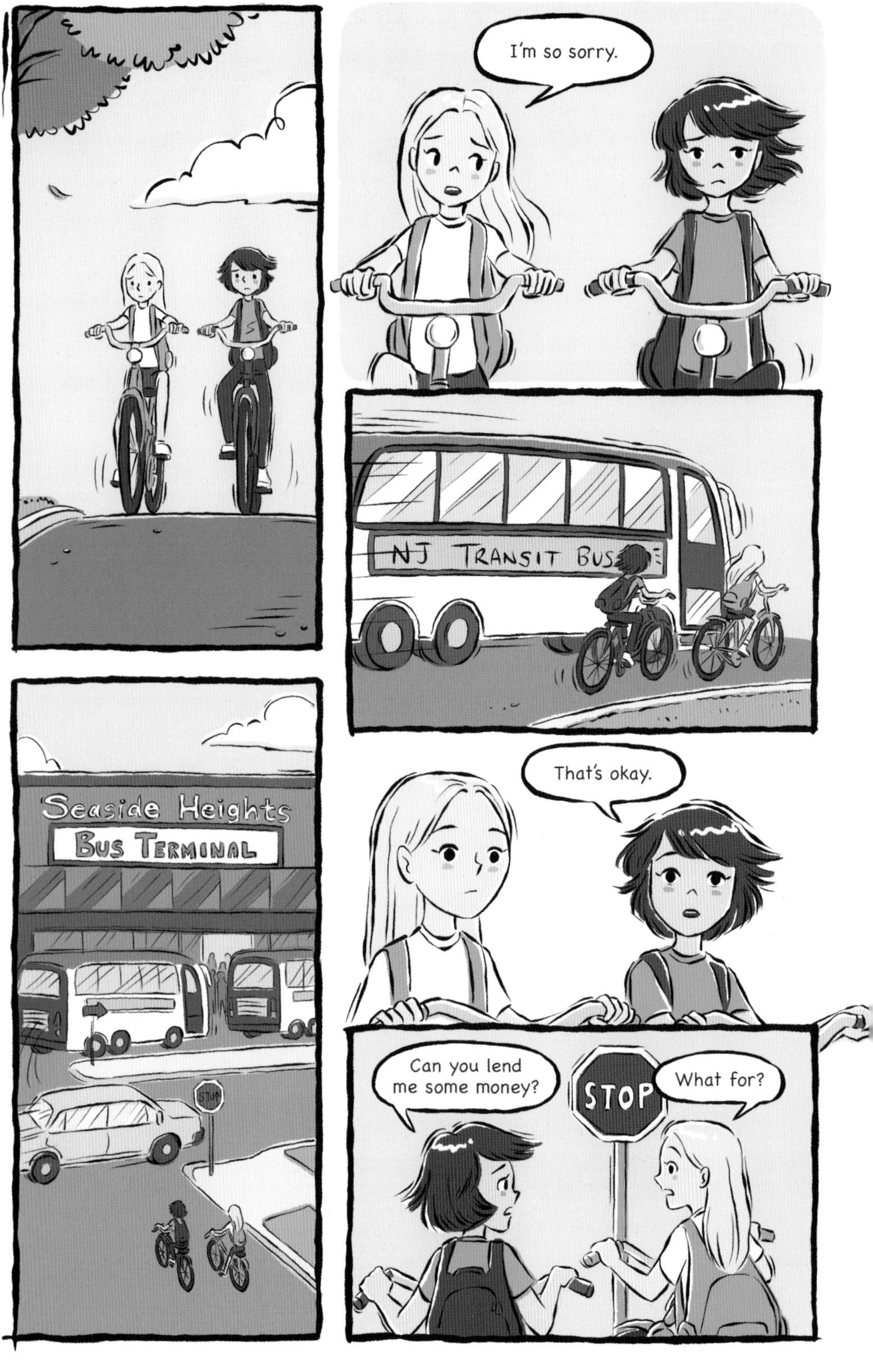
I'm so sorry.
NJ TRANSIT BUS
Seaside Heights
BUS TERMINAL
STOP
That's okay.
Can you lend me some money?
STOP
What for?

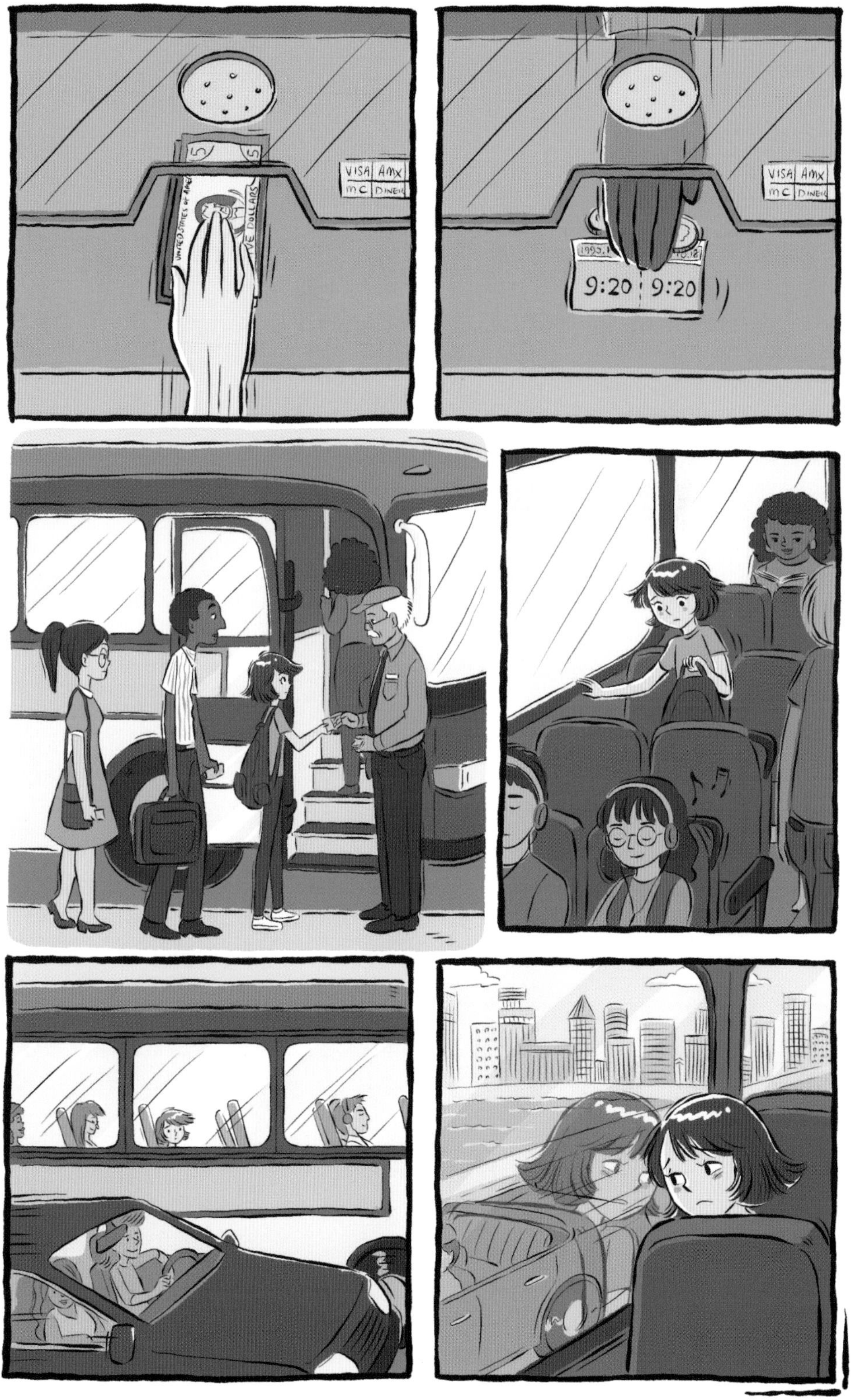

5
VISA AMX
MC DINER
VISA AMX
MC DINER
9:20 9:20

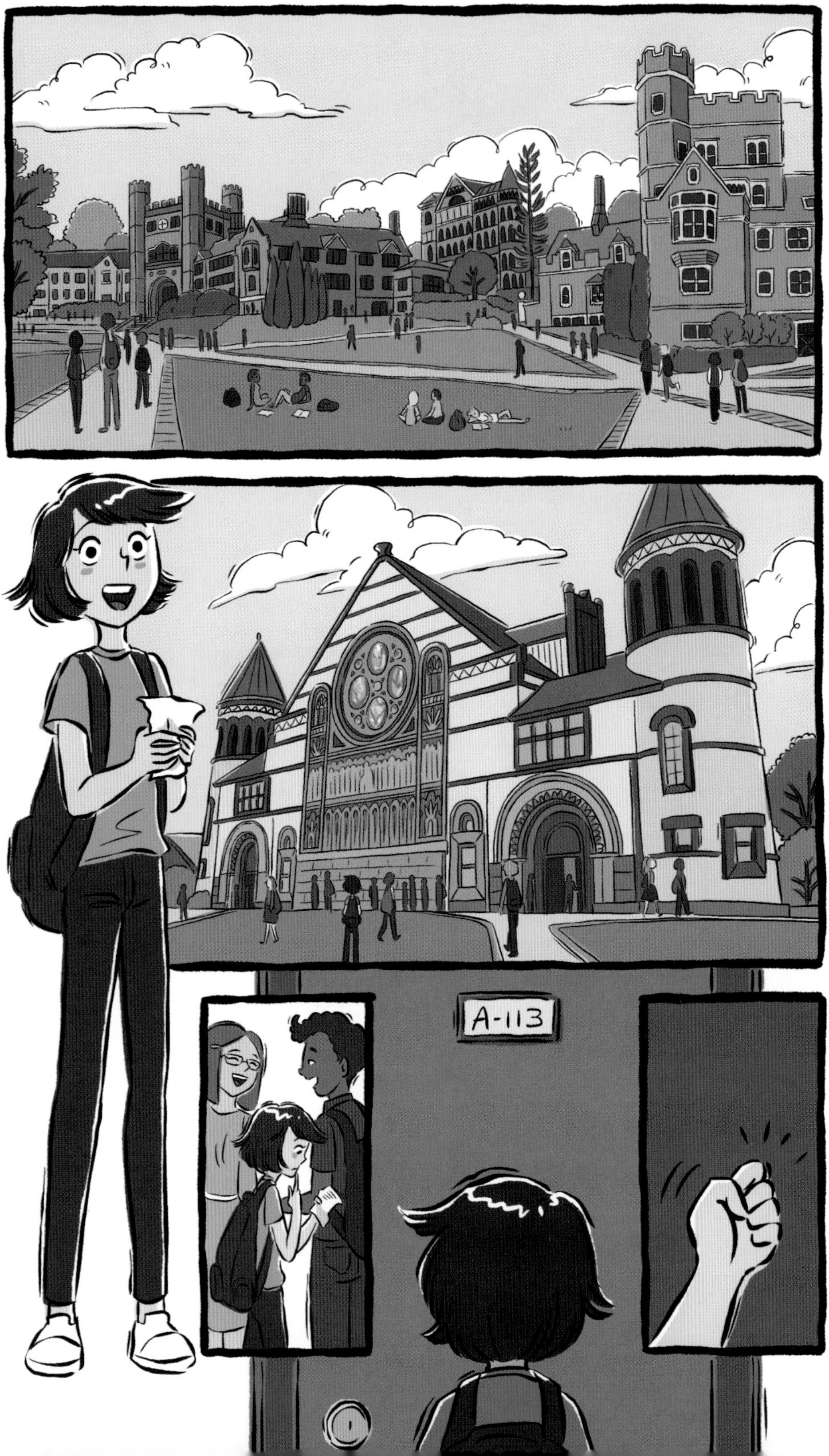
A-113

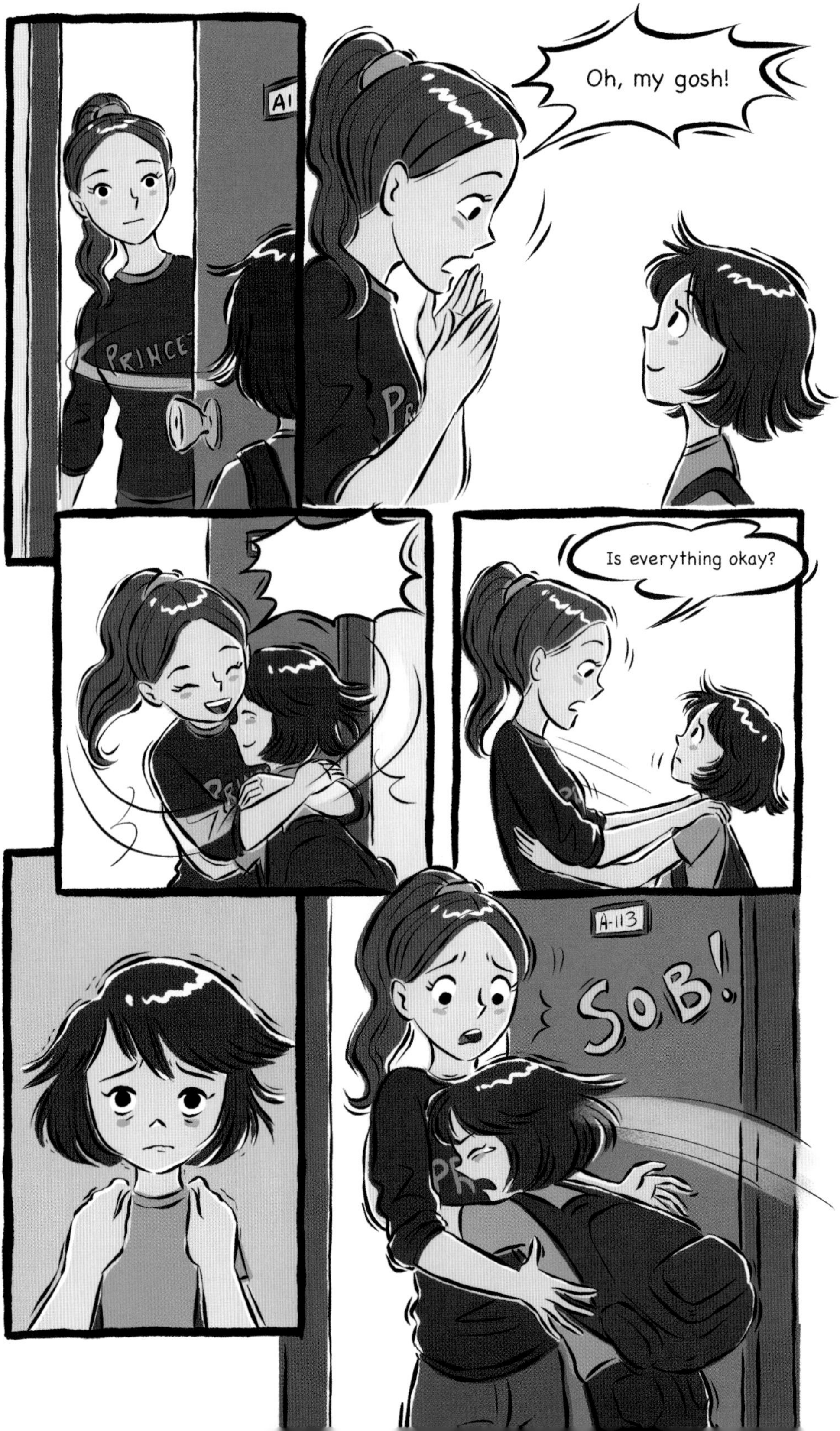
Oh, my gosh!
Is everything okay?
SOB!

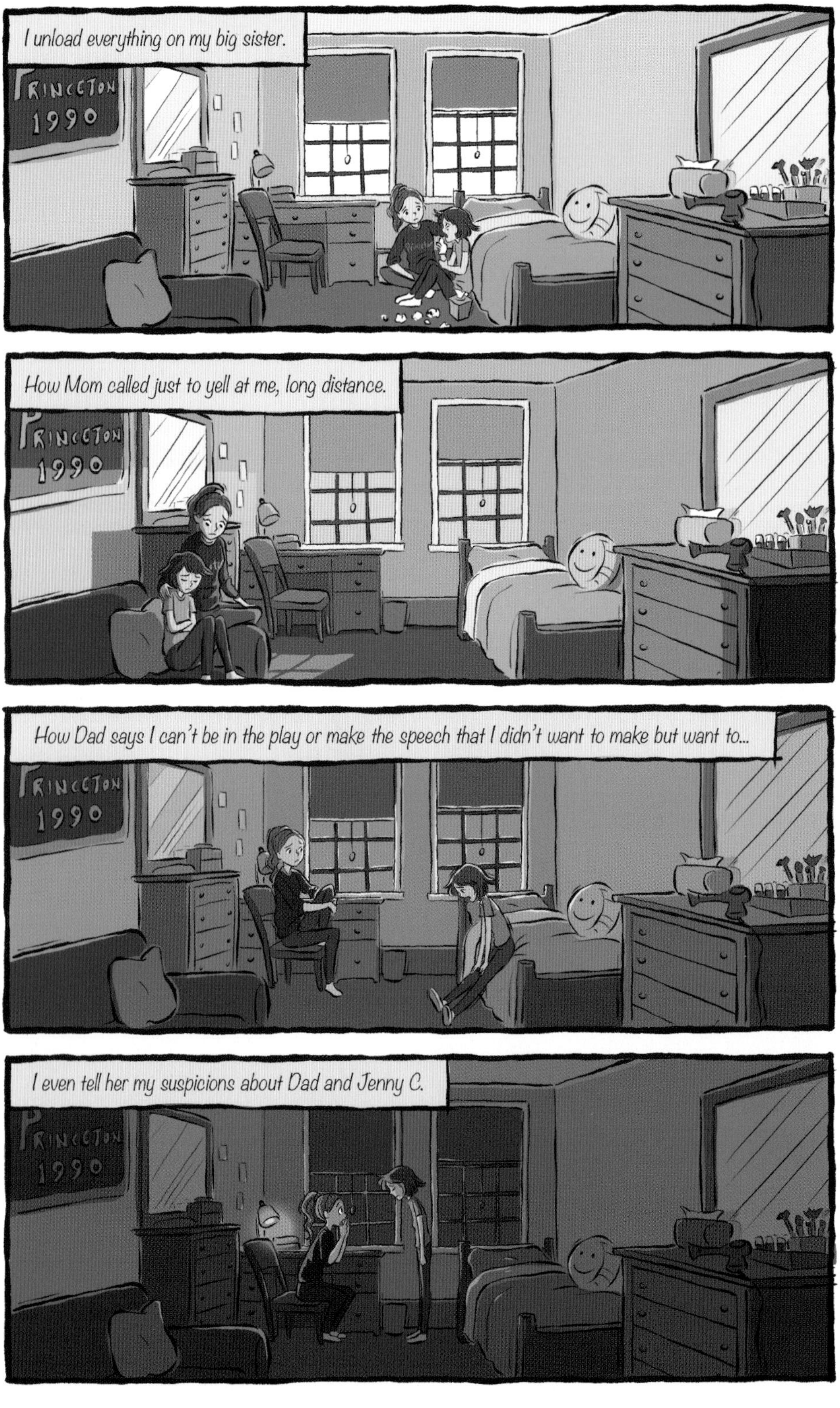
I unload everything on my big sister.
PRINCETON 1990
How Mom called just to yell at me, long distance.
How Dad says I can't be in the play or make the speech that I didn't want to make but want to...
I even tell her my suspicions about Dad and Jenny C.

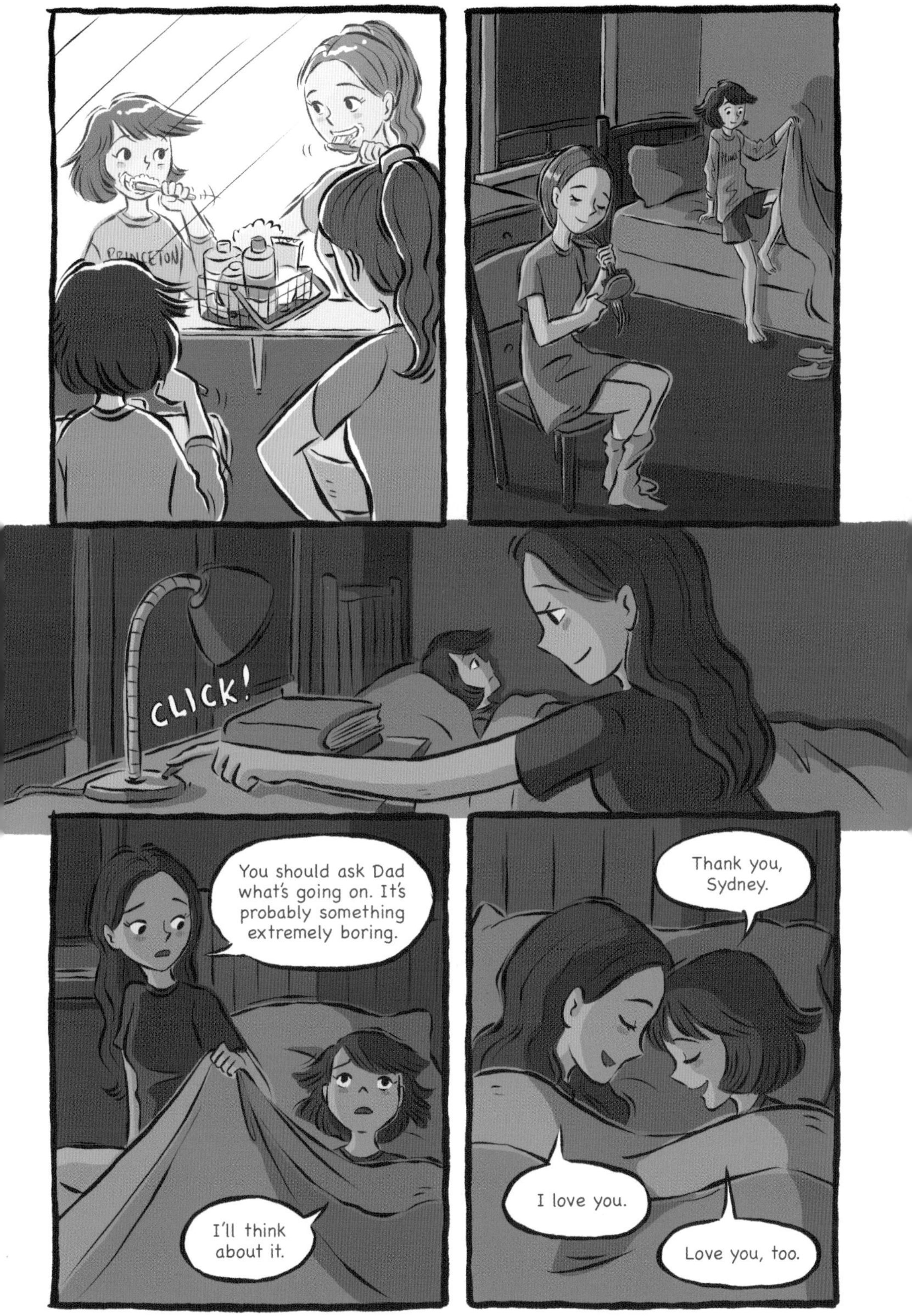
PRINCETON
CLICK!
You should ask Dad what's going on. It's probably something extremely boring.
I'll think about it.
Thank you, Sydney.
I love you.
Love you, too.

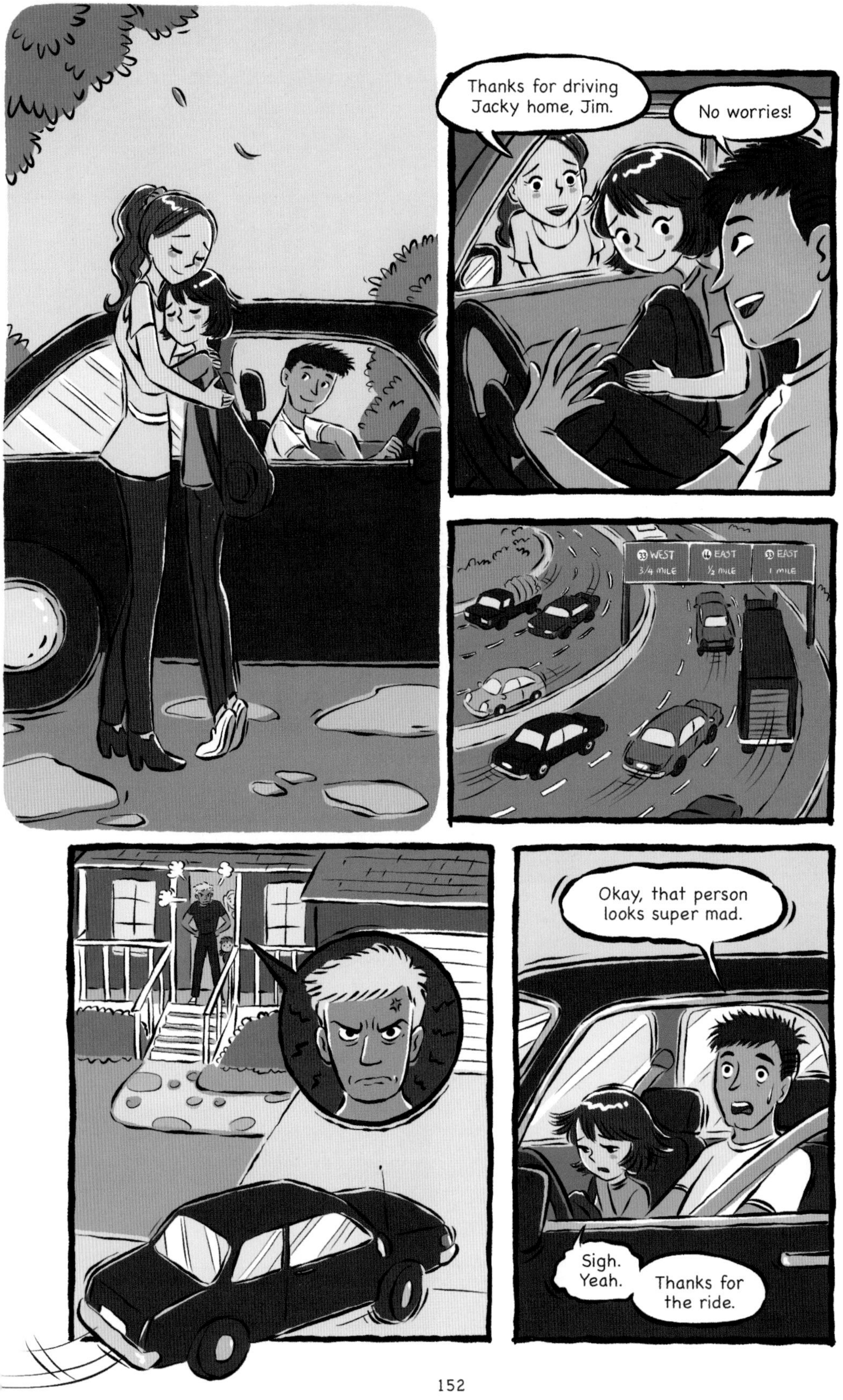
Thanks for driving Jacky home, Jim.
No worries!
33 WEST 3/4 MILE
14 EAST ½ MILE
33 EAST 1 MILE
Okay, that person looks super mad.
Sigh. Yeah.
Thanks for the ride.

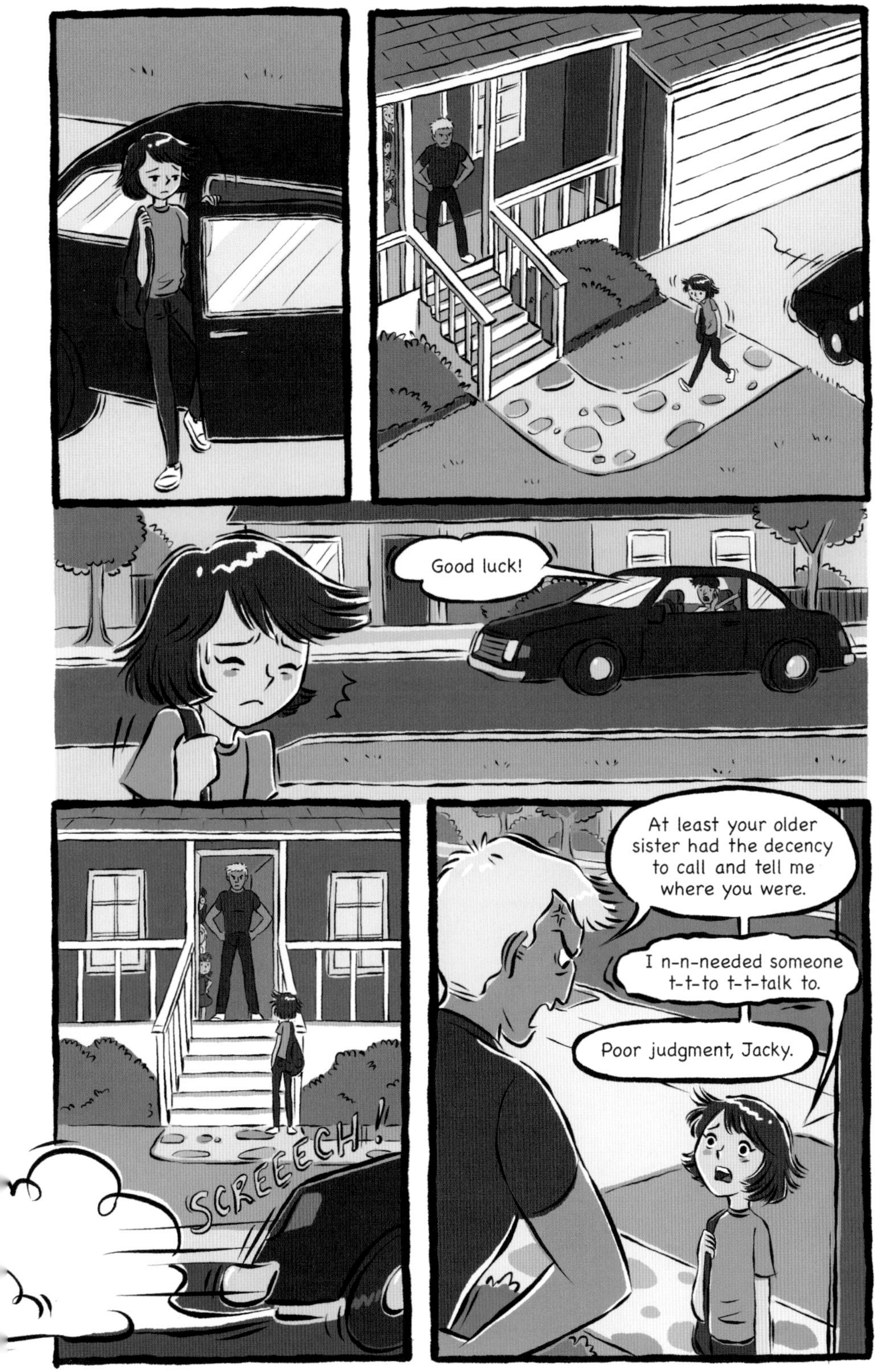
Good luck!
SCREEECH!
At least your older sister had the decency to call and tell me where you were.
I n-n-needed someone t-t-to t-t-talk to.
Poor judgment, Jacky.

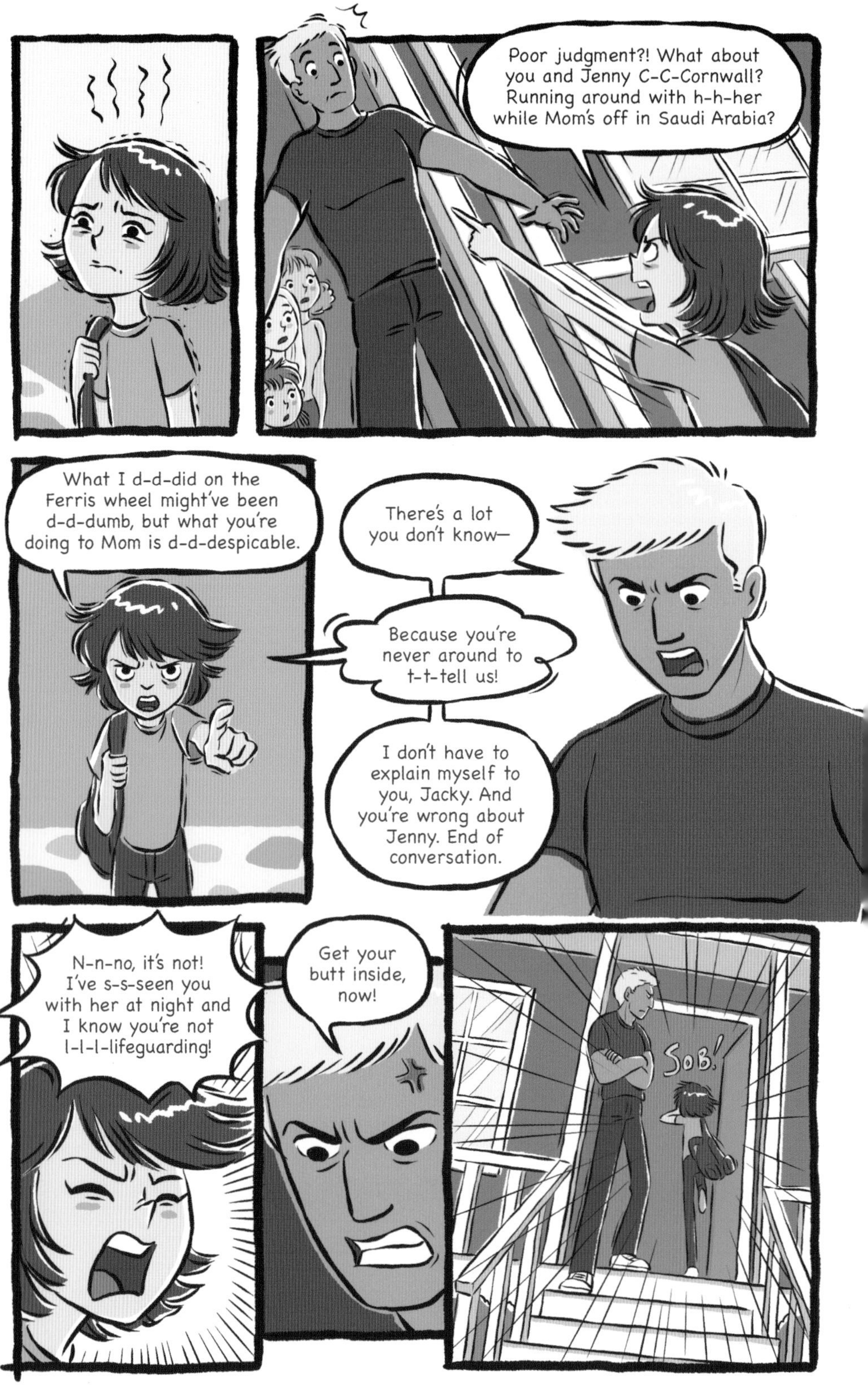
Poor judgment?! What about you and Jenny C-C-Cornwall? Running around with h-h-her while Mom's off in Saudi Arabia?
What I d-d-did on the Ferris wheel might've been d-d-dumb, but what you're doing to Mom is d-d-despicable.
There's a lot you don't know—
Because you're never around to t-t-tell us!
I don't have to explain myself to you, Jacky. And you're wrong about Jenny. End of conversation.
N-n-no, it's not! I've s-s-seen you with her at night and I know you're not l-l-l-lifeguarding!
Get your butt inside, now!
SOB!

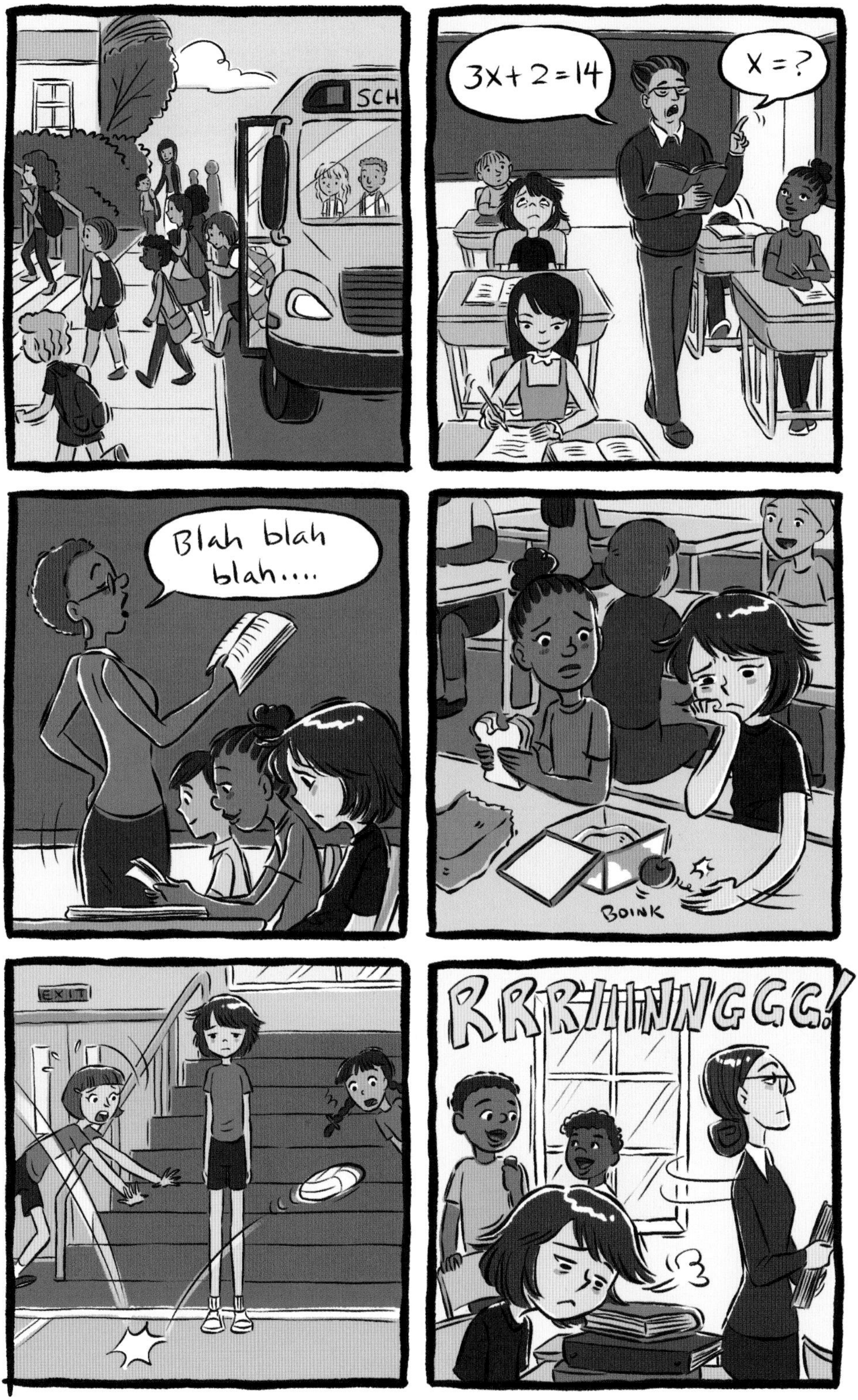
SCH
3x+2=14
X=?
Blah blah blah....
BOINK
EXIT
RRRIIINNGGG!

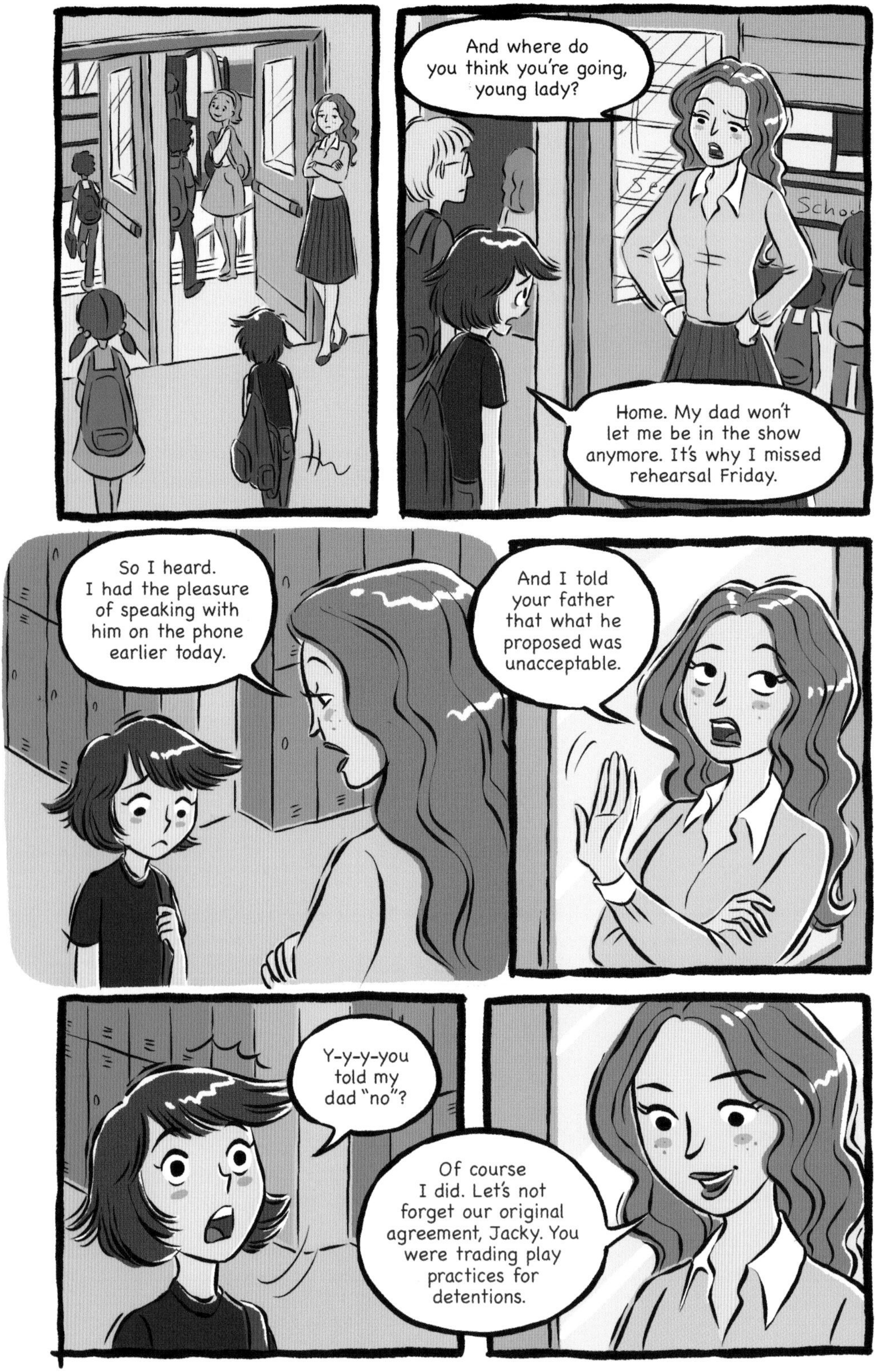
And where do you think you're going, young lady?
Home. My dad won't let me be in the show anymore. It's why I missed rehearsal Friday.
So I heard. I had the pleasure of speaking with him on the phone earlier today.
And I told your father that what he proposed was unacceptable.
Y-y-y-you told my dad "no"?
Of course I did. Let's not forget our original agreement, Jacky. You were trading play practices for detentions.

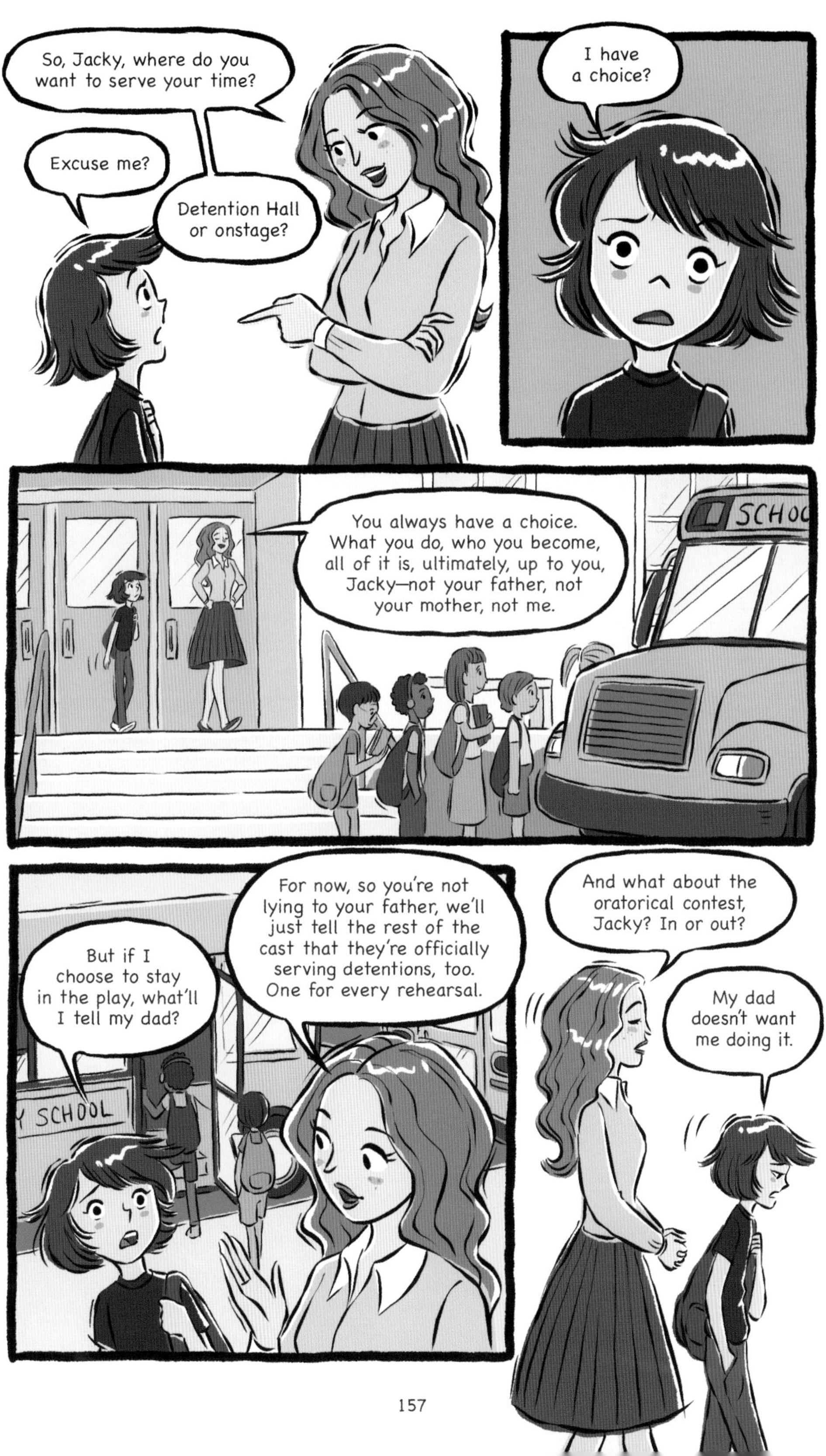
So, Jacky, where do you want to serve your time?
Excuse me?
Detention Hall or onstage?
I have a choice?
You always have a choice. What you do, who you become, all of it is, ultimately, up to you, Jacky—not your father, not your mother, not me.
SCHOO
But if I choose to stay in the play, what'll I tell my dad?
For now, so you're not lying to your father, we'll just tell the rest of the cast that they're officially serving detentions, too. One for every rehearsal.
Y SCHOOL
And what about the oratorical contest, Jacky? In or out?
My dad doesn't want me doing it.

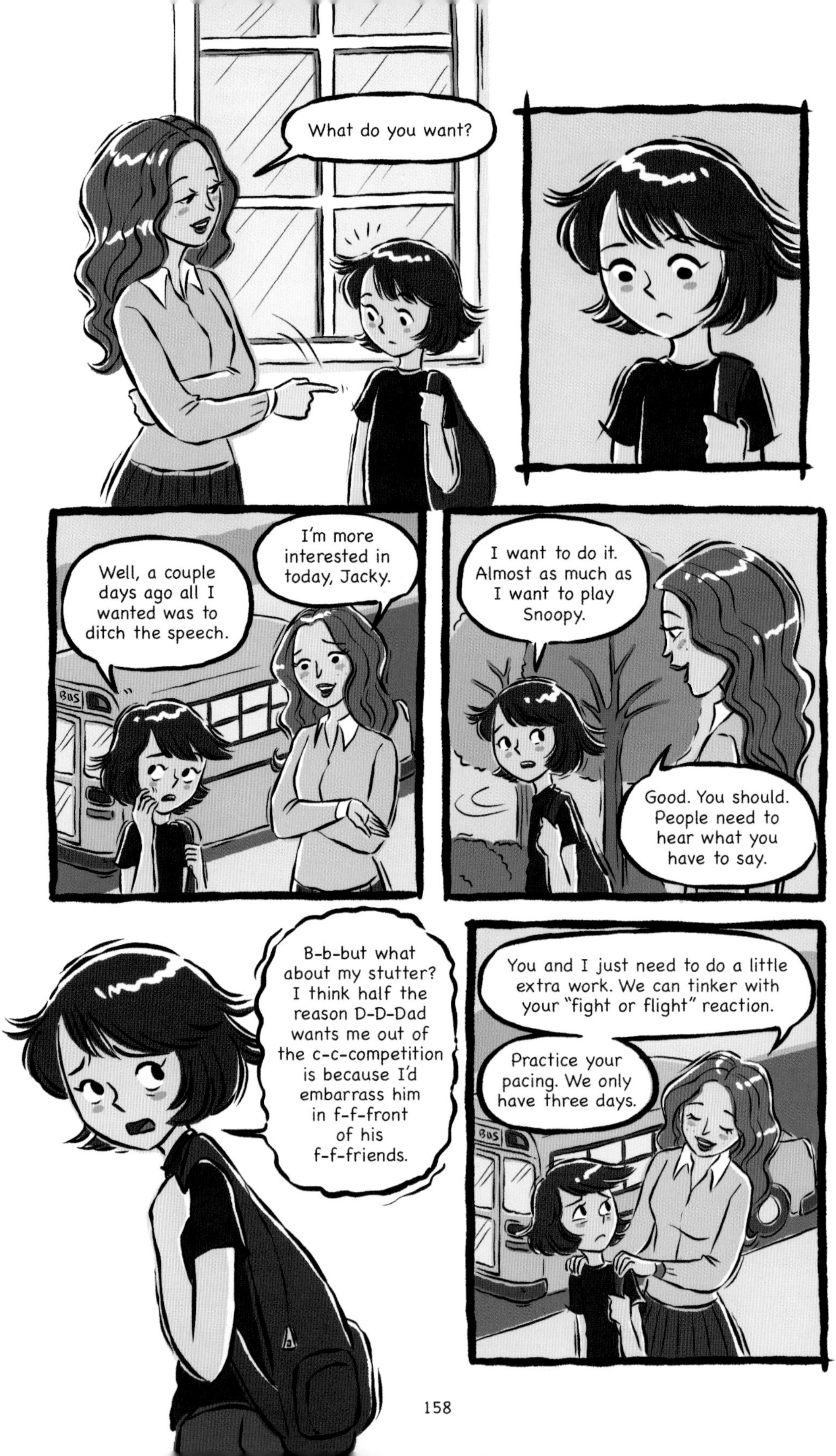
What do you want?
Well, a couple days ago all I wanted was to ditch the speech.
I'm more interested in today, Jacky.
I want to do it. Almost as much as I want to play Snoopy.
Good. You should. People need to hear what you have to say.
B-b-but what about my stutter? I think half the reason D-D-Dad wants me out of the c-c-competition is because I'd embarrass him in f-f-front of his f-f-friends.
You and I just need to do a little extra work. We can tinker with your "fight or flight" reaction.
Practice your pacing. We only have three days.
BUS

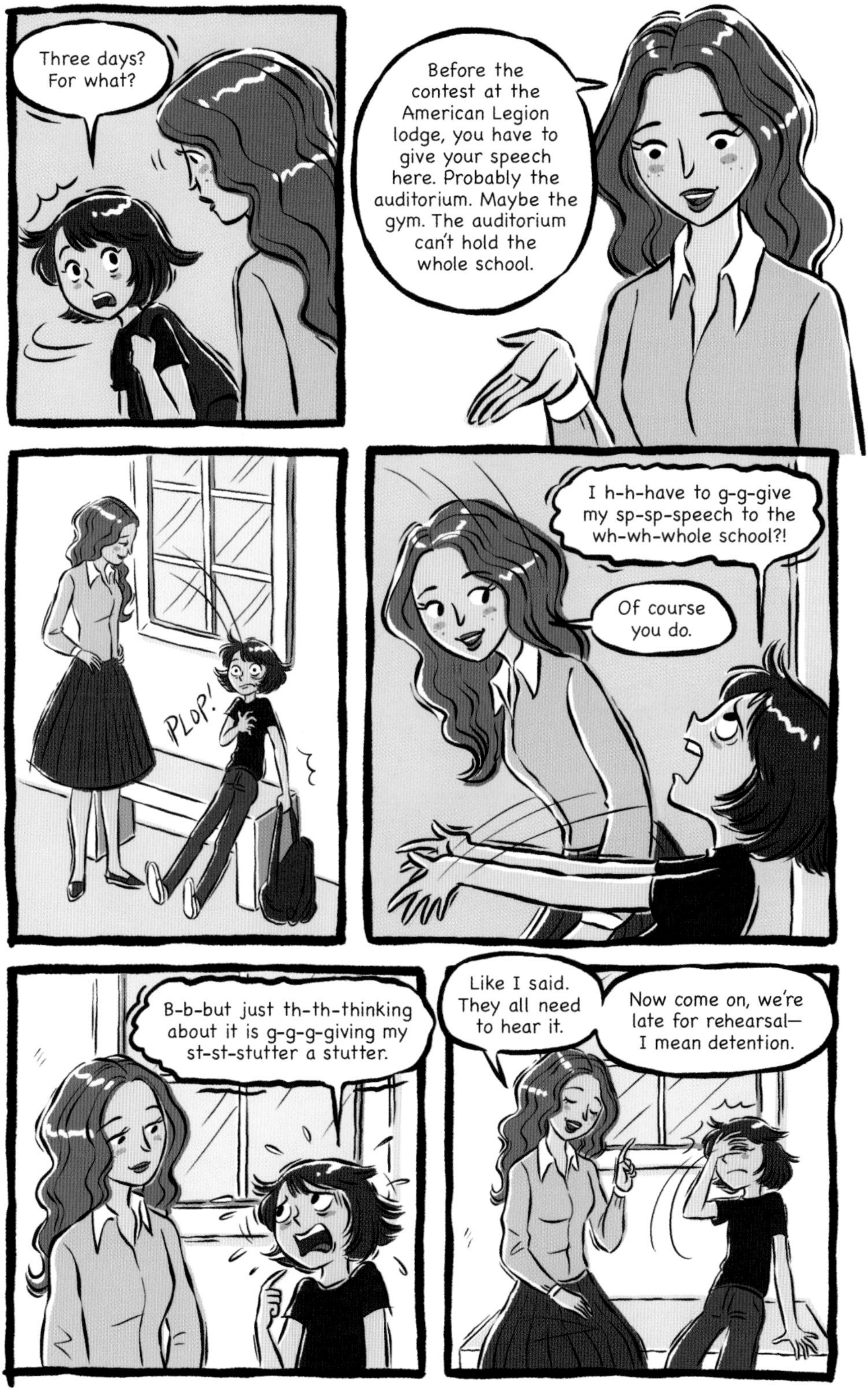
Three days? For what?
Before the contest at the American Legion lodge, you have to give your speech here. Probably the auditorium. Maybe the gym. The auditorium can't hold the whole school.
PLOP!
I h-h-have to g-g-give my sp-sp-speech to the wh-wh-whole school?!
Of course you do.
B-b-but just th-th-thinking about it is g-g-g-giving my st-st-stutter a stutter.
Like I said. They all need to hear it.
Now come on, we're late for rehearsal— I mean detention.

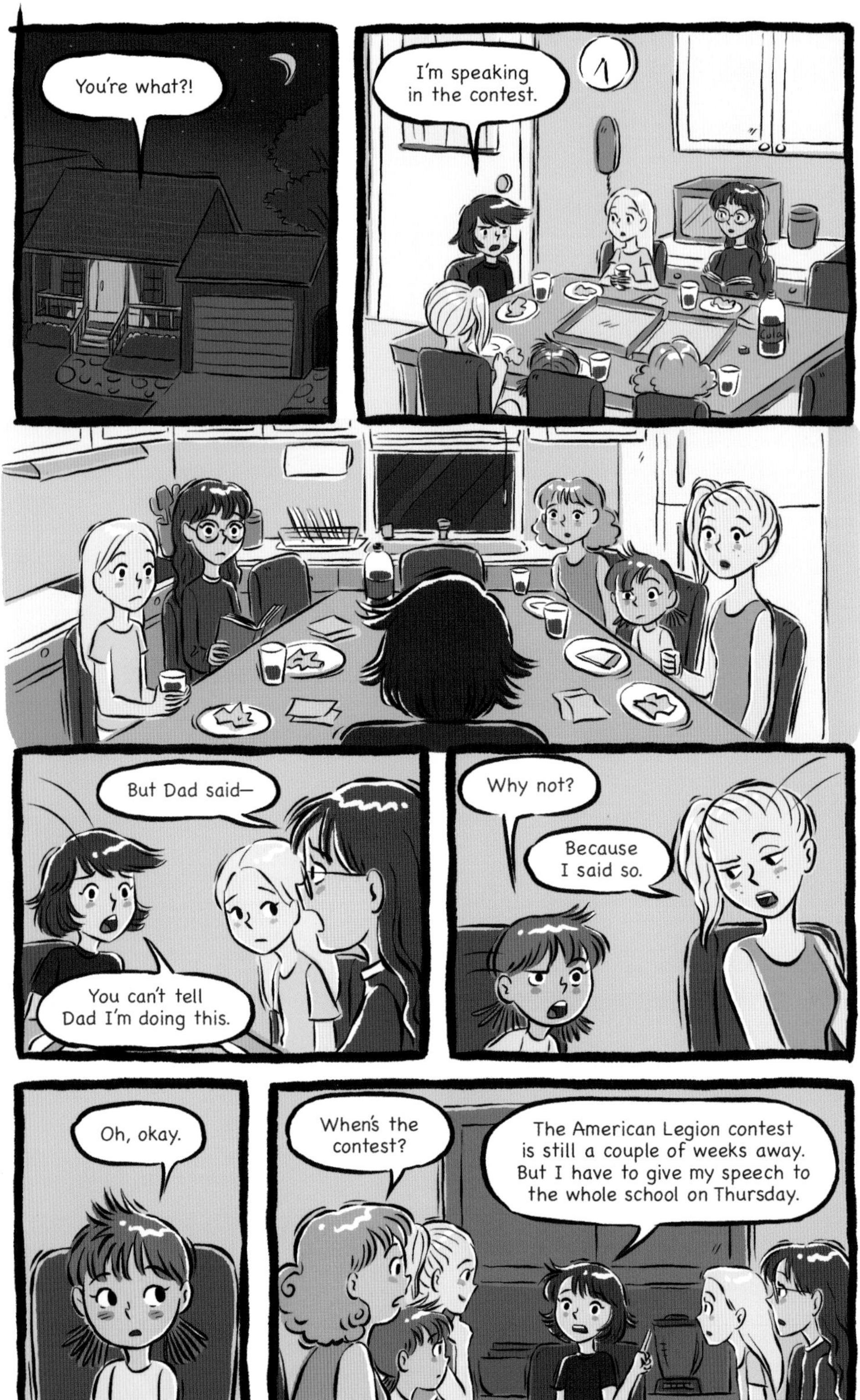
You're what?!
I'm speaking in the contest.
But Dad said—
You can't tell Dad I'm doing this.
Why not?
Because I said so.
Oh, okay.
When's the contest?
The American Legion contest is still a couple of weeks away. But I have to give my speech to the whole school on Thursday.

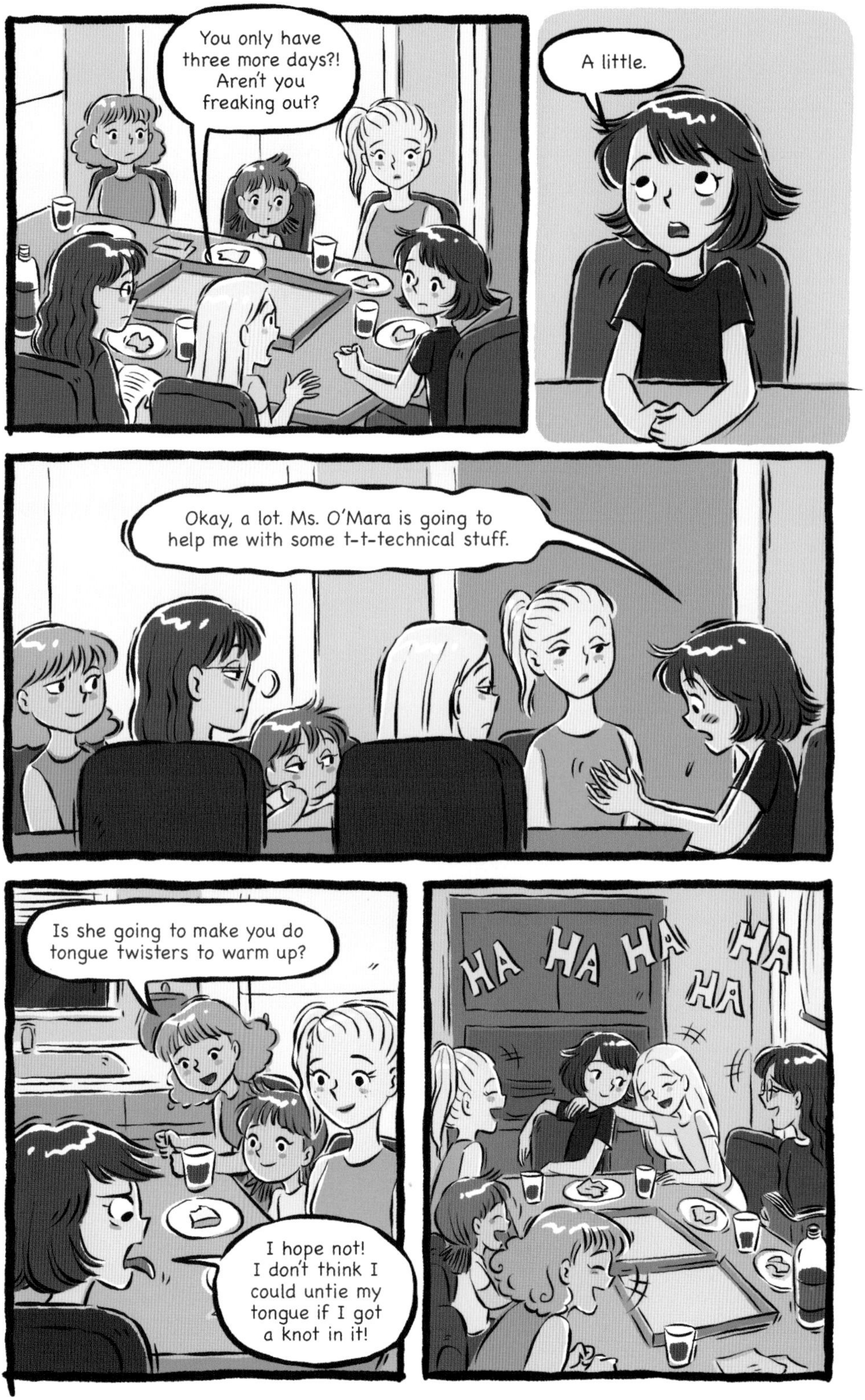
You only have three more days?! Aren't you freaking out?
A little.
Okay, a lot. Ms. O'Mara is going to help me with some t-t-technical stuff.
Is she going to make you do tongue twisters to warm up?
I hope not! I don't think I could untie my tongue if I got a knot in it!
HA HA HA HA HA

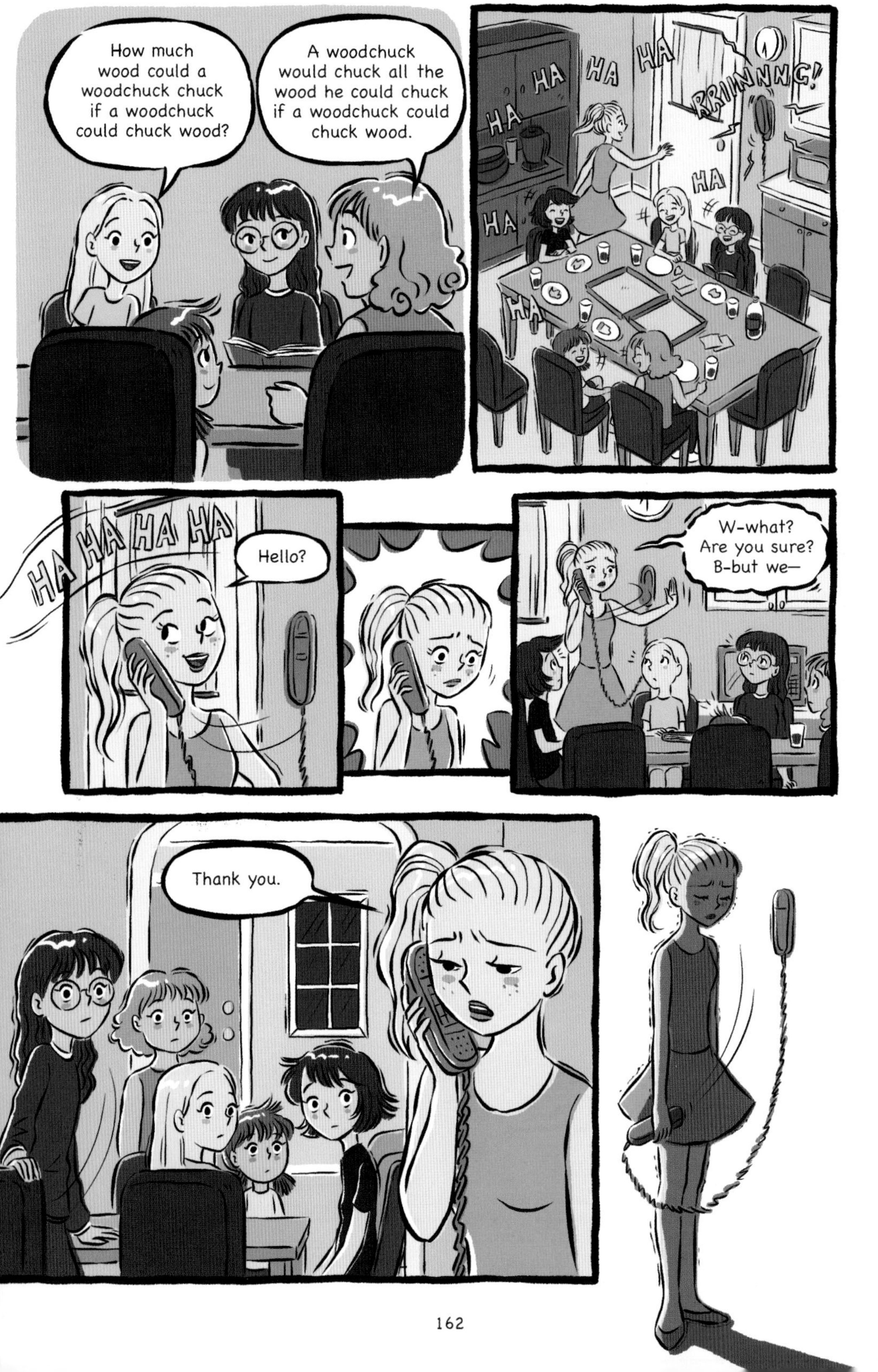
How much wood could a woodchuck chuck if a woodchuck could chuck wood?
A woodchuck would chuck all the wood he could chuck if a woodchuck could chuck wood.
HA HA HA HA
BRRINNNG!
HA HA HA HA
HA HA HA HA
Hello?
W-what? Are you sure? B-but we—
Thank you.

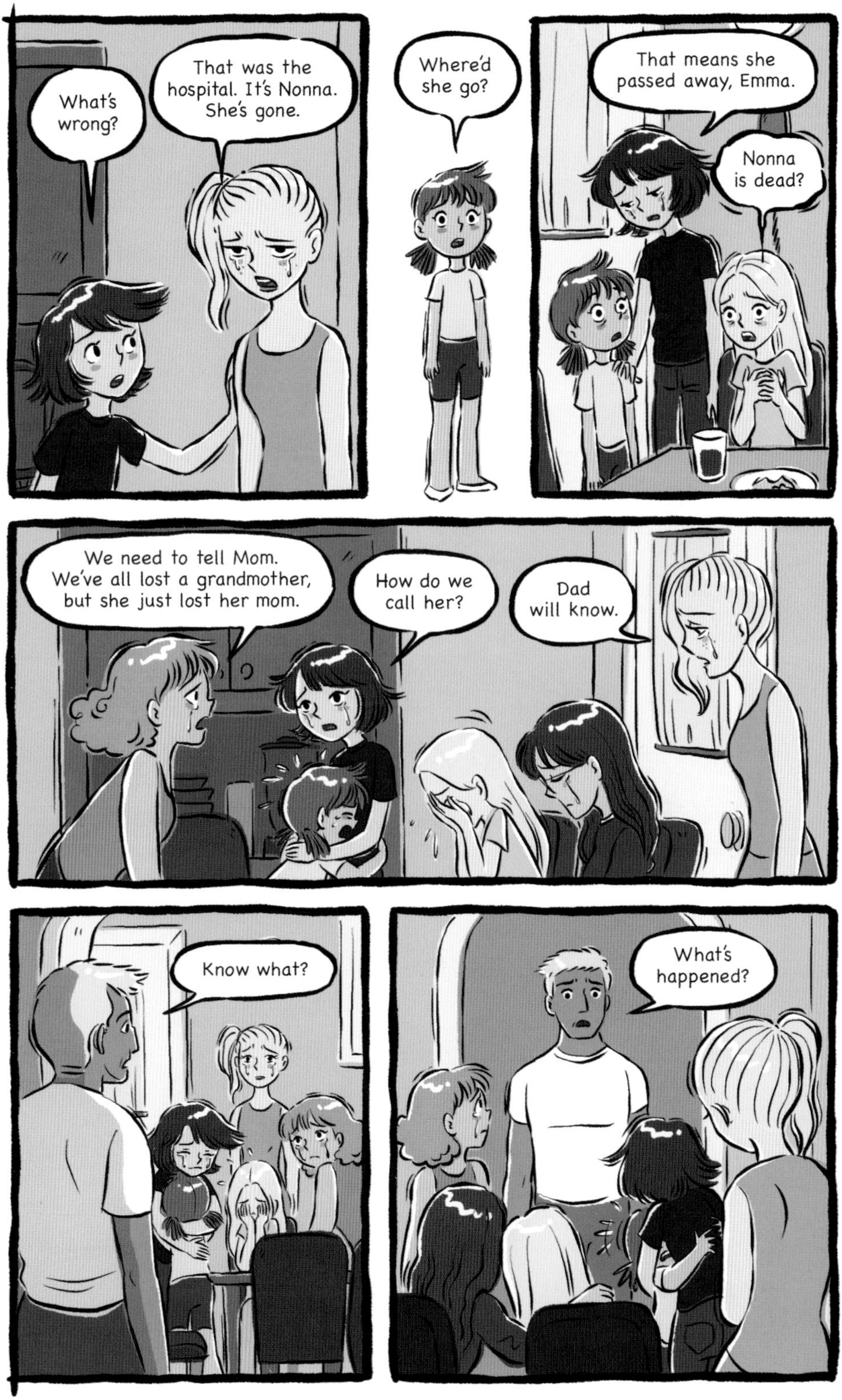
What's wrong?
That was the hospital. It's Nonna. She's gone.
Where'd she go?
That means she passed away, Emma.
Nonna is dead?
We need to tell Mom. We've all lost a grandmother, but she just lost her mom.
How do we call her?
Dad will know.
Know what?
What's happened?

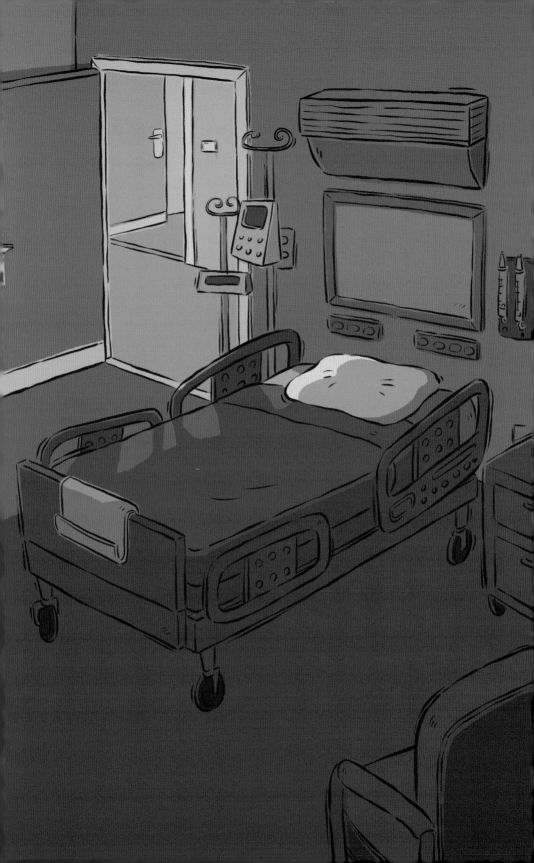

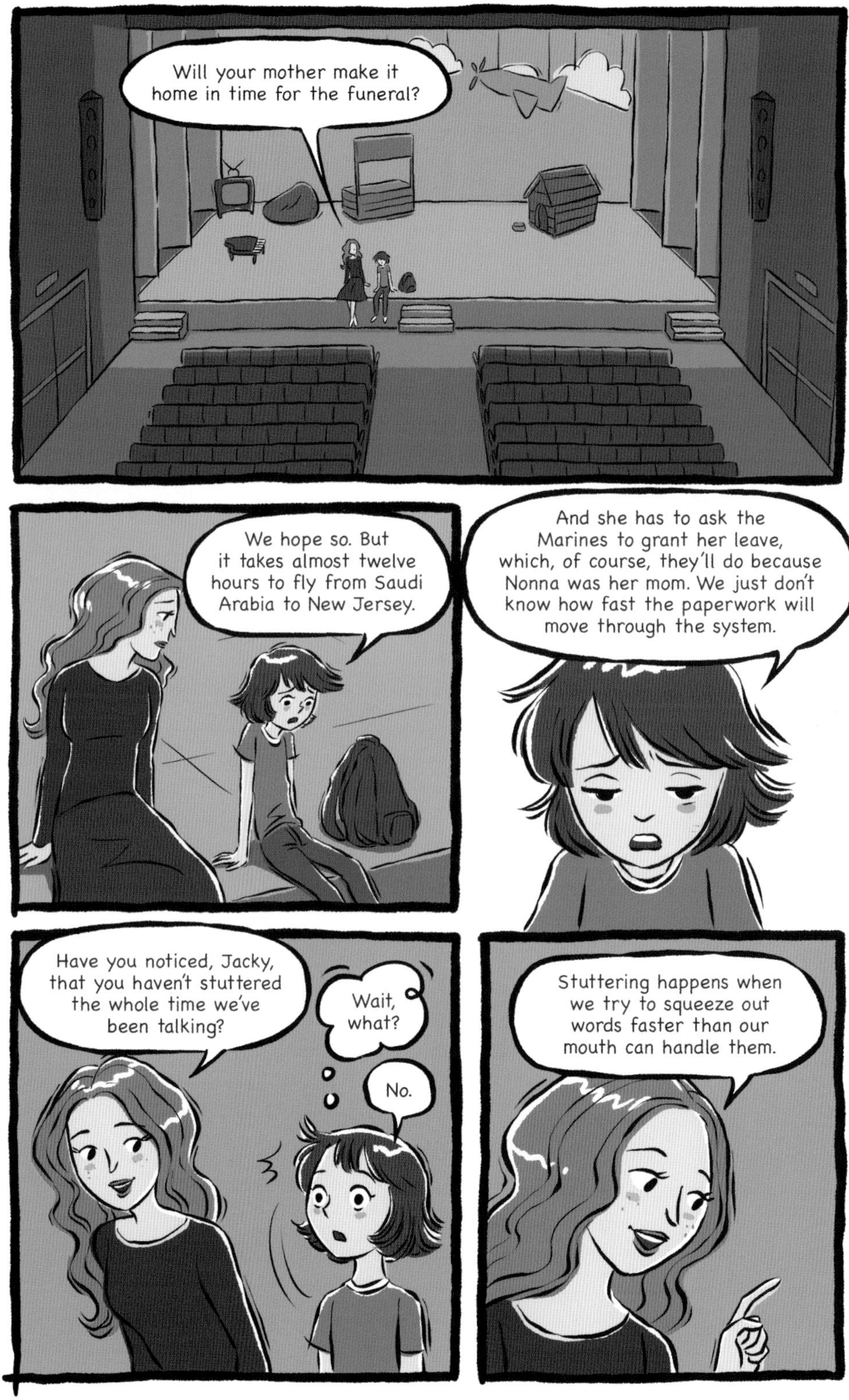
Will your mother make it home in time for the funeral?
We hope so. But it takes almost twelve hours to fly from Saudi Arabia to New Jersey.
And she has to ask the Marines to grant her leave, which, of course, they'll do because Nonna was her mom. We just don't know how fast the paperwork will move through the system.
Have you noticed, Jacky, that you haven't stuttered the whole time we've been talking?
Wait, what?
No.
Stuttering happens when we try to squeeze out words faster than our mouth can handle them.

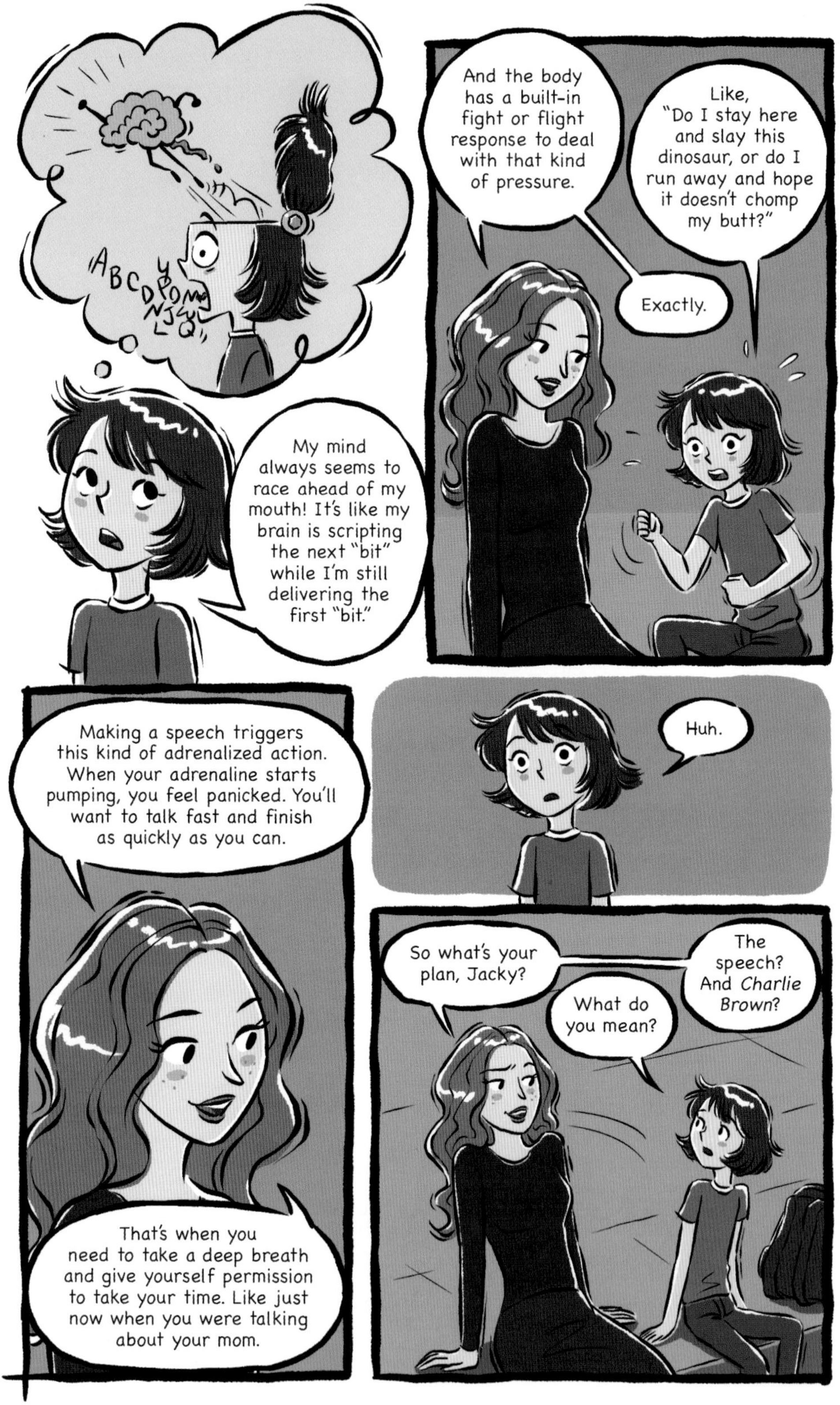
A B C D Y P O M N J L Q
My mind always seems to race ahead of my mouth! It's like my brain is scripting the next "bit" while I'm still delivering the first "bit."
And the body has a built-in fight or flight response to deal with that kind of pressure.
Like, "Do I stay here and slay this dinosaur, or do I run away and hope it doesn't chomp my butt?"
Exactly.
Making a speech triggers this kind of adrenalized action. When your adrenaline starts pumping, you feel panicked. You'll want to talk fast and finish as quickly as you can.
That's when you need to take a deep breath and give yourself permission to take your time. Like just now when you were talking about your mom.
Huh.
So what's your plan, Jacky?
What do you mean?
The speech? And *Charlie Brown*?

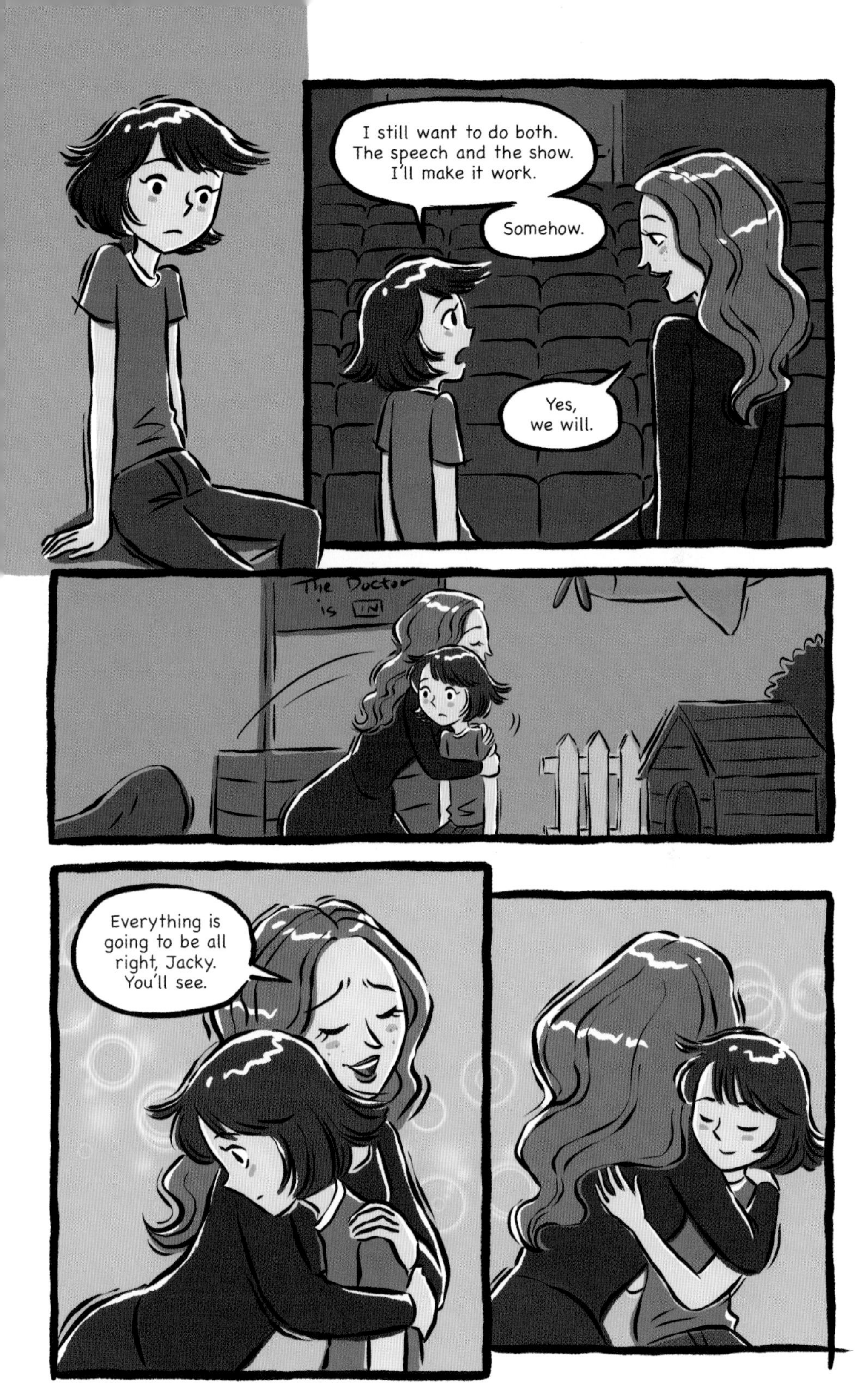
I still want to do both. The speech and the show. I'll make it work.
Somehow.
Yes, we will.
The Doctor is IN
Everything is going to be all right, Jacky. You'll see.

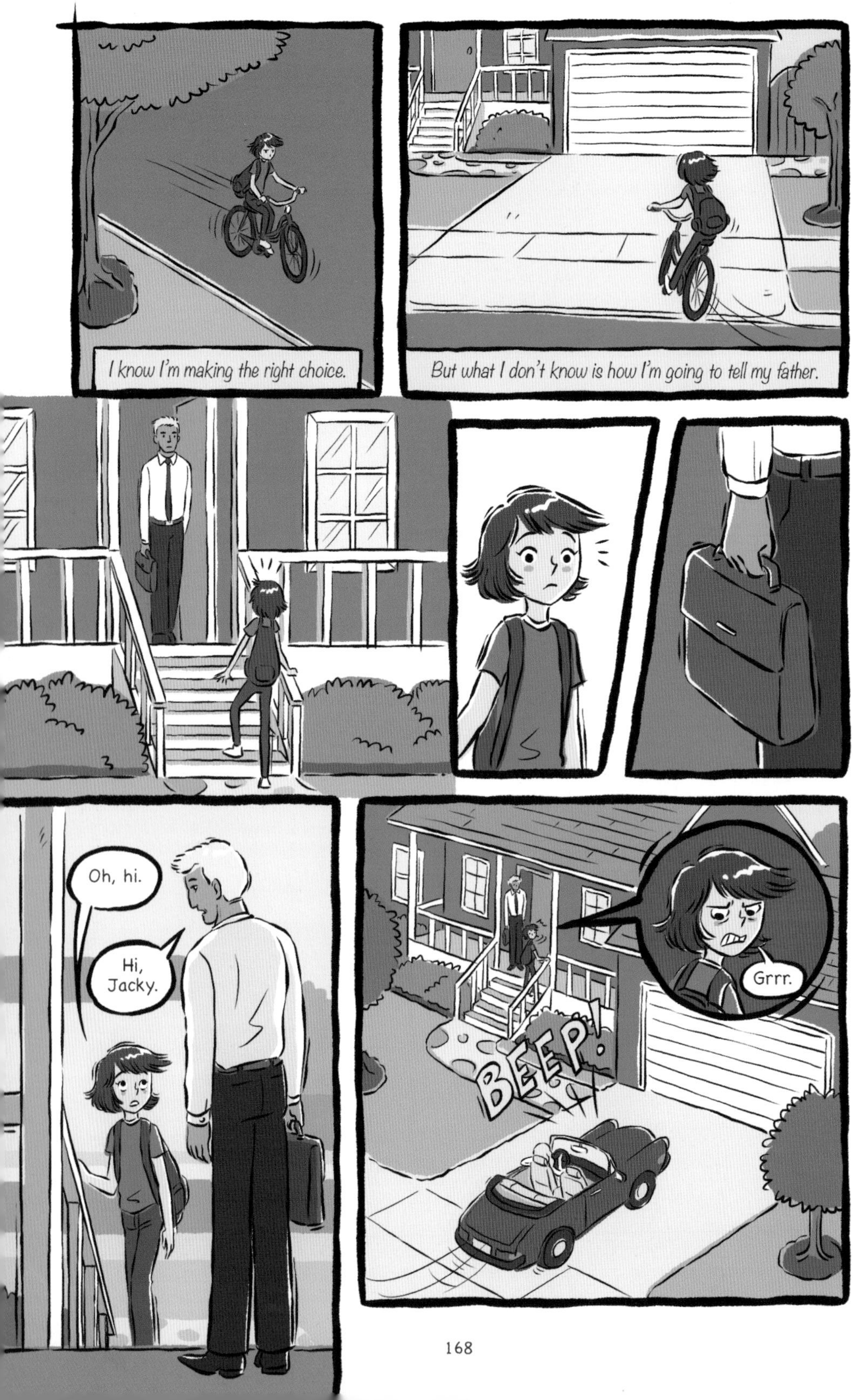
I know I'm making the right choice.
But what I don't know is how I'm going to tell my father.
Oh, hi.
Hi, Jacky.
Grrr.
BEEP!

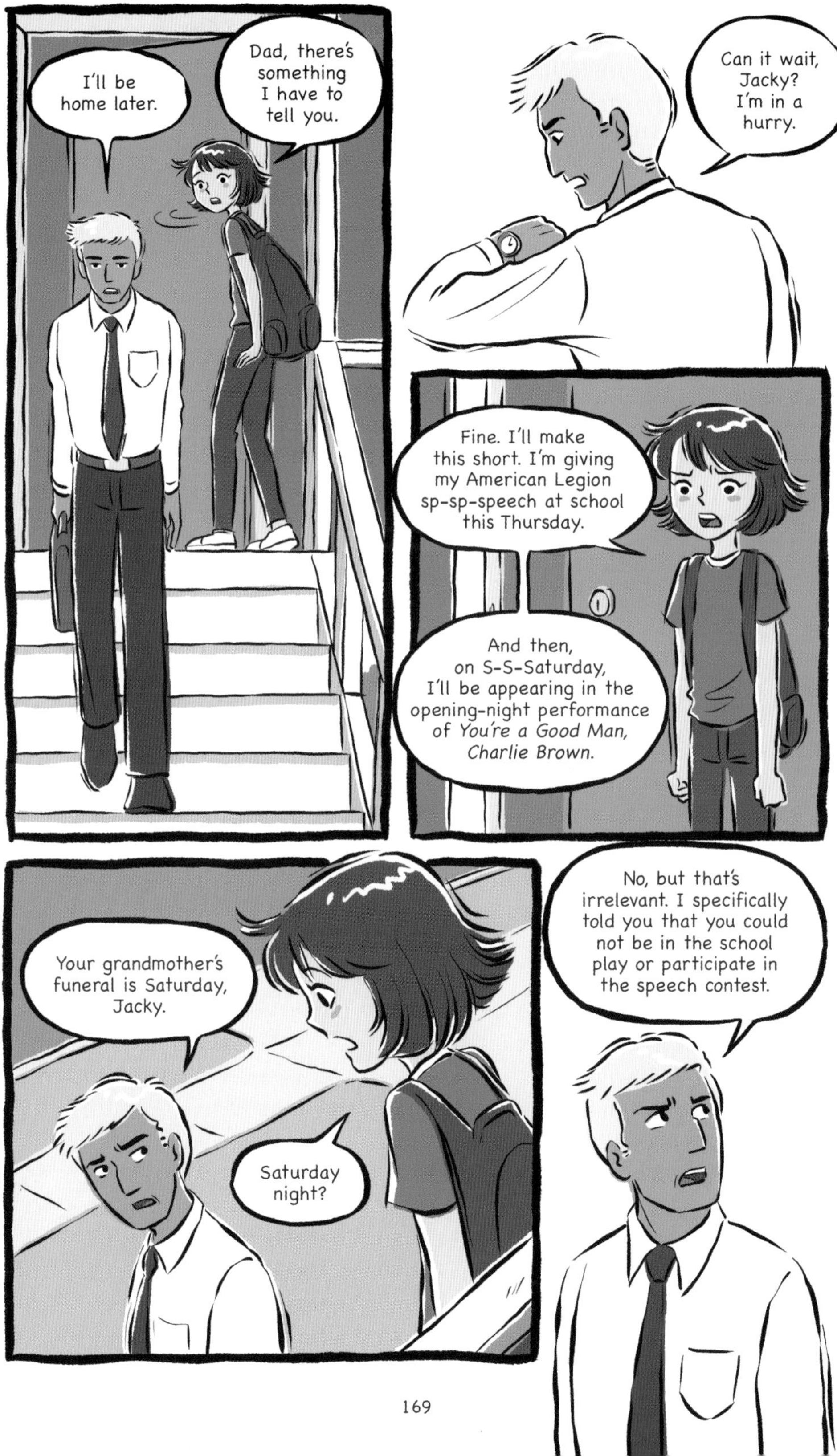
I'll be home later.
Dad, there's something I have to tell you.
Can it wait, Jacky? I'm in a hurry.
Fine. I'll make this short. I'm giving my American Legion sp-sp-speech at school this Thursday.
And then, on S-S-Saturday, I'll be appearing in the opening-night performance of *You're a Good Man, Charlie Brown.*
Your grandmother's funeral is Saturday, Jacky.
Saturday night?
No, but that's irrelevant. I specifically told you that you could not be in the school play or participate in the speech contest.

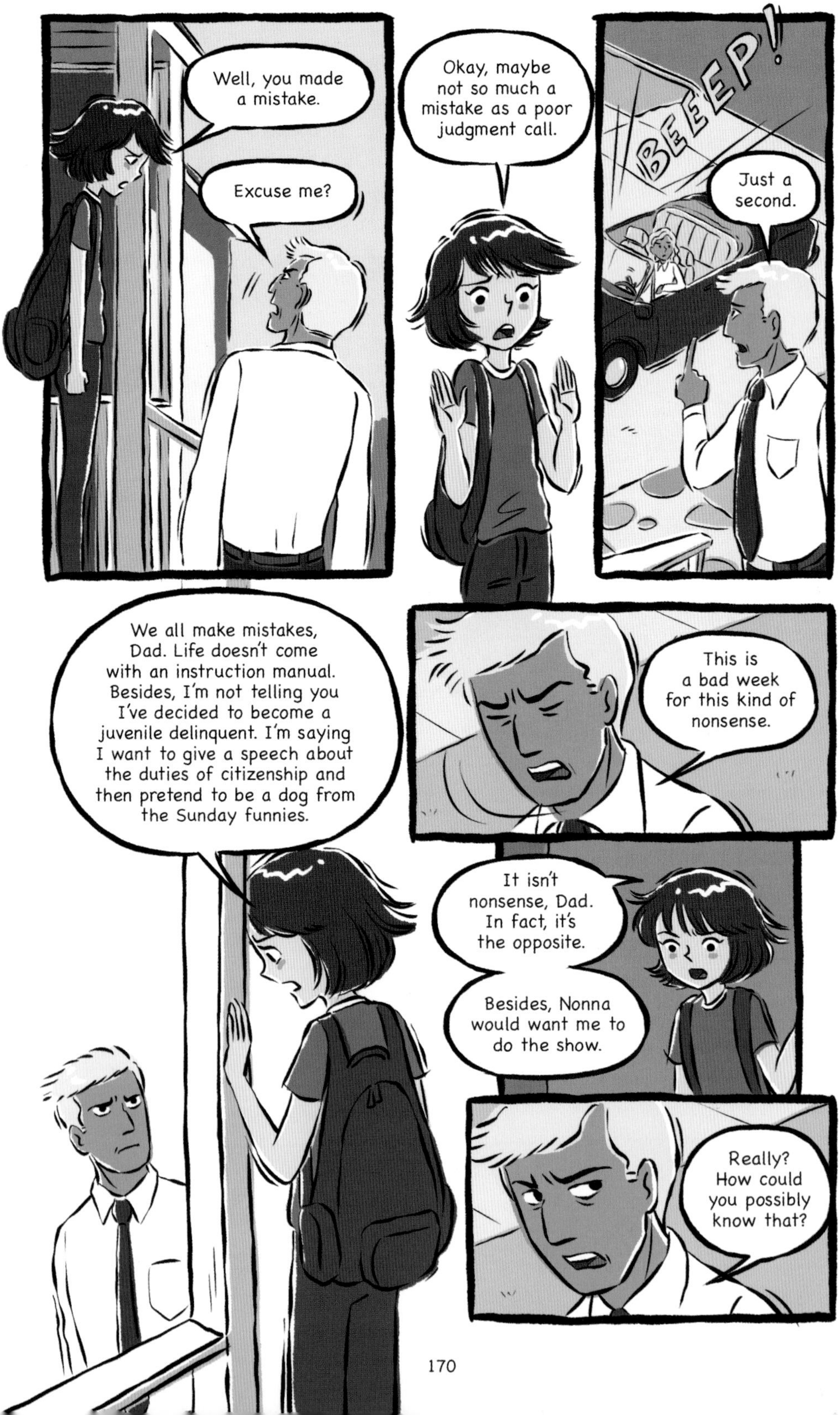
Well, you made a mistake.
Excuse me?
Okay, maybe not so much a mistake as a poor judgment call.
BEEEP!
Just a second.
We all make mistakes, Dad. Life doesn't come with an instruction manual. Besides, I'm not telling you I've decided to become a juvenile delinquent. I'm saying I want to give a speech about the duties of citizenship and then pretend to be a dog from the Sunday funnies.
This is a bad week for this kind of nonsense.
It isn't nonsense, Dad. In fact, it's the opposite.
Besides, Nonna would want me to do the show.
Really? How could you possibly know that?

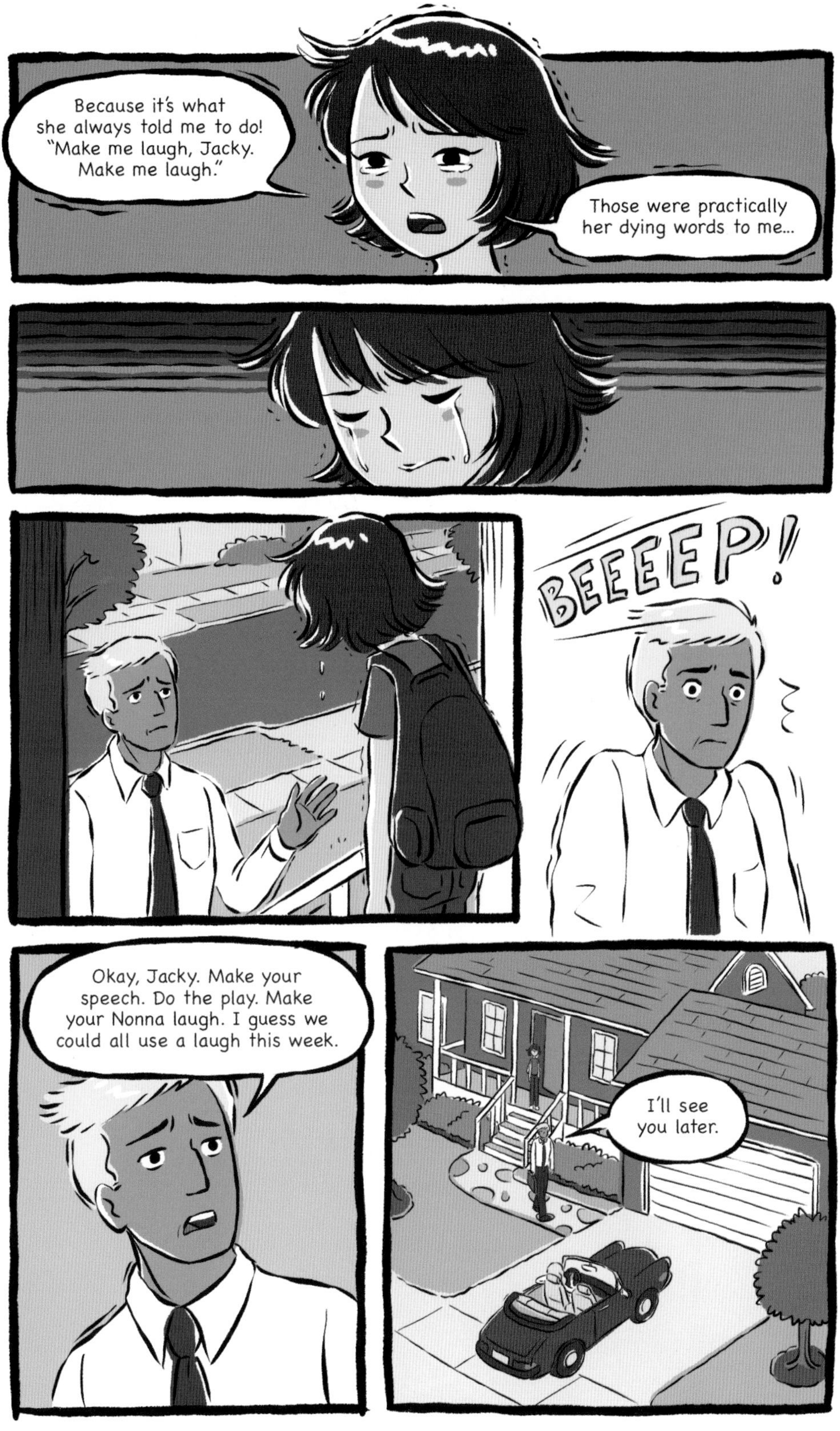
Because it's what she always told me to do! "Make me laugh, Jacky. Make me laugh."
Those were practically her dying words to me...
BEEEEP!
Okay, Jacky. Make your speech. Do the play. Make your Nonna laugh. I guess we could all use a laugh this week.
I'll see you later.

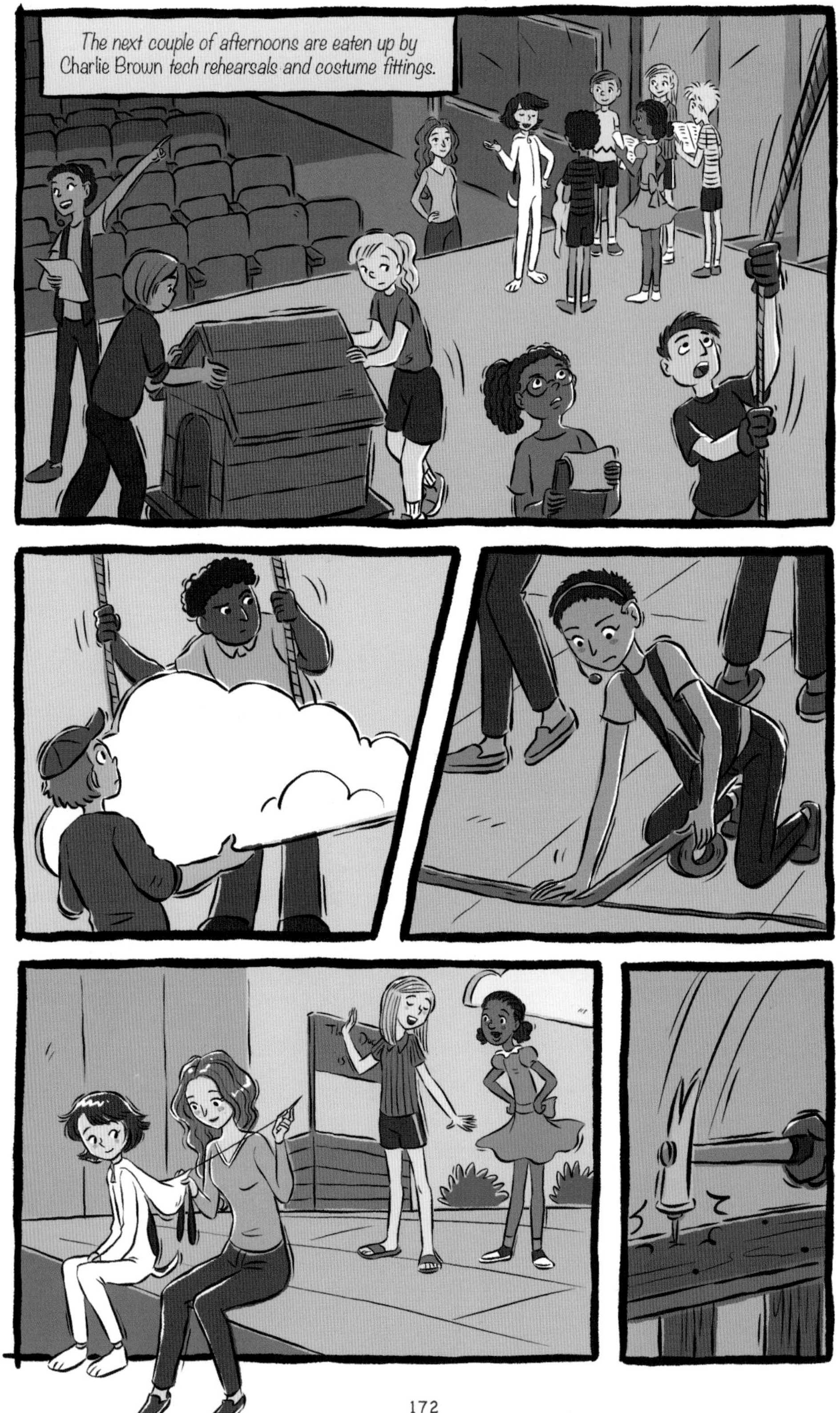
The next couple of afternoons are eaten up by Charlie Brown tech rehearsals and costume fittings.

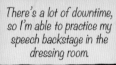

STAGE LIGHT

Dan, you came in just a little early on the last chorus.

Okay.

There's a lot of downtime, so I'm able to practice my speech backstage in the dressing room.

RRRIINNNNNGGG!

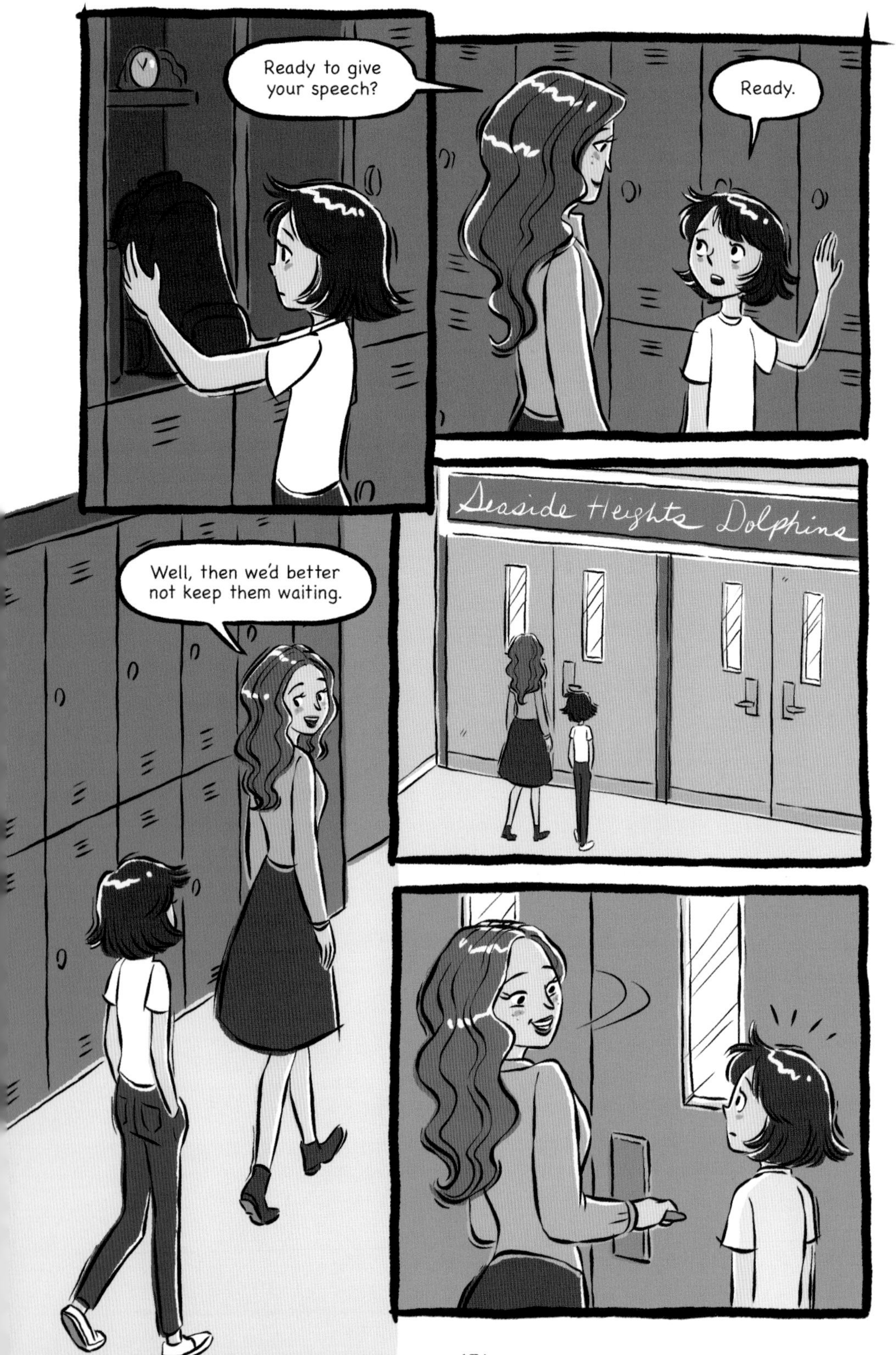
Ready to give your speech?
Ready.
Seaside Heights Dolphins
Well, then we'd better not keep them waiting.

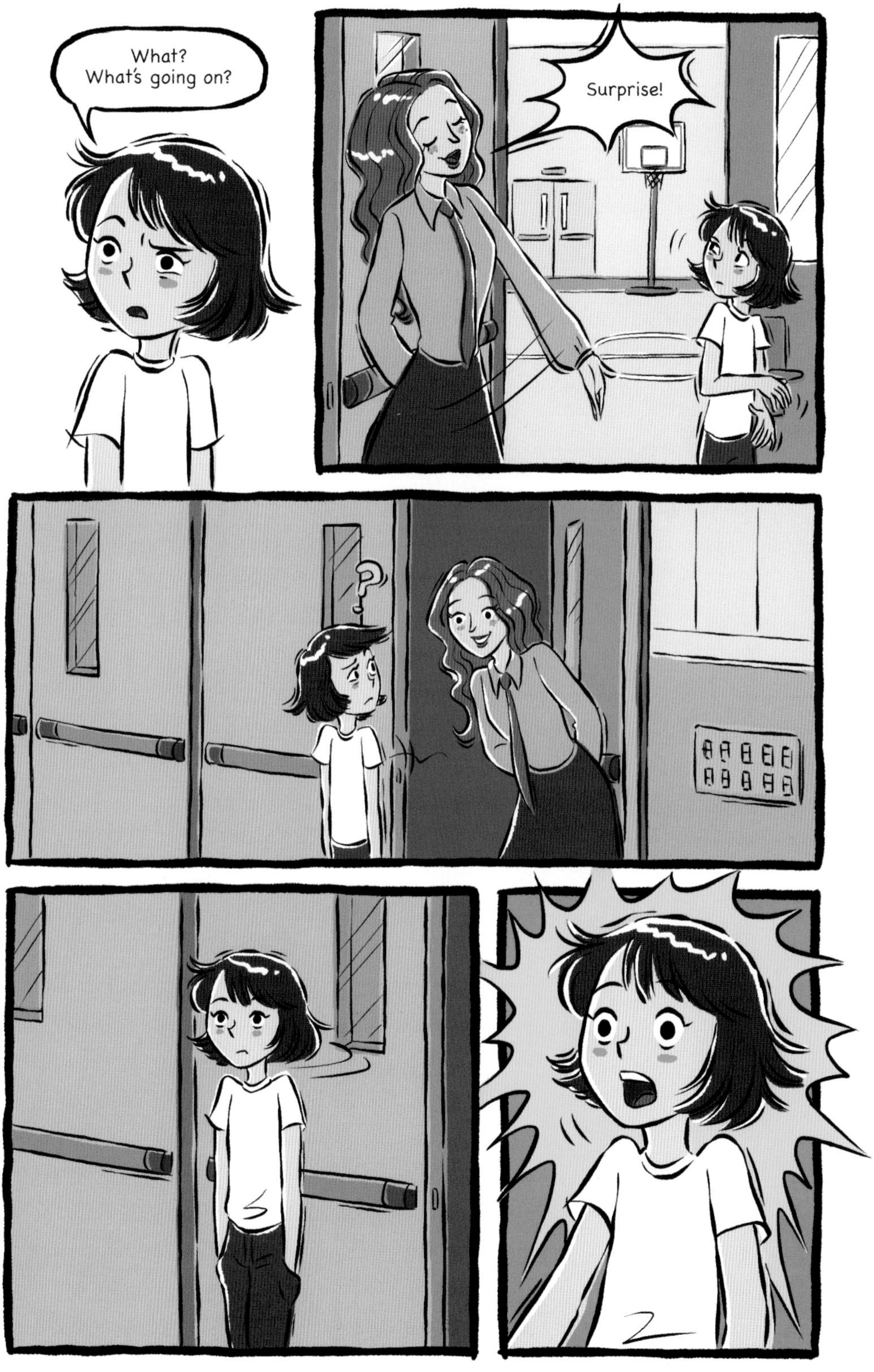
What?
What's going on?
Surprise!
?

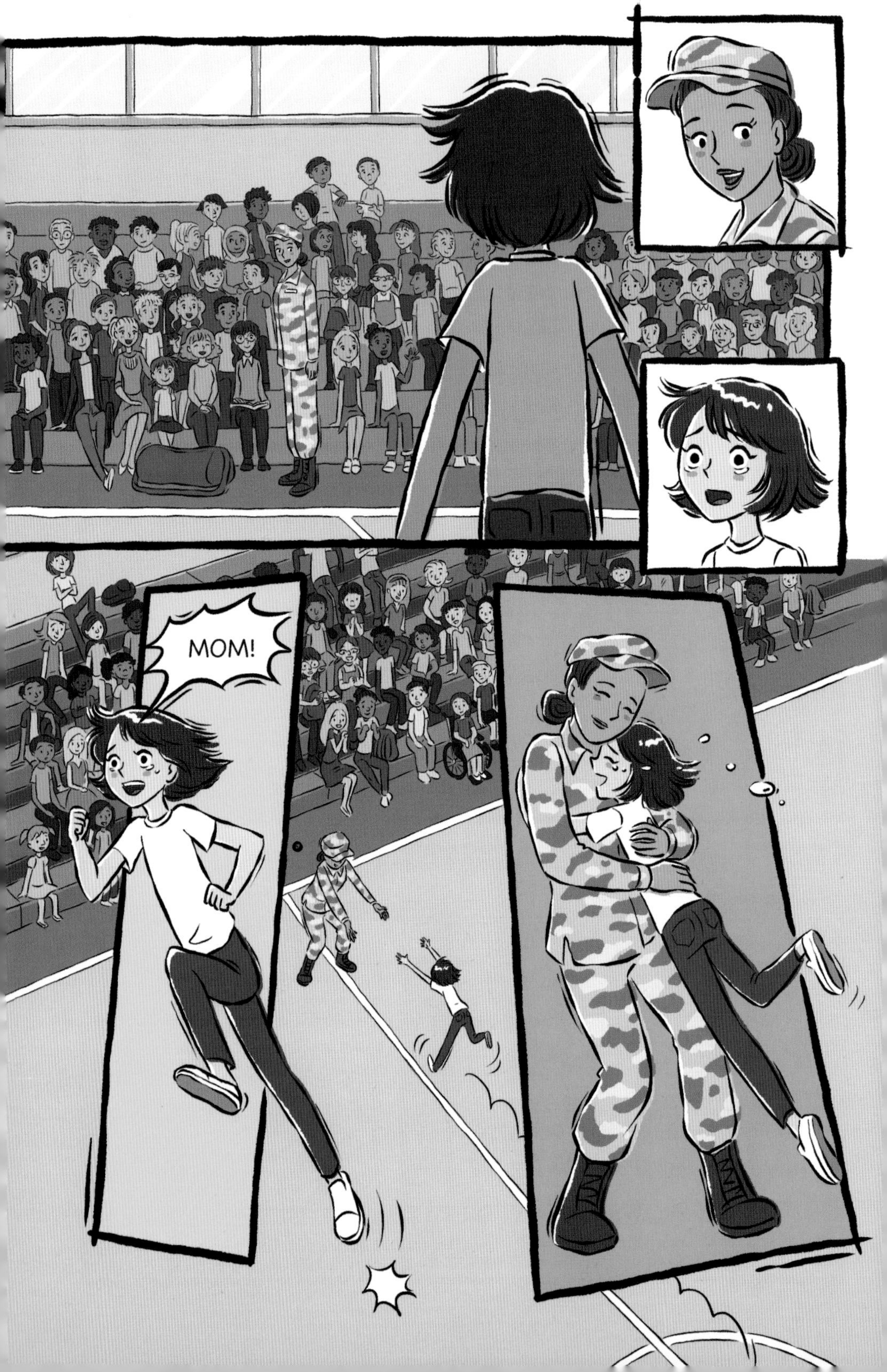
MOM!

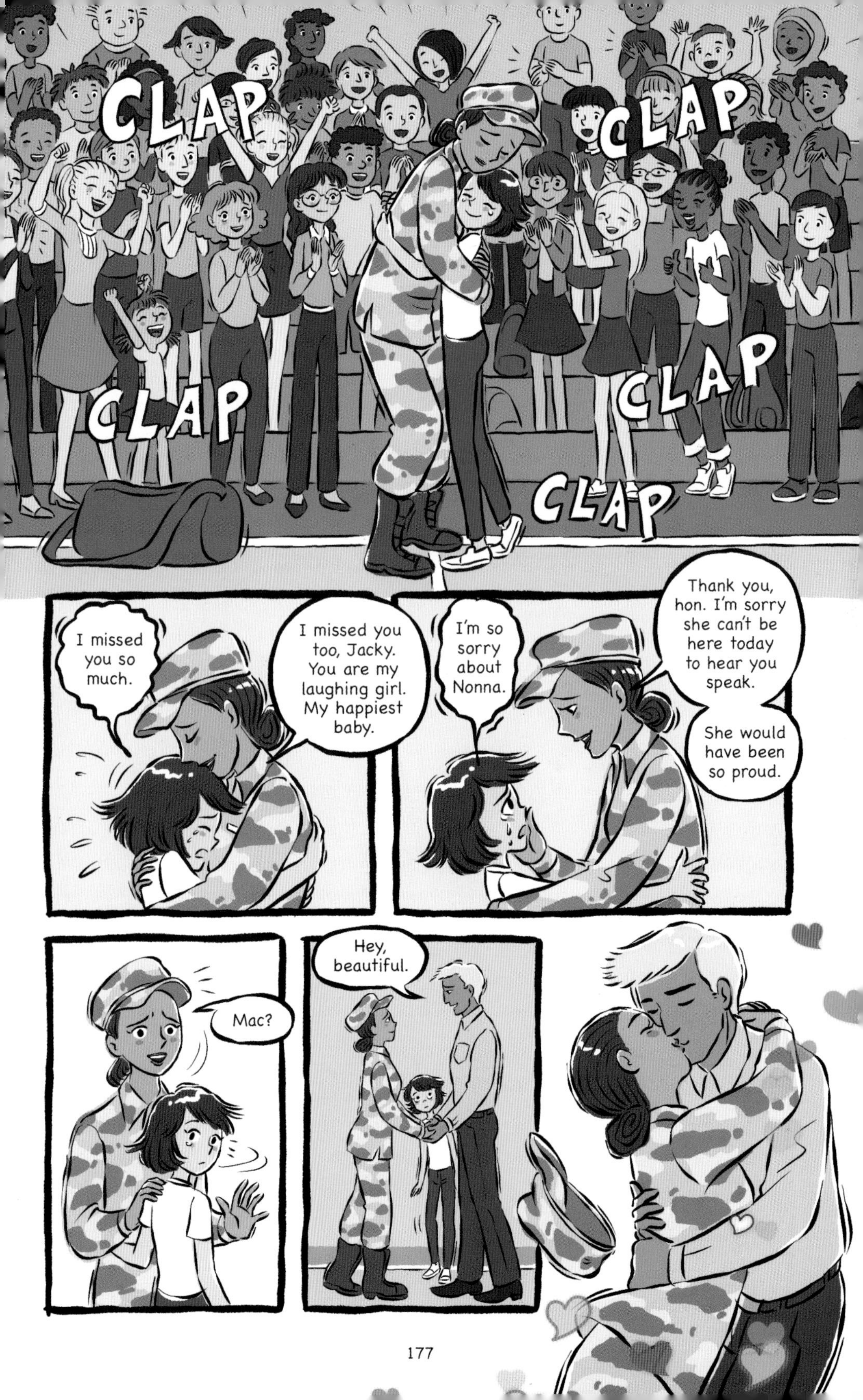
CLAP
CLAP
CLAP
CLAP
CLAP
I missed you so much.
I missed you too, Jacky. You are my laughing girl. My happiest baby.
I'm so sorry about Nonna.
Thank you, hon. I'm sorry she can't be here today to hear you speak.
She would have been so proud.
Mac?
Hey, beautiful.

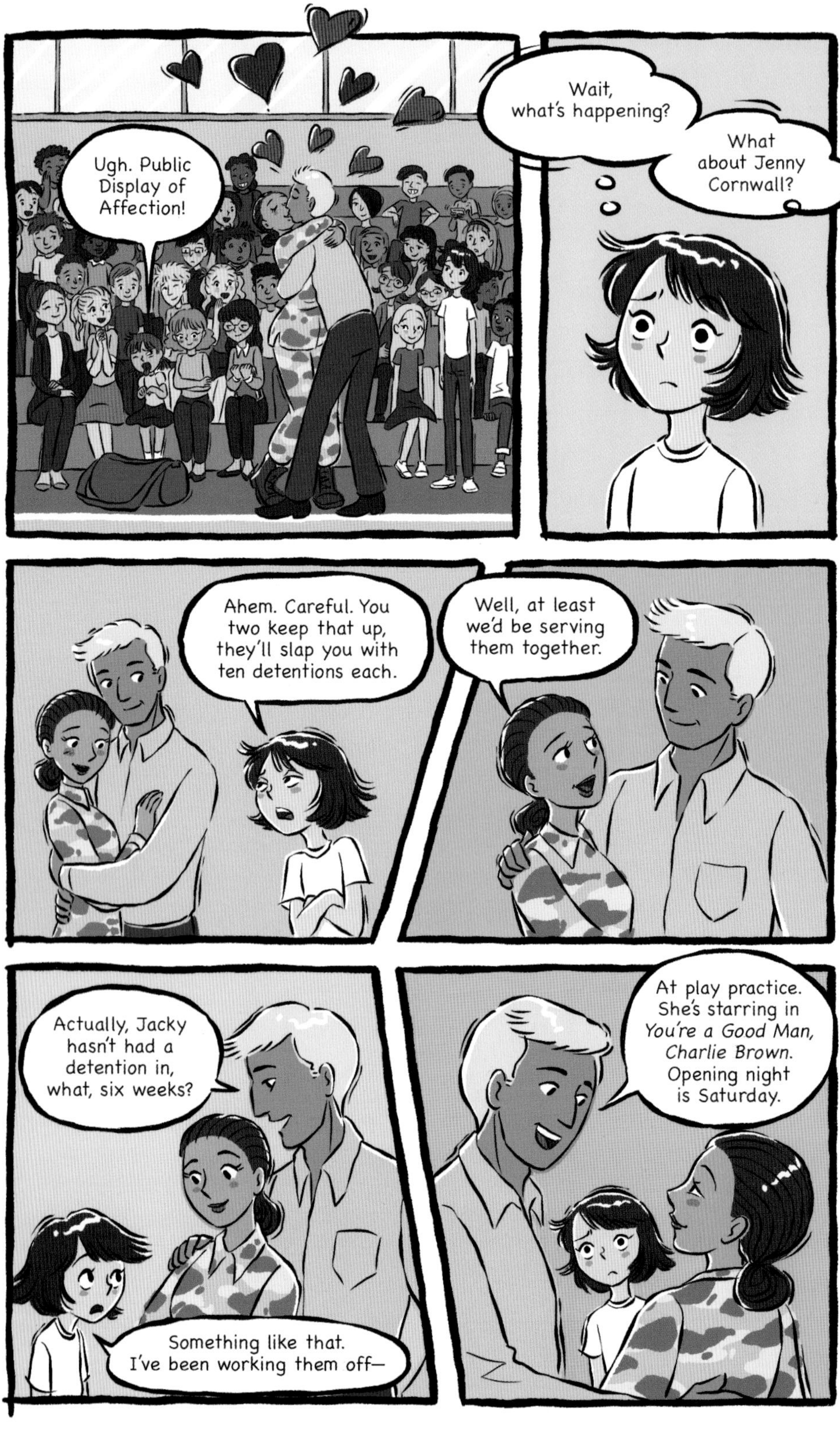
Ugh. Public Display of Affection!
Wait, what's happening?
What about Jenny Cornwall?
Ahem. Careful. You two keep that up, they'll slap you with ten detentions each.
Well, at least we'd be serving them together.
Actually, Jacky hasn't had a detention in, what, six weeks?
Something like that. I've been working them off—
At play practice. She's starring in *You're a Good Man, Charlie Brown.* Opening night is Saturday.

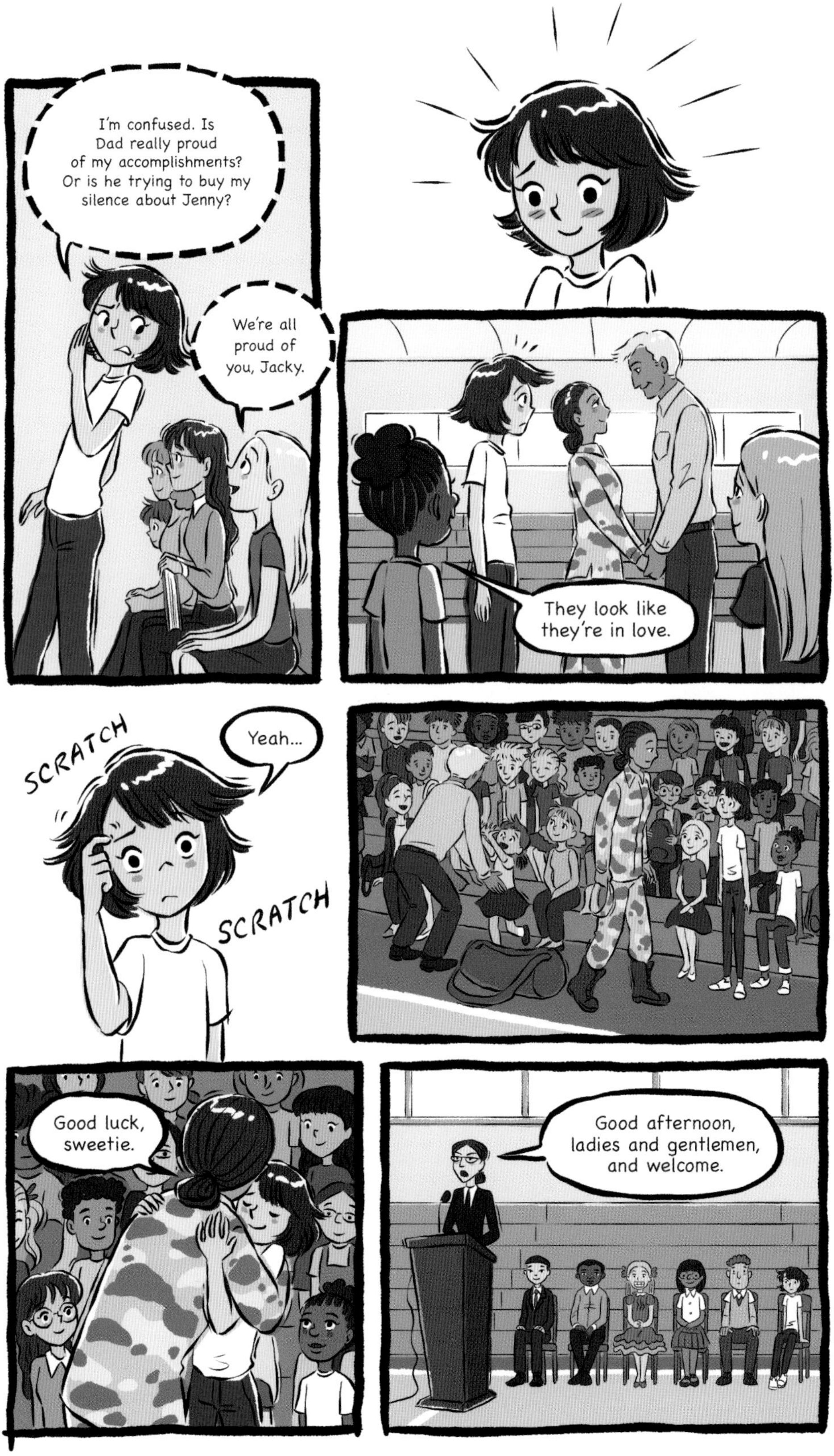
I'm confused. Is Dad really proud of my accomplishments? Or is he trying to buy my silence about Jenny?
We're all proud of you, Jacky.
They look like they're in love.
SCRATCH
Yeah...
SCRATCH
Good luck, sweetie.
Good afternoon, ladies and gentlemen, and welcome.

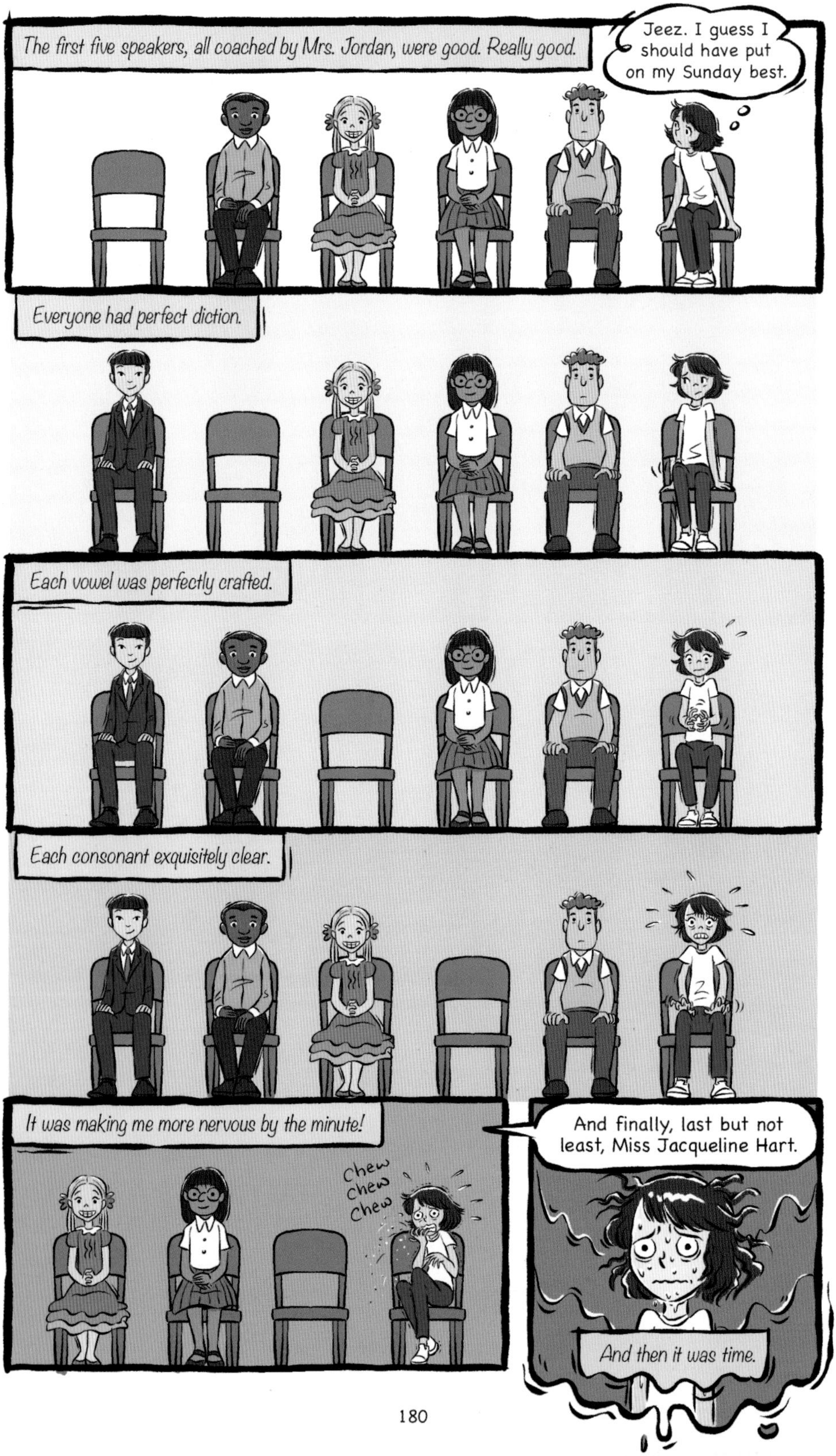
The first five speakers, all coached by Mrs. Jordan, were good. Really good.
Jeez. I guess I should have put on my Sunday best.
Everyone had perfect diction.
Each vowel was perfectly crafted.
Each consonant exquisitely clear.
It was making me more nervous by the minute!
Chew chew chew
And finally, last but not least, Miss Jacqueline Hart.
And then it was time.

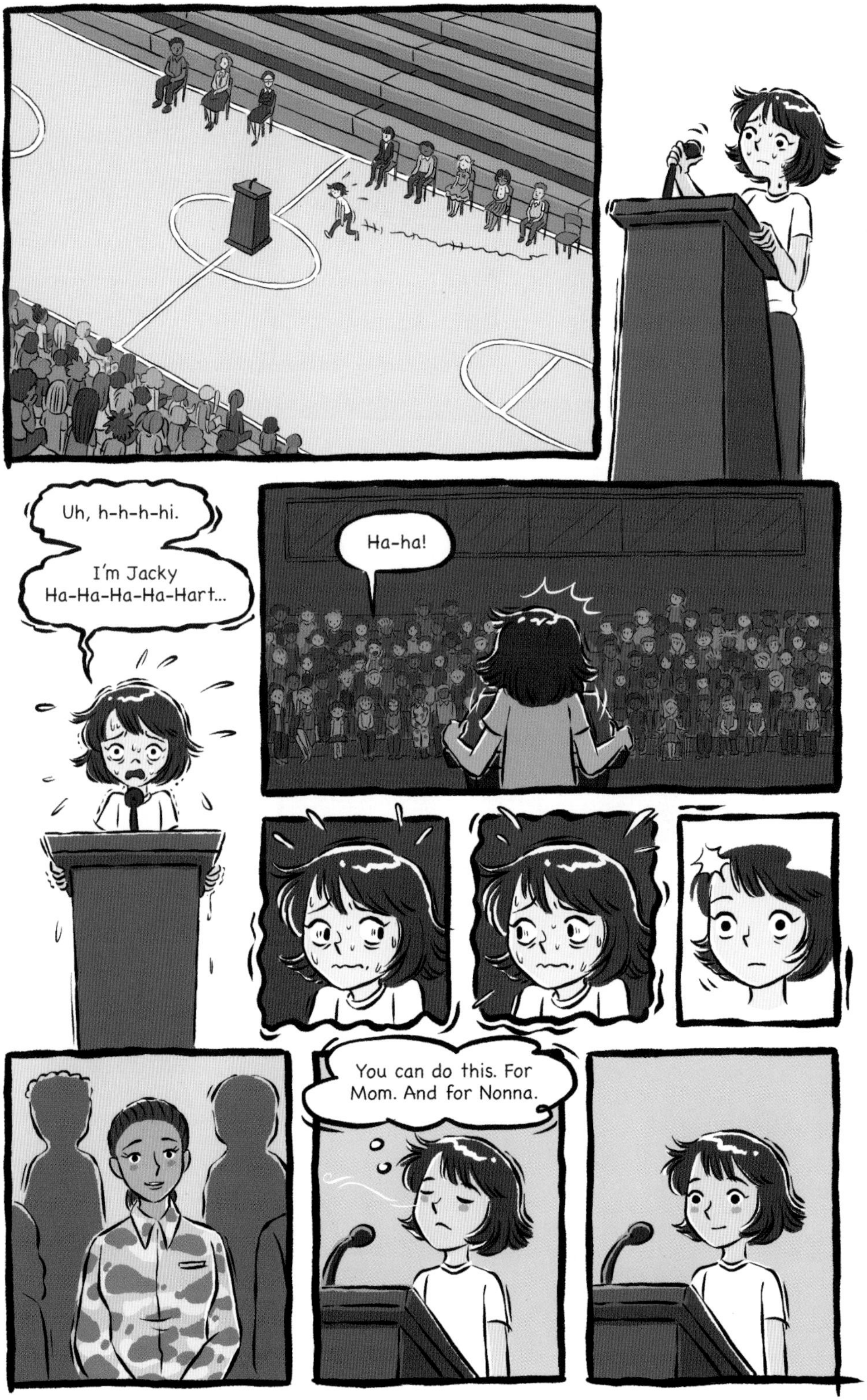
Uh, h-h-h-hi.
I'm Jacky Ha-Ha-Ha-Ha-Hart...
Ha-ha!
You can do this. For Mom. And for Nonna.

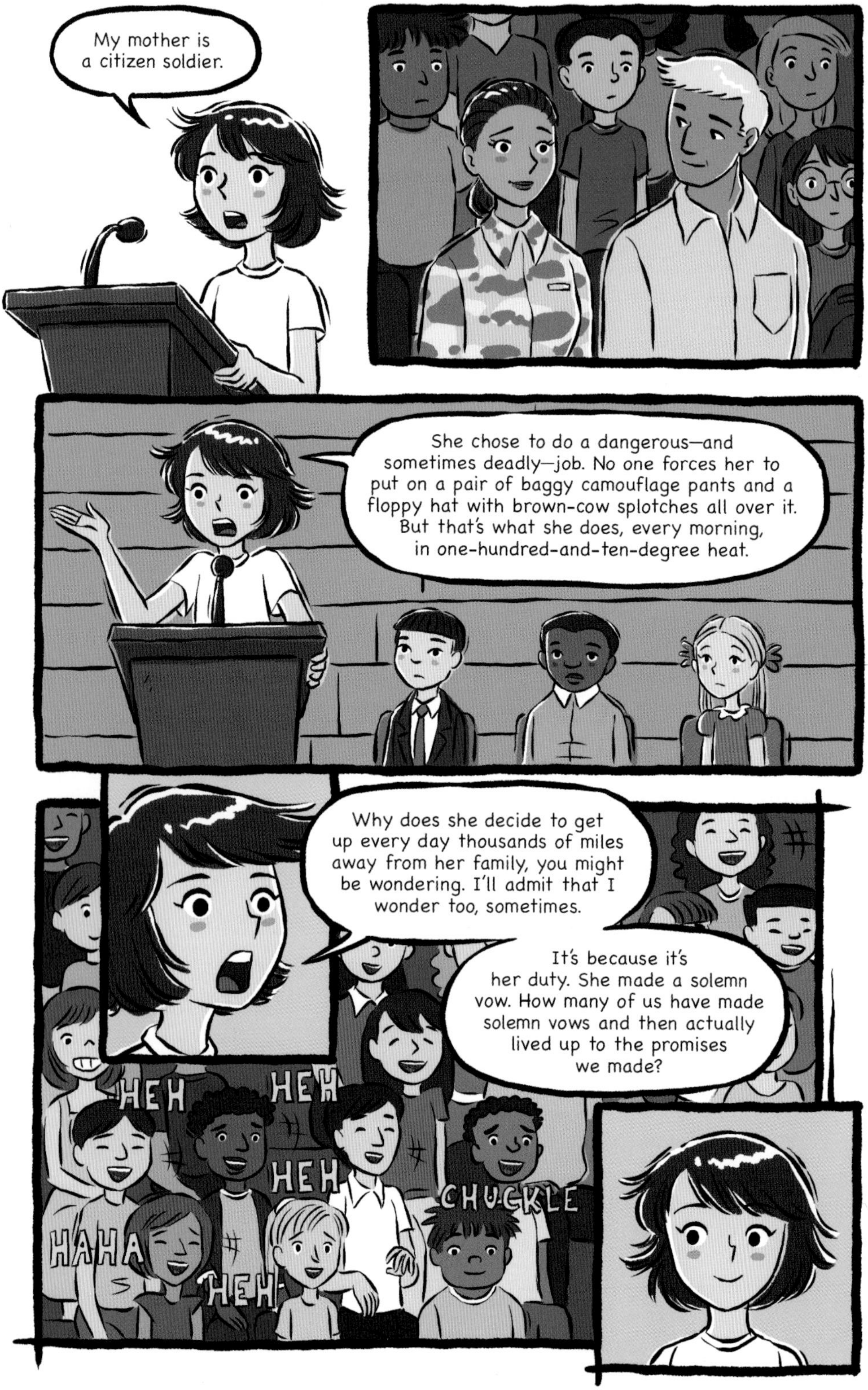

My mother is a citizen soldier.
She chose to do a dangerous—and sometimes deadly—job. No one forces her to put on a pair of baggy camouflage pants and a floppy hat with brown-cow splotches all over it. But that's what she does, every morning, in one-hundred-and-ten-degree heat.
Why does she decide to get up every day thousands of miles away from her family, you might be wondering. I'll admit that I wonder too, sometimes.
It's because it's her duty. She made a solemn vow. How many of us have made solemn vows and then actually lived up to the promises we made?
HEH
HEH
HEH
CHUCKLE
HAHA
HEH

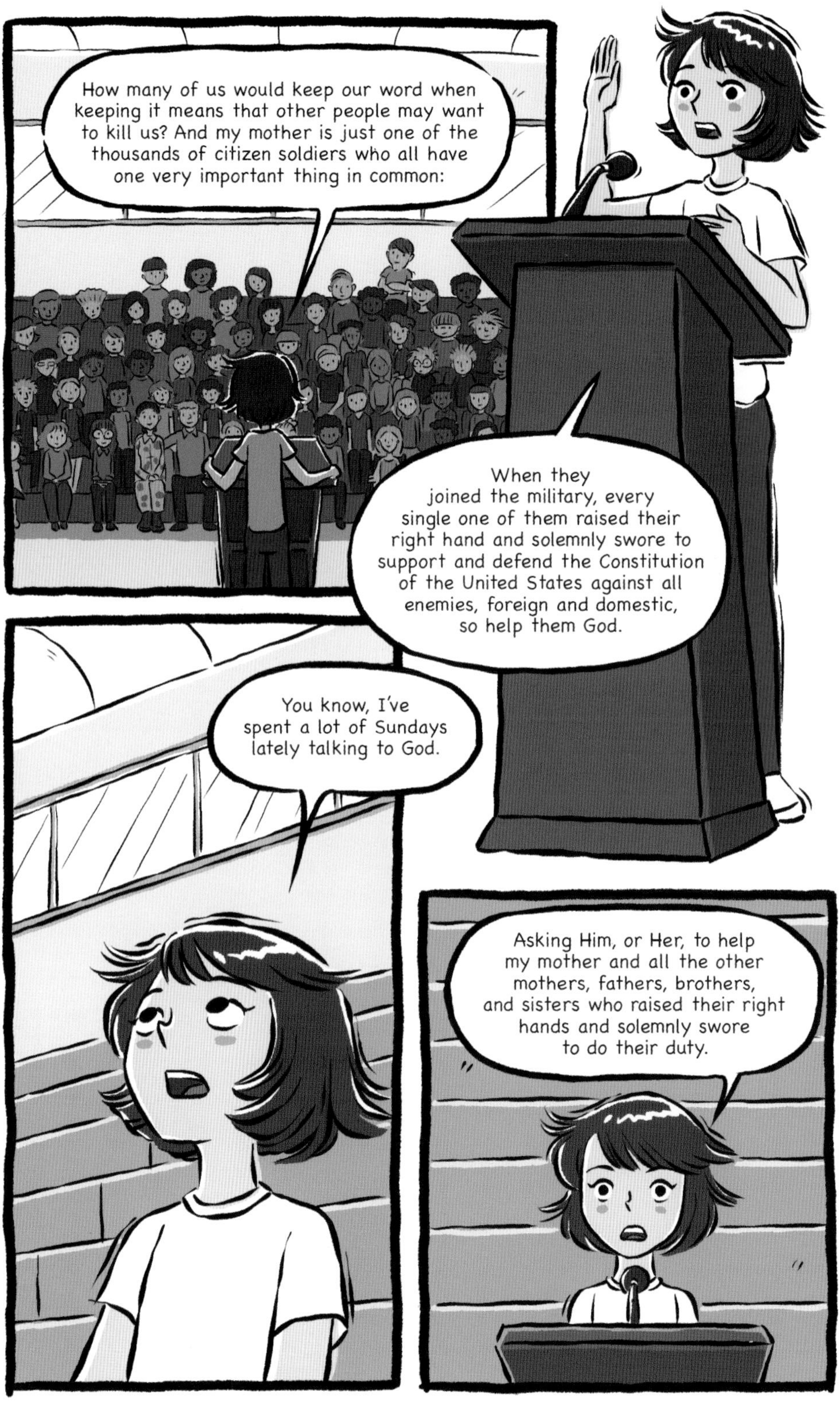
How many of us would keep our word when keeping it means that other people may want to kill us? And my mother is just one of the thousands of citizen soldiers who all have one very important thing in common:
When they joined the military, every single one of them raised their right hand and solemnly swore to support and defend the Constitution of the United States against all enemies, foreign and domestic, so help them God.
You know, I've spent a lot of Sundays lately talking to God.
Asking Him, or Her, to help my mother and all the other mothers, fathers, brothers, and sisters who raised their right hands and solemnly swore to do their duty.

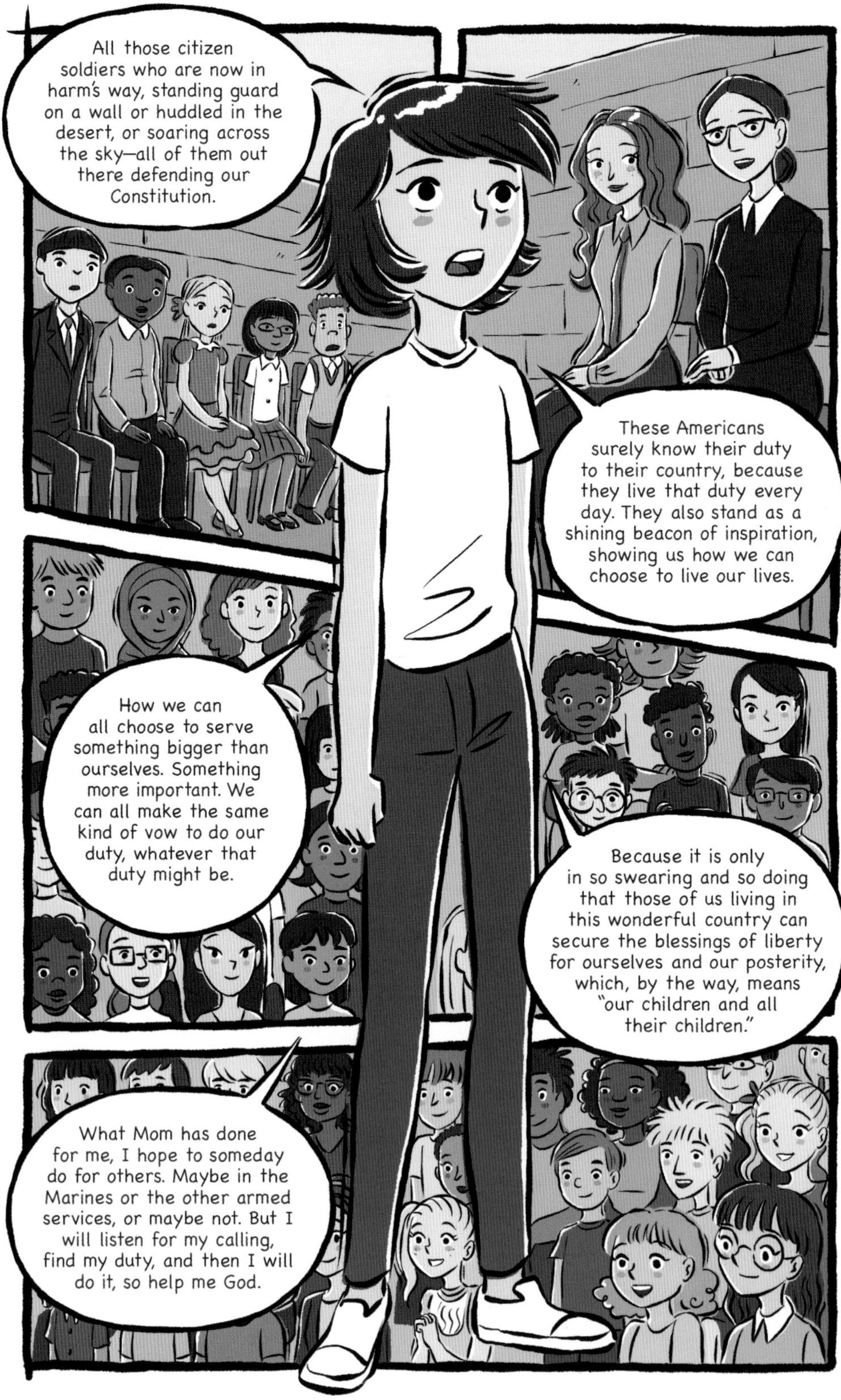
All those citizen soldiers who are now in harm's way, standing guard on a wall or huddled in the desert, or soaring across the sky—all of them out there defending our Constitution.
These Americans surely know their duty to their country, because they live that duty every day. They also stand as a shining beacon of inspiration, showing us how we can choose to live our lives.
How we can all choose to serve something bigger than ourselves. Something more important. We can all make the same kind of vow to do our duty, whatever that duty might be.
Because it is only in so swearing and so doing that those of us living in this wonderful country can secure the blessings of liberty for ourselves and our posterity, which, by the way, means "our children and all their children."
What Mom has done for me, I hope to someday do for others. Maybe in the Marines or the other armed services, or maybe not. But I will listen for my calling, find my duty, and then I will do it, so help me God.

And each of you, as citizens—I implore you to perform your own duties to our country, in whatever way calls to you, big or small.

I need to thank you, Mom, for protecting and defending the Constitution of these United States so that I, and all my sisters, can fully enjoy our blessings of liberty.

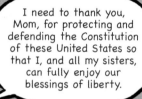

And that's a lot of liberty, folks. There's seven of us!

Thank you.

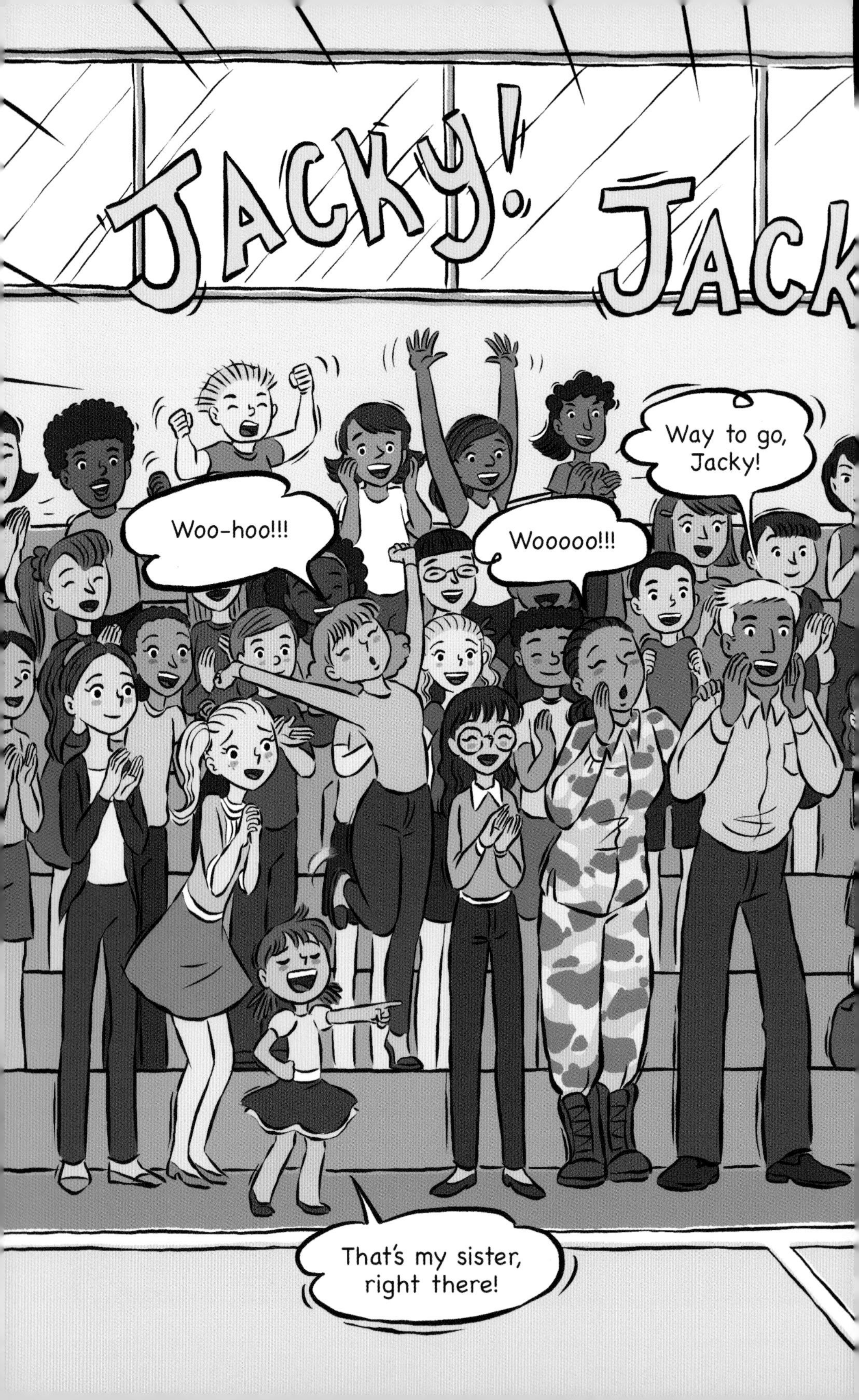
JACKY!
JACK
Woo-hoo!!!
Wooooo!!!
Way to go, Jacky!
That's my sister, right there!

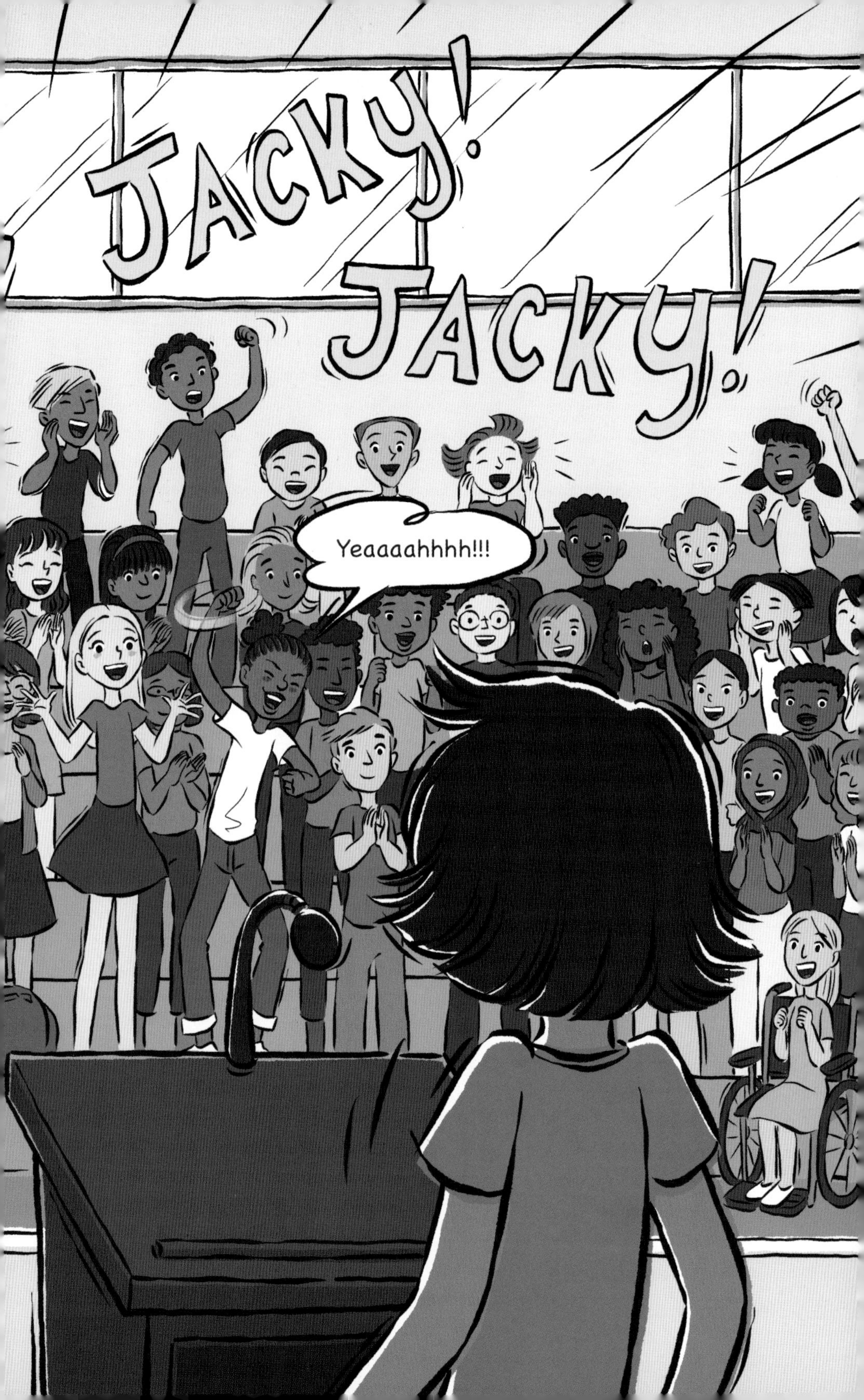
JACKY!
JACKY!
Yeaaaahhhh!!!

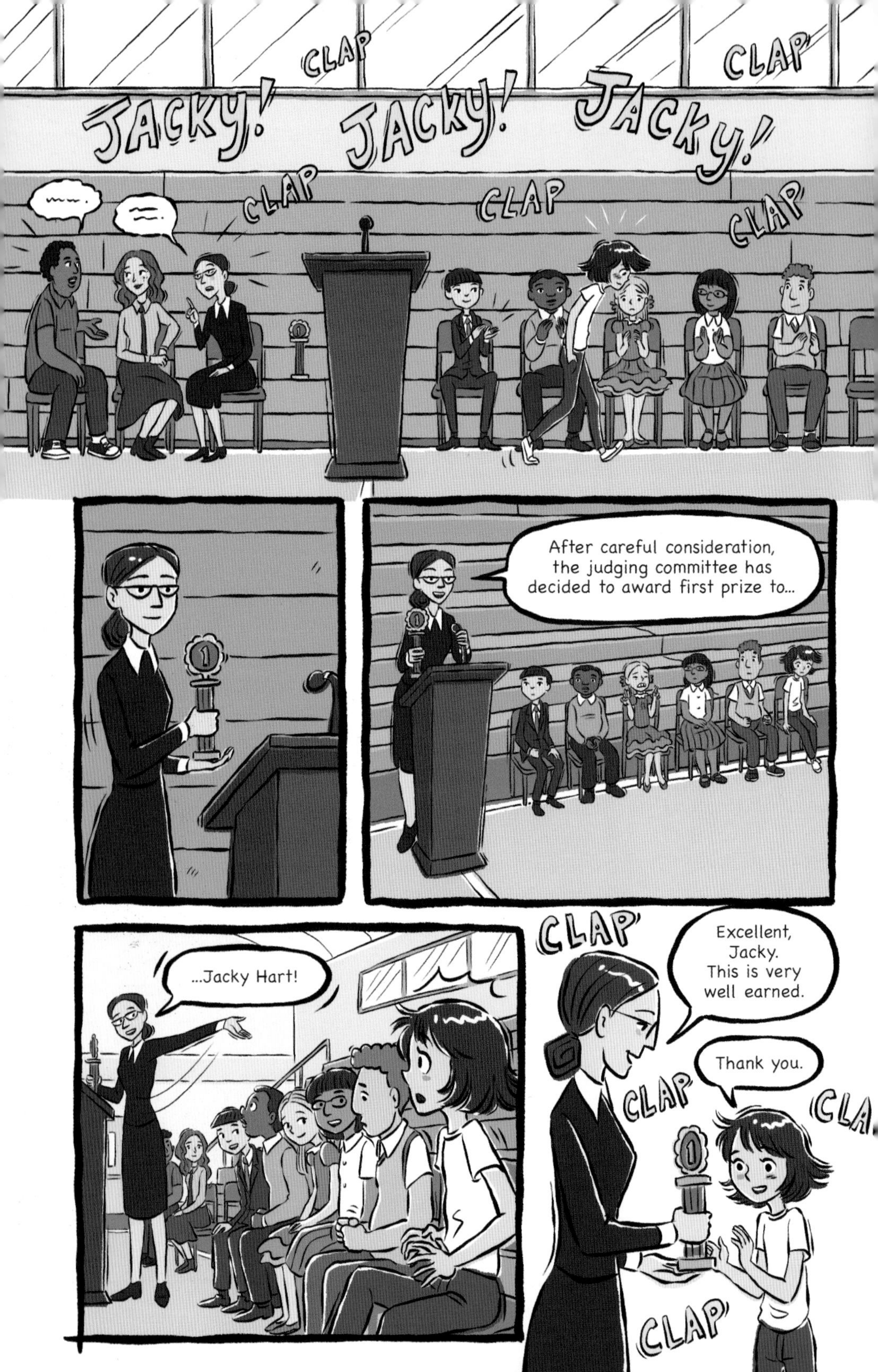
CLAP
CLAP
JACKY! JACKY! JACKY!
CLAP
CLAP
CLAP
After careful consideration, the judging committee has decided to award first prize to...
...Jacky Hart!
CLAP
Excellent, Jacky. This is very well earned.
Thank you.
CLAP
CLA
CLAP

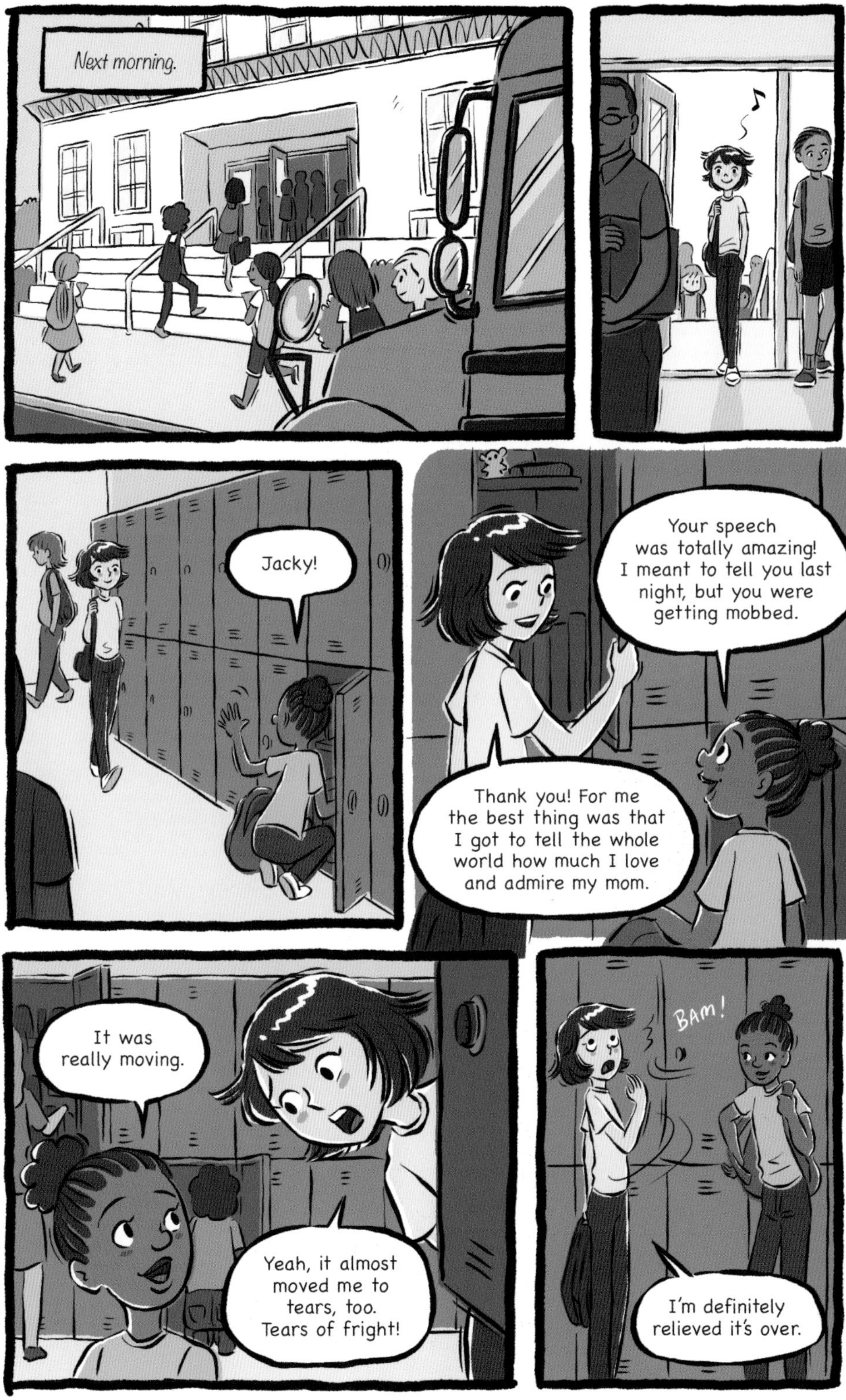

Next morning.
Jacky!
Your speech was totally amazing! I meant to tell you last night, but you were getting mobbed.
Thank you! For me the best thing was that I got to tell the whole world how much I love and admire my mom.
It was really moving.
Yeah, it almost moved me to tears, too. Tears of fright!
BAM!
I'm definitely relieved it's over.

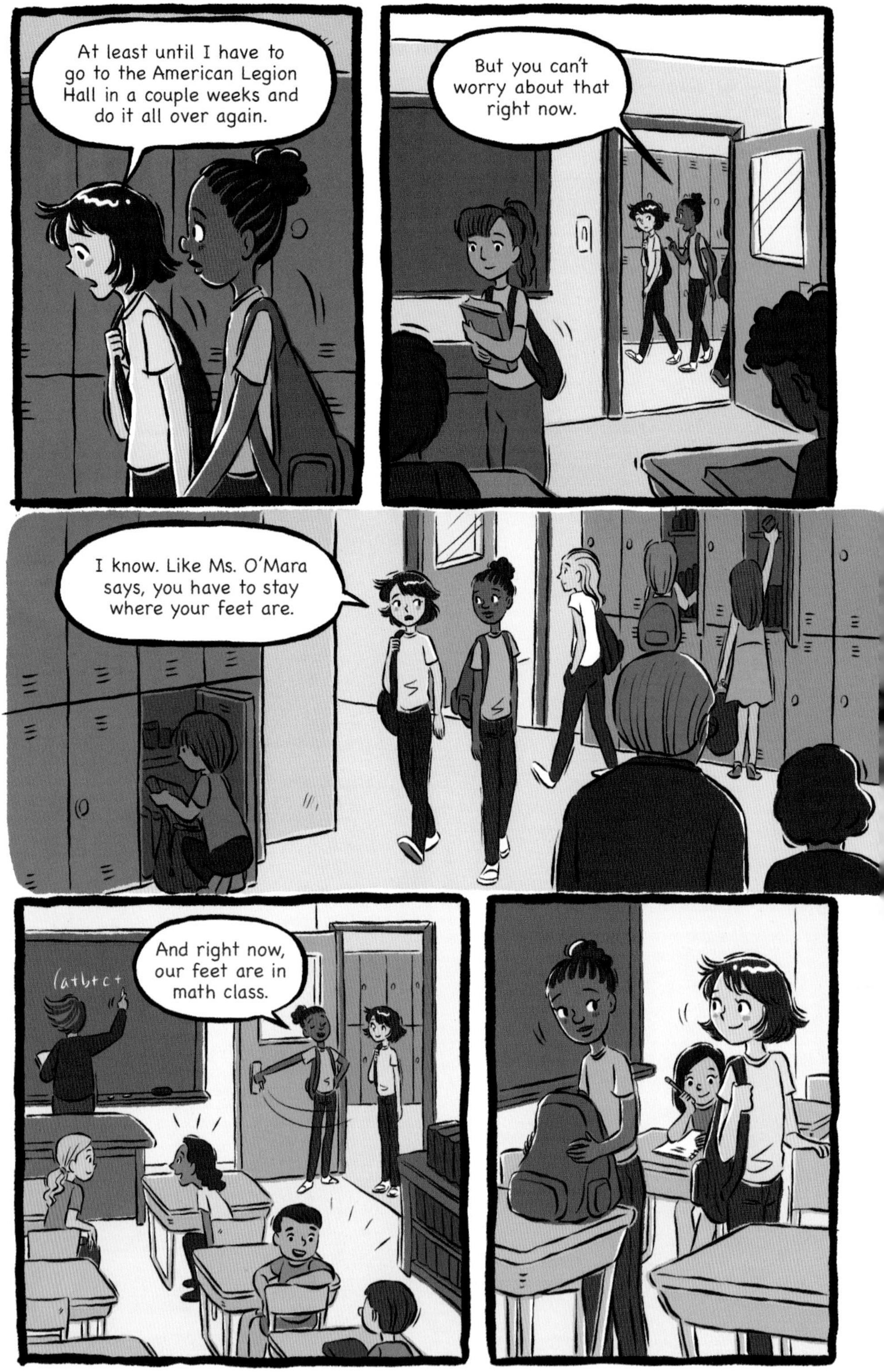
At least until I have to go to the American Legion Hall in a couple weeks and do it all over again.
But you can't worry about that right now.
I know. Like Ms. O'Mara says, you have to stay where your feet are.
And right now, our feet are in math class.

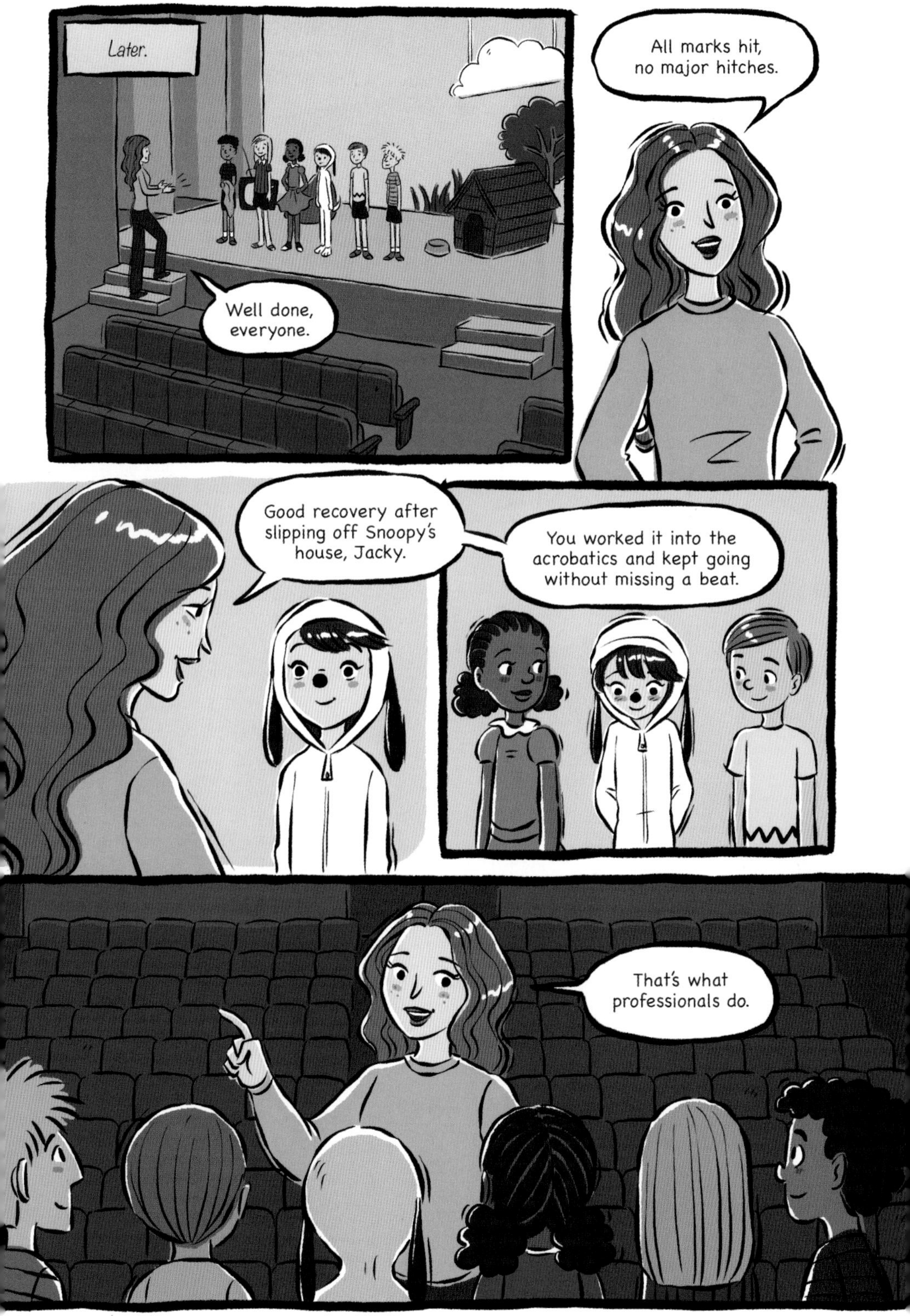
Later.
Well done, everyone.
All marks hit, no major hitches.
Good recovery after slipping off Snoopy's house, Jacky.
You worked it into the acrobatics and kept going without missing a beat.
That's what professionals do.

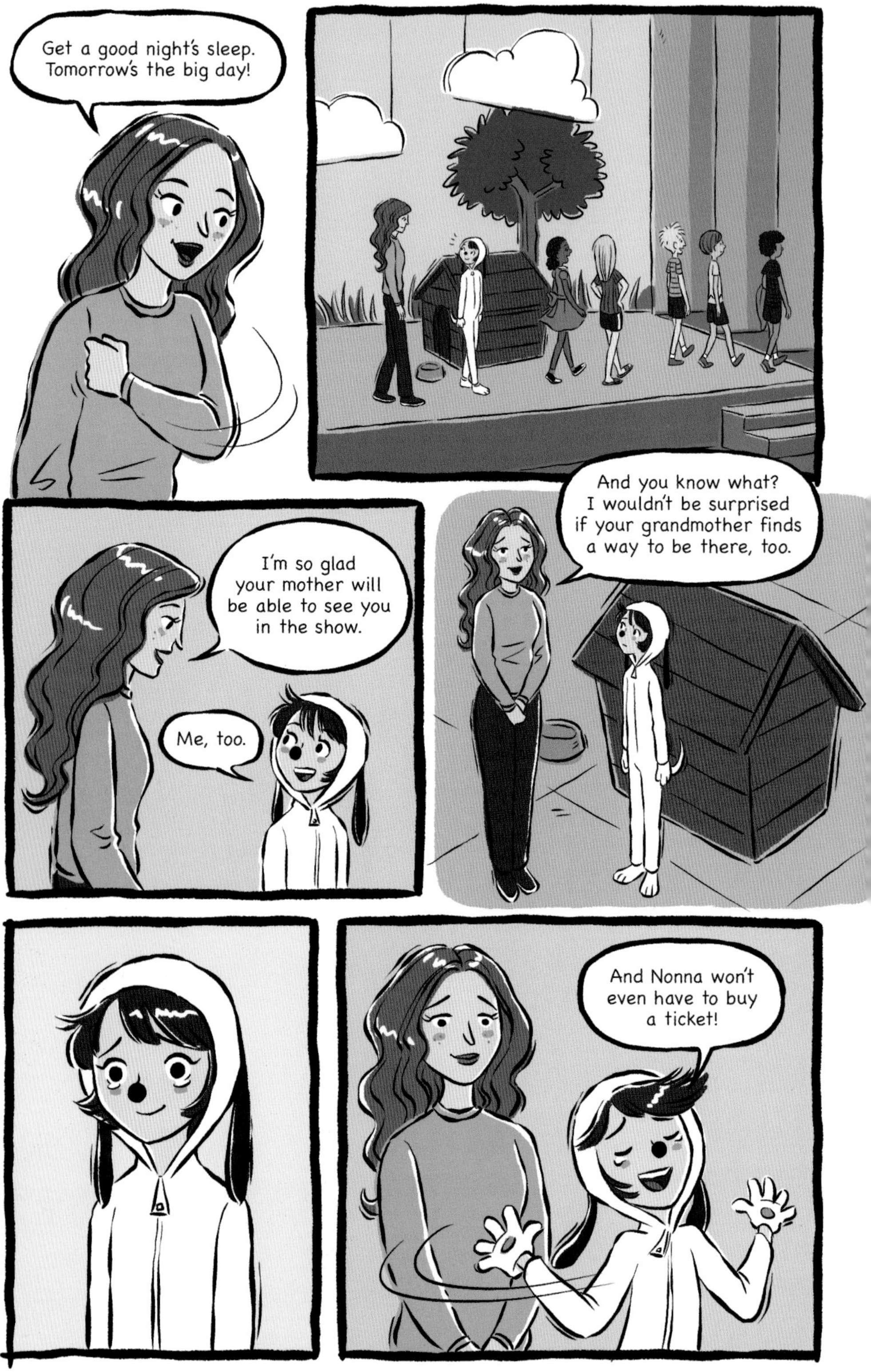
Get a good night's sleep. Tomorrow's the big day!
I'm so glad your mother will be able to see you in the show.
Me, too.
And you know what? I wouldn't be surprised if your grandmother finds a way to be there, too.
And Nonna won't even have to buy a ticket!

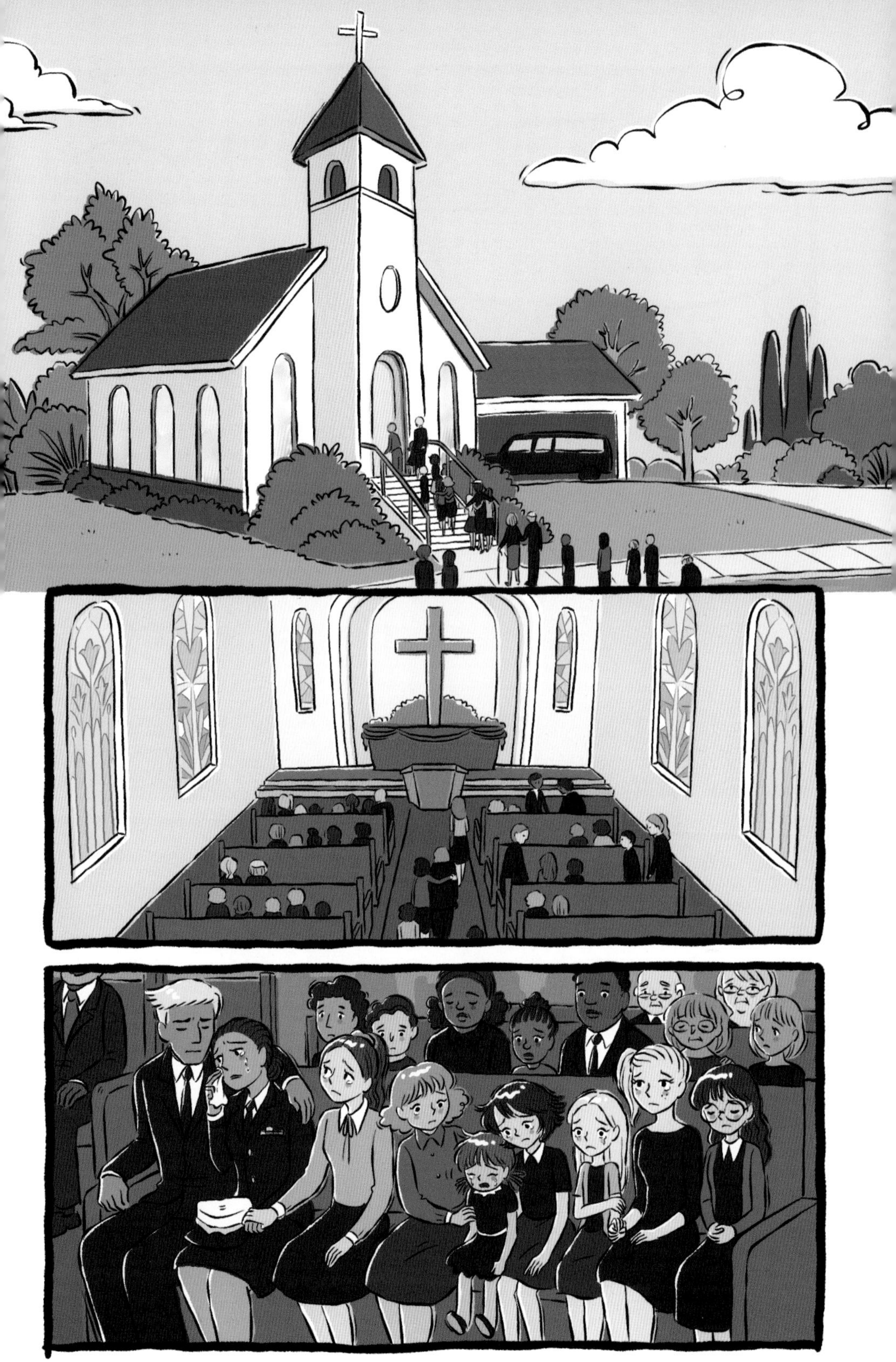

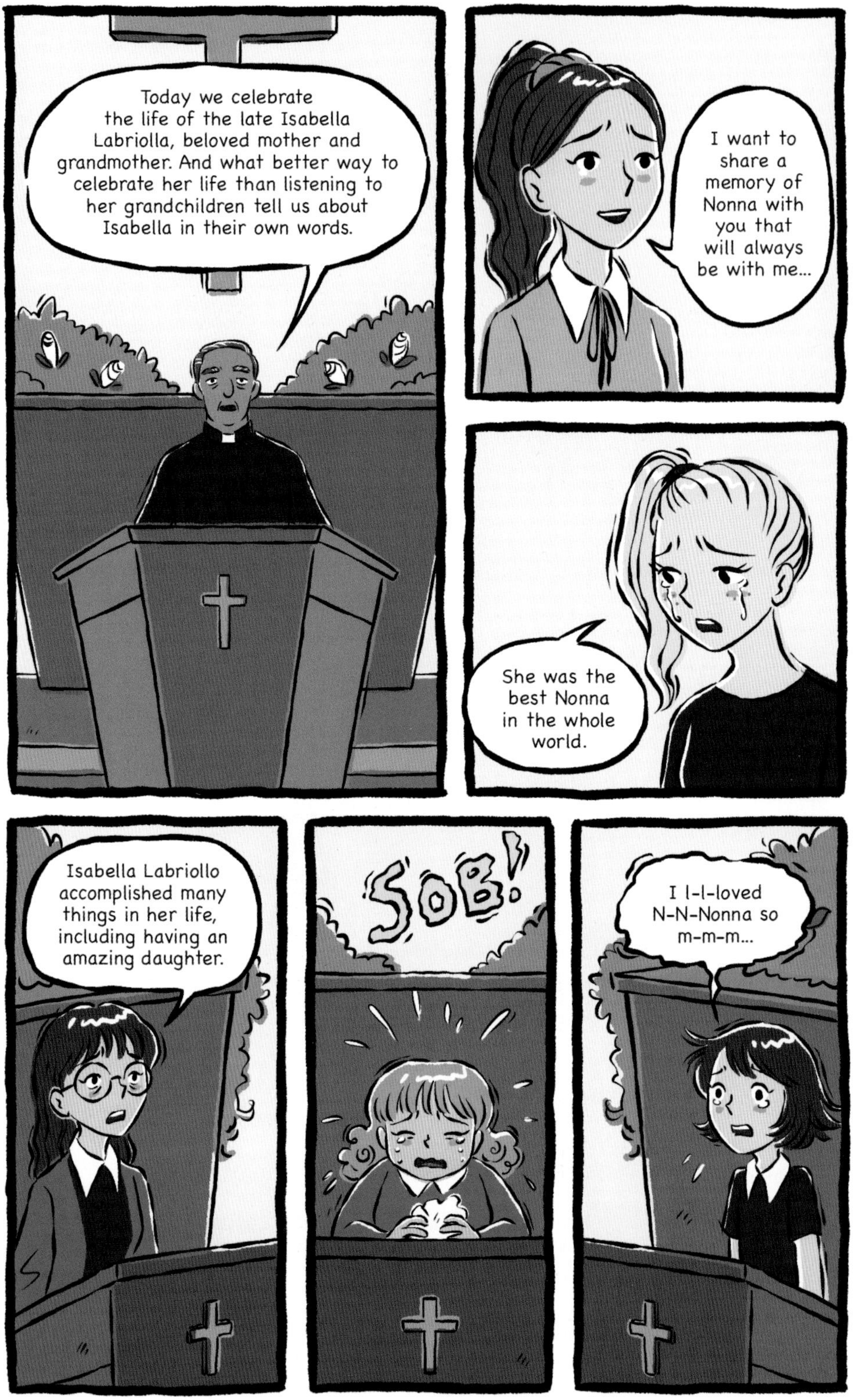
Today we celebrate the life of the late Isabella Labriolla, beloved mother and grandmother. And what better way to celebrate her life than listening to her grandchildren tell us about Isabella in their own words.
I want to share a memory of Nonna with you that will always be with me...
She was the best Nonna in the whole world.
Isabella Labriollo accomplished many things in her life, including having an amazing daughter.
SOB!
I l-l-loved N-N-Nonna so m-m-m...

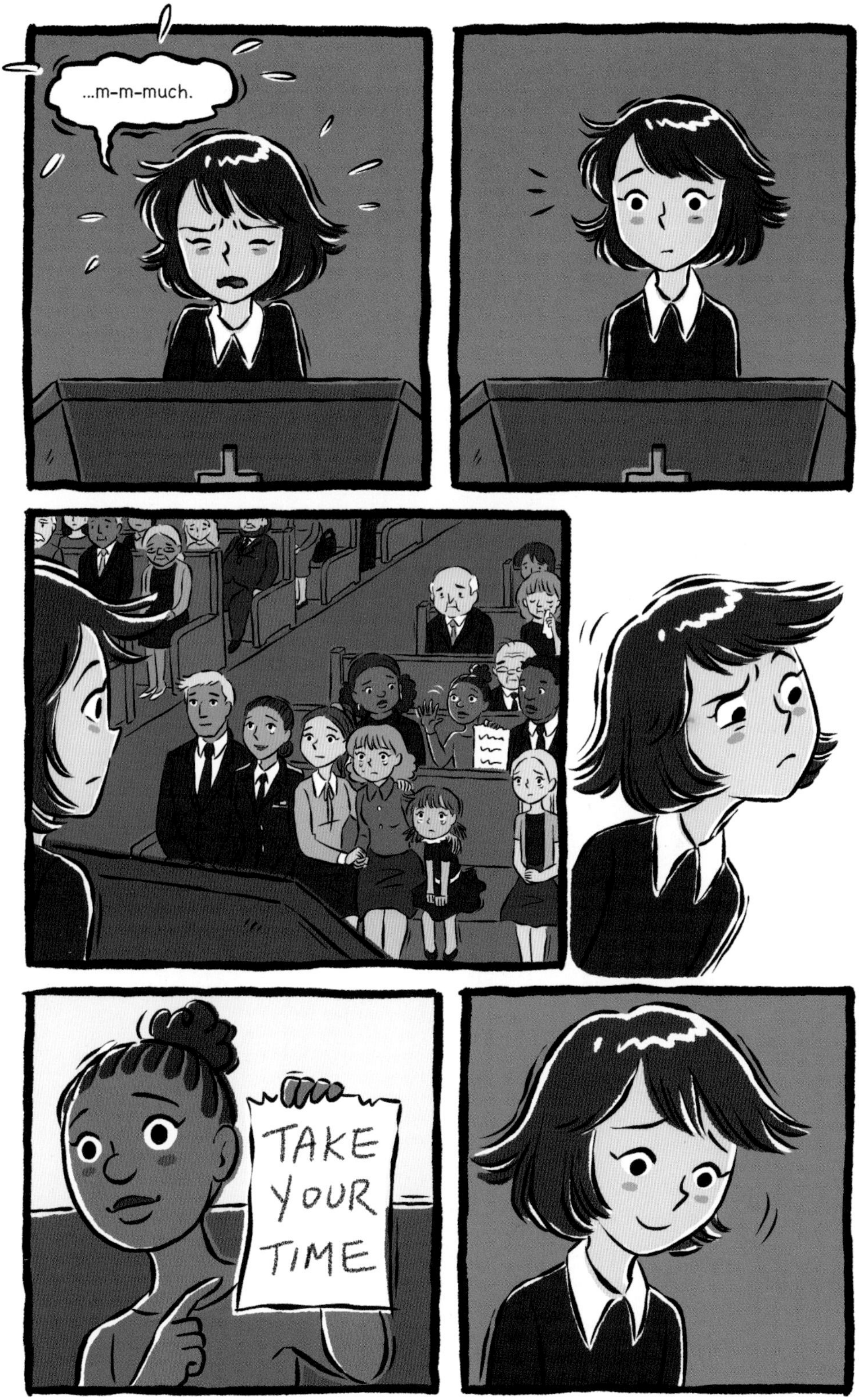
...m-m-much.
TAKE YOUR TIME

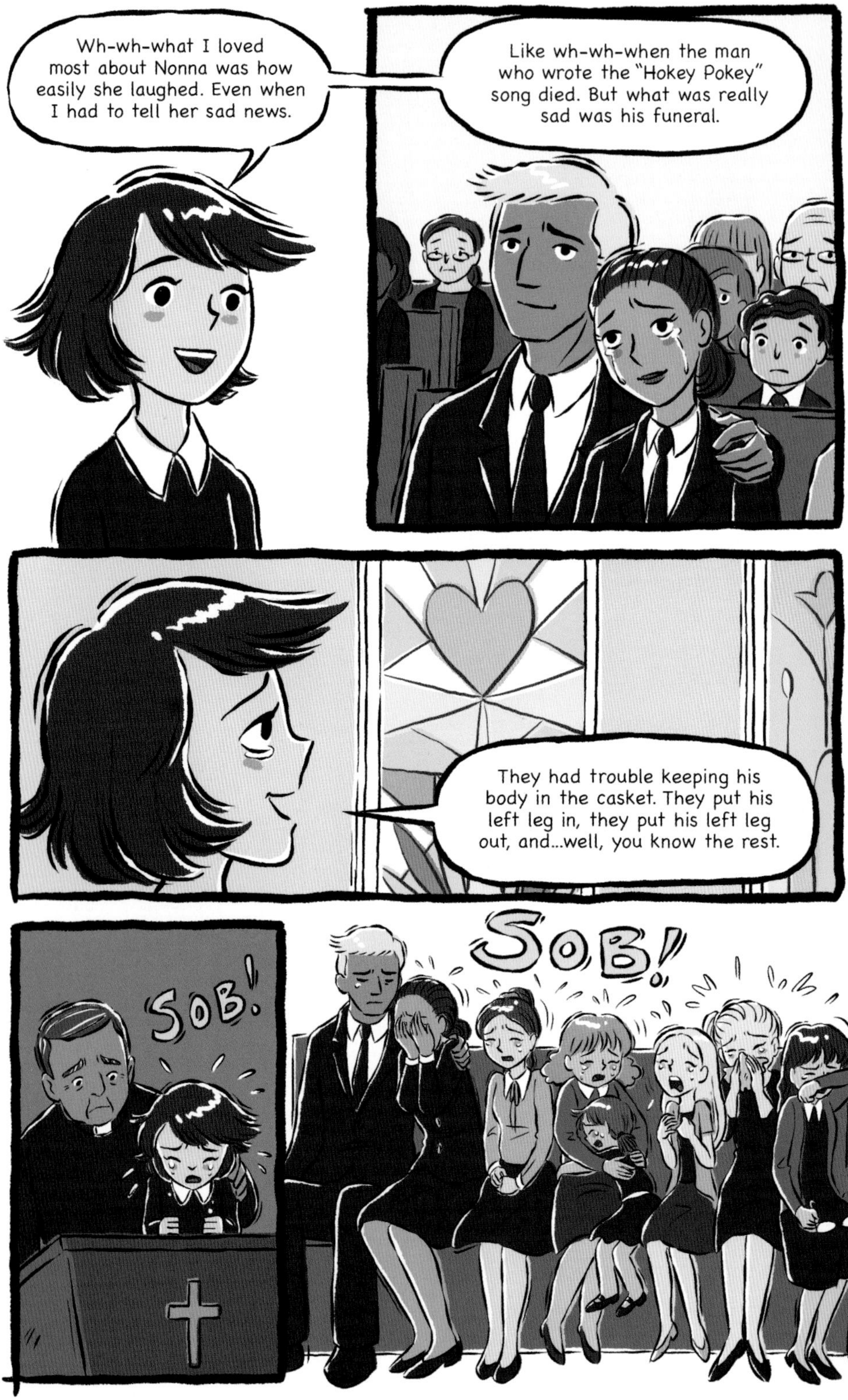
Wh-wh-what I loved most about Nonna was how easily she laughed. Even when I had to tell her sad news.
Like wh-wh-when the man who wrote the "Hokey Pokey" song died. But what was really sad was his funeral.
They had trouble keeping his body in the casket. They put his left leg in, they put his left leg out, and...well, you know the rest.
SOB!
SOB!

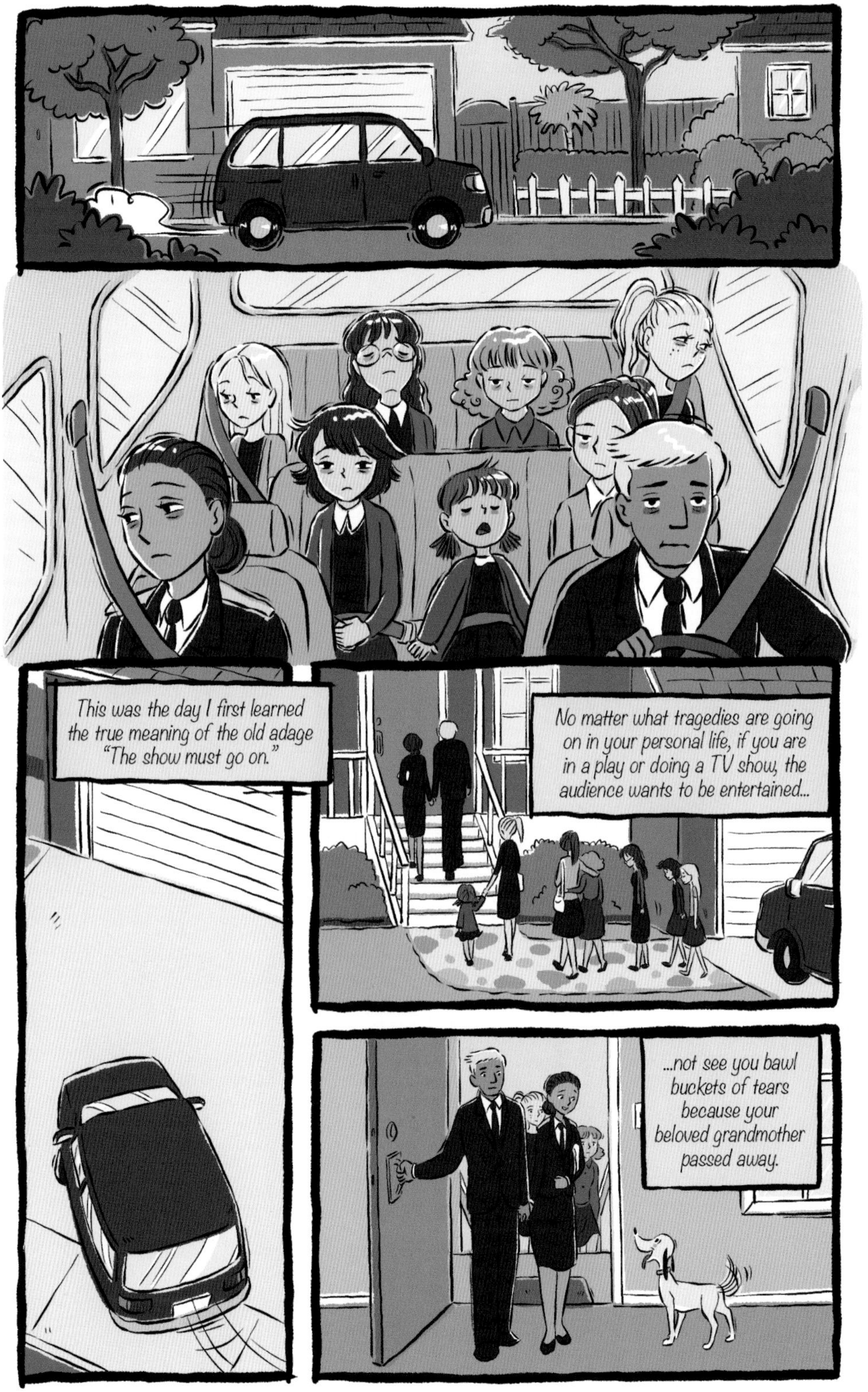
This was the day I first learned the true meaning of the old adage "The show must go on."
No matter what tragedies are going on in your personal life, if you are in a play or doing a TV show, the audience wants to be entertained...
...not see you bawl buckets of tears because your beloved grandmother passed away.

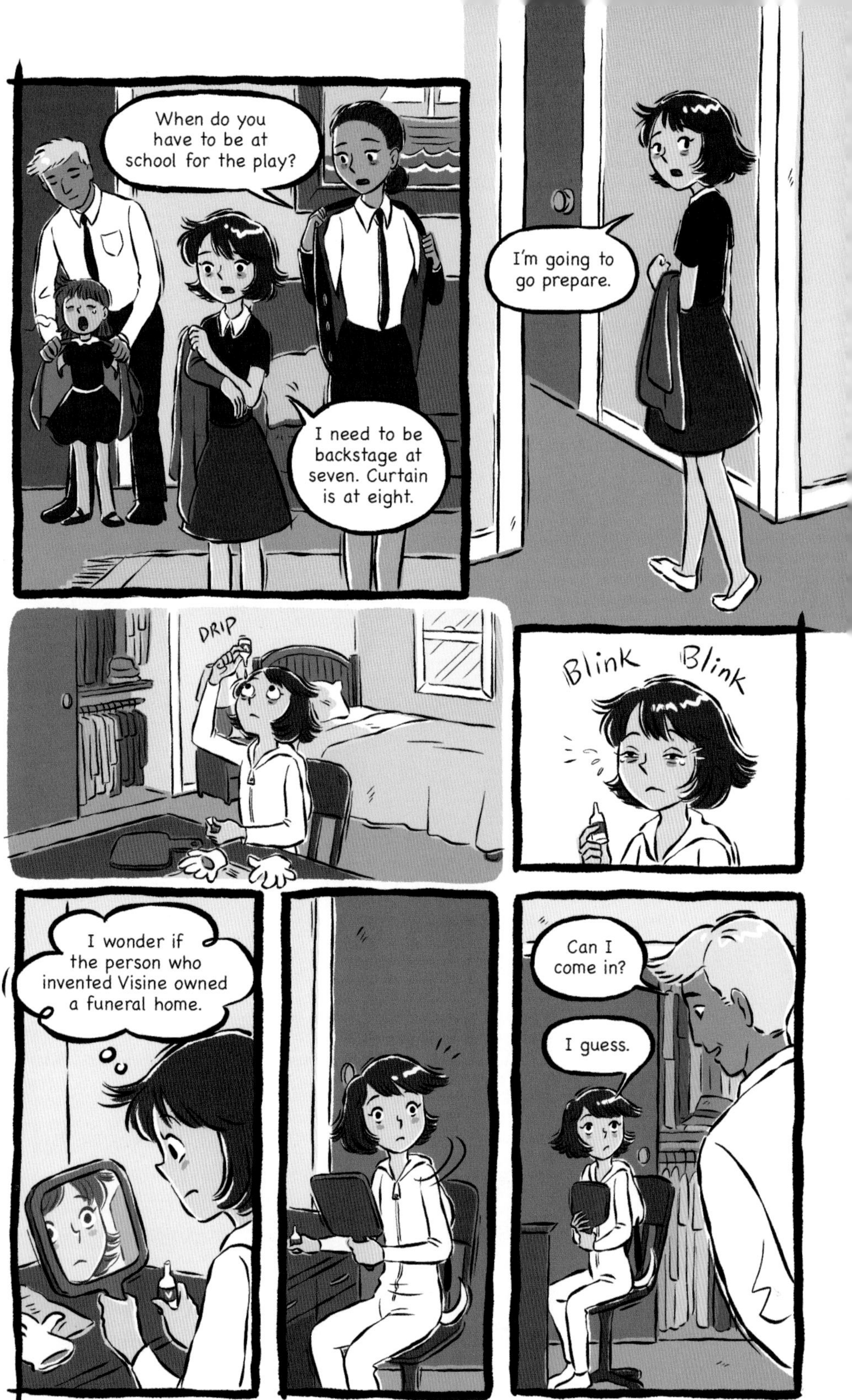
When do you have to be at school for the play?
I need to be backstage at seven. Curtain is at eight.
I'm going to go prepare.
DRIP
Blink Blink
I wonder if the person who invented Visine owned a funeral home.
Can I come in?
I guess.

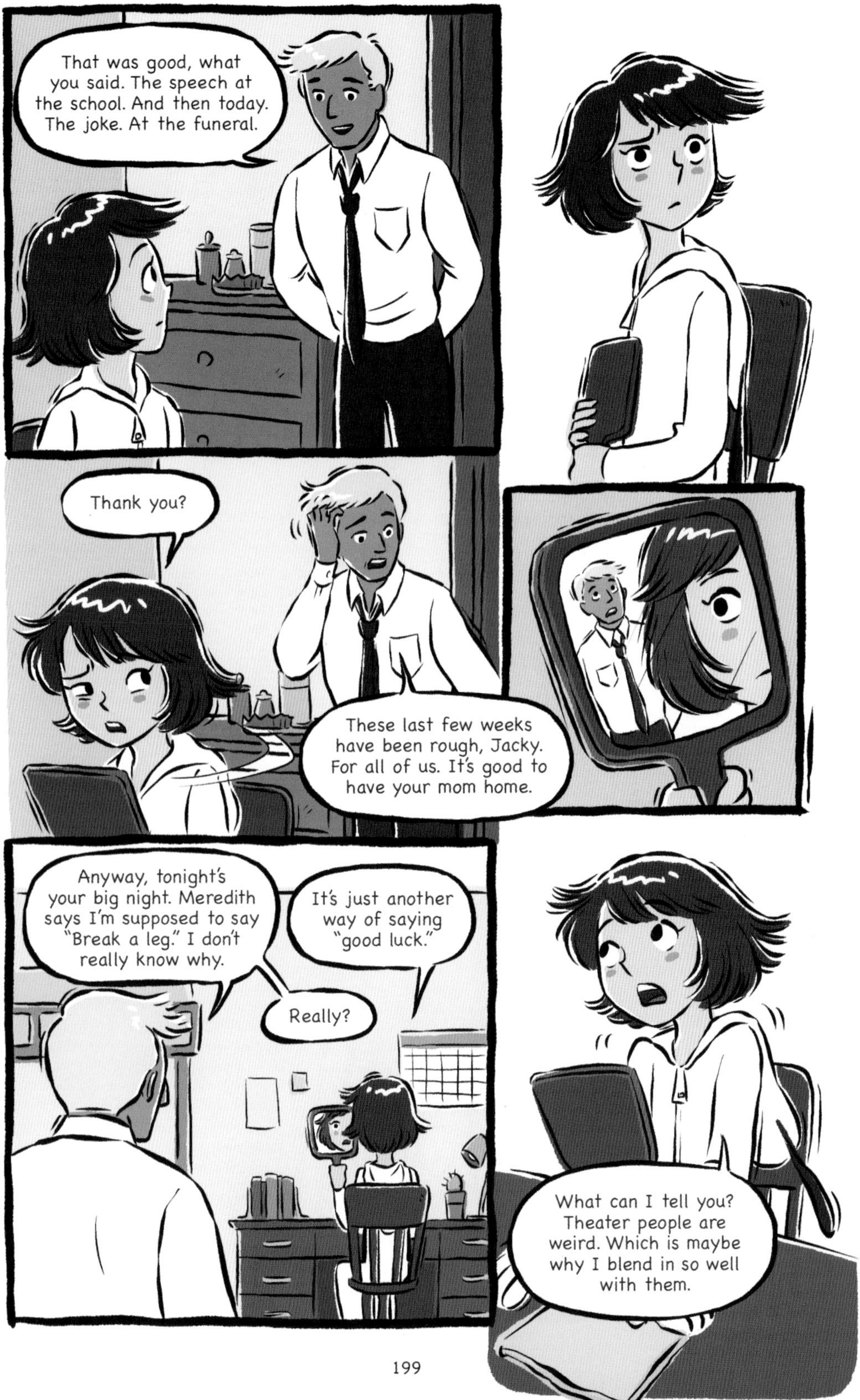
That was good, what you said. The speech at the school. And then today. The joke. At the funeral.
Thank you?
These last few weeks have been rough, Jacky. For all of us. It's good to have your mom home.
Anyway, tonight's your big night. Meredith says I'm supposed to say "Break a leg." I don't really know why.
It's just another way of saying "good luck."
Really?
What can I tell you? Theater people are weird. Which is maybe why I blend in so well with them.

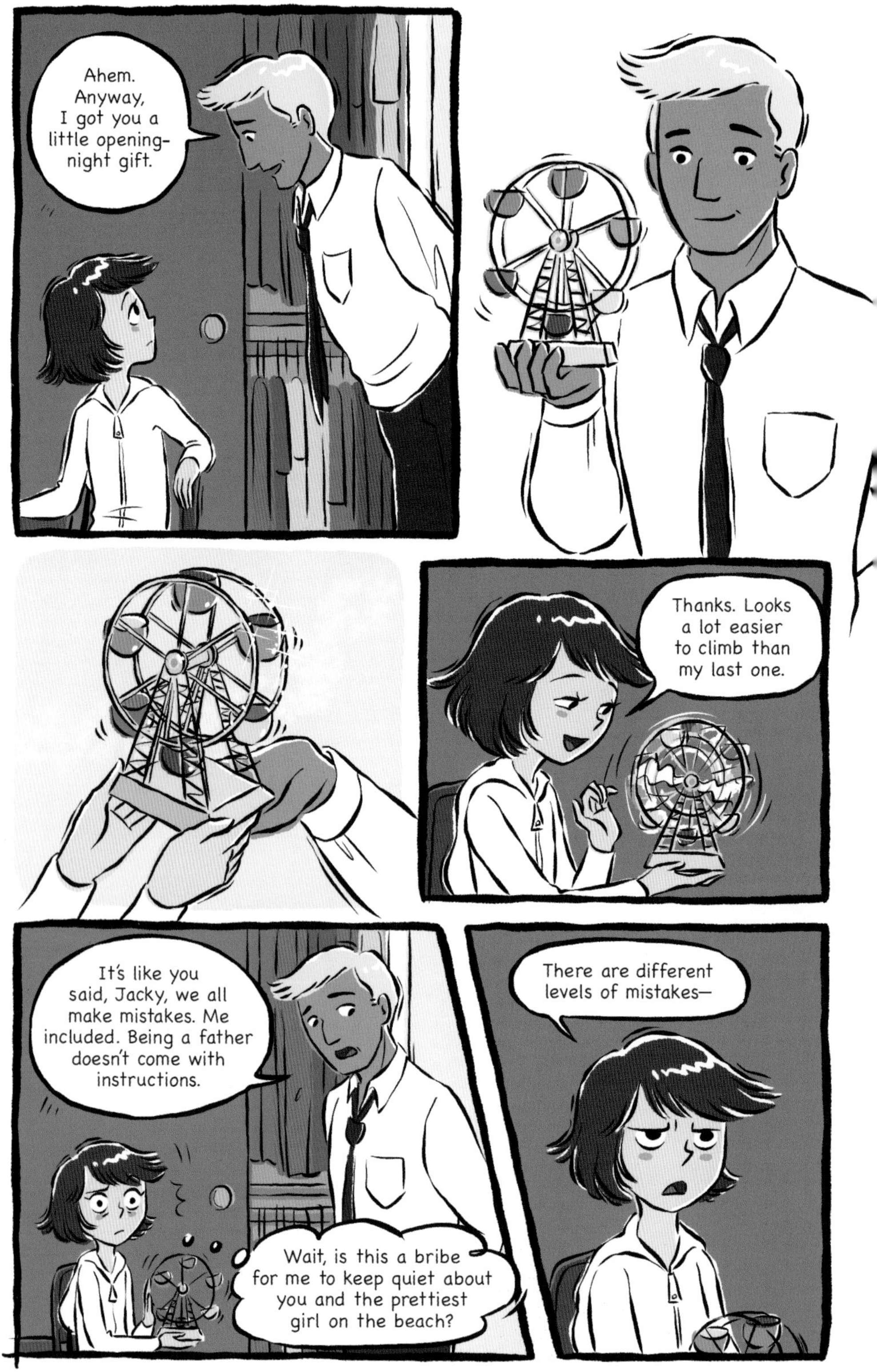
Ahem. Anyway, I got you a little opening-night gift.
Thanks. Looks a lot easier to climb than my last one.
It's like you said, Jacky, we all make mistakes. Me included. Being a father doesn't come with instructions.
Wait, is this a bribe for me to keep quiet about you and the prettiest girl on the beach?
There are different levels of mistakes—

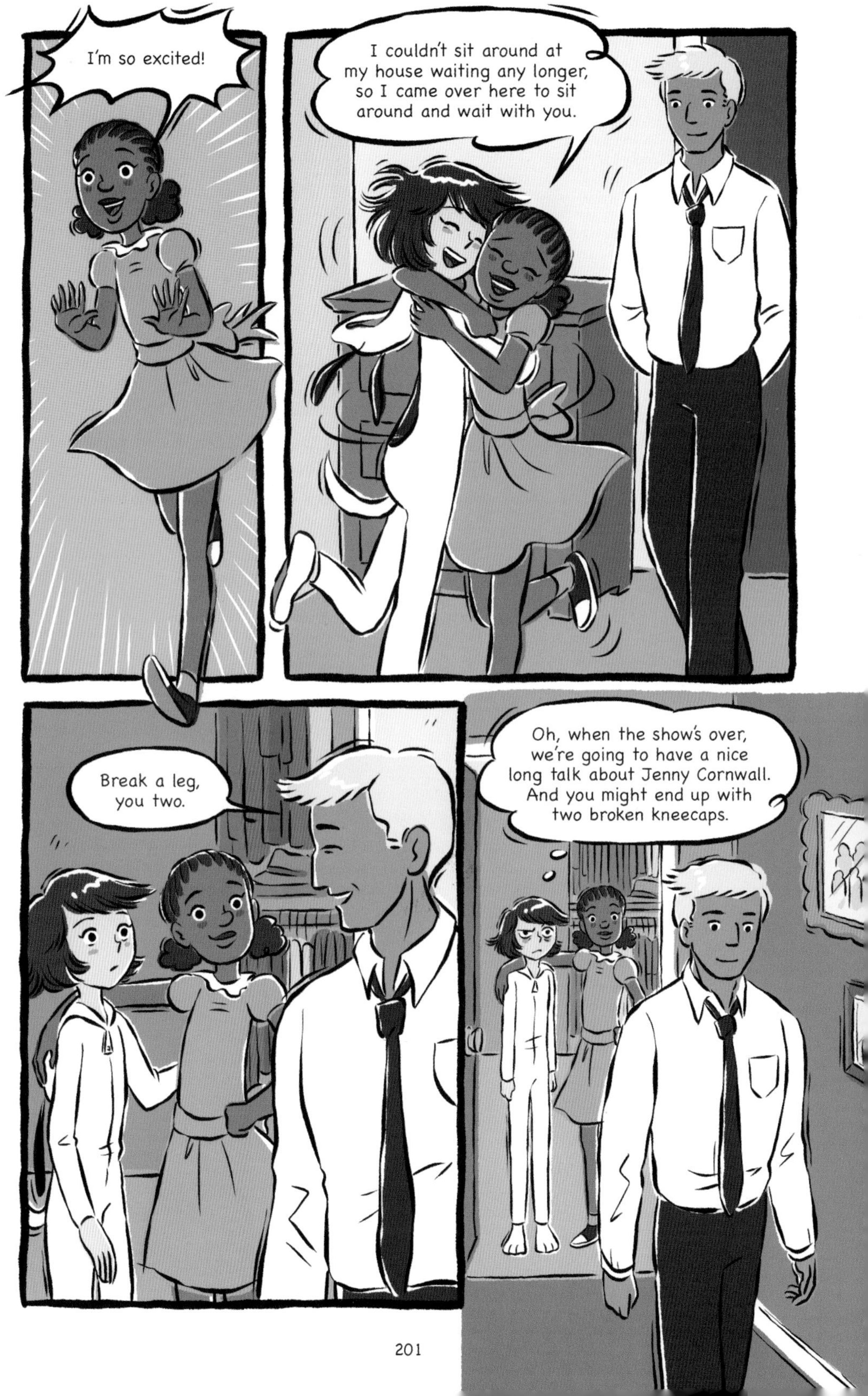
I'm so excited!
I couldn't sit around at my house waiting any longer, so I came over here to sit around and wait with you.
Break a leg, you two.
Oh, when the show's over, we're going to have a nice long talk about Jenny Cornwall. And you might end up with two broken kneecaps.

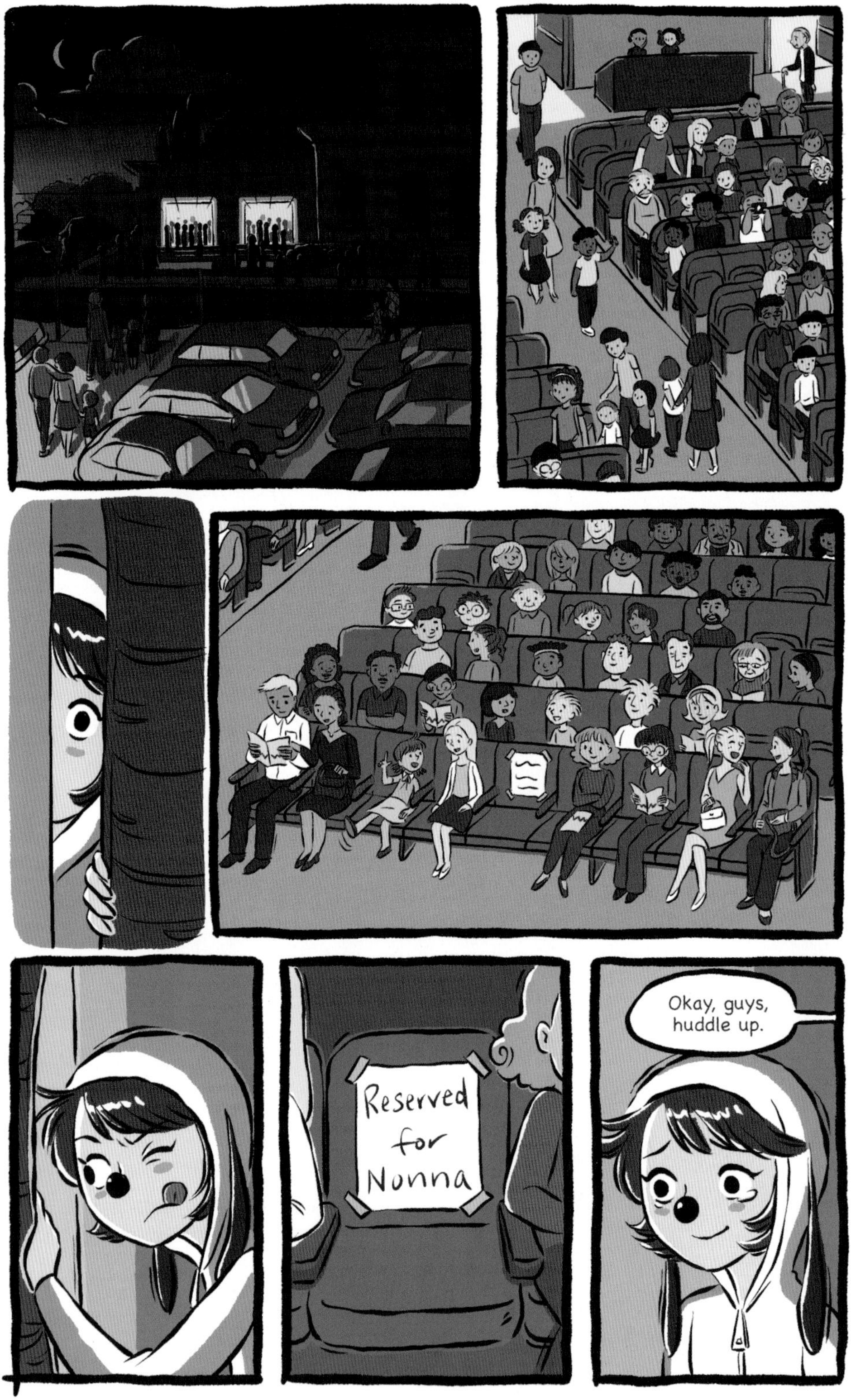
Reserved for Nonna
Okay, guys, huddle up.

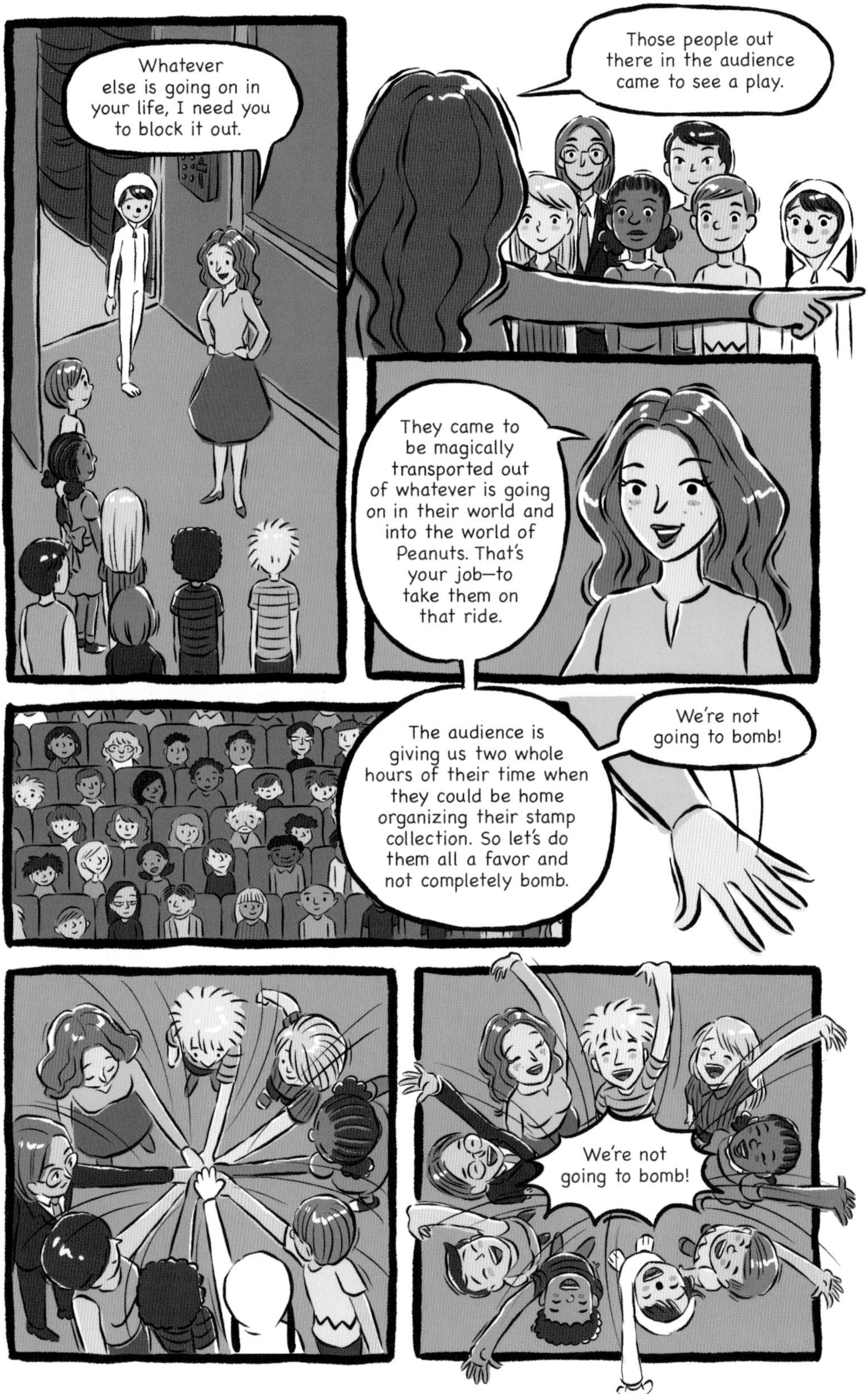
Whatever else is going on in your life, I need you to block it out.
Those people out there in the audience came to see a play.
They came to be magically transported out of whatever is going on in their world and into the world of Peanuts. That's your job—to take them on that ride.
The audience is giving us two whole hours of their time when they could be home organizing their stamp collection. So let's do them all a favor and not completely bomb.
We're not going to bomb!
We're not going to bomb!

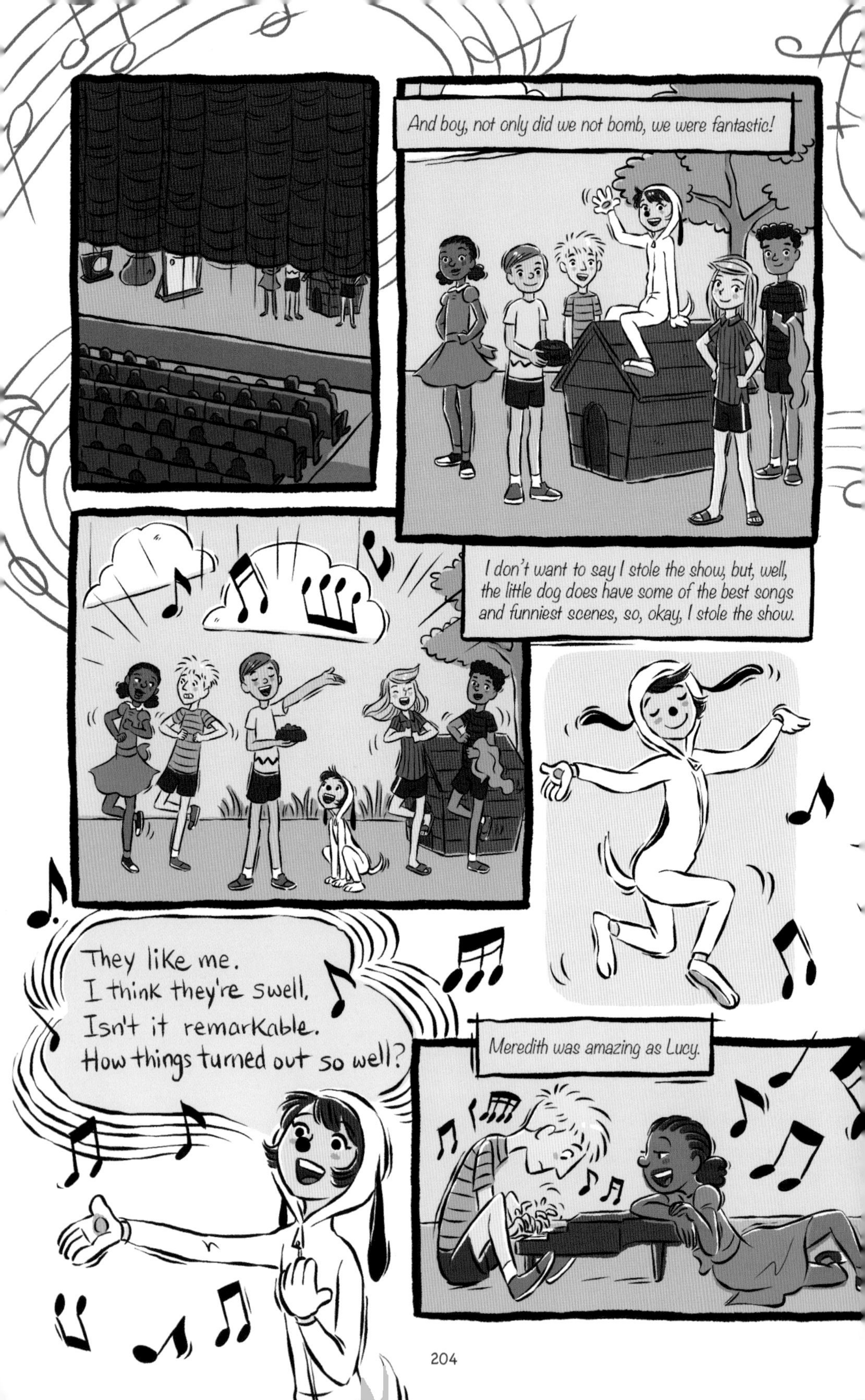
And boy, not only did we not bomb, we were fantastic!
I don't want to say I stole the show, but, well, the little dog does have some of the best songs and funniest scenes, so, okay, I stole the show.
They like me.
I think they're swell.
Isn't it remarkable.
How things turned out so well?
Meredith was amazing as Lucy.

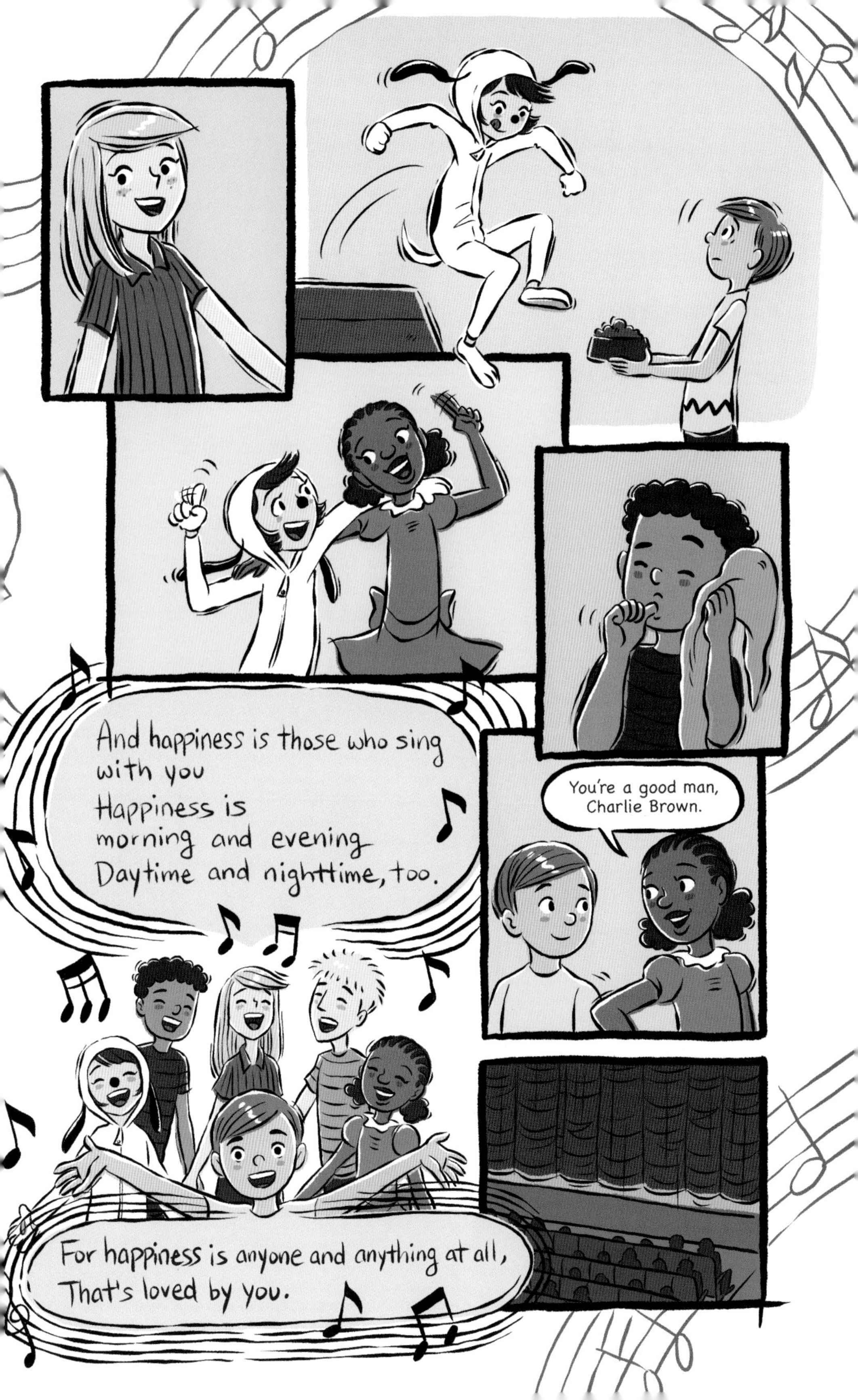
And happiness is those who sing with you
Happiness is
morning and evening
Daytime and nighttime, too.
You're a good man, Charlie Brown.
For happiness is anyone and anything at all,
That's loved by you.

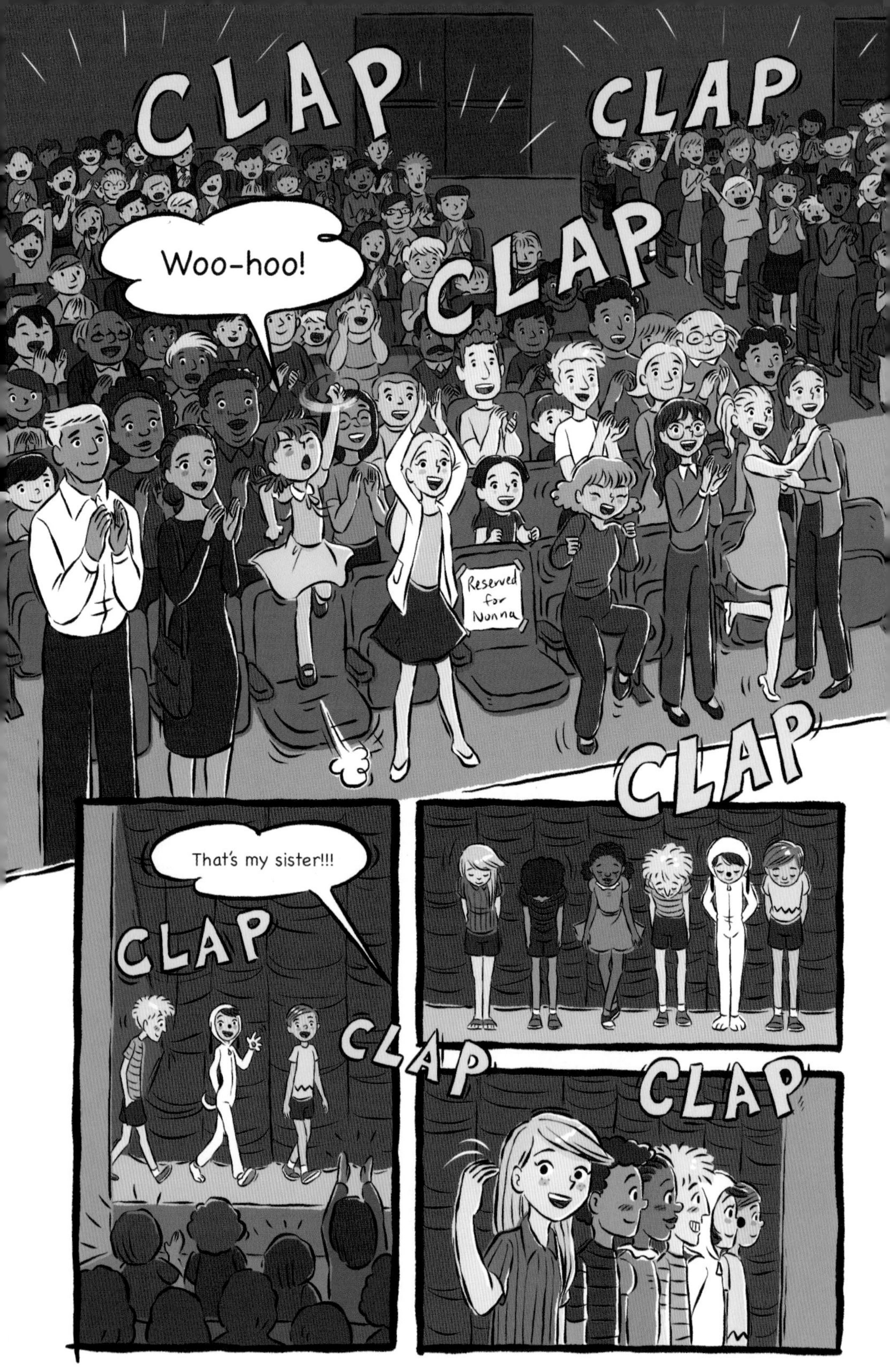
CLAP
CLAP
Woo-hoo!
CLAP
Reserved for Nonna
CLAP
That's my sister!!!
CLAP
CLAP
CLAP

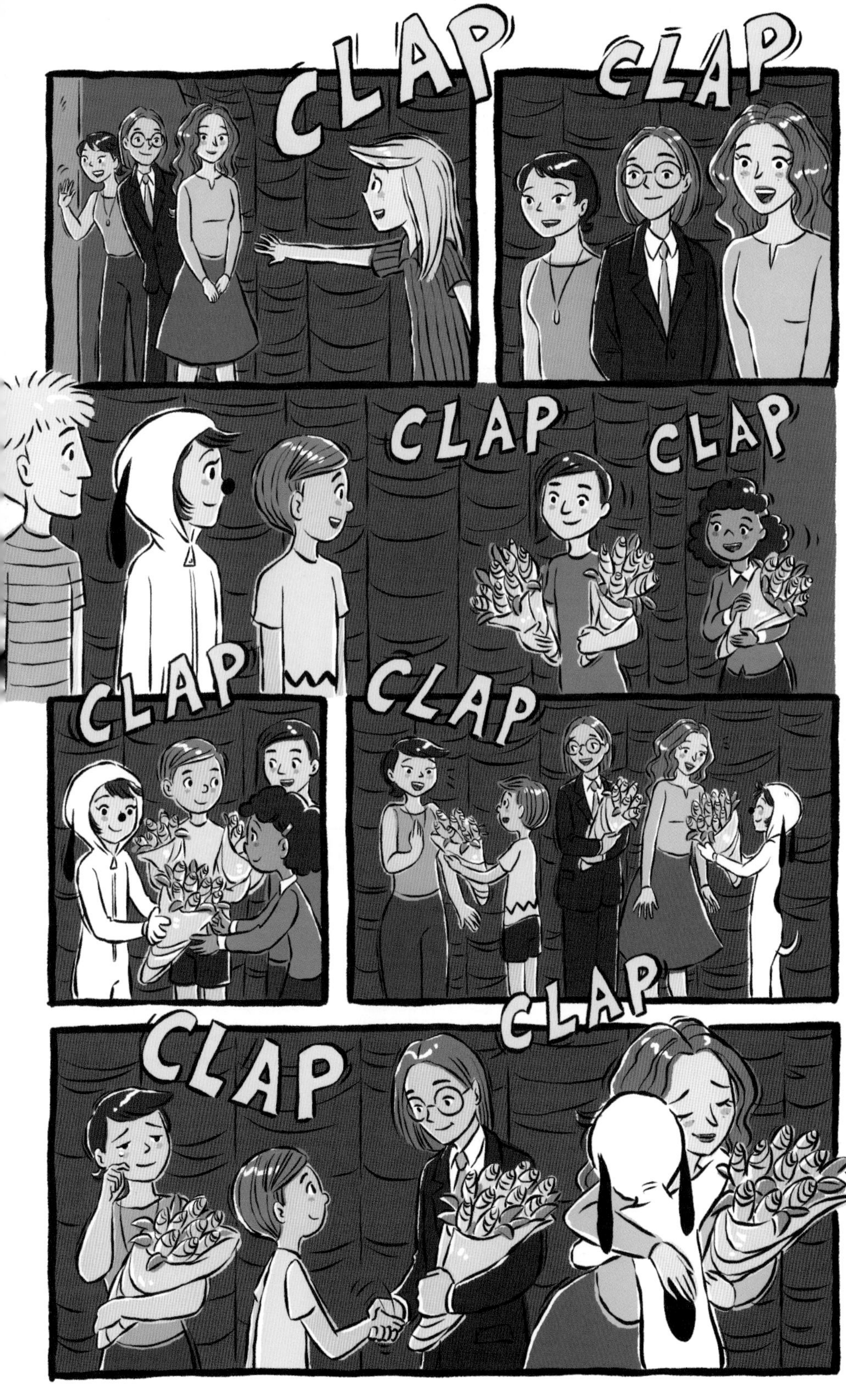
CLAP
CLAP
CLAP
CLAP
CLAP
CLAP
CLAP
CLAP

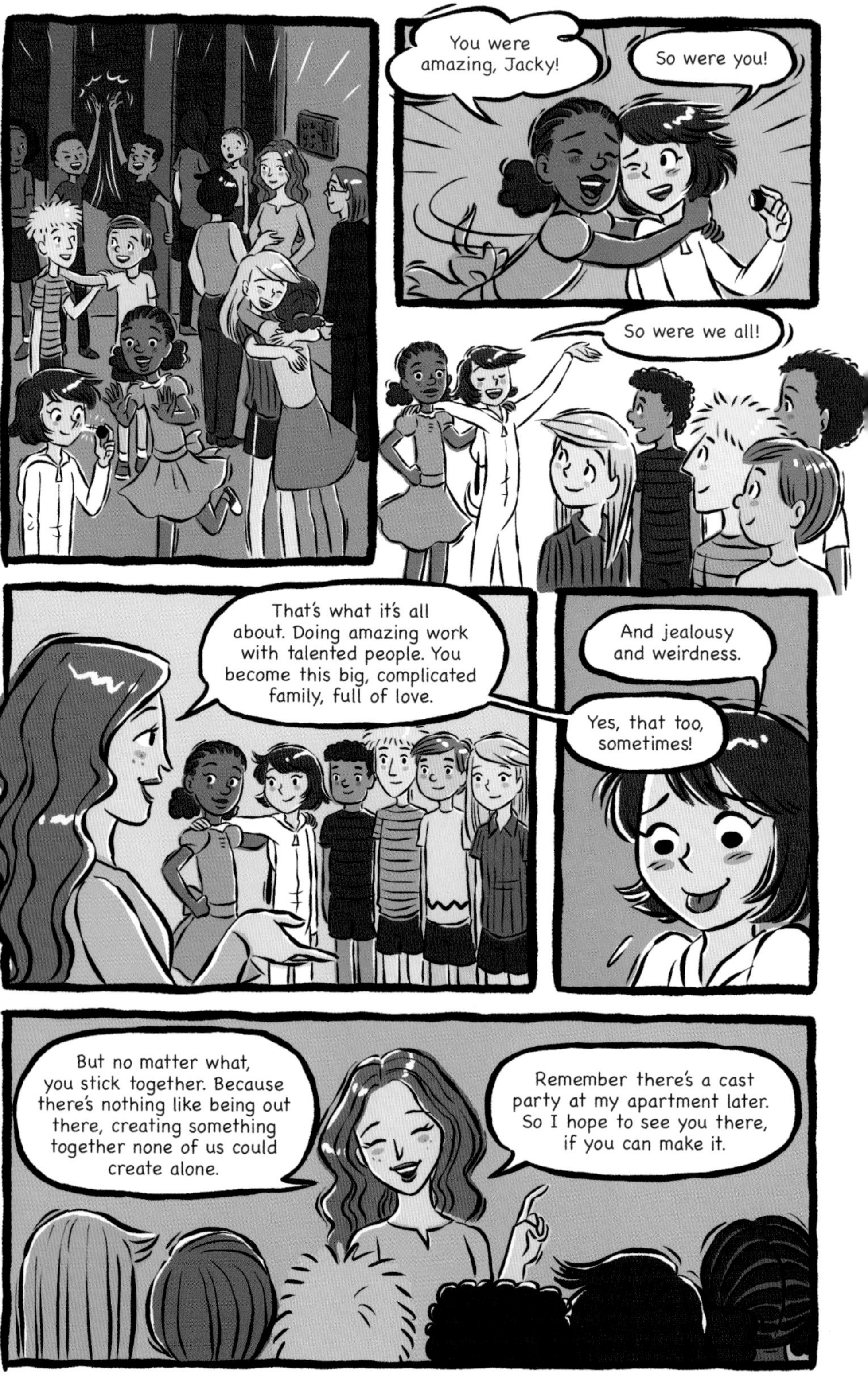
You were amazing, Jacky!
So were you!
So were we all!
That's what it's all about. Doing amazing work with talented people. You become this big, complicated family, full of love.
And jealousy and weirdness.
Yes, that too, sometimes!
But no matter what, you stick together. Because there's nothing like being out there, creating something together none of us could create alone.
Remember there's a cast party at my apartment later. So I hope to see you there, if you can make it.

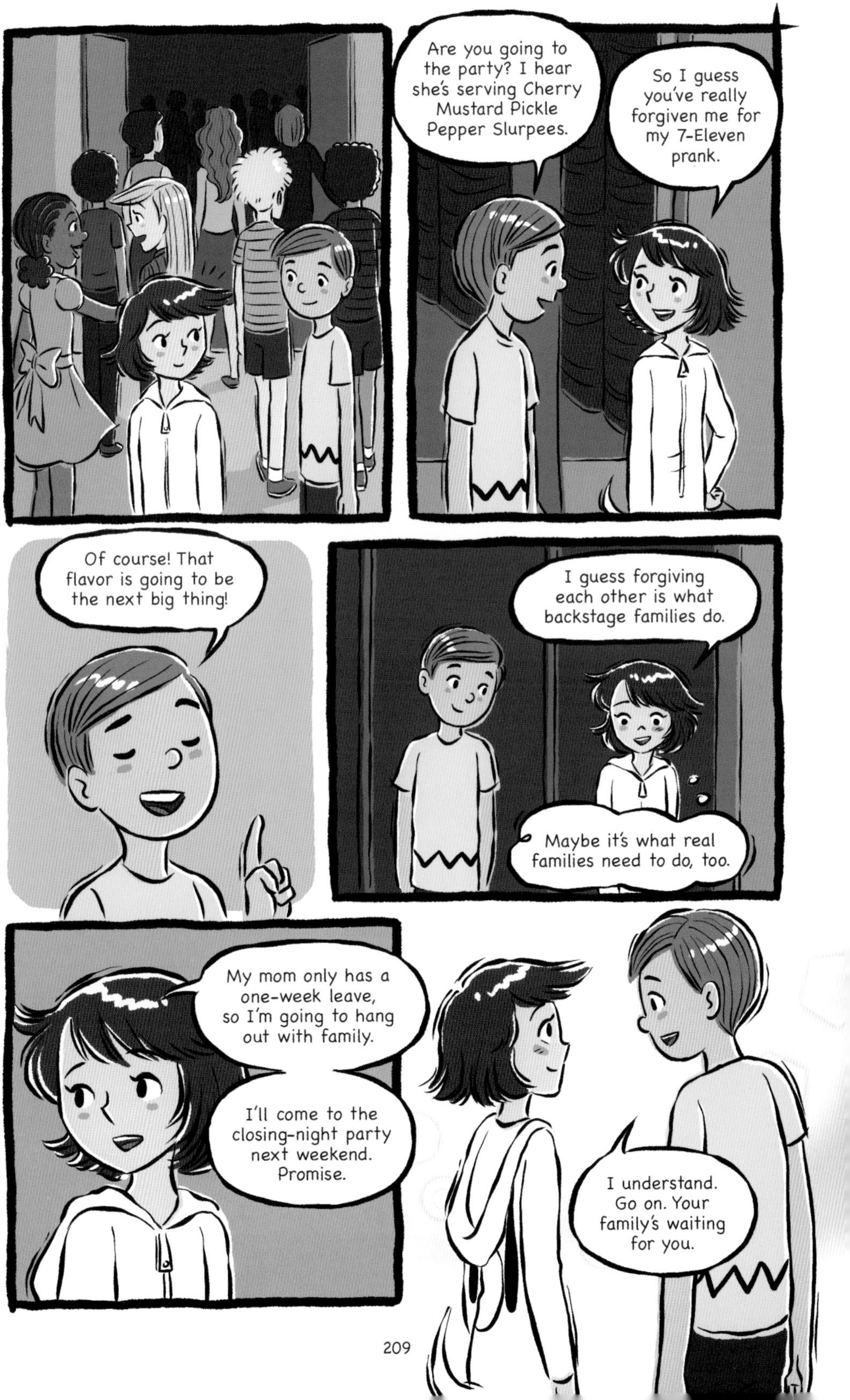

Are you going to the party? I hear she's serving Cherry Mustard Pickle Pepper Slurpees.
So I guess you've really forgiven me for my 7-Eleven prank.
Of course! That flavor is going to be the next big thing!
I guess forgiving each other is what backstage families do.
Maybe it's what real families need to do, too.
My mom only has a one-week leave, so I'm going to hang out with family.
I'll come to the closing-night party next weekend. Promise.
I understand. Go on. Your family's waiting for you.

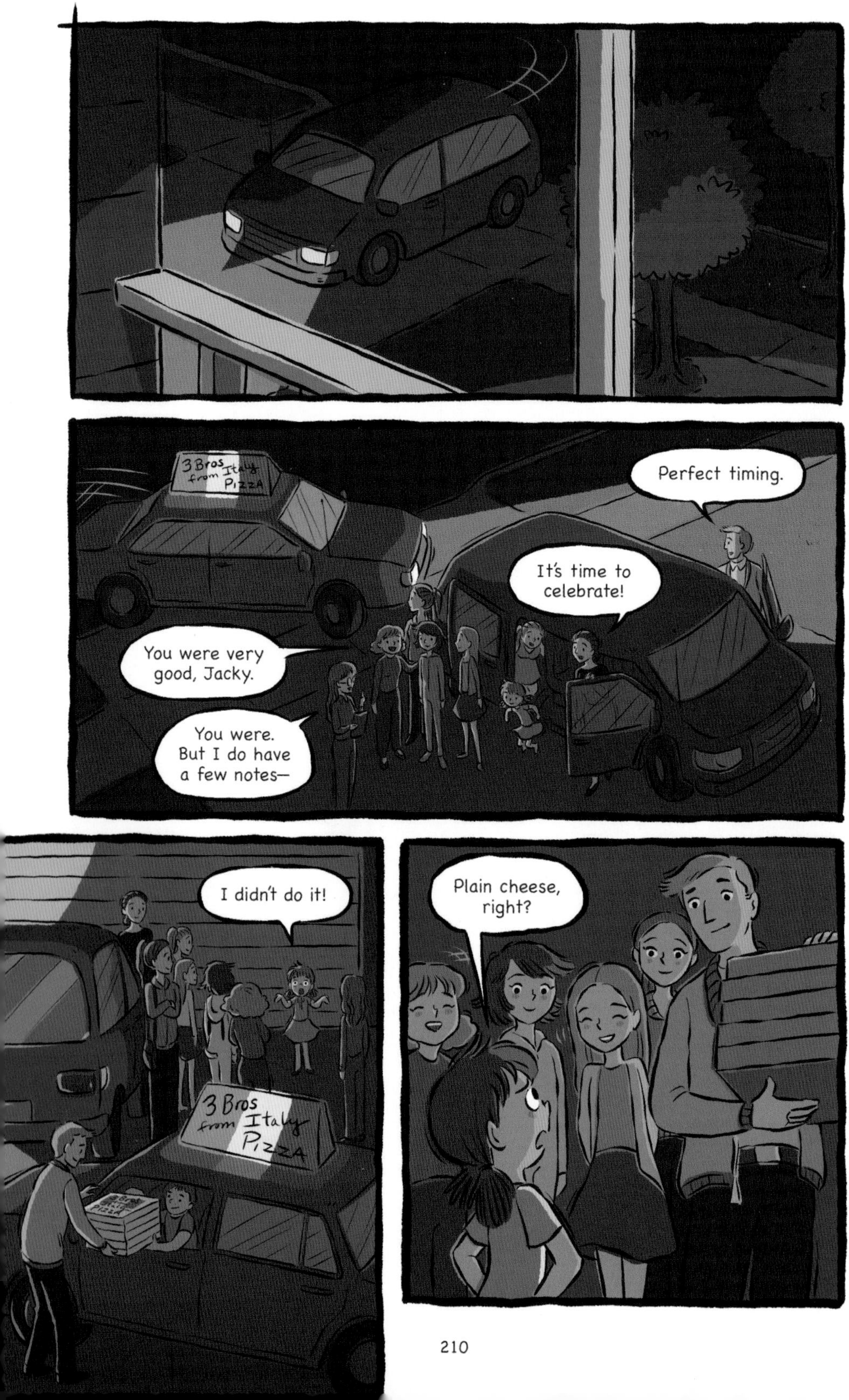
3 Bros from Italy PIZZA
Perfect timing.
It's time to celebrate!
You were very good, Jacky.
You were. But I do have a few notes—
I didn't do it!
3 Bros from Italy PIZZA
Plain cheese, right?

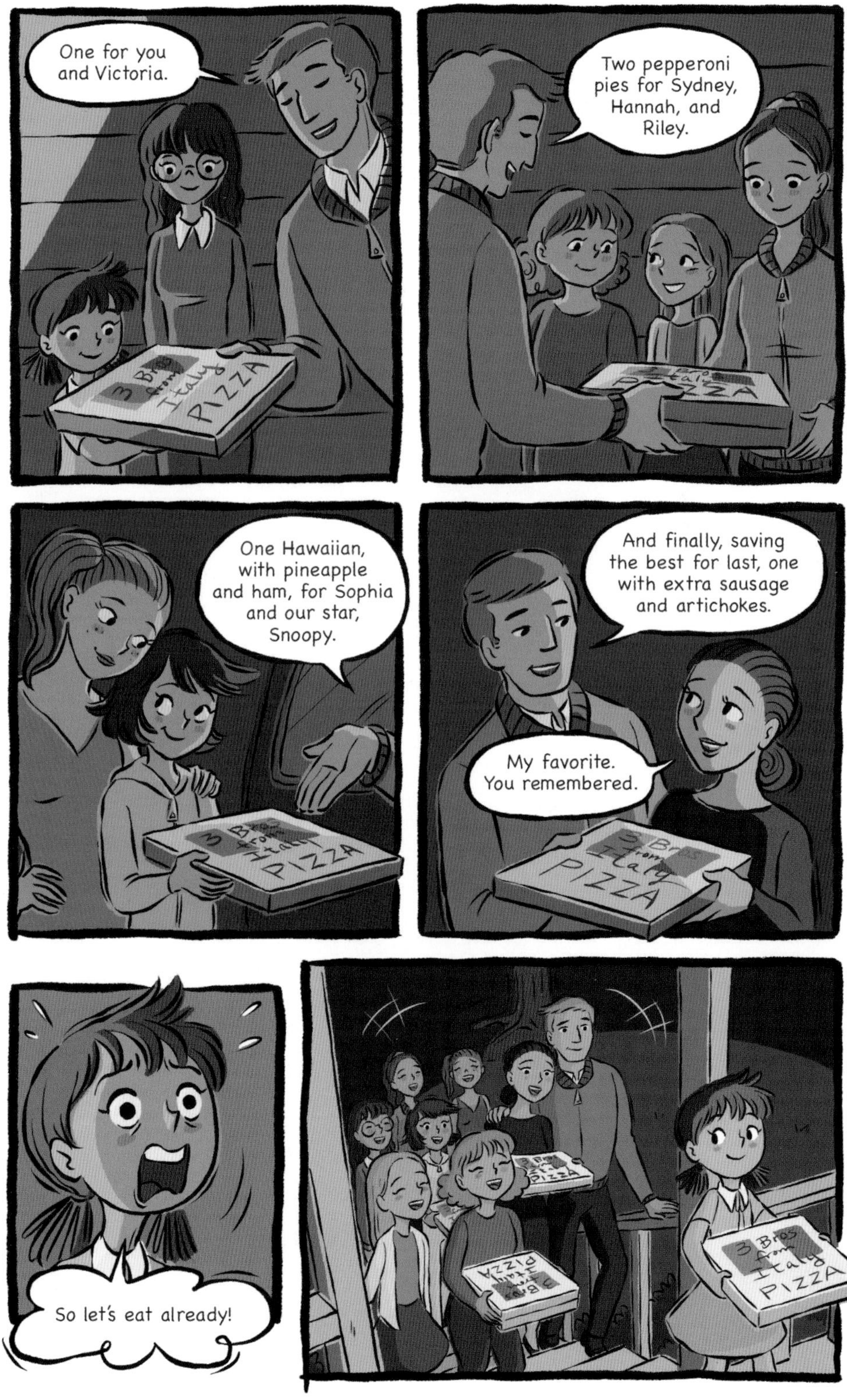
One for you and Victoria.
3 Bros from Italy PIZZA
Two pepperoni pies for Sydney, Hannah, and Riley.
One Hawaiian, with pineapple and ham, for Sophia and our star, Snoopy.
And finally, saving the best for last, one with extra sausage and artichokes.
My favorite. You remembered.
So let's eat already!

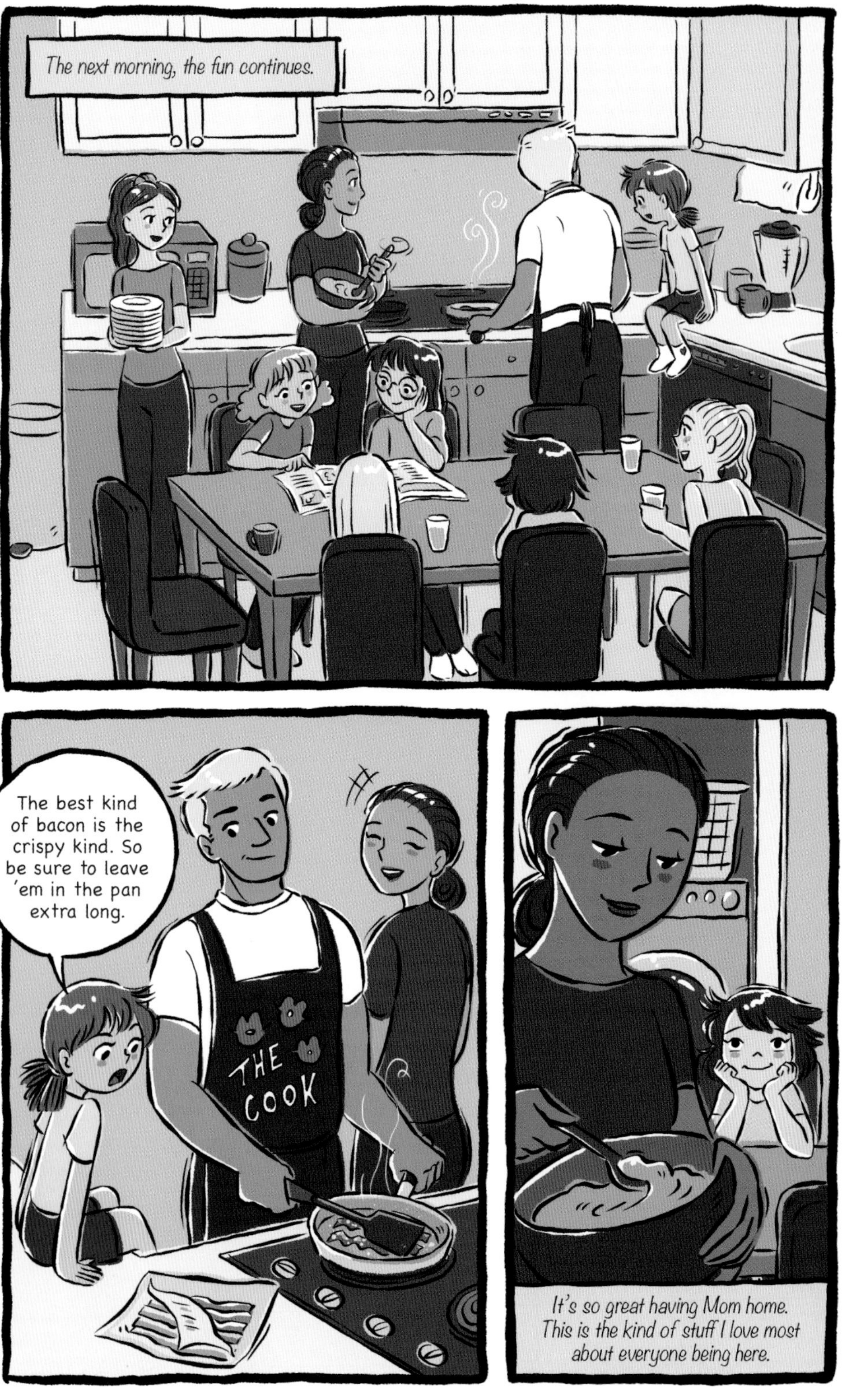

The next morning, the fun continues.
THE COOK
The best kind of bacon is the crispy kind. So be sure to leave 'em in the pan extra long.
It's so great having Mom home. This is the kind of stuff I love most about everyone being here.

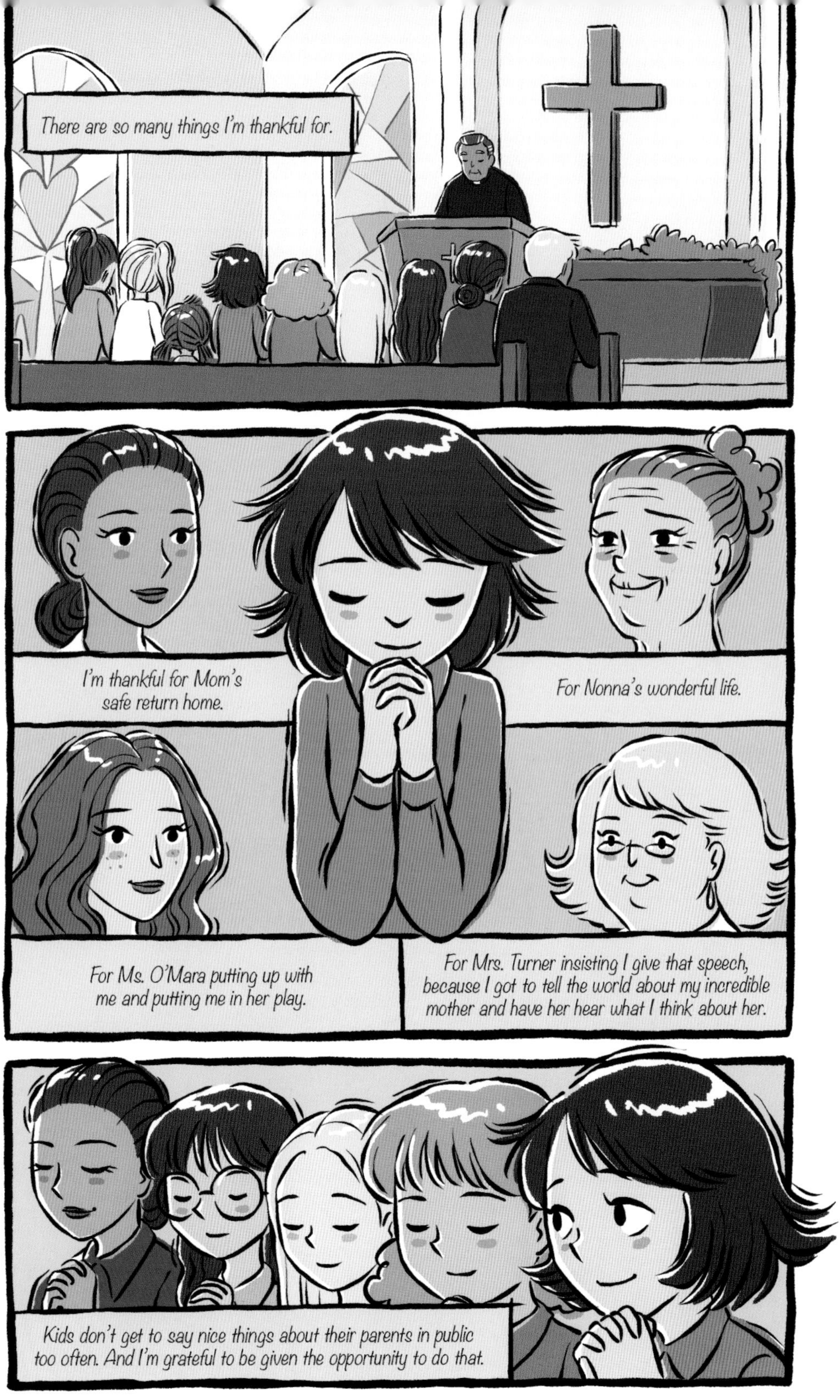
There are so many things I'm thankful for.
I'm thankful for Mom's safe return home.
For Nonna's wonderful life.
For Ms. O'Mara putting up with me and putting me in her play.
For Mrs. Turner insisting I give that speech, because I got to tell the world about my incredible mother and have her hear what I think about her.
Kids don't get to say nice things about their parents in public too often. And I'm grateful to be given the opportunity to do that.

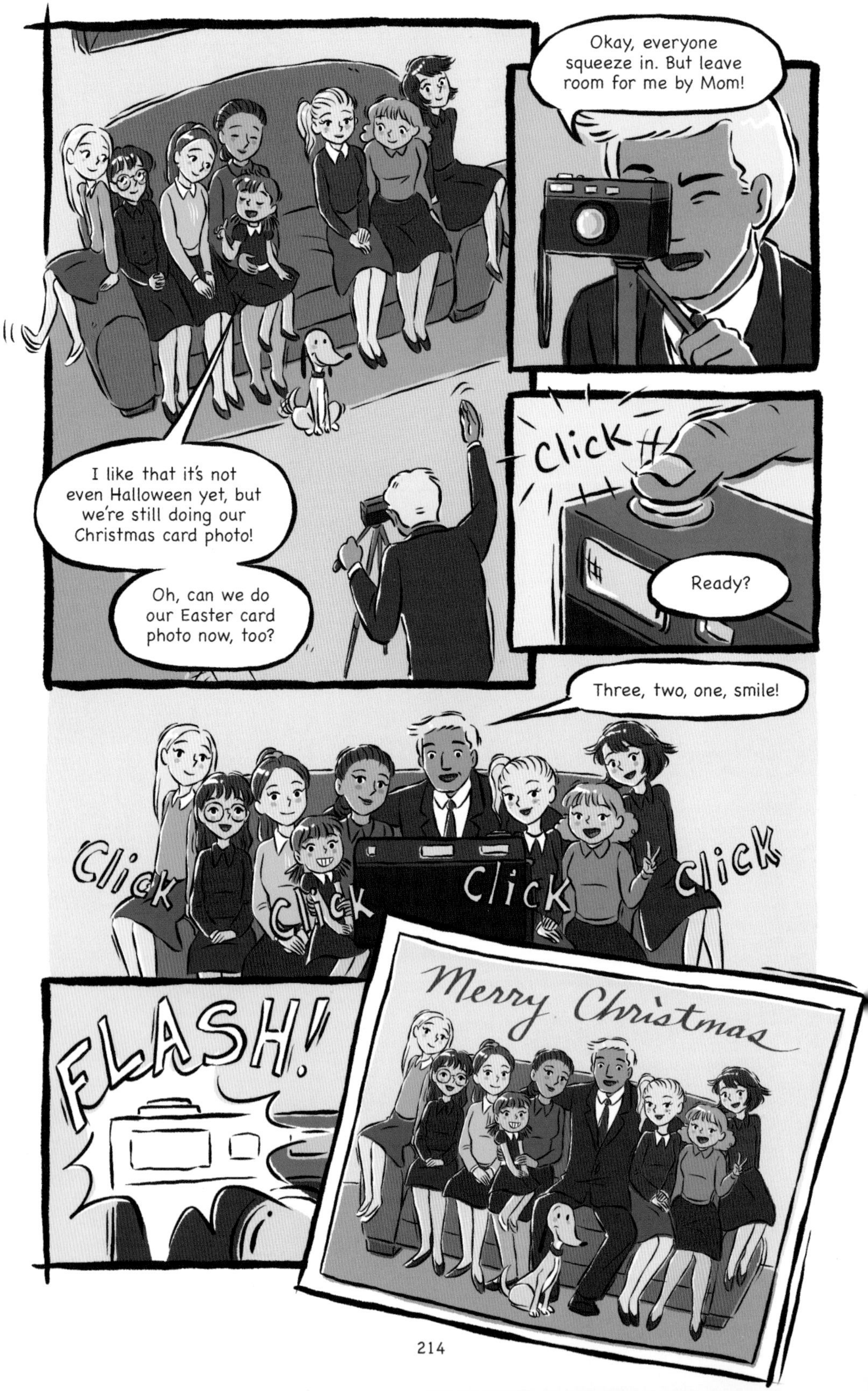
Okay, everyone squeeze in. But leave room for me by Mom!
I like that it's not even Halloween yet, but we're still doing our Christmas card photo!
Oh, can we do our Easter card photo now, too?
Click
Ready?
Three, two, one, smile!
Click
Click
Click
Click
FLASH!
Merry Christmas

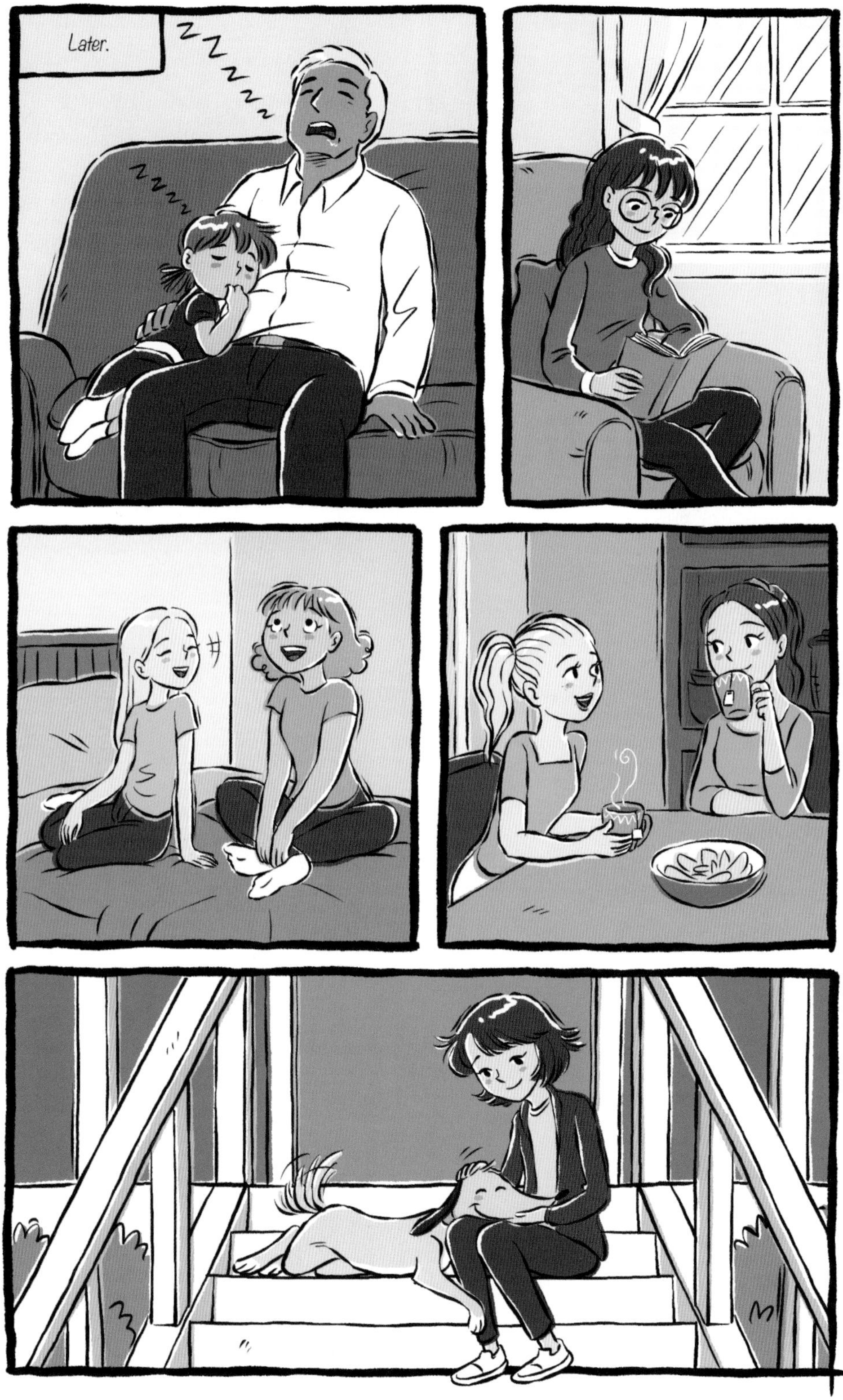
Later.
ZZZZZZ
ZZZZZ

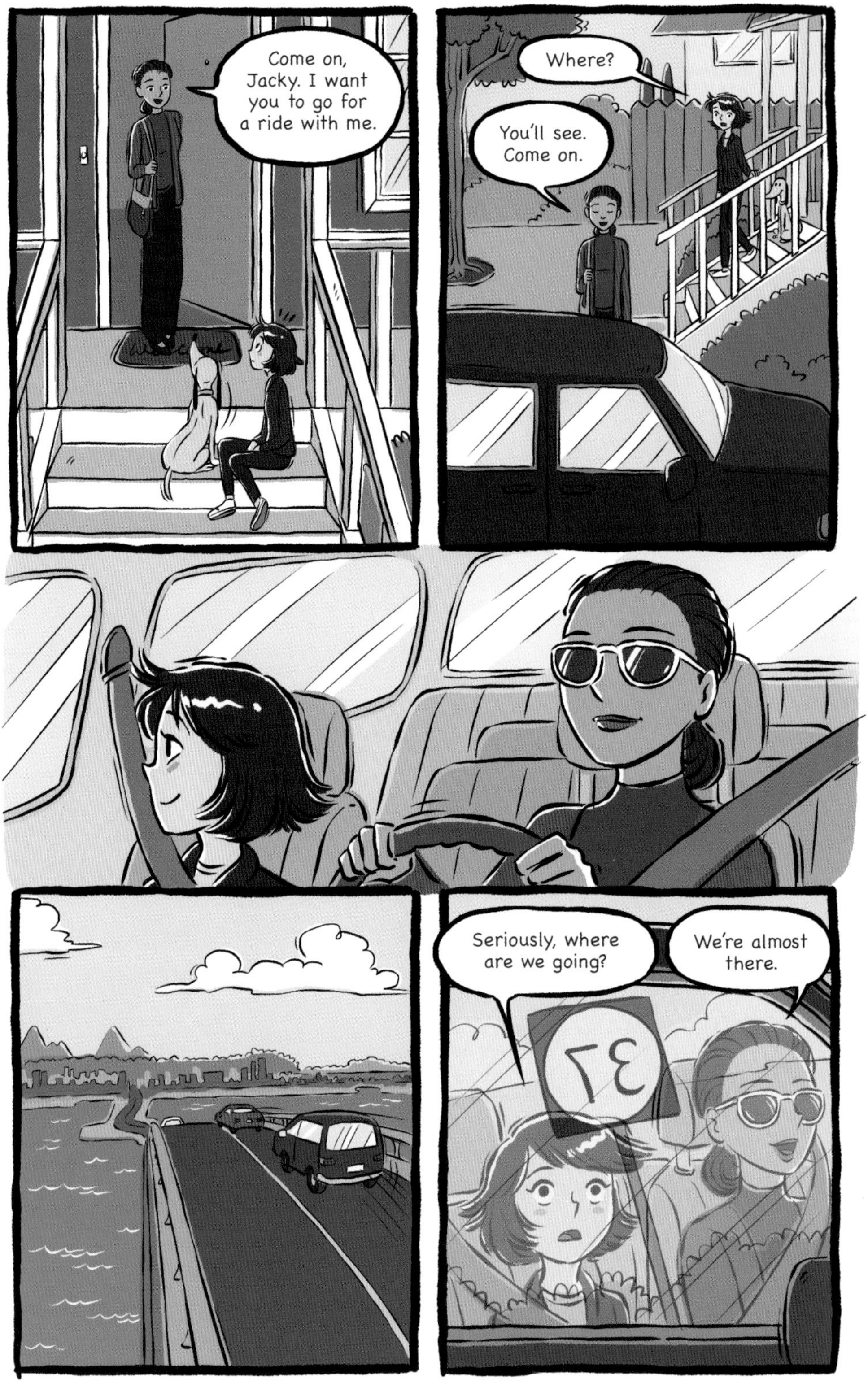
Come on, Jacky. I want you to go for a ride with me.
Where?
You'll see. Come on.
Seriously, where are we going?
We're almost there.
37

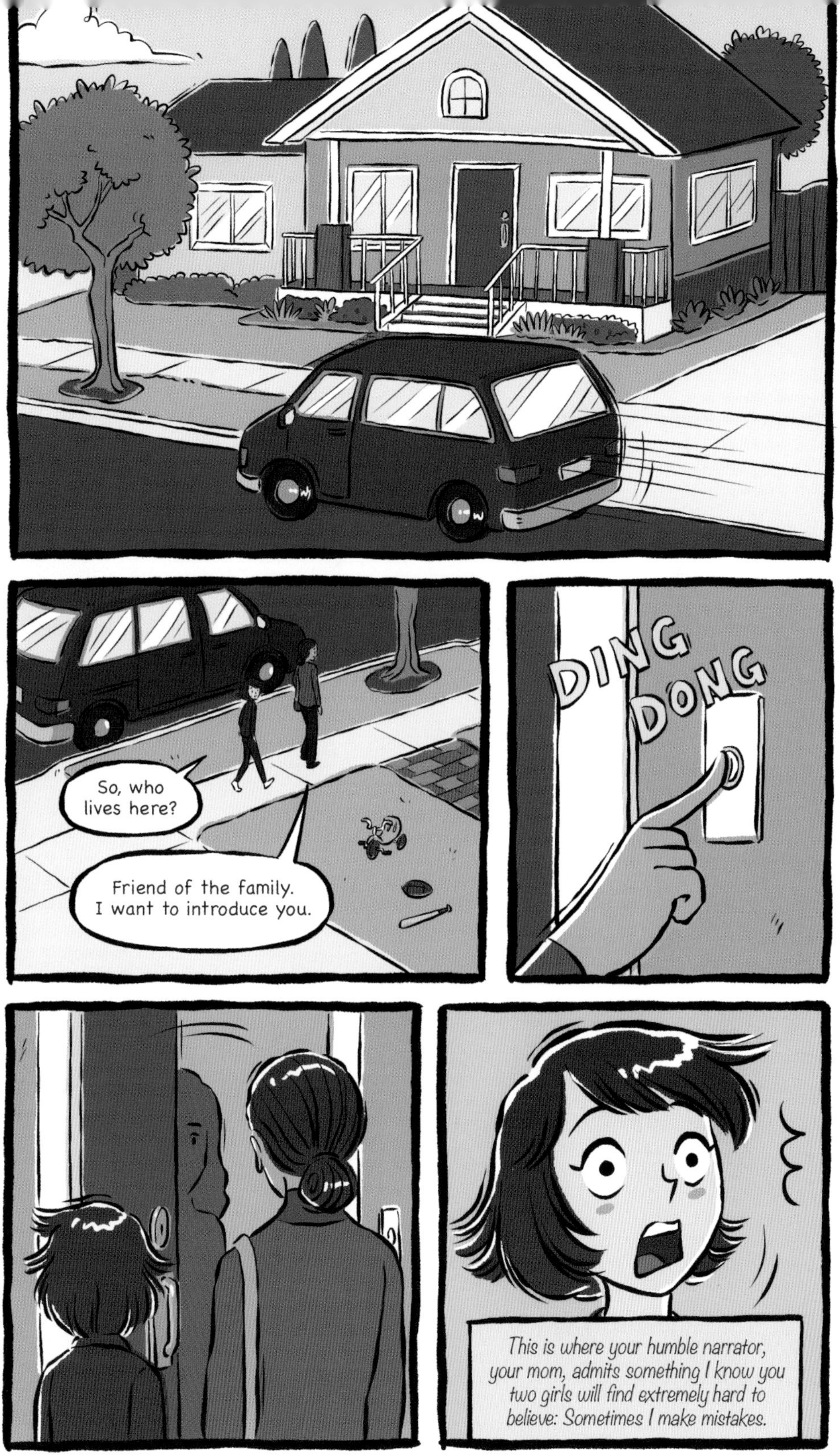
So, who lives here?
Friend of the family. I want to introduce you.
DING DONG
This is where your humble narrator, your mom, admits something I know you two girls will find extremely hard to believe: Sometimes I make mistakes.

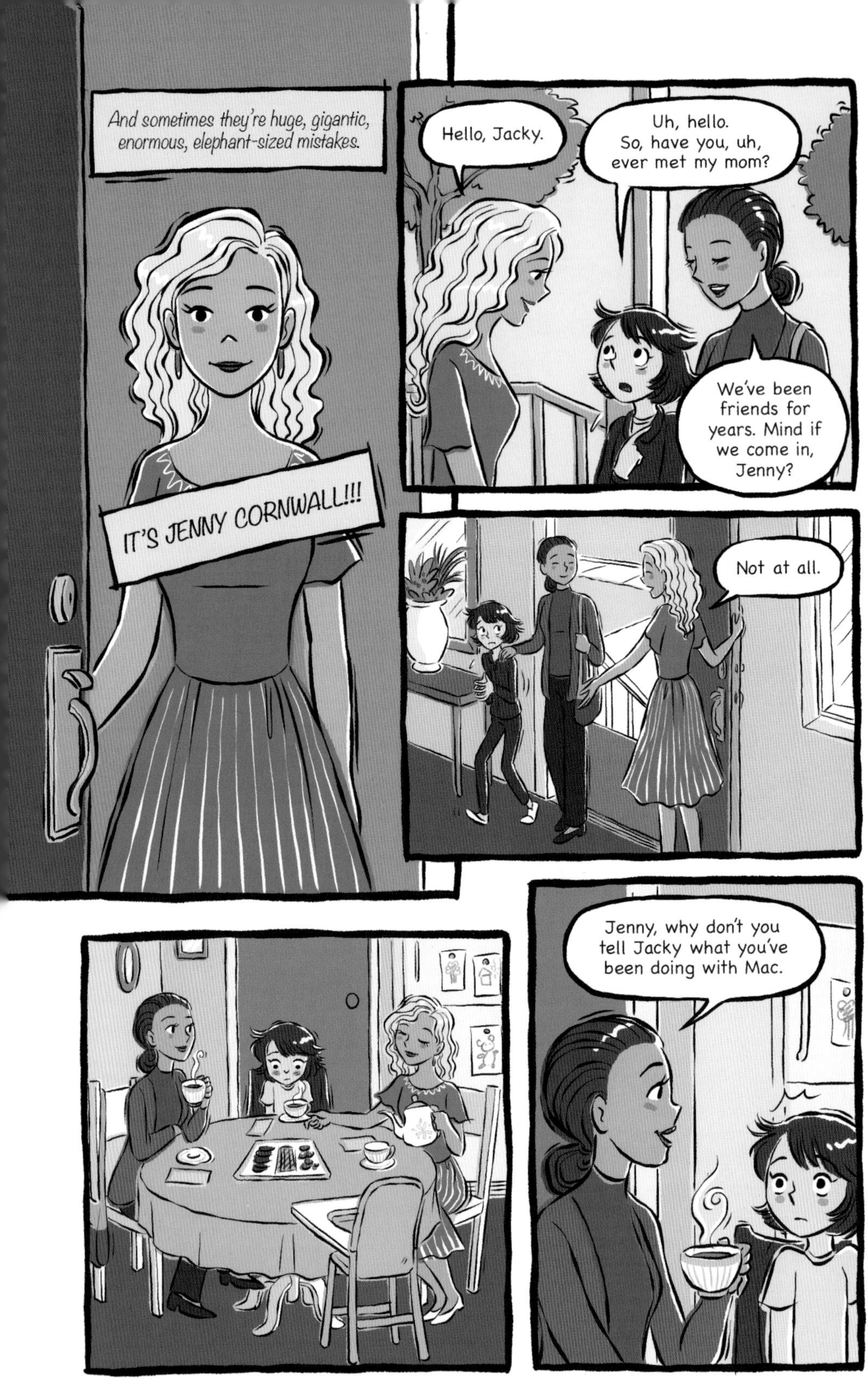
And sometimes they're huge, gigantic, enormous, elephant-sized mistakes.
IT'S JENNY CORNWALL!!!
Hello, Jacky.
Uh, hello. So, have you, uh, ever met my mom?
We've been friends for years. Mind if we come in, Jenny?
Not at all.
Jenny, why don't you tell Jacky what you've been doing with Mac.

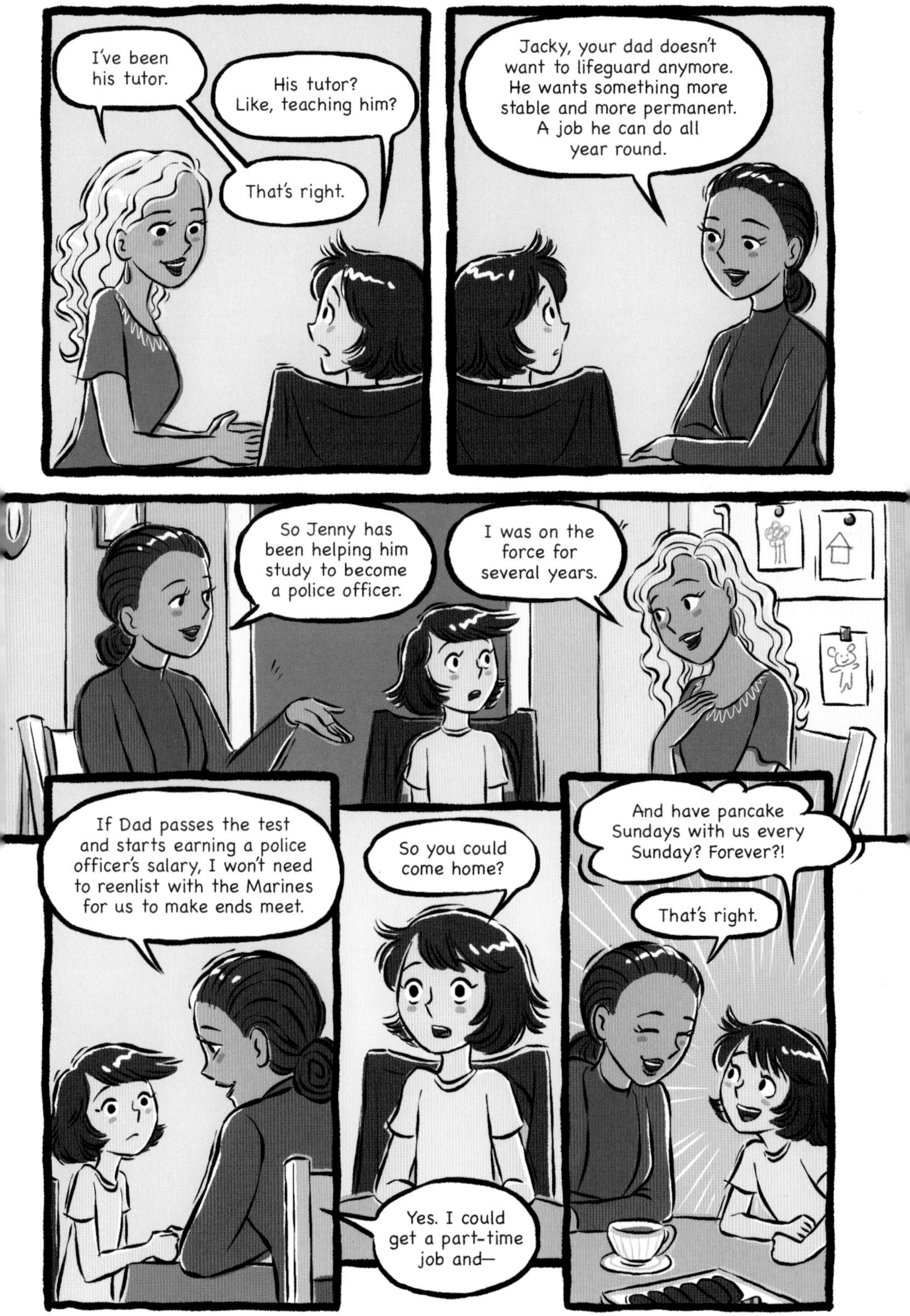
I've been his tutor.
His tutor? Like, teaching him?
That's right.
Jacky, your dad doesn't want to lifeguard anymore. He wants something more stable and more permanent. A job he can do all year round.
So Jenny has been helping him study to become a police officer.
I was on the force for several years.
If Dad passes the test and starts earning a police officer's salary, I won't need to reenlist with the Marines for us to make ends meet.
So you could come home?
Yes. I could get a part-time job and—
And have pancake Sundays with us every Sunday? Forever?!
That's right.

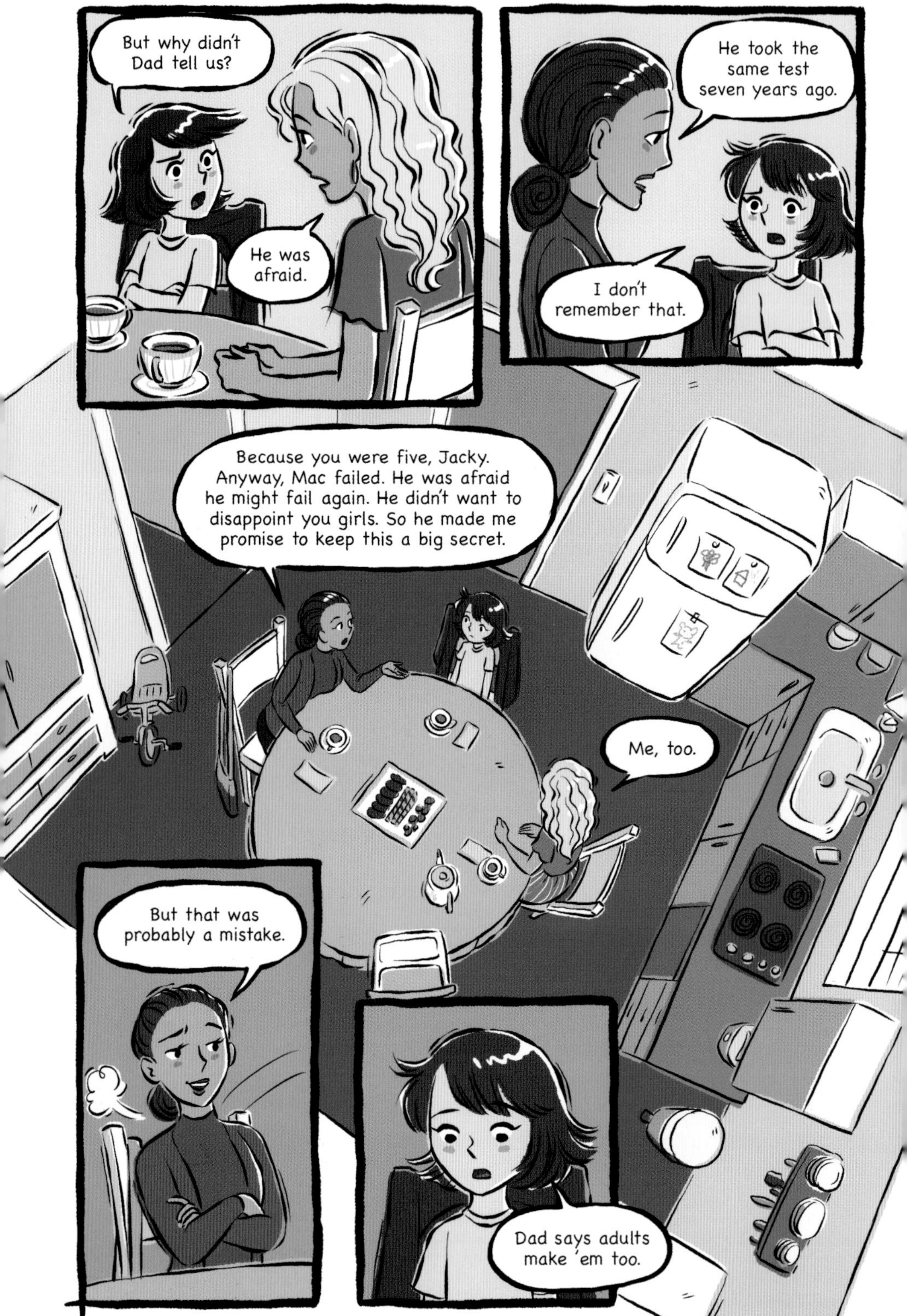
But why didn't Dad tell us?
He was afraid.
He took the same test seven years ago.
I don't remember that.
Because you were five, Jacky. Anyway, Mac failed. He was afraid he might fail again. He didn't want to disappoint you girls. So he made me promise to keep this a big secret.
Me, too.
But that was probably a mistake.
Dad says adults make 'em too.

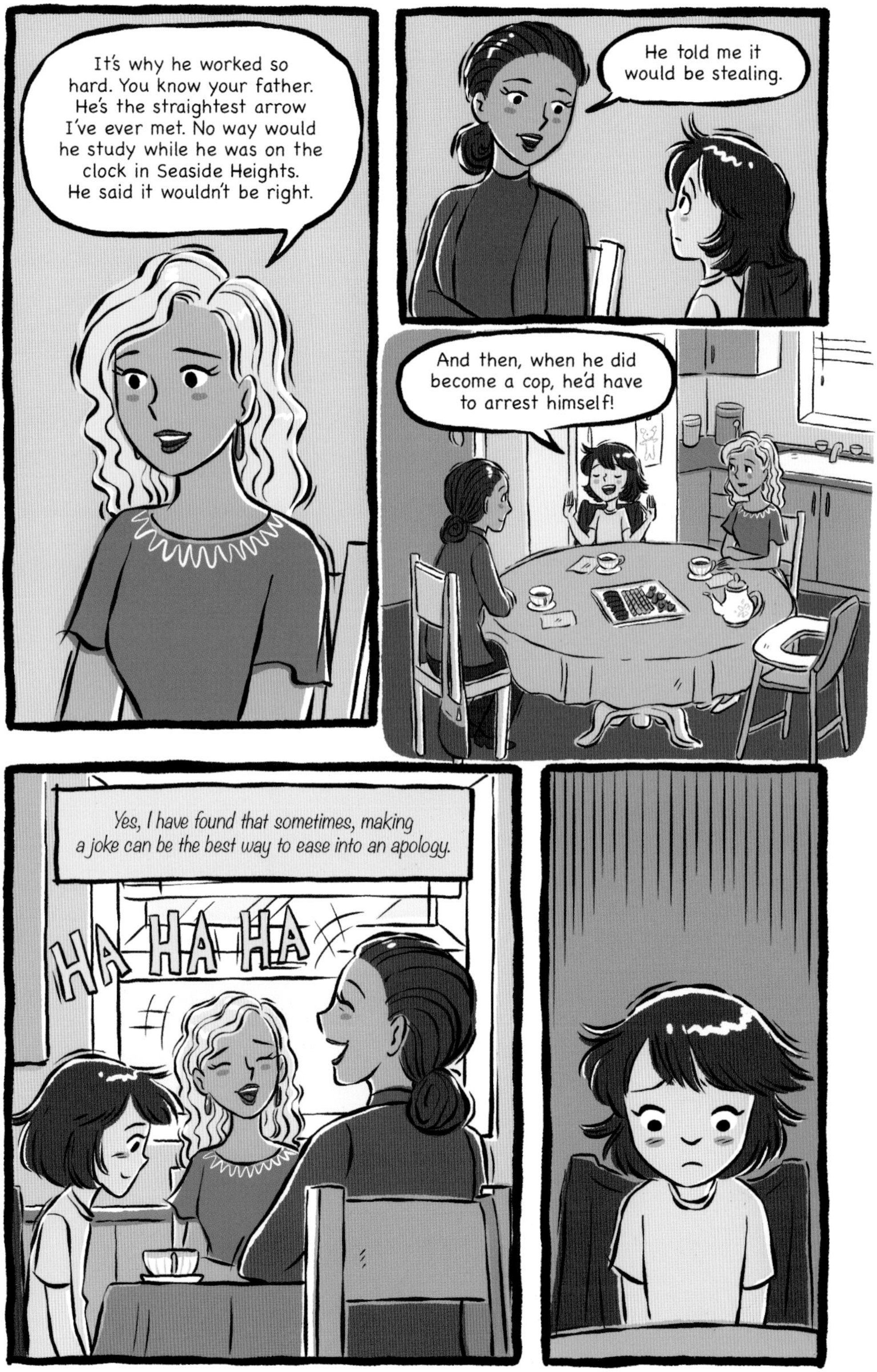
It's why he worked so hard. You know your father. He's the straightest arrow I've ever met. No way would he study while he was on the clock in Seaside Heights. He said it wouldn't be right.
He told me it would be stealing.
And then, when he did become a cop, he'd have to arrest himself!
Yes, I have found that sometimes, making a joke can be the best way to ease into an apology.
HA HA HA

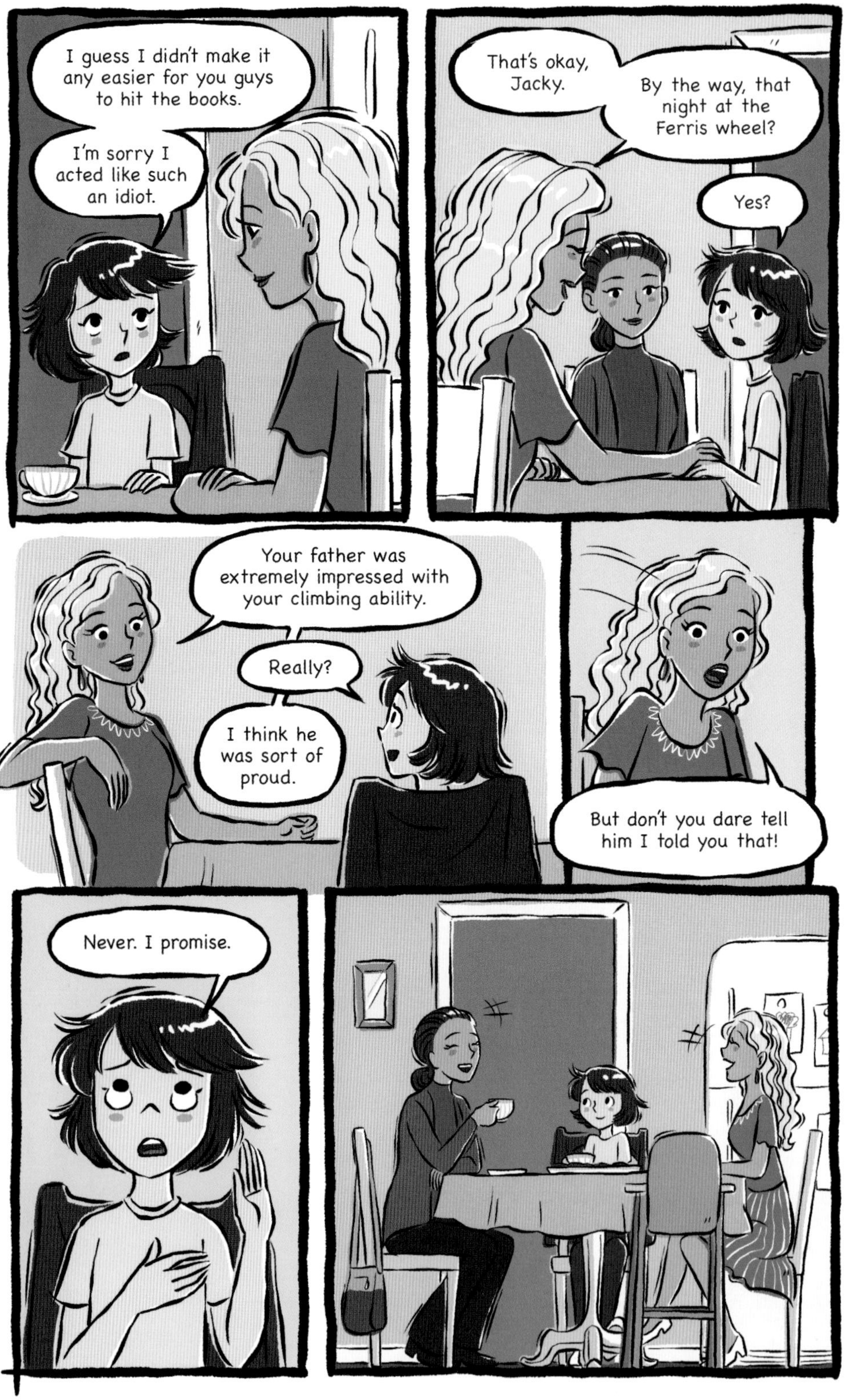
I guess I didn't make it any easier for you guys to hit the books.
I'm sorry I acted like such an idiot.
That's okay, Jacky.
By the way, that night at the Ferris wheel?
Yes?
Your father was extremely impressed with your climbing ability.
Really?
I think he was sort of proud.
But don't you dare tell him I told you that!
Never. I promise.

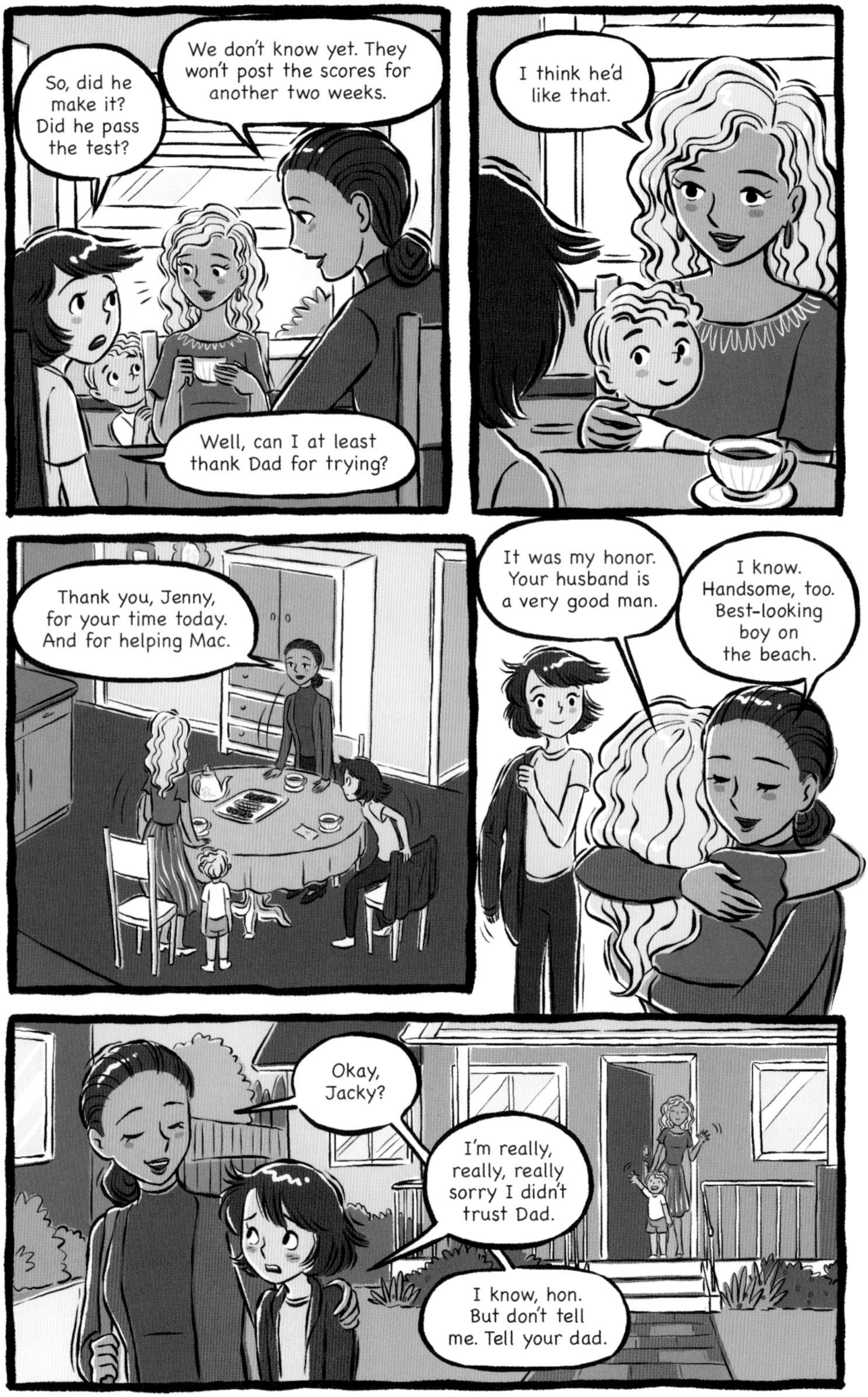
So, did he make it? Did he pass the test?
We don't know yet. They won't post the scores for another two weeks.
Well, can I at least thank Dad for trying?
I think he'd like that.
Thank you, Jenny, for your time today. And for helping Mac.
It was my honor. Your husband is a very good man.
I know. Handsome, too. Best-looking boy on the beach.
Okay, Jacky?
I'm really, really, really sorry I didn't trust Dad.
I know, hon. But don't tell me. Tell your dad.

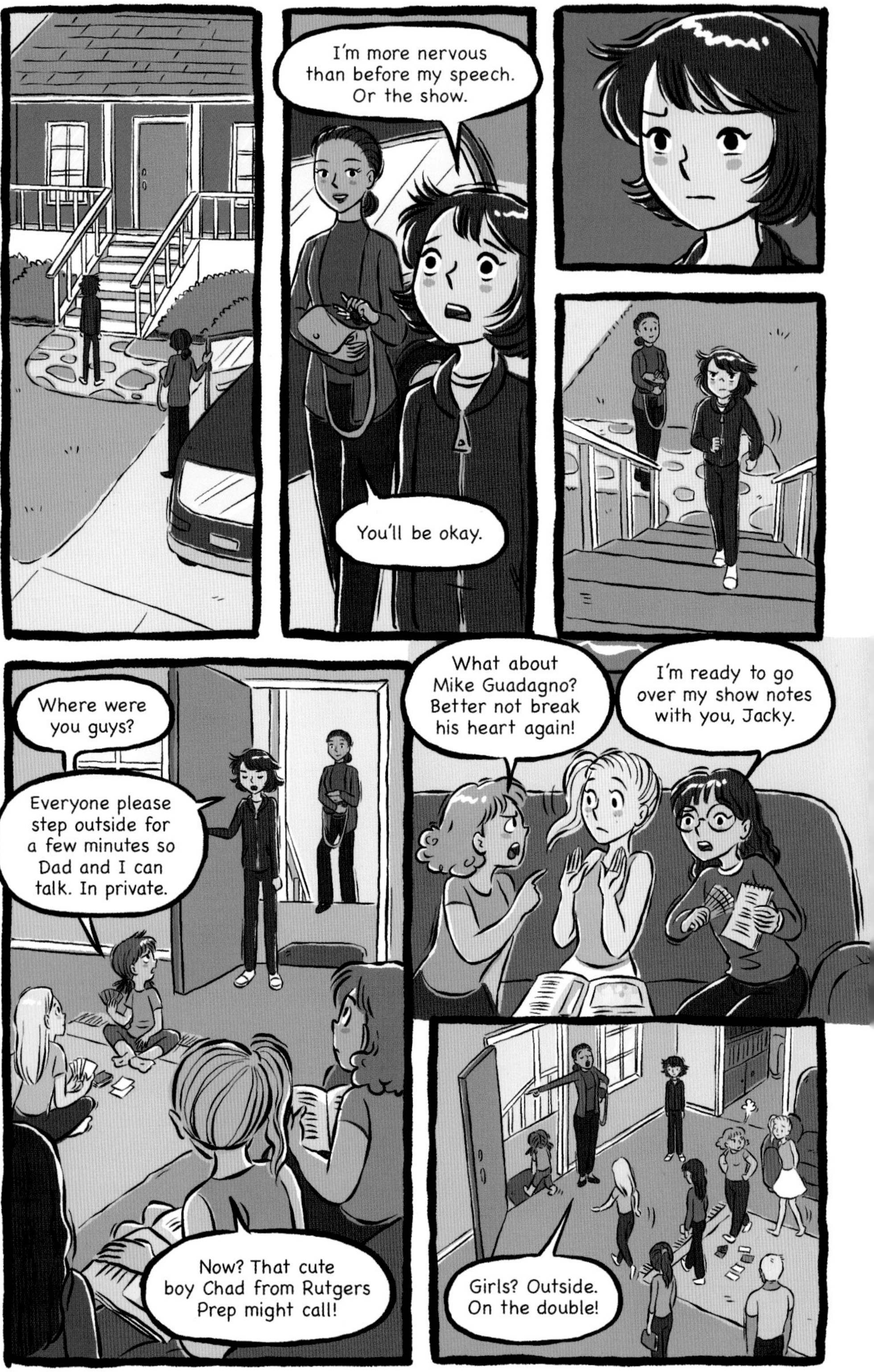
I'm more nervous than before my speech. Or the show.
You'll be okay.
Where were you guys?
Everyone please step outside for a few minutes so Dad and I can talk. In private.
Now? That cute boy Chad from Rutgers Prep might call!
What about Mike Guadagno? Better not break his heart again!
I'm ready to go over my show notes with you, Jacky.
Girls? Outside. On the double!

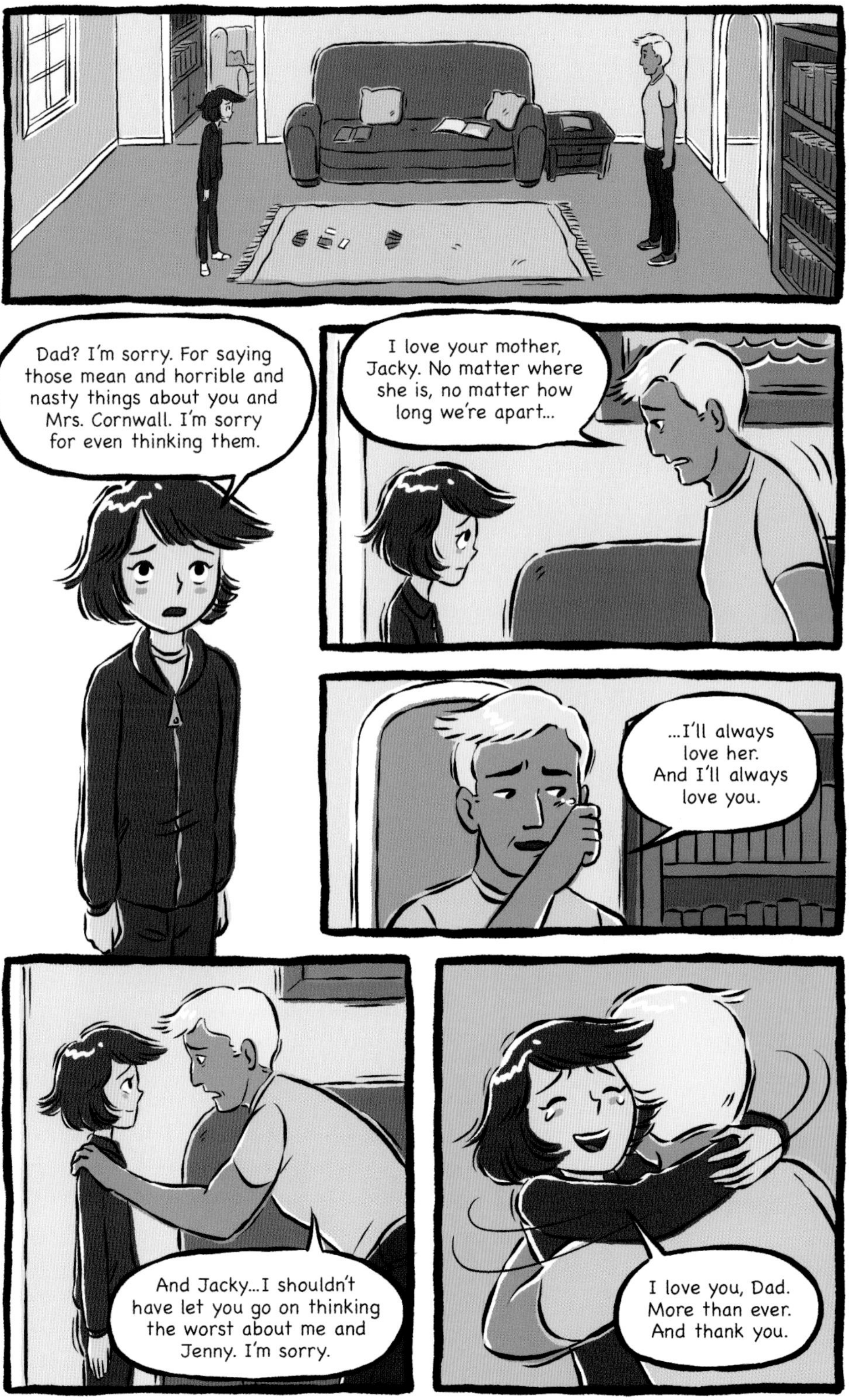
Dad? I'm sorry. For saying those mean and horrible and nasty things about you and Mrs. Cornwall. I'm sorry for even thinking them.
I love your mother, Jacky. No matter where she is, no matter how long we're apart...
...I'll always love her. And I'll always love you.
And Jacky...I shouldn't have let you go on thinking the worst about me and Jenny. I'm sorry.
I love you, Dad. More than ever. And thank you.

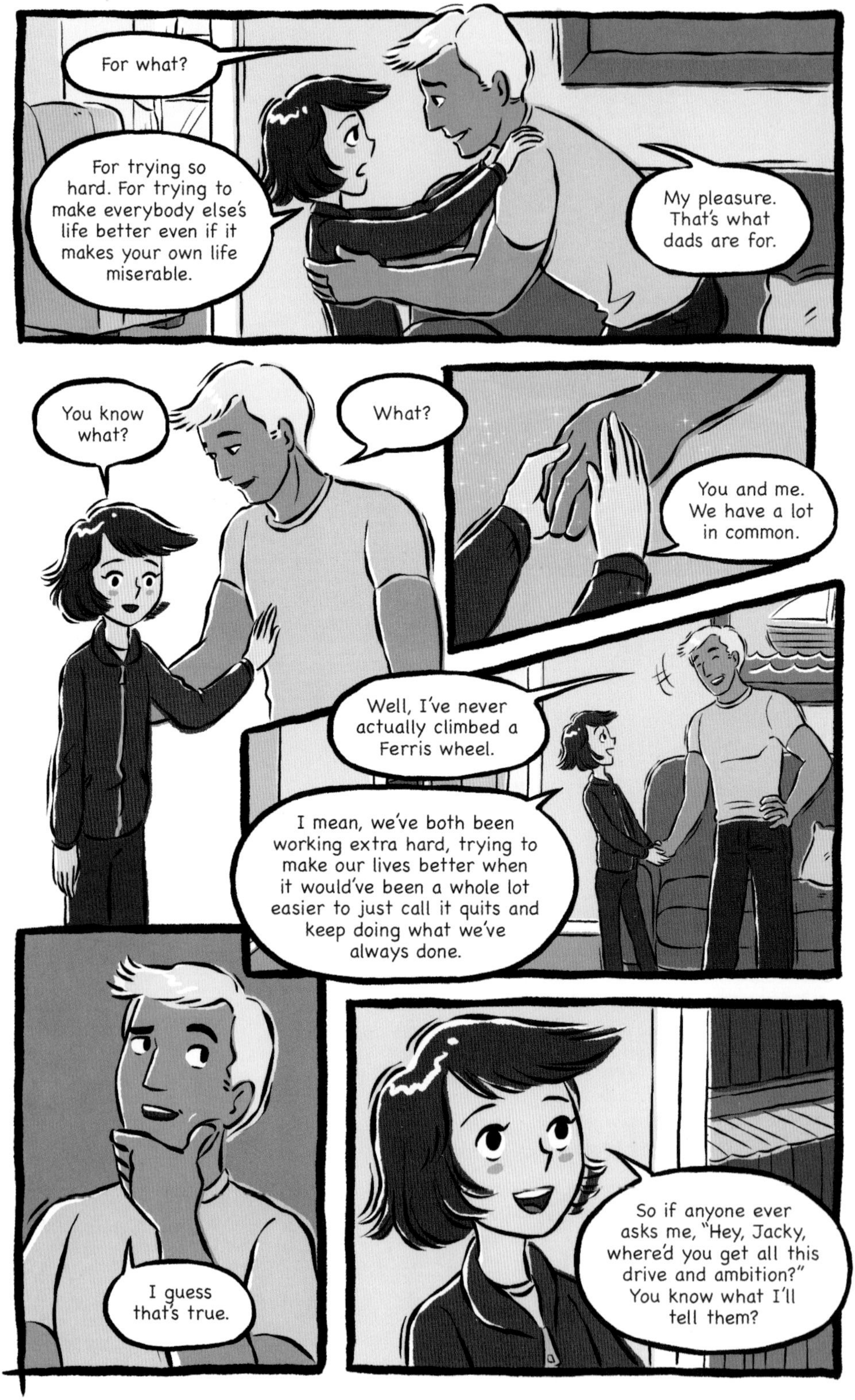
For what?
For trying so hard. For trying to make everybody else's life better even if it makes your own life miserable.
My pleasure. That's what dads are for.
You know what?
What?
You and me. We have a lot in common.
I mean, we've both been working extra hard, trying to make our lives better when it would've been a whole lot easier to just call it quits and keep doing what we've always done.
Well, I've never actually climbed a Ferris wheel.
I guess that's true.
So if anyone ever asks me, "Hey, Jacky, where'd you get all this drive and ambition?" You know what I'll tell them?

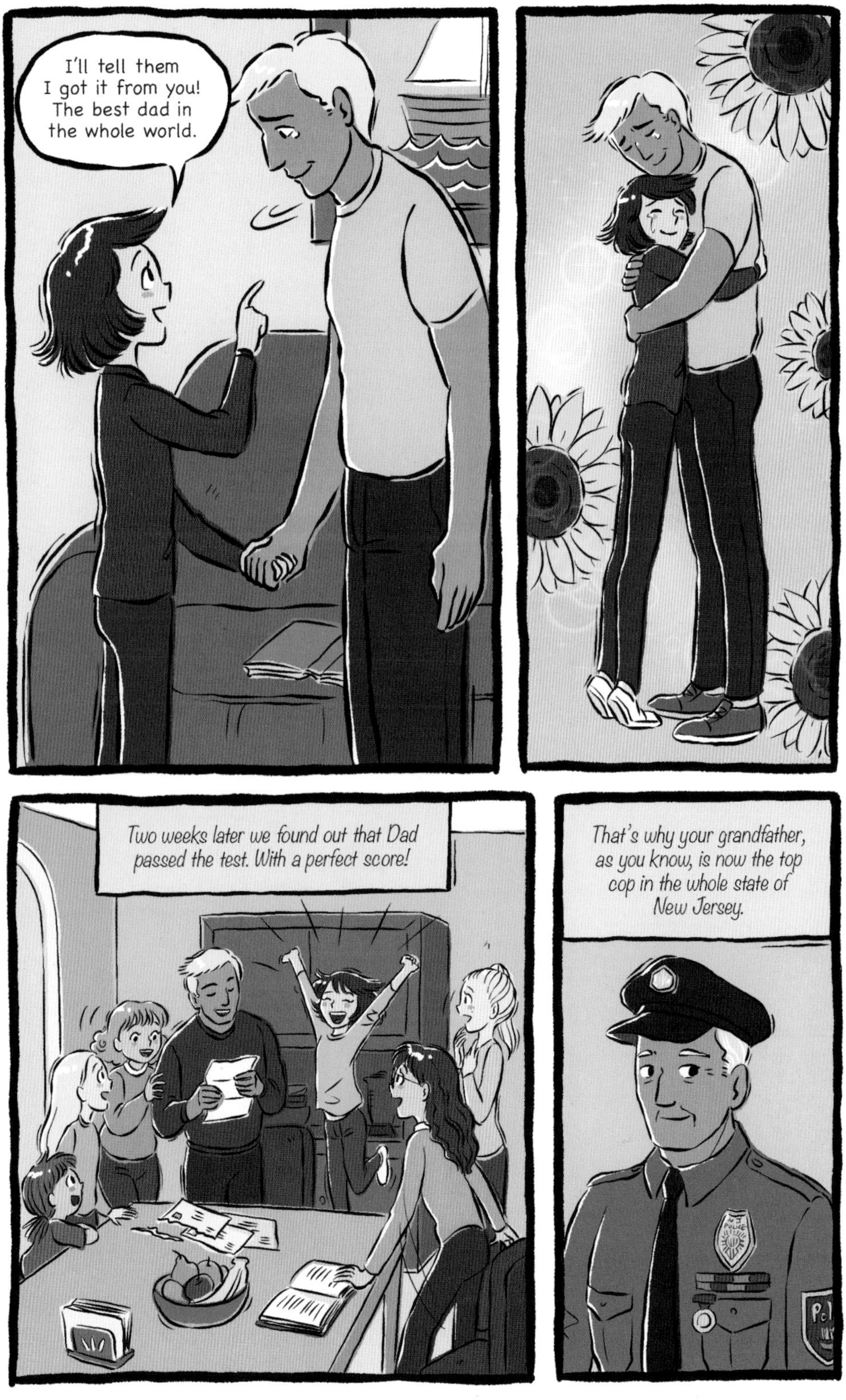
I'll tell them I got it from you! The best dad in the whole world.
Two weeks later we found out that Dad passed the test. With a perfect score!
That's why your grandfather, as you know, is now the top cop in the whole state of New Jersey.

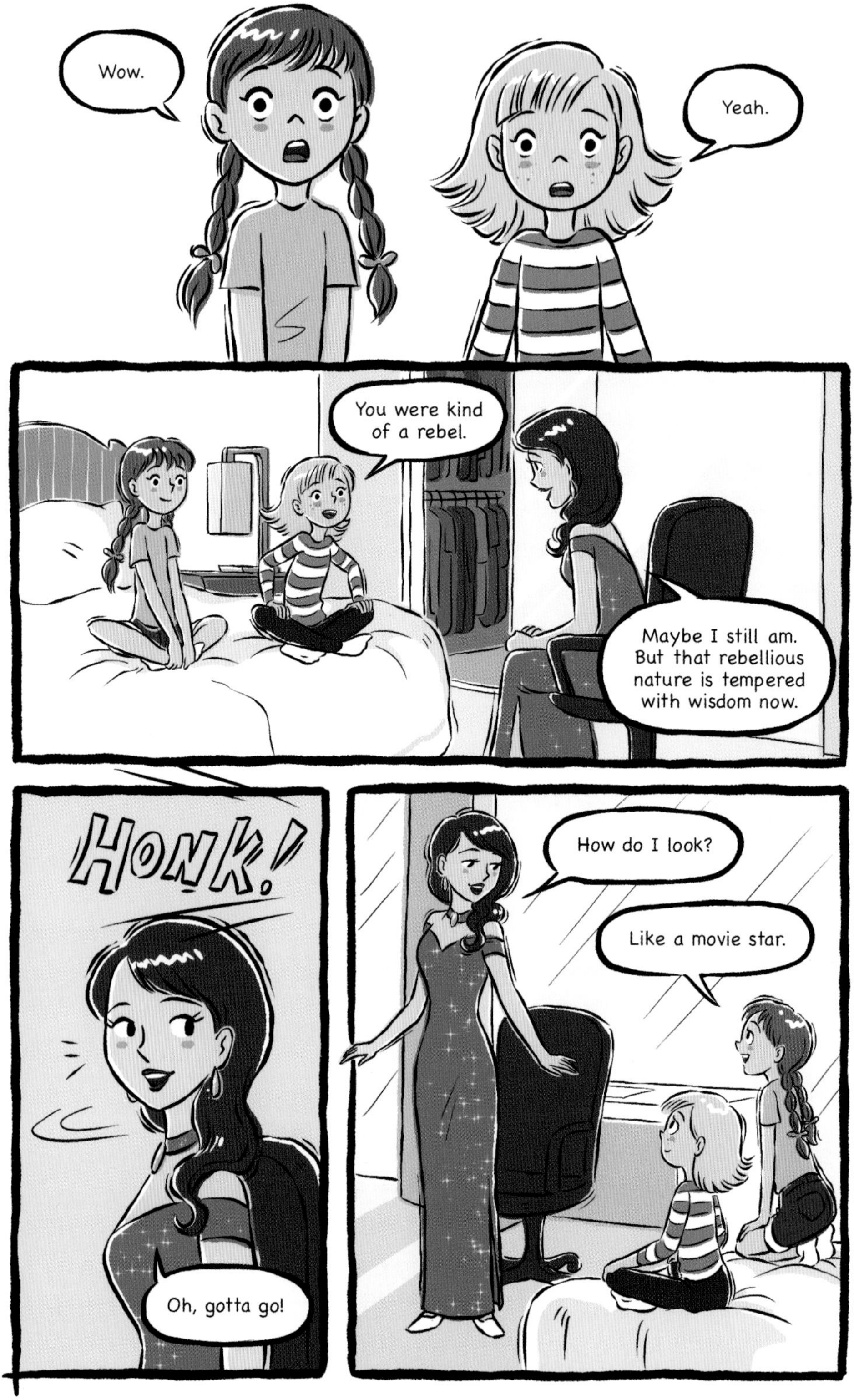
Wow.
Yeah.
You were kind of a rebel.
Maybe I still am. But that rebellious nature is tempered with wisdom now.
HONK!
Oh, gotta go!
How do I look?
Like a movie star.

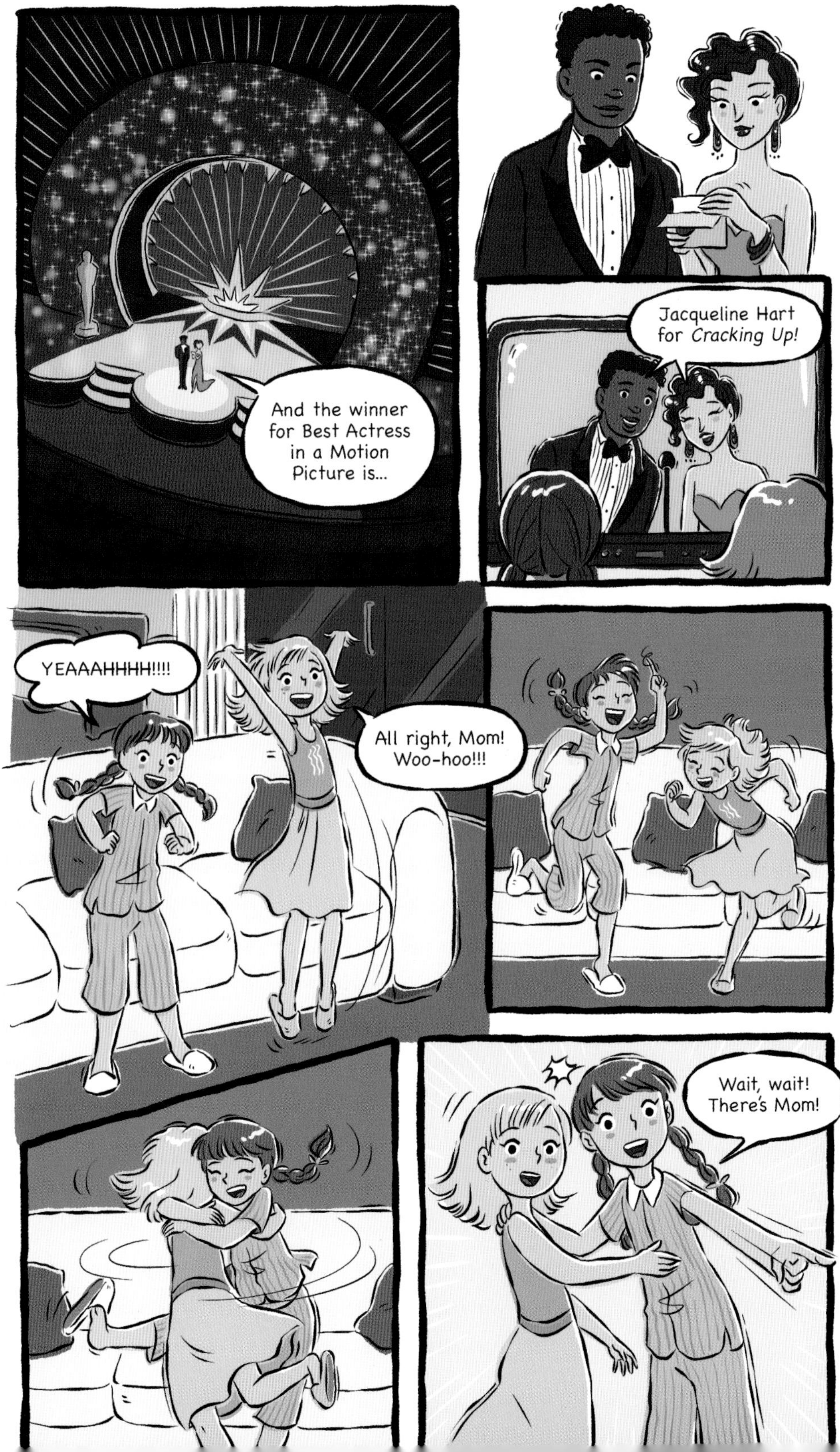
And the winner for Best Actress in a Motion Picture is...
Jacqueline Hart for *Cracking Up!*
YEAAAHHHH!!!!
All right, Mom! Woo-hoo!!!
Wait, wait! There's Mom!

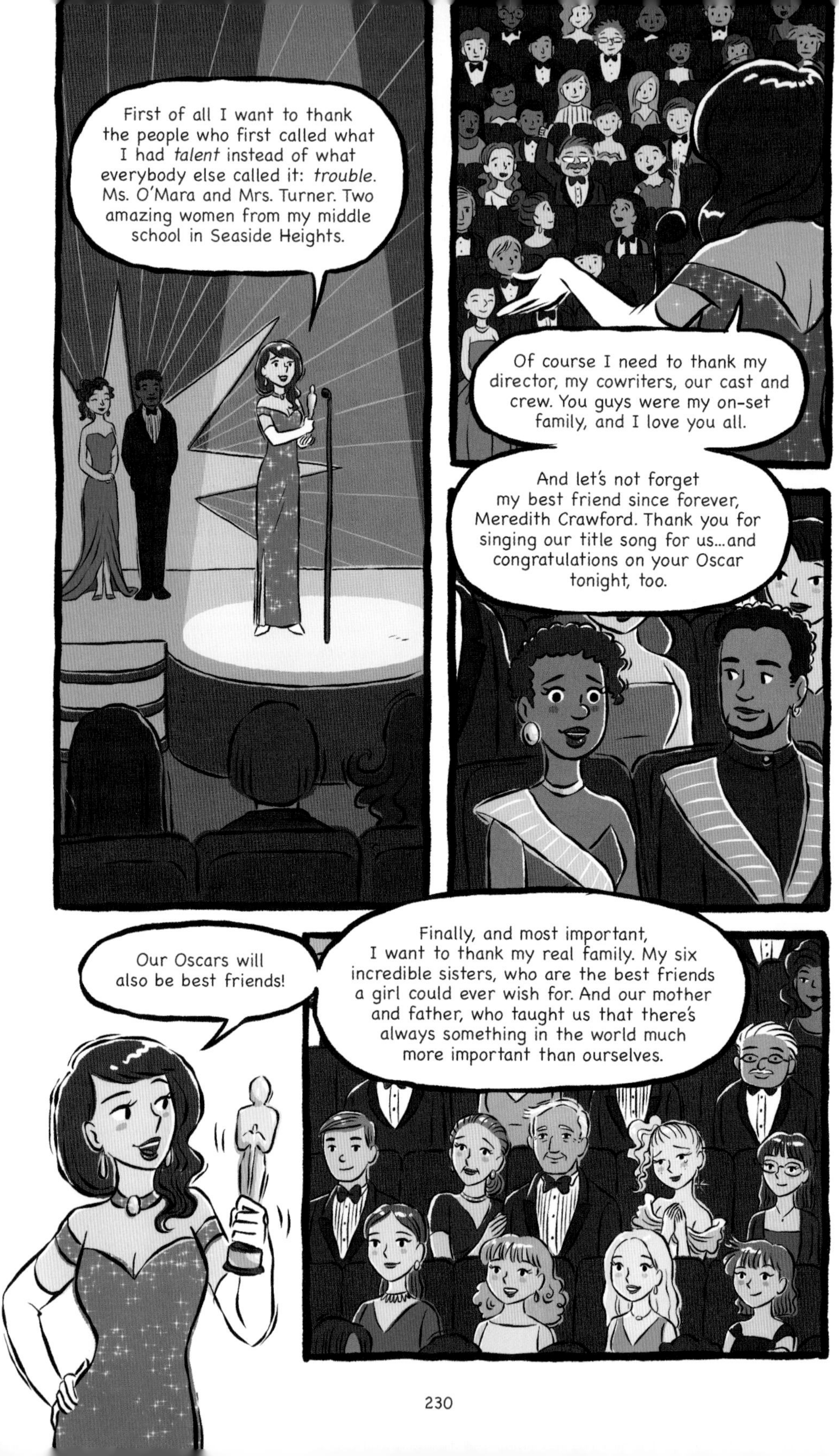
First of all I want to thank the people who first called what I had *talent* instead of what everybody else called it: *trouble*. Ms. O'Mara and Mrs. Turner. Two amazing women from my middle school in Seaside Heights.
Of course I need to thank my director, my cowriters, our cast and crew. You guys were my on-set family, and I love you all.
And let's not forget my best friend since forever, Meredith Crawford. Thank you for singing our title song for us...and congratulations on your Oscar tonight, too.
Our Oscars will also be best friends!
Finally, and most important, I want to thank my real family. My six incredible sisters, who are the best friends a girl could ever wish for. And our mother and father, who taught us that there's always something in the world much more important than ourselves.

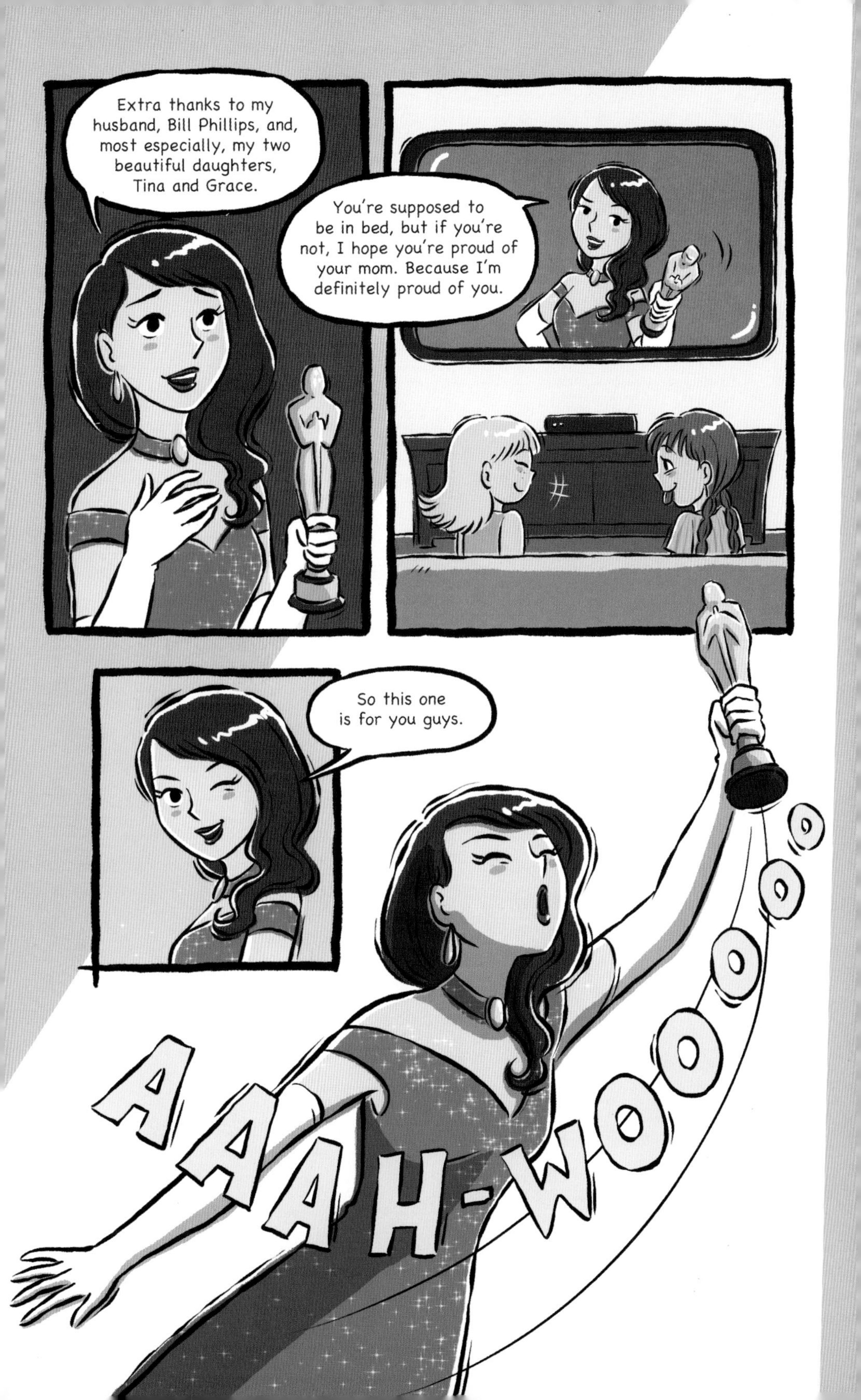
Extra thanks to my husband, Bill Phillips, and, most especially, my two beautiful daughters, Tina and Grace.
You're supposed to be in bed, but if you're not, I hope you're proud of your mom. Because I'm definitely proud of you.
So this one is for you guys.
AAAAH-WOOOOOOOO

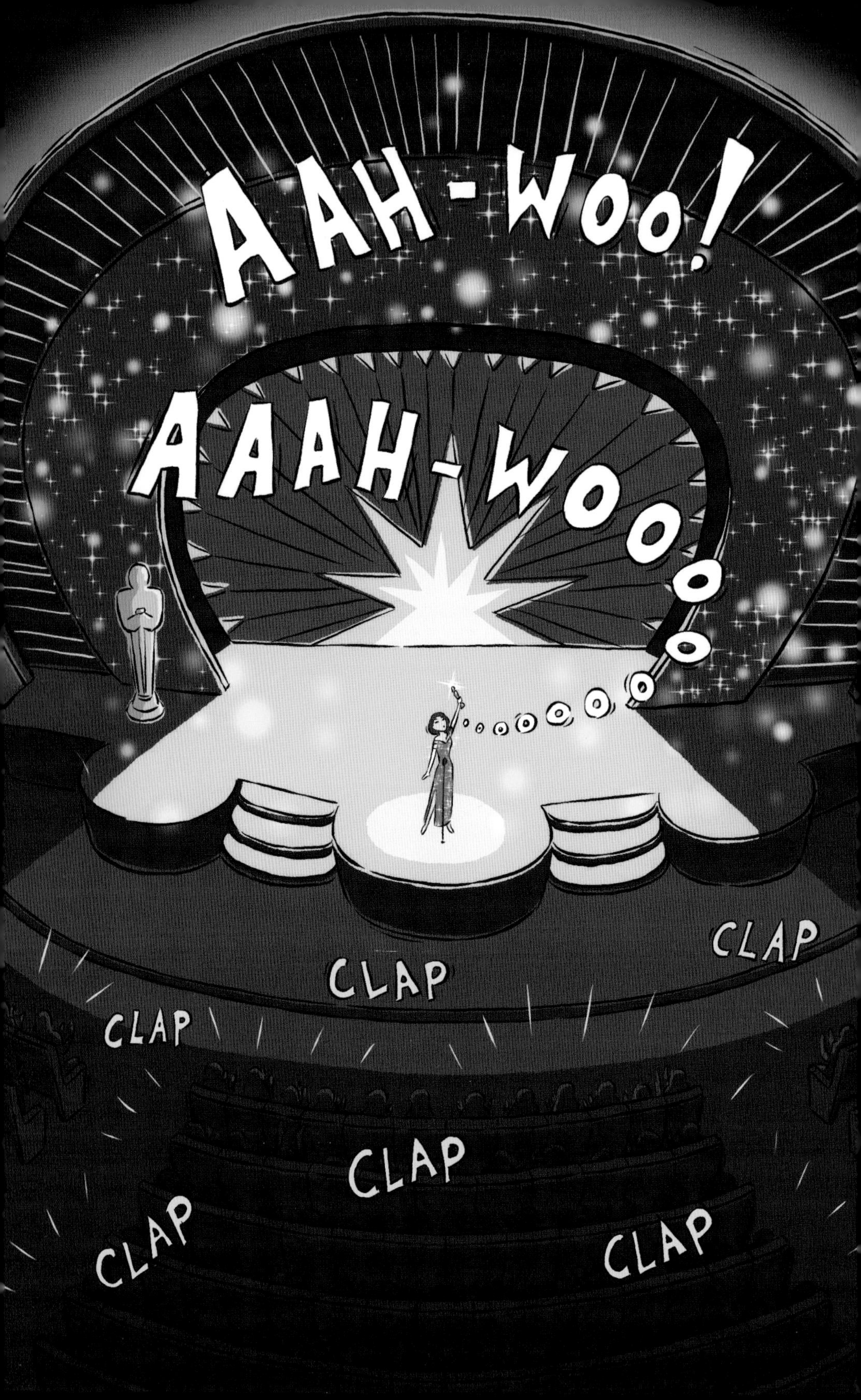
AAH-WOO!
AAAH-WOOOOOOOOOOOO
CLAP
CLAP
CLAP
CLAP
CLAP
CLAP

ABOUT THE AUTHORS

JAMES PATTERSON received the Literarian Award for Outstanding Service to the American Literary Community from the National Book Foundation. He holds the Guinness World Record for the most #1 *New York Times* bestsellers, including *Max Einstein, Middle School, I Funny*, and *Jacky Ha-Ha*, and his books have sold more than 385 million copies worldwide. A tireless champion of the power of books and reading, Patterson created a children's book imprint, JIMMY Patterson, whose mission is simple: "We want every kid who finishes a JIMMY Book to say, 'PLEASE GIVE ME ANOTHER BOOK.'" He has donated more than three million books to students and soldiers and funds over four hundred Teacher and Writer Education Scholarships at twenty-one colleges and universities. He has also donated millions of dollars to independent bookstores and school libraries. Patterson invests proceeds from the sales of JIMMY Patterson Books in pro-reading initiatives.

CHRIS GRABENSTEIN is a *New York Times* bestselling author who has collaborated with James Patterson on the Max Einstein, I Funny, Jacky Ha-Ha, Treasure Hunters, and House of Robots series, as well as *Word of Mouse, Katt vs. Dogg, Pottymouth and Stoopid, Laugh Out Loud*, and *Daniel X: Armageddon*. He lives in New York City.

ADAM RAU was born in Minnesota and moved to New York to attend The School of Visual Arts. In 2004 he landed a job in children's publishing, and before long he was acquiring and editing graphic novels for young readers, which he has been doing for over ten years. Adam lives in Jersey City with his wife and dog.

BETTY C. TANG has been in the animation and illustration world for more than twenty-five years. She has worked for acclaimed studios including DreamWorks Animation and Disney Television Animation, co-directed the Chinese animated feature film, *Where's the Dragon?*, and illustrated for books and magazines. Born in Taiwan, she now lives in Los Angeles, California and writes and illustrates for children.